The Complete Mahabharata
Adi Parva

Ramesh Menon was born in 1951 in New Delhi. He has also written modern renderings of the Mahabharata, Ramayana, Srimad Bhagavad Gita, Siva Purana, Devi Purana and Bhagavata Purana.

The Complete Mahabharata
Adi Parva

Volume 1

RAMESH MENON

RUPA

Published by
Rupa Publications India Pvt. Ltd 2016
7/16, Ansari Road, Daryaganj
New Delhi 110002

Sales centres:
Allahabad Bengaluru Chennai
Hyderabad Jaipur Kathmandu
Kolkata Mumbai

First published in hardback in 2010.

ISBN: 978-81-291-4213-9

First impression 2016

10 9 8 7 6 5 4 3 2 1

Typset by Mindways Design, New Delhi

Printed at Rekha Printers Pvt. Ltd, New Delhi

For Sri RK Mehra,
valued friend, great Publisher

Contents

A Brief Introduction

The last complete version of the Mahabharata to be written in India in English prose was the translation by Kisari Mohan Ganguli in the late 19th century. He wrote it between 1883 and 1896. To the best of my knowledge, it still remains the only full English prose rendering of the Epic by any Indian.

More than a hundred years have passed since Ganguli achieved his monumental task. Despite its closeness to the original Sanskrit and its undeniable power, in more than a hundred years the language and style of the Ganguli translation have inevitably become archaic.

It seemed a shame that this most magnificent of epics, a national treasure, an indisputable classic of world literature, believed by many to be the greatest of all books ever written, is not available in complete form to the Indian (or any) reader in modern, literary and easily accessible English: as retold by Indian writers.

So we, a group of Indian writers and editors, warmly and patiently supported by our publisher Rupa & Co, undertook a line-by-line retelling of the complete Mahabharata, for the contemporary and future reader. Our aim has not been to write a scholarly translation of the Great Epic, but an eminently readable one, without vitiating either the spirit or the poetry of the original, and without reducing its length.

This is not a translation from the Sanskrit but based almost entirely on the Ganguli text, and he himself did use more than one Sanskrit version for his work. However, as will be obvious, the style of this new rendering is very much our own, and our hope is to bring as much of the majesty and enchantment of this awesome epic to you as is possible in English.

Ramesh Menon
Series Editor

Acknowledgements

Sanjana Roy Choudhury, Kadambari Mishra, Deepthi Talwar and Jayashree Kumar edited and proofread this first volume of the Mahabharata. I am most grateful to them for their fine, painstaking work.

CANTO 1

PARVA SAMGRAHA

AUM! I bow down to Narayana and Nara, the most exalted Purusha, and to the Devi Saraswati, and utter the word Jaya.

Ugrasrava is the son of Romaharshana; he is a Suta and a master of the Puranas. One day, bowing reverently, he came to the great Rishis of flinchless austerity who sat at their ease after attending the twelve years' yagna of Saunaka Kulapati, in the Naimisha vana. The Munis were eager to listen to the marvellous legends of Ugrasrava, who had come to their asrama in the forest. The holy ones welcomed him with respect. He greeted those Sages with folded hands and inquired after the evolution of their tapasya.

When the Rishis all sat again, Romaharshana's son also humbly sat upon the seat they offered him. Seeing that he was comfortable, and refreshed, one of the Rishis said, 'From where are you coming, lotus-eyed Sauti, and where have you been spending your time? Tell me, who asks you this, in detail.'

The eloquent Sauti replied appositely and at length in that large conclave of illustrious tapasvins; the language he used was chaste and high, suited to their way of life.

Sauti said, 'I heard the diverse, sacred and marvellous tales, which Krishna Dwaipayana composed in his Mahabharata, and which Vaisampayana narrated at the sarpa yagna of the noble Rajarishi Janamejaya, the son of Parikshit, foremost among Kshatriyas.

Later, I ranged the Earth, visiting many tirthas and other shrines. I journeyed to Samantapanchaka, revered by the Dvijas, where the sons of Kuru and those of Pandu fought their Great War, with all the Kshatriyas of the land fighting for one side or the other.

From there, being eager to meet you, I have come into your presence. Worshipful Sages, you are all like Brahman to me. Most blessed ones, you shine in this yagnashala with the splendour of the Sun. You have finished your dhyana and have fed the holy fire. Now you sit here, at your ease, with no cares.

Tell me, greatest of Dvijas, what would you hear from me? Shall I recount the sacred tales of the Puranas, which tell of dharma and artha, or shall I tell you about the deeds of enlightened Rishis and of the kings of men?'

The Rishis replied, 'The Purana that was first propounded by the great Dwaipayana. When both the Devas and the Brahmarishis had heard it, they said it was the foremost of all Itihasas, histories. It varies in both diction and divisions, has intricate and subtle meanings, logically combined and gleaned from the Vedas, and it is a most holy work. It is composed in elegant language and includes the subjects of every other book. Other Shastras elucidate this Purana, and it reflects the inmost meaning of the four Vedas. We want to listen to that Itihasa, which is also called the Bhaarata, the magnificent Vyasa's holy masterwork, which dispels the fear of evil. We would hear it exactly as the Rishi Vaisampayana told it, joyously, under the direction of Dwaipayana himself, at the sarpa yagna, the snake-sacrifice of Raja Janamejaya.'

Sauti then said, 'I bow to the Primordial Being, Isana, to whom the people all make offerings, whom the multitude adores. He is the true and immortal One – Brahman, manifest, unmanifest and eternal. He both exists and appears not to. He is the Universe and also distinct from the Universe, the creator of all things, high and low, the ancient, exalted, inexhaustible One. He is Vishnu, benign and benignity personified, worthy of all worship, pure, perfect. He is Hari, sovereign of the faculties, the mover of all things, mobile and motionless.

I will now narrate the sacred thoughts of the illumined Muni Vyasa, of marvellous accomplishments, whom all here revere. Some pauranikas have already taught this Itihasa, some now teach it, and others will hereafter disseminate it across the Earth. It is a vast treasure of knowledge, and its fame is established through the three Lokas. The Dvijas, the twice-born, possess it both in detail and in full. The erudite delight in it for being adorned with elegance, with conversations human and divine and with myriad poetic metres.

When this world was without light, plunged in absolute darkness, a Mighty Egg appeared, the First Cause of creation, the single, infinite, inexhaustible seed of all created beings. This is the Mahavidya, formed at the beginning of the Yuga, when, we hear, Brahman the true light, the eternal, inconceivable Being, was present equally everywhere, the unseen and subtle Cause, whose nature is both of being and nothingness.

From this Egg, Pitamaha Brahma emerged, the first Prajapati, along with Vishnu Suraguru and Siva Sthanu. Then the twenty-one Prajapatis appeared – Manu, Vasishta and Parameshthi, ten Prachetas, Daksha, and the seven sons of Daksha.

Then appeared the incomprehensible Purusha, whom all the Rishis know, and also the Viswedevas, the Adityas, the Vasus, the Aswin twins, the Yakshas, the Sadhyas, the Pisachas, the Guhyakas, and the Pitrs.

After these, the wise and most holy Brahmarishis were created, and the numerous Rajarishis distinguished by every noble quality. So too, the waters, the heavens, the earth, the air, the sky, the cardinal points of the heavens, the years, the seasons, the months, the fortnights—called pakshas—with day and night, in proper succession. Thus, all things that are known to man were made.

And when the Yugas end, whatever is seen in the Universe, animate and inanimate, will again be dissolved. When the next Yugas begin, all things will be renewed and like the many fruits of the Earth, succeed one another in the order of their seasons. So the Wheel revolves ceaselessly in the world, without beginning and without end, destroying all things.

The generation of Devas, in brief, was thirty-three thousand, thirty-three hundred and thirty-three. The sons of Div were Brihadbhanu, Chakshus, Atma, Vibhavasu, Savita, Richika, Arka, Bhanu, Asavaha and Ravi. Of these Vivaswans of old, Mahya was the youngest, whose son was Devavrata. Devavrata's son Suvrata had three sons—Dasajyoti, Satajyoti and Sahasrajyoti; each of them sired numerous offspring. The illustrious Dasajyoti had ten thousand progeny, Satajyoti ten times that number, and Sahasrajyoti ten times as many as Satajyoti.

From these descended the clans of the Kurus, the Yadus, and of Bhaarata; the lineage of Yayati and of Ikshvaku, and also all the Rajarishis. Numerous, too, were their generations, and abundant were the creatures and their places of abode. The triune mystery—the Vedas, Yoga and Vijnana Dharma, Artha and Kama; the many books upon the subject of Dharma, Artha and Kama; rules for the conduct of humankind; also, histories and discourses upon various Srutis all these the Rishi Vyasa saw. They are here in their proper order, and mentioned as examples of the Shastras.

The Rishi Vyasa promulgated this vast treasure of knowledge in both a comprehensive and an abridged form. The learned of this world always want to know both versions. Some read the Bhaarata from the invocatory mantra; others begin with the story of Astika, others with Uparichara; while some Brahmanas study the entire epic.

Men of learning exhibit their different knowledges of the text when they comment upon the composition. Some are skilful at expounding its meaning, while others remember its contents in complete detail.

Having, with penance and meditation, tapasya and dhyana, analysed the eternal Veda, the son of Satyavati later composed this sacred history.

When that knowing Brahmarishi, of fierce vows, the noble Vyasa, son of Parasara, finished this greatest of all epics, he considered how he could transmit it to his disciples and leave it behind for posterity. And Brahma, who owns the six attributes, who is the Guru of the world, knew the anxiety of the Rishi Dwaipayana. Brahma appeared in the place where Vyasa was: to grant the Sage what he desired and thus benefit the people of the Earth.

Vyasa sat lost in thought, surrounded by all the tribes of Munis. Seeing Brahma, he rose in astonishment, and standing with joined palms, the Rishi bowed low and ordered a darbhasana fetched for the Pitamaha. Vyasa circumambulated in pradakshina Him who is called Hiranyagarbha, seated upon that especial and lofty grass throne, and came and stood near Him. Brahma Parameshthi commanded him to sit near the asana, and Vyasa did so, his heart full of love, and smiling in joy.

The glorious Vyasa said to Brahma Parameshthi, "Divine Brahma, I have composed a kavya, a poem, which is highly regarded. In it, I have explained the mystery of the Veda and the other scriptures; the rituals of the Upanishads with their angas; the Puranas and Itihasas that I have compiled and named after the three divisions of time, the nature of ageing and decay, of fear, disease, being and non being; a description of different varnas and the various stages of life: laws for the four varnas, the true import of the Puranas; an account of sannyasa and the duties of a brahmacharin; the dimensions of the Sun and Moon, the planets, galaxies, and stars, along with the duration of the four ages; the Rik, Sama and Yajur Vedas; also, the Adhyatma; the sciences of Nyaya, the diagnosis and the treatment of disease; charity and Pasupatadharma; births heavenly and human, for different ends; a description of the tirthas and other holy places, of rivers, mountains, forests, the ocean, of the unearthly cities and the Kalpas; the art of war; the different nations and languages, the nature and customs of the people; and the All-pervading Spirit – all these I have told of in my poem. But now I cannot find anyone to be my scribe for this work, not on this Earth."

Brahma said, "In this gathering of Munis renowned for their sanctity, I honour you for your deep knowledge of divine mysteries. I know you have revealed the Divine Word, from its first utterance, in the language of truth. You have called your present work a kavya, a poem, and so it shall be a poem. No other poet's work shall ever equal this kavya of yours, even as the other three asramas of life are forever lesser than the grihastasrama. O Muni, let us consider Ganesha to become your amanuensis, to write this epic poem down."'

Sauti said, 'Having spoken thus to Vyasa, Brahma left for his own realm, Brahmaloka. Vyasa now thought prayerfully of Ganesha; and Ganesha, remover of obstacles, always ready to fulfil the desires of his devotees, came immediately to the place where Vyasa sat.

When he had been worshipped, welcomed and was seated, Vyasa said to him, "O Guru of the Ganas! I beg you, be the scribe for the Bhaarata, which I have conceived in my imagination, and which I shall narrate to you."

Ganesha answered, "I will be your scribe if my nib does not stop writing for even a moment."

Vyasa said to that Deity, "Wherever there is anything that you do not properly understand, you must stop writing."

Ganesha signified his assent by saying AUM! and was ready to begin. Vyasa began his narration; and to divert Ganesha, and to gain time, he wove the warp and weft of his legend exceedingly close, with many a diversion.

By this ruse, he dictated his work and never allowed Ganesha's nib, which was a tusk he took from his own face, to be still for a moment, for he was always ahead of his scribe.'

'I am,' continued Sauti, 'acquainted with eight thousand and eight hundred verses, and so is Suka, and perhaps Sanjaya. From the mysteriousness of their meaning, O Munis, no one is able, to this day, to penetrate those close-knit and difficult slokas. Even the omniscient Ganesha took a moment to consider; Vyasa, however, continued to compose more verses, abundantly.

As an instrument for applying kohl does, this awesome work has opened the eyes of the inquisitive world, blinded by the darkness of ignorance. As the Sun dispels the darkness, so does the Bhaarata by its treatises on dharma, artha, kama, and final moksha dispel the ignorance of men. As the full Moon unfurls the buds of the water lily with his soft light, so this Purana reveals the light of the Sruti, and makes the human intellect bloom. The torch of this Itihasa destroys the darkness of ignorance, and then the entire mansion of Prakriti becomes illumined.

This work is a tree. The chapter of contents is its seed; the divisions called Pauloma and Astika are its root; the portion called Sambhava is its trunk; the books called Sabha and Aranya are roosting perches; the Parva called Arani, the knots on the bole; the Virata and Udyoga Parvas, the pith; the book named Bhishma, the main branch; the book called Drona, the leaves; the Karna Parva, the fair flowers; the book named Saya, their sweet fragrance; the books entitled Stri and Asthika, the refreshing shade; the book called Shanti, the mighty fruit; the book called Aswamedha, the immortal sap; the Asramavasika, the place where the tree grows; and the book called Mausala is an epitome of the Vedas and held in great reverence by virtuous Brahmanas. The tree of the Bhaarata, as inexhaustible to mankind as the clouds, shall be a source of livelihood to all poets of distinction.'

Sauti continued, 'I will now tell you of the immortal flower and fruit of this tree, whose scent is pure and flavour delicious, and which not the Devas can destroy.

Once, when implored by Bhishma, the wise son of Ganga, and by his own mother Satyavati, the spiritual and virtuous Krishna Dwaipayana fathered three sons, who were like three fires, upon the two wives of Vichitravirya; and having sired Dhritarashtra, Pandu and Vidura, he returned to his asrama to continue his tapasya.

Not until after these three were born, grown and, even, departed on their final journey, did the great Vyasa make the Bhaarata known in this world of men. When Janamejaya and thousands of Brahmanas begged him, he commanded his disciple Vaisampayana, who sat next to him; and

Vaisampayana, sitting with the sadasyas, the guests, recited the Bhaarata, during the intervals in the rituals of the snake sacrifice, for the others repeatedly urged him to do so.

Vyasa has described exhaustively the greatness of the house of Kuru, the virtuousness of Gandhari, the wisdom of Vidura, and the constancy of Kunti. The noble Rishi has dwelt upon the divinity of Krishna, the dharma of the sons of Pandu, and the evil ways of the sons and confederates of Dhritarashtra.

Originally, Vyasa composed the Bhaarata in twenty-four thousand verses, without the digressions and upakathas; the learned recognise only these as the Bhaarata. Later, he composed an outline in one hundred and fifty verses, comprising the introduction and the chapter of contents. This he first taught to his son Suka; and after, he gave it to some of his other sishyas, who possessed the same gifts as his son.

After this, he composed another six hundred thousand verses. Of these, thirty lakhs are known in the world of the Devas; fifteen hundred thousand in the world of the Pitrs; fourteen lakhs among the Gandharvas, and one hundred thousand in the world of men. Narada recited these to the Devas; Devala to the Pitrs; and Suka to the Gandharvas, Yakshas and Rakshasas. In this world, they were recited by Vaisampayana, one of Vyasa's disciples, a man of dharma and foremost among the knowers of the Veda.

Know that I, Sauti Ugrasrava, have also repeated one hundred thousand verses.

Yudhishtira is a vast tree, formed of adhyatma and dharma; Arjuna is its trunk; Bhimasena, its branches; the two sons of Madri are its fruit and flowers; and its roots are Krishna, Brahma, and the Brahmanas.

After he had subdued many kingdoms by his wisdom and prowess, Pandu went to stay with some Munis in a forest. He came to hunt, but brought misfortune upon himself when he killed a stag in the act of mating with its hind. This became a warning that guided the conduct of the princes of his house, his sons, throughout their lives.

To fulfil the laws of grihasta, Kunti and Madri invoked the Devas – Dharma, Vayu, Indra; and the divinities – the twin Aswins, and these gods sired sons upon them. Their sons grew up in the care of their two mothers, in the society of hermits, in the midst of tapovanas and holy asramas of Rishis. Then the Rishis brought the sons of Pandu to Hastinapura, into the presence of Dhritarashtra and his sons; they came wearing the habits of brahmacharis, following their masters as students, with their hair tied in topknots on their heads.

"These sishyas of ours," said the Rishis, "are as your sons, your brothers, and your friends; they are Pandavas." Saying this, the Munis vanished.

When the Kauravas heard they were the sons of Pandu, the noble ones among them shouted for great joy. Others, however, said they were not the sons of Pandu; others said they were; while a few asked how they could be his sons, when he had been dead for so long.

Yet voices on all sides cried, "They are welcome! Through divine Providence we see the family of Pandu again! Let their welcome be proclaimed!"

When the people fell silent, a great applause of invisible spirits rang everywhere, so every direction of the sky echoed. Showers of divinely fragrant flowers fell upon the Earth, and the deep sound of conches and batteries of kettledrums was heard when the young princes arrived. The joy of all the citizens reverberated from Bhumi, the Earth, and reached back up into Swarga, the Heavens.

The Pandavas had already imbibed the Vedas and the other Shastras, and they began living in Hastinapura, respected by all and fearing none.

Men of influence in the city were pleased by the purity of Yudhishtira, the strength of Bhima, the valour of Arjuna, the submissiveness of Kunti to her elders, and the humility of the twins, Nakula and Sahadeva; and the people rejoiced in their noble traits.

Later, Arjuna won the virgin Krishnaa[1] at her swayamvara, in a great gathering of kings, by performing an incredibly difficult feat of archery.

---

[1]Krishnaa is Panchali, the Pandavas' wife, while Krishna is the Avatara. Both are dark.

Then on, he was revered in this world as the greatest bowman; and upon fields of battle, too, like the Sun, his enemies could hardly face him: so brilliant was he, so superior. And having vanquished all the neighbouring Kshatriyas and every considerable tribe, he enabled the Raja Yudhishtira, his eldest brother, to perform the greatest martial sacrifice, the Rajasuya yagna.

With the knowing and shrewd counsel of Krishna and by the valour of Bhimasena and Arjuna, Yudhishtira slew Jarasandha, the hitherto invincible king of Magadha, and the proud Chaidya Sishupala. Then, he had indeed gained the right to perform the grand and superabundant Rajasuya yagna, which bestows transcendent punya, spiritual merit.

Duryodhana came to this sacrifice. He saw the vast wealth of the Pandavas, in evidence everywhere, the bounty of the offerings, the precious stones, gold and ornaments. He saw their wealth in the form of cows, elephants and horses; the rare silks, brocades, garments and mantles; the precious shawls and furs and carpets, made of the skin of the Ranku deer. Envy and grief welled up inside him.

And when he saw the great and exquisite sabha of Mayaa Danava, the Asura architect, as wonderful as any unearthly court, he burned with rage and jealousy. When he was deceived by some cunning architectural illusions that Mayaa had created in his sabha, Bhimasena mocked him heartily in the presence of Krishnaa Draupadi; he laughed at his cousin as he might at a servant.

News came to Dhritarashtra, that, though his son Duryodhana was surrounded by every luxury and indulging in every pleasure, and lived amidst untold riches, he was pale and wasting away, as if from some secret sickness. In a while, out of his excessive fondness for his eldest son, Dhritarashtra gave his consent to their playing a game of dice against the sons of Pandu.

When Vasudeva Krishna heard about this, he was furious. Yet, he did nothing to prevent the game of dice, and the terrible consequences that accrued from it for the Pandavas. Despite Vidura, Bhishma, Drona, and Kripa, the son of Saradwan, Krishna stoked the fire that caused the awesome war that ensued, and consumed the very race of Kshatriyas.

When Dhritarashtra heard the dreadful news that the Pandavas had won the war, he remembered the resolves of Duryodhana, Karna and Shakuni. He pondered in silence for a while, then, spoke to Sanjaya, his sarathy and counsellor.

"Listen carefully, Sanjaya, to everything I am about to say, and let it be beneath you to treat me contemptuously. You know the Shastras well; you are intelligent and wise. I was never in favour of fighting the war, and I took no delight in the destruction of my race. I made no distinction between my own children and the children of Pandu. My sons were wilful and despised me because of my age and infirmity. Being blind and powerless, and because I loved my sons as every father does, I suffered it all.

I was foolish, and my thoughtless Duryodhana's folly grew day by day. In Indraprastha, he saw the wealth and incomparable power of the mighty sons of Pandu. They mocked him for his clumsiness in the Mayaa sabha. He could not bear it, and yet neither could he face the Pandavas in battle. Though he was a Kshatriya, he dared not attempt to find fortune by fighting an honourable war. Instead, he sought the help of the king of Gandhara and contrived a game of dice. It was not a fair game, for the dice Shakuni used were loaded.

Hear, Sanjaya, all that happened thereafter and came to my knowledge. And when you have heard what I say, remember everything as it transpired, and you will know that I had prophetic foresight of what would happen finally.

When I heard that Arjuna bent the bow, pierced the difficult target, brought it down, and took the young woman Krishnaa triumphantly, under the eyes of the assembled Kshatriyas, already, O Sanjaya, I knew we could never hope to prevail.

Then I heard Arjuna had married Subhadra of the race of Madhu, in gandharva vivaha, by the rite of abduction, in the city of Dwaraka. I heard that her brothers, Krishna and Balarama, the two heroes of the race of Vrishni, went to Indraprastha, without any resentment and as friends of the Pandavas, and then, O Sanjaya, I had no hope that we could prevail.

I heard that Arjuna, with uncanny archery, held up the storm sent down by his father Indra, king of the Devas. I heard that Arjuna had pleased Agni by giving him the forest of Khandhava to consume, and then, O Sanjaya, I lost hope of success.

When I heard that the five Pandavas with their mother Kunti had escaped from the house of lac, and that Vidura had helped them effect their escape, then, O Sanjaya, I had no hope of success.

When I heard that, after having pierced the mark in the arena, Arjuna had won Draupadi, and that the brave Panchalas had joined the Pandavas, then, O Sanjaya, I knew we would never have victory.

When I heard that Jarasandha, crown jewel of the royal line of Magadha, and sunlike among all Kshatriyas, had been slain by Bhima with his bare hands, then, O Sanjaya, I knew we had no hope of prevailing.

When I heard that the sons of Pandu had vanquished the kings of all the kingdoms throughout the land and performed the imperial Rajasuya yagna, then, O Sanjaya, I knew our cause was lost. When I heard that Draupadi, her voice choking with tears, full of agony, and in her period, wearing a single cloth, had been dragged into our court, and though she had protectors, had been treated as if she had none, then, O Sanjaya, I had no hope of success. When I heard that my evil wretch Dushasana was trying to strip her of that single garment, but could only pull reams of many-hued cloth from her body into a heap, but not arrive at its end, then, O Sanjaya, I had no hope of success. When I heard that, beaten by Shakuni at the game of dice and deprived of his kingdom, Yudhishtira still had his invincible brothers with him, then, O Sanjaya, I had no hope of ever prevailing. When I heard that the righteous Pandavas wept in shame and torment, when they followed their elder brother into the wilderness and occupied themselves variously to lessen his discomfort, then, O Sanjaya, I had no hope of success. When I heard that Snatakas and other noble Brahmanas, who live by alms, had followed

Yudhishtira into the wilderness, then, O Sanjaya, I had no hope of succeeding. When I heard that Arjuna had pleased the God of gods, Tryambaka, the three-eyed, who came disguised as a hunter, and that he received the Pasupatastra from Siva, then, O Sanjaya, I had no hope of success. When I heard that the honest and renowned Arjuna had gone to Devaloka, and had obtained Devastras there from Indra himself then, O Sanjaya, I knew we could never win. When I heard that Arjuna had vanquished the Kalakeyas and the Paulomas, arrogant with the boon they had which made them invulnerable even to the Devas, then, O Sanjaya, I had no hope of victory. When I heard that Arjuna Parantapa, scourge of his enemies, had been to the realm of Indra to kill those Asuras, and had returned victorious, then, O Sanjaya, I knew we were doomed. When I heard that Bhima and the other sons of Pritha, accompanied by Vaisravana, had arrived in the country that is inaccessible to man, then, O Sanjaya, I had no hope of success. When I heard that my sons, misled by Karna's advice, while on their Ghoshayatra, had been taken prisoners by the Gandharvas and then freed by Arjuna, then, O Sanjaya, I had no hope of succeeding. When I heard that Dharma, the God of Justice, came as a Yaksha and asked Yudhishtira some questions about dharma, then, O Sanjaya, I had no hope of success. When I heard that my sons had failed to discover the Pandavas in disguise, while they lived with Draupadi in the kingdom of Virata, then, O Sanjaya, I had no hope of success. When I heard that the great Kshatriyas of my kingdom had all been vanquished by Arjuna, by himself, in a single chariot, in the country of Virata, then, O Sanjaya, I had no hope of success. When I heard that Vasudeva of the race of Madhu, who covered this Earth with one stride, was committed to the welfare of the Pandavas, then, O Sanjaya, I had no hope of success. When I heard that the king of the Matsyas had offered his virtuous daughter Uttaraa to Arjuna and that Arjuna had accepted her for his son Abhimanyu, then, O Sanjaya, I had no hope of success. When I heard that Yudhishtira, beaten at dice, his wealth and kingdom snatched from him, exiled and his old connections severed, had still assembled an army of seven Akshauhinis, then, O Sanjaya, I had no hope of victory. When I heard Narada declare that Krishna and Arjuna were Nara and Narayana and that he, Narada, had seen them together in Brahmaloka, then, O Sanjaya, I had no hope of being victorious. When I heard that Krishna was anxious to make peace, for the good of humankind, and came to the Kurus, but went away without having been able to accomplish his mission, then, O Sanjaya, I had no hope of success. When I heard that Karna and Duryodhana resolved on imprisoning Krishna, but he revealed his Viswarupa, his body the Universe, then, O Sanjaya, I had no hope of success. When I heard that as he was leaving Hastinapura, Pritha stood, sorrowing, near his chariot and Krishna consoled her, then, O Sanjaya, I had no hope that we could have victory. When I heard that Vasudeva and Bhishma, son of Shantanu, counselled the Pandavas and that Drona, son of Bharadwaja, blessed them, then, O Sanjaya, I had no hope of succeeding. When Karna said to Bhishma, 'I will not fight while you are fighting', and left the field, then, O Sanjaya, I had no hope of winning the war. When I heard that Krishna, Arjuna, and the bow Gandiva of untold prowess these three of fearsome tejas, energy had come together, then, O Sanjaya, I had no hope of victory. When I heard that Arjuna was seized by compunction in his chariot and ready to abandon the war, but Krishna showed him all the worlds within his body, then, O Sanjaya, I had no hope that we could prevail. When I heard that Bhishma, the desolator of our enemies, who killed ten thousand warriors every day in battle, had not slain any of the Pandavas, then, O Sanjaya, I had no hope. When I heard that Bhishma, the righteous son of Ganga, himself told the sons of Pandu how he could be slain in battle, and that the Pandavas slew him joyfully, then, O Sanjaya, I had no hope of succeeding. When I heard that Arjuna placed Sikhandin before himself in his chariot, and shot the invincible Bhishma of boundless courage with a torrent of arrows, then, O Sanjaya, I had no hope of success. When I heard that the aged Kshatriya Bhishma, having all but razed the race of Shomaka, was felled and lay upon a bed of arrows, then, O Sanjaya, I had no hope of being victorious. When I heard that upon Bhishma's being thirsty and asking for water, Arjuna pierced the ground with the Parjannyastra and quenched his thirst, then, O Sanjaya, I had no hope of success. When Vayu, with Indra and Surya, united as allies for the success of the sons of Kunti, and beasts of prey terrified our legions by their inauspicious presence, then, O Sanjaya, I had no hope of success. When the exceptional warrior Drona, though he showed a myriad marvellous varieties of the art of war, did not slay any of the Pandavas, then, O Sanjaya, I lost hope that we might win. When I heard that the Maharatha Samsaptakas of our army who meant to bring Arjuna down were all killed by Arjuna, then, O Sanjaya, I had no hope of success. When I heard that our impenetrable vyuha, guarded by the mighty Drona, had been cloven, singly, and entered by Subhadra's valiant son, O Sanjaya, I lost hope of victory. When I heard that our Maharathas, unable to vanquish Arjuna, had surrounded and murdered the boy Abhimanyu, and crowed over this slaughter with beaming faces, then, O Sanjaya, I lost hope of success. When I heard that the foolish Kauravas shouted for joy after killing Abhimanyu and that the enraged Arjuna swore to kill Jayadratha, then, O Sanjaya, I had no hope of succeeding. When I heard that Arjuna fulfilled his vow in the face of all his enemies, then, O Sanjaya, I had no hope. When I heard that when Arjuna's horses were overcome with tiredness, Krishna unyoked them, made them drink and harnessed them again before he brought them back into battle, Sanjaya, I lost every hope. When I heard that while his horses were exhausted and went to drink, Arjuna remained in his chariot and held all his attackers at bay, Sanjaya, I knew our cause was lost. When I heard that Satyaki of the race of Vrishni struck panic into the invincible elephant legions of the army of Drona and rode easily to the side of Krishna and Arjuna, then, Sanjaya, I had no hope of victory. When I heard that after having Bhimasena helpless and in the eye of his arrow, Karna allowed him to escape with his life, only taunting him and dragging him a short way with the end of his bow, then, O Sanjaya, I had no hope of success. When I heard that Drona, Kritavarma, Kripa, Karna, Aswatthama, and the heroic Salya, king of Madra could not prevent the slaying of Saindhava Jayadratha, then, O Sanjaya, I had no hope of success. When I heard that Krishna's cunning made Karna use the celestial Sakti, given him by Indra, against the Rakshasa Ghatotkacha of the dreadful visage, then, Sanjaya, I had no hope of success. When I heard that in the duel between Karna and Ghatotkacha, that Sakti, which could surely have slain Arjuna, had been cast at Ghatotkacha, Sanjaya, I lost hope again. When I heard that Dhristadyumna broke every law of honourable battle, and slew Drona who sat alone, unresisting and determined to die in his chariot, then, O Sanjaya, I lost every hope. When I heard that Madri's son Nakula engaged Aswatthama in single combat before both armies, proved equal to Drona's son and drove his chariot in circles around Aswatthama, then, O Sanjaya, I had no hope of victory. When, upon the death of Drona, his son invoked the Narayanastra but failed to consume the Pandavas, then, Sanjaya, I had no hope. When I heard that Bhimasena drank the blood of his brother Dushasana on the battlefield without anybody being able to stop him, then, O Sanjaya, I had no hope of victory. When I heard that the boundlessly valiant, invincible Karna was slain by Arjuna in that duel between brothers, mysterious even to the gods, then, Sanjaya, I had no hope of success. When I heard that Yudhisthira Dharmaraja defeated the ıameless Aswatthama, Dushasana, and the fierce Kritavarma, too, then, O Sanjaya, I had no hope of victory. When I heard that Yudhishtira killed the brave king of Madra, who always dared Krishna to do battle with him, then, O Sanjaya, I had no hope of success. When I heard that the evil Shakuni, who owned occult powers, who was the very root of the gambling, and indeed, all the bitter feud, was slain by Pandu's son Sahadeva, then, O Sanjaya, I lost hope of success. When I heard that the exhausted Duryodhana fled to a lake and sought sanctuary in its waters, lying there alone, his strength gone and without a chariot, then, O Sanjaya, I had no hope of succeeding. When I heard that the Pandavas arrived at that lake with Krishna, and standing on its shore, called out contemptuously, tauntingly to my son, who could never tolerate an insult, then, O Sanjaya, I had no hope of prevailing. When I heard that while, after showing in circles a dazzling array of innovative styles of gada yuddha, he was unfairly struck down, at Krishna's behest, then, Sanjaya, I had no hope of victory. When I heard that Aswatthama and his confederates slaughtered the Panchalas and the sons of Draupadi in their sleep, a horrible and dastardly deed, then, O Sanjaya, I had no hope of victory. When I heard that, pursued by Bhima, Aswatthama discharged the first of weapons, Aishika, which direly wounded the embryo in the womb of Uttaraa, then, O Sanjaya, I had no hope of winning. When I heard that Arjuna repulsed Aswatthama's astra, the Brahmashira, with another weapon over which he pronounced the word Sasti, and that Aswatthama had then to give up the jewel-like growth on his head, then, O Sanjaya, I lost all hope. When I heard that upon the embryo in the womb of Virata's daughter being wounded by Aswatthama with a mahastra, Dwaipayana and Krishna pronounced curses on Drona's son, then, O Sanjaya, I lost every hope.

Alas! I must pity Gandhari, childless now, all her grandchildren slain, her parents, brothers and kindred gone. Oh, hard indeed has been the achievement of the Pandavas: they have recovered a kingdom and left no rival to challenge them.

Alas! I have heard that the war has left only ten alive: three from our side, and from the Pandavas', seven; that dreadful war has claimed eighteen Akshauhinis of Kshatriyas, all slain! All around me is darkness, and a swoon comes over me. Consciousness leaves me, Sanjaya, and my mind is far from me."'

Suta said, 'Thus bemoaning his fate, Dhritarashtra was overcome by anguish and swooned for a while; when he revived, he addressed Sanjaya again.

"After what has happened, Sanjaya, I want to put an end to my life at once; I find not the slightest advantage in preserving it any longer."'

Suta said, 'Sanjaya, wise son of Gavalgana, now interrupted the distraught lord of Earth, who lamented thus and sighed like a serpent, repeatedly fainting. Words of deep import spoke Sanjaya.

"You have heard, O Rajan, of the mighty men of immense valour, spoken of by Vyasa and the Rishi Narada: Kshatriyas born of royal families, splendid with every quality, versed in astras, glorious like amsas of Indra; men who conquered the world with dharma and performed sacrifices with offerings to Brahmanas, who having obtained renown in this world, at last succumbed to time. Such men were Saibya, the valiant Maharatha; Srinjaya, great amongst conquerors; Suhotra; Rantideva and the magnificent Kakshivanta; Balhika, Damana, Saryati, Ajita, and Nala; Viswamitra, destroyer of foes; Ambarisha, of matchless strength; Marutta, Manu, Ikshvaku, Gaya, and Bhaarata; Rama the son of Dasaratha; Sasabindu and Bhagiratha; Kritavirya, the fortunate, and Janamejaya; Yayati of untold punya who performed mahayagnas, in which the Devas themselves assisted him, and by whose vedis and stambas this entire Bhumi, with her peopled and uninhabited realms, is marked. The Devarishi Narada spoke of these twenty-four kings once to Saibya, when that king grieved over the loss of his children.

Besides these, other rajas had gone before, still more powerful, Maharathas of noble mind, resplendent with every worthy quality: Puru, Kuru, Yadu, Sura and Viswasrava of great glory; Anuha, Yuvanaswa, Kakutstha, Vikrami, and Raghu; Vijaya, Vitihorta, Anga, Bhava, Sweta, and Vripadguru; Usinara, Sataratha, Kanka, Duliduha, and Druma; Dambhodbhava, Para, Vena, Sagara, Sankriti, and Nimi; Ajeya, Parasu, Pundra, Sambhu, and holy Devavridha; Devahuya, Supratika, and Brihadratha; Mahatsaha, Vinitatma, Shukratu, and Nala, the king of the Nishadas; Satyavrata, Santabhaya, Sumitra, and Subala; Janujangha, Anaranya, Arka, Priyabhritya, Chuchi-vrata, Balabandhu, Nirmardda, Ketusringa, and Brhidbala; Dhrishtaketu, Brihatketu, Driptaketu, and Niramaya; Abikshit, Chapala, Dhurta, Kritabandhu, and Dridheshudhi; Mahapurana-sambhavya, Pratyanga, Paraha and Sruti. These, O Rajan, and other kings, we hear enumerated in hundreds and thousands, and still others in millions, princes of power and wisdom, who renounced abundant kingdom and pleasures and met death just as your sons have done. Their dharma, valour and generosity, their magnanimity, faith, truth, purity, simplicity and mercy have been recorded for the world by holy pauranikas of bygone ages, men of great gyana. Though endowed with every noble virtue, they yielded up their lives. Your sons were malevolent, inflamed by passion, greedy and evil. You are versed in the Shastras, O Bhaarata[2], and are intelligent and wise; those whose hearts are guided by the Shastras never succumb to misfortune. You, O Kshatriya, know both the kindness and severity of fate; this anxiety for your children does not become you. It does not befit you to grieve over the inevitable: for who can avert the dictates of inelucatable fate? No one can escape the path marked out for him by Providence. Existence and non-existence, pleasure and pain, all have Time as their root. Time creates all things and Time destroys all creatures. It is Time that burns living beings and Time that extinguishes the fire. All conditions, good and evil, in the three worlds, are caused by Time. Time cuts short all things and creates them anew. Time is awake when all other things sleep; Time cannot be overcome. Time passes over all things without being slowed by any. Knowing, as you do, that all things past and future and all that is in the present moment are children of Time, it does not befit you to cast aside your reason."'

Sauti said, 'Thus, Sanjaya comforted the king Dhritarashtra, overwhelmed by grief for his sons, and restored some calm to his mind. And using these arguments of Sanjaya for his subject, Dwaipayana composed a holy Upanishad that has been given to the world by learned and holy Pauranikas in the Puranas they composed.

The study of the Mahabharata is an act of piety. He that reads a mere foot of it, with faith, has his sins washed away entirely. Here, Devas, Devarishis, and immaculate Brahmarishis of punya have been spoken of; likewise, Yakshas and great Uragas, the Nagas. Here also the eternal Vasudeva, possessed of the six attributes, is described. He is the truth, and just, the pure and holy, the eternal Brahman, the Paramatman, the constant light, whose divine deeds the Sages recount; from whom the manifest and unmanifest Universe, with its principles of generation

[2]Bharata is used for the great king of that name, and Bhaarata for his descendants. Of course, the land of Bharata, Bharatavarsha, is named after King Bharata, the Great.

and evolution, and birth, death and rebirth issue. That which is called Adhyatma, the Sovereign Spirit of nature, that partakes of the attributes of the Panchamahabhuta, the five elements, is described here. Adhyatma has also been called Purusha, being above such names as 'unmanifest' and the rest; it is also that which the greatest Yatis, who are exempt from common destiny and endowed with the power of dhyana and tapas, behold abiding in their hearts,rather like a reflected image in a mirror.

When the man of faith, devoted to piety, and constant in virtue, reads this canto, he is set free from sin. The believer who constantly hears this canto of the Bhaarata, the Introduction, being recited, from the beginning, never falls into difficulties. The man that repeats any part of the introduction during the two sandhyas of dawn and dusk is freed from the sins he commits during the day or the night. This canto, the very body of the Bhaarata, is truth and nectar. As butter is to curd, the Brahmana among bipeds, the Aranyaka among the Vedas, and Amrita among medicaments, as the sea is among water bodies, and the cow among quadrupeds, so is the Bhaarata among Itihasas, great legends.

He that causes it, even a single metre of it, to be recited to Brahmanas during a sraddha, his offerings of food and drink to the manes of his Pitrs become inexhaustible.

With the help of Itihasas and the Puranas, the Veda might be expounded; but the Veda fears the man of small intellect lest he should try to expound the scripture. The learned man who recites this Bhaarata Veda of Vyasa finds great gain; why, he is saved from the sin of killing a child in the womb, apart from other heinous sins. He that reads this holy chapter of the Moon as good as reads the entire Bhaarata. The man who listens daily, with reverence, to this sacred work acquires long life and renown, and finds Swarga for himself.

In elder days, the Devas placed the four Vedas on one side of a balance and the Bhaarata on the other, and weighed them against each other. Since the Bhaarata was found to be weightier than the four Vedas with their mysteries, then on it was called the Mahabharata, the great Bhaarata. It has been judged to be superior to the Vedas both in substance and gravity. He who fathoms its meaning is released from all his sins.

Tapa is innocent, study is harmless; the codes for living that the Vedas prescribe for all the tribes are harmless; the acquisition of wealth by exertion is not injurious; but when these are abused in their practice, they become sources of evil.'

CANTO 2

Parva Samgraha Continued

The Rishis said, 'O son of Suta, we want to hear in detail from you about the place that you called Samanta-panchaka.'

Suta said, 'Listen, O Brahmanas, to these sacred descriptions. Best of men, you deserve to hear about the place known as Samanta-panchaka. In the hiatus between the Treta and Dwapara Yugas, the mighty Rama, son of Jamadagni, greatest among those that ever bore arms, was infuriated by the sins of the noble race of Kshatriyas and savaged them repeatedly. And when that meteorlike Brahmana annihilated the entire race of Kshatriyas, single-handedly, he formed at Samanta-panchaka five lakes of blood. We hear that he lost his reason from anger and offered oblations of blood to the manes of his ancestors, standing in the sanguine waters of those lakes.

His Pitrs, of whom Richika was first, arrived there and said to him, "Rama, O blessed Rama, O scion of Bhrigu, we are appeased and gratified by the worship that you have offered your ancestors. We are pleased by your valour, O mighty one! Our blessings are upon you. Illustrious one, ask for any boon that you want."

Rama said, "If, O Sires, you are favourably disposed towards me, the boon I ask is that I be absolved from the sins born of my having slaughtered the Kshatriyas in fury, and that these lakes that I have made become famed in the world as holy tirthas."

The Pitrs said, "So be it, but now be pacified."

And Rama was pacified. From that time, the region around those lakes of blood has been Samanta-panchaka, a holy tirtha. The wise have said that every country must have a name significant of some special circumstance that might have made it renowned. The Great War between the armies of the Kauravas and the Pandavas was fought at Samanta-panchaka, on the cusp between the Dwapara and the Kali Yugas. In that holy place, even and without ruggedness of any kind, eighteen Akshauhinis of warriors gathered, eager for battle. And, O Brahmanas, having come there, they were all slain: hence the name Samanta-panchaka for that sacred and most delightful place, which is renowned and celebrated through the three Lokas.'

The Rishis said, 'We want to know, O son of Suta, what the term Akshauhini means. Tell us in detail how many horses, footsoldiers, chariots and elephants comprise an Akshauhini, for you certainly know this.'

Sauti said, 'One chariot, one elephant, five footsoldiers, and three horses form one Patti; three pattis make one Sena-mukha; three sena-mukhas are called a Gulma; three gulmas, a Gana; three ganas, a Vahini; three vahinis together are called a Pritana; three pritanas form a Chamu; three chamus, one Anikini; and ten anikinis form, as it is called by the experts, an Akshauhini. O Brahmanottama, best among Brahmanas, mathematicians calculate that the number of chariots in an Akshauhini is twenty-one thousand eight hundred and seventy. The number of elephants is the same. Pure ones, the number of footsoldiers is one hundred and nine thousand, three hundred and fifty; the number of horses is sixty-five thousand, six hundred and ten. These, O Brahmanas, are the numbers of an Akshauhini, as decided by those that know numbers. Best of Brahmanas, the eighteen Akshauhinis of the Kaurava and the Pandava armies were made up according to these numbers. Time, Kaala, whose acts are wonderful, gathered them in that place and, making the Kauravas the cause for the war, slew them all.

Bhishma, master of astras, fought for ten days. Drona led the Kaurava Vahinis for five days. Karna, the desolator of his foes, was the Kaurava Senapati for two days; and Salya for half a day. Then, the gada yuddha between Duryodhana and Bhima lasted for half a day. When that day ended, Aswatthama and Kripa massacred the remnants of Yudhishtira's army, while the Panchalas and Draupadi's sons slept with no fear of danger.

O Saunaka, this best of narrations called the Bhaarata, which I have begun to relate at your yagna, was once told at the sacrifice of Janamejaya by a most intelligent disciple of Vyasa. It is divided into many cantos. In the beginning are the Paushya, Pauloma and Astika Parvas, which describe in detail the valour and fame of kings. This is a work whose descriptions, diction and meanings are varied and extraordinary. It contains accounts of numerous customs and rituals. It is accepted by the Sages as the state called Vairagya by men who wish for mukti. As the Atman among things to be known, as life among things that are dear, so is this Itihasa, which provides the means of coming to the knowledge of Brahman, the first among all the Shastras. There is not a story that exists in this world that does not depend on this legend, even as the body depends upon the food that it consumes. As masters of noble lineage are always served by servants that desire advancement, so is the Bhaarata cherished by all poets. Words that form the numberless branches of knowledge that pertain to the world and the Veda show just vowels and consonants; this excellent legend displays only the highest wisdom.

Listen, O Rishis, to the outlines of the several Parvas of this Itihasa called the Bhaarata, replete with deep wisdom, of chapters and meters that are varied and wondrous, of subtle meanings and logical interconnections, and embellished with the essence of the Vedas.

The first Parva is called Anukramanika; the second, Sangraha; then Paushya; then Pauloma; then Astika; then Adivansavatarana. Then comes the Sambhava of enthralling events. Then comes the Jatugri-hadaha (the burning of the house of lac) and then the Hidimba-vadha (the killing of Hidimba) Parvas. Next comes Baka-vadha (the slaying of Baka) and then Chitraratha. The next Parva is called Swayamvara (where Panchali chooses a husband), in which Arjuna won Draupadi's hand. Then comes Vaivahika (marriage), followed by Viduragamana (the advent of Vidura), Rajyalabha (the acquisition of a kingdom), Arjuna-vanavasa (the exile of Arjuna) and Subhadra-harana (the abduction of Subhadra). After these we find Harana-harika, Khandava-daha (the burning of the Khandava forest) and Mayaa-darshana (the meeting with Mayaa, the Asura architect). Then we come to Sabha, Mantra, Jarasandha, Digvijaya (the conquest of the four quarters). After Digvijaya come Rajasuyaka, Arghyaviharana (the theft of the Arghya) and Sisupala-vadha (the killing of Sisupala). After these, Dyuta (gambling), Anudyuta (the second game of dice), Aranyaka (in the forest), and Krimira-vadha (the killing of Krimira). The Arjuna-vigamana (the journeys of Arjuna), Kairati, in which the battle between Arjuna and Mahadeva in the guise of a Kirata hunter is described. After this Indraloka-vigamana (the journey to the realm of Indra); then follows that treasure trove of dharma and virtue, the Nalopakhyana (the story of Nala, full of pathos). After this, there follows Tirtha-yatra or the pilgrimage of Yudhishtira, the death of Jatasura, and the battle with the Yakshas. Then the battle with the Nivatakavachas, Ajagara, and Markandeya-samasya (the meeting with Markandeya). Then the meeting of Draupadi and Satyabhama, Ghoshayatra, Mriga-swapna (the dream of the deer). Then comes the story of Brihadaranyaka and then Aindradrumna; then Draupadi-harana (the abduction of Draupadi), Jayadratha-vimoksana (the release of Jayadratha). Then the story of Savitri, which illustrates the great punya and power of marital chastity. After this, we shall come to the story of Rama. The next Parva is called Kundala-harana (the theft of the earrings), and after that Aranya and then Vairata. Then the arrival of the Pandavas in the Matsya kingdom, and how they kept their ajnatavasa, of living undiscovered for one year. We come next to the killing of the Kichakas, then the attempt by the Kauravas to steal to take the cattle of Virata. The next Parva is named after the marriage of Abhimanyu to Uttaraa, the daughter of Virata. The next is a wonderful Parva called Udyoga, of deliberations, followed by Sanjaya-yana (the journey of Sanjaya). Then comes Prajagara (the insomnia of Dhritarashtra from anxiety). Then Sanatsujata, which contains the mysteries of spiritual philosophy. Then Yanasaddhi, and then the arrival of Krishna. Then the story of Matali and then of Galava. Then follow the stories of Savitri, Vamadeva, and Vainya; after which we find the story of Jamadagnya and Shodasarajika. Next, Krishna arrives in the Kuru court, and then Vidulaputrasasana. Then the mustering of the armies and the story of Sheta. Then comes the quarrel of the noble Karna with Bhishma, after which both armies march on Kurukshetra. The next has been named for the enumeration of the Rathis and Atirathas. Then the messenger Uluka comes to the Pandavas, bringing Duryodhana's message that kindles the wrath of the sons of Pandu. Then we come to the story of Amba, followed by the enthralling description of the installation of Bhishma as the Kaurava Senapati. The next Parva deals with the creation of Jambudwipa; then of Bhumi; then the description of the formation of all the dwipas, the island continents. Then, the Bhagavad-Gita; followed by the fall of Bhishma. Drona is made Senapati; after which Arjuna razes the Samsaptakas. The death of Abhimanyu, followed by the vow of Arjuna to kill Jayadratha before the Sun sets. The death of Jayadratha is followed by the killing of Ghatotkacha. Then, you must know, comes the story of the extraordinary death of Drona, and after that the loosing of the Narayana astra. Then, as you know, is the command of Karna, and that of Salya. We come to Duryodhana's immersion in the lake, and the gada yuddha between Bhima and Duryodhana. This is followed by Saraswata, then the descriptions of holy shrines and tirthas, and then genealogies. Then comes Sauptika that tells of events that bring disgrace upon the honour of the Kurus, followed by the Aisika of harrowing events in the night. Next comes Jalapradana, oblations of water offered to the manes of the dead, and then the lamentation of the women, in Stree Parva. The next Parva must be called Sraddha since it describes the funeral rites performed for the slain Kauravas. Next the Rakshasa Charvaka, who disguised himself as a Brahmana to deceive Yudhishtira, is slain. Then the wise and gentle Yudhishtira is crowned in Hastinapura. The next Parva is Grihapravibhaga, followed by Santi, Rajadharmanusasana, Apaddharma, and Mokshadharma. The Parvas that follow are Sukaprasna-abhigamana, Brahmaprasnanusana, the origin of Durvasa, and the disputations with Mayaa. The next is the Anusasanika Parva, which is followed by the ascension of Bhishma. Then the account of the Rajasuya yagna, listening to which all one's sins are washed away. The next Parva is the Anugita. Those that follow are called Asrainvasa, Puttradarshana (meeting the spirits of the dead), and the arrival of Narada. The next Parva is Mausala, full of dreadful and savage happenings. Then comes Mahaprasthanika Parva and the ascension into Swarga. Then comes the Purana called Khilvansa, which contains Vishnuparva, Vishnu's games and exploits as a child, the killing of Kamsa, and finally, the truly amazing Bhavishyaparva, with its uncanny prophecies about the future.

The Maharishi Vyasa composed a hundred Parvas (the above are only some of them). Dividing them into eighteen books, large Parvas, Ugrasrava, the son of Suta Romaharshana narrated them in the Naimisha vana.'

Said Suta, 'The Adi Parva contains Paushya, Pauloma, Astika, Adivansa-vatara, Sambhava, Jatugrihadahana, Hidimbavadha, Bakavadha, Chitraratha, Draupadi Swayamvara, Vaivahika, Viduragamana, Rajyalabha, Arjuna vanavasa, Subhadraharana, Harana harika, Khandava dahana, and Mayaa darshana.

The Paushya Parva deals with the greatness of Utanka, and the Pauloma Parva, of the sons of Bhrigu. The Astika describes the birth of Garuda and of the Nagas, the churning of the Ocean, the birth of the celestial steed Uchchaishrava, and finally, the dynasty of Bhaarata: all as described during the Sarpa yagna of King Janamejaya.

The Sambhava Parva describes the birth of numerous kings and heroes, and that of the Rishi Krishna Dwaipayana: the amsavataras of the devas, the generation of Danavas and Yakshas of great power, and

Nagas, Gandharvas, Avians, and indeed of all creatures; and finally, the life and adventures of King Bhaarata—progenitor of the royal line named for him—the son born to Shakuntala in the asrama of the Rishi Kanva. This Parva also describes the greatness of Ganga, the births of the Vasus into the house of Shantanu and their ascension into heaven. This Parva also tells of the birth of Bhishma, who had in himself amsas of the divine energies of the other Vasus, his renunciation of the throne and his vow of brahmacharya, his guardianship of Chitrangada, and after the death of Chitrangada, his stewardship of the younger brother, Vichitravirya, and his crowning of Vichitravirya. This Parva tells of the birth of Dharma among men because of the curse of Animandavya; of the births of Dhritarashtra and Pandu through the seed of Vyasa, and the birth of the Pandavas.

Jatugriha Parva decribes Duryodhana's plot to send the sons of Pandu to Varanavata, and the evil intentions of the sons of Dhritarashtra towards the Pandavas. We shall hear the advice that Vidura, their well-wisher, gave Yudhishtira as the Pandavas left for Varanavrata, in the mlechchha bhasha. The Parva goes on to describe the excavation of a tunnel, the immolation of Purochana and the woman of the fowler caste, with her five sons, in the house of lac.

Hidimba-vadha Parva continues with the Pandavas meeting Hidimbi in the dreadful jungle, and how Bhima of untold strength kills her brother Hidimba. The birth of Ghatotkacha follows; the meeting of the Pandavas with Vyasa, who sends them to the town called Ekachakra to live disguised as Brahmanas themselves in the house of a Brahmana.

Baka-vadha Parva tells of the slaying of the Asura Baka, and of the amazement of the people at the sight of his corpse. The tale of the extraordinary births of Krishnaa and Dhrishtadyumna follows; upon hearing about the swayamvara from a wandering Brahmana, the Pandavas leave for Panchala, also at Vyasa's behest, and equally because they are powerfully stirred to win Draupadi on learning the tidings of the swayamvara.

Chaitraratha Parva tells of how, on the way, Arjuna defeats a Gandharva called Angaraparna on the banks of the Ganga; he befriends his adversary, and the Pandavas hear the history of Tapati, Vasishtha and Aurva from Angaraparna.

Swayamvara Parva describes the journey of the Pandavas towards Panchala, how Arjuna pierces the matsya yantra, while all the rajas fail, and wins Draupadi; in the battle that follows, Salya, Karna and all the other crowned kings are routed by Bhima and Arjuna; Balarama and Krishna see this remarkable performance and realise that these are the Pandavas; the Yadava brothers come to the house of the potter, where the Pandavas are living.

Vaivahika Parva tells how Drupada is horrified to hear that Draupadi will marry five husbands; consequently, Vyasa tells the wonderful story of the five Indras; the extraordinary wedding of Draupadi.

Viduragamana Parva tells how Dhritarashtra's sons send Vidura to the Pandavas as their messenger; Vidura arrives and is overwhelmed at seeing Krishna; the Pandavas in Khandavaprastha, from where they rule over half of the Kuru kingdom.

Rajyalabha Parva tells of how Narada comes to Indraprastha and, at his advice, the Pandavas decide that each of them will spend a year, by turns and exclusively, as Draupadi's husband. Here Narada tells the tragic tale of Sunda and Upasunda.

Arjuna-vanavasa Parva then tells of Arjuna's exile when he intrudes on the privacy of Yudhishtira and Draupadi, when he is forced to enter his brother's apartment to fetch his bow to rescue the cattle of a Brahmana from some thieves. Arjuna meets Ulupi, the Naga Princess, on the way; Arjuna's tirtha yatra; the birth of Babhruvahana; Arjuna delivers five Apsaras from the curse of a Rishi that turned them into ferocious crocodiles.

Subhadra-harana Parva describes Arjuna's meeting with Krishna at holy Prabhasa; encouraged by Krishna, he abducts Subhadra in a wondrous chariot that flies over sea and land, and through the air, at the very thought of the one that rides in it.

Harana-harita Parva tells of how Arjuna leaves for Indraprastha with his wife and her dowry; Subhadra conceives Abhimanyu, the prodigy; Draupadi Yagnaseni gives birth to her children.

Khandava-daha Parva tells how Krishna and Arjuna come to the banks of the Yamuna and acquire the Sudarshana Chakra and the famed bow Gandiva; Arjuna burns the Khandava vana; he rescues Mayaa; Aswasena the Naga escapses the inferno; the Rishi Mandapala fathers a son in the womb of the bird Saringi. Vyasa divided this Parva into two hundred and twenty-seven cantos, containing eight thousand eight hundred and eighty-four slokas.

The second great Parva is the dense Sabha Parva. This Parva tells of the creation of the splendid Mayaa sabha in Indraprastha; Narada describes the Lokapalas and the realms of heaven, which he knows well; the Pandavas prepare for the Rajasuya yagna; the killing of Jarasandha; Krishna delivers the Kshatriyas incarcerated in the mountain-pass; the digvijaya; the Kshatriyas come to the Rajasuya yagna bringing tribute; the death of Sisupala during the sacrifice, over the dispute about the purodasa; Bhimasena ridicules Duryodhana in the sabha; Duryodhana's grief and envy at seeing the grandeur of Indraprastha and the lavishness of the Rajasuya yagna; the preparations for the game of dice; the wily Shakuni beats Yudhishtira at dice; Dhritarashtra releases the grief-stricken Draupadi from the bondage of servitude that Yudhishtira incurs during the gambling; she is like a skiff in a tempest. Duryodhana contrives to engage Yudhishtira in a second game of dice; Yudhishtira loses again and is exiled, with his brothers. These events constitute what Maharishi Vyasa has named the Sabha Parva. This Parva is divided into seventy-eight cantos, O noblest of Brahmanas, of two thousand, five hundred and seven slokas.

The third Parva is called Aranyaka, of the forest. This Parva tells of the Pandavas leaving for the forest; some Brahmanas follow them; at Dhaumya's telling him to, Yudhishtira worships Surya Deva, God of Day, so he can feed the Brahmanas; the gift of the Sun: the magical platter; Dhritarashtra expels Vidura for speaking on the Pandavas' behalf, and for his brother's own good; Vidura goes to the Pandavas and returns to Dhritarashtra when the remorseful king calls him back; incited by Karna, the evil Duryodhana plots to kill the forest-dwelling Pandavas; Vyasa appears and frightens Duryodhana, prevents him from prosecuting his plan; the history of Surabhi; the arrival of Maitreya; Maitreya's discourse to Dhritarashtra on dharma and karma; Maitreya curses the haughty Duryodhana; Bhima kills Kirmira in the forest; the Panchalas and the Vrishni princes learn of the false game of dice, rolled by the deceitful Shakuni, and arrive in the jungle to meet Yudhishtira; Arjuna allays the wrath of Krishna; Draupadi laments before Krishna; Krishna consoles her; the Rishi also describes the fall of Sauba here; Krishna takes Subhadra and her son to Dwaraka; Dhrishtadyumna brings the sons of Draupadi to Panchala; the sons of Pandu enter the charmed Dwaitavana; the exchange of words between Bhima, Yudhishtira, and Draupadi; Vyasa comes to the Pandavas and endows Yudhishtira with the occult power of Pratismriti; the Pandavas repair to Kamyakavana; mighty Arjuna goes in quest of astras; he duels with Siva who comes in the guise of a kirata; Arjuna meets the Lokapalas and receives divine weapons from them; he journeys to Devaloka to receive astras from Indra; the anxiety of Dhritarashtra when he hears this; Yudhishtira laments to the Maharishi Brihadaswa, who tells the sacred and sad story of the noble Nala and Damayanti, who is the very embodiment of patience. Yudhishtira learns the arcane secrets of dice-play from Brihadaswa; Rishi Lomasa arrives from Devaloka, bringing word of and from Arjuna to his noble brothers; the Pandavas journey to the various sacred tirthas across Bharatavarsha, at the word of Indra that Lomasa brings, during which pilgrimage they gain great punya; Narada's pilgrimage to Putasta is described. The magnificence of Gaya; the story of Agastya, where the Rishi devoured the Asura Vatapi, and his union with Lopamudra from the desire for children. The story of Rishyasringa who was a brahmachari from his very boyhood; the legend of Jamadagni's son Rama of untold glory and prowess, which tells of the slaying of Kartavirya and the Haihayas; the Pandavas and the Vrishnis meet at sacred Prabhasa; the story of Sukanya, where Bhrigu's son Chyavana Maharishi makes the

Aswini twins drink Soma rasa, during the sacrifice of king Saryati, while the other Devas had so far kept them away from it; the grateful Aswini twins bless Chyavana with permanent youth. The Parva then tells the story of King Mandhata; the tale of Prince Jantu, who was King Somaka's only son, who his father offered in a sacrifice and received a hundred sons in return; the excellent story of the hawk and the pigeon; Indra, Agni and Dharma test King Sibi; the story of Ashtavakra, where a dispute arises during Janaka's sacrifice, between that Rishi and the great logician, Varuna's son Vandi; Ashtavakra has the better of Vandi, and releases his father from the ocean deep. There follows the story of Yavakrita, then of the great Raivya; the Pandavas leave for Gandhamadana and the asrama called Narayana; for Draupadi, Bhimasena goes after the saugandhika; he meets Vayu's son the mighty Hanuman in a grove of banana trees; Bhima bathes in the pool on the river and devastates the flowers growing there to gather the exotic saugandhikas; he battles the powerful Rakshasas and the Yakshas, and Hanuman with them; Bhima kills Jatasura; the Pandavas meet the Rajarishi Vrishaparva; they depart for the hermitage of Arshtishena and live there for a time; Draupadi incites Bhima to revenge. Now Vyasa narrates how Bhima climbs Kailasa and his tremendous battle with the Yakshas headed by Hanuman; the Pandavas meet with Vaisravana Kubera. Arjuna returns after he has obtained many diverse devastras to use for Yudhishtira; he describes his encounters with the Nivatakavachas of Hiranyaparva, with the Paulomas and the Kalakeyas: how he slew them all; Arjuna is about to reveal the divine and awesome weapons for Yudhishtira, when Narada appears to prevent him from bringing disaster down upon them; the Pandavas come down from Gandhamadana; a python big as a mountain seizes Bhima in the jungle; Yudhishtira answers the great snake's questions to secure his brother's release; the Pandavas return to the Kamyaka vana. Krishna returns to meet the sons of Pandu; Markandeya arrives there, and regales them with many legends; the story of Prithu, son of Vena; the stories of Saraswati and the Rishi Tarkhya. The legend of Matsya; other ancient tales Markandeya tells: those of Indradyumna and Dhundhumara; then the story of the chaste wife; the story of Angira. Draupadi and Satyabhama meet and speak together; the Pandavas return to the Dwaita vana. Duryodhana's ghoshayatra to gloat over the Pandavas' plight; he is captured by the Gandharva and rescued by Arjuna: a terrible humiliation. Yudhishtira's dream of the deer. The Pandavas return to the Kamyaka vana; the long story of Brihidraunika; the story of Durvasa; then Jayadratha abducts Draupadi from the asrama; Bhima, swift as the wind, chases Jayadratha, catches him and shames him dreadfully by shaving half his hair and moustache. Now follows the long story of Rama, during which that immaculate prince kills Ravana. The story of Savitri appears here; then Indra takes Karna's golden kundala from him, and compensates Karna with an inexorable shakti, which, however, can be used only against one enemy, whom it will certainly kill; then comes the story called Aranya, where Dharma Deva advises his son Yudhishtira; the Pandavas receive a boon and journey towards the west. All these comprise the third Parva, called Aranyaka, of two hundred and sixty-nine cantos, and eleven thousand, six hundred and sixty-four slokas.

The next great Parva is the Virata. The Pandavas arrive in the kingdom of Virata and see a great sami tree in a burial ground on the outskirts of the city. They hide their weapons in this tree, then enter the city in disguise. In Virata, Bhima kills the vile Kichaka, who, mad with lust, tries to molest Draupadi. Duryodhana sends forth his spies in every direction to scour the land for the Pandavas, but they fail to discover the mighty sons of Pandu. The Trigartas make off with Virata's herd and a fierce battle is fought; Virata is taken by the enemy and rescued by Bhimasena; Bhima retrieves the herd, as well. The next day, the Kurus make off again with Virata's kine; Arjuna vanquishes the Kuru host single-handed and releases the cattle; Virata offers his daughter Uttaraa to Arjuna, who accepts her to become the bride of his son and Subhadra's: Abhimanyu, destroyer of his foes. These are the contents of the fourth Parva. The Maharishi Vyasa composed the Virata Parva in sixty-seven cantos, with two thousand and fifty slokas.

Listen now to the outline of the fifth Parva, which is known as Udyoga. While the Pandavas stayed at Upaplavya in the Matsya kingdom and prepared for war, Duryodhana and Arjuna both went at the same time to Dwaraka, and said, "Fight on our side in the war". The Mahatman Krishna replied, "Choose between me—and I will carry no weapon nor strike a single blow during the war—and one whole Akshauhini of my troops. Which of these shall I give to which of you?" The foolish Duryodhana asked for the troops, while Arjuna eagerly accepted just Krishna, as a counsellor who would not fight. We will see how, when the king of Madra rode to join the Pandavas, Duryodhana cunningly entertained him on his way, with lavish hospitality and gifts, never revealing himself until he asked for a boon: which was that Salya would fight for him.

Having given his word, Salya cannot refuse. But he goes to the Pandavas and comforts them by recounting the tale of how Indra triumphed over Vritrasura. The Pandavas send a purohita to the Kauravas. Mighty Dhritarashtra listens to the message of the priest and to the story of Indra's victory and sends Sanjaya to the Pandavas suing for peace. We shall see the terrible insomnia and anxiety that ravages Dhritarashtra, when he hears about the army that the sons of Pandu have collected and about their allies, Krishna and the others. Now Vidura expounds dharma to his brother. Sanatsujata appears and discourses on the atman and dharma for the benefit of the terrified and grieving sovereign. The next morning, Sanjaya speaks, in the court of the king, about Arjuna and Krishna being Nara Narayana. Moved by compassion, Krishna, the illustrious one, comes himself to Hastinapura, to sue for peace. Duryodhana dismisses the embassy of Krishna. The story of Dambodbhava is related, as well as that of the noble Matuli's search for a husband for his daughter; then the story of the Maharishi Galava; the story of the training and discipline of the son of Vidula. Then, before the assembled kings, Krishna learns that Duryodhana and Karna are plotting to take him hostage and reveals his cosmic powers of Yoga. While leaving Hastinapura, Krishna takes Karna apart in his chariot and, telling him who he, Karna, truly is, asks him to join the Pandavas, who are his brothers. Karna refuses the offer, out of pride and loyalty to Duryodhana. Krishna, scourge of the evil, returns to Upaplavya, and tells the Pandavas everything that happened in Hastinapura. Then the Pandavas, having heard all, and having deliberated and discussed the matter deeply, begin to prepare in earnest for war. From Hastinapura, for battle, footsoldiers, horses, charioteers and elephants set forth. The legions of both sides are described. On the day before the commencement of battle, Duryodhana sends Uluka as his messenger to the Pandavas. The charioteers, rathikas, of different classes are described. The story of Amba is told. All this comprises the fifth Parva, Udyoga, of the Bhaarata, full of events relating to both peace and war. O Munis, the great Vyasa composed one hundred and eighty-six cantos in this Parva, with six thousand, six hundred and ninety-eight slokas.

Then comes the Bhishma Parva, which abounds with marvellous events. Here Sanjaya describes the formation of Jambudwipa, followed by an account of the dejection of Arjuna before the battle, his crisis at the prospect of killing his own flesh and blood. Krishna expounds the Sanatana Dharma to him and the path to mukti, and reasons with him to discard his doubts and to fight. The first ten ferocious days of battle. Krishna sees Bhishma slaughtering the Pandava army, while Arjuna hardly fought him, and jumps down from their chariot, whip in hand, and runs at Bhishma to kill him himself. Krishna scathes Arjuna, bearer of the Gandiva, most valiant and gifted of all Kshatriyas, with a tirade. Greatest among archers, Arjuna sets Shikandin before him and shoots Bhishma with his most potent arrows, felling him. Bhishma falls onto a bed of arrows, upon which he lies. This is the sixth Parva of the Bhaarata, of one hundred and seventeen cantos and five thousand, eight hundred and eighty-four slokas, recited by Maharishi Vyasa, master of the Vedas.

Next we recite the excellent Drona Parva, thick with incident. First, the great Acharya Drona is made Senapati of the Kaurava army; delighted, he vows, that master of arms, to take Yudhishtira his captive during the battle, to please Duryodhana; the Samsaptakas draw Arjuna away from the field; Arjuna kills Bhagadatta, who bestrode the field upon the elephant Supritika like a second Indra; the slaying of the teenaged Abhimanyu by Jayadratha and the Maharathas, while the heroic youth fought alone;

Arjuna razes seven Akshauhinis of the enemy and fulfils his vow to kill Jayadratha; Bhima Mahabaho and that best of Maharathas, Satyaki Yuyudhana, penetrate deep into the Kaurava army, impregnable even by the Devas; the two come at Yudhishtira's command, in search of Arjuna; the massacre of the remaining Samsaptakas. The Drona Parva tells of the death of Alambusha, of Srutayus, of Jalasandha, of Shomadatta, of Virata, of the Maharatha Drupada, of Ghatotkacha and countless others; in this Parva, stirred beyond reason by the death of his father, Aswatthama looses the dreadful Narayanastra. The glory of Rudra is told and the burning of the Tripura described. Vyasa arrives and sings the glory of Krishna and Arjuna. This is the seventh Parva of the Bhaarata, in which all the mighty Kshatriyas mentioned are slain. This Parva contains one hundred and seventy cantos, and eight thousand, nine hundred and nine slokas composed after much dhyana by Rishi Vyasa, son of Parasara, owner of true gyana.

Then comes the truly exhilarating Karna Parva, in which Salya, wise king of Madra, is persuaded to become Karna's sarathy. The history of the fan of the Anita Triputa is told. Karna and Salya favour each other with harsh words as they set out into battle; Salya makes the insulting comparison of the swan and the crow; the lofty Aswatthama kills the Pandya king; Dandasena dies; Darda dies; Yudhishtira's duel with Karna before both armies, in which Karna shames the Pandava; Yudhishtira and Arjuna quarrel, and Krishna pacifies an angry Arjuna. In this Parva, Bhima keeps his vow by tearing open Dushasana's chest and drinking the blood from his heart. Arjuna kills the great Karna in single combat. Those that know the Bhaarata call this eighth Parva the Karna Parva. It contains sixty-nine cantos and four thousand, nine hundred and sixty-four slokas.

Next, the wondrous Salya Parva; after all the Maharathas are dead, the king of Madra becomes Senapati of the Kaurava army. One after another, the duels of the remaining rathikas are described. Yudhishtira Dharmaputra kills the great Salya. Sahadeva kills Shakuni. When a mere smattering of troops remained alive after the great slaughtering, Duryodhana went to the lake and submerging himself, as he knew how, lay underwater for a while. Bhima learns from the fowlers where Duryodhana is; the knowing Yudhishtira taunts the sensitive Duryodhana until he emerges from the lake. Duryodhana and Bhima fight the gada yuddha, a mace battle, during which Balarama arrives at Samanata-panchaka; a description of the sacred Saraswati; the mace fight continues; Bhima hurls his gada with tremendous force to break Duryodhana's thighs. All this is contained in the ninth Parva, which Vyasa, who spread the renown of the Kauravas, composed in fifty-nine cantos and three thousand, two hundred and twenty slokas.

Next I will relate the Parva called Sauptika, in which horrible incidents occur. When the Pandavas leave Duryodhana to die slowly, painfully, of his mortal injury, the Maharathas Kritavarma, Kripa and Aswatthama come to Samanta-panchaka in the evening and see King Duryodhana lying on the ground, his thighs broken, and covered with blood. Then Maharatha Aswatthama swears in terrible fury that he will never remove his armour until he has killed all the Panchalas and Dhrishtadyumna, and the Pandavas and all their allies. The three warriors leave Duryodhana and enter the great forest just as the Sun sets. They sit, shocked, under a large pipal tree in the night, when they see one great owl killing a number of crows asleep in the branches, one after the other. Taking this as an omen, Aswatthama, his heart full of rage to think of his father Drona's death, decides to murder the Panchalas in their sleep. Arriving at the gates of the enemy camp, he sees there a Rakshasa of frightful countenance, the demon's head in the very sky, guarding the entrance. The Rakshasa is proof against all the astras of Drona's son, who then quickly worships three-eyed Rudra. And then, with Kritavarma and Kripa, he kills all the sons of Draupadi, all the Panchalas with Dhrishtadyumna and the rest of their kinsmen, all of whom slept unsuspectingly in the night, since the war was over. On that night, all of them perish except the five Pandavas and the Maharatha Satyaki. These escape because Krishna advises them to sleep away from the camp that night and to be on their guard. Dhrishtadyumna's sarathy brings word of the night's savage massacre to the Pandavas. Demented by the death of her sons, her father and her brothers, Draupadi sits before her husbands, resolved to fast unto death. Dreadful Bhima, stirred by what Draupadi says, hefts his mace and rides after the son of his Acharya, to take revenge on Aswatthama for Draupadi's sake. From fear of Bhima and moved by fate and anger, Aswatthama looses a final astra, crying, "This will be the end of all the Pandavas". But Krishna cries, "That shall not be!" and makes Aswatthama's words ineffectual. Arjuna counters Aswatthama's astra with an identical missile of his own. Seeing Aswatthama's vile intention, Dwaipayana and Krishna curse him and he curses them back. The Pandavas take the jewel that grew in Maharatha Aswatthama's head, and are delighted. Boasting of their triumph they come back to the battlefield and give it to Draupadi to assuage her grief. This is the tenth Parva, called Sauptika, which Maharishi Vyasa, peerless Pauranika of revelations, composed in eighteen cantos and eight hundred and seventy slokas. In fact, in this Parva he has combined two Parvas: Sauptika and Aishika.

After these comes the heartrending Parva, Stri, in which stricken and enraged by the killing of his precious Duryodhana, blind Dhritarashtra crushes an iron statue of Bhima, adroitly given to him by Krishna. Vidura consoles the king with a discourse on dharma and moksha. Sad Dhritarashtra and the women of his house make their way to the tragic field of Kurukshetra. The wives of the dead Kshatriyas lament. Gandhari and Dhritarashtra swoon from grief and wrath. The Kshatriya women see their sons, brothers and fathers lying dead on the field, never to return to them. Krishna calms the wrath of Gandhari, raging when she sees the corpses of her sons and grandsons. Yudhishtira of dharma, best among men, has the bodies of the dead kings and princes cremated. While tarpana is being offered for the Kshatriya princes, Kunti confesses her long kept secret that Karna was her son. Maharishi Vyasa describes these events in the eleventh Parva, full of pathos, which moves any feeling heart and even brings tears to one's eyes. It has twenty-seven cantos and seven hundred and seventy-five slokas.

Twelfth is the Santi Parva, which deepens understanding and wisdom. It tells of the dejection of Yudhishtira at having killed his elders, cousins, nephews, uncles and relatives by marriage, at having seen his sons slain. Lying on his bed of arrows, Bhishma expounds Kshatriya dharma and the dharma of kings; he tells of how to deal with crises, in detail, discussing occasion and cause. Understanding these discourses can lead one to true gyana. The mysteries of moksha are delved into and expatiated upon. This twelfth Parva is the favourite Parva of wise men. It has three hundred and thirty-nine cantos, and fourteen thousand, seven hundred and thirty-two slokas.

Next comes the fine and exalted Anusasana Parva. It describes how Yudhishtira, king of the Kurus, finds peace of mind and reconciliation upon hearing Bhishma, the son of Ganga's exposition on dharma. This Parva deals in detail with the codes of dharma and artha; it deals with dana, charity, and its merits; it defines the qualities required to give charity and the laws pertaining to the giving and receiving of gifts. This Parva also describes the rituals of individual dharma, the codes of conduct and the unequalled punya of truth. This Parva dwells on the great merit of Brahmanas and sacred cows, and unravels the mysteries of dharma with relation to time and place. All this is enshrined in the excellent Parva Anusasana, of numerous tales and events. It goes on to narrate Bhishma's ascension into Swarga. This thirteenth Parva, which lays down in detail the dharma for men, has one hundred and forty-six cantos, and eight thousand slokas.

The fourteenth Parva is Aswamedhika. We will tell the fine tale of Samvarta and Marutta; then describe the unearthing of the golden treasure trove; the birth of Parikshit follows, and how Krishna revives the stillborn infant after Aswatthama's astra had killed him in his mother's womb. Arjuna, the son of Pandu, follows the sacrificial horse across Bharatavarsha and gives battle to the Kshatriyas who dared seize the animal. We shall describe the duel between Arjuna and his own son Babhruvaha by Chitrangada, daughter of the king of Manipura. There follows the story of the mongoose during the Aswamedha yagna. This

Aswamedhika Parva contains one hundred and three cantos, and three thousand, three hundred and twenty slokas composed by the most knowing Vyasa.

The fifteenth Parva is called Asramvasika. Here, Dhritarashtra abdicates his kingdom, and sets out for the forest with Gandhari and Vidura. The virtuous Kunti, who always loved and served her elders, also leaves the court of her sons, to follow the old couple. This Parva describes the supernatural meeting of Dhritarashtra with the spirits of his slain children, grandchildren and other princes, returned from the other world by the power and grace of Vyasa. Then the king abandons his grief and, with Gandhari, finds the highest punya of his good deeds. In this Parva, Vidura, who always lived in virtue, attains moksha in the forest. The learned son of Gavalgana, Sanjaya, also restrains his passions perfectly, and that foremost of ministers attains the blessed condition. Yudhishtira of dharma meets Narada, who tells him about the destruction of the Vrishnis. This wonderful Parva Asramvasika has forty-two cantos, and one thousand five hundred and six slokas composed by Vyasa who knows the highest truth.

After this, as you know, comes the Maushala Parva, full of pain. The lion-hearted Vrishnis, who wore the scars from countless fields on their bodies, are cursed by a Brahmana. Drunk out of their wits, urged by fate, they slew one another on the shores of the salt sea with the eraka reeds, which turned in their hands into deadly thunderbolts. After provoking the extermination of their race, Balarama and Krishna, their own hour having come, succumb to all-consuming kaala. Arjuna, best of men, comes to Dwaravati and finds Dwaraka empty of Vrishnis. Grieftsricken, he performs the last rites for his uncle Vasudeva, noblest of the Yadus. Arjuna comes to the place where the Vrishnis had drunk and sees them lying in the postures of death. Arjuna cremates the bodies of Krishna the lustrous and of Balarama, as well as the other Vrishni chieftains. Taking the women and children, the old and the decrepit—all that remained of the Yadu race Arjuna journeys towards Indraprastha and meets disaster on the way in the form of murderous and rapacious highway bandits.

He can no longer use the mighty Gandiva nor summon any astra to defend his wards. The downcast Arjuna goes to the Rishi Vyasa, and following his advice, comes home to Yudhishtira and seeks his leave to adopt sannyasa. This is the sixteenth, Maushala, Parva, which contains eight cantos and three hundred and twenty slokas, composed by the Muni Vyasa, who knows the supreme truth.

Mahaprasthanika is next, the seventeenth Parva. Here, those greatest of men, the Pandavas, relinquish their kingdom and, taking Draupadi with them, set out on their final journey, Mahaprasthana. They arrive on the shore of the sea of red water, and meet Agni Deva. Agni tells Arjuna to worship him and to return the unearthly bow Gandiva to the Fire God, which Arjuna does. In this Parva, the Pandavas embark on their last journey up the great mountain. One by one, his brothers and his wife fall to their deaths, leaving Yudhishtira to climb on alone, never once looking back for them. This seventeenth Parva Mahaprasthanika has three cantos and three hundred and twenty slokas, composed by Vyasa, knower of the truth.

The eighteenth Parva is the exceptional Swarga, in which celestial events are described, happenings in Devaloka. Seeing the heavenly vimana come to fetch him bodily to Swarga, Yudhishtira is full of pity for the brown dog that accompanied him through his journey from the gates of Hastinapura. He refuses to ascend in the vimana without his companion. Dharma Deva sets aside his canine form and reveals himself to his son of perfect virtue. Yudhishtira comes into Swarga and experiences a taste of hell. A celestial servitor takes him through an illusory naraka, where Yudhishtira, soul of righteousness, hears the heart-rending lamentations of his brothers and Draupadi, who appear to be dwelling in that realm, being tormented by Yama. Dharma and Indra show Yudhishtira the zone of sinners. Then Yudhishtira abandons his body by bathing in the Ganga as she flows through Swarga, and attains the heaven that his dharma deserves, where he lives in joy, honoured by Indra and the other Devas. This is the eighteenth Parva as told by the illumined Vyasa; it contains two hundred and nine slokas.

Such in brief are the contents of the eighteen Parvas. The appendix (Khila) contains the Harivamsa and the Vavishya. The Harivamsa contains twelve thousand holy slokas.'

These are the contents of the canto called Parva-samgraha.

Sauti continues, 'Eighteen Akshauhinis of warriors came together for battle. The dreadful war lasts for eighteen days. He that knows the four Vedas with all the Angas and Upanishads but does not know this Itihasa cannot be regarded as having wisdom. Vyasa of fathomless intellect has called the Mahabharata a treatise on Artha, Dharma and Kama. Those who have listened to his awesome legend can never bear to listen to others, even as they who have heard the sweet song of the male kokila cannot stand the raucous cawing of the crow. As the Universe is formed from the Panchamahabhutas, the inspiration of every poet is derived from this wonderful Bhaarata. O Brahmanas, as the four kinds of creatures depend on space to exist, the Puranas depend upon this Itihasa. As the senses depend on the modes of the mind for their functioning, so does all karma and dharma depend upon this treatise. There is not a story in the world but it depends on this legend, even as the body does upon the food it consumes. All poets cherish the Bhaarata, even as servants that desire advancement serve masters of noble descent. Just as the blessed grihastasrama, of the householder, can never be excelled by the other three asramas, no poet or poets can surpass this poem.

O Munis, shake off all inertia. Fix your hearts on punya, for virtue is the only friend that accompanies a man out of this world. The most intelligent man can never really possess wealth or wife, not by cherishing them to distraction; they are fleeting. The Bhaarata uttered from the lips of Dwaipayana is unequalled; it is, verily, dharma, and it is sacred. It destroys sins and generates goodness. He that listens to it being recited does not need to bathe in the holy waters of Pushkara. Whatever sensual sins a Brahmana might commit during the day, he is freed of them by reading the Bhaarata in the evening. Whatever sins he may commit in the night, of deed, word or thought, he is freed from those by reading the Bhaarata at dawn, during the first sandhya. He that gives a hundred cows, their horns covered in gold, to a Brahmana versed in the Vedas and all the Shastras, and he that daily listens to the sacred stories of the Bhaarata, acquire equal punya, spiritual gain. As ships help men who own them, easily cross the Ocean, so does this canto Parva-samgraha help those who study this extensive legend of great beauty and profound meaning.'

CANTO 3

PAUSHYA PARVA

Suta said, 'Once, Janamejaya, the son of Parikshit, and his brothers conducted a great and extended yagna on Kurukshetra. His three brothers were Srutasena, Ugrasena and Bhimasena. And as they sat at the sacrifice, a whelp of Sarama, the celestial she-dog, arrived there. Beaten by Janamejaya's brothers, he ran to his mother, crying in pain. And Sarama asked, "Why are you crying like this? Who beat you?"

He replied, "The brothers of Janamejaya."

His mother said, "You have done something wrong that you were beaten."

He answered, "I have done no wrong. I did not lick the sacrificial ghee, nor did I even look at it." Hearing this, his mother Sarama grew distraught and went to the place where Janamejaya and his brothers were at their extensive sacrifice.

Angrily she cried to Janamejaya, "My son has done no wrong; he has neither looked at your sacrificial ghee, let alone lick it. Why, then, was he beaten?"

They did not reply, at which she said, "You have beaten my son who committed no fault, and evil will come upon you when you least expect it."

Janamejaya was terribly alarmed and depressed to hear this imprecation. After he completed his yagna and returned to Hastinapura, he began to search high and low for a purohita who could absolve his brothers and himself of their sin and turn away the curse.

One day, Janamejaya, while hunting in a forest that was part of his kingdom, saw the asrama of the renowned Rishi Srutasrava. Srutasrava's son, Somasrava, was a most accomplished priest and sat in deep dhyana there. Wanting to make this Sage his purohita, Janamejaya, son of Parikshit, saluted the Rishi Srutasrava and spoke to him, "O owner of the six great qualities, let your son be my purohita."

The Rishi answered, "Janamejaya, my son of deep tapasya, a master of the Vedas, and blessed with the full potency of my sannyasa, was born of a Nagina, who drank my semen. He can free you from every sin except one committed against Mahadeva. Yet, he has one trait that he will never abandon: he must give a Brahmana whatever he asks for. If you can countenance that, certainly take him with you."

Janamejaya replied, "Let me then take him."

Accepting Somasrava as his purohita, he returned to his capital, where he said to his brothers, "This is the man that I have chosen for my Guru; you must do whatever he says, unquestioningly." And his brothers did as they were told. The king marched to Takshashila and conquered that country.

Around this time, there was a Rishi called Ayoda-Dhaumya, and he had three disciples, Upamanyu, Aruni and Veda. The Rishi told one of these sishyas, Aruni of Panchala, to go and stop a leak in the watercourse in a field. At his Guru's command, Aruni of Panchala went to the place and saw that he could not stop the breach in the watercourse in any common fashion. He was distressed because he could not do his Guru's bidding.

He thought for a while and said, "Well, there is one way by which I can stem the leak."

He climbed down into the breach and lay there, and the water was contained by his body. After a while, the Guru Ayoda-Dhaumya asked his other disciples where Aruni of Panchala was. They replied, "Master, you sent him to stop the leak in the watercourse in the field."

Dhaumya remembered and said, "Let us all go to the place where he is."

Arriving there, he shouted, "Ho, Aruni of Panchala! Where are you? Come here, my child."

Hearing his Guru's voice, Aruni quickly emerged from the watercourse, and stood before his master. Aruni said, "I lay in the breach where the water leaked, since there was no other way to do as you said. But now I heard your voice and came to you, allowing the water to escape again. I salute you, Guru, command me."

The Guru said, "Because you rose from the ditch at my command, I bless you to be called Uddalaka. Because you have obeyed me, you shall find great fortune. The Vedas shall shine in you and all the Dharmashastras also."

And blessed by his Guru, Aruni went to the country that he loved.

Upamanyu was another of Ayoda-Dhaumya's sishyas. Dhaumya said to him, "Go, Upamanyu my child, and tend the herd." And Upamanyu took the cattle to pasture. Having watched and grazed them all day, he returned to his master's house in the evening, and saluted him respectfully.

His Guru saw him healthy and untired, and asked, "Upamanyu, my child, what did you feed on that you look so healthy and plump?"

He answered, "Lord, I ate by begging alms."

His Guru said, "You should not eat the alms you get without first offering them to me."

The next day, Upamanyu brought the alms he begged to his master. His Guru took all the food and Upamanyu went to graze the herd. He watched the cattle all day and returned in the evening to his master's asrama. He stood before his preceptor and saluted him with reverence. His Guru saw that he was still in fine fettle, and said, "Upamanyu, my child, I took all that you begged as alms from you, then how do you still look so healthy, even fat?"

Upamanyu said, "Guru, I gave you all the alms I begged the first time, then went begging a second time for food."

His master then said, "This is not how you should honour my command to you. By begging alms twice, you are depriving someone else that lives by alms for their subsistence. You have proved yourself to be greedy."

Upamanyu bowed to acknowledge what his master said, and went away. The next morning, too, he took the herd out to pasture and was with them all day. In the evening, he returned to his Guru's home and stood, hands folded reverently, before his master. His preceptor observed that he was still fat, and said, "Upamanyu my child, I take all the alms you beg and you do not go begging a second time, and you are still in robust health, and fat. How is this?"

Upamanyu replied, "Master, I drink the milk of the cows now."

His Guru said, "You may not drink the milk without my permission."

Again, Upamanyu agreed to do what his Guru asked, and the next day took the herd to pasture. When he returned to his master's dwelling in the evening, he stood before him and saluted him as usual. His master saw that he was still fat, and said, "Upamanyu my son, you do not eat the alms you beg anymore, nor do you go begging a second time, nor do you drink milk from the cows. How do you remain healthy and fat?"

Upamanyu replied, "Master, I sip the froth that drips from the mouths of the calves as they drink from their mothers' teats."

The master said, "The loving calves must drip a good deal of froth for you to drink. But you are depriving the young ones of their nourishment. I forbid you to drink the froth." And Upamanyu, bowing his assent, went away.

The next day, he took the cows to graze. Obeying his Guru, he did not feed on alms, nor drink any milk or froth. Savaged by hunger in the forest, he ate the leaves of an arka[3], which are pungent, saline and poisonous. He became blind. He crawled sightless on the forest floor and fell into a disused well. When he did not return to his Guru's asrama by evening, when the Sun sank over the western mountains, his master asked his other sishyas where Upamanyu was. They said that he had gone out with the cattle.

The Guru said, "I have prevented him from eating anything, and he must be annoyed. Let us then go looking for him." The Guru went with his sishyas into the forest and began to shout, "Ho Upamanyu! Where are you?"

Upamanyu heard his master's voice and answered loudly, "Here I am at the bottom of this well." His Guru asked how he got there. Upamanyu replied, "I ate the leaves of an arka plant and they made me blind. I could not see anything and I fell into the well."

His Guru then said, "Give praise to the Aswin twins, who are the physicians to the Devas, and they will restore your sight." At his master's word, Upamanyu began to hymn the Aswini twins, in slokas from the Rig Veda.

"You have existed since before creation! O first-born beings, it is you that are displayed in this marvellous Universe of five elements. I wish to attain to you by the faculty of hearing and of dhyana, for truly you are infinite. You are the very course of Prakriti and of the intelligent Purusha that pervades that unfolding. You are birds of exquisite plumage perched on the body that is like a tree. You are without the three attributes that are base in every soul. You are incomparable. Your spirit is in every created thing; you pervade the Universe.

You are golden eagles! You are the divine essence into which all things dissolve! You are free from faults and know no decay. Your beaks are beauty embodied, and never strike unjustly. You are victorious in

---

[3]Asclepias gigantea

every battle. You are immortal, and prevail over time. Having created the Sun, you weave the wondrous cloth of the years with the white thread of day and the black thread of night. And with the cloth woven, you have established two ways of karma, one for the Devas and the other for the Pitrs. You set the bird of Life, seized by Time, which has the strength of the Infinite Atman, free and deliver her to endless joy. They that are plunged in ignorance, deluded by the senses, think of you, who transcend matter and its attributes, as having form. Three hundred and sixty cows that are three hundred and sixty days produce one calf between them: the year. That calf creates and destroys all things. Seekers of truth, treading myriad paths, draw the milk that is true knowledge from the calf. O Aswins, you are the creators of that calf!

The year is just the hub of a wheel to which seven hundred and twenty spokes are attached: days and nights. The circumference of this wheel of twelve months is endless. The wheel is full of delusions and knows no decay. It affects all creatures, of this and the other worlds. Aswins, you set this wheel of time in motion!

The wheel of Time, in the year, has a nave of six seasons. The spokes attached to that nave are twelve, the signs of the Zodiac. This wheel of Time manifests the fruit of all karma. The Devas who rule Kaala abide in the wheel. O Aswins, I am bound by the misery of the wheel; liberate me from the wheel of Time. Aswins, you are this Universe of the Panchabhutas. You are the objects that are enjoyed in this and in the next world. Set me free from the five elements! Though you are the Supreme Brahman, yet you move over the Earth with bodies and forms, enjoying the pleasures that the senses afford.

In the beginning, you created the ten cardinal points of the Universe! Then you set the Sun and the sky on high. The Rishis perform their yagnas by the movement of the same Surya, and the Devas and men, as well, according to their svadharma, perform sacrifices and enjoy the fruit of those rites. You mixed the three colours, and produced all that is seen. From these creations the Universe issued, in which the Devas and men perform their svadharma, and, indeed, all creatures receive life!

Aswins, I worship you! I also adore the Akasa, which you made. You are the bestowers of the fruit of karma, the laws of which bind even the Devas. Yet you yourselves are free from the results of whatever you do!

You are the father and mother of us all! As male and female, you consume food, which then develops into life-creating seed and blood. The newborn drinks at its mother's breast. You take the shape of the infant. O Aswins, return my sight to me that I may protect my life!"

The twin Aswins appeared and said, "We are pleased. Here is a sweet cake for you. Eat it."

Upamanyu said, "Your words, O Aswins, have never proved untrue. But I cannot eat your cake without first offering it to my Guru."

The Aswins now told him, "Once, your Guru invoked us just as you have. We gave him a cake just like this one, and he ate it without offering it to his master. Do as your master did."

Upamanyu said to them, "Aswini Devas, I beg your forgiveness, but I cannot eat your cake without first offering it to my master."

The Aswins now said, "O, we are pleased by your Guru bhakti. Your master has iron teeth for eating the cake without offering it to his Guru. You shall have teeth of gold. Your eyes will see again and great fortune will attend upon you."

With this blessing from the Aswins, Upamanyu recovered his sight. He came before his master and, saluting him reverently, told him all that had happened. His Guru was pleased with him and said, "You shall have great fortune, as the Aswins have said. The Vedas shall illumine you, and all the Dharmashastras."

This was the trial of Upamanyu.

Then Ayoda-Dhaumya called his third sishya, Veda, and said to him, "Veda, my son, stay awhile in my house and serve your Guru. You will gain from it."

Veda readily agreed, and remained in his master's house, serving him and his family. Like an ox bearing its master's burdens, he suffered heat and cold, hunger and thirst, always without a murmur of complaint.

Before long, his Guru was satisfied and blessed Veda to have good fortune and universal knowledge. This was the trial of Veda.

Taking his Guru's permission, when he had finished his tutelage, Veda left his master's house and entered grihastasrama, became a householder. In his own house, he had three sishyas. But he never treated them harshly, or had them obey him unquestioningly or perform rough tasks for him, but was the kindest master because of his own difficult experiences in his Guru's house.

The two Kshatriyas Janamejaya and Paushya came to this Veda's home and asked him to be their Upadhyaya, their spiritual guide and mentor. One day, when he had to go out on some work, Veda told one of his disciples, Utanka, to take charge of his household.

"Utanka," said Veda, "you must do whatever needs to be done in my home without neglect, even as I would." And he set out on his journey.

Utanka began living in his Guru's house and was heedful of his master's command in every particular. One day, the women of the household came to Utanka and said, "Utanka, your mistress is in her fertile time. Your master is away, and it falls to you to take his place."

Utanka said to the women, "I cannot do this at you women's bidding. My Guru did not tell me to commit a sin."

After a while, his Guru came home, and when he heard what had happened, Veda was pleased.

He said, "Utanka, my child, what boon do you want from me? You have served me faithfully and my affection for you has grown. You may leave now, and let your every wish come true."

Utanka said, "Let me do something for you, Guru. For I have heard told of the master who teaches without receiving dakshina and the sishya who receives instruction without giving dakshina, that enmity springs up between them, and one of them dies. You have taught me and I must give you some gurudakshina."

His master replied, "Utanka, my son, wait a while."

Some days passed, then Utanka again asked his master, "Command me, Guru, what dakshina shall I bring for you?"

His Guru said, "Dear Utanka, so often you have asked me what dakshina I want from you for what I taught you. Go inside then, and ask my wife what you should bring as dakshina. Bring whatever she says."

Utanka went to his master's wife and said, "Mistress, my Guru has given me leave to go home, and I want to give you something as dakshina for the instruction I have received, something that will please you, so that I do not leave with a debt to my Guru. I beg you tell me what dakshina I should give."

His Guru's wife replied, "Go to King Paushya and beg him for the earrings that his queen wears, and bring them here. The fourth day from today is a sacred day and I want to wear those earrings when I serve the Brahmanas who will dine with us. Do this for me, Utanka! If you succeed, you will find good fortune; if you fail, what fortune can you expect?"

Utanka went away to fetch the earrings, if he could. As he went along, he saw a bull of extraordinary size and a man of huge stature mounted upon it. That man said to Utanka, "Eat the dung of this bull." Utanka refused. The man said again, "Utanka, eat it. Your master ate it before you." Now Utanka agreed and ate the dung and drank the urine of the bull. Then he rose respectfully, washed his hands and mouth, and went to meet King Paushya.

Arriving at the palace, Utanka saw Paushya upon his throne. Utanka approached the king and greeted him by pronouncing formal blessings over him. He said, "I have come to you as a supplicant."

King Paushya returned Utanka's greeting and asked, "Brahmana, what can I do for you?"

Utanka said, "I have come to beg a pair of earrings for my Guru's wife, to be my dakshina to my master. I ask you to give me the earrings that your queen wears."

King Paushya replied, "Go, Utanka, into the antahpura, and ask the queen for the earrings."

Utanka went into the harem, but he could not find the queen. He came back to the king and said, "It is not right that you treat me deceitfully. Your queen is not in the antahpura, I could not find her there."

The king thought a moment, then said, "Recollect, Brahmana, whether you have defiled yourself with something that you ate or drank on your way here. My queen is a chaste wife and cannot be seen by anyone who is sullied from partaking of leftovers. She will not appear before someone that is impure.

Utanka now thought for a moment, then said, "Yes, it must be. Being in a hurry, I must have performed my ablutions while standing."

King Paushya said, "You cannot purify yourself properly while standing, not even while you are on a journey."

Utanka agreed. He sat down facing the east and washed his face, hands and feet thoroughly. Then, without making a sound, he thrice sipped clean water, free of froth and dirt, and not warm, in achamana: just enough to reach his stomach, and he wiped his face twice. He touched the apertures of his organs with pure water.

Having done all this, he went to the women's quarters again. Now he saw the queen. As soon as the queen saw him, she greeted him respectfully and said, "Welcome Brahmana, tell me what I can do for you."

Utanka said, "Give me your earrings, I wish to give them to my Guru's wife as my daskhina to him."

The queen was pleased with Utanka's deportment and his intentions. She felt that he was deserving of this charity, and immediately took off her earrings and gave them to him.

The queen said, "Takshaka, the serpent king, has always coveted these earrings. So be very carfeul how you go with them."

Utanka said to the queen, "Lady, do not worry, Takshaka cannot catch me."

He took solemn and grateful leave of the queen, and went back into the presence of Paushya. Utanka said, "Paushya, I am gratified."

Paushya said to Utanka, "Someone truly deserving of daana comes along once in a rare while. You are a worthy guest, a qualified sadasya, and I want to conduct a sraddha. Stay a while with me."

Utanka replied, "I will stay, but I beg you to have the food for the sraddha fetched quickly."

The king assented readily and began to entertain Utanka as the atithi for his sraddha. Utanka saw that the food set before him had hair in it and felt that it was cold, and deemed it unclean. He said to Paushya, "You have given me unclean food and you will go blind for it."

Paushya retorted, "And because you say that clean food is unclean, you will have no children!"

Utanka rejoined, "It does not become you to curse me back, after offering me unclean food. Look for yourself."

Paushya looked closely at the food and found that it was indeed unclean, being cold and mixed with hair, because it had been prepared by a woman with long braids.

The king sought to pacify Utanka, "Brahmana, the food set before you is indeed cold, and does contain hair. It was prepared without proper care and I beg you, forgive me. Let me not become blind."

Utanka replied, "What I say must come to pass. However, though you go blind you can recover your sight soon, provided your curse does not affect me."

Paushya said to him, "I cannot revoke my curse, for my wrath is not appeased. But you cannot know this because a Brahmana's heart is as soft as freshly churned butter, even if his words carry a sharp razor. But this is not so with the Kshatriya, whose words are soft as freshly churned butter, but his heart is like a razor, and hard. Because I am a Kshatriya and unforgiving, I cannot withdraw my curse. Go your way now."

Utanka said, "I showed you that the food was unclean, and just now you were pacifying me. Besides, you first said that because I said the food was unclean when it was in fact clean I would not have children. But the food is unclean, so your curse cannot affect me. Of this I am certain."

And Utanka left with the earrings.

On the road, Utanka saw a naked beggar coming towards him, most strangely: for sometimes he was visible and at others he vanished. Utanka put the earrings on the ground and went to bathe in a wayside tank. The beggar flashed up, seized up the earrings and ran away. Utanka completed his ablutions, purified himself, bowed worshipfully to the gods and his Gurus and went after the thief as fast as he could. With some effort he overtook him and laid hold of the fellow.

At once, the naked one was no longer a beggar but Takshaka, who dived down into a hole in a ground. Once in, Takshaka sped down into his realm, Nagaloka, the under-world of serpents.

Utanka remembered what the queen had told him and tried to pursue the Naga. With a stick, he tried to excavate the hole into which Takshaka had vanished but could not make any headway. Indra saw his distress and sent his Vajra to help him. The thunderbolt entered the stick and plunged along the hole, tunnelling its way like lightning. Utanka went in and down after the Vajra. He saw Nagaloka, amazing and magnificent, seemingly infinite in extent, with hundreds of palaces and elegant mansions, with turrets, domes and high arched gates, full of the most enchanting parks and gardens for sport and for love.

Awestruck, Utanka sang the praises of the serpents with these slokas:

"O Nagas, subjects of King Airavata, splendid in battle, pouring forth astras in battle like clouds full of lightning driven by the winds! Many-formed, radiant and handsome, with ear-studs of many colours, O children of Airavata, you shine like the Sun in the sky! On the northern banks of the Ganga are many habitations of Nagas. I regularly worship the great serpents there. Who but Airavata would want to move about under the burning Sun? When Airavata's brother Dhritarashtra goes forth, twenty-eight thousand and eight serpents follow him in train. You who move near him and you that remain at some remove: I worship all of you that have Airavata for your elder brother.

I worship you also, O Takshaka, who once lived in Kurukshetra and the Khandava vana: to have the queen's earrings from you! Takshaka and Aswasena, O constant companions that dwell in Kurukshetra on the banks of the Ikshumati! I worship Takshaka's younger brother, the lustrous Srutasena, who lived in the tirtha Mahadyumna in order to become lord of the Nagas."

Though he paid homage to all the great Nagas, the Brahmana Rishi Utanka did not get the earrings. He fell thoughtful. He looked around and saw two young women at a loom weaving a piece of cloth with a fine shuttle, using black and white threads. He saw a wheel with twelve spokes, turned by six boys. And he also saw a man astride a blazing magnificent steed. And he addressed these mantras to them, resonantly:

"This wheel that has twenty-four cantos, for the changes of the Moon, also has three hundred spokes! Six boys, the seasons, keep it always turning! These women are Prakriti, ceaselessly weaving their cosmic cloth with threads of black and white, creating countless worlds and the beings that live on them. And you who send down the thunder, who protect the Universe, who slew Vrita and Namuchi, O Illustrious one wearing a black robe, riding Uchchaisravas churned up from the bottom of the sea, the horse that is an amsa of Agni Deva Lord of Fire, I bow to you, Paramatman, Lord of the three worlds, O Purandara!"

Then the man on the horse said to Utanka, "I am pleased with your worship. What boon shall I give you?"

Utanka replied, "Let me have power over the Nagas."

The man said, "Breathe upon this horse."

Utanka blew his breath onto that horse. From every aperture of the horse's body, dreadful flames and smoke issued to consume Nagaloka. Shocked, singed and terrified, Takshaka flew out from his palace with the earrings, and gave them to Utanka.

"I beg you," said the Naga king, "take back the earrings." And Utanka did.

But having recovered his earrings, Utanka realised, "This is the holy day of which my Guru's wife spoke. I am so far from their home; how will I give her the dakshina in time?"

The man in black said to him, "Ride this horse, Utanka, and he will bring you to your master's home in a moment."

Utanka mounted the horse and immediately arrived at his Guru's house.

It was morning. His master's wife had bathed and sat combing her hair, thinking of how she would curse Utanka if he did not return in time with the earrings. Utanka entered his Guru's home, greeted his master's wife and respectfully gave her the earrings.

"Utanka," said she, delighted, "you have arrived at the right time in the right place! Welcome my child, you have done what you set out to do, and I will not curse you. Good fortune is written for you. Let all your wishes come true and success attend your every endeavour!"

Utanka went to his Guru. His master said, "Welcome! Where were you all these days?"

Utanka replied, "Master, Takshaka kept me from returning sooner. I had to go to Nagaloka, where I saw two women at a loom, weaving a fabulous cloth with black and white threads. What was it? I also saw a wheel with twelve spokes turned endlessly by six boys. What did that mean? Who was the man that I saw, mounted upon the horse of awesome size?

And while I was on the road, I saw a man mounted on a gigantic bull. He said affectionately to me, 'Utanka, eat of the dung of this bull, which your Guru also ate.' So I ate the bull's dung. But who was the man? I beg you, enlighten me about all these."

His Guru said to him, "The two young women you saw are Dhata and Vidhata; the black and white threads are nights and days; the wheel of twelve spokes was the year and the boys that turned it, the six seasons. The man was Parjannya, Lord of rain, and the horse was Agni, the Fire God. The bull on the road was Airavata, Lord of elephants; the man riding the bull was Indra; and the dung of the bull, which you ate, was Amrita, which saved you from certain death in Nagaloka. Indra is my friend and showed you favour. That is how you have come back safely with the earrings. Good child, I give you leave to go now. You will find fortune."

With his Guru's leave and blessing, Utanka went grimly toward Hastinapura. Anger stirred his heart and he wanted to avenge himself on Takshaka. The excellent Brahmana soon reached Hastinapura. Utanka came into the presence of Raja Janamejaya, who had returned victorious from Takshashila some days ago. Utanka saw the triumphant king surrounded by his ministers. He blessed them all, formally.

Utanka spoke to the king at an apposite moment, in fine language and a mellifluous voice. "Rajarishabha, best of kings! How is it that you waste your time childishly, when another critical matter demands your attention?"'

Sauti said, 'Janamejaya saluted the noble Brahmana and replied, "I am discharging the dharma of my royal line by spending time with my subjects. Tell me, what is the urgent matter which has brought you here?"

The great Brahmana Utanka, distinguished by his fine deeds, replied to that munificent king, "O Raja! the matter is urgent because it concerns you. So make haste to attend to it. King of kings, Takshaka took your father's life, and you must take revenge against the vile snake. The time has come, I believe, for the vengeance ordained by fate. So avenge the death of your great father whom the vicious Naga stung, without cause, and burned him into the Panchabhutas like lightning striking a tree. Takshaka, most evil of Nagas, is so drunk with power that he dared bite your godlike sire, scion of your race of Rajarishis.

Cunning beyind measure, he persuaded Kashyapa, prince among physicians, to turn back when that Rishi was on his way to save your father. It will be fitting for you to burn Takshaka in the fire of a sarpa yagna, a sacrifice of serpents!

Rajan! Command the sarpa yagna to begin instantly, it is the only way to avenge your father. And with this sacrifice, you will do me also a great favour. For, most virtuous Kshatriya, the malignant Takshaka once obstructed me when I was on a crucial errand for my Guru."'

Sauti continued, 'Hearing this, the king's fury against Takshaka was kindled. What Utanka said inflamed the Kshatriya like ghee poured into an agnikunda. Grief welled up inside Janamejaya, and he asked his ministers for an account of his father's journey to Swarga. When he heard the circumstances of his father's death from Utanka he was stricken with pain and sorrow.'

Here ends the canto named Paushya, of the Adi Parva of the blessed Mahabharata.

CANTO 4

PAULOMA PARVA

Suta Ugrasrava, son of Romaharshana and a master of the Puranas, stood before the Rishis of Naimisha vana, during the twelve-year sacrifice of Saunaka Kulapati. He had studied the Puranas with meticulous devotion and knew them thoroughly. Hands folded, he said respectfully to the Sages, 'I have told you the story of Utanka in detail, and his tale was one of the reasons for King Janamejaya's sarpa yagna, his snake sacrifice. What, holy ones, do you wish to hear now? What shall I narrate?'

The Rishis replied, 'Son of Romaharshana, we will ask you whatever we most want to hear, and you must recount the stories, one by one. Our master Saunaka is at worship in the sacred agnigriha. He knows the divine legends of the Devas and Asuras. He knows well the Itihasas of men, the Nagas and Gandharvas. Further, Sauti, the learned Saunaka is the chief priest at this yagna. He is able, keeps his vratas faultlessly, he is wise, a master of the Shastras and the Aranyaka, speaks only the truth, is a lover of peace, mortifies his flesh, and performs tapasya by the laws laid down for austerity. All of us revere him. It is only proper that we wait for him. And when he sits upon this darbhasana, you shall answer whatever that best of Dvijas wants to know from you.'

Sauti said, 'So be it. When that mahatman sits with us and asks me to, I will tell you sacred tales that deal with a variety of subjects.'

After a while, having finished all his karma, having worshipped the Devas with prayers and the Pitrs with tarpana, the great Brahmana Saunaka returned to the yagnashala, where the other Rishis of stern vows sat relaxed, with Sauti before them. And when Saunaka sat among the Ritviks and Sadhyas, he spoke to them.

CANTO 5

Pauloma Parva Continued

Saunaka said, 'Child, son of Romaharshana, your father studied all the Puranas and the Bhaarata, with Krishna Dwaipayana. Have you imbibed them, as well? Those ancient chronicles contain fascinating stories and the history of the first generations of Rishis, all of which we heard from the lips of your father. First of all, I want to hear the history of the race of Bhrigu. Recount that lineage, and we will listen carefully to you.'

Sauti said, 'I have learnt everything that the noble Brahmanas of old, Vaisampayana among them, once studied and recounted. I have gleaned all the knowledge that my father possessed. O scion of the race of Bhrigu, listen then to everything that relates to that lofty race, honoured by Indra and all the Devas, by the tribes of Rishis and Maruts. Mahamuni, first of all, I will relate the history of this clan as told in the Puranas.

The blessed Maharishi Bhrigu, we are told, was created by Swayambhuva Brahma from the agni during the sacrifice of Varuna. And Bhrigu had a son named Chyavana, whom he loved dearly. Chyavana had a virtuous son called Pramati. Pramati had a son named Ruru by Ghritachi the Apsara, and to Ruru, by his wife Pramadvara, was born a son named Sunaka. He, O Saunaka, was your great, exceptionally virtuous ancestor. He was devoted to sannyasa, had wide renown, was proficient in dharma, and pre-eminent among those that knew the Vedas. He was honest and self-controlled.'

Saunaka said, 'O son of Suta, why was the illumined son of Bhrigu called Chyavana? Tell me all.'

Sauti answered, 'Bhrigu had a wife named Pauloma, whom he loved. She became pregnant by him. One day, while the chaste Pauloma was in that condition, Bhrigu, foremost among those that are true to their dharma, left her at home and went out to perform his ablutions.

At this time, a Rakshasa whose name was Puloma came to Bhrigu's asrama. Entering, the Rakshasa saw Bhrigu's irreproachable wife and was filled with lust, quite losing his reason on seeing her. The beautiful Pauloma entertained the Rakshasa with roots and fruit of the forest. The Rakshasa, aflame, was so delighted, good Rishi, he decided to carry her away, who was so pure and faithful.

"I shall have what I want," said the Rakshasa, and seizing the beautiful woman, carried her away. And it was true that her father had once betrothed her of the lovely smile to the same Rakshasa, though later he gave her to be Bhrigu's wife with Vedic ritual. O Saunaka of the race of Bhrigu, this hurt rankled deep in the Rakshasa's mind and he found the moment now to abduct her.

The Rakshasa saw the agnishala in which the sacred fire always burned bright, and he asked the Fire God, the blazing elemental, "Tell me, O Agni, whose wife this woman is. You are the mouth of the Devas, you must answer me. Was this woman with skin soft as petals not first offered to me by her father? And did I not accept her? But then her father married her to the deceitful Bhrigu. Tell me truly if this beautiful woman is indeed the wife of Bhrigu, because I have found her alone today and mean to take her from this asrama by force, if she is the same woman. My heart burns to think that Bhrigu has this slender-waisted woman who was my betrothed."'

Sauti continued, 'Again and again, the Rakshasa asked flaming Agni if the woman was Bhrigu's wife. And the god was afraid to answer.

"O Agni," said the Rakshasa, "you dwell within every creature, as the witness of their paapa and punya. Worshipful Agni, answer me truly. Has Bhrigu not stolen the woman that I chose to be my wife? Tell me truthfully, having been given first to me, is she not rightfully mine? When I have your answer, I will carry her away from this asrama, even before your eyes of fire. So answer me with the truth."'

Sauti continued, "The Seven-flamed Deva listened to the Rakshasa and was dismayed, being afraid to tell a lie and equally afraid of being cursed by Bhrigu. At length, the god replied, hesitantly and slowly:

"You did indeed first choose Pauloma, O Rakshasa, but you did not marry her with sacred rites and mantras. Her father gave this renowned beauty to Bhrigu because he wanted Bhrigu's blessing. She was not formally given to you, Rakshasa; rather, Rishi Bhrigu made her his wife with Vedic ceremony and me for witness. This is she. Yes, I know her. I dare not tell a lie. O best of Rakshasas, lies never find honour in this world."'

CANTO 6

Pauloma Parva Continued

Sauti said, 'O Brahmana, the Rakshasa heard what Agni said, in a flash assumed the form of a boar and carried Pauloma away as fast as the wind, even as quickly as thought. It was then that Bhrigu's son, lying in his mother's womb, was outraged by the violence and fell out of her body. For this he was called Chyavana. The Rakshasa saw the infant drop from his mother's womb, shining like the Sun, and he instantly released Pauloma, fell down and became a mound of ashes. And the beautiful Pauloma, grief-stricken, O Brahmana of the race of Bhrigu, took up her child, Chyavana, the son of Bhrigu, and walked away. And Brahma, the Grandsire, Pitamaha of all, saw her, the blameless wife of his son, weeping pitiably. And Brahma comforted her, seeing how she loved her baby. The tears that streamed down Pauloma's face became a great river. And that river followed the Maharishi Bhrigu's wife. And the Pitamaha of the worlds saw that river flowing after Pauloma and he called it Vadhusara. And it flowed beside the asrama of Chyavana, her son. This was how Chyavana of great tapasya, the son of Bhrigu, was born.

Bhrigu saw his child Chyavana and its beautiful mother. And the Rishi flew into a rage and demanded, "Who told the Rakshasa about you that he came to carry you away? O you with the sweet smile, the Rakshasa could not know that you were my wife. Tell me who told him, that I can curse the one who did."

Pauloma replied, "Owner of the six gunas! Agni Deva identified me for the Rakshasa, who carried me away, while I wailed like a kurari.[4*] Your splendid son saved me, for when the Rakshasa saw him being born he released me, fell down and turned into ashes."

Bhrigu heard this and was furious. In rage, he cursed Agni, saying, "You shall eat all things, clean and unclean!"'

[4]Female osprey

CANTO 7

PAULOMA PARVA CONTINUED

Sauti said, 'Enraged by the curse of Bhrigu, Agni Deva roared at the Rishi, "Brahmana, what is this rashness that you have shown me? What was my fault, who did everything, both to keep dharma and to speak the truth, impartially? The Rakshasa questioned me and I answered truthfully. A witness who lies about something that he knows ruins his ancestors and his descendants for seven generations, above and below. He who suppresses the truth that he knows is equally guilty. I could also curse you, except that I hold Brahmanas in high regard. You do know all about me, Bhrigu, yet I will tell you about my attributes again. So listen.

Multiplying myself with tapasya, I assume myriad forms: at the daily hotra everywhere, at sacrifices that last for years, where any holy rites are performed: births, upanayanams, weddings, deaths, and at other yagnas. The Devas and Pitrs are worshipped and appeased by the ghee that is poured into my flames as offering, as prescribed in the Veda. The Devas are the sacral waters; the Pitrs are also the waters. The Devas and the

Pitrs have equal rights to the Yagnas, Darshas and Purnamasas. The Devas are the Pitrs, and the Pitrs the Devas. They are identical beings, worshipped together and separately, too, during the different phases of the Moon. The Devas and the Pitrs consume what is poured into me. I am known as the mouth of the Devas and the Pitrs. On Amavasya, the new Moon, the Pitrs, and during Paurnima, the full Moon, the Devas are fed through my mouth, partaking of the ghee poured into me. Bhrigu, being as I am, the mouth of the Devas and Pitrs, how shall I then eat all things, clean and unclean?"

Then Agni thought deeply for a while and withdrew from every place in which he burned: from the daily homa of Brahmanas, from all long sacrifices, from all holy rites, and every other ceremony. Deprived of their AUMS and Vashats, their Swadhas and Swahas, all the living were plunged in grief at losing their sacrificial fire.

The panic-stricken Rishis went to the gods and said to them, "Immaculate ones! The three worlds are in turmoil that Agni has abandoned them and they cannot perform their sacrifices anymore. We beg you, say what must be done, without delay."

The Rishis and the Devas went together to Brahma. They told him about Bhrigu's curse on Agni, and how the Fire God had withdrawn from every sacrifice and ritual.

They said, "Master of Fortune, Bhrigu has cursed Agni to eat all things clean and unclean. But Agni is the mouth of the Devas and he first partakes of every sacred offering. He drinks the sacrificial ghee. How can he consume all things, clean and unclean?"

The Creator of the Universe heard them and he summoned Agni. Gently, Brahma said to Agni, who was also the creator of all, and immortal, "You create and destroy the worlds. You preserve them. You support every sacrifice and ritual throughout the three worlds. You must not flout your dharma so the sacred rites are interrupted. You who consume the sacrificial ghee, who are the Lord of all things, why are you being so foolish? You alone are always pure in the Universe, and you are its only eternal foundation. I say to you, not all of you shall partake of all things, clean and unclean. Only the flames of your baser parts shall devour all things alike. Your body which, dwelling in the bellies of carnivores, devours flesh, shall also eat all things, clean and unclean. And as everything touched by the Sun's rays becomes pure, so shall everything that is burnt in your flames be purified. O Agni, you are the supreme energy born from your own power. Then, O Deva, by your own tejas let the Rishi's curse come to pass. Continue to receive the havis offered into your mouth: the offering that is yours and that which is for the other Devas."

Agni replied to the Pitamaha, "So be it," and he left to follow Brahma's dictate. The Devas and the Rishis also went to their homes, quite delighted. The Rishis performed their rituals and sacrifices as before. And the gods in heaven and all creatures of the world rejoiced. And Agni also rejoiced because he was free from having to sin.

Thus, O Saunaka, owner of the six qualities, the Maharishi Bhrigu cursed Agni once in time out of mind. This is the ancient legend about Pauloma, the death of the Rakshasa, and the birth of Chyavana.'

CANTO 8

PAULOMA PARVA CONTINUED

Sauti said, 'O Brahmana, Bhrigu's son Chyavana Muni fathered a son by his wife Sukanya, and that was the illustrious Pramati of dazzling vitality. Pramati sired in Ghritachi a son called Ruru. Ruru begot on his wife Pramadvara a son called Sunaka. I will tell you in detail, O Rishi, the entire story of Ruru of boundless clan. Listen to it now, in full.

Once there was a great Rishi called Sthulakesa of great tapasya shakti, deep gyana and compassion toward all creatures. Brahmana Muni, this was the time when Viswavasu, king of the Gandharvas, is said to have enjoyed sexual relations with the celestial Apsara Menaka. Bhargava, when her time came, Menaka delivered her child near the asrama of Sthulakesa. Abandoning the newborn baby on the banks of the river, O Brahmana, Menaka, who had neither pity nor shame, went away.

The Rishi Sthulakesa, of great dhyana, found the infant lying forsaken in a lonely place on the riverside. He saw that it was a girl, bright as the child of an immortal, ablaze with beauty! Maharishi Sthulakesa, foremost of Munis, was filled with compassion. He took the child and raised her. The exquisite child grew up in his holy asrama, and the noble and blessed Rishi performed all the sacred ceremonies for her, beginning with the one at birth, as laid down in the divine Shastras.

She excelled all those of her sex in goodness, beauty and every noble quality, so the maharishi called her Pramadvara. The pious Ruru once saw Pramadvara in Sthulakesa's hermitage and his heart was pierced by Kama Deva's arrow; he was stricken with love for her. Through his friends, Ruru told his father Pramati, son of Bhrigu, about his love. Pramati went to Sthulakesa of renown and asked for Pramadvara's hand in marriage for his son. Her foster-father gave the maiden Pramadvara in betrothal to Ruru, and fixed the wedding for the day when the Varga-Daivata nakshatra, Purva-phalguni, was rising.

A few days before the one appointed for the wedding, Pramadvara was at play with her sakhis and, her time come, stepped on a snake, which bit the lovely girl. She fell to the ground unconscious; colour drained from her face and all the vital signs of life fled her person, one by one, as she writhed in pain. Her hair limp and wild, she who had been so beautiful and attractive in life was the very opposite in death's throes; her companions could hardly bear to look at her.

In a while, calm came over her face and the reed-waisted girl, quelled by venom, lay as if asleep. Now she was even more beautiful in death than she had been alive. Sthulakesa and the other Rishis of the forest came and saw her lying there bright as a golden lotus. Many noted Brahmanas came to that place and they sat around the dead girl in pity and sorrow. Swastyatreya, Mahajana, Kaushika, Sankhamekhala, Uddalaka, Katha and Sweta of great fame; Bharadwaja, Kaunakutsya, Arshtishena, Gautama, Pramati, his son Ruru and other forest-dwellers came there as the news spread and, seeing Pramadvara lying dead, her life quenched by the snake's poison, they sat there and wept. But Ruru could not stand the sight and stumbled away in agony.'

CANTO 9

PAULOMA PARVA CONTINUED

Sauti said, 'While the illustrious Brahmanas sat around Pramadvara's corpse, Ruru ran deep into the jungle and he sobbed aloud; he wailed out his grief.

Thinking of his love, he cried, "Ah, she that was so beautiful and delicate lies unmoving on bare ground. What could be more dreadful for us who knew her? If I have been charitable, if I have performed any tapasya, if I have ever revered and served my elders, let all my punya be spent in bringing my love back to life. If since my birth I have restrained my passions, kept my vratas, let sweet Pramadvara rise alive from where she lies!"

While Ruru lamented the loss of his bride to have been, a messenger from heaven came to him in the forest. Said the divine one, "O Ruru, you rail in vain against time. Blessed one, she whose days in this world have run out can never return. The mortal days of this daughter of a Gandharva and an Apsara are exhausted. So, child, snatch your heart back from sorrow."

Then he paused, before adding softly, "But, there are exceptions and the gods have already provided one condition by which life might be restored to her. If you can fulfil that condition, you might have your Pramadvara back."

Ruru asked, "Messenger from Swarga, what is the condition of the Devas? Tell me, tell me in detail, that I might fulfil it. Ah, good Duta, save me from this grief!"

The divine messenger said to Ruru, "Ruru of Bhrigu's clan, give up half your own life to her and Pramadvara shall live again."

Never hesitating, Ruru cried, "I gladly offer half my life if my bride returns to me, lovely as she used to be!"

Then the Gandharva king and the divine messenger, both of them splendid and great, went to Dharmaraja, the Lord Death, and said to him, "If it please you, Lord, let Pramadvara's life be restored with a portion of Ruru's life."

Dharmaraja replied, "Devaduta, messenger of the gods, if it is your wish, let Pramadvara, Ruru's betrothed, live again with a portion of Ruru's life."

Even as Dharmaraja said this, Pramadvara of exquisite complexion rose from death as if from sleep: with a portion of Ruru's life. Of course, his offering would shorten Ruru's own life.

On the auspicious day, their fathers joyfully married Ruru and Pramadvara with the proper rituals. The couple was devoted to each other. Ruru had a rare wife, lovely and bright as the filaments of a lotus, and he swore to wreak vengeance on all serpents for the snake that had bitten Pramadvara. Whenever he saw a snake, he would become furious and kill it with some weapon.

One day, O Brahmana, Ruru went into a great forest, and he saw an aged serpent of the species called Dundubha lying on the ground. Ruru raised his staff in wrath, even like the Yama danda, to kill it, when the Dundubha spoke to Ruru, "I have done you no harm, O Brahmana! Why do you want to kill me in such anger?"'

CANTO 10

Pauloma Parva Continued

Sauti continued, 'When Ruru heard what the snake said, he answered, "A snake bit my wife, dear to me as life. And I swore then that I would kill every serpent I saw. That is why I will now kill you with my staff."

The Dundubha said, "O Brahmana, the snakes that bite man are a different species from us. Why should you kill Dundubhas, who are serpents but in name? We are prey to the same misfortunes as other snakes but do not share their venom. We have the same sorrows but not the same strengths or joys. It is a mistake for you to kill the Dundubhas."

Rishi Ruru listened to the snake and saw how it trembled with fear, unlike a serpent, though it was indeed a snake, but more like a human; and he did not kill it. Ruru, owner of the six great attributes, asked the snake, "Tell me, O Dundubha, who are you really that lie here as a snake?"

The Dundubha replied, "Ruru, I was once a Rishi and my name was Sahasrapat. The curse of a Brahmana transformed me into a snake."

Ruru asked, "O best of snakes, why did a Brahmana curse you? How long will you be a snake?"

CANTO 11

PAULOMA PARVA CONTINUED

Sauti continued, 'The Dundubha said, "Long ago, I had a friend called Khagama. He had considerable spirtual power by his tapasya and was short-tempered and rash of speech. One day, while he performed the Agni-hotra, I made a snake of grass and playfully tried to scare him with it. He fainted from fright. But when he regained consciousness, that honest Rishi, who always kept his vows, cursed me in anger, 'Since you made a snake of grass to frighten me, become a snake yourself, and as powerless as a grass snake, for you shall have no venom!'

O Muni, I knew how powerful he was by his penance. I bowed low before him, with folded hands and a pounding heart, and said, 'My friend, it was only a jest to make you laugh. I beg you, pardon me and take back your curse.'

Seeing me desperate, the Sage was moved to pity. Still breathing hard he said, 'I cannot revoke my curse and you must become a snake. But Muni, when Pramati's pure-hearted son Ruru appears before you, the curse will end.'

You, my friend, are that same Ruru. When I have my true form back, I will tell you something that will benefit you." The Dundubha was transformed before Ruru's eyes and he was again an illustrious Brahmana, radiant as the day.

He said to the powerful and peerless Ruru, "Best among created beings, sparing a life is the highest virtue, and a Brahmana should never kill any creature. A Brahmana should always be gentle and non-violent. This is the most sacred injunction of the Vedas. A Brahmana should be versed in the Vedas and Vedangas, and should inspire all men with faith in God. He should be kind to all creatures, truthful and forgiving. His prime dharma should be to study and remember the Veda. The dharma of the Kshatriya is not for you. To be stern, to wield a sceptre and to rule his subjects is the dharma the Kshatriya.

Listen, O Ruru, to how the race of serpents perished at Janamejaya's sarpa yagna of old, and how a great Brahmana, Astika, master of the Vedas and potent with spiritual powers, delivered the Nagas."'

CANTO 12

Pauloma Parva Continued

Sauti continued, 'Ruru asked, "Best of Dvijas, why did King Janamejaya want to slaughter the race of serpents? Why did Astika save them, and how? Tell me in detail."

The Rishi replied, "Other Brahmanas will tell you the wonderful story of Astika." Saying this, he vanished.

Ruru ran here and there in the jungle looking for the disappeared Rishi. But he did not find him, though he ran far and hard; he fell exhausted on the ground. He thought of what the Rishi had said and was bewildered. The world spun round and he fainted. Regaining consciousness, he went home and asked his father to tell him the story of Astika. And his father told him that tale.'

CANTO 13

Astika Parva

Saunaka asked, 'Why did that tiger among kings, the magnificent Janamejaya, decide to sacrifice the race of snakes in the fire of a sarpa yagna? Suta, tell us every detail. Tell us why Astika, best among the twice born, best among Rishis, rescued the Nagas from the blazing flames. Whose son was the king that undertook the terrible snake sacrifice? Whose son, also, was Astika?'

Sauti said, 'Most eloquent Saunaka, the story of Astika is a long one. I will tell it in full, if you will listen.'

Saunaka said, 'I am eager to hear every detail of the enchanted tale of the Rishi Astika, best among Brahmanas.'

Sauti said, 'This tale was first told by Krishna Dwaipayana, and Brahmanas call it a Purana. Vyasa's sishya, my Sage father Romaharshana once narrated the story when asked by the Munis of the Naimisa vana. I was there on that occasion and, great Saunaka, since you now ask me I will repeat the tale of Astika exactly as I heard it. Listen to the entire sin-destroying story.

Astika's father was as powerful as Prajapati. He was a brahmacharin, always in tapasya. He ate very little, was a great sannyasi, and his lust was under complete control. His name was Jaratkaru. Foremost among the Yayavaras, virtuous, keeping stern vratas, blessed with great taposhakti, Jaratkaru once went on a yatra through the world. Diverse places he visited, bathed in many sacred tirthas, and rested where night fell. Possessing enormous vigour, he practised such austerities as few men can, who are not souls of deep self-restraint. The Rishi lived imbibing only air, and he never slept at all. Ranging across the Earth like fire, one day he saw his ancestors, hanging in a great pit with their heads pointing down and their feet up.

Jaratkaru addressed them, "Who are you that hang upside down by a rope of virana fibres being gnawed all round and all the time by the rat that lives in this pit?"

The ancestors said, "We are Rishis of stern vows; we are the Yayavaras. We sink down into the Earth because we have no descendants. We have a son named Jaratkaru. Alas, the wretched child lives a sannyasi's life. He does not even think of becoming a grihasta, of taking a wife and having children! We fear that our clan will become extinct and that is why we are hanging in this hole. We have every wealth but live like indigents, in this misery.

Noble stranger, who are you that grieve for us like a friend? Tell us who you are, best of men, that stands here and tell us why you grieve for us miserable ones."

Jaratkaru said, "You are my sires and grandsires, for I am Jaratkaru. Tell me how I can serve you."

The fathers answered, "Do everything in your power, child, to beget a son to continue our line. Then, noble boy, you will gain punya for yourself and for us. Not by good deeds or by long tapasya does a man acquire the punya that he does by becoming a father. Therefore, son, we command you: marry a wife and beget children. In this lies our highest welfare."

Jaratkaru said, "I shall not marry for my own sake, nor earn wealth for my enjoyment, but I will do both for your felicity. My condition, by the Shastras, is that I find a bride who bears my own name, and that her friends and family give her willingly to be my bride. But then, who will give his daughter to a poor man like me? I will cetainly accept any woman given to me as alms. O my fathers, I will do everything in my power to marry! I give you my word, and will not break it. Once I marry, I will have children so you might be saved and attain to the realms of eternal bliss.'"

CANTO 14

Astika Parva Continued

Sauti said, 'Jaratkaru of great vratas ranged over the Earth in search of a bride, but found none. One day, he went into a jungle and, remembereing his ancestors, prayed thrice in a weak voice for a wife. Vasuki rose up before him and offered his sister to the Rishi. The Brahmana hesitated: did she have the same name as himself? Noble Jaratkaru thought, "I will not marry any woman that does not bear my own name."

The wise Rishi, of severe penance and great wisdom, asked mighty Vasuki, "Tell me, O Naga, the name of your sister."

Vasuki replied, "Jaratkaru, my younger sister is called Jaratkaru. I offer her to you; take the slender-waisted one to be your wife. I have kept her for you, O best among Brahmanas, so take her."

And he brought the lovely Jaratkaru, his sister, to the Rishi, who married her with proper rites.'

CANTO 15

Astika Parva Continued

Sauti said, 'O foremost among the knowers of Brahman, the mother of the Nagas had cursed them once: "Agni, whose sarathy is Vayu the Wind, shall burn all of you at Janamejaya's sarpa yagna!" It was in order to nullify that curse that Vasuki, king of snakes, married his sister to the Rishi Jaratkaru. When Jaratkaru had married the Nagina Jaratkaru with Shastraic rituals, a great soul was born to them, a son they named Astika. Astika was an illumined Rishi, who knew the Vedas and all their Angas. He regarded all beings with an equal eye, and allayed the anxieties of both his mother and his father.

When, some time after Astika's birth, a king from the Pandava line undertook a great sarpa yagna, it was Astika who delivered the Nagas, his brothers, maternal uncles and other serpents, too, from dying in the flames of Janamejaya's snake sacrifice.

Thus Jaratkaru delivered his father's ancestors by begetting children. By his tapasya, O Brahmana, and by keeping many vratas and studying the Veda, he freed himself from all debt. Performing diverse yagnas, at which different kinds of offerings were made, he worshipped the Devas. By practising brahmacharya, he pleased the Rishis, and by fathering children, he gratified his Pitrs.

Jaratkaru repaid the debt he owed his sires, who then rose into Swarga from the pit where they had hung. Acquiring profound spiritual merit, punya, after a long life of many years, Jaratkaru left his body and found heaven for himself, leaving Astika behind.

This is the story of Astika. O Tiger of the race of Bhrigu, what would you hear from me next?'

CANTO 16

Astika Parva Continued

Saunaka said, 'Sauti, tell us in more detail about the life of the learned and sage Astika. We are agog to hear more, for, O most pleasant one, you speak sweetly, with immaculate intonation, and your narration pleases us. Why, you speak as well as your father, who was always ready to please us. Tell us the whole story of Astika, even as your father told it to you.'

Sauti said, 'O Chiranjivis, blessed with long lives, I will indeed tell you the story of Astika as I heard it from my father. Brahmana, in the Krita Yuga, the golden age, Prajapati had two daughters. Sinless Muni, the sisters were wonderfully beautiful. Kadru and Vinata became the wives of Kashyapa. Kashyapa found great pleasure in his two wives and he, who resembled Prajapati himself, granted them each a boon.

When they heard this they rejoiced. Kadru wished for a thousand Nagas to be born as her sons, all of them equally splendid. Vinata wished for two sons stronger, greater, more powerful, having more vitality and splendour than Kadru's thousand.

Kashyapa said, "So be it!" granting Kadru her boon of a thousand sons, and Vinata hers for two. Vinata was delighted with her two superior sons, as was her sister with her thousand. "Carry the embryos carefully," said Kashyapa, and then he went away into the forest, leaving his two wives pleased.

Noblest of Dvijas, after a long pregnancy, Kadru brought forth a thousand eggs, and Vinata two. Their maidservants placed the eggs separately in warm vessels. Five hundred years passed; then one day Kadru's thousand eggs cracked open, resonantly as thunder, and her thousand splendorous sons were born. But Vinata's sons did not appear.

Vinata was jealous, and she broke open one of her eggs before time. Inside, she found a child whose upper limbs were fully formed, but not the lower part of his body, which was still undeveloped, stunted. The child in the egg cursed his mother, "Since you broke my egg prematurely, you will be a slave. If you wait five hundred years and not try to crack open the other egg, the lustrous child within it will deliver you from slavery. If you truly want a strong child, you must lavish tender care on the egg for all these five hundred years."

Having cursed his mother, the child rose into the sky. Brahmana, he was Aruna, the charioteer of Surya, whom we see every morning at dawn. When five hundred years passed, the other egg burst open, and from it emerged magnificent Garuda, the serpent-eater. Bhriguvyaghra, as soon as he saw light of day, Vinata's son left his mother. The Lord of all birds felt hungry and took wing in quest of the food that the Creator of all things had ordained for him.'

CANTO 17

Astika Parva Continued

Sauti said, 'Muni, about this time the two sisters saw the marvellous jewel among horses, the calm and magnificent Uchchaisravas, whom the Devas worship. He arose when the Kshirasagara was churned for the Amrita, and he was divinely graceful, ever-young, Creation's masterpiece, irresistibly vigorous and bearing every auspicious sign and mark upon his person.'

Saunaka asked, 'Why did the Devas churn the Ocean for the nectar? How and when did the mighty and resplendent Uchchaisravas come forth from its waves?'

Sauti said, 'There is a mountain called Meru, which appears like a great stack of blazing light, for its peaks reflect the golden rays of the Sun that fall upon them. Devas and Gandharvas come regularly to the Golden Mountain, past compare, immeasurable and unapproachable by men, to expiate their many sins. Terrible beasts of prey range over it, and numerous magically life-giving herbs illumine its sides. Meru is the first of mountains and stands towering, and kissing Devaloka, as it were.

Ordinary folk cannot even dream of climbing Meru. Mystic trees of wishes and enchanted streams abound upon Meru, and its slopes and valleys ring with the songs of choirs of fabulous birds. Once the Devas met upon its jewelled peak in conclave. They had performed severe penance to obtain the Amrita, the nectar of immortality, and it seemed that the time had come for them to seek it.

Seeing the celestial gathering's anxiety, Narayana said to Brahma, "You must churn the Ocean with the Devas and the Asuras, and you will find divine medicament and jewels you cannot imagine, and many other wonders. O Devas, churn the Kshirasagara and you will discover the Amrita."'

CANTO 18

ASTIKA PARVA CONTINUED

Sauti said, 'There is a mountain called Mandara whose peaks seem like clouds. It is the best of mountains, and cloaked by herbs growing thickly all over it. Countless birds sing their sweet songs upon it, and dangerous predators range its slopes. The Devas, Apsaras and Kinnaras come to sport and make love upon Mandara. It rises eleven thousand yojanas into the sky, and its roots plunge down as many yojanas into the earth. The Devas wanted to uproot it to use for their churning rod, but they could not. They came to Vishnu and Brahma, who sat together, and said, "Lords, tell us how we can dislodge Mandara to serve our purpose."

Son of Bhrigu, Vishnu and Brahma agreed. Lotus-eyed Vishnu gave the difficult task to the mighty Ananta, Prince of snakes. O Brahmana, Ananta tore up the mountain, with its forests and all the denizens of those forests.

The Devas came to the shore of the Ocean with Ananta and said to the Sea of Milk, "Ocean, we have come to churn your waters to have the Amrita."

The Ocean replied, "Tathaastu! So be it, since I will have my share. I can bear the prodigious churning with the mountain."

The Devas went to the king of tortoises and said to him, "O Kuurmaraja, you must support the mountain on your back!"

The Tortoise-king agreed, and Indra set the mountain on his shell.

The Devas and the Asuras made a churning rod of Mandara, Vasuki their rope, and began churning deep for the nectar. The Asuras held Vasuki's hood and the Devas held his tail. Ananta, who was with the gods, would at times suddenly lift the Naga's hood and lower it as abruptly. Flames and black smoke spewed from Vasuki's jaws. These turned into clouds, charged with lightning, and poured down rain that refreshed the tired Devas. Flowers also rained from every side over the gods, flying from the trees of whirling Mandara, covering them in cool fragrances.

Then, O Brahmana, from the ocean deeps came a tremendous roar like the thunder of the clouds of the Pralaya, the Apocalypse. Countless fish and other creatures of the Sea were crushed by Mandara and perished in the salt water. Numberless denizens of Patala, the under-world, and of the world of Varuna, died.

Great trees, with birds in their branches, upon spinning Mandara were torn up by their roots and flung into the water. Rubbing roughly against one another, many of these caught fire; fires broke out all round the churning and upon the mountain itself, licking through its forests. The mountain looked like a mass of black clouds veined with lightning. O Brahmana, the fire spread to the mountain, and immolated lions, elephants and the other creatures that lived on Mandara.

Then Indra put out the fire with some lashing rain.

After the churning had been underway for some time, O Brahmana, the extrusions of some herbs and treees, which were nectarine, mingled with sea-water, as did the liquid gold from the belly of the mountain.

And the Devas drank this water and felt immortal. Slowly, the milky water of the churned Kshirasagara turned into ghee, because of those rare extrusions. But the Amrita itself still did not appear.

The gods came before Brahma, Granter of boons, upon his Lotus throne, and said, "Sire, we are spent and have no strength left to continue churning. The Amrita has not yet surfaced and we must resort to Narayana to help us now."

Hearing them, Brahma said to Narayana, "Lord, bless the Devas with strength to churn on."

Narayana said, "Devas, I will infuse you with my own strength. Go, put the mountain back in place and churn the sea again."

Their strength renewed, the gods began churning again. In a while, the softly luminous Moon emerged, thousand-rayed, from the Ocean. Then the Devi Lakshmi, incomparable, clad in white, rose out of the waves, followed by the dazzling white Uchchaisravas, and the celestial ruby Kaustubha that Narayana wears upon his breast.

Lakshmi, Soma and the Horse swift as the mind all came before the Devas. Now, the divine and original physician Dhanvantari rose from the waters, bearing a pale chalice with the Amrita.

The Asuras saw him and roared, "It is ours!"

Airavata, of mammoth body and with four gleaming white tusks, came forth. Indra who wields the Vajra, the thunderbolt, took him. The churning continued and, last of all, the dreaded poison Kalakuta appeared, smoking, staining the waves black. In a trice, it engulfed the Earth, blazing up like a fire. The toxic fumes of the Kalakuta stupefied the three worlds, Swarga, Bhumi and Patala. Brahma begged Siva to save the worlds, and Siva quaffed the poison to preserve creation. Maheswara held the Kalakuta in his throat, which was burnt blue, and from that time Siva is also called Nilakanta, blue-throated.

Seeing all these wonders, the Asuras despaired, and prepared to fight the Devas for Lakshmi and the Amrita. Narayana summoned his Maya, his feminine power of illusion. He assumed the form of Mohini, a dark and irresistible seductress, and flirted with the Danavas, arousing them past reason. Enchanted by her, the Demons gave the chalice of Amrita, which they had snatched from Dhanvantri, into her hands.'

CANTO 19

ASTIKA PARVA CONTINUED

Sauti said, 'The Daityas and Danavas, the Asura sons of Diti and Danu, clad in superb armour and bearing unworldly weapons, were ready to attack the Devas for the ambrosia. But Mohini, the Enchantress, deceived the Demons and gave the Devas all the Amrita, which they greedily drank, in their terror of the Asuras, and they became immortal.

While the gods were drinking the nectar of immortality, a Danava called Rahu assumed the guise of a Deva and, sitting among them, he also drank the Amrita. But Surya and Soma discovered him and Vishnu lopped off Rahu's head with the Sudarshana Chakra when the Amrita had only reached his throat. And the grisly head of the Demon Rahu, big as a mountain, rose into the sky and began to cry out dreadfully.

The Danava's headless body fell on the Earth, making her tremble, all her mountains, forests and islands. From that time, Rahu has hated Surya and Soma, and to this day he swallows them during the eclipses of the Sun and the Moon.

Then Narayana was no more the Mohini of untold temptation, but Himself again, and cast inexorable astras at the Danavas, weapons that made them tremble, weapons that killed thousands of them in a wink.

Thus, on the shore of the salt-water Sea, the dreadful battle between the Devas and Asuras, the Devasura yuddha broke out. Sharp javelins and spears, and thousands of every kind of weapon filled the air on every side, darkening the sky. Dismembered by the Sudarshana Chakra, mangled by swords, crushed by maces, pierced through by arrows, burned by astras, Asuras beyond count lay dead upon the Earth in pools of blood from their wounds and blood they had vomitted. A rain of heads glinting golden crowns and ornaments, hewn from their necks with razor sharp blades, fell onto the ground. Drenched in gore, great Asuras lay dead everywhere like ruddy peaks of mountains, so huge were they.

And when the Sun rose in glory, thousands of warriors hacked at one another with diverse weapons. Screams rang out on all sides, and roars. Warriors that fought from a distance struck each other with arrows and iron javelins; those that fought hand to hand slew one another with blows of their fists.

The air was thick with shrieks of pain. Everywhere deep voices roared, "Cut him down!", "Run him through!", "Off with his head!", "At them!", "Burn him!", "Kill!", and "Forward!"

As the battle raged, Nara and Narayana entered the fray again. Narayana saw the celestial bow in Nara's hand and remembered his own weapon, the Sudarshana Chakra, scourge of the Danavas. No sooner did he think of it, that the Disc, bane of his enemies, bright as Agni, truly dreadful in battle, flared down from the sky. Receiving it, Narayana of limitless energy, his arms like the trunks of elephants, cast that blinding weapon, which could consume enemy cities in a flash, at the Asuras. Burning like the Fire that devours the world when the Yuga ends, the Chakra, wheeling everywhere, slew millions of Demons all around.

At times it burnt them into ash mounds, at others desiccated them, flashing through phalanxes and whole legions in a wink; and sometimes, it went among them like an army of pisachas and drank their blood!

On the other side, white as clouds from which the rain has fallen, having untold strength and fearless hearts, the Danavas flew up into the sky, and from a great height, hurled down a thousand mountain peaks over the Devas, harrying them constantly. Those huge mountains, like banks of thunderheads, flat-topped and mantled with trees, collided as they fell from the sky, with so many claps of thunder.

And when a million warriors roared without pause and those wooded mountains clashed together, the Earth and all her forests trembled.

Then Nara the divine appeared at the terrific battle between the Asuras and Siva's Ganas. With golden-headed arrows, he smashed the falling mountains to dust, and covered the firmanent in a haze. Repulsed by the Deva legions, and seeing the blazing Sudarshana consuming their forces on every side and in the fields of heaven, many doughty Asuras plunged down into the Patalas in the bowels of the Earth, while others dove down deep into the salt-water Sea.

The victorious Devas worshipped Mount Mandara and set him back in his place, so he was rooted again. Having the Amrita for themselves, the Devas shouted for joy, making Swarga echo with their shouts, and returned on high to their own realms. Great were their celebrations when they returned to Devaloka, and Indra and the other gods gave the chalice of Amrita to Narayana for safekeeping.'

CANTO 20

ASTIKA PARVA CONTINUED

Sauti said, 'This is the tale of how the Amrita was churned up from the Ocean, and that was when Uchchaisravas, the original and peerless steed, also arose. It was this horse about which Kadru asked Vinata, "Tell me, good sister, briefly, what colour is Uchchaisravas?"

Vinata answered, "The prince of all horses is perfectly white. What do you think, my sister? You say what colour he is, and let us make a wager upon it."

Kadru replied, "O my sister of the sweet smile, I think the horse has a black tail. Beautiful one, let us make a bet and let she that loses become the other's slave!"

Having made their wager, the sisters went to their homes, resolving to ascertain who was right about the colouring of Uchchaisravas the next day, by examining him closely.

Kadru was bent upon winning the wager, and she commanded her thousand sons to become a thousand black hairs and immediately cover the divine steed's tail. She would not become a slave!

But when her sons, the Nagas, refused to do as she asked, she cursed them, "During the sarpa yagna of the wise Pandava king Janamejaya, Agni will devour you!"

Brahma Pitamaha heard this savage curse of Kadru and knew that fate had subtly influenced the entire episode, for he saw that the race of serpents multiplied with alarming swiftness and threatened the rest of his creatures. Brahma and the other Devas gave their sanction to the curse of Kadru. The snakes were virulently poisonous, had great speed and strength and were vicious in the extreme; and it might be said that their own mother's curse was for the good of the rest of creation.

Fate punishes those that seek the death of other beings with death: with such observations, the Devas did not oppose Kadru's curse, and went away to their realms.

Brahma called Kashyapa and said gently to him, "Pure one, vanquisher of all your enemies, their mother Kadru has cursed your sons the Nagas, huge and their venom virulent and always intent on biting other creatures. Do not grieve over the curse, my son, for the burning of the race of serpents in the sarpa yagna was written long ago."

The Creator of the Universe consoled Kashyapa and also taught him the secret vidya of rendering snakebites harmless.'

CANTO 21

ASTIKA PARVA CONTINUED

Sauti said, 'When the night ended and dawn broke, O you who are rich in tapasya, Kadru and Vinata went impatiently to inspect Uchchaisravas. On their way, they saw the Ocean, into which all waters flow, vast and deep, rolling with waves, roaring mutedly, teeming with whale-eating timmingalas, monstrous crocodiles and thousands of other species, gigantic tortoises and other monsters of the deep.

The Ocean was a veritable mine of all kinds of gems: the home of Varuna Deva, the wonderful abode of the Nagas, the Lord of all rivers, where the submarine fire of the Apocalypse slumbered, the refuge of the Asuras, the terror of all creatures, the majestic reservoir of water: the immutable Ocean.

Holy is the Sea, benign to the Devas, the source of the Amrita, boundless, inconceivable, and altogether wonderful. Dark is the Ocean, subtly sounding with the speech of marine creatures, its waves roaring endlessly, and spinning with fathomless whirlpools.

All creatures fear the Ocean. Stirred by the winds blowing from its shores, rising up agitatedly, it appears to dance with wave hands raised everywhere. Swelling and ebbing with the waxing and waning of the moon, father of Vasudeva's mighty conch shell Panchajanya, treasure trove of jewels, the Ocean was once cloven and tossed about violently when Vasudeva of incalculable strength plunged into the depths of the Sea as Varaha, the Great Boar, to retrieve the Earth, Bhumi Devi, lying submerged on the bed of the Ocean, which is lower than the Patalas, the realms of nether.

The Rishi Atri of vast tapasya and stern vratas could not fathom the deeps of the Ocean, not when he had toiled for a hundred years. Whenever a Yuga ends, the Ocean becomes the Ekarnava, the bed of Vishnu Padmanabha, while that God of measureless power lies plunged in Yoga Nidra, his plumbless sleep, his profound cosmic meditation.

Sagara is the refuge of Mainaka, who fears Indra's Vajra, and the sanctuary of the Asuras whenever they are vanquished in war. The Ocean offers water as ghee into the fire blazing out from the mouth of Badava, the Fire of the End, who has the form of a Sea Mare. Fathomless he is, and limitless, immense, immeasurable, the Lord of rivers.

Kadru and Vinata saw thousands of mighty rivers plunging with haughty currents into the Ocean – even like rivals in love, each one wanting to be the first to unite with the beloved, each wanting to stop the others.

They saw that the Ocean was always full, ever dancing with waves. They saw it was as deep as time and as wide as the sky, that awesome receptacle of water!'

CANTO 22

ASTIKI PARVA CONTINUED

Sauti said, 'The Nagas consulted among themselves and decided to do as their mother wanted, for if they did not she might well withdraw her love and burn them up. If, on the other hand, they pleased her, she might release them from her curse. They said, "We will make the horse's tail black," and they became the hairs on the tail of Uchchaisravas.

Brahmanottama, best among Brahmanas, the sisters Kadru and Vinata, the daughters of Daksha, flew along in some delight to see the far shore of the Ocean. On their way they saw the calm, redolent and wonderful Ocean being suddenly agitated by the wind, and roaring. They flew quickly over it.'

CANTO 23

Astika Parva Continued

Sauti said, 'Having crossed the Ocean swiftly, Kadru and Vinata alighted near Uchchaisravas. They saw that first of steeds, fleetest of all, was white as the rays of the Moon; however, its tail was black. Kadru made Vinata, who had lost their wager, her slave, and Vinata grieved very much and was dejected past telling.

Meanwhile, when his time came, resplendent Garuda cracked open the egg in which he had lain so long and burst forth from it, dazzling the Universe. Ah, magnificent he was, beyond compare. He could assume any form at will, fly anywhere with a thought, and summon limitless strength and energy.

He was like a mass of fire; he was terribly brilliant. His lustre was that of the fire at the end of the Yuga; his eyes were like streaks of lightning. As soon as he was born, he grew immeasurably and flashed up into the sky. Fierce he was, and his keening cries shook the firmament; he seemed as dreadful as a second Badava.

When the Devas saw him, they were terrified and flew to Agni Vibhavasu. Bowing low to that deity of many forms upon his throne, the Devas said, "Agni, why have you spread your body out? The mass of flames you have extruded spreads everywhere to consume us!"

Agni replied, "Enemies of the Asuras, it is not as you imagine. This is not I but great Garuda, as strong and as splendid as I am. He has been born to be the joy of Vinata and the mount of Vishnu. Why, the very sight of his refulgence has made you afraid! He is the son of Kashyapa, bane of Nagas, guardian of the Devas, and an enemy of the Daityas and Rakshasas. Come, let me show you."

The Devas said, "you are a Rishi, a knower of every mantra. You receive the largest portion of the havis from every sacrifice, always glorious."

Agni and the Devas cautiously approached Garuda. They worshipped him, the Lord of birds, why, the sovereign spirit of everything animate and inanimate in the Universe.

"You are the destroyer of all things, the creator of all! You verily are Hiranyagarbha; you are Daksha and the other Prajapatis, the progenitors of creation; you are Indra; you are Hayagriva; you are the astra that Vishnu became in Siva's hands when Rudra burned the Tripura; you are the Lord of the Universe; you are the mouth of Vishnu; you are the four-faced Padmaja; you are the Brahmana, wise; you are Agni, Vayu and the gods of everything in the Universe.

You are gyana; you are maya, which binds us all; you are the pervasive Brahman; you are the Lord of the Devas; you are the great Truth; you are fearless; you are immutable; you are Nirguna Brahman; you are the energy of the Sun; you are the intellect; you are our great guardian; you are the sea of holiness; you are purity; there is no darkness in you; you own the sashta lakshana, the six lofty qualities; you are invincible in battle.

All things came from you, O you of the magnificent deeds; you are everything that has been and all that has not yet been. You are pure knowledge; as Surya does the world with his rays, you illumine this Universe, animate and unmoving. You dim the splendour of the Sun, each moment, and you are the destroyer of all things. You are all that is mortal and all that does not perish as well. You are as splendent as Agni, and you burn up everything even as Surya burns the fallen creatures in anger when the age ends.

O terrible one, you are proof against the fire that devours the Universe at the Dissolution, the Mahapralaya. Mighty Garuda, who range the firmament, we seek refuge in you. Lord of birds, awesome is your vitality, your irradiance that of fire, your brilliance that of lightning, which no darkness can approach. You are as lofty as the clouds; you are cause and effect, of matchless prowess and the granter of boons.

Lord, the Universe is heated by your splendour of molten gold. Give refuge to the noble Devas, who are terrified by you and dash about hither and thither through the sky in their vimanas from that fear. Greatest of birds, Lord of all, you are the merciful Rishi Kashyapa's son; be not wroth but take pity upon the Universe. You reign supreme; O, quieten your anger and watch over us.

Your voice is like thunder and, at your cries, the ten cardinal points, the firmament, Swarga, Bhumi and our minds quail, O Avian. We beg you diminish your body that resembles Agni. Dim your lustre, which is like Yama's when he is angry; for at the sight of your brilliance, our hearts lose their calm and pound out of all control.

Lord of birds, be propitious to us that solicit your mercy. O lambent one, bless us with fortune and joy."

When the Devas and Rishis worshipped him, that bird of fair feathers dimmed both his energy and his fearsome brilliance.'

CANTO 24

Astika Parva Continued

Sauti said, 'In truth, when it heard about its size and looked at itself, the Bird made itself smaller.

Garuda said gently, "Since you fear this dreadful form of mine, I will diminish myself. Let no creature be afraid."

Then Garuda, sky ranger, who could travel anywhere at will, who could call upon any degree of energy, set his brother Aruna upon his back and flashed away from his father's asrama to his mother upon the far shore of the Ocean. He set the shining Aruna down in the east, just at a time when Surya had decided to consume the worlds with his blazing rays.'

Saunaka asked, 'When did Surya want to burn the three worlds? What did the Devas do to provoke his wrath?'

Sauti said, 'Anagha, sinless, Surya and Soma pointed Rahu out to the Devas, while he sat among them and drank the Amrita, when the Ocean was churned. Since then he hated them. When Rahu tried to devour Surya Deva, the Sun God became furious. He thought, "What I did benefited all the gods, but I alone must suffer for saving them, and no one comes to help me when the Demon is about to swallow me before their very eyes; instead, they watch calmly, as spectators. I will destroy the worlds for this callousness!"

He journeyed to the western mountain. From there, he began to burn fiercely, to spew forth dreadful heat to consume the worlds.

The great Rishis went to the Devas and said, "A terrible heat has arisen in the middle of the night, striking terror in every heart and threatening to destroy the three worlds!"

The Devas and the Rishis went to Brahma and said, "Pitamaha, what is this terrible heat at midnight that makes the worlds panic? Surya has not yet risen but it already seems as if the Apocalypse is here. Lord, what will happen when he rises?"

The Grandsire replied, "Truly, Surya is preparing to rise today and burn the worlds. As soon as he rises, everything will become ashes. But I have a solution. We all know Kashyapa's intelligent son Aruna. He has a vast body and great splendour. Let him sit before Surya as his charioteer, and he will absorb the dreadful heat of the Sun. By this the worlds, the Rishis and the dwellers in Swarga shall find their remedy."

At Brahma's command, Aruna sat before Surya, and the Sun rose with his heat dimmed by Aruna's huge form. This is the story of Surya's wrath and how Garuda's brother Aruna became his sarathy. Listen next to the answer to your other question.'

CANTO 25

Astika Parva Continued

Sauti said, 'As I told you, the many-splendoured Garuda flew across the ocean to his mother's side, where Vinata lived in misery, as her sister's slave. Once Kadru called Vinata and said to her in the presence of her son, "Gentle Vinata, in the midst of the Ocean is an enchanting island where the Nagas dwell. Take me there!"

Vinata, mother of the Bird of splendid feathers, carried her sister, the mother of the serpents, upon her shoulders to that island. Commanded by his mother, Garuda carried the Nagas on his back. Vinata's sky-ranging son flew high, near the Sun, whose heat scorched the snakes and they fainted. Kadru saw her sons unconscious and began to pray to Indra.

"I bow to you, Lord of all the Devas. I bow to you, slayer of Vritra. I bow to you, slayer of Namuchi. O thousand-eyed, O Consort of Sachi. I beg you to protect my sons from searing Surya with your rain! Best of the Devas, you are our great Guardian. Purandara, you pour down torrents. You are Vayu, the clouds, fire, and the lightning in them. You are the propeller of clouds, and you have been called the Great Cloud, which will darken the galaxies at the end of the Yuga. You are deafening thunder and the roaring thunderheads. You are the Creator of the worlds and their Destroyer. You are unvanquished. You are the light of all creatures, Aditya, Vibhavasu, and the Panchamahabhutas. You are the king of the Devas. You are Vishnu. With your thousand eyes, you are the final recourse. You are, O Deva, Amrita and the most precious Soma.

You are the moment, the day, the bala, the kshana. You are the bright fortnight of the waxing Moon, and the dark fortnight, too. You are kaala, kashta, and truti. You are the year, the seasons, the months, the nights, and the days.

You are the Earth with her mountains and forests. You are the sky, resplendent with the Sun. You are the vast Ocean, heaving with waves, teeming with whales, timmingalas that eat whales, and makaras, and countless fish. You have great fame, always worshipped by wise men and Maharishis, with their minds focused in dhyana.

For the weal of all creatures, you drink Soma rasa at yagnas and the clarified butter offered with holy mantras. Brahmanas worship you with sacrifices to fulfil their desires. O incomparably strong one, the Vedas and Vedangas sing your praises, which is why wise Brahmanas who want to perform sacrifices study the Vedas carefully.'"

CANTO 26

Astika Parva Continued

Sauti said, 'Upon having his praises sung by Kadru in worship, Indra, king of Devas, who rides Uchchaisravas, finest of steeds, covered the sky with bank upon bank of rainclouds, and commanded them, "Let fall your sacred and life-giving rain!"

Crackling with lightning, roaring at one another in the firmament, the clouds loosed their rain in torrents. In that deluge, the sky looked as if the end of the Yuga had come. It seemed as if the sky danced madly with the waves risen into it, the roar of the clouds, the gashes of lightning, the violent winds that blew. Pitch darkness fell, which no ray of Sun or Moon pierced. Only the deluge raged on.

The Nagas revived and were overjoyed by Indra's downpour. The Earth was covered by water, and the cool, clear liquid flowed down into the Patalas. Bhumi Devi was covered by waves and waves of water, everywhere.

The snakes and their mother arrived safely on the island called Ramaniyaka.'

CANTO 27

Astika Parva Continued

Sauti said, 'Yes, drenched by Indra's deluge, the Nagas felt cool and happy. Borne by the Eagle of white feathers, they arrived swiftly upon the island. The Creator had appointed that island to be the home of the makaras.

First they saw the eerie Lavana Samudra, the Ocean of Salt. Then they beheld an exotic forest, washed by the waves of that Sea. They heard the heavenly music of Gandharvas and Apsaras. Wondrous trees grew thickly, bearing rare flowers and fruit. They saw magnificent mansions upon the island, with tanks brimming with lotuses. They saw shimmering, azure lakes, and scented fine breezes laden with the fragrance of incense. They saw that the trees here were those that grow only upon the Malaya Mountain, and they reached into heaven, so tall were they. Other trees, as lovely, had their vivid flowers blown everywhere by the breeze.

That enchanted forest was dear to the Gandharvas, and they came to it always for it delighted them. The bees all around seemed drunk and maddened by the sweet honey they drank from the flowers. And the sight of all this was exceedingly delightful. In every way, that forest was charmed and full of rare delight and sacredness, and the sons of Kadru rejoiced to see it and to listen to the sweet songs of its birds.

The Nagas commanded Garuda of great energy, "Fly us to another island as beautiful as this one and where the water sparkles pure. Sky ranger, you must have seen many exquisite places while flying through the air!"

Garuda thought for a moment then asked his mother Vinata, "Why must I do the bidding of the snakes?"

Vinata said to her son, who possessed every virtue, and enormous vitality and power, "Best of birds, I have fallen on bad times and become my sister's slave. The snakes deceived me so that I lost my wager with my sister, which left me as her slave."

Hearing this, the dejected Garuda said to the serpents, "Tell me Nagas, what can we do to become free from our bondage to you?"

The snakes replied, "Bring us the Amrita and then, O Bird, you will be free."'

CANTO 28

ASTIKA PARVA CONTINUED

Sauti said, 'When the snakes said this to him, Garuda said to his mother, "I will go and fetch the Amrita. But I want to eat something on my way. Tell me where I can feed."

Vinata replied, "On a remote island in the midst of the Ocean, the Nishadas have their beautiful home. Eat the thousands of Nishadas that live there, and then bring the Amrita. Remember never to harm a Brahmana, for of all creatures, a Brahmana must never be killed. An angry Brahmana is like Agni or Surya, like poison or a sword. A Brahmana is the master of all creatures, and is worshipped by the virtuous. Not even in anger must you kill a Brahmana; enmity with a Brahmana is a sin. My sinless child, neither Agni nor Surya is as devastating as an austere Brahmana when provoked to wrath. A good Brahmana can be known by various signs. He is the firstborn of all creatures, the foremost among the four varnas, the sire and master of all."

Garuda asked, "Mother, what is a Brahmana's form, how does he behave and what is his strength? Does he blaze like fire, or is he of tranquil disposition? Mother, tell me the auspicious signs by which I can recognise a Brahmana."

Vinata replied, "My child, if you swallow a good Brahmana, he will savage your throat like a fish-hook or burn it like a live coal. O, never must you kill a Brahmana, not even in anger."

Out of her love for him, Vinata repeated herself to Garuda, "Your stomach will not receive or digest a good Brahmana."

Though she knew the incomparable strength of her son, she still blessed him with all her heart, for, having been deceived by the snakes, she was still grief-stricken. She said, "May Vayu protect your wings, and Surya and Soma your back; may Agni watch over your head, and the Vasus your whole body.

I will also sit here, performing constant rituals for your wellbeing and success. Go, my son, and fulfil your mission."

Garuda spread his wings and flew up into the sky. Soon he fell upon the Nishadas on their island home, with terrible ferocity, like a ravenous Yama. He raised a squall of dust with his wingbeats, covering the sky; he drained a great part of the Sea, and lashed the forests of the mountains of that island with the waters. Then he spread his gigantic beak wide and blocked every highway of the Nishadas' city. Not knowing where they ran, the panic-stricken Nishadas, blinded by the pall of dust, rushed into that yawning maw, even as birds in a forest swarm into the open sky when their trees shake in a gale.

The hungry Lord of birds, serpent-eater, sky rover, of limitless strength and thought-like speed, clamped his beak shut, swallowing thousands of the Nishada fisherfolk in a blink.'

CANTO 29

Astika Parva Continued

Sauti continued, 'Now it happened that a Brahmana and his wife also went down the throat of Garuda, and began to burn him like live coals.

Garuda said to him, "O best of Brahmanas, I will open my beak and you must come out quickly, for I must never kill a Brahmana even if he sins."

The Brahmana said, "This Nishada woman is my wife. Let her come out with me."

Garuda said, "Bring the woman with you, but come out at once! Hurry, before the blazing juices of my belly digest you."

The Brahmana and his Nishada wife emerged in a trice and went their way, singing Garuda's praises. Now Garuda spread his wings again and flew up once more into the sky, quick as a thought.

He saw his father, and greeted him reverentially. The Maharishi Kashyapa asked him, "Are you well, my child? Do you have enough to eat daily? Is there enough food for you in the world of men?"

Garuda replied, "My mother is well, as is my brother, and so am I. But father, I do not always get enough to eat, and am at poor peace for that. Now the Nagas have sent me to fetch the Amrita. I mean to find it and bring it back even today, so my mother's slavery will end. My mother said to me, 'Eat the Nishadas.' I ate thousands of them but my hunger is not appeased.

Holy one, tell me what else I can eat to find the strength to wrest the Amrita away by force from the Devas. Tell me what I can consume, by which I can both satisfy my hunger and quench my thirst."

Kashyapa Muni replied, "This lake before you is sacred. It has renown even in Swarga. In it is an elephant, his head turned down, ceaselessly battling a great tortoise who is his elder brother. I will tell you about their enmity from another life. Listen to why they are here.

Once, long ago, there was a great Rishi called Vibhavasu. He was a Sage with a quick and fiery temper. He had a younger brother called Supritika. Supritika did not want to hold his inheritance jointly with his brother and always spoke of partitioning it.

Vibhavasu told Supritika, "Only fools who are blinded by the love of wealth ever think of partitioning their patrimony; for once the patrimony is divided the wealth will delude them and they will fight over it. After the division, invariably false friends will poison the selfish ones' minds against one another, confirming their enmity. Further divided, they will surely fall, and complete ruin will swiftly overtake them.

The wise never endorse the partitioning of a patrimony between brothers, because once that happens the brothers live in constant fear of one another and cease to honour the most sacred Shastras. But Supritika, you will not listen to my counsel but always want to cleave our inheritance. I say to you, you shall become an elephant!'

Supritika cursed Vibhavasu back hotly, 'You will become a tortoise and live in water!'

And so, out of the love for wealth and property, these two have become an elephant and a tortoise. Both are proud of their great bodies and strength, and fight each other with unremitting hatred, without pause. Look, here comes the handsome and enormous elephant Supritika, as always in anger."

The giant tortoise heard him trumpeting and surfaced, agitating the lake violently. Seeing him, the elephant curled his trunk and rushed into the water. The mighty pachyderm beat the water roughly with his trunk, his head and tail; he stamped it angrily with his massive feet, so waves rose and the numberless fish in the lake were swept along upon them, panic-stricken. And the mountainous tortoise lifted his huge head high and, accepting the elephant's challenge, swam eagerly forward for the encounter.

The elephant was six yojanas tall and twice that measure around. The tortoise was three yojanas high and ten around. Wildly, full of wrath, the two began to butt and strike each other, their roars filling the air.

Said Kashyapa Muni to his son Garuda, "Eat both these, bent upon killing each other. Eat that savage elephant who looks like a mountain and the ferocious tortoise like a bank of clouds, and then go forth to fetch the Amrita."

Kashyapa blessed Garuda, "I bless you for your battle against the Devas. May all things auspicious shower their blessings upon you – vessels brimful of holy water, Brahmanas, sacred cows, and everything else that can bless you. My mighty son, when you fight the Devas let the Riks, the Yajus, the Samas and all the profound mysteries of the Upanishads be your strength!"

Garuda went to the side of the lake, and looked at the expanse of lucid water upon which waterbirds floated. Remembering what his father said, Garuda, swift as the mind, seized the elephant in one claw, the tortoise with the other, and soared into the sky.

He came to a sacred place called Alamba, and saw many divine and lustrous trees there, kalpavrikshas. Those trees trembled in the gusts of wind that his wings raised. The trees of golden branches feared they would be broken. Seeing the kalpavrikshas shaking with fright, Garuda flew to some other trees, indescribably beautiful. They were gigantic, and their branches were made of many shimmering jewels and their fruits were of gold and silver. Water from the sea washed their trunks.

Among these, and even loftier than the others, stood a great patriarchal Nyagrodha. Seeing Garuda flaring towards it, swift as the mind, that Pipal said, "Sit upon this branch of mine, a hundred yojanas long, and eat the elephant and the tortoise."

Garuda, best of birds, big as a mountain, alighted on that prodigious bough, and at once the great leafy branch, home to thousands of lesser birds, broke with a sound like a clap of thunder.'

CANTO 30

ASTIKA PARVA CONTINUED

Sauti said, 'As soon as Garuda's feet rested upon it, that branch snapped like a twig. Garuda cast his gaze around him in wonder and saw Balakhilya Rishis hanging, head down, from the branch, in deep dhyana. Fearing that they would die if the branch fell on the ground far below, in a wink, still clutching the elephant and the tortoise in his claws, Garuda also seized the falling branch of a hundred yojanas in his beak. He rose into the sky with his new burden and the old one. The Rishis were wonderstruck at what the Avian had done, which no Deva could have achieved.

They said, "Let this greatest of birds be called Garuda, for the impossible burden that he bears."

At his ease, Garuda flew through the sky and whenever he passed above a mountain it shook in the gusts from his wingbeats. Many lands and wonders he saw beneath him as he flew along at his great leisure. Then he spied a place where he could land softly, saving the tiny thumb-sized Balakhilyas: it was Mount Gandhamadana, dwarapalaka to the heavens.

He saw his father Kashyapa sitting in tapasya upon the fragrant mountain. Kashyapa also saw his radiant and vital son, big as a peak, quick as light, deadly as a Brahmana's curse, inconceivable, ineffable, fearsome, blazing like Agni, invincible so not the Devas, Danavas and the greatest Rakshasas could vanquish him; that sky ranger who could crush mountains, drain away whole seas, and, indeed, destroy the three worlds, looking as fierce as Yama.

Seeing Garuda approach and knowing what his son wanted to achieve, the illumined Kashyapa warned him, "Be very careful, my son, for you might have to suffer if you are rash or impatient. If you annoy the Balakhilyas, who live by imbibing the rays of the Sun, they might smite you with their tapasysa shakti."

Then, for his son's sake, Kashyapa addressed the Balakhilyas of great fortune, whose sins had been consumed in the fire of their asceticism.

Kashyapa said, "You whose wealth is tapasya, Garuda is on a mission for the welfare of every living creature. Great is the task upon which he goes forth. Bless him, great ones."

When they heard what Kashyapa said, the little Munis relinquished the branch and went away to the sacred mountain Himavat to continue their tapasya. After the Rishis had gone, Vinata's son spoke to his father, and his voice was unclear for the massive bough in his beak.

Garuda asked, "Illustrious father, where shall I let down the arm of the tree? Show me a place where there are no men."

Kashyapa now told Garuda about a mountain, always covered with snow, full of sheer valleys and deep caves, where no ordinary creatures could go even in imagination. Kashyapa gave his son directions to find that mountain. Carrying the branch, the elephant and the tortoise, Garuda flashed away towards that inaccessible hidden mountain. The branch of the tree that he carried in his beak could not be circumscribed by a rope made from the stretched hides of a hundred cows.

For lakhs of yojanas flew Garuda, in a mere moment. And following Kashyapa's directions, he arrived over the isolated mountain and dropped the tremendous branch from his beak. It fell with a great sound, and that prince of mountains shook when the storm that Garuda's spanless wings raised struck it. Its trees poured down their flowers in a helpless rain. Its jewelled peaks were themselves loosened and came crumbling down all its sides.

The bough felled countless trees with dark leaves and golden flowers, which seemed like clouds with lightning in them. The fallen trees, dyed in mountain metals, shone as if the Sun bathed them in his light.

Garuda now perched on the summit of that mountain, and ate both the elephant and the tortoise. Finishing his great meal, he spread his wings and rose into the sky, quick as a thought.

In Devaloka, frightening omens appeared and the Devas trembled. Indra's Vajra blazed as if in terror. Flaming meteors fell out of the sky, smoking, as plain by daylight as they might be in the night. The weapons of the Vasus, the Rudras, the Adityas, the Sadhyas, the Maruts and other Devas began to spend themselves in contention against one another. Why, nothing like this had happened even during the war against the Asuras, the Devasura yuddha.

Rough winds blew, peals of thunder threatened to crack open the sky, and meteors continued to stream down in thousands. Without a cloud in its vacancy, the sky roared and roared. Blood flowed copiously from the body of the king of the Devas. The divine garlands the other Devas wore faded and they felt weak in all their limbs.

Then clouds scudded into the sky and poured down a heavy rain of blood. The dust raised by the winds dimmed the lustre of the crowns the Devas wore. Indra, of a thousand yagnas, and the other gods trembled with fright and said to their Guru Brihaspati, "Master, what are these dreadful omens? I see no enemy on the horizon, then why do the very elements assail us?"

Brihaspati replied, "O Indra of a thousand eyes, you have been careless and have sinned. And a being born by the tapas of the Balakhilyas, the mighty son of Kashyapa and Vinata, one who is a sky ranger and can assume any form he chooses, is coming to take the Amrita from you.

The bird is the strongest of the strong and can do what seems impossible. He will indeed take the Amrita from you."

Indra said to the guardians of the Amrita, "Brihaspati says that a bird of measureless strength and energy is on his way to steal the Amrita. I am warning you, so he does not take it by force."

The Devas were amazed, but they prepared to defend the Amrita. All of them stood around the Nectar, and Indra who wields the Vajra of thunder stood with them. The Devas wore priceless golden breastplates, jewelled, and impenetrable armours of hide. They carried sharp blades and numberless other strange and powerful weapons, which gave off sparks of fire, and smoke. They carried chakras and spiked gadas, trisulas, khatvangas, all great and awesome: weapons suited to each great god, mystic astras: supernatural missiles.

Wearing unearthly ornaments, splendid with the brilliant armour and weapons, the Devas waited, now calmly determined, those peerless ones, to protect the Amrita. They who could devastate the cities of the Asuras stood there in forms as awesome and bright as fire. The battlefield to be sparkled with thousands of spiked and jewelled maces, even as the sky was lit by the rays of the Sun.'

CANTO 31

ASTIKA PARVA CONTINUED

Saunaka asked, 'Sauti, son of Suta, what was Indra's sin, his carelessness? How was Garuda born by the tapas of the Balakhilyas? How did Kashyapa Muni, a Brahmana, have the king of birds for his son? How was Garuda invincible and the strongest of creatures? How could he go anywhere at will? How did he have such boundless vitality? If the Purana has answers to these questions, I would hear them.'

Sauti said, 'Indeed, the Purana deals with what you ask. Listen, O Dvija, to the answers to your questions.

Once upon a time, Kashyapa Prajapati undertook a yagna to have children, a putrakama yagna, and the Devas, the Rishis and Gandharvas all came to help him. Kashyapa gave Indra charge of fetching the sacrificial fuel for the fire, and with him the Balakhilyas and all the other Devas. Indra of untold strength easily hefted a mountainous portion of firewood and was bringing it to the yagnashala. On his way, he saw a number of tiny, less than thumb-sized Rishis, who together carried along a single strand of a palasa leaf. Those Rishis were obviously starving, for they were skin and bones. Suddenly, they staggered into a pool of water collected in the indentation on the path made by the hoofprint of a cow. They flailed about and struggled in that minuscule pool.

Purandara, Indra proud of his strength, looked at them bemused; then, laughing uproariously, calling out to the little Munis in mockery, he left them there: why, he stepped right over their heads. Those Rishis blazed with sorrow and wrath. They prepared to perform a great yagna to have their revenge, and hearing about it Indra became terrified.

Listen, O Saunaka, to what those excellent and austere Balakhilyas did. They poured ghee into a fire of sacrifice, chanting mantras loudly:

"Let there be another Indra among the gods, who can fly anywhere at will, summon limitless strength and energy, and strike fear into the Deva king. By the fruit of our tapasya, let such a one arise, swift as the mind, and fierce!"

And the king of the Devas, he of a hundred yagnas, heard about the Balakhilyas' sacrifice, and flew to Kashyapa of the austere vrata for protection. When Prajapati Kashyapa heard what Indra said, he went to the Balakhilyas and asked them if their sacrifice had been successful.

And those honest Rishis replied, "Let it be as you say!"

Kashyapa pacified them, "At the word of Brahma, Indra has been made Lord of the three worlds. You Munis want to create another Indra, but it does not become you, noble Sages, to render Brahma's word false. Yet, let not your sacrifice become futile: let there come into being another Indra, but a king of birds, a Pakshiraja of untold strength, vitality and speed. Indra begs you to take pity on him."

The Balakhilyas first offered Kashyapa Prajapati worship, then said to him, "Prajapati, our yagna is for an Indra! It is also a putrakama yagna for you to have a son. We leave its completion to you; do what you see as being proper and wise."

Meanwhile, Daksha's chaste, fortunate, virtuous daughter Vinata wanted to have children and, having completed her worship and bathed, she came to her husband Kashyapa, in her fertile time.

Kashyapa said to her, "Devi, the yagna I undertook has borne fruit, and you shall have what you want. Two heroic sons you will bear, who shall become lords of the worlds. Because of the tapasya of the Balakhilyas and by my own penance, your sons shall have great fortune and be worshipped throughout Swarga, Bhumi and Patala."

Kashyapa and Vinata came together and then he said to her, "Bear these auspicious seeds with great care. Your two sons will be the lords of all winged creatures. These valiant rangers of the sky will be revered in every realm, and have the gift of assuming any form they choose.

The gratified Prajapati then said to Indra, "You will have two brothers of boundless tejas and strength, who will never harm you but be friendly towards you. Do not grieve anymore, you will continue to be Lord of the worlds. But never again slight those that worship the Brahman, nor dare insult the Munis, who are wrathful and whose curses are more potent than your thunderbolt."

Hearing this Indra's fears were stilled, and he returned to Devaloka.

Her purpose fulfilled, Vinata was also joyful, and, in time, she gave birth to two sons, Aruna and Garuda. And Aruna, of the flawed limbs, became the charioteer of the Sun. And Garuda was given sovereignty over the race of birds. O you of the line of Bhrigu, Bhargava, now hear about the great achievement of Garuda.'

CANTO 32

ASTIKA PARVA CONTINUED

Sauti said, "Great Brahmanas, the Devas prepared for battle, and soon enough Garuda appeared before those ones of light. When the gods saw how great he was, how bright and strong, they shook with fright; why, they began to strike one another with their weapons.

Among those guarding the Soma was a certain Brahmana, the divine architect, measureless in might, bright as a bolt of lightning and terrifically vital. The encounter between Garuda and him lasted a mere moment, before, devastated by talons, beak and wings, the Deva lay dead on the field.

Garuda raised such a squall of dust with his massive wings that the three Lokas were darkened by it, and the Devas swooned in that stormy darkness of dust. The immortal guardians of the Amrita were blinded and no longer saw Garuda. Then, freely, at his will, he raked them with beak and claw; he swatted them like flies with his wings; he mangled them as he chose in Swarga.

Indra, God of a thousand eyes, commanded Vayu the Wind, "Scatter the dust quickly, Maruta, or we are lost!"

Vayu blew away the pall of dust and, when they saw again, the Devas attacked Garuda. He began to roar like the stormclouds of the Pralaya, terrifying every creature alive. He spread his wings, and the king of birds rose into the sky, and the Devas armed with every conceivable weapon, including chakras bright as suns, saw him above them. Never pausing, Garuda attacked them from above, and indeed from every side, with a storm of many weapons, with talon, beak and wing.

Raked by his claws, savaged by his beak, the Devas bled in rills. Overwhelmed by the lord of birds, the Sadhyas and the Gandharvas fled eastward, the Vasus with the Rudras to the south, the Adityas to the west, and the Aswins towards the north. Having great tejas, they retreated while fighting, always gazing back at their redoubtable enemy.

Garuda battled the Yakshas, Aswakranda of great valour, Rainuka, the bold Krathanaka, Tapana, Uluka, Swasanaka, Nimesha, Praruja and Pulina. And the son of Vinata smashed them with wings, talons and beak, like punitive Siva himself, who wields the Pinaka in wrath when the Yuga ends. Those dreadful and fearless ones soon looked like great black clouds raining blood from all their limbs.

Having slain the Yakshas or put them to flight, Garuda came to the chalice of Amrita. He saw that it was surrounded by fire on all sides. And the hissing flames of that fire covered the very sky and, fanned by gusts of wind, they seemed to want to devour the Sun himself.

Shining Garuda sprouted ninety times ninety beaks, drained the waters of many rivers with them, flew back to the fire that guarded the Amrita, and doused it with those waters.

Now he became diminutive, very small indeed, so he could enter into the niche where the chalice of Amrita was kept.'

CANTO 33

ASTIKA PARVA CONTINUED

Sauti said, 'Having assumed a golden body, bright as a Sundrop, the bird king flashed into the chamber of the Amrita like a cataract into a sea. He saw that a wheel, its edges sharp as razors, spun at great speed, endlessly around the Amrita. The Devas had created it to cut any hopeful thieves into slivers. Garuda made himself smaller still and easily flew through the deadly wheel. Now he saw two huge blazing serpents, forked tongues like streaks of lightning, jaws spewing fire, eyes aflame, restless and hissing like twin storms, their venom deadly. Their lidless unwinking eyes burned with quenchless ferocity. Either of them would have instantly made ashes of any intruder they spied.

The bird of fair plumage threw dust into their eyes and, when they could not see, he set upon them, beak and talons flashing, from every side. In moments, Vinata's son ripped those Nagas into shreds.

Immediately, he took the chalice of Amrita from its niche, smashing the uncanny humming contrivance that surrounded it with a blow of his beak, and rose away with the nectar, at speed of thought. He emerged with the Amrita, but did not drink it, and tireless as ever, he flew homewards, dimming the light of the Sun in the sky.

On his way, Vinata's son met Vishnu in the firmament. Narayana was gratified that Garuda had not drunk the Amrita. That God who knows no decay said to the sky crosser, "I want to grant you a boon."

Garuda replied, "Let me then stay above you." He said again, "Let me be immortal and free from every sickness without drinking Amrita."

Vishnu said to the son of Vinata, "So be it."

Garuda received the two boons, and said to Vishnu, "I also grant you a boon, so ask me for something, O owner of the six gunas."

Vishnu asked mighty Garuda to become his vahana, his mount. He made the Pakshiraja sit upon the flagstaff of his vimana, saying, "Even so you shall stay above me."

And King Bird replied to Narayana, "So be it," and flashed away, racing the wind.

As Garuda coursed along with the Amrita, Indra cast his Vajra at him. But Garuda only laughed when the thunderbolt fell on him. He said to Indra, sweetly, "I worship the Rishi Dadichi from whose bones the Vajra is made. I worship the Vajra and you, too, O Lord of the thousand yagnas. I feel no twinge of pain from your thunderbolt, but now I cast off one feather of mine, and you shall not find its end."

The Pakshiraja gave up one of his feathers and every creature saw that shining feather and felt incredibly glad, for it was so beautiful and radiant. They said, "Let this bird be called Suparna, he of the fair feathers."

Thousand-eyed Indra Purandara watched this magical happening and felt the bird was truly some very great Being, and spoke to him. Indra said to Garuda, "Pakshishreshta, O best of birds, I want to know the extent of your awesome strength, and I want to have eternal friendship with you."

CANTO 34

Astika Parva Continued

Sauti continued, 'Garuda said, "Purandara, let there be friendship between us, just as you wish. You know my strength is hard to resist. Indra of a thousand yagnas, the virtuous never extol their own prowess, nor do they praise themselves.

But since we are now friends and you ask me, I will tell you about my strength, though I repeat that never do the good speak of their own merits.

O Sakra, I can bear the Earth, with all her mountains, forests, oceans and you yourself standing upon her, on a single feather of mine. I am blessed with such strength that I can bear the three worlds, and all they contain, mobile and unmoving, and never feel tired."

O Saunaka, when Garuda said this, Indra, king of the Devas, who wears the crown of the three worlds and always works for their weal, said, "Truly it must be as you say, for anything is possible with you. Accept my deep and heartfelt friendship now, and if you have no need for the Amrita, return it to me: for those to whom you are taking it will always be our enemies."

Garuda answered, "There is a reason why I am taking the Amrita. I shall not give it to anyone to drink, O thousand-eyed; as soon as I set it down you can make away with it again, O Lord of Swarga!"

Indra said, "Greatest Avian, I am satisfied and I thank you. Ask me, O Pakshiraja, for any boon you want."

Garuda remembered how the sons of Kadru turned the tail of Uchchaisravas black, making his mother Vinata a slave.

He said, "I will always do your bidding, O Indra. Let snakes become my food!"

The slayer of the Danavas said to him, "So be it!" and flew to Hari, Devadeva, God of gods, Mahatman, and Lord of Yogins. Vishnu sanctioned everything Garuda had said.

The lustrous King of Swarga said to Garuda, "I will bring away the Amrita as soon as you set it down," and with that bid farewell to Suparna.

Garuda flew like an arrow to his mother, and cried in joy to the serpents, his half-brothers, "I have brought the Amrita; let me set it down on some kusa grass.

O Nagas, you must bathe and perform your worship, then come back here and sit down to drink it. And from today, as you promised, let my mother no longer be a slave, but free, for I have done what you asked, I have brought the Amrita."

The snakes said, "So be it," and went to perform their ablutions.

Meanwhile, Indra took the chalice of Amrita and flew back to Swarga. The Nagas bathed, performed their nitya karma, their daily devotions, and other sacred rites, and hurried back, in great excitement to drink the Amrita. They found the bed of kusa grass, on which the chalice had been placed, empty. In frenzy, they fell to licking the sharp grass and their tongues, bisected by the kusa blades, have been forked ever since.

Having been touched by the Amrita, the kusa grass was sanctified and has been sacred ever after. This is how Garuda fetched the Amrita from Devaloka, and how the serpents had their tongues divided.

Then Suparna sported in delight in the surrounding forest, in the company of his mother. Mighty and worshipped by all beings that traverse the sky, he further pleased his mother by feeding on the snakes.

The man who listens to this story, or recites it to a gathering of pious Brahmanas, surely finds heaven for himself, for great is the punya to be gained by recounting the legend of Garuda.'

CANTO 35

ASTIKA PARVA CONTINUED

Saunaka said, 'Son of Suta, you have told us why Kadru cursed her sons the serpents, and also why Aruna cursed his mother Vinata. You have told us how Kashyapa, their husband, blessed Kadru and Vinata with boons. You have told us the names of Vinata's sons, but you have not told us the names of the sons of Kadru. We are keen to hear the names of the greatest among Kadru's sons.'

Sauti said, 'Great Munis, to name all the serpents would be a lengthy task, and I will tell you the names only of the main among them. Listen, O you whose wealth is tapasya.

First born was Sesha, after him Vasuki. Then came Airavata, Takshaka, Karkotaka, Dhananjaya, Kalakeya, Mani, Purana, Pinjaraka, Elapatra, Vamana, Nila, Anila, Kalmasha, Savala, Aryaka, Ugra, Kalasapotaka, Suramukha, Dadhimukha, Vimalapindaka, Apia, Karotaka, Samkha, Valisikha, Nisthanaka, Hemaguha, Nahusha, Pingala, Vahyakarna, Hastipada, Mudgarapindaka, Kamvala, Aswatara, Kaliyaka, Vritta, Samvartaka, Padma, Mahapadma, Sankhamukha, Kushmandaka,

Kshemaka, Pindaraka, Karavira, Pushpadanshtraka, Bilwaka, Bilwapandara, Mushikada, Sankhasiras, Purnabhadra, Haridraka, Aparajita, Jyotika, Srivaha, Kauravya, Dhritarashtra, Sankhapinda, Virajas, Subahu, Salipinda, Prabhakara, Hastipinda, Pitharaka, Sumuksha, Kaunapashana, Kuthara, Kunjara, Kumuda, Kumudaksha, Tittri, Halika, Kardana, Bahumulaka, Karkara, Akarkara, Kundodara, and Mahodara.

These, O best of Dvijas, are the main Nagas. The sons of these and their sons are beyond counting: they are thousands of millions.'

CANTO 36

Astika Parva Continued

Saunaka said, 'Child, you have named many of the most powerful Nagas. What did they do when they heard about the curse?'

Sauti said, 'Sesha, first among them, of great renown, left his mother and performed rigorous tapasya. Observing stern vratas, he sat in penance upon Gandhamadana, at Badari, at Gokarna, the forest of Pushkara, and the foothills of Himavat. He dwelt in those sacred places, some holy for their waters and others for their earth.

Never swerving from his vows, single-mindedly, his passions under perfect control, he did tapasya. Brahma, Pitamaha of all, saw that ascetic with matted jata, wearing rags, and his body and skin shrivelled and parched by his severe austerities.

Brahma said to the fortunate hermit of rare fortitude, "What are you doing, O Sesha? Think also of the well-being of the creatures of the worlds. Sinless one, you are afflicting every creature with your searing penance. Sesha, tell me what desire impels this tapasya."

Sesha replied, "All my full brothers are evil-minded, and I do not want to live among them. Grant me this boon, Lord. They are like enemies, always envious of one another, and that is why I am sitting alone in tapasya. I do not want to even see them. They are cruel to Vinata and her son.

Is Vinata's son, who ranges the sky, not another brother of ours? But they envy him. He is also much stronger than us through our father Kashyapa's boon to him. Because of my brothers' envy and their viciousness I am sitting here in tapasya, and I mean to cast off this body so that I never need to be with my evil brothers, even at another stage of our lives."

Brahma said, "Sesha, I know what your brothers are and they are in mortal danger from your mother's curse: this I have ordained. Don't grieve for them, but ask me for a boon. I am pleased with you and I will give you anything. You are set on the path of virtue; may your heart journey far down this high way and become ever more established in goodness and tapasya."

Sesha said, "Divine Pitamaha, Lord of all, this is the boon I want: that my heart always delights in goodness and in sacred tapas."

Brahma said, "Sesha, I am gratified with your self-denial and love for peace. But I have a task for you, O Naga: bear this world, unsteady with her mountains and forests, her seas, cities and asramas, so that she becomes stable."

Sesha said, "Lord of all creatures, bestower of boons, Lord of the Earth, Lord of the Universe, I will do as you say. Set Bhumi upon my head."

Brahman said, "Nagottama, best of snakes, burrow beneath the Earth; she will give you a tunnel to pass through. O Sesha, by bearing the Earth upon your head and holding her steady, you shall certainly do something that I will greatly value."

Then the elder brother of Vasuki, king of the snakes, entered a hole in the ground and passed through to the other side of the Earth. He supported the Goddess Bhumi Devi upon his head, with her girdle of seas.

Brahma said, "Sesha, best of snakes, you are Dharma Deva himself, because you support the Earth, with all that she bears, by yourself, even as I might, or Indra."

The Naga Sesha, the Lord Ananta, of untold might, lives under the Earth, supporting her at the word of Brahma. The illustrious Grandsire, foremost of immortals, then gave Vinata's son Suparna to Ananta, to help him.'

CANTO 37

Astika Parva Continued

Sauti continued, 'Vasuki, best among Nagas, heard his mother's curse and wondered how to escape it. He consulted with his brothers, Airavata and the rest.

Vasuki said, "Sinless ones, you know about the curse of our mother, and we must try to escape it. There is a remedy for every other curse, but none for one pronounced by one's mother.

When I think that this curse was spoken in the presence of the Almighty, Infinite and True One, my heart trembles. Ah, surely we are as good as dead. Otherwise, why did the Lord not prevent our mother from cursing us?

We must waste no time, but think how we can escape the curse. You are all wise and intelligent. Together, we can surely find a remedy: why, even as the Devas found Agni of old, when the Fire God hid himself in a cave, we must find a way to stop Janamejaya from undertaking his sarpa yagna, a way to save our lives!"

The assembled Punnagas, all wise sons of Kadru, then gave their counsel for avoiding death at the snake sacrifice.

One group of serpents said, "We will disguise ourselves as lofty Brahmanas and go and tell Janamejaya, 'This yagna of yours is sinful and you should not undertake it.'"

Other Nagas said, "We should turn ourselves into his closest counsellors. He will certainly ask for our advice, and we shall tell him to avoid the sarpa yagna at all costs, listing the many evils it will bring down upon the world."

Another vicious Naga advised, "Let one of us bite the sacrificial priest who is to conduct the sarpa yagna. Indeed, let us kill every Brahmana alive that knows how to conduct a sarpa yagna and might become the Ritvik at the king's sacrifice!"

One more virtuous and kindly said, "This is evil counsel, and nothing is as dangerous as killing a Brahmana. When one's life is threatened, one must depend on the ways of virtue to save oneself, for evil ways finally destroy the very world."

Another Naga suggested, "We will turn into clouds full of lightning, and pouring down rain onto the yagna fire, extinguish it!"

Other snakes, the best of their kind, said, "Let us go in stealth by night and steal the vessel with the Soma rasa. That will interrupt the sacrifice."

"Let us unleash millions of our kind around the yagna, to bite men everywhere and spread terror and panic."

"Let us defile the sanctified offerings of food with excrement and urine."

"Let us become the king's Ritviks, and ask for our dakshina when the yagna begins. He will be in our power and give us whatever we ask for. We can ask that the yagna be stopped."

"When the king swims in the river, let us bind him and carry him away to Patala. That way the yagna will never be performed."

Other Nagas, who thought themselves sage, said, "Let us go and bite Janamejaya. When he dies, the threat will have been torn up by its root. O you that hear with your eyes, this is our counsel, and let us decide on the best course and act immediately."

Now silence fell, and they waited for Vasuki to decide. After some moments' thought, Vasuki said, "I do not like the counsel of any of you; I do not think any of it will benefit us. I think that only the grace of Kashyapa can save us. Nagas, my heart does not believe that there is another way that will truly bring welfare upon my race and me. I am anxious, for I am the one who must decide what to do, and I must take responsibility for the decision, the praise or blame for it."'

CANTO 38

Astika Parva Continued

Sauti said, 'When the other snakes and Vasuki had spoken, Elapatra said, "We cannot prevent the sarpa yagna. Also, it is not from King Janamejaya of the Pandavas that this terror issues, so that we can avoid calamity by attacking him. O Vasuki, one cursed by fate has recourse only to fate; nothing else can save him. Fate is the root of our fear and anger.

Listen to me. When she uttered her curse, I lay trembling in our mother's lap. O Best among Nagas, O splendid Lord Vasuki, coiled there I heard what the shocked Devas said to Brahma Pitamaha.

The Devas said, 'Pitamaha, Devadeva, who but the vicious Kadru could give birth to such precious children and then curse them, even in your holy presence? And you, O Brahma, endorsed her curse, saying, "So be it." Tell us why you did not prevent her, instead.'

Brahma replied, 'The Nagas have multiplied. They are cruel, terrible and venomous. I did not stop Kadru because I wish the welfare of my other creatures. The serpents that are poisonous and those that otherwise sin, biting men and beasts for no reason other than the pleasure they take from inflicting pain and death, shall indeed be killed. But the serpents that are virtuous and harmless shall not be affected.

Listen to how, when the time comes, the good snakes might escape death. In the race of the Yayavaras a great Rishi called Jaratkaru shall be born, wise and his passions controlled. Jaratkaru shall have a son called Astika. He will stop the sarpa yagna, and all the good snakes will escape death.'

The Devas said, 'O knower of truth, on whom will the Mahamuni of great asceticism and virility father his illumined son?'

Brahma replied, 'That best of Brahmanas shall beget a son of great tejas on a wife bearing the same name as him. Vasuki, king of the Nagas, has a sister called Jaratkaru. Astika shall be born to her, and he will save the race of snakes.'

Elapatra continued, "The Devas said to Brahma, 'So be it then,' and the Pitamaha returned to Brahmaloka, loftiest world.

O Vasuki, I see your sister Jaratkaru here. I say to you, to save us all give her to the Rishi Jaratkaru as alms, to be his wife. For I heard that this shall be the means to our release from the curse, and the Sage is abroad seeking a wife who bears his own name."'

CANTO 39

ASTIKA PARVA CONTINUED

Sauti said, 'Dvijottama, best of the twice-born, the serpents were delighted when they heard what Elapatra said.

"Well done!" they cried, and "Well said!"

From that time, Vasuki raised his sister Jaratkaru with the greatest care and joy. Not long after, the Devas and Asuras churned the Kshirasagara together, Varuna's domain. Vasuki, the mighty, became their churning-cord.

As soon as the churning was over, the serpent king came before Brahma Pitamaha, with the Devas. The Devas said, "Lord, Vasuki suffers terribly for fear of his mother's curse. He wishes for the deliverance of his race, and we beg you to remove his grief. This king of the Nagas has always been our friend and helpmate. Devadeva, be kind to him, assuage the fever in his heart."

Brahma replied, "Devas, let Vasuki do as Elapatra told him. The time has come, and only those that are evil shall die, not the good. Jaratkaru has been born, and the Brahmana sits in stern tapasya. At an auspicious time, Vasuki should give his sister to the Muni. Devas, Elapatra spoke the truth and nothing less."

Vasuki, king of the Nagas, ordered his people, who were gathered there in great numbers, "Keep a close watch on the Rishi Jaratkaru. As soon as he asks for a wife, come and tell me. The salvation of our people depends on it."

CANTO 40

ASTIKA PARVA CONTINUED

Saunaka said, 'Son of Suta, tell me why the brilliant Muni whom you call Jaratkaru, was so named in the world. Tell us the etymology of that name.'

Sauti said, 'Jara means to waste, and Karu implies vastness. This Rishi's body was once enormous, and he gradually wore it away with relentless penance. O Brahmanas, Vasuki's sister was called Jaratkaru for the same reason.'

Saunaka, the virtuous, said with a smile, 'Yes, this is true, I have heard what you say before. But tell me how Astika was born.'

Sauti replied from what he knew from the Shastras. 'After Vasuki commanded his Nagas to inform him the moment Rishi Jaratkaru asked for a bride, many days passed but the Sage continued his tapasya. His seed retained within his body in brahmacharya, he wandered the Earth without fear and showed no sign that he wanted to take a wife.

Later, O Brahmana, a king named Parikshit was born into the race of the Kurus. Like his great-grandsire Pandu, he was mighty-armed, the greatest bowman of his time, and he was fond of the hunt.

He ranged the jungles at will, hunting deer, boar, wolf, wild buffalo and many other beasts as well. One day, he shot a deer with an arrow and that creature ran from him, which no deer had ever done before. He chased it deep into the forest, even as Rudra once pursued the deer Yagna through the skies, bow in hand.

This deer plunged deeper and deeper into the forest and the king after it. Exhausted and thirsty, Parikshit broke into a clearing and saw an emaciated Rishi who sat drinking the froth from the milk that some calves sucked from their mother's teats. Running up to the Muni, and raising his bow, the tired and hungry king demanded, "Brahmana, I am Parikshit, son of Abhimanyu, and king of the Kurus. I shot a deer with my arrow and it escaped me. Have you seen the animal?"

But that Muni had sworn a mowna vrata, a vow of silence, and did not reply. The king saw a dead snake lying nearby. In anger, he picked up the carcass with the end of his bow and draped it across the silent Muni's shoulders. The Sage made no protest, and still spoke no word, good or bad. Parikshit's anger left him; he was full of remorse.

He turned back to his capital, while the Muni sat on in dhyana. The Sage knew that Parikshit was a tiger among kings, and a sovereign of dharma. Though he had been insulted, the Muni forgave the king and did not curse him. Parikshit of the race of Bhaarata did not know that the one he had insulted was a Rishi, otherwise he would never have behaved as he did.

That Rishi had a son called Sringin, a youth gifted with great tejas, of solemn vows and profound penance, but easily angered and difficult to appease. He invariably sought to work for the good of all creatures and often sat rapt before his Guru, in dhyana and worship.

At his Guru's word, he was on his way home when, O Brahmanottama, a friend of his, another Sage's son called Krisa told him what had happened to his father while he was away: how Parikshit had draped the dead snake round his neck.

Sringin blazed up in anger, smoking like poison.

Krisa said laughing, "Be not proud ever again, Sringin; though you are a Muni and have great tejas, your father wears a dead snake round his neck! Dare not speak haughtily to us true Rishis' sons, ever again. You have lost your manhood today when you see your father with a dead snake round him and can do nothing about it. Ah, but your father has done nothing to deserve such humiliation, and that saddens me most of all, even as if I myself have been punished for some crime I did not commit."'

CANTO 41

Astika Para Continued

Sauti said, 'Mighty Sringin's eyes burned in wrath. He asked Krisa in a soft, dangerous voice, "How does my father wear a dead snake today?"

Krisa replied, "King Parikshit draped the snake round your father's neck."

Sringin asked, "What wrong did my father do that evil king? Krisa, answer me this, and I will show you the power of my tapasya shakti."

Krisa said, "The son of Abhimanyu was out hunting and wounded a stag with his arrow. The creature escaped him and he chased it through the forest and came upon your father sitting in dhyana. The excited and tired king demanded to know if your father had seen the wounded deer.

Your father had taken a mowna vrata, and did not reply. Hungry, thirsty and tired, Parikshit repeatedly asked your father the same question and he got no reply. In anger, the king picked up the snake's carcass with the tip of his bow and draped it round your meditating sire's shoulders.

Sringin, your father has yet to stir from his dhyana, and Parikshit has returned to his capital Hastinapura, city of elephants."

Sringin's eyes turned red and, in the grip of fury, the Rishi's son touched some holy water and cursed Parikshit. "In seven nights' time, the serpent Takshaka will take the sinner Parikshit, who dares defile a Brahmana with a snake's carcass, to the land of Yama!"

When he had cursed the king, Sringin went home and saw his father sitting in dhyana, the dead snake still around him. Sringin's anger and grief flared up again. He sobbed and said, "I have cursed the wretched Kuru king for what he dared do to you, and in seven days Takshaka's bite will take him to the land of the dead."

But his father said, "My son, I am not pleased with you. Rishis should never give in to anger. We live in that great king's country; he protects us with his dharma. We should forgive him any transgression. If you break dharma, my child, I say to you, dharma will break you. If the king did not protect us, we could never pursue our spiritual lives in peace and safety, and find the great punya that we do; he deserves a portion of our punya.

Parikshit protects his subjects even as his great-grandsire did, and he should be forgiven anything he does. The Rajarishi was tired and hungry, and he did not know about my vow of silence. My son, a country without a king is plagued with all kinds of evil and disasters.

The king punishes criminals, and the fear of punishment creates peace. In peace, the people pursue their svadharma, their natural duty, undisturbed, just as we do our spiritual lives and perform our sacred rites. The king establishes dharma; he brings Swarga to Bhumi. He protects yagnas from being desecrated or disturbed, and this pleases the Devas. They send down timely rains, which grow grains and herbs, which nourish and preserve men.

Manu says that a sovereign Kshatriya ruler of the destinies of men is equal to ten Brahmanas who know the Veda. Parikshit did what he did because of exhaustion, hunger and ignorance of my vow. O, why have you cursed that great one in rash childishness? My son, in no way does the king deserve a curse from us.'"

CANTO 42

Astika Parva Continued

Sauti said, 'Sringin said to his father, "Whether I have been rash or childish, my father, whether you like it or not, whether what I have done is dharma or adharma, my curse shall not be proved vain. For I have never lied in my life, not even in jest."

His father Samika said, "My son, I know that you have great power and you are truthful. I know your curse will be fulfilled. Yet, even a grown son must always seek his father's advice so the good son might find great fame. You are just a boy, how much more you need wise counsel.

You are always at tapasya, but the wrath of even the illumined, who own the six lofty qualities, only grows. You do certainly keep your vows and observe dharma. But you are young, still rash and prone to anger, and I know that I must counsel you.

You live eating the fruit and roots of the forest, and it is your nature to do so. You must not murder the punya that accrues from your asceticism, but kill this dreadful anger instead. You acquire your merit with great pain and effort; anger robs you of so much virtue.

Those who lose their punya cannot find calm, and only calm bestows success on the long labours of Rishis. You must conquer your passions, especially your anger; you must become forgiving. With forgiveness a man gains worlds that even Brahma cannot have.

I live the way of peace, and I must do whatever good I can. I must send word to the king and tell him that my son, a callow youth of undeveloped intellect, has cursed him in anger, at seeing what Parikshit did to me."

That Maharishi sent his disciple Gaurmukha of gentle manners and deep tapasya to Hastinapura, telling him that he must first enquire formally and politely after the king's health and well-being, and only then deliver his dreadful message.

Soon, Gaurmukha came to the city and the palace of the monarch of the Kuruvamsa. He first sent word of his arrival to Parikshit through a palace guard at the gate.

When he entered the king's sabha, Parikshit duly honoured the Dvija. When he had refreshed himself after his journey that Brahmana delivered his terrible message, exactly as his Guru Samika had instructed him to, in the presence of all the king's ministers.

Gaurmukha said, 'Rajadhiraja, king of kings, in your kingdom there lives a Rishi called Samika, virtuous of soul, his passions controlled, peaceful, and given to stern penance. O tiger among men, while the Rishi kept a mowna vrata, you draped a dead snake around his neck with the tip of your bow.

Samika himself forgave what you did, but not his son. Rajadhiraja, his son cursed you, without his father's knowledge, that within seven nights the Naga Takshaka will kill you. Samika repeatedly asked his son to save your life, but, alas, there is no one who can undo the boy Sringin's curse.

Sringin still remains enraged, O King, which is why Samika has sent me to you, for your welfare."

The Kuru Rajarishi heard the savage message, and remembered his own angry sin. He became dejected and remorseful, especially when he heard that the Maharishi Samika had sworn a vow of silence. Parikshit felt doubly contrite when he realised how kindly and forgiving Samika was that he had sent Gaurmukha to warn him about the curse.

The king, who looked like a Deva, did not grieve as much for his impending death, as he did for what he had done to the Rishi Samika.

He sent Gaurmukha back, saying, "Let Samika Muni bless me."

When the messenger left, anxiety struck Parikshit like an arrow. He consulted his ministers and decided to immediately erect a mansion in the air, supported upon a single smooth column. Night and day, it would be closely guarded. All around it and within, too, there would be the finest physicians with the most potent herbs, and Brahmanas that were experts in the mantras of healing.

Protected on every side, the king, surrounded by his ministers, discharged his dharma from that mansion. No one could approach him; why, they say the very air could not come near Parikshit.

When the seventh day arrived, Rishi Kashyapa was on his way to Parikshit, to cure him after Takshaka inevitably struck: for the knowing Brahmana had heard all about the curse.

The Prajapati thought, "I will cure the king after he has been bitten, and I shall gain punya by what I do and wealth also."

But Takshaka, who had assumed the guise of an aged Brahmana, accosted Kashyapa on his way. The prince among snakes said to that bull among Munis, "Where are you going in such haste? What urgent business makes you hurry so?"

Kashyapa replied, "Today Takshaka will consume Parikshit of the House of Kuru, bane of his foes, with his venom. I am in haste because I am going to cure the great Pandava king after the snake, virulent as Agni, bites him."

Said Takshaka, "O Brahmana, I am the same Takshaka who will burn that Lord of the earth. Turn back Kashyapa, because you cannot cure one that I bite."

Kashyapa retorted, "I know the most powerful mantras for snakebite, and I will go to the king and cure him."'

CANTO 43

ASTIKA PARVA CONTINUED

Sauti said, 'Takshaka said, "If what you say is true, let me see you revive this pipal tree after I bite it. Brahmanashreshta, I will show you the power of my venom. You show me the potency of your mantras."

Kashyapa replied, "Bite the pipal then, O King of serpents, and I will bring it back to life."

Takshaka bit the tree, and his venom reduced the pipal to ashes. Takshaka said to Kashyapa, "First among Brahmanas, let me see you bring the lord of the forest back to life!"

Kashyapa gathered the ashes in his hands and said, "By the power of my mantras, I will revive the nyagrodha before your eyes."

Chanting arcane incantations over the ashes, Kashyapa first sprouted a green shoot from the ashes; two leaves grew from the sprout. He set these down, and continued to chant. In no time, a full grown trunk appeared, branches, leaves and all, and the pipal, lord of the forest, stood there exactly as before.

Takshaka breathed, "A miracle! O Mahamuni whose wealth is your tapasya, what other wealth do you desire that you go to cure the king? Difficult as it might prove, I will give you whatever you are after.

Besides, remember that, because the king has been cursed by a Rishi to die of my bite, his lifespan has been shortened. O Kashyapa, your fame and honour pervade the three worlds. If you fail to restore Parikshit to life after I sting him, your fame will vanish like the splendour of the Sun during an eclipse."

Kashyapa said, "I am going for gold. If you give me the gold I seek, O Naga, I will not go to Parikshit for it."

Takshaka said, "Dvijottama, I will give you more gold than you expect from the king. So do not go to Hastinapura."

Kashyapa, best of Brahmanas, sat down for a moment and was plunged in dhyana. He meditated upon Parikshit and saw in his mystic heart that the lifetime of the Pandava monarch was indeed exhausted. He asked Takshaka for a great deal of gold and the serpent gave it to him. Taking the gold, Kashyapa turned back.

Now Takshaka flashed on towards Hastinapura. On his way, he heard how Parikshit was living in a mansion in the air, protected by potent mantras and yantras that rendered snake venom ineffective, and by rare herbs and other specifics for curing snakebite.

The snake thought, "I must use some deception to approach the king. What shall I do?"

Takshaka sent some of his snakes disguised as Rishis to Parikshit. They brought gifts of fruit, kusa grass, and holy water. Takshaka said to these, "Go to the king, calmly, just as if you only want to give him the flowers, fruit and holy water. Show no anxiety or impatience."

Those snakes did as they were told; they brought those offerings to Parikshit, and he accepted the fruit, the grass and the water. Then he said to them, "Now leave me."

When the snakes disguised as Rishis had left, Parikshit said to some ministers and friends that were with him, "Come, eat these excellent fruit that the Rishis brought."

Indeed, Fate impelled the king and his companions to eat those fruit. Fate made the king select for himself the fruit in which Takshaka had hidden himself. As the king bit into the fruit, O Saunaka, an ugly worm appeared from it, its eyes glittering black with coppery slits.

The king saw the worm and laughed. Great Parikshit said, "The sun is setting on this seventh day, and I need not fear poison anymore. Takshaka has not come. Let this worm become the serpent king and bite me so the words of the Rishis are not proved false!"

His time had come and his ministers laughed with him. Smiling, Parikshit put the tiny worm on his neck. In a flash the worm turned into gigantic Takshaka, eyes blazing, and wrapped his gargantuan coils around the king's neck. With a roar, Takshaka bit that Kshatriya.'

CANTO 44

ASTIKA PARVA CONTINUED

Sauti said, 'The king's ministers saw Parikshit in Takshaka's coils and turned white with terror, and cried out. When Takshaka roared, they fled as a man. And as they ran, screaming, sobbing, they saw awesome and wondrous Takshaka flying through the sky above them, like the scarlet streak in a blue lotus, like the vermillion-filled parting that divides the hair on a woman's head.

The mansion in the air blazed up with Takshaka's poison, and the king fell dead, burnt to ashes as if he had been struck by lightning. When Takshaka's poison had consumed the king, his main minister and his royal priest, a most holy Brahmana, performed the last rites for him, though there was nothing left of the noble Parikshit for them to cremate.

The citizens all gathered and crowned the dead sovereign's minor son the new king. Janamejaya they called that scion of the race of Kuru. Though he was still a boy, Janamejaya was mature and wise in his mind. With the guidance of his counsellors and the royal priest, Parikshit's eldest son ruled the kingdom even like his great-grandfather Yudhishtira.

The ministers saw how he kept his enemies at bay, and went to Suvarnavarman, king of Kasi, and asked him for his daughter Vapushtama to be Janamejaya's bride. Having made some enquiries about the young Kuru monarch, Kasiraja gave Vapushtama to be Janamejaya's queen, with every proper ritual and ceremony. Janamejaya was delighted in his wife and he never gave his heart to any other woman, ever.

Youthful and energetic, he ranged the world cheerfully with his lovely queen, journeying on rivers and lakes, and in forests and through fields of flowers, steeped in pleasure and joy. He enjoyed his life even as his ancestor Pururavas of old had, when the Apsara Urvashi became his. Vapushtama was the most beautiful of women and she pleased him in every way, as he did her.'

CANTO 45

Astika Parva Continued

'Meanwhile, the Rishi Jaratkaru ranged the Earth, making his home for the night wherever he found himself when the Sun set. He roamed at will, observing the most difficult vratas, which only evolved Sages can keep, and bathing at many holy tirthas. The Muni lived on just air for his food, and had no sensual desires of any kind. Daily, he grew more emaciated.

One day, he saw the spirits of his ancestors, hanging heads down in a hole, by a cord of virana roots, of which only one strand remained unbroken. And that thread was gradually being eaten away by a large rat also living in that pit. And the Pitrs in the hole were starving, macilent, pathetic, and eager for salvation.

Jaratkaru approached the pitiable ones humbly, and asked, "Who are you hanging by this cord of virana roots? Just one strand remains and the rat living in the hole gnaws away at it, and soon it will give way and you will plunge down into this bottomless pit, headfirst.

Ah, my heart is moved to pity seeing you like this. Tell me how I can help you; I am prepared to sacrifice a quarter, nay a third, why a full half of my tapasya for you. No, take all my penance if you will, if that can save you from your plight."

His Pitrs said, "Brahmacharin, you want to save us but you cannot do that by your tapasya. Child, eloquent of speech, we have our own considerable tapasya, but we have no children, and that is why we are hanging here and shall soon plunge headfirst into hell.

Brahma himself has said that having a son is great punya. We are bewildered as our time runs out swiftly. Child, we don't know you though, no doubt, your fame is spread across the Earth. You are fortunate and venerable, who take such pity on us and grieve over our plight so sincerely.

Brahmana, listen to who we are: we are Rishis of the Yayavara clan, of flinchless vratas. Muni, we have fallen into this pit from a lofty realm because we have no offspring. All our tapasya has not yet been consumed; we still have a single thread, by which we hang.

Our one strand, our last hope, is called Jaratkaru. That unfortunate has mastered the Vedas and their Angas and he is a lone ascetic. He keeps lofty vows, engages in the most difficult penance, controls his desires perfectly, and has no desire for the fruit of his rigours.

He just as well might not exist, as far as we are concerned: it is because of him that you find us in this condition. He has no wife, no son, no kin! And so we hang in this hole, barely sentient, men who have no one to look after them.

If you ever meet him, be kind enough to tell him, 'Your Pitrs hang head down in a hole in great sorrow. Jaratkaru, take a wife and beget children. Brahmana, you are the single thread by which your ancestors hang.'

Brahmana, the once many-stranded rope of virana roots by which we hang is the rope of our clan. The strands that have been eaten away are we whom time has devoured. The single root that remains is Jaratkaru, who has chosen brahmacharya. The rat you see is inexorable time. The rat gradually gnaws away at the wretched Jaratkaru, who thinks only of himself.

Brahmana, his asceticism will not save us. Look how we have been uprooted from higher worlds and fallen down into this pit: barely conscious beings any more, gnawed incessantly by kaala, devolving like the worst sinners. And when the last strand gives way and we plunge into hell, Jaratkaru will go with us. Dear friend, no tapasya, yagna or any sacred pursuit can compare with a son.

Child, you have seen us; we beg you, tell Jaratkaru about us in detail. Brahmana, since you are kindly disposed towards us, persuade him to marry and father children. Ah, we feel how lovingly you grieve for us, and we wonder who you are: a friend of Jaratkaru's or, perhaps, even one of our own? Tell us, O fine one, who are you that remain here so patiently?'"

CANTO 46

Astika Parva Continued

Sauti said, 'Hearing all this, Jaratkaru was plunged in gloom. His voice choking, tears in his eyes, he said to his Pitrs, "You are my sires and grandsires! I am the sinner Jaratkaru; so chastise me, wretch that I am, and command me what to do."

The Pitrs replied, "O son, son, truly it is our great fortune that you have arrived here on your wanderings. Brahmana, why have you not married?"

Jaratkaru said, "My fathers, I have always wanted to keep my vital seed inside my body and thus take my body into the next world. So I decided that I would never marry, but always remain celibate.

But now I have seen you hanging here like bats, I have turned my heart away from brahmacharya. I will do as you ask. I will marry if I can find a girl who has the same name that I do. She must give herself to me without my asking, as alms, and I should never have to maintain her. Sires, if I find such a woman I will marry, not otherwise. And the child that I beget on her shall be your salvation, O my fathers, and you shall live in grace forever, without fear."

Having given his word to his manes, Jaratkaru set out once more, wandering the face of the Earth again. O Saunaka, he was old and could find no wife, and he thought of his Pitrs hanging in their hole and he grieved terribly. However, he continued seeking a bride.

Once, in a deep jungle, he was quite unmanned by sorrow and began to sob loudly. The Brahmana cried out loud, "I want a wife!" three times. "All of you that can hear, mobile and unmoving, and all that are here invisibly, hear me! My stricken manes have commanded me to marry and father a son. I range the world at my Pitrs' word, in poverty and in dire sorrow, to find a wife who will be given to me as alms.

If any among you has a daughter who bears the same name as I do, and one that I will not have to support, let him give her to me. O let him give her to me so I can save my fathers who hang precariously in the hole in the ground!"

The snakes that had been following Jaratkaru, waiting for just this moment, sped back to Vasuki and told him what had happened. The Naga king took his sister Jaratkaru with him, decked in her finest ornaments, and went to the jungle where the Rishi was.

Brahmana, there Vasuki offered his sister Jaratkaru as alms to the noble Sage. He did not accept her immediately: he was not certain that she had his name and also the matter of upkeep had not been settled. He was silent for a few moments, then, he asked, "What is the girl's name? You must know that I shall not maintain her."'

CANTO 47

ASTIKA PARVA CONTINUED

Sauti said, 'Vasuki said to the Rishi Jaratkaru, "Best of Brahmanas, she has the same name as you do. She is my sister and has done tapasya. I will look after her, so take her for your wife. I swear that I will protect her with all my resources. Greatest of Maharishis, I have nurtured her carefully just for you."

The Rishi replied, "Do we agree that I shall not maintain her and also that she will always obey me? If she displeases me once, I will leave her."

Vasuki gave the Muni his solemn word on both counts. Jaratkaru now entered Vasuki's home and took the hand of the serpent king's sister, offered to him with all proper Shastraic ritual. Then, Jaratkaru Muni took his bride and went into the lavish apartment and bedchamber that Vasuki showed him.

And in the private chamber was a great bed covered with priceless sheets of silk. The Rishi said to his wife Jaratkaru, "You must never say or do anything that is against my wishes or liking. If you ever displease me in the least thing, I will leave you and go away. Remember this well."

The Nagina princess, Vasuki's sister, quickly agreed, in anxiety and some sadness, "So be it". Wanting to be useful to her clan, for she knew why she had been married to the Rishi, that chaste princess served her husband with the wakefulness of a dog, the timidity of a deer, and the uncanny sensitivity to his mood, which a crow has.

And one day soon, after her period was over, Vasuki's sister purified herself with a ritual bath, went to her husband the Muni, and she conceived. The embryo was like a flame in her womb, of terrific tejas, and shone like fire. It grew inside her like the waxing moon.

One afternoon, during her pregnancy, Jaratkaru of great renown, tiredly put his head in his wife's lap and fell asleep. While he slept, the Sun entered his mansion in the Western Mountain and began to set.

Brahmana, Vasuki's sister became worried, she was afraid that her husband might lose his punya. She thought, "What should I do? Shall I wake my husband or not? He is exacting and meticulous in his rituals, and must say his twilight sandhya prayers before the Sun sets. But if I wake him, I risk his wrath. Which is worse: that he is angry with me or that he loses his punya?"

Deciding that losing his punya was worse than risking his fury, Vasuki's sister said in the softest voice to her great husband lying like a flame with his head in her lap, "Most fortunate, illustrious one, you must wake up. The Sun is setting and you must bathe, say the name of Vishnu, and perform your sandhya vandana. Twilight is upon us, my lord, awake."

Jaratkaru opened his eyes, his lips quivered in anger, and he said to his wife, "You have insulted me, O lovely Nagina, and I will no longer live with you but go back to where I came from. O woman of the soft thighs, the Sun cannot set while I am asleep in your lap. No one should continue to live where he has been insulted, least of all a Brahmana like me."

Jaratkaru, his wife, trembled with fear. She said to him, "Oh, Brahmana, I did not wake you from any wish to insult you. I only woke you so that you would not lose your punya by not observing your sandhya vandana."

Rishi Jaratkaru was furious and he wanted to abandon his wife. Said he, "Beautiful one, I have never spoken a lie, and leave you I shall. I have been happy with you but I did tell your brother that the day you displeased me I would go. When I have left, tell Vasuki that I have gone, and do not grieve for me."

Jaratkaru of faultless features was grief-stricken and terrified. Somehow, she mustered the courage to speak to her husband. Her heart trembled and she had gone pale.

Folding her hands to him, tears streaming down her lovely face, she said, "It is not right that you leave me when I have done no wrong. You walk the way of virtue and so do I, with my heart set upon saving my race. Best of Brahmanas, the purpose for which I was given to you has not yet been fulfilled. What will Vasuki say to me?

Brahmana, the son that my kinsmen want from me to save them from our mother's curse is not yet born. I beg you do not leave me until you give me children. I am sinless, why are you being cruel to me?"

The Muni Jaratkaru said to his wife, "You have conceived and the being in your womb is a Maharishi, brilliant as Agni himself, a master of the Veda and the Vedangas."

With that, Jaratakaru Rishi went away, his heart set on resuming his tapasya.'

CANTO 48

Astika Parva Continued

Sauti said, 'O you that have such great punya, when her husband left, Jaratkaru the Nagina went straight to her brother Vasuki and told him what had happened. Vasuki turned paler than his sister on hearing her news.

He said in despair, "You know why you were given to be the Rishi's wife. Only if a son is born to you by your husband can our race be saved from Janamejaya's sarpa yagna. Brahma himself said so, with the Devas present.

Sister, it is not proper for me to ask, but have you been with the Sage? Has he made you pregnant? I dare not follow the Rishi, for he might curse me if I do. But tell me everything that transpired between you two. Ah, remove the arrow of terror that has lain buried in my heart for so long."

Jaratkaru consoled her brother, saying, "My husband said to me that I have conceived, and then he went away. I have never known him to tell a lie, even jokingly. He would surely not have lied about such a grave matter. He said that I should not grieve, because I will have a son who blazes like Surya Deva.

He said this much to me before he went away. So be comforted, my brother, and let the deep sorrow in your heart vanish."

Vasuki, king of snakes, cried in joy, "Tathaastu, so be it!" And he gave his sister the finest gifts and wealth, and praised her to the skies. Brahmana, the splendid foetus inside her grew like the Moon waxing during the bright fortnight.

When her time came, the Nagina Jaratkaru gave birth to a child who was dazzling as a Deva child, and by his birth he assuaged the fears of his ancestors and his mother's people. The child grew up there in the house of Vasuki, king of snakes.

He studied the Vedas and their Angas from Chyavana Muni, Bhrigu's son. And even when he was a mere boy, he kept the most stringent vratas. He was gifted with great intelligence, with virtue, knowledge and freedom from mundane indulgences. He was a saintly child.

They called him Astika, which meant "There is", for that was what his father had said before leaving, when his mother asked him if there was a child conceived in her. He was a solemn and grave child, endowed with exceptional intellect. The Nagas raised him with the greatest care, and they said that he resembled golden Mahadeva, who wields the trisula. As he grew, day by day, he was the delight of his entire clan.'

CANTO 49

Astika Parva Continued

Saunaka said, 'Tell me again in detail everything that King Janamejaya asked his ministers about his father's death.'

Sauti said, 'O Brahmana, listen to what Janamejaya asked them and also to what they said in reply about the death of Parikshit.

Janamejaya asked them, "You know what happened to my father. Tell me how that king of great renown met his end. Once I hear the truth from you I shall decide what is to be done, if it benefits the world. Otherwise, I will do nothing and let the matter pass."

One of the ministers replied, "Hear, O Rajan, about the life of your illustrious father, and also how he left this world.

He was the most virtuous and noble Kshatriya, who always protected his people. Listen to how he conducted himself, why, like an embodiment of dharma, watching over the four varnas, each discharging their svadharma, and watching over Bhumi Devi. He was blessed with untold prowess and immense fortune.

No one disliked Parikshit and he disliked no one. Like Brahma himself, he was equal-minded towards all the living. Rajan, your father protected Brahmana, Kshatriya, Vaishya and Sudra, impartially. Widows and orphans, the deformed and the poor, he supported.

He was as handsome as another Soma Deva. The matchless Saradwat was his Guru at arms. Janamejaya, your father was always dear to the Lord Govinda. He was born to Uttaraa when the Kuru race was almost extinct and, because he was tested with death while in his mother's womb, Abhimanyu's mighty son was named Parikshit.

He knew the Shastras that describe the dharma of kings, in detail, and virtue was part of his nature. His passions were under his control; he had a profound and powerful intellect and a prodigious memory, the matchless Parikshit.

He knew the nuances of dharma and politics as well, and he ruled over his people for sixty glorious years. Then he died tragically and was mourned by all his subjects. After him, you, great Janamejaya, were crowned when you were a mere child, and you have ruled the Kuru kingdom for a thousand years. Like your father, you are virtuous and protect every creature that lives in your land."

Janamejaya said, "Never has a king been born in the House of Kuru who did not seek the good of his people, or one that his people did not love. Consider especially my grandsires, the Pandavas of awesome deeds.

But tell me again, how did my father, with all his virtues, meet his death? Describe everything to me as it happened. I want to hear it all."

Commanded by their sovereign, his councillors told him all that had happened.

"Rajan, your father, guardian of the very Earth, foremost among those that live by the Shastras, became addicted to hunting, just like his ancestor Pandu Mahabaho, greatest among archers. He would leave the governance of the kingdom to us, from the most trivial to weighty matters, and be off hunting in the forest.

One day, he shot a deer with an arrow and when it did not die, he followed it deep into the jungle, armed with his sword and his bow and quiver. However, he could not find the stag. Being sixty years old, he was soon tired and hungry.

Suddenly, he saw in the heart of the forest a radiant Rishi. The Sage had sworn a mowna vrata, a vow of silence. The king asked him repeatedly if he had seen the deer, but the Muni made no reply. Suddenly, the king lost his temper at the Sage who sat like a block of wood. Parikshit did not, in fact, know that this was a Rishi observing a vow of silence. O Bharatarishabha, your father scooped up a dead snake that lay on the ground with the tip of his bow and draped it round the neck of the Rishi at his dhyana. The Sage still did not say a word, and no hint of anger touched his pure and tranquil heart. He sat on in silence, now with the dead snake around him."'

CANTO 50

Astika Parva Continued

Sauti continued, 'The ministers said, "Maharaja Parikshit returned to Hastinapura. The Muni had a son, who was born of a cow; his name was Sringin. He was famed for his great spiritual powers and brilliance, and also his quick temper.

He would go every day to the house of his Guru to worship and serve him. Released for the day by his master, Sringin was on his way home, when a friend of his told him what your father Parikshit had done to his father. Sringin heard that his sinless father now sat in meditation, as still as a statue, with a dead snake around his neck. Rajan, the Rishi whom your father mocked was a great Sannyasin, his passions restrained, always absorbed in tapasya and also performing many wonderful deeds. He was an illumined one, all his senses under perfect control.

All that he did and said was invariably full of grace and sweetness. No greed or desire came near him; he was a contented one. No envy or pettiness touched him, or rage, never. He was old now and frequently kept a vow of silence. Most of all, he was a sea of kindness in whom any creature in distress could seek sanctuary.

This was the Sage that your father insulted, and he did not react at all to what Parikshit did. However, when his son Sringin heard what had happened, he cursed your father in fury. Sringin was a mere youth, but he had potent spiritual powers. Touching holy water with his fingers, blazing in anger, he said, 'Wretched king, behold the power of my tapasya shakti! I curse you that, within seven days, Takshaka will burn you with his poison, that you dared drape a dead snake around my father.'

Then Sringin went to where his father sat with the snake still around him. He told his father that he had cursed Parikshit. At once, his father sent a disciple of his, Gaurmukha, a good-natured, virtuous and well-mannered young man, to your father's court, to warn him.

Arriving in Hastinapura, Gaurmukha rested a while, and then delivered his master's message to the king: 'O Rajan, my callow son has cursed you that, in seven days, Takshaka will burn you with his poison. Be warned, Parikshit, take every care.'

Janamejaya, when your father heard the terrible message, he quickly made arrangements to take all precautions against Takshaka.

When the seventh day arrived, Kashyapa Muni was on his way to your father, when Takshaka, disguising himself as a Brahmana, accosted him on the road.

The Naga king said to Kashyapa, 'Where are you going in such a hurry? On what business are you going?'

Kashyapa replied, 'Brahmana, I am going to meet King Parikshit, best of the Kurus, for today Takshaka will burn him with his poison, and I shall restore him to life with my power.'

Takshaka said, 'Why do you want to revive the king, Brahmana? I am Takshaka, and I say to you, you will fail to restore Parikshit to life after I have bitten him. You do not know how virulent my poison is. Let me show you.'

Takshaka buried his fangs in a great nyagrodha tree, a looming king of the jungle. At once, the tree was burnt to ashes. But Kashyapa, O King, revived it with his mantras.

Takshaka was wonderstruck and said to the Sage, 'Tell me what you want from Parikshit for saving his life.'

Kashyapa, said, 'I am going to him for gold.'

Takshaka said softly, 'Sinless, I will give your more gold than you expect from Parikshit. Take it and go home.'

Kashyapa Prajapati accepted a fair treasure from Takshaka, gold and jewels to his heart's content, and turned back home.

Takshaka disguised himself again, and going into the presence of your good father, who was living in a mansion in the air supported on a single column, blasted him with his poison, burning him to ashes.

When your father's last rites had been performed, O tiger among men, you were made the king. This is the story of how your father died, and we have told it to you as it happened, savage though it was. You have heard about how Maharaja Parikshit draped the snake around the Rishi Samika's neck, how Sringin cursed him, and how horribly he died. Now you must decide what you want to do."

King Janamejaya, Parantapa, bane of his enemies, said to his ministers, "How did you know about the meeting between Takshaka and Kashyapa, about the pipal tree being burnt to ashes and then revived by the Muni?

It is certain that Kashyapa could have saved my father's life with his mantras. But fearing the world's ridicule if he failed to kill noble Parikshit, the vile snake bribed the Rishi to return home.

I have already thought of how I mean to punish Takshaka. However, the meeting between Takshaka and the Sage occurred in the heart of the jungle, on a lonely path. How do you know in such detail everything that was said and done on that occasion?"

The ministers said, "Rajan, a Brahmana's servant had climbed that pipal tree to break some dry branches for his master's sacrificial fire. He told us about the meeting between the Sage and the Serpent king, and neither saw him.

When Takshaka burned the tree, Rajadhiraja, this man was also reduced to ashes. When Kashyapa gave life to the tree, the fellow lived again, and came to tell us what had happened in the forest's heart. Now you must decide what you will do to avenge your great father."

Janamejaya heard what his ministers said, and began to cry and to wring his hands in anguish on hearing how his father had died. The lotus-eyed king sighed and gasped; he sobbed and even screamed aloud. His eyes blazed, and he touched holy water with his fingers to sanctify what he was about to say.

Composing himself somewhat, Janamejaya said to his ministers, "I thank you for telling me how my father perished. I have decided to take revenge on the malignant Takshaka. It is true that Sringin first cursed my father, but for what reason except the evil and pride in his heart did Takshaka turn Kashyapa back? If he had allowed the Sage to come to Hastinapura, my father's life would have been saved.

Takshaka did not know what my wrath would be when I discovered what he did. He gave gold to the Brahmana and turned Kashyapa back. In what way had my father offended Takshaka that he did this? Why, the Rishi Samika forgave my father easily. I will have terrible revenge on Takshaka, for my own satisfaction, for Samika's and for the satisfaction of all of you that loved Parikshit."'

CANTO 51

ASTIKA PARVA CONTINUED

Sauti continued, 'The ministers approved as a man, thunderously. Janamejaya, Lord of the Earth, that tiger of the race of Bhaarata, called his chief priest and his Ritviks. In chaste language, he said to them, "I must avenge myself on Takshaka for killing my father. Do you know how I can cast the low snake and all his clan into a fire? I want to burn the serpent just as he did my father."

The chief priest answered, "Rajan, there is a yagna by which you can accomplish your desire, a great sacrifice created by the Devas. It is called the sarpa yagna and has been described in the Puranas. Scholars that know the Puranas have told us that only you, mighty king, can perform the sarpa yagna."

O Saunaka, Janamejaya felt exhilarated as if Takshaka had already been burnt and flung into the blazing maw of Agni, which consumes the havis of every sacrifice.

The king said to those Brahmana masters of mantras, "Let us prepare for the sarpa yagna! Tell me what you need for the snake sacrifice."

The king's learned Ritviks measured out land for the yagnashala, as prescribed in the Shastras. The platform was adorned with auspicious and priceless articles required for the yagna, and with Brahmanas.

Jewels in abundance, and paddy decked the yagnashala. The Ritviks sat upon it in comfort. When the dais was built, in strict accordance with Shastraic injunction, the Brahmanas installed Janamejaya as the Sacrificer, so that he could fulfil his purpose.

Just before the sacrifice got underway, something happened that did not portend well for the completion of the sarpa yagna. As the yagnashala was being built, a professional Suta builder of great intelligence, an expert in the craft of laying foundations, and a master of the Puranas, declared, "The soil upon which this dais is erected and the time the measurements for it were taken both indicate that the yagna will not be completed, and a Brahmana shall cause its obstruction."

When the king heard this, he ordered his dwarapalakas not to let anyone enter the yagnashala without his permission.'

CANTO 52

ASTIKA PARUA CONTINUED

Sauti said, 'The snake sacrifice began at the proper time, and the priests, wearing black robes and their eyes red from the smoke that issued from the agnikunda, poured ghee into the fire, chanting the prescribed mantras.

They said the names of the Nagas aloud, as they poured clarified butter into the mouth of Agni, and chanted the dire incantations. Wherever they were, the hearts of the serpents quailed in fright. Drawn helplessly into the blazing fire, the snakes came from wherever they were, and piteously crying out to one another, fell into the flames.

In millions, their bodies swollen, panting and hissing, they came and, twining around one another in their final moments, plunged headlong into the agni kunda. White, black, blue, old and young fell alike into the blaze, crying out in various voices. There were those measuring a krosa, others a yojana long, those of the length of a gokarna; and all of them fell in a torrent into that greatest of fires.

Millions upon millions of Nagas died, with no control over their own bodies, pulled inexorably into the flames by the fell mantras of the priests. Amongst those that perished were some Nagas like horses, others like the trunks of elephants, and yet others as big as elephants and with the strength of pachyderms in musth. Varicoloured, their venom smoking and virulent, always vicious, looking like great maces with spikes, those Nagas cursed by their mother Kadru streamed into the leaping jaws of the flames and died.'

CANTO 53

Astika Parva Continued

Saunaka asked, 'Which Maharishis were the Ritviks during the sarpa yagna of Janamejaya of the line of the Pandavas? Who were the Sadasyas at the sacrifice so fearsome and tragic for the serpents? O son of Suta Romaharshana, tell us in detail so that we might discover which Rishis knew the rituals for that yagna.'

Sauti replied, 'I will recite the names of the Sages who became Janamejaya's Ritviks and Sadasyas. The Brahmana Chandabhargava was the Hotri. Great was his renown, and he was born into the lineage of Chyvana and was among the foremost masters of the Veda.

The learned old Brahmana, Kautsa, was the Udgatri, and chanted the Vedic hymns. Jaimini was the Brahmana, and Sarngarva and Pingala the Adhvaryus. Vyasa with his son and disciples was present, and Uddalaka, Pramataka, Swetaketu, Pingala, Asita, Devala, Narada, Parvata, Atreya, Kundajathara, Kalaghata, Vatsya, old Srutasravas always absorbed in japa and the study of the Vedas.

Kohala, Devasharman, Maudgalya, Samasaurava, and many other Brahmanas, all Vedic masters, became the Sadasyas, the guests of honour at that sacrifice of Parikshit's son.

When the Ritviks began to pour ghee into the fire, the most dreadful Nagas, who struck terror into every creature, began to pour into the flames. The fat and marrow of the snakes consumed by the fire flowed in streams. The air was filled with a fearful stench as the snakes burned. The screams of the snakes in the flames and those of the serpents about to fall into the flames were a single incessant cry.

Meanwhile, Takshaka, prince of snakes, heard that Janamejaya had begun his sacrifice and he flew to Indra's palace. Shaking in terror, confessing his sin, he sought sanctuary from Purandara.

Indra said to him, 'Takshaka, while you are here you have nothing to fear from the sarpa yagna. I worshipped Brahma for your sake, so have no fear.'

Sauti continued, 'Taking heart from this, Takshaka began living in Indra's realm, joyfully. But Vasuki, king of the Nagas, saw how his people died without let, how his family was being reduced moment by moment, and he was full of sorrow, his heart breaking.

Calling his sister Jaratkaru, he said to her, "My body burns and I cannot see the cardinal points of the sky anymore. My mind is a whirl, my sight fails me, my heart is breaking and I am about to faint. I feel certain that Janamejaya's fire, kindled to consume our race, draws me irresistibly, and I too will fall into it today. I feel certain that I will also find Yama's realm for myself. The time has come, sister, for the purpose to be fulfilled for which you were married to the Rishi Jaratkaru. Best among Naginas, Astika must put an end to the sarpa yagna. Brahma himself told me this, long ago. Tell your son, my child, who is a master of the Vedas and so esteemed even by his elders, that he must save me and those that depend on me."'

CANTO 54

ASTIKA PARVA CONTINUED

Sauti said, 'The Nagina Jaratkaru called Astika and said, "The time has come for you to fulfil your destiny, the reason why my brother gave me in marriage to your father. My son, do what you have to."

Astika asked, "Why did my uncle give you in marriage to my father? Tell me everything so that I might do what I feel needs to be done."

Jaratkaru, who remained calm though she was anxious for the lives of her people, said, "My son, Kadru is the mother of all the Nagas. Do you know that she cursed her sons in anger? She cursed them saying, 'You have refused to become black hairs on the tail of Uchchaisravas, so that Vinata becomes my slave. I curse you that Agni, whose sarathy is Vayu, shall consume you all during Janamejaya's sarpa yagna! And dying, you shall find hell for yourselves, where unredeemed souls dwell.'

And Brahma himself ratified her curse, saying, 'So be it.'

Vasuki heard that curse and also Brahma approving it. My brother sought the protection of the Devas, by becoming their churning rope when they churned the Ocean for the Amrita. When they had the Amrita, the Devas took Vasuki to Brahma Pitamaha. They beseeched the Lotus-born One to nullify the curse of Kadru.

The Devas said, 'Lord, Vasuki, king of the snakes, is dejected for his people. How can his mother's curse be turned away?'

Brahma replied, 'Rishi Jaratkaru will marry a wife who bears his own name. The Brahmana born from her will save the Nagas.'

And so, Vasuki gave me to your noble father well before the sarpa yagna began. My child, radiant as a god, you were born from that union. That time of your destiny has come, and you must save my brother and me from Janamejaya's fire. Tell me what you think, Astika my son."

Astika said simply to his mother, "Yes, I will."

He turned to the pale and terrified Vasuki and, as if breathing new life into him, said, "Great Vasuki, best of snakes, I will save you from the curse. Abandon your anxiety, there is nothing to fear anymore. Never have I spoken a falsehood, even in jest, so I certainly do not lie now. Let me go to Janamejaya's sacrifice and pacify him with sweet words and blessings, too, and make him stop the sarpa yagna. O Nagaraja, trust me, for I will do as I have said."

Vasuki breathed, "Astika, my head spins and my heart is breaking. I cannot see the cardinal points anymore. Ah, my mother's curse is upon me."

Astika said, "Nagottama, best of snakes, do not worry, for I will dispel your fear of Janamejaya's fire. I will extinguish the flames of revenge that burn like the fire at the end of the Yuga."

Astika now sped away to the king's sacrifice, taking, as it were, his uncle's terror with him; the Nagas felt relieved. Arriving, Astika saw the wonderful yagnashala and the many Sadasyas seated upon the dais, holy men as bright as Surya and Agni.

Janamejaya's dwarapalakas refused to let Astika enter. Astika won them over with sweet words and blessings. Entering the yagnashala, that great Brahmana began to fulsomely praise the king of vast power and accomplishments, as well as the Ritviks, the Sadasyas, and the sacred fire.'

CANTO 55

Astika Parva Continued

Astika said, "Soma, Varuna and Prajapati performed yagnas in time out of mind at Prayaga. O Bharatarishabha, son of Parikshit, your sacrifice is in no way inferior to theirs. Ah, may it bless those dear to me!

Indra performed a hundred yagnas, but this one yagna of yours is equal to ten thousand of Sakra's sacrifices, O Bharatarishabha, son of Parikshit. Ah, may it bless those dear to us!

Your yagna is like the yagna of Yama, of Harimedha, or Rantideva, O Bharatarishabha, son of Parikshit. Let those dear to us be blessed!

Like the sacrifice of Mayaa Danava, of King Sasabindu, or of King Vaisravana (at which he was himself the chief priest), is this sacrifice of yours, O Bharatarishabha, son of Parikshit. Let those dear to us be blessed!

Your yagna equals the sacrifices of Nriga, of Ajamida, of Dasaratha's son Rama, O Bharatarishabha, O son of Parikshit. Let those dear to us be blessed!

Like the yagna of King Yudhishtira, the son of a Deva, of Ajamida's race, renowned even in Swarga, is this sacrifice of yours, O Bharatarishabha, O son of Parikshit. Let those dear to us be blessed by it!

Like the yagna of Krishna Dwaipayana, the son of Satyavati, in which he himself was the chief priest, is this sacrifice of yours, O foremost of Bharata's race, O son of Parikshit. Let those dear to us be blessed by it!

These Ritviks and Sadasyas who attend your yagna are as magnificent as Indra who slew Vritrasura, as splendid as Surya. There remains nothing that they do not know, and the gifts offered them produce inexhaustible punya.

I am convinced that no Ritvik in the three worlds can equal your Ritvik Dwaipayana. Why, all his sishyas become matchless Ritviks and range the Earth performing their dharma. I see how Agni Deva—gold his seed and black smoke marking his path, Agni who is called Vibhavasu and Chitrabhanu—blazes with flames that sway to the right and bears your libations of ghee to the other Devas.

O Janamejaya, no king on Earth protects his people as you do. O, I am pleased with your abstinence and your restraint. I feel that you are either Varuna or Yama the Lord of dharma. Why, you watch over the creatures of the Earth even like Indra, with his Vajra in hand. In this world, you have no equal for greatness and for sacrifice. I say that you are like Khatvanga, Nabhaga and Dilipa.

You are as strong as Yayati and Mandhatri, as splendorous as Surya; your vows as stern as Bhishma's, your hidden tejas like Valmiki's, who sat covered by an anthill. Like Vasishtha you have mastered your anger. Your sovereignty is as Indra's. Your grandeur and lustre are like Narayana's. You dispense justice like Yama. Like Krishna, every virtue adorns you.

You are as fortunate as the Vasus; you are the home of yagnas. You are as mighty as Dambodbhava. You are as much a master of the Shastras and arms as Jamadagni's son Parasurama. Your tejas matches that of Aurva and Trita. Your gaze inspires terror even as Bhagiratha's did."

With such fulsome adoration, Astika addressed Janamejaya, the Sadasyas, the Ritviks and the sacrificial fire. Janamejaya saw omens all around.'

CANTO 56

ASTIKA PARVA CONTINUED

Suta said, 'Janamejaya said, "This is a boy, but he speaks like a wise old man. He is not a boy but wise, an old soul. I think I want to grant him a boon. Brahmanas, I ask your leave to do that."

The Sadasyas said, "A Brahmana, even if he is a boy, deserves the respect of kings. A learned Brahmana more so. This boy deserves to have every desire of his satisfied, but not before Takshaka comes into your fire."

But the king was eager to grant the young Brahmana a boon. "Ask for a boon," he said.

The Hotri did not approve, "Takshaka has not yet come to our sarpa yagna."

Janamejaya said, "Let us strive to complete the yagna quickly. Takshaka must come and die, for he is my enemy."

The Ritviks said, "Rajan, the signs of the Shastras and the fire both say that Takshaka dwells in Indra's realm, in fear for his life."

The illustrious Suta Lohitaksha, master of the Puranas, had already told the king this.

When Janamejaya asked again why Takshaka had not appeared, the Suta replied, "Sire, the Brahmanas speak truly. I know the Puranas and I say to you that Indra has granted Takshaka a boon. Indra said to the Naga, 'Remain hidden with me and Agni will not burn you.'"

Hearing this, Janamejaya the Sacrificer was dejected. He urged the Hotri to bend his will to his task. The Hotri chanted mantras, and poured more ghee into the fire, and Indra came there on high.

The Deva came in his vimana, covered by thick clouds, with all the gods around him, and following him, Gandharvas and bevies of Apsaras. Takshaka, terrified, hid in Indra's robe.

In rage, Janamejaya cried again to his mantra-chanting Brahmanas, "If Takshaka hides with Indra, then cast him into the fire with Indra himself!"

The Hotri poured more libations into the fire, calling Takshaka's name. As the ghee fell into the flames, the terrified Takshaka was revealed in the sky with Indra. Purandara saw the yagna and grew afraid. He abandoned Takshaka in a trice and flew back to his world. Slowly, ineluctably, the potent maledictions drew the trembling Takshaka toward the flames."

The Ritviks said, "Maharaja, your yagna is complete. You may now grant the excellent Brahmana a boon."

Janamejaya said to Astika, "O Brahmana, so handsome and boyish, I want to grant you a worthy boon. Ask me for whatever you want, and I swear you shall have it even if it is something well nigh impossible to give."

The Ritviks said triumphantly, "Rajan, look how Takshaka draws close. Listen to his screams and roars as he nears the flames. Indra has forsaken him and, weakened by the mantras, he falls out of heaven. Look where he falls swooning, and hissing like a storm!"

Just before Takshaka fell into the sarpa yagna fire, Astika asked Janamejaya for his boon.

"O great King, if you want to grant me a boon, let this sacrifice of yours cease at once, and not another snake fall into the flames!"

O Brahmana, Parikshit's son was dismayed and pleaded with Astika, "Illustrious one, I will give you gold, silver, cows, and whatever else you want, but don't let my yagna stop."

Astika replied, "I do not want gold, silver, cows or anything else, O King, but only that this sacrifice ends and that my mother's kinsmen are spared."

Again and again, Janamejaya begged Astika, "Brahmana ask me for another boon, and my blessings be upon you!"

But, O Saunaka of Bhrigu's race, he would not ask for another boon. Finally, the Sadasyas, all knowers of the Veda, said to Janamejaya in one voice, "Give the Brahmana the boon he wants!'"

CANTO 57

Astika Parva Continued

Saunaka said, 'Sauti, tell me the names of all the Nagas that fell into Janamejaya's fire."

Sauti replied, "Billions of snakes fell into the fire, most excellent Brahmana, beyond count. But listen to the names of the main Nagas, as many as I can remember.

First listen to the names of the kindred of Vasuki, who were coloured red, blue and white, all of them ferocious and their venom deadly. Helplessly afflicted by their mother's curse, they poured into the flames and sizzled to death, just like libations of ghee.

Kotisa, Manasa, Purna, Chala, Pala, Halmaka, Pichchala, Kaunapa, Chakra, Kalavega, Prakalana, Hiranyabahu, Charana, Kakshaka, Kaladantaka – all these sons of Vasuki fell into the fire.

Brahmana, besides them, numberless other serpents, highborn, terrible and powerful, burned to ashes in the fire. Listen to those that died which belonged to Takshaka's clan: Puchchandaka, Mandalaka, Pindasektri, Ravenaka; Uchochikha, Charava, Bhangas, Vilwatejas, Virohana; Sili,

Salakara, Muka, Sukumara, Pravepana, Mudgara, Sisuroman, Suroman and Mahahami.

Of Airavata's kin, Paravata, Parijata, Pandara, Harina, Krisa, Vihanga, Sarabha, Meda, Pramoda and Sauhatapana perished. Brahmanashreshta, from the clan of Kauravya those that were burned to ashes were Eraka, Kundala, Veni, Veniskandha, Kumaraka, Vahuka, Sringavera, Dhurtaka, Pratara and Astaka.

Of the kinsfolk of Dhritarashtra, who are as swift as Vayu and their poison virulent, Sankukarna, Pitharaka, Kuthara, Sukhana, Shechaka, Purnangada, Purnamukha, Prahasa, Shakuni, Dari, Amahatha, Kumathaka, Sushena, Vyaya, Bhairava, Mundavedanga, Pisanga, Udraparaka, Rishabha, Vegavat, Pindaraka; Raktanga, Sarvasaranga, Samhriddha, Patha, Vasaka, Varahaka, Viranaka, Suchitra, Chitravegika, Parasara, Tarunaka, Maniskandha and Aruni were consumed.

Brahmana, these were the most prominent snakes that perished, known for their mighty deeds and accomplishments. I cannot begin to name all the snakes that died, for they were truly beyond count: the sons of the great Nagas that I have named died, and their sons. So many those flames devoured!

Some had three heads, some had seven, others ten, and their poison was like the fire at the end of the Yuga and they were all dreadful to behold.

There were others, immense, swift as lightning, lofty as mountain peaks, long as a yama, a yojana, even two yojanas, who could assume any form at will, and who were as strong as they wanted to be, their venom like Agni – all cursed by a mother, all of them became ashes in the flames of that great yagna.'

CANTO 58

ASTIKA PARVA CONTINUED

Sauti said, 'Listen to something else rather wonderful that Astika did. When Janamejaya was about to grant Astika's boon, Takshaka, abandoned by Indra and hurtling towards the Earth, suddenly stopped falling and remained suspended in the air. Janamejaya was puzzled by this since the Ritviks still chanted mantras and poured butter into the agni that blazed in his name.'

Saunaka asked, 'Suta, were the mantras impotent that Takshaka stopped falling?'

Sauti replied, 'While Takshaka plunged firewards, by now unconscious with weakness and fear, Astika said thrice, "Stay! Stay! Stay!" And at this, Takshaka remained suspended in midair.

Then, urged repeatedly by his Sadasyas, Janamejaya said, "Let the yagna end and no more snakes perish. This is my boon to Astika."

Shouts of joy and praise rang through the air. Thus the sarpa yagna of the son of Parikshit, king of the Pandava race, stopped. Janamejaya, scion of the race of Bharata, was pleased with his sacrifice, and gave away untold wealth to the Ritviks and Sadasyas who had attended his great sacrifice.

He also gave gold beyond count to the Suta Lohitaksha, the expert at building foundations, who had said before the yagna began that it would be interrupted by a Brahmana. The munificent king also gave Lohitaksha fine garments and food, and was gratified.

Finally, that king concluded his yagna with the prescribed rituals. Showing Astika all reverence, Janamejaya sent him home in joy that his mission had been accomplished.

Janamejaya said to Astika, "You must come again and be a Sadasya at my Aswamedha yagna, my imperial horse sacrifice."

Astika replied that he would, and returned home, the king and he both satisfied. Arriving home in delight, he touched the feet of his mother and his uncle, and he told them all that had happened.

All the Nagas there heaved a great sigh of relief and were delighted with Astika that he had removed their fear. They said to him, "Gifted child, wise Astika, ask us for any boon."

Astika promptly said, "Let anyone who reads this holy story of what I did, either at dawn or dusk, with concentration and a cheerful heart, never have to fear anything from you."

The snakes said happily, "Let it be exactly as you want, nephew! Anyone that recalls the names of Astika, Artiman and Sunitha, by day or by night, shall have no fear of snakes. He who says, 'I remember Jaratkaru's son Astika, who saved the race of Nagas from perishing at the sarpa yagna, so do not harm me and go away, O Naga!' shall be safe from every one of our kind.

The snake that still bites such a man shall have his hood spilt in a hundred pieces like the fruit of the Sinsa tree."

That great Brahmana was satisfied and pleased. Now the Mahatman set his heart upon leaving the world, and when his time came, he rose into Swarga, leaving his son and grandsons behind.

This is the tale of Astika, exactly as it happened. It is certainly true that relating this story dispels the fear of snakes. O Brahmanas, O

Maharishi of Bhrigu's line, I have told you the legend of the holy Astika just as your ancestor Pramati told it to his son Ruru. Listening to this tale fetches great punya, O Saunaka, and I hope that having told it from the beginning, I have satisfied your curiosity.'

CANTO 59

ADIVAMSAVATARANA PARVA

Saunaka said, 'Child, Suta, I am very pleased with you that you have told me this story beginning with the sons of Bhrigu. Now I ask you again, to narrate for us, O Ugrasravas, the Bhaarata that Vyasa composed. I want to hear all the myriad and exciting stories told among those illumined Sadasyas who came to Janamejaya's sarpa yagna, during the intervals between the rituals they performed at the prolonged sacrifice – the tales and the lessons to be learnt from them: tell me both, O Sauti, in full.'

Sauti said, 'Those Brahmanas spoke of many matters derived from the Veda, when they had the time, but Vyasa recited the magnificent Itihasa called the Bhaarata.'

Saunaka said, 'I want to hear that sacred history called the Mahabharata, which has spread the fame of the Pandavas across the world, the Itihasa which Krishna Dwaipayana recited when Janamejaya asked him, after the sarpa yagna was over.

That legend was conceived in the oceanic mind of Maharishi Vyasa, his soul purified by yoga. You have whetted my thirst with whatever you have said so far, but not appeased it, O Suta.'

Sauti said, 'I will narrate Vyasa's great Itihasa, the Mahabharata, for you, from beginning to end. Nothing will give me more pleasure, O Saunaka.'

CANTO 60

ADIVAMSAVATARANA PARVA CONTINUED

Sauti said, 'When the Rishi Krishna Dwaipayana heard that Janamejaya had been installed as the Sacrificer for the sarpa yagna, he came to that yagna. Vyasa, grandfather of the Pandavas, had been born on an island in the Yamuna, to the virgin Kali by Shakti's son Parasara Muni. As soon as he was born, miraculously, he was a full-grown Sage, who already knew the Vedas and the Vedangas and all the Itihasas.

Naturally he possessed vast inborn knowledge and illumination that no other could hope to have through tapasya, studying the Veda, keeping vratas, fasting, having sons or by performing yagnas. Greatest among those that knew the Veda, Vyasa divided the single Veda into four. The Brahmana had knowledge of the Parabrahman, knew the deep past by intuition, was a truly holy one, and treasured the truth. His ways sacred and his fame great, he sired Pandu, Dhritarashtra and Vidura, so that the line of Shantanu might not be extinguished.

With his disciples, all knowers of the Vedas and their Angas, this Mahatman walked into the yagnashala of Rajarishi Janamejaya. He saw

Janamejaya sitting there like Indra himself, surrounded by his Sadasyas, by numberless kings who had all performed sacred ablutions, and by masterly Ritviks who were like Brahma himself.

When Bharatottama Rajarishi Janamejaya saw Vyasa Muni, he rose quickly and came with his guests and his kinsmen to welcome the Sage in great joy. With his Sadasyas' warm approval, the king offered the Rishi a lofty golden seat, just as Indra had to Brihaspati.

When Vyasa, who is worshipped by the Devas and can grant great boons, sat on the golden seat, the king of kings worshipped him with rites set down in the scriptures. The king offered his grandsire Krishna Dwaipayana water to wash his feet and rinse his mouth, arghya and gifts of sacred cows. Vyasa accepted the formal offerings, asked for the cows to be protected, and was pleased with the Pandava.

After these adorations, Janamejaya bowed to his great grandsire, then sat down with him in joy and asked after his well-being. The illumined Muni looked at the king with love, asked in turn after his welfare, and offered homage to the Sadasyas who had all already adored him.

When all this was done, folding his hand reverentially, Janamejaya asked that great Brahmana, "Lord you saw with your own eyes the lives of the Kurus and the Pandavas. I want to hear their story from you. What caused the enmity between them, which resulted in such extraordinary events?

Also, what led to the Great War between my grandsires, which killed countless men? Why was their good sense dimmed by fate? Best among Brahmanas, I beg you, tell me in full all that happened."

Krishna Dwaipayana turned to his disciple Vaisampayana seated at his side, and told him, "You tell the king all about the enmity that sprang up between the Kurus and the Pandavas, exactly as I told it to you."

At his guru's dictate, the blessed Vaisampayana narrated the entire story to Janamejaya, his Sadasyas and the other Kshatriyas and Brahmanas gathered there. He told them all about that enmity and the Great War that devastated the Kurus and the Pandavas.'

CANTO 61

Adivamsavatarana Parva continued

'Vaisampayana said, "I first prostrate in sashtanga namaskara, eight limbs touching the ground, before my guru, with absolute devotion in my heart. I also worship this sacred assembly of learned Brahmanas. I will now narrate all that I heard from the Mahamuni Vyasa, greatest among geniuses in the three worlds. O King, surely, since the Bhaarata has come to you, you deserve to hear the awesome epic. My heart might otherwise tremble to undertake this immense narration, but having my guru's command I feel no trace of fear.

Listen, O Janamejaya, to why discord broke out between the Kurus and the Pandavas; hear about the envious lust for kingdom that led to the game of dice and how the Kurus sent the Pandavas into exile in the forest. I will tell you everything that happened, O best among kings.

When their father Pandu dies, those young Kshatriyas, the Pandavas, come home to Hastinapura. In quick time, they become masters of archery. The Kurus see that the sons of Pandu are exceptionally gifted with strength, vitality, intelligence and fortune, and that the people love them; and the Kurus are stricken with envy.

The devious and perfidious Duryodhana, with Karna and Duryodhana's uncle Shakuni, son of Subala, begins to persecute the sons of Pandu, and to plot to have them exiled. Swayed by Shakuni's evil counsel, Duryodhana schemes to kill the Pandavas, so that he can have undivided sovereignty. Dhritarashtra's demonic son feeds poison to Bhima, mixed in some sweets, but Bhima of the stomach of the wolf digests the poison, and only falls asleep from it on the banks of the Ganga.

Duryodhana binds Bhima hand and foot and, casting him into the river, walks away. But Kunti's enormously strong son awakes, easily breaks the thongs that bind him and Bheemasena Mahabaho surfaces, all his sluggishness gone.

While he falls, sleeping, into the water, black watersnakes bite him all over his great body, their venom deadly. But that nemesis of his enemies still does not die.

All the while that their cousins plot to murder them, their noble uncle Vidura helps the sons of Pandu in every way that he can, frequently saving their lives. As Indra watches over the world from Swarga does Vidura watch over the Pandavas and keeps evil away from them.

By many means, covert and open, Duryodhana attempts to do away with his cousins. Time and again he fails, for the fates protect the Pandavas, keeping them safe for the great destiny they have been born to fulfil – the very annihilation of the race of kings.

Duryodhana sits in dark conclave with his coterie—Karna, Dushasana and some others—and, with Dhritarashtra's knowledge, has a house of lac built in Varanavrata, in Kasi. Out of inordinate love for his son, as well as blind ambition to keep the throne, Dhritarashtra colludes with Duryodhana to send the innocent Pandavas to Varanavrata. As the sons of Pandu are leaving Hastinapura with their mother Kunti, Vidura discreetly warns them of mortal danger and tells them how to escape it.

Kunti and her sons arrive in Varanavrata and begin living in the lacquer palace; Duryodhana's agent Purochana, who has built the edifice, takes them there. For a year they live in the deadly mansion, on their guard all the while, watching Purochana's every move.

Meanwhile, Vidura sends them an expert tunneller, who secretly excavates an underground passage leading out of the house of lac. One night, the Pandavas set fire to the palace, immolating Duryodhana's spy within, and escape through the secret tunnel.

In great anxiety at the murderous plot hatched against them, the sons of Pandu flee with their mother. In the forest, near a natural fountain, they see a Rakshasa, but do not slay him for fear of giving themselves away to their enemies, whom they want to think them dead, burnt alive in the lacquer palace at Varanavrata. Instead, they flee into the deep jungle, from fear of Duryodhana and his brothers.

In that vana, Bhima takes Hidimbi for his wife, for some time, after killing her brother, the Rakshasa Hidimba. He sires Ghatotkacha on her. The Pandavas, knowers of the Vedas, observing their vratas, find their way to the town called Ekachakra. Disguising themselves as Brahmanas, those bulls among men live in the house of a Brahmana, begging alms for a living.

Here the tigerish Bhima Mahabaho slays the ferocious Rakshasa Baka, the man-eater, and delivers the people of Ekachakra from their constant terror. Here, too, they hear about Krishnaa, the princess of Panchala, for whom her father is to hold a swayamvara, at which she would choose a husband for herself.

The Pandavas go to Panchala and win the hand of Draupadi to be the wife of all five of them. After living in Panchala for a year, their presence is discovered and they return to Hastinapura with their bride.

King Dhritarashtra and Shantanu's son Bhishma say to them, 'We have learned sadly of the rancour between yourselves and your cousins. We have decided to bestow ancient Khandavaprastha on you as your patrimony, half the kingdom, so there is no further cause for dispute. Go without envy in your hearts, for great is Khandavaprastha, its highways broad and its expanse wide.'

Without argument, the sons of Pandu leave for Khandavaprastha, with some friends and followers, taking many precious jewels, ornaments and gold with them. For many years, the Pandavas live in peace in Khandavaprastha which they now call Indraprastha.

They subdue many kingdoms and Kshatriyas by force of arms, and live in constant dharma, and truth. Always serene and humble, unmoved by wealth, crushing many forces of evil in their kingdom, the Pandavas rise to great power.

Now mighty Bhima conquers the kingdoms of the East, the heroic Arjuna, the North; Nakula, the West; Sahadeva, doom to his enemies, the South. When this is done, they hold sway over all of Bharatavarsha. Why, with the five Pandavas, the Earth seems as if six Suns shine upon her!

Then, Yudhishtira Dharmaputra is forced to send his brother Arjuna, greatest and ambidextrous bowman, dearer to him than life, into the forest for twelve years. That Purushavyaghra, tiger among men, resolute, gifted with every virtue, lives in the wilderness for eleven years and as many months.

During his exile, Arjuna visits Krishna in Dwaravati. In Dwaraka, Ocean City, he takes Krishna's younger sister, the lotus-eyed Subhadra, her voice sweet like honey, to be his wife. She marries him joyfully, even as Sachi married Indra; she unites, in gladness, with Arjuna, the son of Pandu, as Sri did with Vasudeva.

Later, O best of kings, Kunti's son Arjuna and Krishna please Agni, who bears the havis from every yagna to the Devas, by burning the Khandava vana with its potent herbs, and that cures Agni of indigestion. Arjuna, with Kesava to help him, finds the task of burning the forest easy, for nothing is difficult for Vishnu of infinite resources.

Agni gives Kunti's son the divine longbow, the Gandiva, and an inexhaustible quiver, and a war-chariot that flies Garuda on its banner. It is then that Arjuna saves the great Asura Mayaa from being consumed by the fire.

The grateful Mayaa builds an unearthly sabha for the sons of Pandu, adorned and encrusted with every kind of priceless jewel and gemstone.

When the evil Duryodhana sees the Mayaa Sabha he wants to own that palace.

Duryodhana arranges to play a game of dice with Yudhishtira, at which Subala's son Shakuni uses loaded dice, rolling them with his cunning fingers. Beating the eldest Pandava at the false game of dice, Duryodhana sends the Pandavas into exile for twelve years and a thirteenth year to be spent in disguise, so no one discovers them: on pain of going back into exile.

In the fourteenth year, O King, the Pandavas return to claim their kingdom, but Duryodhana refuses to return it. War is declared, and the Pandavas regain their ravaged kingdom, but only after the very race of Kshatriyas perishes on the field of Kurukshetra, and finally Duryodhana also dies.

This is the story of the Pandavas, who never allowed adharma, evil, to rule them, and of their enmity with their cousins the Kauravas, and of the Great War with which the sons of Pandu recover their kingdom," said Vaisampayana,' says Sauti to Saunaka and his rishis.

CANTO 62

ADIVAMSAVATARANA PARVA CONTINUED

'Janamejaya said, "Most excellent Brahmana, you have now briefly told me the Itihasa known as the Mahabharata, which is about the great deeds of the Kurus. O Muni rich in tapasya, now narrate the entire epic in full, for I am desperately eager to listen to its every detail.

Hearing an abbreviation of this awesome legend does not satisfy me. I feel certain that there must have been great cause for the virtuous and mighty Pandavas to kill their own kin, something for which they are still praised.

Why did those tigerlike men, themselves innocent and capable of destroying their cousins, quietly suffer the persecution and ignominy dealt out to them?

Why, O Brahmana, did the mighty-armed Bhima, strong as ten thousand elephants, restrain his anger, though he was so wronged? Why did Drupada's daughter, the chaste Krishnaa, not consume the Kauravas with fire from her eyes? Why did Pritha's sons Bhima and Arjuna, and

Madri's princes Nakula and Sahadeva, obey Yudhishtira, who had such a weakness for gambling?

Why did Yudhishtira Dharmaputra, the very embodiment of rectitude, quietly endure the extravagance of injuries heaped upon himself and his family? Why did Dhananjaya, whose sarathy was Krishna himself, Arjuna who later sent teeming hosts of dauntless Kshatriyas to the next world, suffer in silence?

O mighty Tapasvin, tell me everything that happened, exactly as it did, and describe whatever those Maharathas did."

Vaisampayana said, "O Rajan, appoint a time for the narration of the entire Mahabharata, for the legend wrought by Krishna Dwaipayana is long indeed; this is just the beginning. I will certainly recite the entire epic of the illumined Vyasa of fathomless intellect, who is worshipped in all the worlds.

The Bhaarata contains a hundred thousand sacred slokas, composed by Satyavati's son of untold genius. He that recites it, and they that listen to it, attain Brahmaloka and become like Devas. The Mahabharata is equal to the Vedas; it is sacred and beautiful; it is the most wonderful of all legends; it is a Purana, which the rishis worship.

It dwells in depth on artha and kama, profit and pleasure. This sacred epic makes the heart yearn for mukti. Men that narrate this Veda of Krishna Dwaipayana to men of liberality, honesty and faith earn great wealth. The most grievous sins, even killing an embryo in the womb, are burnt to ashes by this Itihasa. However vicious and sinful a man might be, if he hears this legend, he escapes from his sins as the Sun does from Rahu when the eclipse ends.

This Itihasa is called Jaya; those that wish for victory should listen to it or read it. A king who hears the Mahabharata with a heart full of faith vanquishes all his enemies and conquers the world. This history is a Mahayagna on its own, and yields the most auspicious and blessed fruit.

A young king should always listen to it in the company of his queen, for the couple shall then beget heroic and noble children, heirs to the throne. This Bhaarata is the exalted and holy science of Dharma, Artha and Moksha, as well: Vyasa of immeasurable intelligence says so.

This Itihasa is recited today and shall be told and read in the dim future. They that hear it or read it have children and servants who are always obedient to them. Every sin, of body, word or mind, immediately leaves them that listen to this legend. Those who hear, without mockery or criticism, the story of the birth of the Bhaarata princes will never have to fear any sickness, let alone fear dying or the world to come.

Krishna Dwaipayana composed this epic to spread the fame of the Pandavas and of the other Kshatriyas, noble, learned, of great repute; he wished also to bring welfare to the world through his profound and monumental work.

Reading the wonderful Bhaarata bestows fame and blesses a man with long life, for it is a divine and sacred legend. He that retells this epic to holy Brahmanas gains inexhaustible punya; he who recites the advent of the renowned Kuru generations is instantly purified, acquires a large family and honour in the world.

The Brahmana who regularly studies the sacred Mahabharata during the four months of the monsoon is redeemed from all his sins. He who has read the Bhaarata can be regarded as knowing the Vedas.

This epic contains accounts of the Devas, Rajarishis, Brahmarishis, the immaculate Krishna, of Mahadeva Siva, God of gods, and the Devi Parvati, of the birth of Karttikeya born from the union of Siva and Parvati and raised by six mothers. The Mahabharata tells of the greatness of Brahmanas and of the sacredness of cows.

The Bhaarata is a compendium of all the Srutis and every virtuous person should listen to it. The learned man who recites it to Brahmanas during the sacred months is washed of all his sins; he ceases to care about the pleasures even of Swarga, and attains union with Brahman, the Ultimate Reality.

He who tells even a single foot of this Kavya, this epic Poem, to Brahmanas performing a sraddha, makes the ritual immortal, since then the Pitrs become deeply gratified with all the offerings made to them.

Listening to the Mahabharata destroys every sin, conscious and unconscious, which we commit daily with our senses or in our hearts.

The legend of the lofty births of the Bhaarata princes is called the Mahabharata; he who knows the etymology of that name is saved from all his sins. Indeed, this Itihasa of the race of Bhaarata is so extraordinary that it purifies anyone, who hears it, of every sin.

The Maharishi Krishna Dwaipayana took three years to compose his epic. Rising early, performing his sacred ablutions and daily worship, he would sit down to compose this Mahabharata. Therefore, Brahmanas must listen to it with the formal reverence of keeping a vow.

He who narrates Vyasa's sacred epic and those that hear it are all saved from being affected by the fruit of their karma, good and bad. He who truly wants to gain lasting punya should listen to the entire Bhaarata, for this single Kavya is equal to all the others, and hearing it purifies the heart.

The joy and satisfaction that a soul experiences upon attaining Swarga is hardly equal to those to be had from hearing this holy legend. The virtuous man who narrates the Mahabharata with faith in his heart gains the punya derived from an Aswamedha or a Rajasuya yagna.

The Bhaarata is a treasure trove of precious jewels to rival the endless Ocean and golden Meru. Surely, surely, this legend is sacred; it is exquisite and magnificent; it is equal to the Vedas; it must be heard; it is pleasing to the ear and the heart; it washes away every sin and confers great virtue.

O King, he who gives a copy of the Mahabharata as a gift, gives the very Earth as a present with her girdle of seas. O son of Parikshit, this is the beautiful Poem, which bestows virtue and victory, which I am going to recite for you in full. Listen.

Yes, the Rishi Krishna Dwaipayana woke early every day for three years and composed this epic full of wonders: the Mahabharata. O Bharatrishabha, bull among the Bhaarata kings, whatever has been said about dharma, artha, kama and moksha might surely be found elsewhere; but nothing that is not contained in the Mahabharata is to be found anywhere.'"

CANTO 63

ADIVAMSAVATARANA PARVA CONTINUED

'Vaisampayana said, "There is once a Paurava king of dharma called Uparichara. He is also called Vasu and is addicted to hunting. Commanded by Indra, he conquers the beautiful kingdom of Chedi. Later, he renounces the use of weapons and, living in an asrama, practises the most rigorous penance. Indra and the Devas, fearing that Uparichara's tapa would make him king of Devaloka, manifest themselves before Vasu, and with honeyed words and flattery make him abandon his penance.

The Devas say, 'Lord of the Earth, you must protect this world lest dharma fades from her face while you sit here in tapasya. If you protect dharma in the world, dharma in return will protect the Universe.'

Indra says, 'Rajan, be the vigilant guardian of dharma on Earth. You are virtuous and, after this life, you will discover many marvellous and sacred realms. Though I belong to Swarga and you to Bhumi, you are my friend and precious to me.

Lord of men, you live in a land of many delights, sacred, abounding in game, fertile and rich, safe and well guarded even like Devaloka, its climate kindly, and furnished with every object of enjoyment and pleasure.

King of Chedi, mines of gold and silver embellish your lands, as do a plenitude of precious stones of every kind. Your cities and towns live in dharma; your people are honest and contented; they do not lie even in jest.

Sons never ask for their patrimony to be divided, and are always mindful of their parents' welfare. Lean or weak cattle are never yoked or made to haul or bear burdens. They are first fed, kindly and generously.

In Chedi the four varnas always adhere to the performance of their svadharma, their natural and inherent duties.

Vasu, I mean to allow you to range the three worlds at will, for I will give you a crystal vimana such as only the Devas have. Among mortal men, only you shall own such a vimana and fly in it like a god.

I will also give you a garland of unfading lotuses, which will make you invincible in battle, for, while you wear it no weapon shall injure you. And, O King, this holy and peerless garland, known in the world as Indra's mala, shall be your emblem.'

Indra, slayer of Vritra, also gives Uparichara Vasu a bamboo staff with which to protect the good and men of peace. When a year passes, Uparichara plants this bamboo stick in the ground to worship the one that has given it to him.

From then on, Rajan, every king of the Earth begins to plant a pole in the ground to worship Indra. Having erected the stamba, they adorn it with cloth made of gold thread, garlands and precious ornaments, and daub it with rare perfumes. This is how the Deva Indra comes to be worshipped with garlands and precious ornaments.

Indra comes as a swan to accept the worship of Uparichara Vasu.

Delighted with the adoration, Indra says, 'All kings, and any men who worship me in the way the king of Chedi has done, and observe this festival of mine, shall bring glory and victory to their countries and kingdoms. Their cities shall grow and be prosperous, and their streets and homes flow with joy.'

Thus Indra blesses King Vasu; and it is true that all men who observe the festival of Indra with gifts of land, gold and precious stones, find success, honour and fame throughout the world. Vasu, Lord of the Chedis, is always magnanimous and performs countless great yagnas; and Indra honours him and blesses him generously so that he rules the world from Chedi, with dharma as his sceptre. And to worship Indra, he unvaryingly observes the festival that he himself has begun.

Vasu has five sons of great strength and energy. He makes them rulers of various provinces of his boundless kingdom. His son Brihadratha becomes the ruler in Magadha; he is also known as Maharatha. His other sons are Pratyagraha, Rusamba—also called Manivahana—Mavella, and the invincible Yadu.

These, O King, are the five sons of the Rajarishi of dazzling tejas. The five sons of Vasu founded kingdoms named after themselves and separate dynasties that endure through long ages.

When Vasu sits in his crystal ship of the air, Indra's gift to him, and flies through the sky, Gandharvas and Apsaras fly to greet him. It is because he ranges the higher realms that he is named Uparichara.

The river Suktimati flows beside Uparichara, Vasu's capital. An animated and lust-maddened mountain called Kolahala once attacks the gentle river, and forcibly embraces her. Vasu sees the attempted molestation and kicks the mountain. The river escapes from Kolahala's sinister embrace through the hole in the mountain made by Uparichara's kick.

But Kolahala begets twin children, a boy and a girl, on the river he has forced. In gratitude, for having freed her from Kolahala, Suktimati gives the children to Vasu. That Rajarishi makes the boy the Senapati of his army, and the girl Girika he marries himself.

One day, after her period is over, Girika bathes and comes alluringly to her husband wanting a child from him. However, that same day

Vasu's Pitrs have appeared to him and told him to kill a deer for their sraddha.

Not wanting to disobey his ancestors' spirits, the king goes into the jungle to hunt a deer, but his mind is full of thoughts of the luscious Girika, as lovely as Sri herself. It is spring, and the forest is as enchanting as the garden of the king of the Gandharvas.

Asokas, Champakas, Chutas and Atimuktas abound, as do Punnagas, Karnikaras, Bakulas, Divya Patalas, Patalas, Narikelas, Chandanas and Arjunas, all sacred trees, ancestral plants splendorous with scented flowers and shining fruit.

The sweet, haunting songs of the kokila hold the forest in thrall; the ecstatic drone of honeybees is their sruti.

The king is stricken by desire and he sees his Girika before his mind's eye, but not before him in the flesh. Maddened, he ranges that charmed forest and spots a lovely Asoka tree, its foliage rich and its branches covered in a riot of flowers. The king sits down at the foot of the tree, and excited beyond measure by the heady fragrances of spring all around him, by the caressing breeze that whispers through the forest aisles, his mind full of images of his wife, Uparichara Vasu spills his seed into the palm of his hand.

He sees a falcon in a branch quite near him. Vasu, knower of the nuances of artha and dharma, says to the bird, 'Friend, take this seed to my wife Girika, for her season has come.'

The falcon takes the precious semen in its beak and flashes away towards the king's capital, quick as a thought. A fishing hawk, perched in a tree beside the Yamuna, sees the falcon winging along with the royal seed in its beak and thinks the falcon is carrying a shred of meat.

The hawk flies at the falcon. Locking wings, they fight in the air and Uparichara Vasu's seed falls from the falcon's beak down into the waters of the Yamuna below.

An Apsara called Adrika lives in the river; she has been turned into a fish by a Rishi's curse. She sees Vasu's shimmering seed strike the water, and swimming to it in a flash, she swallows the king's semen. Ten months after she swallows the seed, she is taken by some fishermen. In their very boat, the great fish gives birth to resplendent human children: a boy and a girl.

At once, the curse ends, just as the Brahmana who cursed her said it would, and the fish is a celestial nymph again. She rises into the sky along the path that Rishis, Siddhas and Charanas tread, and vanishes.

The wonderstruck fishermen bring the children to King Uparichara and tell him what has happened. They cry, 'My Lord, we found these two human children inside the body of a fish!'

Uparichara takes the male child and raises him. Later, he would become the King Matsya of great dharma.

The king gives the girl child, who smells of fishes, to the fishermen, saying, 'Let her be your daughter.'

The chief of those fishermen adopts the girl and calls her Satyavati. The Apsara's daughter, and the king's, grows into an exceptionally beautiful girl, with a lovely smile and a friendly nature, though she still smells of fishes. She plies a ferry across the Yamuna for her foster-father.

One day, the Maharishi Parasara, abroad on his pilgrimage, sees the girl, and is struck by love's thunderbolt, at least by irresistible desire. Riding in her ferry, Parasara Muni says to the girl with the smooth skin and exquisite thighs, 'Lovely girl, give yourself to me!'

Satyavati replies, 'Holy one, look at the Rishis standing on either bank of the river. How can I give myself to you with them watching?'

Parasara raises his hand in an occult mudra, and they are plunged in thick fog. It covers the river and both banks in darkness and fills Satyavati with awe.

She blushes now, and says shyly, 'Muni, I am a virgin living with my father. Sinless one, if I give myself to you, my virginity will be lost. Rishi, how will I face my father? Indeed, how will I live with that shame? I beg you, Holy One, think of this and then do as you decide.'

Parasara Maharishi replies, 'You will have your virginity back after you grant my desire. Also, you shall have any other boon you want from me, bashful and beautiful girl, and my words have never proved false.'

Satyavati says, 'Let my body smell sweet and not of fish anymore.'

'So be it,' says mighty Parasara.

She is so pleased with her boon that Satyavati straightaway comes into season. She allows the Rishi to embrace her. She now becomes so wonderfully fragrant, that men calls her Gandhavati, and they can smell the heavenly scent of her body from a yojana away. She is also called Yojanagandha, while they had called her Matsyagandhi before.

Having slaked his desire, Parasara goes away.

Satyavati rows to an island in the Yamuna and gives birth immediately, magically, to Parasara's child. He is splendid, and a full-grown Rishi as soon as he is born, and seeks his mother's permission to go and perform tapasya.

As he leaves, he says to her, 'If you ever have need of me only think of me and I shall come to you.'

So it is that Vyasa is born to Satyavati and Parasara Muni. Because he is born on a dwipa, an island, he is called Dwaipayana, island-born, and Krishna because he is dark complexioned.

The island-born Sage knows that dharma loses one leg in every yuga, beginning with four and finally standing on just one in the Kali Yuga. He knows that the lifespan, the strength and intellect of men also wane with the passing yugas. Having worshipped Brahma and the great Brahmarishis so he could divide the Veda to suit the coming age, Dwaipayana makes four Vedas out of one. For this he is called Vyasa, the arranger, or compiler, and Veda Vyasa, compiler of the Veda.

The Maharishi teaches Sumanta, Jaimini, Paila, his own son Suka and Vaisampayana the four Vedas, and the Mahabharata is like the fifth. Of course, the Mahabharata is his own composition.

Some years after this, Bhishma, of stunning vigour, fame and untold splendour is born to Ganga and his father is King Shantanu of the Kurus. He is an amsavatara of the Vasus of heaven.

There is a renowned Rishi calls Animandavya. He is a master of every interpretation of the Vedas, an illustrious one of great tejas and high repute. Once, he is falsely accused of theft, and the old and innocent Muni is impaled upon a spike.

He summons Dharma and says to the Deva of justice, 'When I was a boy I pierced a little insect with a blade of grass. O Dharma, I remember that one sin I committed but cannot recall any other. But since then I have done penance, thousandfold. Has my sin not been removed by all that tapasya?

Also, killing a Brahmana is the most heinous of all sins, and you, O Dharma, have sinned. You shall be born on Earth as a Sudra for this sin.'

From that curse Dharma is born as a Sudra –the wise Vidura, pure in body and perfectly virtuous.

The Sutaputra Karna is no Suta but born of Kunti while she is a maiden in her father's house, and Surya Deva is his father. He comes out of his mother's body wearing a natural coat of armour like his skin and golden earrings like sundrops: kavacha and kundala.

Vishnu, worshipped by all the worlds, is born to Devaki and Vasudeva to bless the three Lokas. He is Un-born and immortal, of untold splendour, the Creator of the Universe and the Lord.

He is the invisible cause of all things, undecaying, the pervasive Atman, the still universal centre around which everything revolves, the primal essence in which the three gunas of Nature, Sattva, Rajas and Tamas, are born, the Viswatman, the unchanging One, the substance from which the Universe is made, the Creator of the Universe of the Panchamabhutas, the Sovereign, the Antaryamin who abides unseen in everything, who owns the six lofty qualities, who is Pranava, Aum of the Vedas, infinite, moved only by his own will, lustrous, the embodiment of Sannyasa, who floats upon the waters of eternity before the creation, who is the germ of this cosmic plant, the great combiner, Un-created, invisible essence of everything, transcendent, Nirguna who cannot be known by the senses, the Universe, who has no beginning, birth or decay, infinitely wealthy, the Ancestor of every creature He incarnates into the race of the Andhaka Vrishnis to promote dharma in the world.

Satyaki and Kritavarman, masters of astras, warriors of fierce tejas, learned in the Shastras, servants of Narayana in all things: these two are born to Satyaka and Hridika.

From the seed of Maharishi Bharadwaja (of profound tapasya), which he ejaculates into an earthen pot, a drana, Drona is born. The seed of Rishi Gautama, spilt into a clump of reeds, grows into twins the mighty and sage Kripa, and his sister Kripi, who will marry Drona and become the mother of Aswatthama.

Dhrishtadyumna, blazing like Agni, born to become the nemesis of Drona, comes forth from a yagna fire, as does his sister Krishnaa: Draupadi whose dark and unrivalled beauty will cause the war upon the crack of two Yugas.

Prahlada's sishya Nagnajit, and Subala are born into the world. Subala's son is Shakuni, who is cursed by the Devas and becomes the enemy of dharma in the world, and a slaughterer of men. Subala also has a daughter called Gandhari, who becomes the mother of Duryodhana and his brothers. Shakuni and his nephew are experts at amassing wealth, and inexhaustibly avaricious.

Vyasa begets upon the widows of Vichitravirya the Kuru princes Dhritarashtra, who would become king, and the valiant and mighty Pandu. Dwaipayana also fathers, upon a Sudra woman, the sagacious and intelligent Vidura, sinless and a master of both artha and dharma.

Pandu's two wives, Kunti and Madri, give him five sons, like Devas. The eldest, Yudhishtira, is the natural child of Dharma: Yama who is the God of Justice. Bhima, his stomach a wolf's, is the son of Vayu the Wind. Arjuna, Dhananjaya the fortunate, greatest of archers, is Kunti's third son and Indra himself, king of the Devas, is his father.

Nakula and Sahadeva, the handsome twins always obedient to their elders, are born to Madri, and their fathers are the Aswins.

The wise Dhritarashtra sires a hundred sons, Duryodhana and his brothers, by Gandhari, and also Yuyutsu, who is born of a Vaisya woman. Among those hundred and one, eleven are Maharathas: Duryodhana,

Dushasana, Duhsaha, Durmarshana, Vikarna, Chitrasena, Vivimsati, Jaya, Satyavrata, Purumitra and Yuyutsu.

Krishna's sister Subhadra gives birth to Abhimanyu; Arjuna is the prince's father, making Pandu his grandfather. The five Pandavas each has a son by their wife Panchali. Radiant and handsome are these princes and masters of the Vedas and the Shastras.

Yudhishtira's son is Prativindhya; Bhima's, Sutasoma; Arjuna's, Srutakirti; Nakula's, Shatanika; and Sahadeva's son is the powerful Srutasena. In the forest, Bhima also begets Ghatotkacha, the Rakshasa prince, on Hidimbi.

Drupada also has another daughter, Shikhandin, who later turns into a male child. Sthuna the Yaksha effects the transformation in the jungle to help Shikhandin accomplish her life's obsession.

Why, hundreds of thousands of Kshatriyas fight the Great War of the Kurus. Ten thousand years would be too few for me to name all their names. But the main protagonists, with whom this Itihasa deals, I have told you about."'

CANTO 64

ADIVAMSAVATARANA PARVA CONTINUED

Janamejaya said, "Brahmana, tell me in detail about those you have named and those that you have not. Tell me what happened to those thousands of crowned kings, and why they are born into the world, those Maharathas."

Vaisampayana said, "It has been said, O King, that what you ask is mysterious even to the gods! However, I bow to Narayana, and shall do my best to answer your question.

Jamadagni's son Parasurama massacres the Kshatriyas in twenty-one savage encounters, so the Earth is rid entirely of the race of kings, and then he makes his way to Mahendra, most excellent mountain, and sits there in tapasya to expiate his sins of violence.

When Parasurama has exterminated the Kshatriya men, thousands of women of the royal race resort to Brahmana men, austere Rishis, in order to have sons. It must be said that intercourse takes place between them only when the princesses and queens are ovulating, never otherwise or from mere lust.

The Kshatriya women conceive and give birth to countless children, sons and daughters, of great vitality and lustre, and it seems that Kshatriya kind will flourish once more. This is the new generation of the Kshtariya race, sired by Brahmanas of mighty tapasya.

Indeed, the new Kshatriyas thrive, and live in dharma, accumulating great punya. The four varnas, with the Brahmanas at their head, are re-established. During this time, lust vanishes and men go to their wives only when the women are in season, and never out of carnal desire.

Why, O Bharatarishabha, at this time the same is true of every species on Earth, even birds of the air. Thus, O Protector of the world, lakhs and crores of creatures are born, all virtuous, living in a burgeoning swath of dharma, and free from sickness and sorrow.

O King with the elephant's gait, once more the Kshatriyas rule Bhumi, with her mountains, jungles and cities. They rule with dharma as their sceptre and joy is upon the world and the four varnas, of whom the Brahmanas are pre-eminent.

Free from every vice generated by lust and anger, the Kshatriya kings rule justly, punishing those that deserve chastisement. Thousand-eyed Indra, of a hundred Mahayagnas, sees how righteously the Kshatriyas rule, and he sends down timely rains, which bless all creatures.

Rajan, those are days when no one dies prematurely, but only in the fullness of time, and when no man knows a woman carnally before he has come of age Bharatrishabha, the Earth is filled from sea to sea, coast to coast, with long-lived men of dharma.

The Kshatriyas perform great sacrifices and give away vast wealth as charity. All Brahmanas study the Vedas and the Vedangas religiously, Bharatarishabha, and the Upanishads, as well. In those days, no Brahmana ever teaches for gold, or ever reads the Veda aloud in the presence of a Sudra.

The Vaisyas dutifully till the Earth with their bullocks, and they never yoke their beasts themselves, but their servants, the Sudras, do.

The herd is cared for lovingly, and every cow and bull and calf fed well. Men never milk cows before their calves are weaned.

No merchant ever tampers with his scales of measure in those days. Purushavyaghra, O tiger among men, all men cleave to dharma, and whatever they do, they do with dharma in mind. All the varnas live by their svadharma alone, and dharma is maintained and does not decay or diminish, but indeed only grows.

Bharatarishabha, human women and cows give birth when their time is full, not before or after. Trees bear flowers and fruit in their proper season. Rajan, the Krita Yuga having begun, Bhumi teems with myriad species, all in harmony.

Then, O Bull of the race of Bhaarata, the Asuras begin to take birth in the royal Houses. The sons of Aditi, the Devas, repeatedly crush the sons of Diti, the Daityas, and those of Danu, the Danavas, in battle. Their unearthly kingdoms lost, Swarga gone, the Demons begin to incarnate on Earth.

The powerful Asuras, wanting sovereignty over Bhumi, begin to be born not only among Kshatriyas and other humans, but among all the species: as cows and bulls, horses, donkeys and asses, camels, buffaloes, among the Rakshasas and the other magical races, among elephants and deer. Through the passage of the Yugas, owing to these demonic births, Bhumi Devi's burden of evil increases to the extent that she feels she cannot support the weight anymore and will plunge down into the Narakas, into hell.

Some of the sons of Diti and of Danu, cast out of heaven, are born on Earth as kings of terrible hubris. With terrific energy, the forces of evil swarm over the Earth in various forms and shapes. They teem in the world, from sea to sea.

With their undeniable strength, they begin to persecute Brahmana and Kshatriya, Vaisya and Sudra, and indeed every virtuous creature of the Earth. Striking terror into every heart, they go about committing rapine, pillage and murder. They range the world in great bands, of hundreds of thousands, veritable armies of the night. Mocking truth and virtue, intoxicated by their strength and arrogance, they even desecrate and slaughter holy Rishis in their asramas in the hearts of sacred forests.

Oppressed and ravaged by these unrestrained, powerful, wealthy and daily swelling legions of evil, Bhumi Devi thinks in despair of Brahma. Only the combined strength of awesome ones like Sesha Naga, the Kuurma Avatara and the great Diggajas is able to continue to support the weight of the Earth with her mountains and oceans.

O King, now terrified by the burden of the Asuras upon her, the dreadful load of their wantonness and savagery unleashed, Bhumi frantically seeks Brahma's help to save her from plunging down into the void.

She sees Brahma, the Creator, Pitamaha of all creatures, undecaying Grandsire, surrounded by the Devas, Brahmarishis of great fortune, being worshipped by Gandharvas and Apsaras, who are the eternal servitors of the gods.

Wanting protection, the Earth begins to tell Brahma her woes, in the presence of those Regents of the worlds. Rajan, the omniscient, Svayambhuva, Self-created, and supreme Lord already knows her petition. Bharatarishabha, being the Creator and Sovereign of the Universe, shall He not always know whatever is in the hearts of his creatures, including the Devas and the Asuras?

Rajan, the Lord of the Earth, the Creator of all creatures, who is calls Isa, Sambhu, Prajapati, speaks to Bhumi Devi. Brahma says, 'Bhumi Devi, womb of wealth, I will appoint all the celestials to accomplish what you wish. Now go back.'

When she has gone, Brahma says to the Devas, 'Go, be born in amsa on Earth and seek war with the Asuras who hold sway over her and torment her.'

The Creator calls all the Gandharva tribes and all the Apsaras and says to them, 'Go be born into the world in amsa in whatever forms you like.'

Indra and his Devas decide they will do as Brahma commands. They first go to Narayana in Vaikuntha, He that bears the Chakra and the

Gada, whose skin is the hue of a thundercloud, who wears pitambara robes, of blinding splendour, Padmanabha from whose navel the Lotus grows in which Brahma is born, whose lotus eyes gaze down at his great chest, looking within, ever in dhyana, who is the bane and the slayer of the Asuras, who is the Lord of Prajapati himself, Devadeva the mighty who bears the Srivatsa whorled upon his breast, who animates the faculties of all beings and whom all the Devas worship.

Indra says to that most exalted Purusha, 'Lord, be incarnate!'

Hari replies, 'Tathaastu! Be it so.'"

CANTO 65

SAMBHAVA PARVA

Vaisampayana said, "Indra and Narayana speak together about how He would be born on Earth, and how the Devas, too, would incarnate in amsa. When every Deva knows his role, Indra returns from Vaikunta.

One by one, over time, the Devas are born on Earth in amsa to kill the Asuras already born there and to remove the burden of Bhumi, Swarga and Patala. They incarnate as they please as Kshatriya kings, as Brahmarishis and Rajarishis, and they kill the Asuras born as Rakshasas and Gandharvas, as Nagas, and as other dreadful creatures. The Danavas cannot resist the avenging Devas, so mighty are the gods."

Janamejaya said, "I want to hear from the beginning about the births of the Devas, the Danavas, the Gandharvas, the Apsaras, the men who are more than men, the Yakshas and the Rakshasas."

Vaisampayana said, "I bow down to the Svayambhuva, and will tell you what you wish to know.

Brahma has six sons born immaculately of his spirit: Marichi, Atri, Angiras, Pulastya, Pulaha and Kratu. Marichi's son is Kashyapa, and from Kashyapa all the creatures are born.

One of the original Prajapatis, Daksha has thirteen daughters of great beauty and fortune. Tiger among men, O Scion of the race of Bhaarata, these thirteen are called Aditi, Diti, Danu, Kala, Danayu, Simhika, Krodha, Pradha, Viswa, Vinata, Kapila, Muni and Kadru.

The sons and grandsons of these, all of burning tejas, are beyond count. Aditi gives birth to the twelve Adityas, Lords of the Universe. They are Dhatri, Mitra, Aryaman, Sakra, Varuna, Ansa, Vaga, Vivaswat, Usha, Savitri, Tvashtri and Vishnu. The youngest is the greatest of them all.

Diti has one son called Hiranyakashyipu, and he has five sons, renowned throughout the worlds. The eldest is Prahlada, the next Sahradha, then Anuhrada, Sibi and Vashkala.

O Bhaarata, Prahlada has three sons Virochana, Kumbha, and Nikumbha. Virochana's son is Bali, the Great. And the son of Bali is the great Asura Bana. The blessed Bana is a bhakta of Rudra, and is also known as Mahakala.

O Janamejaya, Danu has forty sons. The eldest of them is Viprachitti of great fame, then Sambara, Namuchi and Pauloman; Asiloman, Kesin and Durjaya; Ayahsiras, Aswasiras, and the powerful Aswasanku; Gaganamardhan, Vegavat and Ketumat; Swarbhanu, Aswa, Aswapati, Vrishaparvan and Ajaka; Aswagriva, Sukshama, Tuhunda of vast strength, Ekapada, Ekachakra, Virupaksha, Mahodara, Nichandra, Nikumbha, Kupata, Kapata; Sarabha, Sulabha, Surya, and then Chandramas these are the best known in the race of Danu.

The Devas Surya and Chandramas, the Sun and the Moon, are different beings, not the sons of Danu of the same names. These other ten, also of untold strength and vigour, are also, O Rajan, the sons of Danu: Ekaksha, Amritapa of fathomless valour, Pralamba and Naraka, Vatapi, Satrutapana, the great Asura Satha; Gavishtha, Vanayu and the Danava Dirghajiva.

Bhaarata, the sons and the grandsons of these are countless. Simhika gives birth to Rahu, the tormentor of the Sun and the Moon, and to three others: Suchandra, Chandrahantri and Chandra Pramardana.

The numberless progeny of Krura, also called Krodha, are as devious and as vicious as she is. Hers is a clan full of wrath, and merciless to its enemies.

Danayu has four sons who are bulls among the Asuras. They are Vikshara, Bala, Vira and Vritrasura the Great. The sons of Kala are all like Yama himself, boundlessly vigorous smiters of their foes. Kala's sons are calls Vinasana, Krodha, Krodhahantri and Krodhashatru.

Kala has many other sons, as well. Shukra, the son of a Rishi, is the chief priest and Acharya of the Asuras. Shukra has four sons, also priests of the Asuras. Tashtadhara and Atri are two, and there are two others, fierce tejasvins. They are like the Sun himself, and ambitious enough to want to conquer Brahmaloka.

These are the sons of the Devas and the Asuras as told in the Purana. The progeny of these are past counting, O King.

Vinata's sons are Tarkhya and Arishtanemi, Garuda and Aruna, and Aruni and Varuni.

Kadru's sons are Ananta Sesha, Vasuki, Takshaka, Kumara, and Kulika.

Bhimasena, Ugrasena, Suparna, Varuna, Gopati, Dhritarashtra, Suryavarchas, Satyavachas, Arkaparna, Prayuta, Bhima and Chitraratha - the famed, learned one, master of his passions - Kalisiras, Parjannya Kali and Narada these Devas and Gandharvas are the sons of Daksha Prajapati's daughter Muni.

Anavadya Manu, Vamsa, Asura, Marganapria, Anupa, Subhaga, Vasi are the daughters of Pradha, and her sons are Siddha, Purna, Barhin, Purnayus of wide renown, Brahmacharin, Ratiguna, Suparna, Viswavasu, Bhanu and Suchandra. All these are Gandharvas of heaven.

Pradha also bears her husband Kashyapa the delectable Apsaras Alambusha, Misrakesi, Vidyutparna, Tilottama, Arunaa, Rakshita,

Rambha, Manorama, Kesini, Subahu, Surata, Suraja and Supriya. Her most famous sons are Atibahu, Haha and Huhu, and Tumburu.

The Amrita, Brahmanas, sacred cows, the Gandharvas and Apsaras, are born to Kapila Deva, as the Purana says.

This account of the birth of the Gandharvas and Apsaras, of the Nagas, Suparnas, Rudras, and the Maruts, of cows, Brahmanas of great fortune and holy deeds, is sacred and extends the life of he that reads it, and delights the ear and the mind.

He who reads or narrates the birth of the exalted beings in the presence of the Devas and Brahmarishis has many excellent children, finds fortune, fame, and attains to the best of worlds in the hereafter."

CANTO 66

Sambhava Parva Continued

Vaisampayana said, "We have seen how the six Maharishis are the mind-born sons of Brahma. He has another son called Sthanu. Sthanu, of huge tejas, has eleven sons—Mrigavayadha, Sarpa, Nirriti of great fame, Ajaikapat, Ahivradhna, Pinaki - bane of his enemies, Dahana, Iswara, the splendorous Kapali, Sthanu, and the illumined Bharga. These are the eleven Rudras.

Marichi, Angiras, Atri, Pulastya, Pulaha and Kratu are the brilliant sons of Brahma. The world knows that Angiras has three sons—Brihaspati, Utathya and Samvarta, all profound tapasvins.

Rajan, the sons of Atri are many, all of them Maharishis, masters of the Veda, Sannyasis, Atmaramas, their souls at perfect peace.

Rajavyaghra, tiger among kings, the sons of the wise Pulastya are Rakshasas, Vanaras, Kinnara fauns and Yakshas.

O King, the sons of Pulaha are the Salabhas (winged insects), lions, Kimpurushas (manticores), tigers, bears and wolves.

The sons of Kratu, sacred as yagnas, are the devout Balakhilyas, mighty tapasvins, who are the companions of Surya.

Protector of the Earth, the illustrious Rishi Daksha, peerless Sannyasi, his soul absorbed in infinite peace, springs from the big toe of Brahma's right foot. And from the big toe on his left foot, Daksha's chaste and noble wife emerges. The Muni begets fifty daughters upon her, all of them flawless of face and limb, their eyes like lotus petals.

Having no sons, he makes Putrikas of his daughters, which meant that their sons would be his sons as well as the sons of his daughters' husbands. Daksha marries, with sacred rites, ten of his daughters to Dharma, twenty-seven of them to Soma the Moon, and thirteen he gives to Kashyapa.

The ten wives of Dharma are Kirti, Lakshmi, Dhriti, Medha, Pushti, Sraddha, Kriya, Buddhi, Lajja and Mali.

Soma Deva's twenty-seven wives are they that show the time they are the Nakshatras, the asterisms of the Moon. They are Yoginis because they help maintain the worlds.

Brahma has another son called Manu. Manu has a son called Prajapati, who has eight sons, known as the Vasus. They are Dhara, Dhruva, Soma, Aha, Anila, Anala, Pratyusha and Prabhasa.

Of these, Dhara and the enlightened Dhruva are born from Dhumra; Chandramas (Soma) and Swasana (Anila) are born to the intelligent Swasa; Aha is the son of Rata; Hutasana (Anala) is Sandilya's son; Pratyusha and Prabhasa are the sons of Prabhata.

Dhara has two sons, Dravina and Hutahavyavaha. Dhruva's son is Kaala (Time) who devours the worlds. Soma's son is the splendent Varchas. Varchas begets Sisira and Ramana on his wife Manohara.

Aha's sons are Jyotih, Sama, Santa, and also Muni. Agni's son is the many-splendoured Kumara, born in a forest of sara reeds; he is Saradvata. He is also calls Karttikeya since the six Krittikas raised him.

Agni's other sons are Sakha, Visakha and Naigameya. Anila's wife is Sivaa, and their sons are Manojava and Avijnataagati.

The son of Pratyusha is the Rishi Devala. Devala has two sons, famed for their forbearance, forgiveness and their great intellects.

Brihaspati's sister, who always speaks the truth, performs tapasya and ranges over the Earth, becomes the wife of Prabhasa, the eighth Vasu. And she bears him the illustrious Viswakarman, from whom all the arts began: a thousand of them. He is the architect of the Devas, fashioner of the first and matchless ornaments among the stars; he is indeed the original artist. Viswakarman creates the celestial vimanas of the gods; and humankind lives on because of the countless precious inventions of Viswakarman, the universal artist. Men worship him for this reason, and he is an eternal one and changeless.

Dharma, who bestows joy, takes a human face and emerges from Brahma's right breast. Ahasta (Dharma Deva) has three sons who can enchant everyone; they are Sama, Kama and Harsha: Peace, Desire and Joy. They support the worlds with their activity.

Kama's wife is Rati, Sama's is Prapti, and the wife of Harsha is Nanda. Yes, indeed, upon these the worlds depend.

Kashyapa is the son of Marichi, and the Devas and Asuras are the sons of Kashyapa. Hence, Kashyapa is the Father of the worlds.

Tvashtri, who assumes the form of Badava, a mare, becomes the wife of Savitri. She gives birth in the sky to twins of great fortune and fame: the Aswini Kumaras.

Rajan, Aditi has twelve sons, Indra being the eldest. The youngest is Vishnu in whom the worlds are founded.

There are thirty-three Devas eight Vasus, eleven Rudras, twelve Adityas, Prajapati, and Vashatkara.

Let me tell you about the sons of these, by their Pakshas, Kulas and Ganas. The Rudras, the Sadhyas, the Maruts, the Vasus, the Bhargavas and the Viswedevas are each reckoned as being one Paksha. Garuda the son of Vinata, the mighty Aruna, and the illustrious Brihaspati are counted among the Adityas. The Aswin twins, all perennial plants and the lesser animals are counted among the Guhyakas.

These are the Ganas of the Devas, O King! Listening to this recitation washes away his every sin from a man.

Lustrous Bhrigu comes forth, tearing open Brahma's breast. Shukra, learned and wise, is Bhrigu's son. Shukra becomes a Graha, a Planet, and, traversing the sky, commanded by Brahma, sends down and withholds the rain, looses and holds back calamities, and nurtures the lives of every creature in the three worlds.

Shukra of unfathomed intellect and sagacity, of stern vratas, always a Brahmacharin, cleaves himself in two with his tapasya shakti, and becomes a spiritual Guru to both the sons of Diti and of Aditi.

When Brahma has thus gainfully employed great Shukra, Bhrigu begets another son Chyvana who blazes like the Sun, and is virtuous and famed. He emerges from his mother's womb in anger and rescues her from the clutches of the Rakshasas.

Chyvana marries Manu's daughter Arushi, and sires Aurva of matchless fame on her. Aurva tears open his mother's thigh to be born. Aurva begets Richika, who, even as a child, possesses awesome spiritual power and brilliance, and every virtue as well.

Richika's son is Jamadagni, who has four sons, the youngest being Parasurama, who is his older brothers' superior in every way, and a master of his passions. A master also of astras and of every weapon, he slaughters the race of Kshatriyas.

Aurva has a hundred sons, Jamadagni being the eldest. These hundred father thousands of children, across the Earth.

Brahma has two other sons, Dhatri and Vidhatri, who stay with Manu. Their sister is the auspicious Lakshmi, who dwells amidst lotuses. Lakshmi's spiritual sons are the horses that go through the sky.

Shukra's daughter Divi becomes Varuna's first wife. She bears him a son called Bala and a daughter Sura, the goddess of wine, much to the delight of the Devas.

Adharma, Sin, is born when creatures felt hungry and began to eat one another. Adharma is a destroyer of every being. Adharma's wife is Nirriti, and the Rakshasas that are their children are calls Nairritas. She has three other savage sons, always sinful and cruel: Bhaya who is fear, Mahabhaya who is terror, and Mrityu who is Death, forever killing. Because he is such a ceaseless killer, Mrityu has no wife or child.

Tamra gives birth to five daughters, known throughout the worlds Kaki the crow; Shyeni the eagle; Phasi the hen; Dhritarashtri the goose, and Suki the parrot. Kaki generated crows, Shyeni eagles, falcons, hawks and vultures, Dhritarashtri ducks, geese, swans and the fabled chakravakas, and the sweet and auspicious Suki brings forth parrots and parakeets, and their ilk.

Krodha gives birth to nine daughters, eight of them wrathful by nature Mrigi, Mrigamanda, Hari, Bhadramana, Matangi, Sarduli, Sweta, Surabhi, and the ninth, the virtuous and good-natured Surasa.

King of men, Mrigi's children are deer; Mrigamanda's are bears and also srimaras, of the sweet feet. Bhadramana begets the celestial elephant Airavata. Hari's children are monkeys, and also horses and all bovine creatures: golangulas,-the cow-tailed ones.

Sarduli begets lions and tigers in vast numbers, leopards and other powerful predators. Rajan, Matangi's progeny are the elephants of the Earth. Sweta bears one elephant of extraordinary size and speed, named Sweta after her.

Surabhi gives birth to two daughters, the sweet-natured Rohini and the famous Gandharvi. O Bhaarata, she has two other daughters, Vimala and Anala.

Rohini is the mother of all kine, and Gandharvi of all equine beasts. Anala gives birth to the seven kinds of trees that yield soft fruit the date, the palm, the hintala, the tali, the little date, the nut and the coconut. She has another daughter called Suki, the mother of parrots.

Surasa bears a son calls Kanka, a species of long-feathered birds. Shyeni, the wife of Aruna, gives birth to two sons of great tejas and strength: Sampati and the mighty Jatayu. Surasa also bears the Nagas and Kadru, the Punnaga snakes. Vinata has two sons, Garuda and Aruna, whose fame is limitless.

Great King, of the mighty intellect, this is the genealogy of all the main species. Listening to this, a man is purified of his sins, finds great knowledge, and finally attains to the most exalted condition in the life to come."

CANTO 67

Sambhava Parva Continued

Janamejaya said, "Holy One, I want to hear in detail about the advent as men of the Devas, the Asuras, the Gandharvas, Rakshasas, lions and tigers, the other animals, the Nagas, the Pakshis, and indeed all creatures. I want to hear everything that they did when they had human forms."

Vaisampayana said, "Lord of men, I will first tell you about the incarnations of the Devas and Danavas that were born as men. The great Danava Viprachitti is born as that bull among men, Jarasandha of Magadha.

Diti's son, the Daitya Hiranyakashyipu, is born as Sishupala of Chedi. Samhlada, the younger brother of Prahlada, comes down as Salya, that tiger amongst the Balhikas. The spirited Anuhlada, the youngest, becomes Dhrishtaketu.

Rajan, the Daitya Sibi, incarnates as King Druma, while the great Asura Vashkala becomes the mighty Bhagadatta. The five ferocious great Asuras – Ayahsira, Aswasira, Aysanku, Gaganamurdhan and Vegavat are all born in the House of Kekaya and all become powerful kings.

The other indomitable Demon Ketumat incarnates in the world as the terrible King Amitaujas. The Asura Swarbhanu becomes the fierce King Ugrasena.

The Asura Aswa is born as the King Asoka, invincible in battle and choleric. Aswa's younger brother, the Daitya Aswapati, is born into the world as the Kshatriya King Hardikya.

The formidable and fortunate Asura Vrishaparvan becomes King Dirghaprajna. His younger brother Ajaka is born as Shalva, dark sorceror. The powerful Aswagriva comes to the world as King Rochana.

Rajan, the Asura Sukshma, of subtle intelligence and great achievements, becomes the famous Brihadratha.

The noted Demon Tuhunda becomes the King Senabindu. Ishupa becomes Nagnajita; Ekachakra becomes Pritivindhya; Virupaksha, master of a thousand arts of war, is born as Chitravarman.

The valiant Danava Kara, who shatters the pride of his enemies, is born as Suvahu; Suhtra, of great energy, destroyer of his enemies, becomes the King Munjakesa of glowing fortune. Invincible, intelligent Nikumbha is born to become King Devadhipa.

The Asura known amongst Diti's sons as Sarabha becomes on Earth the Rajarishi Paurava, while Kupatha is born on Earth as the famed monarch Suparshva. The Asura Kratha incarnated as the royal Sage Parvateya, splendid as a golden mountain.

The Asura called Salabha becomes the King Prahlada in the country of the Balhikas. Chandra, the Daitya who is as handsome as the Lord of stars who also has his name, the foremost among the sons of Diti known by the name of Chandra, becomes Chandravarman in this world, the Kambhoja king.

Arka, Danavarishabha, becomes the Rajarishsi Rishika. That best of Asuras, Mritapa incarnates as Paschimanupaka; Garishtha becomes King Drumasena. Mayura becomes King Viswa; his younger brother Suparna becomes Kalakriti.

Chandrahantri becomes the Rajarishi Sunaka; Chandravinasana comes as the king called Janaki. That bull among the Danavas, Dhirghajihva, becomes Kasiraja; Simhika's son Rahu, tormentor of Surya and Soma, is born as Kratha.

Danayu's eldest son, Vikshara, becomes Vasumitra on Earth. Her second son Bala becomes the Pandya king; her third Vira, also called Balina, becomes Paundramatsyaka. Rajan, Danayu's fourth son, the great Vritrasura, incarnates as the Rajarishi Manimat. Vritra's younger brother Krodhahantri becomes known in this world as the King Danda. Krodhavardhana becomes Dandadhara.

The eight sons of the Kaleyas are all born as kings, strong as tigers. The eldest becomes King Jayatsena in Magadha; the second, mighty as Indra, becomes Aparajita; the third is born a matchless king of the Nishadas, strong and devious; the fourth is to become the royal sage Srenimat. The fifth becomes King Mahanjas, destroyer of his enemies; the sixth, of huge intelligence, becomes Abhiru, another famed Rajarishi; the seventh has boundless fame and is the King Samudrasena, knower of the Shastras. The eighth of the Kaleyas becomes Brihat, a king of dharma, always working for the welfare of all beings.

The mighty Danava Kukshi, incarnated as Parvatiya, is named for his lustre, which is that of a golden mountain. The Asura Krathana becomes King Suryaksha in the world; the handsome Demon Surya becomes a king of the Balhikas called Darada.

Rajan, I told you about the tribe of Asuras called the Krodhavasas. Many fearless Kshatriya kings of the Earth are Demons of that tribe – Madraka, Karnaveshta, Siddhartha, Kitaka, Suvira, Subahu, Mahavira, Balhika, Kratha, Vichitra, Suratha, the handsome Nila, Chiravasa, Bhumipala, Dantavakra, Durjaya, Rukmi the tigerish Kshatriya, your namesake Janamejaya, Ashada, Vayuvega, Bhuritejas, Ekalavya the brilliant Nishada, Sumitra, Vatadhana, Gomukha, the Kshatriyas of the clan of Karushakas, Khemadhurti, Srutayus, Udvaha, Brihatsena, Kshema, Ugratirtha, the Kalinga king, Matimat, the King Iswara. Yes, all these are Krodhavasa Asuras, incarnated as human kings.

A most powerful Demon called Kalanemi is born as the son of Ugrasena of Mathura, and he becomes Kamsa, the Great and the Terrible.

The Asura Devaka, lustrous as Indra, is born into the world as a king of the Gandharvas.

Rajan, you must know that Bharadvaja's son Drona is not born from any woman, but is an amsavatara of Brihaspati. He is a peerless archer, with power over every astra, of great tejas and greater achievements. He is also a master of the Vedas, the pride of his kind.

O King, Drona's son is the heroic Aswatthama, his eyes like lotus-petals, a terror to his enemies, of tremendous energy, is an amsavatara of equal embodiments of Siva, Yama, Kama and Krodha.

Because of Vasishta's curse and also Indra's dictate, the eight Vasus are born into the world as the sons of Ganga and Shantanu. The youngest Vasu, Prabhasa, is Bhishma, of the grand vow. He is the light of the House of Kuru, a knower of the Vedas, of lofty intellect, the most eloquent speaker, who melts the legions of his enemies in battle. Why, Jamadagni's son Parasurama Bhargava could not vanquish Bhishma when he fought a duel with him.

The Brahmana Sage Kripa, a man among men, is an amsavatara of the Rudras.

Shakuni, O King, who crushed his foes, is none other than Dwapara, the third Yuga incarnate!

Satyaki, pride of the Vrishnis, whose aim never falters, is an amsavatara, an incarnation of the Maruts, who are Vayu's companions. The Rajarishi, the Panchala King Drupada, greatest among bowmen, is also an incarnation of the Maruts, as indeed is the Vrishni Kritavarman, that bull among bulls among Kshatriyas; so, too, is King Virata.

Arishta's son Hamsa is also born into the clan of the Kurus and becomes a king of the Gandharvas.

Dhritarashtra, born of the seed of Krishna Dwaipayana, and blessed with long and mighty arms and unrivalled strength, he of prophetic vision, is blind because of his mother's indelicacy and the consequent anger of the Rishi Vyasa.

Pandu is Dhritarashtra's younger brother, of prowess that defies description, devout and truthful; why, purity incarnate. Their brother Vidura, I have told you, O King, is an avatara of the son of Maharishi Atri: Dharma, Lord of Righteousness and Justice.

As for Duryodhana, incalculably evil king, who ruins the honour of the Kuruvamsa, he is an amsavatara of the Kali Yuga, the Demon Kali. He is the cause of the Great War that devastated the Earth; he lit the fire that finally consumed everything.

The Rakshasas, who are once born as the sons of Pulastya Muni, now take birth as Duryodhana's hundred evil brothers, Dushasana being the first of them. Bharatrishabha, Durmukha, Duhsha and others of these hundred, who always supported Duryodhana's most treacherous and murderous schemes, are all sons of the same Pulastya Muni.

Of course, Dhritarashtra has another son, not by Gandhari but by a Vaishya woman in his palace, and we have seen that this is the virtuous Yuyutsu, who always sided with his cousins the Pandavas of dharma."

Janamejaya said, "Illustrious Suta, tell me the names of Dhritarashtra's sons in order of birth, beginning with the eldest."

Vaisampayana said, "O King, Duryodhana is the first, then Yuyutsu, Dushasana, Duhsaha, Duhshala, Durmukha, Vivimsati, Vikarna, Jalasandha, Sulochna, Vinda, Anuvinda, Durdharsha, Subahu, Dushpradharshana, Durmarshana, Dushkarna, Karna, Chitra, Vipachitra, Chitraksha, Charuchitra, Angada, Durmada, Dushpradharsha, Vivitsu, Vikata, Sama, Drananabha, Padmanabha, Nanda, Upanandaka, Sanapati, Sushena, Kundodara, Mahodara, Chitrabahu, Chitravarman, Suvarman, Durvirochana, Ayobahu, Mahabahu, Chitrachapa, Sukundala, Bhimavega, Bhimabala, Balaki, Bhimavikrama, Ugrayudha, Bhimachara, Kanakayu, Dridhayudha, Dridhavarman, Dridhakshatra, Somakirti, Anadara, Jarasandha, Dridhasandha, Satyasandha, Sahasrabahu, Ugrasravas, Ugrasena, Kshemamurti, Aparajita, Panditaka, Visalaksha, Duradhara, Dridhahasta, Suhasta, Vatavega, Suvarchasa, Adityaketu,

Bahvasin, Nagadatta, Anuyaina, Nishangi, Kuvachi, Dandi, Dandadhara, Dhanugraha, Ugra, Bhimaratha, Vira, Virabahu, Alolupa, Abhaya, Raudrakarman, Dridharatha, Anadhrishya, Kundaveda, Viravi, Dhirghalochana, Dirghabahu, Mahabahu, Vyudhoru, Kanakangana, Kundaja and Chitraka[5].

Dhritarshtra also has a daughter by Gandhari called Duhsala, who is not of the hundred, and neither is Yuyutsu, the Vaishya woman's son. I have recited the names of the hundred in order of their births.

All these are mighty Kshatriyas, great warriors. All of them knew the Vedas, and, Rajan, all the other Shastras besides. They are invincible, in attack and defence, and truly learned besides.

When they are of age, they marry suitably beautiful and accomplished princesses; and the Kaurava king gives his daughter Duhsala to be the wife of Jayadratha, king of the Sindhus. This is done on the advice of Dhritarashtra's brother-in-law, Shakuni.

O King, Yudhishtira is an amsa of Dharma; Bhimasena of Vayu; Arjuna of Indra; Nakula and Sahadeva, handsomest of men, their looks unrivalled on Earth, of the Aswin twins.

Soma Deva's son, Varchas the strong, becomes Arjuna's son of stunning genius, the dashing Abhimanyu. When Varchas is to be born, Soma says to the other Devas, 'I cannot live without my son. So let him incarnate on Bhumi, but live a short human life before returning to me after killing countless Daityas.

Nara, whose companion is Narayana, will be born as Indra's son Arjuna the Pandava. Let my Varchas be born as Arjuna's son and become a Maharatha. Let him be away on Earth for sixteen years, and when he is sixteen the Great War shall be fought, and, Devas, all your amsavataras shall raze the Asuras and the very race of Kshatriyas.

Yet, one day during the war, a great encounter will occur inside a cunning Chakravyuha. Krishna and Arjuna, Nara Narayana, will not have part in that battle, but my son shall pierce the impenetrable spinning wheel of warriors and take devastation to the enemy.

---

[5]These do not add up to a hundred, and there seem to be two Mahabahus.

On his own, my son will send a quarter of the entire enemy army to Yama's realm, in the space of half a day. None will be able to stand before him, but finally, near dusk, a ring of Maharathas will combine to slay my mighty child with treachery, and Varchas shall return to me.

Abhimanyu will beget the single heir to the Kuru throne, and prevent the royal line of Bhaarata from becoming extinct.'

The Devas assent, 'So be it.' Why, they applaud him all together and offer him worship, that Lord of the stars. This, Rajan, of course, is the story behind the birth of your father's father.

The fireborn Maharatha Dhrishtadyumna is an amsa of Agni. Prince Shikhandin, who was once a princess, is the amsavatara of a Rakshasa.

Bharatarishabha, the celestial Risis are born as the five sons of Draupadi – Prativindhya, Sutasoma, Srutakirti, Satanika, Nakula and Srutasena, endowed with terrific energy.

Vasudeva's father is Sura, a great Yadava chieftain. He has a daughter called Pritha, whose beauty is unmatched in this world. Sura has vowed, with Agni as his witness, that he would give his firstborn child to his cousin Kuntiboja, who is childless.

He gives Pritha to Kuntibhoja, who adopts her as his daughter. She becomes a charming and attentive young hostess in the palace of her adoptive father, especially to visiting Rishis and Brahmanas. Once, she waits graciously upon the Rishi Durvasa, a master of the profoundest mysteries of the spirit, but his temper also a legend.

Pritha, now called Kunti by her doting foster-father, looks after the irascible Sage's every wish and whim with such affection and care, that, as he is leaving, he says to her, 'I am pleased with you, my child. I am going to teach you a secret mantra with which you can summon any Deva you wish. By their grace, one day you shall bear divine children.'

He teaches her the recondite incantation, and then leaves.

Some days pass; then seized by curiosity, the young Kunti, still a maiden living in her father's home, chants Durvasa's mantra one morning and summons Surya Deva, the Sun God. You might imagine her surprise when the blazing Deva actually appears before her and begets a child on her, a son who becomes without equal among the archers of the world.

Kunti gives birth in magical secrecy, with Surya's blessing, and from fear of the censure of the world and her relatives, she floats her Sun-child, irradiant and handsome as the Sun himself, and born wearing golden armour and earrings, his body of perfect proportions, away on the river that flows at the bottom of her father's palace garden.

The husband of Radha sees the wooden box of that shining infant floating downstream, and takes him home to his childless wife to be their son. They name him Vasusena, and when he grows up he becomes a master of weapons, of all the Shastras and sciences, learns the Veda, and, the truth being his strength, there is nothing he would not give away as alms to a Brahmana who comes begging to him, so generous is he.

Then, Indra, who is the origin of all things, comes to that mighty son of Surya and asks him for his natural kavacha and kundala as alms. Indra wants to disadvantage Vasusena against Arjuna, who of course is Indra's own son.

Promptly, that unequalled warrior strips off his armour, removes his magical earrings, both of which are his father Surya's protection to him, and gives them to Indra. Astonished by his truthfulness (for he has sworn not to refuse anyone that comes to him at high noon for whatever they ask of him as alms), and moved by his fearless generosity, Surya gives Vasusena his own Shakti, saying, 'Invincible hero, anyone at whom you cast this Shakti will die, be he not a Deva, an Asura, a Manava, a Gandharva, Naga, Rakshasa or any other celestial or earthly being.'

Surya's son is first called Vasusena, but later, because he has cut his coat of golden mail from his body to give it as alms to Indra, Surya's prince, Kunti's eldest son, is called Karna.

However, that natural Kshatriya grows up in the home of a Suta; Radha and her husband are the only parents he ever knows. Later, O King, Karna, noblest of men, greatest of archers, slayer of his enemies, the finest amsa of the God of Day, becomes the closest companion and advisor of Duryodhana the Kaurava.

Then there is born into the world Vaasudeva Krishna, indomitable and unrivalled in every way, an Avatara of Narayana, Devadeva the Eternal One. His brother Baladeva is an amsa of Sesha Naga.

Rajan, mighty Pradyumna is Sanatkumara incarnate. Many other dwellers in Swarga incarnate themselves in the race of the Vrishnis, swelling its glory.

And, O King, the portions of the tribe of Apsaras which I have mentioned already, also becomes incarnate on Earth according to Indra's commands. And sixteen thousand portions of those goddesses become, in this world of men, the wives of Vasudeva. And a portion of Sri herself becomes incarnate on Earth, for the gratification of Narayana, in the line of Bhishmaka. She is the chaste Rukmini.

And the faultless Draupadi, slender-waisted like the wasp, is born of a portion of Sachi (the queen of the Devas), in the line of Drupada. She is neither short nor tall; she is of the fragrance of the blue lotus, of eyes large as lotus-petals, of thighs fair and round, of dense masses of black curly hair. And endowed with every auspicious feature and her complexion like that of the emerald, she enchants and steals the hearts of the five Pandavas, greatest among men of the world.

The two goddesses Siddhi and Dhriti are born as Kunti and Madri to become the mothers of those five. The Devi Mali incarnates as Gandhari, daughter of Subala, who becomes blind Dhritarashtra's wife.

This, Rajan, is the narration of the incarnation of the Devas, the Asuras, Gandharvas, Apsaras and Rakshasas as invincible kings and lovely queens of the Earth.

I have told you about the exalted ones born as Yadavas and Vrishnis, the others born as powerful kings in other royal houses, and those who take birth as Brahmanas, Kshatriyas and Vaishyas.

This account of the incarnation as amsavataras of the God and Demons can bestow wealth, fame, children, longevity and success, if one listens to it with faith. He that hears it learns the true nature of the creation, preservation and destruction of the world, and thus finding wisdom, he is never conquered even by the gravest sorrow."

CANTO 68

SAMBHAVA PARVA CONTINUED

Janamejaya said, "Brahmana, you have indeed told me about the incarnations in amsa of the Devas, the Danavas, the Rakshasas, the Gandharvas and Apsaras. But I want to hear the genealogy of the Kuruvamsa again, from its inception. I beg you, Vaisampayana, relate this to me before all these auspicious and illumined Rishis."

Vaisampayana said, "O noblest of Bhaarata's race, Dushyanta of blazing tejas is the founder of the Paurava line. He is the Guardian of the Earth bounded by four seas, and has complete sway over the Four Quarters of this world. Moreover, he is sovereign of myriad islands in the midst of the ocean. Bane of his enemies, he even holds sway over the distant countries of the Mlechchas.

While Dushyanta rules, the varnas remain pure and there are no children born of mixed caste. No one tills the soil, because the Earth herself yields every manner of produce, spontaneously, as she does precious metals and gemstones: magically.

There are no sinners and all men are good, and live in dharma and virtue; whatever they do their motives are pure and selfless. There is no fear from thieves, famine, or disease – for none of these exist. The four varnas delight in their svadharma, for its own sake, not performing any karma from desire for gain.

His people feel perfectly secure during the golden reign of Dushyanta, and Indra sends down the rains in proper season and the Earth flourishes. Rich is the yield of the field and the bough. The world abounds in wealth of every kind and every species of animal, bird and plant, great and small.

Brahmanas perform their sacred dharma punctiliously; they are truthful to a fault. The young king is marvellously strong, his body hard as Indra's Vajra, and he can lift Mount Mandara, with all its forests, and hold it up, easily.

He is a master of the four forms of gada-yuddha, mace fighting – hurling it from afar, striking with it at close quarters, whirling it around to strike many adversaries, and staving off a combatant with it. He is an expert at every form of warfare, a master of every weapon; he rides an elephant and a horse with equal skill.

Dushyanta is as strong as Vishnu, brilliant as Surya, deep and grave as Varuna, and as patient as Bhumi Devi. His contented people love their king and he rules with dharma as his sceptre."

CANTO 69

SAMBHAVA PARVA CONTINUED

Janamejaya said, "Tell me now about the birth and the life of Mahatma Bharata and about the birth of Shakuntala. Holy one, tell me how Dushyanta, that lion among kings, married Shakuntala. O most erudite among men, great Vaisampayana, tell me all."

Vaisampayana said, "Once, Dushyanta Mahabaho sets out for the forest with a large complement of soldiers. Hundreds of horses and elephants go with the king. Footsoldiers, chariots, cavalry and elephant mounted warriors travel with Dushyanta – Kshatriyas bearing swords and spears, maces and heavy cudgels.

Yes, surrounded by hundreds of great warriors, that king sets out and the Earth and Sky echo with the tigerish roars of those warriors, and with booming conches, batteries of drumrolls, the clatter of chariot wheels, the trumpeting of elephants, the whinnying of horses, the din of weapons being clashed together and against breastplate and armour – it is deafening, the noise that force makes as it goes forth.

Beautiful and noble women line their sprawling terraces to watch the grand march of mighty King Dushyanta. The women see how magnificent he is, like Indra himself.

They say, 'This tiger among men is a match for the Vasus in battle; no enemy can stand before him.'

The women shower flowers down on their king in joy. Followed by the greatest Brahmanas, chanting out their blessings ceaselessly, the king proceeds towards the jungle in some delight. He goes to hunt deer. Not only Brahmanas and Kshatriyas, but Vaishyas and Sudras follow Dushyanta who rides a haughty elephant even as the king of the Devas does. The people follow him until he forbids them to go with him any further.

Then Dushyanta climbs down from his royal elephant and into his chariot, yoked to steeds swift as thoughts, and the sound of his chariot wheels fill Earth and Sky. Soon, he sees a great forest before him and, entering it, sees that it is like the heavenly garden Nandana.

Bilwa, Arka, Khadira, Kapittha and Dhava trees he sees and that the ground is strewn with crags that have come loose and fallen from surrounding hills. He sees no water anywhere, no humans, and the jungle stretches away on every side for yojanas. There are deer in plenty in that forest, as well as lions and other fierce predators.

Dushyanta and his men begin to hunt in that forest, slaughtering countless beasts. That tiger among kings kills many a tiger, within range, with unerring arrows; he wounds many others that he sees at great distances; then he leaps on other striped terrors that are too near to be slain by arrows and kills them with his sword.

There are beasts he kills by casting spears at them that pierce their hearts, and others he fells with mace and club. Fearlessly, he ranges through that jungle, strewing carcasses everywhere. The forest is in turmoil.

Lions flee that jungle in prides; elephant herds, their tuskers slain, crash away in panic in every direction, trunks raised high, screams filling the air, spraying urine and dung in terror, some vomiting blood. Some wounded beasts trample many of the king's men who are not quick enough to escape their wild charges.

Exhausted, the mastodons soon fall down, for there is no water anywhere to drink. The king's hungry warriors eat many of those that have died, some raw and some roasted over spits.

That jungle, which teemed with animals a short while ago, is quickly filled with dead beasts and hardly any that live, because those that do live flee for their lives, so savage is the hunt of Dushyanta and his men."

CANTO 70

Sambhava Parva Continued

Vaisampayana continued, "Having slaughtered thousands of innocent beasts in that forest, until there is no game left in it to hunt, Dushyanta goes towards another forest, to hunt on.

By now, his force has scattered and he has just two of his men with him – his priest and his minister. Tired, hungry and thirsty, the king stumbles upon a desert at the edge of the second forest. Crossing this plain of sand, where no green thing grows, Dushyanta and his men enter the second forest, like a garden in heaven, full of Rishis and their asramas.

Dark, deep and enchanting this forest is, with cool and fragrant breezes whispering through stands of trees laden with flowers in every colour. Velvet grasses cover the ground, as far as they can see, and the sweetest songs of birds fill the air most of all, the inspired melodies of the male kokila and also the twanging of cicadas.

Ancient and magnificent are the trees of this forest, their lofty branches entwining high above the jungle floor to form a verdant awning.

Flowering vines cling to many of these and bees hum over them, drinking their nectar.

No tree here but that which bears some luscious fruit; none without the bees swarming over its flowers; and none that has any thorns. Yes, truly the whole forest rings with the symphonies of feathered choirs. And the flowers? A carnival, a riot of them, from every season, in every colour, some from dreams. After the march through the arid sands, the green shade is like balm to the king and his men.

The breeze seems to welcome Dushyanta, gently dislodging a small rain of flowers to fall over his head as if in benison. So lofty are those patriarchs of the jungle, clad in rainbow flower garments of every hue, honey-throated songsters perched on their branches, that their crowns surely must thrust themselves into Swarga above.

Their branches, though, are bent with the weight of the flowers they bear. Gazing at all this, hearing the drone of the bees like the sruti to the song of the birds, great Dushyanta is enchanted.

Bands of Siddhas, Charanas, tribes of Gandharvas, Apsaras, Vanaras and Kinnaras come to this charmed forest, to sport, to make love and become inebriated with its enchantment.

The soft breezes scented with flowers blow everywhere, with no method, as if they play with the trees. The king sees that this forest grows in a great loop of a river and, looking at a singularly lofty stand of trees, like some great and incredible column, he is reminded of a gaudy stamba erected at Indra's festival.

Wandering in that forest, Dushyanta comes closer to that auspicious grove of trees in which there is an asrama of some Rishis, serene and brimming, as it were, with the joy of the Spirit. A sacred fire burns solemnly in the agnikunda at its heart. The king sees that many Yogis, Balakhilyas and other Munis sit around the fire and offer worship there. There are many kutilas that comprise the hermitage, each with a holy fire alight within it. The flowers fallen from the trees form a thick bright carpet over the ground.

Perhaps even more lovely than the rest of that forest is this asrama nestling in the grove of lofty trees, their boles so wide and great. The limpid river Malini flows beside that asrama, waterbirds of every kind swimming, playing, on her transparent current.

The Rishis bathe in her, and she suffuses their hearts with bliss. On her banks Dushyanta sees herds of deer that seem fearless and even tame; he sees chakravakas on her wavelets crested with the purest white foam; he sees the abodes of Kinnara fauns on the far bank of the sacred Malini. Monkeys and bears he sees in large numbers, elephants, tigers and snakes.

Of course, there are numerous asramas that dot the course of the river, where Rishis live in dhyana, imbibing the Scriptures. The fine asrama on the banks of that river, which Dushyanta sees first, belongs to the Maharishi Kashyapa, and many of his disciples live therein, Rishis of profound tapasya.

Dushyanta sees the river, many islands on her stream, her banks gorgeous, and the asrama that seems truly like the hermitage of Nara Narayana upon the banks of the Ganga; and he decides he would enter that asrama. In some transport at everything he sees and feels, Dushyanta, whose chariot is inexorable to his enemies, walks into that sanctuary as lovely as a bit of Devaloka fallen into this world.

The forest, which is even like the garden of Chitraratha, the Gandharva king, echoes with the cries of peacocks. Dushyanta wants to meet the Maharishi Kanva of the line of Kashyapa, a Sage whose lustre is such that it is difficult to even look at him.

Earlier, when they rejoined him at the hem of the second forest, Dushyanta had said to his flagbearers, the horsemen and the elephant riders, 'I will go alone to see the mighty Rishi of Kashyapa's race, the one without darkness. Wait here for me.'

Going into the blessed jungle with just his priest and his minister, Dushyanta immediately forgets his hunger and thirst; indeed they leave him. Great joy surges through him. He puts aside all his royal insignia, his armour and weapons, and goes forward without ornaments to see that Sage who is an immortal sea of the Spirit.

The forest is like a piece of Brahmaloka. Above the birdsongs and the nectar-drunk bees, Dushyanta hears the chanting of Riks by sonorous and beautifully modulated Brahmana voices. Elsewhere, he sees Yagnas, and hears the Vedangas and the Yajur mantras being chanted. Other asramas resonate with the harmonies of the hymns of the Saman being sung by Rishis of deep tapasya. Still other zones of that jungle are adorned with Munis who are masters, obviously, of the Atharva Veda.

The king walks on, in awe, and hears the Samhitas being recited, exquisitely. Other Brahmanas, healers, are chanting other arcane mantras. Truly, this is equal to being in Brahmaloka, thinks Dushyanta.

He sees Brahmanas that are experts at creating yagnashalas; others that are masters of the rules of krama for sacrifices; others are master logicians and adept at all the sciences of the mind, all these fully knowing the Veda; masters of language and grammarians; those that know the most secret rituals; those that tread the path of Moksha Dharma; dialecticians and metaphysicians with minds like rapiers that quickly cut away any dross and arrive at the truth of a philosophical proposition.

The king sees Brahmanas who know prosody, Nirukta; astrologers; men that know the nature of matter and its underlying illusion; those learned in the fruit to be obtained from various yagnas; those that can converse with birds and monkeys; those that know vast treatises on every subject, backwards – in short, men who know all there is to be known.

Dushyanta hears their melodious and strong voices at japa, chanting the sacred names of God; he sees them performing homa, making burnt offerings in the holy fire.

He is received respectfully wherever he goes, and he wonders at the delectable carpets those Brahmanas offer him to sit upon. Seeing and hearing all that he did in that forest, he truly feels that he has entered Brahmaloka. Yet, he wanders on because he has not found the asrama of the Muni Kanva.

Finally, that tiger among kings arrives, with his minister and his priest, at the hermitage of Kashyapa, where the loftiest Sages of incomparable asceticism and vows live."

CANTO 71

SAMBHAVA PARVA CONTINUED

Vaisampayana said, "Now, the king leaves his two companions at the entrance to that asrama and goes in alone. He does not see the Rishi Kanva or any other Sage, and calls out loudly, 'Is anyone here?'

His deep voice echoes like thunder in that silent place. Then, a young woman, a girl as beautiful, surely, as the Devi Sri herself, appears. She is wearing the simple, rough clothes of a hermit's daughter. She is fair and her eyes are black, and she receives the king with honour and welcomes him.

She brings him a darbhasana to sit upon, gives him padya, water to wash his feet, and offers him arghya. Respectfully, she inquires after his health and his peace of mind.

With utmost reverence she says, 'O Rajan, tell me what I can do for you. I await your command.'

The king says to that flawless beauty, her voice and speech so sweet, 'I have come to worship the most exalted Rishi Kanva. Lovely one, tell me where he is.'

Shakuntala replies, 'He has gone into the forest to gather fruit. He will return shortly. I beg you, wait for him here.'

The king gazes at her, helplessly, and sees that she is beautiful past reason; her face and form are perfect. He sees how sweet her smile is, and how she is radiant with her tapasya, and her humility. Besides, she is in the bloom of lush youth.

Captivated, Dushyanta says, 'And who are you? Whose daughter are you? Why do you also live in the forest when you are so beautiful, and obviously so chaste? Ah, you have stolen my heart and I want to know all about you, everything.'

She smiles and says sweetly, 'Rajan, I am the daughter of Maharishi Kanva.'

Dushyanta says, 'That Sage, whom the Universe worships, is a Brahmachari. Dharma Deva might break a vow, but not the Rishi Kanva. How can you be his daughter, beautiful one?'

Shakuntala replies, 'I will tell you, Rajan, how I became the Muni's daughter. Once, another Rishi came here and asked the same question. I will tell you what my father said to him.

My father Kanva said to that Rishi, "Once, long ago, Viswamitra performed such an awesome tapasya that Indra became anxious that the Rishi blazing with tejas would usurp his throne in Amaravati, and cast Indra down from Swarga.

Indra called the Apsara Menaka and said to her, 'You are the most beautiful of your kind, Menaka, and I want you to do me a small service. The Rishi Viswamitra blazes like the Sun with the power of his tapasya. I fear his penance will cast me down from my throne.

Sweet Menaka of the slender waist, I want you to seduce the Sage from his dhyana, and interrupt his penance. Go and tempt him; use all your weapons: your youth, your beauty, your charms, your smile, your sidelong glances, your soft voice.'

Menaka replied, 'Lord, you know how powerful Viswamitra is and he is quick to anger, too. Why, he has made even you anxious. Then shall I not fear him? He caused the death of Vasistha's children. You know that Viswamitra is born a Kshatriya and only later became a Brahmana through tapasya.

Why, when he wanted a holy river near him, in which to perform his ablutions, he created the deep and swift Kausiki. You know how the Rajarishi Trishanku, whom a father's curse turned into a Vetala, fed Viswamitra's wife during a famine, while Viswamitra was away at his penance.

When Viswamitra returned after the famine was over, he changed the name of the Kausiki near his asrama to Para, and then became Trishanku's priest to help him rise bodily into Swarga.

Why, you refused to drink the Soma rasa from that yagna, O Indra, and when you commanded the rising Trishanku to fall back to the Earth, Viswamitra in fury created a second Universe (with all the stars beginning with Sravana), for Trishanku to rule.

I am terrified of such a one, my Lord. If you want me to do what you ask, you must tell me how I can escape being consumed by his wrath. He can burn the three worlds with his tejas, or make the Earth quake with a stamp of his foot. He can pluck up Meru by his roots and cast him as far as he pleases. He can fly around the Earth, all her ten cardinal points, in a moment.

How can even an Apsara like me hope to move such a one, alight with his tapasya like a fire, his virtue perfect, his passions controlled? His mouth is like Agni; the pupils of his eyes are like Surya and Soma; his tongue is like Yama.

O Devendra, how will I dare touch him? Yama, Soma, the great Rishis, the Sadhyas, the Visis and Balakhilyas are terrified of Viswamitra! How can I dare even look at him?

But because you command it, I will go to the dreadful Rishi, to accomplish your purpose. But O Indra, devise a plan by which you can protect me from his anger if it is roused. Vayu should go with me, as well, and fill the asrama with the scents of spring, snatch my garment from my body so that I stand naked before the Rishi, and let Manmatha, Kama, roiler of minds, be there as well to turn the Sage's heart to me.'

When Indra gave her all that she asked for, and said that he would be at hand himself near Viswamitra's asrama, invisibly, to rescue her if the Sage became angry, Menaka went to Kaushika's hermitage to seduce Viswamitra from his penance.'"

CANTO 72

SAMBHAVA PARVA CONTINUED

"Shakuntala continues, 'My father Kanva said, "Indra commanded Vayu, who goes wherever he pleases, across the Earth, to be with Menaka when she approached Viswamitra, as also Kama Deva.

Timidly, her heart pounding, the exquisite Menaka went into the Rishi's asrama and saw Viswamitra sitting there in dhyana, bright as a fire himself, he that had burnt his sins to ashes in the other fire of his tapasya; and he still sat on, in intense dhayna.

She folded her hands and greeted the Sage, then began to dance before him, and to sing softly. In a moment, Vayu whisked the single white garment from her body, leaving her bare. With a cry, as if in terrible bashfulness and annoyance, she ran after the flying cloth, white as the moon.

Viswamitra, his tejas like cosmic fire, gazed upon her naked body and saw how perfect she was, and youthful, no blemish upon her ravishing nakedness. He saw how graceful she was, and shot by Kama Deva with one of his subtle flowery shafts of love, that bull among Sages was pierced through by lust.

Hoarsely he called to her, and she went to him willingly and he took her ardently to himself. They were together for many years, and so happy were they that those years passed like a single day.

Viswamitra begot a child on Menaka. As her time drew near, Menaka went to a secluded place on the banks of the Malini, gushing through a verdant valley of Himavat. There she gave birth to a daughter, and, Apsara that she was, she abandoned her child beside the river and went away.

A flock of vultures saw that baby lying there helpless in a forest that teemed with lions, tigers and leopards, and the great birds flew down and sat around the infant in a protective ring, and no predator approached her, no Rakshasa or carnivore took her life.

Later that day, I went to the river for my ablutions and saw the strange sight of the vultures guarding Menaka's daughter in the heart of the wilderness. I brought her home and made her my daughter.

You know that they who create the body, who protect life and who provide food are all fathers, according to the Shastras. Because birds, Shakuntas, protected her in the jungle, I named her Shakuntala. Brahmana, this was how Shakuntala became my daughter and the sinless child also looks up to me as being her father."

This, O King, is what my father said to the Rishi who asked him the question that you have asked me. I have never known my natural father and I do indeed think of Kanva Muni as being my only father. This is my story, O Dushyanta!'"

CANTO 73

SAMBHAVA PARVA CONTINUED

Vaisampayana continued, "King Dushyanta says, 'This is wonderful! I love you Shakuntala, and want you to be my wife. Whatever your heart desires you shall have: golden necklaces and earrings, priceless robes of silk, great moon pearls from distant lands, golden coins, the finest carpets, and whatever else you want. Why, let all that I have, and my kingdom, be yours from today.

Only come to me now, marry me in Gandharva vivaha, beautiful one. It is considered to be the first form of marriage and the best. Be mine now, this very moment!'

Shakuntala says, 'O King, my father has gone to gather fruit in the forest. Wait but briefly and he will give me to you to be your wife.'

Beside himself, Dushyanta replies, 'Flawless, perfect one, exquisite one, I want you to be my life's companion. From now I live only for you and my heart is yours.

One belongs first and last to oneself; each of us depends finally on himself or herself. And so it is lawful for you to give yourself to me. The eight kinds of marriages are Brahma, Daiva, Arsha, Prajapatya, Asura, Gandharva, Rakshasa and Paisacha.

Brahma's son Manu, the Lawgiver, has said that all these are proper depending on who one is. The first four are proper for Brahmanas, and the first six for Kshatriyas. For kings even Rakshasa vivaha is allowed. Asura vivaha is allowed only to Vaishyas and Sudras.

Of the first five, three are sattvik, while two are not. The Paisacha and Asura vivahas are violent and unsafe. These are the laws of dharma, and they must be followed.

To Kshatriyas, Gandharva and Rakshasa vivaha are allowed. You must not be afraid; for us either of these, or even a mixture of both, is perfectly lawful. Fair one, I am full of desire for you, and if you feel the same for me, let us marry now by Gandharva vivaha, and consummate our love!'

Shakuntala listens to the impatient king, then says, 'If it is indeed true that we are allowed to marry by Gandharva vivaha, if I can truly give myself to you in dharma, listen O Purushottama, to my conditions, and you must swear solemnly to give me what I ask.

The son that you beget in me must become the Yuvaraja and king after you. Grant this one condition, Dushyanta, and let us marry and be one flesh.'

The king does not think a moment before crying, 'So be it! I will even take you, my beauty with the sweetest smile, to my capital. I swear this to you, lovely one, for you deserve no less.'

With that he takes her to be his wife in Gandharva vivaha, and possesses her immediately. Then he leaves her, after repeatedly reassuring Shakuntala, 'Beloved, I will send my finest legion, of the four varnas, to fetch you to my city.'

Having sworn this, Dushyanta leaves that asrama and that forest like a bit of heaven on earth. As he rides home, he begins to think of Kanva. He wonders, 'What will the Rishi say when he discovers what happened?' With this thought, he arrives in his capital.

As soon as Dushyanta leaves the asrama, Kanva returns. Ashamed and feeling guilty, Shakuntala does not go out to meet him as she usually does. But that great Sage is a mystic and already sees everything that has transpired with his inner eye.

Not annoyed, but pleased, he says, 'My child, there is no sin in what you did today, secretly, without waiting for me to return. You have been with a man, but you have not broken dharma by giving yourself to him. Why, the Shastras say that Gandharva vivaha between a man and a woman who desire each other is the highest form of marriage for Kshatriyas.

Dushyanta is a noble and virtuous king, and you have taken him for your husband with all your heart. Your son by him shall be mighty and illustrious. He will be invincible in battle and have sway over Earth and Sea.'

Shakuntala now goes to her tired father and washes his feet. She takes the load of fruit he has brought, and sets it down. She says softly, 'I beg you, bless Dushyanta and his ministers, too.'

Kanva replies, 'Sweet child, for your sake I will bless him. Also, ask me for any boon you want.'

Shakuntala thinks of Dushyanta whom she loves, and says, 'May every Paurava king be virtuous and may they never lose their kingdom or their throne.'"

CANTO 74

SAMBHAVA PARVA CONTINUED

Vaisampayana continued, "Dushyanta leaves the asrama, promising Shakuntala that he will send for her. But the months pass, her time comes and she delivers a magnificent child, a boy of shining tejas. When the child is three years, he blazes like agni. He is handsome, generous, and quickly, very accomplished as well.

Kanva performs all his rites of passage and teaches the child of great intelligence everything that he needs to know, so day by day he grows more splendid. His teeth are pearls, his locks shine, and even as a young boy he is so strong that he can kill lions. He has every auspicious line and mark in his palms, his brow is broad and lofty, his beauty and strength swell like the Moon waxing during the bright fortnight.

He grows like the son of a Deva. When he is just six, he seizes lions and tigers, bears, bison and even elephants and ties them to the great trees around the asrama. Some of these beasts he rides, and others he chases for sport.

The Rishis in Kanva's asrama name him Sarvadamana because he subdues any beast, however strong. Boundless are his strength and vigour.

When Kanva sees all this, he tells Shakuntala that the time has come for Sarvadamana to be crowned the Yuvaraja of his father's kingdom.

Kanva says to his disciples, 'Take Shakuntala and her son to her husband's city. Women should not live so long in their parents' homes, for it tarnishes their reputation, even their virtue. Take her to Dushyanta, without delay.'

The disciples set out with Shakuntala and her son for Hastinapura, city of elephants. Thus, the lovely forest woman and her son, handsome and radiant like a god, his eyes like lotus petals, leave the forest where both have grown, and where Dushyanata first met and knew Shakuntala.

Arriving in Hastinapura, she enters the king's palace and presents their son, who looks like the rising sun, to his father. Maharishi Kanva's sishyas bring Shakuntala to the king and immediately return to their hermitage.

Shakuntala greets the king, formally, love shining in her eyes. She says to Dushyanta, 'My Lord, this is your son, now make him the Yuvaraja. You, Rajan, sired this child like a Deva in me, and it is time you fulfilled the oath you swore that he would become your heir. Remember, O Dushyanta, everything that you said to me in my father Kanva's asrama.'

The king remembers her well, but he says harshly, 'I do not remember anything. Who are you, evil woman, dressed as a Sannyasini? I do not recall having any relations with you, not of dharma, artha or kama. You may go or stay here, as you please. I have nothing to do with you.'

Stunned, stricken, Shakuntala stands as if she has turned to stone, or a wooden post. Then rage grips her and her eyes turn the colour of copper and her lips quiver. The looks she gives the king seem as if they would burn him to ashes. But she restrains herself and, with a great effort, quenches her rising fury.

Composing herself, though her heart seethes with rage and sorrow, equally, she looks straight at Dushyanta and says to him in a quiet and dangerous voice, 'Dushyanta, you remember very well everything that happened between us. How do you now say, like some lowborn man,

O King, that you do not know me? Your heart is my witness, whether I speak truly or not.

Do not demean yourself, for the liar is one who robs his own soul. He is capable of every sin. You think that you are the only one who knows what you did with me. Don't you know that the Ancient, Omniscient Narayana dwells in every heart and every moment?

He knows your every sin, and yet you dare to sin in his presence. Every sinner thinks that his sins pass unnoticed; but the Devas see everything as does He who lives in every heart. The Sun, the Moon, the Air, the Fire, the Earth, the Sky, Water, the heart itself, Yama, the day, the night, both sandhyas, and Dharma – all these witness everything that any man ever does.

Surya's son Yama ignores the sins of a man with whom Narayana, the omniscient witness, is pleased; but Yama torments the man with whom Narayana is not pleased. The Gods never bless those that degrade themselves with falsehood; why, his own soul will not bless such a man.

I am a devoted wife. It is true that I come here myself; but do not insult me because of that, O King. I am your wife and I deserve respect from you. Dare you dishonour me because I come here myself? Dare you treat me like some prostitute in the presence of all your court?

I want for nothing in the forest, and neither do I lead a sorry life. Do you hear me Dushyanta? If you refuse to do what I ask, my curse will burst your head open, in a hundred pieces. A husband enters his wife's womb as seed, and emerges again as his son. This is why the Sages who know the Vedas call a wife Jaya: she of whom one is born.

And a son born to those that know the mantras of the Veda becomes the saviour of departed ancestors. A son rescues his manes from the hell called Put, and so Brahma has named a son as Putra. Begetting a son, one conquers the three worlds; with a son's son a man finds eternity. Through a great grandson, his grandsires obtain everlasting joy.

A true wife is skilled in household matters: she who bears a son is a dharmapatni, a good wife, as is she who is devoted to her husband. The good wife is chaste and knows no man other than her husband.

His wife is half of a man; she is his dearest friend; she is the very root of dharma, artha and kama; she is the seed of moksha.

Married men perform their dharma, living contentedly in grihastasrama. They are cheerful that have wives; they find fortune. Sweet-spoken wives are like friends in whose company a man is joyful; in the performance of dharma, they are like fathers; when a man is ill or sad, they are like mothers.

Even when he travels through deep and dangerous forests, a good wife is a man's companion and solace. Everyone trusts a man who has a good wife. O Rajan, a wife is a man's most treasured possession. Why, even when a man leaves this world for Yama's realm, his wife, if she is devoted, goes with him. A wife who departs before her husband waits for him; but if the husband goes first, the chaste wife follows close.

Rajan, this is why marriage exists; a man enjoys his wife's companionship not only in this world but in the next. Then, the Rishis all say that a man himself is born as his son: so he whose wife bears him a son must look upon her as his mother. Why, when a man sees the face of his son, like looking into a magical mirror, he feels as joyful as a virtuous man who attains Swarga.

Men suffering in the world, from all its trials of body and mind, feel as refreshed by their wives' company as one does having a cool bath on a hot and sweaty day. Not in anger should a man ever displease his wife, for, everything his joy, fortune and virtue depend upon her.

A wife is the sacred field in which the husband sows his seed and is born again. Not Rishis can procreate without having wives. Which happiness can match what a father feels when he sees his son running into his arms and hugging him, be the child covered in dust and dirt?

Ah, then why are you so callous to your child who has come to you and looks with such longing at you, to take him onto your lap? Even ants nurture their eggs with tender care; then why do you, a great king of dharma, refuse to acknowledge your son?

Not the touch of the softest sandalwood paste, of the most feminine woman, of the purest, coolest water on a hot day, can equal the feeling of clasping one's child in one's arms. A Brahmana is the first among all creatures that walk on two legs; the cow, the best of those that walk on four; a king, the foremost among one's guardians; and one's own son is the best of all beings and objects to touch and to hold.

Embrace your beautiful son, O Dushyanta, and you will find no sensation on Earth can equal that joy. O Parantapa, I bore this child in my womb for a full three years before I brought him forth to become the dispeller of all your sorrows. O Paurava king, when I gave birth to him, an asariri from the sky said: "He shall perform a hundred Aswamedha Yagnas!"

Why, men that travel to distant lands, take other men's children onto their laps, sniff their heads and feel great joy.

Dushyanta, you know the Vedic mantras that Brahmanas chant when a son is born: "You are born, O son, of my body. You have sprung from my heart. You are my own self come as my son. Live to be a hundred years. My life depends on you, and the continuation of my family. O son, live in great joy for a hundred years!"

Yes, this lustrous child has sprung from your body; look at him and see yourself as you would your image in a still lake. He has been kindled by you: even as a sacrificial fire is from a domestic one. You are but one; through him you have made yourself two.

Rajan, you came hunting in the wilderness. I was a virgin living in my father's asrama and you importuned me. The six most beautiful Apsaras are Urvasi, Purvachitti, Sahajanya, Menaka, Viswachi and Ghritachi. Among them, Brahma's daughter Menaka is the first. She came down to the Earth and Viswamitra begot me on her.

She gave birth to me in a valley of Himavat, and then, feeling no maternal love, she abandoned me as if I was someone else's child. Ah, I wonder what sin I committed in some other life that first my parents abandoned me, and now you, my husband, do the same. For myself, I am content to return to my father Kanva's asrama, but you must not renounce this child, your son.'

Dushyanta listens to all this, but then says savagely, 'Shakuntala, women are given to lying, and I do not remember having begotten any child on you. Who will believe what you say? The promiscuous Menaka, who knows no affection even for her own child, is your mother, as you yourself say. She abandoned you upon Himavan's slopes just as one discards the flowers offered to the Devas during worship, when the worship is over.

Your father, the lustful Viswamitra, was a Kshatriya but chose to become a Brahmana; he, too, is cruel and heartless that he abandoned you. But it is true that Menaka is the first among the Apsaras, and your father foremost of Rishis. You are their daughter, yet you talk like a whore, obscenely.

You do not deserve to be believed. Aren't you ashamed of yourself, casting aspersions, especially against me? Leave at once, you harlot dressed as a Sannyasini. Where is the Maharishi Viswamitra and where is the Apsara Menaka? Why are you, deceiving, vile woman, dressed as an ascetic? As for your son, he is grown up, while you insist on calling him a child.

You say he is a boy, but look how strong and powerful he is. If he is just six, as you claim, how is he so big, like a Sala tree? For sure, you are a lowborn, lying whore. You are begotten lustfully by Menaka, and not in love.

I don't know you or anything that you say. Go away, go wherever you like!'

Shakuntala replies, 'O King, you see the faults of others, be they not as small as a mustard seed, but not your own which are bigger than a bilwa fruit! Menaka is an Apsara, indeed she is reckoned to be the most beautiful of the Apsaras, their queen. Dushyanta, I am of much nobler and higher birth than you. You walk upon the Earth, O Rajan, but I rove the Sky at will. The comparison between you and me is as between a mustard seed and a mountain. Such is my power, mortal king!

I can fly to the worlds of Indra, Kubera, Yama and Varuna. What I came here to tell you, King of dharma, is from the purest motives and not from any greed. Listen to me and forgive me for these comparisons between yourself and me.

But an ugly man thinks of himself as being better looking than other men and mocks them – until he looks at his own face in a mirror for the first time. Then he sees the truth, and the real difference of nature between himself and other men. The truly handsome man does not mock anyone.

The evil man is always a reviler. Just as swine look for filth even in a garden of flowers, the mocker always hears only vileness in anything that another tells him, whatever it is. However, a wise man listens to the speech of others, good and evil mixed, but like the goose, which knows how to drink only the milk from a mixture of milk and water, he takes only the good.

The honest man always hesitates to speak ill of others, but the evil ever delight to do so. The good always delight in showing regard to their elders, but the evil always find pleasure in disparaging the good. The good are happy in never seeking faults; the evil are happy only in finding them. The wicked always speak ill of the good and the honest; yet, even if hurt by them, the good do not wound the evil.

What can be more absurd than those that are themselves evil accusing the good of being so? When even atheists grow angry at those that abandon truth and virtue, and become like virulent serpents, what shall I say about myself, who have grown in faith?

He who begets a son who is his very image, and yet does not accept or love him, never attains to the worlds that he desires, for the Gods destroy his fortune and take his possessions from him. The Pitrs have said that a son continues the race and bloodline, and so a son is the greatest yagna and dharma. No man should abandon his son.

Manu tells of five kinds of sons: a son begotten upon one's own wife, one gained as a gift from another, one bought for a consideration, a child who becomes a son from love, and sons begotten upon women other than one's wife. All these are sons.

Sons support the dharma and the achievements of their fathers, enhance their joy, and save the spirits of dead ancestors from hell. So, O tiger among Kshatriyas, it does not become you to abandon a son like yours. Accept and cherish your child, O Dushyanta, like your own self. Lion among kings, you degrade yourself by being deceitful.

The creation and dedication of a tank brings more punya that digging a hundred wells. Performing a yagna confers more merit than creating a sacred tank. A son is far more auspicious than a sacrifice, and the truth more sacred than a hundred sons.

Once, the punya from a hundred Aswamedhas was weighed against the truth, and the truth was found to be immeasurably heavier. Dushyanta, the truth is equal to the study of all the Vedas and bathing at all the sacred tirthas together. There is no other virtue to equal the truth, and nothing superior to the truth. The truth is God himself, O Kshatriya; truth is the highest vrata.

So do not break your word to me, and be one with the truth. If you set no value by what I say I will go away with no protest; indeed, I must avoid the company of a man like you. But, Dushyanta, when you die, this son of mine shall surely rule all this Earth surrounded by the four seas and be crowned by the king of mountains.'

With this, Shakuntala turns on her heel and walks out of the king's presence. No sooner has she left, than a great asariri, a disembodied voice, speaks echoingly from the air to Dushyanta who sits amidst his priests, his Gurus and ministers.

The voice says, 'A mother is only the sheath of flesh; the son born from her is the father himself. O Dushyanta, cherish your son and do not demean Shakuntala. Best of men, a son is a form of the father's seed and he rescues the spirits of the ancestors from the realm of Yama.

You are this child's father, and Shakuntala spoke the truth. The husband cleaves his body and is born from the wife as a son. Dushyanta, accept and love your son by Shakuntala. To try to live by forsaking one's living son is a terrible misfortune. Paurava, cherish your lofty son born to Shakuntala. And because you will accept and nurture this child at our word, he shall be called Bhaarata, the precious and cherished one.'

In that voice the very gods speak thunderously to Dushyanta before all his court and people. Suddenly, Dushyanta's face lights up with great joy.

That king cries, 'Did you all hear what the asariri says? The command of the Devas! I always knew that this child was mine. Yet, if I had accepted him merely at what Shakuntala said, my people would have been suspicious, and always harboured a doubt that the prince was not mine.'

O Bharatottama, once the heavenly voice has established that the child Bharata is indeed his son, Dushyanta is full of joy. He rises and clasps the powerful boy in his arms, and performs every ritual that a father should for his son. He never stops hugging him and sniffing his head in adoration.

The Brahmanas shower their blessings over the child and the bards of the court, the Sutas, sing his praises. Dushyanta feels the unearthly delight that any father does when he touches his child.

Dushyanta calls Shakuntala back and now welcomes her with fond and great love. Pacifying her for the ordeal he has subjected her to, he says, 'Devi, O Goddess, you and I were married in seclusion, with no witness. I was afraid that my people would think that it is no proper vivaha but a chance encounter of lust, and hence our son illegitimate.

They would have resented him being crowned the Yuvaraja. Oh my love, I forgive everything you said to me in anger because I love you more than my life and have since I first saw you!'

The Rajarishi Dushyanta now welcomes his queen with offerings of perfumes, food and drink. Thus, the Paurava names his son Bharata, and crowns the magnificent child his heir. In time, the brilliant and famed wheels of the chariot of Bharata the Great would fill every corner of the Earth with their sound, even like the vimanas of the Devas.

The son of Dushyanta subjugates every other King of the Earth, and he rules with dharma and unequalled is his fame. Becoming a king of kings, the invincible Bharata becomes known as Sarvabhauma, Lord of all the world, and Chakravarti.

Countless sacrifices he performs, even like Indra, lord of the Devas. Maharishi Kanva is the chief priest at those Mahayagnas, at which Bharata gives bounteous gifts to Brahmanas. The Cow Sacrifice and the Horse Sacrifice Bharata performs, and gives Kanva a thousand coins of gold as the Ritvik's dakshina.

This is the mighty Bharata, of numberless great achievements, after whom the lordly race of kings into which you are born is named. And in that royal house, godlike kings of great lustre are born, kings like Brahma himself. Their number is past counting. But, Scion of the race of Rajarishi Bhaarata, I will name the main ones for you, kings blessed with fortune to rival that of the Devas, men of dharma, devoted to the truth."

CANTO 75

SAMBHAVA PARVA CONTINUED

Vaisampayana said, "Listen to this sacred genealogy of those Rajarishis, which enhances dharma, artha and kama.

Daksha Prajapati, Manu, the son of Surya, Bharata, Ruru, Puru and Ajamidha. Sinless King, I will also recite the genealogies of the Yadavas, the Kurus and kings of the line of Bharata. These are sacred indeed, and their narration is an act of worship, which confers wealth, fame and a long life. Rajan, the men I have named are radiant as Maharishis, and as powerful.

Prachetas has ten sons, all of them ascetics and righteous. In the most ancient times, they consume with fire from their mouths, forests of poisonous plants and fell trees that covered the Earth.

Prachetas' eleventh son is Daksha, and from him all the creatures originated, and so he is called Prajapati.

The Muni Daksha takes Virini to be his wife and begets a thousand sons upon her, all great tapasvins. Narada teaches Daksha's thousand sons the Samkhya marga as a way to moksha, and they never become creators or progenitors themselves, but wander the galaxies to find the ends of the Universe, for Narada Muni subverts their minds.

O Janamejaya, Daksha Prajapati then begets fifty daughters, for his intention is to further creation, have it multiply and flourish. He says that their sons would belong to him as well as to their husbands. He gives ten of his daughters to Dharma, thirteen to Kashyapa and twenty-seven to Soma, and these Nakshatras chart the course of the Moon.

Marichi's son Kashyapa begets the Adityas, among whom Indra is the eldest and the Lord, on Daksha's eldest daughter; he also fathers Surya, who is also called Vivaswat, in her.

Vivaswat, who is also called Martanda, begets Yama. He then sires another son, of brilliant and fathomless intellect, called Manu. Manu possesses profound wisdom and is devoted to dharma. He becomes the father of the human race, and they are called Manavas or Manushyas after him. Be they Brahmanas, Kshatriyas or any other humans, they are called Manavas for they are all descended from Manu.

Later, O King, the Brahmanas and Kshatriyas mix their races. Manu's Brahmana sons devote themselves to studying the Veda.

Manu sires ten other children: Vena, Dhrishnu, Narishyan, Nabhaga, Ikshvaku, Karusha, Saryati, a daughter named Ila, Prishadhru and Nabhagarishta. All these live as Kshatriyas.

Manu has fifty other sons on Earth, but they die fighting one another. The learned Pururavas is Ila's son, and it is told that Ila is both his father and his mother. Pururavas the Great holds sway over thirteen Dwipas, continents, and though he is a man, his companions are all celestials.

Drunk with power, his reason lost, Pururavas crosses the Brahmanas and robs them of their wealth, without fearing their anger. Sanatkumara comes down from Brahmaloka to advise him against this rashness, but Pururavas ignores his counsel. The Maharishi grows angry and with a curse destroys that greedy king in a moment.

Pururavas first brings from the realm of the Gandharvas the three kinds of sacred fires for worship. He also brings the Apsara Urvashi to be his wife, and the son of Ila fathers six sons on Urvashi – Ayus, Dhimat, Amavasu, Dhridhayus, Vanayus and Satayus.

Ayus begets four sons, Nahusha, Vriddhasarman, Rajingaya and Anenas, on the daughter of Swarbhanu. Of all the sons of Ayus, Nahusha is the most intelligent and powerful, and rules his vast kingdom with dharma.

Nahusha has the support of the Pitrs, Devas, Rishis, Brahmanas, Gandharvas, Nagas, Rakshasas, Kshatriyas and Vaisyas, for he is friendly towards all of them. He puts down crime and bands of brigands ruthlessly, and peace pervades his kingdom.

But in his arrogance, he once commands the greatest Rishis to carry him upon their backs in his palanquin, like beasts of burden, and they curse Nahusha. Before that he fascinates the Devas themselves with his charm and beauty, his asceticism, his strength and his brilliance. He rules like another Indra.

Nahusha begets six sons, all well-spoken, called Yati, Yayati, Sanyati, Ayati and Dhruva. Yati takes Sannyasa and becomes a Muni, like Brahma himself. Yayati becomes a sovereign of great power and dharma. He rules all of the Earth, performs innumerable sacrifices, worships his Manes and the Devas unfailingly, and is never vanquished in battle.

Yayati's sons are all great archers, and splendid with every virtue. He sires them in his two queens Devayani and Sarmishta. Devayani's sons are the twins Yadu and Turvasu, and Sarmishta's are Drahyu, Anu and Puru.

When he has ruled wisely and justly for many many years, suddenly one day, through a curse, the infirmity of old age strikes Yayati like some dread disease: gone is his splendour, his handsomeness, his virility.

He calls his sons Yadu, Puru, Turvasu, Drahyu and Anu, and says to them, 'My sons, I want my youth back to enjoy the company of young women. You must help me.'

His eldest son by Devayani says, 'What do you want us to do?'

Yayati replies, 'Take my age and give me your youth, my son. Ah, Rishi Usanas cursed me and I have aged overnight. I have not satisfied my desires and they torment me. Oh, give me your youth to take my pleasures with it!'

At first, none of those sons would do what he asks. Then his youngest son Puru says, 'I will take your infirmity upon myself and let you have my youth. I will rule your kingdom as you command, while you satisfy your every desire.'

The Rajarishi Yayati uses his tapasya shakti to take Puru's youth and give the young man his own old age. Yayati is young again and Puru is an old man, and Puru rules the kingdom in his father's name.

A thousand years pass, and Yayati, Rajavyaghra, remains as strong and virile as a tiger. He enjoys his wives to his heart's content, and in the gardens of the Gandharva king Chitraratha, he enjoys the Apsara Viswachi. But even after a thousand years and more, the king finds that his desires rage on, undimmed.

Yayati remembers something he has read in the Purana: 'Desire can never be quenched by indulgence. It is like pouring ghee into a fire to extinguish it; the flames only burn more fiercely.

Not he that owns all the wealth in the world, all its gold, diamonds, beasts and women will find himself satisfied, but will only crave for more. Only the man who does not sin in thought, deed or word attains to the purity of Brahmana, and finds joy and peace in his own soul.

When a man fears nothing, and is feared by nothing and no one, when he wishes for nothing but is content, when he harms no living thing, he attains eternal peace, Brahmanirvana.'

After his long years of every indulgence, Yayati is wise enough to realise that desire can never be satisfied with indulgence. Yayati stills his mind with dhyana. He takes his old age back from his son and returns Puru's youth to him. He crowns Puru king, and says to him, 'You are my true heir, my only real son. From now let our royal line be known by your name. Let my vamsa be called the Pauravas.'

Then Yayati leaves for the mountain of Bhrigu to devote himself to Sannyasa. After years of tapasya, and acquiring great spiritual punya, his wives and he fast until their spirits leave their bodies, and they attain Swarga."

CANTO 76

Sambhava Parva Continued

Janamejaya said, "Profound Muni, rich with ascetic wealth, tell me how my ancestor Yayati, born in the tenth generation from Prajapati, manages to make the daughter of Shukra his wife. Tell me of this in detail. Also, tell me about all the kings that founded the different dynasties."

Vaisampayana said, "King Yayati is as splendid as Indra himself. I will tell you, O Janamejaya, how both Shukra and Vrishaparvan give him their daughters to be his wives; I will tell you especially about Devayani.

Of old, the Devas and the Asuras fight for the sovereignty of the three worlds and everything in them. The Devas make Angiras' son Brihaspati their priest to perform their yagnas for them, and the Asuras make Shukra, also called Usanas, theirs. Between the two Brahmanas there is always rivalry, each deriding the other and extolling himself.

Shukra knows the Mritasanjivini vidya, the arcane art of bringing the dead back to life, and during any Devasura yuddha—a war between the gods and the demons—he would revive the Asuras that are slain, and the Danavas and Daityas would come roaring back to fight.

The Asuras also kill many of the Deva warriors, but Brihaspati does not know the Sanjivini and cannot bring them back to life. The Devas despair; they are in terror of Usanas' vidya.

They go to Brihaspati's eldest son Kacha, and say to him, 'We bow to you, and ask you to do us a service that we consider a great one. We beg you learn the Mritasanjivini from Shukra Bhargava, O that mighty Brahmana. You will find him in the court of Vrishaparvan; he always protects the Asuras, but not us.

You are younger than he is, and you can worship him reverently. You can also pay tribute to Devayani, who is Shukra's favourite daughter. Surely, only you, Kacha, can please both of them, and by flattering Devayani with every sweetness, fawning on her, you can acquire the Sanjivini from her father.'

Brihaspati's son says, 'So be it,' and goes to Vrishaparvan, the Asura king's, capital. Seeing Shukra in the Danava's lavish court, Kacha folds his hands and says humbly, 'I am the grandson of Rishi Angiras and the son of Brihaspati. I am called Kacha; take me for your sishya. If you become my Guru, I will be a brahmacharin for a thousand years, and your disciple. Command me, O Brahmana!'

Shukra, who is called Kavya or Usanas as well, says, 'You are welcome Kacha. I will take you to be my disciple and treat you with regard, for I will be showing Brihaspati regard if I do.'

Kacha says, 'I thank you, my lord,' and at once swears a vow of Brahmacharya, celibacy, for a thousand years. With that he becomes Shukra's sishya and begins to serve and please both his master, as well as Shukra's daughter Devayani.

Kacha is young, as is Devayani, and he would sing and dance for her, and play on several instruments. O Bharatottama, devoting himself, he brings her flowers and fruit, and does her bidding with alacrity, whatever she wants done. She, too, sweet-natured maiden, would sing for him and look after his every need, when they are alone together, even as he kept his vow unflinchingly.

When five hundred years pass, the Danavas learn Kacha's true intention. They are furious, and seeing him alone in the forest one day with Shukra's cows, they kill him, cut his body into pieces and feed him to wolves and jackals. They have no compunction about killing a Brahmana. They detest Brihaspati, and of course they want to keep Kacha from acquiring the secret of the Mritasanjivini, the art of reviving the dead.

Come twilight and the cows return to their fold without Kacha. Devayani says to her father Shukra, 'Your evening fire has been lit and the Sun has set, father. The cows have come home, but Kacha is not with them. He is either lost or dead, and I cannot live without him!'

Shukra says, 'I will bring him back.'

With the Sanjivini vidya, Shukra calls Kacha to return. The shreds of the disciple's body tear open the bodies of the jackals and wolves that have eaten him, and unite into a living Kacha, who, full of joy, appears before his Guru.

Devayani demands of him, 'Why are you so late?'

Kacha says to Bhargava's daughter, 'I was dead. I was coming home with fuel for the fire, with kusa grass and wood. I sat under a nyagrodha tree, and the cows also cropped grass in the shade. Some Asuras saw me and asked, "Who are you?" I replied, "I am Brihaspati's son." As soon as I said this, the Danavas killed me, cut my body into pieces and fed it to wolves and jackals. Then they went away, singing for joy. Sweet Devayani, then your father called out to me and I have returned to you from the dead.'

Another day, Kacha goes into the forest to gather flowers for Devayani. The Danavas see him, kill him again and, pounding him into a paste, dissolve him in the sea.

When he does not come home, Devayani again goes in tears to her father. Once more, Shukra calls Kacha with his Sanjivini and the disciple appears whole and alive before his Guru, and recounts what had had happened.

The third time the Asuras kill Kacha, they burn his body to ashes, and then mix those ashes in wine and give the wine to Shukra himself to drink.

Come night, and when Kacha does not return, Devayani says to her father, 'Father, Kacha went to pick flowers for me, but he has not come home. He is either lost or dead, and I will not live without him.'

Shukra says, 'Child, Brihaspati's son has been killed again. Each time I bring him back from Yama's realm, and again he is killed. I am afraid I can do nothing for Kacha.

Devayani, don't cry. You should not grieve over a mortal. Why, because of my power, the Brahmanas, the Devas with Indra, the Vasus and Aswins, the Asuras, and indeed all the Universe worship you, during the three sandhyas. Forget Kacha now, because he is killed as often as I revive him.'

Devayani replies, 'How can I forget him, and not grieve for him, whose grandfather is the ancient Angiras, whose father is Brihaspati, both great Rishis, and who is himself an ocean of tapasya. Kacha is a Brahmacharin and a Sannyasi, always caring, and skilled in everything that he does. I mean to fast to death and follow Kacha where he has gone. Oh father, I love the handsome Brahmana!'

Maharishi Shukra sees his daughter grief-stricken, and grows angry. He says, 'The Asuras dare kill my sishya who lives in my house! Killing a Brahmana is the worst of all sins and would consume Indra himself. The Rudrabhakta Asuras make me a party to their crime when I revive Kacha and they kill him again. They want me to lose my character as a Brahmana.'

Compelled by Devayani, Shukra is about to call Kacha back again from the dead. But Kacha fears what might happen to his Guru, and says from his master's belly, 'O Master, I am Kacha who worships you. Treat me like your own son, be kind to me Lord.'

Shukra says, 'How did you enter my stomach? I will leave the Asuras this moment and join the Devas!'

Kacha says, 'By your grace, I remember everything that happened. My punya is intact, and my tapasya shakti. With these, I am able to endure the pain that savages me. O Guru, the Asuras killed me, burnt me to ashes, then mixed the ashes in your wine. That is how I am in your belly. But as long as you are alive, the craft of the Asuras will never prevail over the science of the Brahmana.'

Shukra says to Devayani, 'My child, how can I help you now? Kacha is inside me. The only way he can live again is if I die. He cannot emerge unless he rends my belly and kills me.'

Devayani sobs, 'Both your lives are equally precious to me, and both your deaths would savage me equally! If either of you dies, so will I.'

Then Shukra says, 'O son of Brihaspati, you can count yourself successful in all your endeavours, because Devayani loves you well. If you are not Indra disguised as Kacha, learn the Mritasanjivini from me today. No one can come out alive from my stomach. But a Brahmana must not be killed.

So learn the Sanjivini from me, then be born even as my son, rending my belly. But be sure that when you are alive again, you act with grace.'

Kacha learns the secret art of reviving the dead from Shukra; then he tears open his master's belly and emerges as luminous as the Moon on the fifteenth day of the bright fortnight. He sees his Guru's remains lying before him like a heap of tapasya, and using the Sanjivini, Kacha restores Shukra to life.

Worshipping him with love, Kacha says to his Guru, 'I was ignorant until you poured Gyanamrita, the nectar of knowledge, into my ears. You are my father and my mother, Lord. He who is ingrate enough to take knowledge from his Guru, who is the most precious of all precious things in the world, who must be worshipped, and then causes his master injury, shall be hated in the world and damned to find hell for himself.'

Shukra looks at the handsome Kacha, and thinks of how he had drunk him mixed with wine. He thinks furiously of how the Asuras had deceived him when he was drunk.

Rising in anger, Mahatman Shukra cries, 'From this day, any Brahmana who drinks wine shall lose all his punya and be considered as having committed Brahmahatya. He shall be despised in this world and all the others.

I, Shukra Bhargava, declare this, and let the Brahmanas, honest men, the Devas, men that revere their superiors, and the three worlds hear this edict of mine, which shall regulate the conduct and preserve the dignity of Brahmanas everywhere.'

Then he summons the Asuras, whom fate has robbed of their reason. He says to them, 'Foolish Danavas, Kacha has what he wants. He has learnt the Sanjivini Vidya and is now as powerful as Brahma himself. He will live with me.'

With that Shukra fell silent. In some disarray, the confounded demons return to their homes. Kacha has now spent a full thousand years with his Guru and prepares to return to Devaloka, with his master's leave."

CANTO 77

SAMBHAVA PARVA CONTINUED

Vaisampayana said, "When the thousand years of his vow end, Kacha, with his Guru's permission, is about to depart for Devaloka, when Devayani says to him, 'O Kacha, grandson of Angiras Muni, resplendent are your birth and conduct, your learning, humility and your asceticism. Even as my father worships and honours the Muni Angiras, I adore and revere your father Brihaspati.

Remember this and listen to what I have to say. Recall how I disported myself with you during the years of your vow of Brahmacharya. Now the time of your vrata is over. Now I ask you to turn your love towards me. I ask you to marry me with mantras from the Veda.'

Kacha replies, 'I respect and worship you just as I do your father! Why, beautiful and faultless Devayani, I adore you even more than him. My Guru Shukra Bhargava loves you more than his own life. As his daughter, you merit my worship. I beg you do not ask me to marry you!'

Devayani replies, 'You, also, are the son of a great father and deserving of my reverence and worship. O Kacha, best among Brahmanas, have you forgotten the love I showed for you when the Asuras killed you time and again? Recall that affection, and my devotion, and do not now abandon me for no fault of mine. I truly love you.'

Kacha says, 'Punyavrata, do not ask me to commit such a sin! Lovely one, be kind to me instead. I hold you in higher esteem than I do my master. Virtuous one, your face like the moon, your eyes long as lotus petals, you are Shukra Kavya's child; do not forget that I, too, was born from his body. You are my sister, and we have passed our days happily together.

We understand each other perfectly and I now beg you to allow me to return to my home in the sky. Bless me that I have a safe journey. Whenever you think of me, or speak of me, you must remember me as one who did not break dharma. I ask you to always serve my Guru readily and single-mindedly.'

Devayani replies in anger, 'If you refuse to make me your wife, even after I have begged you, O Kacha, may all your tapasya and gyana be fruitless!'

Kacha says, 'I have refused you only because you are my Guru's daughter, and not because you have any flaw or fault. Also, my Guru has not said anything to me about marrying you. If it pleases you, curse me.

I have told you what I must do, being a Rishi. I do not deserve your curse, Devayani, but you have cursed me. You have cursed me from passion and not from any sense of dharma. What you want shall never happen, and I say to you that no Rishi's son will ever marry you. You have said that my learning will prove fruitless. So be it. But I say that it shall prove fruitful to whomever I teach the Vidya.'

With that, Kacha flies back to Devaloka, where Indra and the other Devas come out to worship him, with padya and arghya.

Indra says, 'You have achieved what seemed impossible and you shall have immortal fame for this. O Kacha, you will have a share in the havis from every sacrifice.'"

CANTO 78

SAMBHAVA PARVA CONTINUED

Vaisampayana said, "Indeed, the celestials are overjoyed that Kacha has acquired the Sanjivini Vidya. Immediately, he teaches them the secret science of bringing the dead back to life, and the Devas are certain that they can vanquish the Asuras in battle.

Gathering around Indra of a hundred Mahayagnas, they cry to him, 'The time is here to show our might. Kill your enemies, O Purandara!'

Indra Maghavat roars, 'So be it!' and goes forth with his celestial army. On his way he sees some lovely women bathing in a lake in the charmed gardens of the Gandharva Chitraratha. Becoming invisible, he quickly mixes up the women's clothes, which they have arranged neatly on the bank of the lake.

When the women finish bathing, it happens that Vrishaparvan's daughter Sarmishta mistakenly wears Devayani's clothes. Devayani is furious. She cries at Sarmishta, 'Asuraputri, daughter of an Asura, you are my sishya, my inferior. How dare you wear my clothes? You are presumptuous and no good will ever befall you.'

Stung, Sarmishta flashes back, 'Your father is like a hired chanter of praises, a vabdhi in my father's court! He fawns over my father, while Vrishaparvan sits at his ease or even lies stretched out upon his couch. You are just the daughter of a singer of the praises of my father, and one who lives on alms besides.

My father, on the other hand, is the king whose praises your father sings. He is a giver of alms, not a receiver. You are a beggar's daughter and a beggar yourself. Swear at me, if you like, swear to be my enemy; cry in anger, I do not care. You live by the alms of my father, and I can harm you if I choose, but not you me. You want to pick a fight with me, but I do not consider you my equal, beggar!'

Devayani is beside herself. She runs at Sarmishta and tries to tear her clothes from her body. The Asura princess pushes her into a well and goes home, fuming, believing that she has killed her friend and quite pleased with what she has done.

Nahusha's son Yayati is out hunting nearby. His horses are tired and thirsty, and so is he. He sees the well and rides up to it. Peering over its edge, he sees it is shallow and dry, but he also sees a young woman inside who is bright and beautiful as a flame, her skin shining like a goddess'.

Gently, he says to her, 'Who are you? Your fingernails gleam like burnished copper, and the jewels in your earrings are not of this world. Why are you crying? How did you fall into this well covered with grass and reeds? Say, slender-waisted beauty, whose daughter are you?'

Devayani replies, 'I am the daughter of Shukra, who gives life again to the Asuras that the Devas kill in battle. My father does not know what has happened to me. O King, you are wellborn, wellbred and noble. Great are your prowess and your fame. Here is my right hand, its nails as you say like burnished copper. Take my hand and pull me out of the well.'

King Yayati hears that she is a Brahmana's daughter and he draws her out of the well by her right hand. He gazes for a long moment at her long and fine legs, her soft thighs that are exposed; then bowing and smiling at her, he goes back to his capital.

When Yayati has gone, Devayani sees her sakhi Ghurnika who has come in search of her. Sobbing, Devayani tells her what has happened, how Sarmishta pushed her into the well and left her for dead.

'Tell my father everything, Ghurnika, and tell him that I will never enter Vrishaparvan's city again.'

Trembling with rage, Ghurnika stamps back into the Asura's palace and finds Shukra there. Her mind clouded by anger, Ghurnika says to Kavya, 'Great Brahmana, Vrishaparvan's daughter insulted Devayani in the woods and even tried to kill her!'

Shukra, who dotes on Devayani, hurries to the woods, and when he sees his daughter he clasps her in his arms. His voice choking, the wise Shukra Bhargava says, 'My child, whatever fortune or misfortune befalls any of us is because of our own karma. You must have sinned at some time, and this has been the retribution and expiation for you.'

Her eyes still full of fire, Devayani replies, 'Retribution or not, listen to me, father. Listen to what Vrishparvan's daughter Sarmishta dared say to me. Her eyes red as plums, she says viciously that you, O my father, are only her father Vrishaparvan's hireling, a chanter of his praises, a mere vabdhi.

She said, "You are just the daughter of a singer of the praises of my father, and one who lives on alms besides. My father, on the other hand, is the one whose praises your father sings. He is a giver of alms, not a receiver. You are a beggar's daughter and a beggar yourself."

Not once but many times she said this to me, that arrogant princess, her eyes burning. Father, if what she says is true and I am indeed the daughter of a hired chanter of praises, of one who lives on alms, then I must offer worship to Sarmishta and hope to receive her grace.'

Shukra says, 'Devayani, you are no daughter of a hired adorer, and neither do I take alms or receive gifts. You are the daughter of one who worships none but is worshipped by everyone. Vrishaparvan knows this, as do Indra and Yayati also. The ineffable Parabrahman, the Ultimate and sovereign Godhead, is my support and strength. Brahma himself has said that I am the master of all things in Heaven and Earth. I send down the rains, Devayani, to nourish all creatures and green plants, to nurture everything that lives.'

Thus, Shukra tries to console his distraught daughter."

CANTO 79

Sambhava Parva Continued

Vaisapayana said, "Shukra continued, 'Devayani, he who masters anger and learns to ignore the meanest words of his enemies, conquers all. The Sages say that the true charioteer never gives slack to his reins. The true man or woman also never gives in to his or her anger. He who subdues his own anger conquers everything.

A Mahatman always forgives, sloughing off his fury as a snake does its skin. He or she who never yields to rage, despite being provoked by evil words or deeds, certainly finds dharma, artha, kama and moksha.

Between the man who ceaselessly performs penance and sacrifices every moon for a hundred years and he that never feels anger, the second is the superior. Children, boys and girls who do not know right from wrong, surely quarrel. The wise do not imitate them.'

Devayani responds, 'Father, I also know the difference between anger and forgiveness and which is superior. But when a disciple is disrespectful, his Guru should never forgive him if the master truly wants his sishya to mend. Therefore, I do not desire to live any longer in a country where evil has such sway. The wise, who live in dharma, will not live among those that speak ill of noble birth and courteous conduct. Father, one should live where pure birth and noble conduct are both respected; indeed, the Rishis have said that this is the best kind of place in which to live. The vicious words of Vrishaparvan's daughter burn my heart, like dry fuel that men use to kindle a fire.

Nothing in the three worlds is more wretched than for a man to adore his enemies, when they are blessed with fortune and wealth while he himself has none. Why, the greatest Sages have said that death is preferable for such a man.'"

CANTO 80

SAMBHAVA PARVA CONTINUED

Vaisampayana said, "Now Shukra Kavya, greatest of Bhargavas, becomes angry. Having lost his temper, he goes to Vrishaparvan, and without weighing his words, says irately, 'O King, like the very Earth, sins do not bear fruit immediately. But gradually, secretly, they destroy the sinners.

The fruit of sins are visited either upon oneself, one's sons or grandchildren, even; for sin must bear fruit. Like heavy food, it cannot be digested. You killed the Brahmana Kacha, Angiras' grandson, a virtuous man, a knower of dharma, again and again, while he lived in my asrama as my dutiful and loving disciple.

O Vrishaparvan, for this crime and for your daughter Sarmishta's intolerable abuse of my daughter Devayani, I am going to leave you and your race. Why do you stare at me, O King; do you think I am lying to you, or that I am a fool? I see that you want to make light of your sins, rather than correct them and find some forgiveness.'

Vrishaparvan says, 'O Bhargava, I have never said that you are a liar or tried to find any fault with you. Indeed, you are the very embodiment of dharma and satya, virtue and truth.

I beg you be merciful to me! O Bhargava, if you actually leave us, we shall plunge down into the Patalas and dwell there in the depths of the Ocean, for there is nothing else we could do.'

Shukra retorts, 'Asuras, go to the bottom of the Sea or fly and scatter in every direction: I do not care! I cannot bear to see my daughter grieve. She is more precious to me than my life; why, my life depends on her.

You must placate her. Even as Brihaspati always seeks the welfare of Indra, so have I always sought yours with my tapasya shakti.'

Vrishaparvan says, 'O Bhargava, you are the absolute master of whatever the Asura lords of this world possess – their elephants, cows, horses, and even myself!'

Shukra says, 'If you speak the truth then you will placate Devayani.'

Shukra goes and tells Devayani what Vrishaparvan said. But she answers him, 'Bhargava, Father, if you are indeed the Lord of the Asura king and all his wealth, let Vrishaparvan come here and tell me so himself.'

Vrishaparvan comes to Devayani and says, 'Lovely Devayani of the sweet smile, I will give you whatever you ask for, do whatever you want, however difficult it might be.'

Devayani says at once, 'I want Sarmishta, with a thousand sakhis, to attend on me as my handmaiden. She must also come with me to my husband's house, wherever my father chooses to give me.'

Vrishaparvan says to a maid that waits on him, 'Go and fetch Sarmishta here at once. She will do as Devayani says from now.'

The sakhi goes to Sarmishta and tells her, 'O Sarmishta, come with me and save our people. Shukra Bhargava has threatened to leave the Asuras unless Devayani is pacified. Princess, you have to become Devayani's handmaiden from now, and serve her in everything.'

Sarmishta replies, 'I will come happily. Shukra and Devayani must not leave the Asuras through any fault of mine. I will become Devayani's handmaiden.'

At her father's command, Sarmishta emerges from her father's great palace in palanquin, with a thousand of her sakhis. She folds her hands to Devayani and says, 'These thousand girls and I are all your servants. I will follow you wherever your father gives you away.'

Devayani replies tartly, 'I am the daughter of one who chants your father's praises and lives by the alms that your father gives him. You, Sarmishta, are the daughter of one whose praises my father sings, who gives alms to my father. How can you become my servant?'

Sarmishta murmurs, 'One must always serve one's family and one's race, and I will do as my father asks, happily. I will be your handmaiden and go with you wherever you are given in marriage.'

When Sarmishta says this, Devayani turns to Shukra and says, 'Father, greatest of Brahmanas, I am satisfied. I know now that your power and your wisdom are not in vain. I will enter the Asura's city again.'

Happily, Shukra goes back into Vrishaparvan's city and the Danavas all worship him, their Guru, devoutly."

CANTO 81

SAMBHAVA PARVA CONTINUED

Vaisampayana continued, "Some weeks pass, then Devayani goes to the same woods to take her pleasure there. She goes with Sarmishta and two thousand sakhis attending on her. Happy together, the young women roam freely through the charmed garden of Chitraratha, drinking nectar from flowers, feasting on rare and delicious fruit. Joy goes with them.

Nahusha's son Yayati, out hunting deer again, arrives there once more, tired and thirsty again. That king sees Devayani, Sarmishta and the other sakhis, all wearing unearthly ornaments, and full of voluptuous languor because of the flower wine they have drunk freely. Devayani, the most beautiful among them, her smile dazzling, her skin the softest and fairest, lies stretched upon some lush grass, while Sarmishta gently massages her feet.

Yayati sees all this, and says to the two of them, 'Lovely ladies, tell me your names and whose daughters you are. It seems to me that these two thousand handmaidens all attend on the both of you.'

Devayani answers him, 'Manavottama, best of men, I am the daughter of Shukra Bhargava, the Asura Guru. This is my sakhi and my handmaiden Sarmishta. She attends on me wherever I go and she is the daughter of Vrishaparvan, king of the Asuras.'

Yayati wants to know, 'How is the lovely princess your handmaiden? I marvel at this.'

Devayani replies, 'Fate is responsible for everything that happens. Do not marvel, because Fate has made Sarmishta my handmaiden. By your face, and from your attire, you seem to be a king. You speak chastely, and nobly; your language is of the Veda. Who are you, whose son, and where have you come from?'

Yayati says, 'While I was a brahmacharin, I heard and studied all the Vedas. I am known as Yayati, a king's son and a king myself.'

Devayani asks, 'King, why have you come here? To gather lotuses, to fish, or to hunt?'

Yayati says, 'Lovely one, I have been out hunting deer and felt thirsty. I came looking for water. I am exhausted, but say a word and I will leave.'

Devayani answers, 'Leave? My two thousand sakhis and my handmaiden Sarmishta are here to serve you. I ask you to become my friend and my lord. And may fortune be with you.'

Yayati replies, 'Beautiful Devayani, I do not deserve you. You are the daughter of a Brahmana, Shukra Bhargava, and you are immeasurably my superior by birth. Your father cannot give you away even to the greatest king.'

Devayani replies, 'Brahmanas have married Kshatriyas before, and Kshatriyas have married Brahmanas. Your father is a Rajarishi and so are you. Son of Nahusha, marry me!'

But Yayati says, 'Most beautiful one, it is true that the four varnas sprang from the same Body. But their dharma and natures are not the same. The Brahmana is the purest and the highest of the four.'

Devayani says, 'No man other than you has ever touched my hand before. You took my hand once and I ask you to take me for your queen. For how will any other man ever touch this hand which you, a Rajarishi, have touched?'

Yayati says, 'The wise know that a Brahmana is more dangerous than an angry snake or a blazing fire, and must be avoided.'

Says Devayani, 'Purusharishabha, why do you say that a Brahmana should be avoided like an angry snake or a blazing fire?'

The king replies softly, 'The snake kills one person, even as the sharpest weapon does. But an angry Brahmana consumes whole cities, why kingdoms, in a moment. Therefore, bashful one, a Brahmana is more dangerous than a snake or fire. I cannot marry you unless your father gives you to me.'

Devayani says, 'I have chosen you to be my husband and you are saying that you will take me for your wife if my father gives me to you. Fear nothing and you will not even have to ask my father for my hand.'

Devayani despatches one of her sakhis to her father, to tell him everything. As soon as he hears what has happened, Shukra arrives in Chitraratha's garden and sees Yayati, who worships him reverently and then stands with folded hands, awaiting the great Bhargava's command.

Devayani says, 'Father, this is the son of Nahusha. He took my hand and saved me when I was in the well. I beg you give me to him to be his wife, for I will not marry any other man.'

Shukra exclaims, 'Splendid Kshatriya, my daughter wants you for her lord. I give her to you freely. O son of Nahusha, take her for your wife.'

The cautious Yayati says, 'O Brahmana, I want your blessing that I shall be spared the sin of begetting a half-breed child upon her.'

Shukra says, 'I will absolve you of the sin. Do not be afraid to marry my exquisite child. Keep her well, and may you enjoy transports of joy in her company.

You must also look after every need of the other young woman, Vrishaparvan's daughter. But you must never call her to your bed.'

Yayati circumambulates the Brahmana in pradakshina, and he marries Devayani with every auspicious ritual prescribed in the Shastras.

Honoured by the great Shukra and his disciples the Asuras, receiving in some joy the precious Devayani, and her sakhis, Sarmishta and the other two thousand, Yayati returns to his kingdom, at Shukra's behest."

CANTO 82

SAMBHAVA PARVA CONTINUED

Vaisampayana said, "Yayati returns to a joyous welcome from his people. His capital is even like Indra's city, and he brings his wife Devayani into his private royal apartments, in his antahpura. Devayani then asks her husband to build a fine mansion for Sarmishta and her thousand sakhis in the asokavana in the palace garden. Yayati has such a mansion built in quick time, and spares no effort in seeing to Sarmishta's every comfort and luxury.

Nahusha's regal son dallies only with Devayani, even like a Deva, for many years, in perfect bliss. Then, one day, Devayani conceives and gives birth to a fine son. A thousand more years pass—for the beings of those days are far longer-lived than in these dwindled times, they are indeed like gods in their years and days and nights—and Vrishaparvan's daughter Sarmishta attains puberty and sees that she is in season.

She becomes anxious, 'My season has come, but I have not taken a husband. Whatever shall I do? My body yearns for a strong man and to have his child. Devayani has become a mother and my youth seems to be doomed.

Shall I take Devayani's husband for my own and bear his child? Yes, that is what I will do. I will ask to meet him in private and the great king will not refuse me.'

As fate is mysterious, just as she is thinking these forbidden thoughts, Yayati strolls through the asokavana, aimlessly. He sees Sarmishta appear from behind a tree and stops in his tracks. She stands silently before him, a flush on her fair cheeks. He sees how her womanhood has bloomed.

Smiling bewitchingly, now that she is alone with him and nobody watching them, she folds her hands and says, 'O son of Nahusha, I have heard that no one can see the women who live in the private chambers of Soma, Indra, Yama, Varuna, and in yours, O King.

You know, Yayati, that I am wellborn and beautiful as well. I have seen you gaze at me. I am in my season, O Rajan. I beg you let my womanhood not be wasted; make a mother of me!'

Yayati replies, 'I know very well how nobly born you are, in the proud race of the Danavas, and you are beautiful almost past compare; why, I see no hint of any flaw in your face or your form. It is true that I desire you powerfully, but you also know what Usanas' command was when I married his daughter: that I would care for your every need, but I would never summon Vrishaparvan's daughter to my bed.'

Sarmishta says, 'O King, it is said that it is no sin to lie: in jest, about a woman a man wants to enjoy, to be married to, when in mortal danger, and if one's entire fortune is about to be lost. A man who lies about these five incurs no sin.

Devayani and I have both come here for your pleasure, and you have sworn to do everything in your power to please us both. When you said that only she would come to your bed, you lied, O King!' says Sarmishta archly.

Yayati replies, 'A king should always be an example to his people. A king who lies will certainly sin, and find his destruction. As for me, I dare not lie, even if the greatest calamity threatens me.'

Says Sarmishta, 'Rajan, a woman can look upon her dear friend's husband as being her own. A friend's marriage is one's own. You have married my friend, and by doing so you have married me. You are my husband, too! Besides, you did swear to do everything in your power to keep me happy.'

Yayati says, still doubtfully, 'I have indeed sworn to give you whatever you want. Tell me what I should do.'

Sarmishta then says, 'Save me from sin, Yayati. Father a child in me, and let me fulfil a woman's highest dharma, of becoming a mother. I am Devayani's slave, and you are her lord and master. You are my lord and master, too, as much as you are hers. I beg you, make love to me, great King, and make me a mother.'

So enticing is she that Yayati allows her to persuade him. There beneath an asoka tree, he grants her wish. When he has made love to her several times, they part affectionately, Sarmishta returning to her mansion and Yayati to his palace.

The lovely Sarmishta conceives, and in due course gives birth to a child as splendid as a Deva child, his eyes as long as lotus petals."

CANTO 83

Sambhava Parva Continued

Vaisampayana said, "When Devayani hears that Sarmishta has had a baby, envy stings her like a serpent, O Bhaarata. Devayani goes to Sarmishta and says angrily, 'You have sinned, lustful woman!'

Sarmishta replies, 'A Rishi of great dharma and a knower of the Vedas came here and I asked him to grant me a boon, and father a child on me, for I was in my time. In dharma, he did as I asked and this child is his.'

Devayani says, 'If this is true, then you have not sinned. But tell me the name and gotra of the Brahmana, if you know them.'

Sarmishta says, 'He is as splendid as Surya Deva. Seeing him was enough; I felt no need to ask for his name or gotra.'

Calming down, Devayani smiles, 'Well, if this is true and you have a child by a noble Brahmana, I have no reason to be angry with you, but to rejoice.'

They embrace and spend some time together happily, talking and laughing, then Devayani returns to her palace. Rajan, Yayati also begets two sons, Yadu and Turvasu, upon Devayani and they are like Indra and Vishnu.

And that Rajarishi fathers three sons on Vrishaparvan's daughter Sarmishta: Drahyu, Anu and Puru.

One day, Devayani and Yayati go walking in a secluded part of the asokavana. Suddenly, they see three children of unearthly beauty playing there, innocently.

Devayani asks in surprise, 'Whose children are these, Rajan, who are so handsome that they seem like a Deva's sons? Why, they are as resplendent and beautiful as you are!'

Without waiting for his reply, Devayani goes up to the trusting children and asks, 'Who are you? Who is your father?'

The children point at Yayati, and say their mother is Sarmishta. They then run to their father and lovingly hug his legs. Yayati dares not caress them back before Devayani, but stands as if turned to stone. Crying that he ignored them, the boys run to their mother.

But Devayani follows them, and rounds angrily on Sarmishta, 'You have betrayed me, you have lied to me, even being my friend and dependent on me. How did you dare, Sarmishta? This is your Asura nature, to lie!'

Sarmishta says, 'Sweet friend, I did not lie to you, what I said about a splendid Rishi is true. I have done nothing to break dharma and I do not fear you.

When you chose the king to be your husband, so did I in my heart. My beautiful Devayani, a dear friend's husband is one's own, as well. You are the daughter of a great Brahmana and I love and respect you. But I love and revere this Rajarishi even more!'

Devayani now turns on Yayati, 'You have betrayed me and I will not live here any more!'

Her tears flowing from eyes red with rage, she turns and walks away. Alarmed and sorry for her, Yayati goes after her. But try as he will to pacify her and persuade her not to leave, she will not listen. Soon enough she comes before Shukra, the son of Kavi, with Yayati right behind her.

Devayani folds her hands to her father and takes the dust from his feet. Yayati does the same, worshipping the Bhargava.

Then Devayani sobs, 'Father, adharma has vanquished dharma. The lowly have scaled great heights and the noble have fallen. This King Yayati has fathered three sons on Vrishaparvan's daughter Sarmishta, while I, my father, have just two.

O Bhargava, Yayati is famed for his knowledge of dharma. But I say to you, O Kavya, he has left the path of righteousness.'

Shukra says angrily, 'Kshatriya, you have embraced vice though you know dharma in every nuance. I curse you that infirmity paralyses you!'

Yayati says, 'Holy One, the Danava king's daughter asked me to make her womanhood fruitful, while she was in her season. I only did as she asked from a sense of dharma, and not from any wantonness or lust. The man who will not beget a child on a woman in her season, who asks him, is called an embryo-killer by those that know the Vedas. O Bhargava, when a man is approached by a woman in her time, full of desire, and he refuses her, surely he is a sinner. I went to Sarmishta in dharma and not from lust.'

Shukra replies, 'Son of Nahusha, you should have first asked me and awaited my command. What you did is a betrayal of dharma, as well as theft. I curse you to lose your youth and become an old man!'

At once, Yayati becomes old and decrepit.

Yayati says, 'Bhargava, I am not yet satisfied with my manhood or with being with Devayani. I beg you, withdraw your curse.'

Shukra answers, 'I can never lie. Even now, O King, my curse is upon you. But you can, if you wish, exchange your decrepitude for the youth of another.'

Yayati says, 'Brahmana, say that whichever of my sons gives me his youth and takes my age shall be my heir and have great virtue and fame.'

Shukra replies, 'So be it. Think of me, O son of Nahusha, when you exchange your age for your son's youth, and he shall be your heir, have a long life, universal fame and many children!'"

CANTO 84

SAMBHAVA PARVA CONTINUED

Vaisampayana said, "His youth gone, trembling with weakness and age from Shukra's curse, he calls his eldest, and also the most accomplished son, Yadu, and says, 'My child, look what Usanas' curse has done to me. I am old and infirm, my skin is wrinkled and my hair all grey.

But I have not yet satisfied the desires of my manhood. Yadu, take this age from me and give me your youth. When a thousand years have passed, I will return your youth to you and take back my age.'

Yadu replies, 'With age one cannot eat and drink as one wants. O King, I cannot do what you ask. White hair, dejection, weakness, wrinkles, emaciation, not being able to work and being defeated by one's companions – these are not for me, I could not bear them.

Father, you have other sons, more precious to you than I am. You know all about dharma: ask one of them to take your age and give you his youth.'

Yayati says, 'You are born from my heart, but you will not give me your youth. I curse you that your sons shall never be kings!'

He now calls Turvasu, 'Turvasu, take this age of mine and give me your youth for a thousand years, for my desires are not fulfilled. After a thousand years, I will return your youth to you and take back my age and weakness.'

Turvasu replies, 'I detest old age, father; it takes away every appetite and pleasure. It robs one of strength and beauty, of intellect and one's very life.'

Yayati says to him, 'You are born from my heart, my son, but you will not give me your youth. Turvasu, your race shall become extinct. Wretched prince, you will be a king of half-breeds, among whom lowborn men father children on blue-blooded women. You will rule tribes of meat-eaters, mean-spirited, who don't think twice before sleeping with their masters' wives, who live like animals and birds, sinners with no trace of nobility in them!'

Yayati now calls Sarmishta's son Drahyu and says, "Drahyu, my child, take my age for a thousand years and give me your youth so I can satisfy all my desires. After a thousand years, I will return your youth to you and take back my infirmity.'

Drahyu replies, 'Father, how can an old man enjoy riding on elephants and in chariots; how can he ride horses or women? I cannot take your age and give you my youth.'

Yayati says to him, 'You are born from my heart, but you will not give me your youth. Your most ardent desires shall never be fulfilled! You will be a king, and only in name, of a land where there are no roads for men, horses, chariots and elephants; not even for mules and goats, or for bullocks or palanquins. You will be a king where the only paths are waterways and the only transport boats and rafts.'

Yayati calls Anu and says, 'My son Anu, take my age and give me your youth for a thousand years. I will return your youth to you after a thousand years, and take back my age.'

Anu replies, 'The old eat like dribbling children and are incontinent. They cannot offer libations into the sacred fire at yagnas. They are unclean and impure. Father, I cannot take your age from you.'

Yayati says to him, 'You are born from my heart, but you will not give me your youth. You find so much wrong with old age that old age will overtake you anyway. Anu, your children shall die as soon as they become youths, and neither will you ever perform any yagna before a sacred fire.'

Finally, Yayati calls his youngest son Puru and says to him, 'You are my youngest son, Puru, but it seems you shall become my heir. Look at this age that the curse of Kavya has brought upon me: my hair turned white, my skin wrinkled. But I have not satisfied the desires of my youth and manhood. Puru, my child, take my age from me and give me your youth. When a thousand years pass, I will return your youth to you and take back my old age.'

Puru replies without hesitating, 'I will do whatever you say, father. O King, I will take your old age upon myself and do you take my youth and enjoy every pleasure of life with it. And I will live as you command.'

Yayati says, 'Puru, I am well pleased in you. And for that I say to you, yours shall be a great reign and everyone in your kingdom will be happy and contented. They shall have their every desire fulfilled.'

The Rajarishi Yayati then thinks of Shukra Bhargava and takes his son Puru's youth from him, giving the young prince his decrepitude."

CANTO 85

SAMBHAVA PARVA CONTINUED

Vaisampayana said, "The great King Yayati begins to enjoy himself, to indulge his every appetite, with his son's youth. O Bhaarata, he lives in dharma while pursuing his pleasure, and never leaves the path of virtue and sanctity.

Yayati worships the Devas with yagnas; he adores his Pitrs with Sraddhas; he pleases the poor with generous daana, charity; he gives munificently to deserving Brahmanas; he entertains everyone entitled to hospitality with a king's food and drink. He protects Vaishyas; he is kind to Sudras.

He puts down crime and criminals in his kingdom, so that it is a haven of safety and order. Yayati is like another Indra to all his subjects, high and low. Powerful like a young lion, he enjoys every happiness and pleasure, but never transgressing dharma; he sates his every desire. His only sorrow is that the thousand years of youth he has taken from his son must end one day.

He is a master of the mysteries of time, its divisions – auspicious and otherwise. Reading the suitable kaalas and kaasthas, he dallies with the

Apsara Viswachi, sometimes in Indra's exotic garden Nandana; at others in Alaka, Kubera's exquisite city; at times, on the peaks of Mount Meru in the North.

When a thousand perfect years have passed, that king of dharma calls his son Puru, who is an aged man, and says to him, 'My son, bane of your enemies, I have enjoyed every pleasure with the youth you gave me, each in its season, indulging my every desire as much I as could.

But I have learnt that desires do not subside with indulgence; they burn more fiercely like fire fed with ghee. Why, if one man owned the Earth and everything that is in her—all her paddy and barley, her silver, gold and gems, her animals and women—he would still not be satisfied.

One should renounce one's very desire, the very hunger for enjoyment. Desire is the deadly enemy, the fatal sickness. Only he that has cast away his desires (hard indeed for sinners and the evil minded to do), which do not wane with age or infirmity, only such a man can be truly happy.

For a thousand years, my heart was bent upon satisfying my every desire. The more I indulge my desires the stronger they grow. Now I mean to cast off desire itself and fix my mind on the Parabrahman. I will go away into the forest and pass the rest of my life among innocent deer, with no thought of possessions or enjoyments of the flesh.

Puru my son, as for you I am well pleased in you, my child, very well pleased. Here, take back your youth. Take my kingdom, as well. You are my truest son, the one who has served me in every way; why, you sacrificed your youth for me.'

Nahusha's son Yayati takes back his old age from Puru and restores his son's youth to him. Now Yayati wants to crown Puru king. But the four varnas, led by the Brahmanas of the kingdom, protest.

They say, 'Lord, how can you make Puru the king, passing over Devayani's son Yadu, who is the great Shukra's grandson? Yadu is your firstborn son, after him Turvasu, and of Sarmishta's sons the first is Drahyu, then Anu, and Puru is indeed the very youngest. How does the youngest prince deserve the throne over his elder brothers? This is not dharma as we see it, and we ask you to observe dharma in this momentous matter.'

Yayati then says to the four varnas, the Brahmanas at their head. 'Listen, my people, to why Yadu, my eldest son, should not have the kingdom. I asked him to do something, but he would not; he disobeyed me. The Rishis say that a disobedient son is no son at all.

But the son who obeys his parents, always seeking their welfare, being agreeable to them, is indeed the true son. Yadu did not do what I asked of him, nor did Turvasu; Drahyu and Anu showed scant regard for my wishes. Puru alone obeyed me; why he gave his youth to me for a thousand years, after Shukra cursed me.

Therefore, my youngest son shall be my heir. He took my age upon himself; why, he is more than a son, he is a true friend. Also, Kavi's son Shukra himself has said that the son that obeys me, and only he, shall become my heir. The Bhargava says that prince would bring the world under his sway. So, I beg you my friends, let Puru become your king. He is the most deserving and righteous among my sons, the only one truly fit to become king.'

The people then say, 'You speak the truth, O King, and even if he is the youngest, the son that seeks the welfare of his parents and obeys them, deserves to prosper. From what you say, Puru deserves the crown; besides, if Shukra himself has commanded it, we have no further argument.'

His people content, Nahusha's son Yayati crowns Puru king. Having made the kingdom over to his youngest, Yayati performs the ritual initiation to take Sannyasa and retires into the jungle. When he has taken the vows, he leaves his great city forever, accompanied by some Brahmanas and Rishis.

The sons of Yadu come to be called the Yadavas; Turvasu's sons become the Yavanas. Drahyu's sons are the Bhojas, while the Mlechchas are the sons of Anu.

However, the progeny of Puru are the noble Pauravas, into which royal house, O Rajan, you have been born: to rule with dharma as your sceptre, and your passions under perfect control."

CANTO 86

SAMBHAVA PARVA CONTINUED

Vaisampayana said, "Having crowned his precious son Puru as king, Nahusha's son Yayati goes away into the vana and becomes a hermit. He lives in an asrama with some Rishis, keeps many severe vratas, eating only fruit and roots, subjecting himself to every privation; and finally Yayati ascends into Swarga.

In Swarga, he spends some years in perfect bliss, but then Indra casts him down from his heaven. I have heard, Rajan, that though he is cast down, Yayati does not fall to the Earth but remains suspended in the firmament. I have heard that, later, he enters Devaloka again with Vasuman, Ashtaka, Pratardhana and Sibi."

Janamejaya said, "Tell me why Indra cast Yayati down from Devaloka, and how he enters Swarga again. O Brahmana, tell me this in the presence of all these Rishis.

Yayati, lord of the Earth, is truly like the king of the Devas himself. The progenitor of the mighty race of the Kurus is as splendorous as the Sun. Tell me everything about his life in Swarga and Bhumi, for he is a lustrous one, his fame known throughout the world, and his deeds and achievements are matchless."

Vaisampayana said, "I will tell you the sacred tale of Yayati's adventures on Earth and in Heaven. The legend consumes the sins of those that listen to it, for it is holy indeed!

Having made Puru the king, Yayati, son of Nahusha, expels his other sons, Yadu the eldest of them, out among the Mlechchas. He then enters the forest and lives there as a Vanaprastha, subsisting on fruit and roots.

He gains immaculate control over his mind and his passions, and performs many sacrifices to gratify the Devas and the Pitrs. He pours libations of ghee into the agni, according to the rites prescribed for Vanaprasthas. He entertains guests and strangers with roots and fruit, and offerings of ghee, and then he himself eats the seeds of wild corn which he forages for in the forest.

For a thousand years, Yayati lives as a forest-dwelling hermit. He keeps a mowna vrata, a vow of silence; and now, his mind perfectly controlled, he eats nothing and lives just on the air he breathes; neither does he sleep at all: for a whole year.

For another year, he intensifies his austerities, sitting amidst five fires, four that he kindles around himself and the fifth is the Sun above. Then, still never eating or sleeping, only breathing (occasionally), he stands on one leg for six months, still as a stone.

Thus, Yayati rises straight into Devaloka, and his sacred fame has spread across Bhumi and Swarga."

CANTO 87

Sambhava Parva Continued

Vaisampayana said, "While Yayati, kings of kings, lives in Devaloka, the Devas, the Sadhyas, the Maruts and the Vasus revere him. His mind perfectly stilled, the king would, from time to time, journey from Devaloka to Brahmaloka. I have heard that long years he spent in the realm of the Devas.

One day, while Yayati is with Indra, the Deva king asks the king of the Earth, 'Yayati, what did you say to your son Puru when he took your decrepit age from you and gave you his youth? What did you say when you gave him your kingdom?'

Yayati replies, 'I told him that all the lands between the Ganga and the Yamuna were his. This was the heart of the kingdom; while his brothers would rule the outlying countries. I also told him that those without anger are always superior to those under its sway; that those who forgive are always better than the unforgiving.

Man, I said to my son, is superior to animals. Among men, the learned are higher than the ignorant. I said that if he was wronged, he should never wrong in return, for a man's anger does not burn his enemy but only himself. Indeed, it takes away his every virtue and bestows it upon the one that he wounds with his fury.

I said to him that he should never injure anyone with harsh or cruel words; never vanquish his enemies by vile means; never speak scornfully of anyone, or utter sinful words that might hurt another.

He that wounds others with sharp words, as if with thorns, I said to my son, is a man that bears Rakshasas upon his tongue. Prosperity and fortune fly at his very sight. I said that he should make men of dharma his models, and always compare what he did with their exalted deeds, while ignoring whatever the evil say.

He must imitate the deeds of the Sages; for those wounded by savage words weep day and night because cruel speech strikes at a man's very entrails. Wise men, gentle men, never loose these barbs at anyone.

Nothing in the three worlds surpasses kindness, friendship, charity and sweet speech to all. Always speak soothingly, never scorchingly. I said to my son that he should always revere those that deserve his reverence; that he should always give and never beg!'"

CANTO 88

SAMBHAVA PARVA CONTINUED

Vaisampayana said, "Now Indra asks Yayati, 'O King, after you had performed your dharma, you became a Vanaprastha and a Sannyasi in the jungle and performed tapasya. Tell me, Yayati, son of Nahusha, who is your equal in penance and austerity?'

Yayati replies, 'Vasava, in tapasya, I see no one who is my equal; not among men, the Devas, the Gandharvas or the Maharishis.'

Indra says sternly, 'King! You disrespect your superiors, your peers and even your inferiors with this hubris. You do not know their true worth in punya or tapasya. Your own punya has dwindled by this and you must fall from my world.'

Yayati says, 'Sakra, if my punya has indeed diminished and I must fall from Swarga, let me, O King of the Devas, fall among the good and the honest.'

Indra says, 'Rajan, you will fall among the wise and the virtuous, and you will find great fame for yourself. But hereafter, Yayati, never underestimate or demean your equals or your superiors.'

Yayati falls from Devaloka. As he is falling, the Rajarishi Ashtaka, protector of dharma, greatest of royal Sages, sees him.

Ashtaka asks, 'Who are you, O youth whose beauty equals Indra's, who blaze like Agni, falling from on high? Are you Surya Deva emerging from behind a cloudbank? Why, seeing you fall by the path of the Sun, brilliant as Agni or Surya, all creatures swoon, while wondering who you are.

We see you upon the path of the gods, your tejas like Indra, Surya or even Vishnu's, and we ask you: who are you? If you had greeted us, we would not have been rude enough to greet you first. But now tell us who you are and why you are falling into our realm.

Ah, be without fear; may all your sorrow and afflictions be over! You are now with the virtuous and the wise; even Indra, who slew Bala, can do you no harm here. O you seem to be as mighty as Indra. We, the wise and the virtuous, always relieve those that are stricken by misfortune and grief.

Everyone here is as wise and honest as you are. So remain here in peace. Only Agni can give heat; only Bhumi can make a seed germinate; only Surya can illumine all things; so, too, only the Sadasya, a Guest, can command the wise and the virtuous.'"

CANTO 89

SAMBHAVA PARVA CONTINUED

"Yayati says, 'I am Yayati, son of Nahusha and the father of Puru. My punya is reduced because I showed disrespect for every creature, and I am cast down from the realm of the Devas, Siddhas and Rishis. I am older than all of you, which is why I did not greet you first. I know that a Brahmana always reveres his elders.'

Ashtaka says, 'You say an elder is worthy of reverence, but the real elder is he that is one's superior in gyana and tapasya.'

Yayati replies, 'Sin devastates the punya from the four kinds of dharma. Vanity contains the seed that leads one to hell. The good never follow the evil, but always live in dharma so their punya increases.

I had great punya myself, but I have lost it all now, and I will hardly be able to recover it, not with the severest tapasya. Seeing my fate, let anyone who seeks his own welfare abjure vanity.

He who acquires great wealth should perform great sacrifices; he that is profoundly learned must remain humble; he who has studied the entire Veda must withdraw his mind from every sensual pleasure and devote himself in dhyana. Such men shall surely find heaven.

Let him who acquires great wealth not exult; let not the man who has studied the Veda in full become proud. Men have different natures, and destiny reigns supreme. Power and effort are both in vain. Wise men know that Fate rules everything and they neither exult nor lament whatever fate might bring them, fortune or misfortune.

When men truly realise that sorrow and joy depend not upon their exertions, nor are these in their power to control, but Fate bestows both, each in its season, they will learn to rise above exulting and grieving.

The Sage is always contented, not celebrating at fortune nor lamenting over misfortune. Destiny is supreme; it is unbecoming to exult or grieve over anything.

O Ashtaka, I never allow myself to yield to fear. I never succumb to grief. I know that I shall be exactly as the Great Lord of all things has ordained that I be. Insects and worms, all plants, snakes and other creatures that crawl, vermin, fish in the water, stones, grass, wood, indeed, all things moving and immobile shall be united with the Parabrahman once they are free from the results of their karma.

Joy and sorrow are ephemeral. Hence, O Ashtaka, why should I ever grieve? We cannot fathom what we must do to avoid misfortune, or why it comes; but we can decide not to grieve over it!'

Yayati of great dharma is in fact Ashtaka's maternal grandfather. Now, in the Sky, Ashtaka asks him, 'Rajadhiraja, King of kings, tell me all about the worlds you have been in and enjoyed; tell me how long you were in each one. You speak of the precepts of dharma like the greatest masters who know the deeds and the teachings of the greatest Beings, intimately.'

Yayati says, 'I was a great king on Earth, and the whole world was my domain. Leaving my kingdom to my son, I sat in tapasya for a thousand years and gained many lofty realms with my punya. I dwelt in these for another thousand years and then attained to a still more exalted realm: Indraloka, of untold beauty, a hundred yojanas on every side, realm of a thousand portals.

There, too, I lived a full thousand years and then attained to a higher world yet: Brahmaloka, of perfect grace and bliss, where there is no ageing or decay. Here, too, I lived for another thousand years, and then ascended to a loftier world, Vishnuloka, realm of the God of Gods. There I spent another thousand years, blissfully.

I have dwelt in countless worlds, which the Devas adore, and I was as powerful and lustrous as a Deva. I could assume any form I chose, and I spent a million years in the enchanted and incomparable Nandana, dallying with Apsaras under trees so grand and wondrous that I can hardly describe them. Their flowers are exquisite and the scents of these truly heavenly.

After countless years, of unalloyed beatitude, one day a grim-faced messenger cried thrice to me in his voice of thunder, 'Ruin! Ruin! Ruin!' O lion among kings, immediately I fell from Nandana, for my punya was ruined. I heard the Devas crying in dismay, 'Alas! Yayati's punya is ruined and the king of dharma is falling.'

As I fell, I cried to them, 'Where, O Devas, are the wise ones amongst whom I can fall?'

They pointed this sacred yagnashala out to me. I saw smoke rising from your fires, I smelt the ghee that is being poured ceaselessly into it; guided by these, I have fallen towards you, and my heart is glad to see you all.'"'

CANTO 90

SAMBHAVA PARVA CONTINUED

"Ashtaka says, 'You lived in the Nandana for a million years and you could assume any form you chose. Then why, O greatest among the kings of the Krita Yuga, have you been forced from that world and come here?'

Yayati answers, 'Just as, on Bhumi, family and friends forsake men who lose their wealth, in Swarga, Devendra and his Devas forsake those who lose dharma and their punya.'

Ashtaka says, 'How can a man lose his dharma and punya in that realm? Also, tell me, mighty King, the various karmas that lead to the various lofty worlds. I know that you have intimate acquaintance with the lives and teaching of Great Beings.'

Yayati says, 'Holy One, men that praise themselves find the hell called Bhauma. Though they are in fact macilent, they grow fat on Earth, and have sons and grandsons, all of whom become food for vultures, dogs and jackals. One should never praise oneself. Tell me, O King, what more you wish to hear.'

Ashtaka says, 'When age kills the body, vultures, peacocks, insects and worms devour it. Where does the man go? How does he return to life? And I have not heard of this hell called Bhauma on Earth.'

Yayati answers, 'When he quits one body the man enters a mother's womb, according to his karma, and remains there formlessly, until his time comes and he becomes an embryo, and then is born again into the world and walks upon the surface of the Earth.

This Earth is Bhauma, the hell into which he falls because he does not regard death or work toward attaining mukti. Some live in Swarga, by their punya, for sixty thousand years, others for eighty thousand; then, inevitably, they fall. When they fall, they suffer attacks from various Rakshasas, who appear as sons, grandsons, and other relatives. Finally, they withdraw their hearts and in despair seek moksha.'

Ashtaka asks, 'For what sin do the Rakshasas attack the fallen? Why are they not destroyed? Why do they enter another womb, and grow organs and develop senses?'

Yayati replies, 'Falling from heaven, the being becomes a subtle fluid. This fluid becomes semen, the seed. The seed enters the mother's womb in her season, develops into an embryo and emerges as a child, just like a fruit from its flower.

Entering trees, plants, water, air, earth and space, the spirit fluid becomes all the creatures that are to be seen.'

Ashtaka says, 'Tell me, O Sire, for I do not know, does the being that is born human enter the womb in human form or some other? How does the foetus acquire its form, with eyes and ears, and the other senses, and consciousness as well? Father, you are one that knows the deeds and the thoughts of Great Beings.'

Yayati says, 'Its karma is already inherent in the subtle being, the sukshma rupa, when he is seminal fluid. In the womb, what is latent develops into physical form, first as embryo, then as the infant born; later, he becomes conscious of himself as a human: the ears hear sound, the eyes see the world of forms and colours, the nose is sensible of various scents and smells, the tongue of taste, the body of touch, and the mind of ideas.

Thus, O Ashtaka, the sthula rupa, the material body, develops from the sukshma, the subtle or spirit body.'

Ashtaka asks, 'On death, the body is burnt or otherwise consumed. Reduced to nothing, how does it take rebirth?'

Yayati says, 'Lion among kings, on dying the man assumes a subtle form, remembering all his deeds and life, as in a dream, and quick as a thought he enters into another body, as seed, then again a mother's womb.

If he has led a good life, he evolves to a higher form, and if he has sinned, a lower one. The worst sinners devolve into worms and insects. I have no more to say on this subject, O pure and noble-souled Ashtaka!

I have told you how beings are born, live, die and are reborn as creatures four-footed, those with six and more legs. What else do you want to ask?'

Ashtaka says, 'How, O Pitr, do men attain to the higher realms from where they do not return to life on Earth? Is it by tapasya or by gyana, asceticism or knowledge? Tell me, can one gradually evolve into these blissful realms? I beg you tell me everything there is to know about this.'

Yayati answered him, 'The Rishis say there are seven gates through which a man may enter Swarga: asceticism, benevolence, tranquillity, self-control, modesty, simplicity and kindness to all creatures. The Sages also say that vanity robs a person of all these seven.

The man who acquires knowledge, then begins to think of himself as a great scholar, and with his learning disparages or destroys the reputation of others, never finds the realms of immortal felicity; neither does his learning lead him to the Brahman.

Study, humility, worshipping before a holy fire, and sacrifices — these four remove every fear. However, when they are contaminated by vanity, they create fear instead. The wise man never exults at being honoured, nor does he chafe at being dishonoured. For only they that are themselves wise honour the wise; the evil will never revere the virtuous, but will insult and try to destroy them.

"I have given so much daana, so much charity; I have performed so many yagnas; I have studied so much; I have kept so many vratas" – this vanity is the very root of fear. Never indulge these feelings; do not entertain these thoughts.

But learned men who know that the changeless, ineffable Brahman is their lone support, the Spirit who always showers his blessings on good men like yourself, such men find perfect peace, here and hereafter.'"

CANTO 91

SAMBHAVA PARVA CONTINUED

"Ashtaka says, 'Knowers of the Veda differ about how the four Varnas should lead their lives, the Brahmacharins, the Grihasthas, the Bhikshus and the Vanaprasthas, so they might acquire punya.'

Yayati replies, 'A Brahmacharin living in his Guru's house must learn from his master only when he is called for a lesson; he must serve his Guru without being called or asked; he must rise before his Guru does, and sleep after his master sleeps.

He must be humble, with his passions controlled, patient, vigilant and devoted to his studies. Only then will he succeed.

The oldest Upanishads say that a Grihastha must acquire wealth legitimately and honestly, and perform sacrifices. He must always give some of what he earns in charity. He must be hospitable to anyone who comes to his home, and should never partake of anything without sharing some portion of it.

A Bhikshu does not seek a forest to sit in tapasya. He roams the world, depends on his own strength, is never vicious, gives some charity always, and never causes pain to any living creature. Only then does he achieve success.

The true Bhikshu lives by alms, is very learned and accomplished, has his passions under perfect control, has no worldly desires, concerns or attachments, does not sleep under a Grihastha's roof, and has no wife. Journeying a little every day, he travels over most of the country.

A learned man becomes a Vanaprastha when he has truly mastered his desire for pleasure and his acquisitiveness; then he embarks upon the path after the prescribed rituals. He that dies in the forest while living the life of a Vanaprastha causes the mukti, the liberation and dissolution into the Brahman of ten generations of his ancestors and his progeny, himself included.'

Ashtaka asks, 'How many kinds of Munis are there, who keep the mowna vrata of silence?'

Yayati answers, 'He is a Muni who lives in a forest though he is near a town, as is he who lives in a town that is near a forest.'

Ashtaka asks, 'What is a Muni?'

Yayati replies, 'A Muni withdraws from the world and lives in a forest. He never seeks to possess worldly goods, but is able to obtain anything at all with his mystical powers. Thus, he lives in a forest with a town or city near him.

Again, a Muni who has withdrawn his mind from all worldly things might well live in a town or village, as a Sannyasi. He never shows any pride of birth, family or learning. He wears threadbare clothes, yet he can imagine that he wears the richest garments.

He eats just enough to support his life. Such a man, even if he lives in a town or village, in truth lives in a forest.

He who restrains his senses and passions, and keeps a vow of silence, refraining from any karma, all action, and allowing no desire to capture his mind, surely succeeds. Why should we not worship a man who sustains himself on pure food, never injures any living being, whose heart is always pure, who is swathed in a halo of asceticism, who is free from the leaden weight of desire, who does not cause injury even when dharma sanctions it?

Emaciated by penance, his very flesh, marrow and blood thinned, such a man conquers not just this world but the highest one. When this Muni sits absorbed in dhyana, indifferent to joy and sorrow, honour and insult, he leaves this world and communes with the Brahman. Why, when the Muni eats and drinks, even wine or the flesh of animals, without relish or desire, but like a baby feeding at his mother's breast, he is still like the pervasive Brahman and one with the Universe. The Muni attains salvation.'"

CANTO 92

SAMBHAVA PARVA CONTINUED

"Ashtaka asks, 'O King, of the man of asceticism and the man of knowledge, both working tirelessly toward moksha, even like the Sun and the Moon, which one first finds communion with the Brahman?'

Yayati replies, 'The Vedas help the learned man quickly realise that the perceived universe is only illusion, maya. Upon this realisation, he immediately attains to the Supreme Brahman, the original font, the only blissful reality.

Those that follow the path of dhyana and Yoga arrive at the same goal, but they usually take a longer time: for they depend upon experience alone to rid themselves of samsara.

If a Yogi does not attain mukti in one lifetime (perhaps having been led astray now and then by the allurements of samsara), whatever evolution he achieves goes with him into his next life. But the Gyani always sees only Immortal Unity, and even if he is steeped in the enjoyments of the flesh, they never affect him or his heart. Nothing impedes his salvation.

He that fails to find knowledge must resort to pious karma, to sacrifices. However, no man who performs a yagna with an eye on its fruit ever achieves moksha. His yagnas remain fruitless, and are indeed rajasic, even cruel by nature.

But a man who performs his dharma seeking no gain, but in a spirit of immaculate detachment, his karma is Yoga itself: it is communion with God.'

Ashtaka says, 'Rajan, you look like a young man; you are handsome and wear a heavenly garland. You are lustrous and splendid. From where are you coming and where do you go? Are you someone's messenger? Are you going down to the Earth?'

Yayati says, 'I have fallen from heaven, having lost all my punya. I am doomed to fall into Bhauma, the hell on Earth. Yes, as soon as I finish speaking with you, I will fall down into the world. Ah, even now the Lokapalas command me to hurry. O Ashtaka, I have a boon from Indra that though I shall fall into the Earth, I will fall among the wise and the virtuous, men of dharma. Surely, all of you here are men of dharma, both wise and virtuous.'

Ashtaka says, 'You know everything. I want to know from you, O Yayati, are there any worlds that I might enjoy in Swarga or in Akasa? If there are, then I say to you, you shall not fall.'

Yayati says, 'O King, there are as many worlds above for you to enjoy as there are cows and horses on Earth, and all the other beasts of the wild and the hills together!'

Ashtaka says, 'Rajan, if indeed there are worlds on high for me to enjoy, as the fruit of my punya, I give them all to you. Thus, you shall not fall. Take all those worlds from me quickly, and grieve no more.'

Yayati replies, 'Best of kings, a Brahmana who knows the Brahman may accept such a gift but not you or I. Rajan, I have myself given gifts to Brahmanas, even as one should. But let no man who is not a Brahmana bring dishonour upon himself by taking alms; let the wife of a learned Brahmana never take alms. While I am in the world below, I shall, as I have done before, perform much dharma. When I have never accepted a gift before, how can I take one from you now?'

Another Rajarishi there says, 'Resplendent one, I am Pratardana. I ask you, are there any worlds in Swarga or Akasa for me to enjoy with my punya? Tell me, for you know everything.'

Yayati says, 'Rajan, there are worlds beyond count, full of bliss, where sorrow and pain cannot enter, for you to enjoy; they are as bright as the face of the Sun. Live in each one for just seven days, and they shall yet never be exhausted.'

Pratardana says, 'Then I give all those to you, so that you will not fall. Let the worlds that I have gained become yours, be they in Akasa or in Swarga. Take them quickly, and be sad no more!'

Yayati answered, 'Rajan, no king should ever accept from an equal what he has earned by Yoga and Tapasya; that is not dharma. No wise Kshatriya should leave the path of dharma, particularly when fate visits him with calamity. A king must keep dharma in view always, and walk in dharma. I would debase myself if I take what you offer. There are others, who seek to acquire punya, who never accept gifts. How, then, shall I?'

Another of those kings of dharma now spoke to Yayati. 'I am Oshadasva's son Vasumat. Tell me, Yayati, are there any worlds that I can enjoy, by my accumulated punya, in Swarga or in Akasa? Mahatman, you know all those sacred realms!'

CANTO 93

SAMBHAVA PARVA CONTINUED

Yayati says, 'There are as many realms for you to enjoy as there are places in the sky, the ten directions of the Universe and on the Earth that the Sun illumines.'

Vasumat then says, 'I give them all to you; let all the worlds meant for me become yours. And you shall not fall anymore. And if it is not proper for you to take them from me as a gift, O King, then buy them from me: their price is a straw.'

Yayati replies, 'I do not remember ever having bought or sold anything usuriously. No king ever has; then how shall I now?'

Vasumat says, 'If you consider buying them as being against dharma, then take them freely from me, as a gift, because I say to you that I will never go to those worlds myself. So let them be yours.'

Now Sibi says to Yayati, 'I am Usinara's son Sibi. O Pitr, are there any worlds in Swarga or Akasa for me to enjoy by my punya? You know all the worlds that a man might gain through tapasya.'

Yayati says, 'You have never failed to help honest and good men who asked for your help. There are infinite worlds for you to enjoy in heaven, all bright as lightning.'

Sibi says, 'If you think it wrong to buy them from me, I give them to you as my gift. Take them all, O King, for I will never go there, to those realms where the wise never feel any disquiet.'

Yayati says, 'O Sibi, powerful as Indra, you have indeed earned an infinity of heavenly realms for yourself. But I have no wish to enjoy worlds given to me by others. I fear I cannot accept your gift.'

Now Ashtaka declares, 'O Pitr, we have all offered you the higher realms that we have earned by our tapasya and dharma. You refuse to accept them. But we are going to leave them to you, and ourselves go down into Bhauma, hell on Earth.'

Yayati replies, 'You are all wise and honest. Give me what I deserve; I cannot do what I have never done before.'

Ashtaka says, 'Whose are these five golden chariots? Do men that fly to the realms of permanent bliss go in them?'

Yayati says, 'Indeed, the five glorious chariots that blaze like fire would bear you to the realms of bliss.'

Ashtaka says, 'Yayati, take the chariots and fly into Swarga. We can wait; we will follow later.'

Yayati says, 'Look! The path to Swarga is revealed before us. We can all go together, for it seems that we have all conquered heaven.'

All those noble kings climb into the chariots of the Devas and fly up into Swarga, illumining all the sky with the radiance of their virtue as they go.

Breaking the silence, as they flash along, Ashtaka asks, 'I always thought that Indra is especially my friend, and that I would enter his realm first. But how does Usinara's son Sibi leave the rest of us behind?'

Yayati says, 'Usinara's son relinquished his every possession to attain Brahmaloka. So he is the first among us. Besides, the liberality, asceticism, truth, virtue, modesty, forgiveness and friendliness of Sibi, as well as his burning desire to do good have been such that no one can measure them.'

Again curious, Ashtaka asks his mother's father, Yayati, who is like Indra himself, 'O King, tell me truthfully who you are, from where you come and whose son you are? Has any other Brahmana or Kshatriya on Earth done all that you did?'

Yayati replies, 'Truly, I am Yayati, Nahusha's son and Puru's father. I was Lord of all the Earth. You are all my daughters' sons, and I am your grandfather. I conquered the world, then gave rich garments to Brahmanas, and also a hundred pedigreed horses that are fit to be sacrificed at Aswamedha yagnas.

Such sacrifices please the Devas and they bless those that perform them. I gifted the Earth that I had conquered to the Brahmanas, the world with all her horses, elephants, gold, every kind of treasure, and also a hundred arbudas of the finest milch cows.

Why, Earth and Sky, Bhumi and Akasa, exist because of my dharma; Agni still burns in the world of men because of my dharma and my truth. I have never spoken a single word that is a lie; and for this the wise worship the truth.

Ashtaka, everything that I have told Pratardana, Vasumat and you is true. I know beyond doubt that the Devas, the Rishis and all the realms and homes of the blessed are full of grace and bliss because they are all founded in Truth.

He that reads or hears this account of our ascent into Swarga, with no evil in his heart, shall himself find the worlds to which we go.'

Thus did mighty King Yayati of old, saved by his grandsons, re-enter Swarga from where he fell, while his fame spread throughout the three worlds."

CANTO 94

SAMBHAVA PARVA CONTINUED

Janamejaya said, "O Vaisampayana, worthy of worship, tell me about the sons of Puru, and the kings that descended from them. Tell me about the power and deeds of each one. I have heard that every king in the line of Puru is a man of dharma and great prowess, and that each one has excellent sons. O you, who are rich in tapasya, tell me the lives of those kings of deep learning and great achievements."

Vaisampayana said, "Listen then to the lives of the heroic kings born into the House of Puru, every one of them as strong as Indra, owning boundless wealth, and the adoration of all in consequence of their dharma and their awesome deeds.

By his wife Paushti, Puru has three sons: Pravira, Iswara and Raudraswa, all of them redoubtable Maharathas. Of these, Pravira begets upon his wife Suraseni a son called Manasyu.

Manasyu, whose eyes are as wide and long as lotus petals, holds sway over the world, bounded by the four seas. Manasyu's wife is Sauviri, and he fathers three sons in her: Sakta, Sahana and Vagmi. And they are great Kshatriyas in battle and Maharathas.

Puru's son Raudraswa begets upon the Apsara Misrakesi ten sons, all great archers. They grow to be tremendous Kshatriyas, performing countless yagnas to worship the Devas. Each of them begets sons who acquire deep learning of every kind and are men of dharma.

The ten sons of Raudraswa are Richeyu, Kaksreyu and Vrikeyu: of great strength; Sthandileyu, Vaneyu and Jaleyu: of great fame; Tejeyu of great strength and intellect; Satyeyu strong as Indra; Dharmeyu and Sannateyu both powerful as Devas.

Of these, Richeyu becomes sovereign ruler of the Earth and is known as Anadhrishti. He is as strong as Indra among the Devas. Anadhristi's son Matinara becomes a renowned king of dharma, who performs the Rajasuya and the Aswamedha yagnas.

Matinara has four sons of untold prowess: Tansu, Mahan, Atiratha and Druhyu the glorious. Among these, the mighty Tansu becomes the perpetuator of Puru's line. He subdues the Earth and gains great fame, honour and splendour.

Tansu's son is the mighty Ilina, who becomes the greatest among all conquerors, and also brings the whole world under his sway. Ilina begets five sons upon his wife Rathantara, and Drohmanta is the eldest; they are as mighty as the five elements, the Panchabhutas.

Ilina's sons are Dushyanta, Sura, Bhima, Pravasu, and Vasu. And, O Janamejaya, the eldest of them, Dushyanta, becomes king.

By his wife Shakuntala, Dushyanta has a fine son, Bharata, who becomes king. The royal race that he founded bears Bharata's name, and because of his greatness its fame spread across the Earth.

Bharata marries three wives and begets nine sons by them. None of them is like his father and Bharata is not pleased. Growing angry, their mothers kill their sons. Finally, Bharata performs a great putrakama, with Bharadvaja as his priest, and begets a son called Bhumanyu.

In this prince, Puru's magnificent descendant Bharata is pleased; he feels that this boy is his worthy heir and crowns Bhumanyu Yuvaraja.

Bhumanyu marries Pushkarini and sires six sons in her: Suhotra, Suhotri, Suhavih, Sujeya, Diviratha and Kichika. The eldest, Suhotra, inherits the throne and he performs many Rajasuyas and Aswamedhas. Suhotra brings the whole world, with her girdle of seas, her forests teeming with elephants, her lands with cows and horses, and her treasure troves of gold and jewels, under his sway.

The Earth, burdened with numberless humans, elephants, horses and chariots seems as if she might sink down into Patala. During the reign of Suhotra of dharma, lakhs of yupastambas, stakes of sacrifice, cover the face of Bhumi. Suhotra begets upon his wife Aikshaki three sons: Ajamidha, Sumidha, and Purumidha. The eldest, Ajamidha, becomes king and he sires six sons: Riksha by Dhumini; Dushyanta and Parameshthin by Nili; and Jahnu, Jala and Rupina are born from Kesini. All the tribes of the Panchalas are descended from Dushyanta and Parameshthin. And the Kushikas are the sons of Jahnu of measureless might.

Riksha, the eldest, becomes king and he begets Samvarana, who furthers the royal line. O King, I have heard that during the reign of Riksha's son Samvarana, famine, pestilence, drought and disease sweep across the Earth, killing millions. For the first time, enemies defeat the Bhaarata princes. The Panchalas, with footsoldiers, cavalry, elephant warriors and chariot fighters, conquer the world. With ten Akshauhinis, the Panchala king vanquishes the Bhaarata king.

Samvarana flees with his wife and ministers, sons and relatives, and hides in the forest on the banks of the river Sindhu, which extends to the foot of the Himalaya. The Bhaaratas live there for a full thousand years, in a fortress they build.

When a thousand years pass, one day the illumined Rishi Vasishta comes to see the Bhaaratas in exile, and they come out to worship him with arghya. Welcoming him reverently, they tell him everything that has happened. When the Rishi sits in a lofty chair, Samvarana himself says to the sage, 'Be our priest, O Holy One! For we wish to regain our kingdom.'

Vasishta replies, 'Aum', consenting.

Vasishta makes Samvarana the sovereign of all the Kshatriyas in the world; with his recondite mantras, he makes the heir of Puru like the horns of the bison, the tusks of the elephant. Becoming Lord of the Earth once more, Samvarana performs many Mahayagnas and the gifts he gives the Brahmanas are magnanimous beyond description.

Samvarana marries Surya Deva's daughter, Tapati, and begets on her a son called Kuru. Kuru's dharma is flawless, he is the soul of rectitude, and the people make him king. The field called Kurukshetra or Kurujungala, renowned in the world, is named after this great sovereign: for he sits in that field in tapasya for long years, and sanctifies it through his penance.

Kuru's wife, Vahini of the lofty intellect, bears him five sons: Avikshit, Bhavishyanta, Chaitraratha, Muni and the celebrated Janamejaya. Avikshit begets the mighty Parikshit, Savalaswa, Adhiraja, Viraja, Salmali of great strength, Uchaihsravas, Bhangakara, and Jitari is the eighth.

From their dharma and tapasya seven Maharathas, Janamejaya their leader, are born into this royal House. Parikshit's sons are masters of dharma and artha. They are Kakshasena, Ugrasena, Chitrasena of enormous vitality, Indrasena, Sushena and Bhimasena.

The sons of Janamejaya are all endowed with inordinate strength and become celebrated the world over. They are Dhritarashtra – the eldest, Pandu, Balhika, Nishadha of tremendous tejas, the mighty Jambunada, Kundodara, Padati, and Vasati is eighth. They too are steeped in dharma and artha, and compassionate to all living creatures.

Dhritarashtra becomes king, he has eight sons: Kundika, Hasti, Vitarka, Kratha, Havihsravas, Indrabha, and the invincible Bhumanyu. Numberless grandsons has Dhritarashtra, but only three of them acquire renown: Prateepa, Dharmanetra and Sunetra.

Of these, Prateepa has no rival on Earth. O Bharatarishabha, Prateepa has three sons, Devapi, Shantanu, and the Maharatha Balhika. Devapi, the eldest, becomes a Sannyasi, for he wants his brothers to have the kingdom. Shantanu and Maharatha Balhika inherit the Earth.

Rajan, besides all these, countless mighty, mighty Kshatriyas are born into the race of Bhaarata, each of them blessed with burning energy and like Devas in their dharma and tapasya.

So, too, many Maharathas, great chariot-warriors, all as irresistible as Devas, are born into the race of Manu. Their numbers increase the Aila dynasty beyond calculation."

CANTO 95

SAMBHAVA PARVA CONTINUED

Janamejaya said, "Brahmana, you have told me the history of my ancestors, and about the great kings born into our royal line. However, you have only told me briefly about this ancestry. I beg you, O Vaisampayana, recount the lives of these great men in some detail, beginning with Manu, Lord of creation.

Who would not be enchanted to listen to such a narration, for it surely is sacred? Why, the fame of these kings has spread across Swarga, Bhumi and Patala, such is their wisdom, their might, their lofty characters and their dharma. Your Itihasa is like Amrita; rare delight fills me when you speak of their liberality, power and strength, their intelligence, their vigour and fortitude!"

Vaisampayana said, "Listen then, O Rajan, in full to the legends of your race, just as I heard it from my master Dwaipayana.

Daksha begets Aditi, who begets Vivaswat, who begets Manu, who begets Ila, and Ila begets Pururavas. Pururavas begets Ayus, who begets Nahusha, and Nahusha begets Yayati.

Yayati has two wives, Usasanas' daughter Devayani, and Sarmishta the daughter of Vrishaparvan. Devayani gives birth to Yadu and Turvasu; and Vrishaparvan's daughter Sarmishta gives birth to Druhyu, Anu and Puru.

The descendants of Yadu are the Yadavas and those of Puru are the Pauravas. Puru has a wife called Kausalya, in whom he begets a son called Janamejaya, who performs three Aswamedhas and another great sacrifice calls Viswajit; after which he goes away into the forest and takes Sannyasa.

Janamejaya has Ananta, the daughter of Madhava, and she bears him a son called Prachinvat. This prince has his name because he conquers all the eastern countries up to the very land where the Sun rises. Prachinvat marries Asmaki, a Yadava princess and fathers in her a son called Sanyati.

Sanyati marries Varangi, the daughter of Drishadwata, and she bears him a son called Ahayanti. Ahayanti marries Bhanumati, the daughter of Kritavirya, and she gives him a son called Sarvabhauma.

Sarvabhauma marries Sunanda, the daughter of the Kekaya king, by abducting her. He fathers Jayatsena in her. Jayatsena marries the Vidarbha king's daughter and she bears him Avachina. Avachina also marries another Vidarbha princess, Maryada. Her son is Arihan. Arihan marries Angi and their son is Mahabhauma. Mahabhauma marries Suyajna, the daughter of Prasenajit. She bears him Ayutanayi. He bears this unusual name because he performs a sacrifice for which the fat of an ayuta of male creatures is specified.

Ayutanayi marries Kama, the daughter of Prithusravas, and their son is Akrodhana, who marries Karambha, the daughter of the king of Kalinga. Their son is Devatithi, who marries Maryada, the princess of Videha, and their son is Arihan.

Arihan marries Sudeva, the princess of Anga, and he sires in her the prince Riksha. Riksha marries Jwala, the daughter of Takshaka, and their son is Matinara, who performs a twelve-year yagna on the banks of Saraswati, a great and potent sacrifice. When it is complete, Saraswati appears before the king and makes him her husband, and their son is calls Tansu.

Tansu marries Kalingi and begets a son called Ilina. Ilina marries Rathantari and they have five sons, of whom Dushyanta is the eldest. Dushyanta marries Viswamitra's daughter Shakuntala, and their son is Bhaarata the Great.

'The mother is only the receptacle in which the father begets the son. The father is himself the son. Therefore, O Dushyanta, accept your son and do not humiliate Shakuntala. God among men, the father becomes the son and rescues himself from hell. Shakuntala speaks the truth when she says that you are this child's father.'

Thus the asariri, the divine voice, spoke in the court of Dushyanta, and Dushyanta then accepts his child; and Bharata has his name for that: the accepted one.

Bharata marries Sunanda, the daughter of Sarvasena, king of Kasi; and their son is Bhumanyu. Bhumanyu marries Vijaya, the daughter of Dasarha, and their son is Suhotra, who marries Suvarna, the daughter of Ikshvaku. Their son is Hasti, who indeed founded this great capital of yours, and it is after him that it is named Hastinapura.

Hasti marries Yasodhara, the princess of Trigarta, and their son is Vikunthana, who marries Sudeva, the princess of Dasarha. They have a son called Ajamidha. Ajamidha has four wives, Raikeyi, Gandhari, Visala and Riksha. And he begets two thousand and four hundred sons upon them.

Of all these, Samvarana becomes king and perpetuates the dynasty. Samvarana marries Vivaswat's daughter Tapati, and their son is Kuru, who marries the Dasarha princess Subhangi, and their son is Viduratha. Viduratha marries Supriya, a Madhava princess, and their son is called Anaswan. Anaswan marries Amrita, another daughter of the Madhavas, and their son is Parikshit, who marries Suvasa, a Bahuda princess, and their son is Bhimasena.

Bhimasena marries the Kekaya princess Kumari, and begets upon her Pratisravas, whose son is Prateepa. Prateepa marries Sunanda, the daughter of Sibi, and they have three sons: Devapi, Shantanu and Balhika. When he is just a boy, Devapi goes away into the jungle and takes Sannyasa. Shantanu becomes king.

Here is a sloka about Shantanu:

'Old men whom this king touched not only felt indescribable joy, but had their youth restored to them.'

Indeed, so is he named Shantanu. And Shantanu marries Ganga, who bears him a son Devavrata, who is later known as Bhishma, of the solemn vow.

Wishing his father to find happiness (for Ganga has left him), Bhishma helps Shantanu marry Satyavati, who is also known as Gandhakali for the fragrance of her body. When she is a young virgin Satyavati bears the Rishi Parasara a son, upon an island in a stream of the Yamuna: he is my Guru Dwaipayana.

She bears Shantanu two other sons, Chitrangada and Vichitravirya. But Gandharvas slay Chitrangada before he grows to manhood. Vichitravirya becomes king, and he marries the two daughters of the king of Kasi, Ambika and Ambalika. But Vichitravirya dies before they can bear him any children.

Satyavati bends her mind to the task of how the race of Dushyanta can be continued. She remembers her first son, the Rishi Dwaipayana. He appears before her, and asks, 'What shall I do for you, mother?'

She says, 'Your brother Vichitravirya has left this world without fathering any sons. Beget sons of dharma for him.'

Dwaipayana fathers three children, Dhritarashtra, Pandu and Vidura, to continue the royal line. By his boon to his son, Dhritarashtra has a hundred sons by his wife Gandhari. Among those hundred, four achieve renown: Duryodhana, Dushasana, Vikarna and Chitrasena.

Pandu has two jewels among women for his wives: Kunti (also called Pritha), and Madri. One day, while hunting in the forest, Pandu sees a stag covering its mate. Callously, the Kshatriya kills that deer with an arrow before its desire is slaked.

Pierced by the king's arrow, the deer suddenly changes into a Rishi (who has taken, with his wife, the form of deer to enjoy lovemaking), and says to Pandu, 'O Pandu, you are a man of dharma and you also know the pleasure a man has satisfying his desire. My desire is not gratified and you have killed me. When you next make love to your wife, you will also die before finding fulfilment!'

With that the Rishi dies, and also his wife and mate as if they shared the same life. Pandu trembles at the curse and from then would not go to his wives.

He says to them in that forest, 'I am cursed through my own fault. But I have heard that the childless never find Swarga or any heaven at all.'

He begs Kunti to bear him sons. She acquiesces; by Dharma Deva, she bears him Yudhishtira; by Vayu, she bears him Bhimasena; and by Indra she gives him Arjuna.

Pandu is delighted with his sons. He says to Kunti, 'Madri has no sons; use your mantra to help her bear children as well.'

'So be it,' says Kunti and speaks the incantation for her husband's second wife, and Madri bears him Nakula and Sahadeva, twin sons by the Aswins of heaven.

One day, Pandu sees Madri wearing just her ornaments and bathing in the river, naked. His long repressed desire kindled, he thrusts himself upon her on the riverbank. Immediately as he does, he dies. Madri burns herself on her husband's funeral pyre, to go with him into Swarga, for his desire remained unsatisfied.

She says to Kunti, 'Raise these twins of mine like your own sons, with love.'

After their father's death, some Rishis of the forest bring Kunti and the five Pandavas to Hastinapura and present them to Bhishma and Vidura. Immediately, the Munis vanish before all eyes, while flowers fall out of the sky when those Sages name the sons of Pandu, saying whose natural child each one is, and divine drumrolls reverberate across the clear blue heavens.

Bhishma takes the Pandavas in. They describe the death of their father, and perform the last rites for him in Hastinapura. When the evil, spoilt Duryodhana sees that his cousins are to be raised in the city, violent jealousy possesses him. Even like a Rakshasa, he does everything in his power to do away with them. But Fate will take its course inexorably, and all Duryodhana's malignant schemes are frustrated.

Finally, in despair, he has the Pandavas sent to Varanavrata by his doting father; they go willingly, and at first innocently. There he tries to immolate them in a cunningly built house of lac, but they are saved yet again by the warning and the help of their uncle Vidura.

Later, the Pandavas kill Hidimba and then go to Ekachakra. Here Bhima kills the Rakshasa Baka, and after that they go to Panchala, where they win Draupadi for their wife, before returning to Hastinapura, and then going to Khandavaprastha, where they live in peace for a while, and beget children.

Draupadi bears Yudhishtira a son calls Prativindhya; Bhima's son is Sutasoma; Arjuna's is Srutakriti; Nakula's is Satanika; and Sahadeva's son by Draupadi is Srutakarman.

Yudhishtira also marries Devika, the daughter of Gobasana of the Saibyas, at her swayamvara, and their son is Yaudheya. Bhima also marries Balandhara, the daughter of the king of Kasi, by offering his strength as dowry, and has a son by her called Sarvaga.

Arjuna goes to Dwaraka, Dwaravati, and carries away Subhadra, Krishna's soft-spoken sister, and brings her home to Indraprastha. Arjuna and Subhadra have a son called Abhimanyu, a splendidly gifted prince and a favourite of Krishna's.

Nakula also marries Karenumati, princess of Chedi, and their son is Niramitra. Sahadeva marries Vijaya, daughter of Dyutimat, king of Madra, being chosen by her at her swayamvara, and they have a son called Suhotra.

Of course, the firstborn of all the sons of the Pandavas is Ghatotkacha, Bhimasena's son by Hidimbi. These are the eleven Pandavaputras, and among them Abhimanyu is the one that continues the royal line.

He marries Virata's daughter Uttaraa and she gives birth to a stillborn child, a premature baby who has been burnt in his mother's womb by Aswatthama's astra. Krishna tells Kunti to take the lifeless child onto her lap, and he says, 'I will revive this child of six months.'

Krishna brings the infant back to life and gives him great strength, vitality and brilliance. Having restored him to life, Krishna says, 'Because this child has faced death before being born, he shall be called Parikshit, the tested one.'

Parikshit marries Madravati, O King, and you, Janamejaya, are their son. You married Vapushtama, and have two sons called Satanika and Sankukarna. Satanika has married the princess of Videha and their son is Aswamedhadatta.

This, Rajan, is the lineage of the House of Puru and the Pandavas. Let Brahmanas that keep vratas, devout Kshatriyas who practise svadharma and protect their subjects, attentive Vaisyas and reverent Sudras, who serve the three higher varnas, all listen to this sacred Itihasa, for it increases punya.

Those that recite this sacred genealogy or listen to it with reverence find Swarga for themselves, and go to the realms of the blessed. The Devas, Rishis and all men honour them.

The enlightened Vyasa composed this holy Itihasa, the Bhaarata. Brahmanas that know the Vedas and other men that listen to it with pure and worshipful hearts gain great spiritual reward and, it is told, conquer the heavens.

Even if they sin, they find honour, for a sloka describes this Itihasa thus: 'This Bhaarata is equal to the Vedas; it is beautiful and it is sacred. It bestows wealth, fame and a long life. Let all men listen to it with absorption.'"

CANTO 96

SAMBHAVA PARVA CONTINUED

Vaisampayana said, "There is a king called Mahabhisha born into the race of Ikshvaku. He is Lord of all the Earth, and always speaks the truth and is mighty indeed. With a thousand Aswamedhas and a hundred Rajasuyas he adores Indra, and finally attains Swarga.

One day, the Devas have gathered to worship Brahma. Several Rajarishis are present at the yagna and so is Mahabhisha. Ganga, queen of rivers, also comes to offer adorations to the Grandsire. Suddenly a gust of wind blows her clothes, white as moonbeams, away from her body and she stands exposed.

The Devas bend their heads, turning their eyes away from her. But Rajarishi Mahabhisha stares brazenly at the queen of rivers.

Brahma curses Mahabhisha, 'Wretch, you forget yourself at the sight of her! You will be born on Earth as a man. She shall also come to you as a woman in the world, and she will cause you anguish, repeatedly. Only when you lose your patience and turn on her in anger will you be free of this curse of her tormenting you. Finally, after a full life as a mortal, Mahabhisha, you will return to Swarga as yourself.'

King Mahabhisha thinks of all the great kings of the world and wishes to be born as the son of the awesome Prateepa. And, if truth be told, Ganga also desires Mahabhisha when she sees him stare at her unabashedly with such desire in his eyes. She, too, wants him, as she leaves that conclave of the Devas and journeys down towards the Earth.

On her way, she sees the eight Vasus of heaven also travelling, forlorn, on the same path as herself. The queen of rivers asks them, 'Why are you so dejected? O Swargavasis, heaven dwellers, is all well with you?'

The Vasus reply, 'O Ganga, Rishi Vasishta has cursed us for a sin we committed against him. He sat at his sandhya vandana and we could not see him in the fading light. We crossed before him, disturbing his worship, and he cursed us in anger, "Be born as men!"

We cannot escape the curse. We ask you, O Ganga, become a human woman and bear us as your children. Queen of all rivers, we cannot enter the womb of a mortal woman.'

Ganga says, 'So be it.' Then she asks them, 'Which great man on Earth will you make your father?'

The Vasus replies, 'Prateepa will have a son called Shantanu whose fame will mantle the Earth even as the rays of the Sun do. We wish to be born from his seed.'

Ganga smiles, 'O Vasus, sinless ones, this is exactly as I wished. I will become Shantanu's wife and you shall be our children.'

The Vasus says, 'O Tripathagaa, who flow through Swarga, Bhumi and Patala, you of the three courses, cast us, as each one of us is born, into the water so we do not have to live long in the dreadful mortal world.'

Ganga says, 'I will do as you ask, but let not my lovemaking with him be entirely fruitless. One of you must survive and live a full life as our son.'

The Vasus says, 'We will each give up an eighth part of our life energy to create a single son for you, one to fulfil your every wish, who will live a full life as a man. But he himself shall beget no children.'

Making this pact with Ganga, the Vasus immediately go on their way; they are in a hurry to see an end to the curse of mortality."

CANTO 97

Sambhava Parva Continued

Vaisampayana said, "There is a king called Prateepa, who is compassionate towards every living thing. He spent many years in tapasya at the source of the Ganga.

One day, Ganga rises from her waters as a ravishing woman and approaches that king. She goes directly to the Rajarishi at his dhyana and sits upon his right thigh, which is as strong as the trunk of a Sala tree.

Opening his eyes and seeing the beauty on his lap, the king says, 'Lovely one, what do you want from me?'

She says, 'I want you for my husband, O King. Kurusthama, best of the Kurus, be mine, for to refuse a woman who offers herself to you is condemned by the Rishis.

Prateepa answers, 'Fair one, I never go to another man's wife or women that are not of my varna from lust. This is my dharma vrata.'

Ganga says, 'I am neither inauspicious nor ugly. I am worthy of being enjoyed. I am a celestial woman, and my beauty is unearthly. I want you for my husband; do not refuse me, Kshatriya.'

Prateepa answers, 'I have sworn a vow of continence; if I break my vrata, sin will consume me. Besides, lovely one, you have sat on my right thigh and put your arms around me. But you must know that the right leg is the place for daughters, while the left lap is for wives. Peerless woman, I am forbidden to enjoy you as a lover, but shall indeed accept you: as my daughter-in-law, as my son's wife.'

Ganga says, 'King of dharma, let it be as you say: I will become your son's wife. Out of my regard for you, I shall be a queen of the hallowed line of Bharata, whose kings are the sanctuary of every other king on Earth. Why, a hundred years would not suffice for me to count the virtues of your royal house.

The majesty and dharma of the renowned kings of your royal line are beyond calculation or compare. But, Lord of the Earth, I must tell you that when I am your son's wife, he shall not be the judge of what I do, be it anything at all. Be assured, though, that I will be a faithful wife to him and please him in every way. Finally, he will find heaven for himself because of the sons that I bear him, and because of his own dharma.'

Ganga vanishes, and Prateepa now waits for the birth of his son to keep the word he has given her. Indeed, at this very time, Prateepa, bull among Kshatriyas, and his wife are performing penance to have a son, for they are childless.

They are quite old when a son is born to them, and he is Mahabhisha whom Brahma has cursed. They call him Shantanu, because his father has already calmed his passions with penance when he is born: Shantanu, the one born of serenity.

Shantanu, finest among the Kurus, realises early that the realm of immortal bliss is gained only by one's deeds; he treads the path of dharma, devoutly.

When Shantanu grows into a youth, Prateepa calls him one day and says, 'Shantanu, some years ago, before you were born, a celestial woman came to me and I gave her my word that you would marry her and beget children upon her. If you happen to meet her, secretly, and if she asks you to sire children in her, take her for your wife.

Also, my pure child, you must never judge what she does, whatever it might be, fair or foul, nor ask who she is, or where she comes from, but take her for your wife. This is my command to you.'

Prateepa makes Shantanu king, and goes away into the forest to become a Vanaprastha. Shantanu, blessed with great intelligence and as splendid as Indra, spends a great deal of his time in the forest: he is an avid hunter, addicted to the sport, numberless deer and bison he kills.

One day, ranging the banks of the Ganga on his hunt, he comes to a place frequented by Siddhas and Charanas. He sees a woman there who seems to be as beautiful as the Devi Sri: faultless of face and form, her teeth like pearls, wearing unearthly ornaments and garments so fine and resonant that they might have been woven from the filaments of lotuses.

Shantanu feels uncanny rapture surge through him; his hair stands on end for delight. He drinks in the sight of her, and, helplessly, drinks on. The woman sees Shantanu, magnificent and brilliant, and feels a pang of love. She also gazes helplessly at him, and gazes on as if she could never tear her eyes away from him.

Shantanu says softly to her, 'You with the waist like a lotus stalk, you whose beauty is divine, I do not know if you are a Devastri or a Danavi, a Gandharvi, an Apsara, a Yakshi, a Nagini or a mortal woman, a Manushi. But I want you to become my wife.'"

CANTO 98

SAMBHAVA PARVA CONTINUED

Vaisampayana said, "She sees his smile, she hears what he says, so tenderly; she remembers her word she gave the Vasus; she remembers Mahabhisha, and she speaks to him, her voice perfect and her every word making his heart quiver in thrall.

She says, 'O King, I will be your wife and obey you in all things. But I have one condition: you must never question what I do, whatever it might be, good or bad, or ask me who I am. You must never say a harsh word to me. As long as you treat me kindly and never question me, I will be a devoted wife to you. But the moment you say a cross word to me or question me, I will leave you forever.'

Shantanu does not hesitate to agree, 'So be it.' He gives his solemn word.

She is delighted to become his wife and he is ecstatic to be her husband. Great joy and pleasure they give each other. Shantanu keeps his word to her: he never asks her who she is, nor questions her ever. And she is a perfect wife to him, and Shantanu, Lord of the Earth, is more than content for she gratifies him in every way, by her beauty, her conduct, her generosity, her loving affection and her ardour, too.

The Devi Ganga, Tripathagaa of the three courses, has assumed an exquisite human form, and she is entirely happy being the wife of that tiger among kings, Shantanu, who is as mighty as Indra himself; it is as if she now enjoys the fruit of all her past punya.

In turn, she delights him, by her unearthly beauty and her love, her womanly wiles and her lovemaking, with her songs and by dancing for him; indeed, theirs is an almost unalloyed happiness, while months, seasons and years fly by and the king hardly notices them pass.

But when Ganga first becomes pregnant and delivers a son as beautiful as a Deva child, she takes the newborn straight to the river and casts him into the foaming current. She says to Shantanu, who is aghast, 'This is for your own good. Trust me, ask me nothing.'

Shantanu does not question his otherwise perfect wife for fear that she will leave him. Seven times this happens, and the king never says a word, though gradually he becomes a broken man, seeing his sons sink in the Ganga.

But when the eighth child is born, and his wife, with a smile, is about to cast the baby into the river, Shantanu cannot bear it anymore. He cries to her, 'Stop! You will not kill my son. Who are you? Whose daughter are you? What are you that can kill your own children? Murderess, your sins are too dreadful to even think of.'

She replies calmly, 'If it is children you want, you are already the most blessed of fathers. I will not kill this child. But you have broken your word that you would never question me or say an unkind word to me and I must leave you now forever. I am Jahnu's daughter Ganga. The greatest Rishis worship me. I lived with you for all these years to fulfil a purpose of the Devas.

Vasishta cursed the eight Vasus to mortal births. On Earth there is none but you that deserved to become their father. Also, there is no one but I who could become their mother. I took this human form to give birth to them. Shantanu, by becoming the father of the eight

Vasus you have gained many Swargas for yourself, realms of permanent bliss.

The Vasus also made me swear that I would set them free from the darkness of mortal bondage as soon as they are born. I did not kill them, as you saw it, but only liberated them from the curse of Apava Rishi, Vasishta.

I must leave you now, O King, my time with you is over. Be blessed and raise this child. Call him Gangadatta for me. He shall be great beyond all measure and bring fame and honour to your royal house.'"

CANTO 99

SAMBHAVA PARVA CONTINUED

"Shantanu asks, 'Who was Apava Muni and what did the Vasus do, that he cursed them to human birth? What has this eighth child of yours done for which he must live a full human life? O Jaahnavi, tell me everything in detail.'

Ganga replies, 'Bharatashreshta, Vasistha, the Sage who was later known as Apava, was the son of Varuna. He had his asrama on Meru, king of mountains, in a green forest. The place was sacred, with birds and animals of every kind abounding. Flowers of every season bloomed perennially in the magical place. Bharatottama, Varuna's son, best among men of dharma, sat in tapasya in that forest, full of streams flowing with sweet water and with sweet roots and fruit aplenty.

Daksha Prajapati had a daughter called Surabhi. Bharatarishabha, she bore her husband Kashyapa Muni a daughter, Nandini, who was born as a radiant and divine cow of wishes, who could fulfil any desire. Vasishta took Nandini to help him with his ritual homa. Nandini lived in his asrama and adored by all the Sages in that sacred forest, ranged through it at will.

One day, O Bharatarishabha, the Vasus, with Prithu at their head, came to that forest which the Devas and Devarishis love. They ranged through that vana at their leisure, with their wives, all of them enchanted by the glorious mountain and the forest of delights.

Then the slender, gorgeous wife of one of the Vasus saw Nandini, the cow of wishes, through the trees. She saw how lovely Nandini was, her eyes large, her teats ample and full of milk, her tail fine, her hooves as beautiful as jewels, bearing every other auspicious sign, and radiant. The Vasu's wife pointed Nandini out to her husband Dyu.

O King who are as strong as the elephant Airavata, Dyu saw Nandini and admired her many excellences. He said to his wife, "O my black-eyed beauty of the tapering thighs, the cow belongs to the Rishi who lives in this tapovana. My wasp-waisted one, do you know that a mortal who drinks Nandini's milk does not age for ten thousand years?"

Best of kings, the reed-waisted and beautiful Devi said to her irradiant husband Dyu, "I have a precious human friend in this world, her name is Jivati. She is so beautiful and young, that daughter of that Deva among Manavas, the Rajarishi of great dharma and intellect, Usinara.

My lustrous husband, I want to give this cow and her calf to my friend. I want Jivati to drink Nandini's milk and be free from age and death. My illustrious lord, grant me my wish, I beg you. Oh, nothing would please me more!"

Dyu wanted to please his wife and, with the help of his brothers Prithu and the others, he spirited away Nandni and her calf. Indeed, when his wife batted her long eyes at him, Dyu forgot to whom Nandini belonged. He forgot dharma and that he might fall terribly through this crime.

When Varuna's son returned to his asrama in the evening with the fruit he had gathered, he did not see Nandini or her calf. Vasishta searched the charmed tapovana for her, high and low. When he could not find the cow, he used his mystic vision and saw exactly what had happened, how the Vasus had spirited her away.

In rage he cursed the Vasus, crying, "They dared to steal my sweet Nandini with her lovely tail, and milk like Amrita. Let the arrogant Vasus be born into the world of men, on Bhumi!"

Bharatrishabha, this was how the Rishi Apava cursed the eight Vasus. Having pronounced his curse, Vasishta sat down to meditate again. When the awesome Brahmarishi cursed them those celestials were instantly aware of it, and flew down to his asrama in distress. They did their utmost to pacify the Rishi, but Apava, knower of dharma, would not relent.

However, the righteous and kindly one said, "Vasus, Dhava and you others, I have cursed you. Yet you shall be free from my curse within a year of being born into the world. But Dyu is he that led you to this sin, and he must spend a full human life in the world of men.

Though I cursed you in wrath, my curse cannot prove vain. Dyu, you shall indeed live on Earth but you will beget no children. You shall know the Vedas and the Shastras and be a man of profound dharma. You will be an obedient son to your father, but you will never enjoy intimate relations with a woman and remain celibate all through your mortal life."

With that, Maharishi Vasishta left the Vasus. They then came together to me and, O King, they implored me for the boon that as soon as I gave birth to them I would set them free from Vasishta's curse by casting them into the river. Best of kings, I only did what they asked so that they could be free from this world. Also, this eighth child, who is Dyu, must live a full mortal life from Vasishta's curse.'

With that, she takes her child and vanishes; she would bring him back to his father when he is older. Shantanu's son is called both Gangeya and Devavrata, and he excels his father in accomplishment.

After Ganga leaves, Shantanu returns sadly to Hastinapura. Let me tell you now about the dharma and the fortunes of this great king of the House of Bharata. For this wondrous Itihasa is known as the Mahabharata."

CANTO 100

SAMBHAVA PARVA CONTINUED

Vaisampayana said, "Well loved by the Devas and all Rajarishis, Shantanu is famous in all the worlds for his wisdom, his dharma and his truthfulness: never would he tell a lie. He is self-controlled, liberal, forgiving, intelligent, modest, patient and energetic, that bull among men.

Blessed with all these qualities, a master of dharma and artha, he protects the race of Bhaarata and indeed all men and women. His throat is marked with three lines, like a sankha, a conch; his shoulders are massive and wide and he is as strong as an angry elephant. It seems that every auspicious royal sign dwells in the person of Shantanu as if they consider him to be their choicest abode.

Men who observe the deportment of Shantanu become convinced that dharma is infinitely superior to artha and kama, that rectitude is loftier than wealth and enjoyment. Truly, there is never another king like Shantanu. When the other kings of the Earth see his absolute devotion to dharma they make him an emperor, a king of kings, and then on, during the reign of Shantanu the Great, those kings are free from fear and sorrow.

They sleep in peace and awake every morning having dreamt beautiful and joyful dreams. Because Shantanu is like Indra himself in tejas, vital and brilliant, every king of the Earth becomes a king of dharma, liberal and always performing yagnas and deeds of deep goodness. When Shantanu and other kings like him rule the Earth, the dharma of every varna, of men and women of every persuasion, grows incalculably. The Kshatriyas serve the Brahmanas; the Vaisyas wait upon the Kshatriyas; and the Sudras, worshipping the Brahmanas and the Kshatriyas, wait upon the Vaisyas.

Shantanu lives in Hastinapura, the wonderful capital of the Kurus, and he holds sway over all the Earth, bounded by the four seas. He is honest and straightforward, and as much a master of dharma as the king of the Devas. He combines in his person such liberality, religion and austerity that great fortune comes to him and, through him, spreads in tides across the world he rules. He knows no malice or anger; he is as handsome as Soma Deva; he is as brilliant as Surya Deva; and as strong as Vayu the Wind God. His wrath, if roused, is like Yama's, yet he is ordinarily as patient as Bhumi Devi, who bears all things upon herself.

Rajan, while Shantanu rules the Earth, no deer, boars, birds, or other animals are killed wantonly. Great kindness towards all living creatures pervades his kingdom, and he himself is the very soul of mercy, knowing neither desire nor anger, but extending his protection to all creatures.

He performs yagnas to the Devas, the Rishis and the Pitrs, and never is any creature killed in sin. Shantanu is king and father to all and, particularly, to those that are wretched, who have no one else to watch over them; a guardian of birds and beasts he is, indeed, of every created thing.

And during the rule of the best of the Kurus, of that king of kings, speech and truth are the same thing, and men's minds flow always towards liberality, virtue and love of their fellow beings. Shantanu enjoys domestic happiness for thirty-six years and then goes away into the forest to become a Vanaprastha.

Shantanu's son, the Vasu Dyu, born of Ganga and named Devavrata, is as handsome as his father and also like him in his dharma and his learning. He is a prodigy at every branch of knowledge, mundane and spiritual, skilful beyond description. Prodigious are his strength and vigour, too. He becomes a Maharatha, effortlessly; indeed, he becomes a great ruler, though he never actually becomes king.

One day, some years after Ganga leaves him, taking their eighth infant with her, Shantanu follows a deer he has wounded with his arrow along the banks of the Ganga, when he suddenly sees the river turned to a mere trickle, indeed, run almost dry. Shantanu gazes at this in wonder: what could do this to that mightiest of rivers?

Then he sees a youth as handsome and radiant as Indra, who holds up the river's flow with his astra, an unearthly weapon. The king watches in astonishment. The youth is Shantanu's son, but having last seen him as a babe in arms, Shantanu does not know him.

However, the boy knows his father at once but he chooses to vanish using his maaya shakti, his power of illusion, making himself invisible. Shantanu now suspects that the boy is his son, and he speaks to the river that flows again, 'Let me see that youth!'

Ganga assumes the form of a beautiful woman and appears before the king, holding the boy, wearing unearthly ornaments and raiment, with her right hand. Shantanu does not recognise the woman, clad in shimmering white robes and also wearing unworldly ornaments. She has been his wife for many years, but this is another form in which she appears.

Ganga says, 'Tiger among men, this is your eighth son that you begot on me. He is a master of astras, and of every other weapon. O King, take him with you now to your city of heroes. I have raised him with great love and care.

Our brilliant son studied all the Vedas and the Vedangas with Vasishta; as an archer, he is Indra's equal. O Bhaarata, the Devas and the Asuras have both blessed him. Whatever Shukra Bhargava knows, my son knows as well, having learnt from him; he also knows all the Shastras that Angiras' son Brihaspati, whom the Devas and Asuras both adore, knows, having studied them from the Guru himself.

He has learnt the use of weapons from Jamadagni's son, the invincible Parasurama Mahabahu. O bravest of kings, I have brought your heroic son to you; he is a matchless bowman and knows the dharma of kings in its every nuance and detail.'

She gives the boy's hand into Shantanu's, and vanishes. Shantanu brings his son, glorious as Surya, back to Hastinapura. That scion of the line of Puru blesses his great fortune as he rides into his capital, which resembles Amaravati in heaven, bringing his radiant boy with him. He calls all the Pauravas together and formally crowns his son Devavrata as the Yuvaraja.

Bharatarishabha, so noble and able is that prince that, quickly, his father and the other members of the Paurava clan, and also the people, see that he is certainly the jewel of that illustrious line, and they love him. As for Shantanu, he dotes on the youth; that powerful king's joy at living with his son knows no bounds.

Four years pass, then one day the king ranges through some woods on the bank of the Yamuna, when suddenly he smells a scent of heaven, and cannot tell what its source is. Here and there he goes, desperate to find what it is that smells so sweet.

Finally, he sees a black-eyed young woman, her beauty unworldly: a fisherman's daughter.

Shantanu says to her, 'Who are you, and whose daughter are you? What are you doing here?'

She answers him, 'Be blessed, stranger! I am the daughter of the chieftain of the fishermen on this river. By his command, I ferry travellers across the river in my boat.'

Shantanu gazes at that beauty, friendly and so fragrant, and for the first time after Ganga left him, he feels desire stir in him, powerfully. He wants her for his wife. Shantanu goes to her father and asks for her hand.

The fishermen's chieftain says, 'O King, I will gladly give my daughter to be your wife, but I have a condition. You are a man of dharma and you must fulfil my condition if you want to marry my daughter. If you give me your word on it, I will certainly give you my daughter for I could never hope to find another husband for her who is your equal.'

Shantanu says, 'Tell me your condition, the word you want from me. If it is in my power to grant what you want, I certainly will. But unless I know what it is, how can I give you my solemn word?'

The fisherman says, 'Rajan, what I want is that the son born to my daughter shall become king after you, and no other.'

O Bhaarata, Shantanu desires the fishergirl desperately, but he thinks of Devavrata and knows he cannot agree to the fisherman's condition. Burning within himself to possess the fragrant girl, his mind full of just her, he sadly turns back to Hastinapura.

Back in his capital, Shantanu is plunged in gloom.

One day, Devavrata goes to his grieving father and says, 'Why do you grieve like this? Every good fortune is yours; all the chieftains and kings obey you. Yet you shut yourself up alone and speak no word to anyone, not even to me.

You do not go out riding anymore. You are pale and losing weight every day; despondency envelops you and you have lost the very spark of life. Father, I beg you, tell me what illness you are suffering from, so that I can find a cure for you.'

Shantanu says, 'It is true what you say, my son, that I have become melancholy. I will also tell you why sorrow is upon me. Gangeya, you are my only son, the only heir to the throne of Bhaarata. You are a Kshatriya and are frequently at arms or sport with weapons.

My child, human life is always uncertain. O Gangaputra, if some danger befalls you, we shall be heirless. To me, you by yourself are worth a hundred sons, and I have no wish to marry again. I only pray that fortune always attends on you, and that our dynasty continues.

The Rishis say that he who has only one son has no son. Sacrifices performed before a holy fire and the knowledge of the three Vedas bestow immortal punya; but such punya does not have a sixteenth part of the spiritual merit that one gains by having a son.

Why, men and beasts are hardly different from each other in this respect. My wise child, I have no shadow of doubt that a man finds Swarga for himself when he has a son.

Even the Devas regard the Vedas, which are the root of the Puranas, as having scriptural authority and the Vedas are full of examples of this. O Bhaarata, you are a Kshatriya and bold and daring, and as I said, always at arms or in battle. I fear that you might be killed one day in battle.

If that happens, my child, what will become of the royal house of Bharata? What will happen to our dynasty? Some pretender, some usurper will sit upon our hallowed throne. This is the thought that dejects me and fills me with sorrow and anxiety.'

Devavrata does not reply immediately, but that perspicacious young man suspects the truth, the real cause of his father's misery. He goes to the old minister who has devoted his life to the king's personal well-being and asks him what causes his father's depression.

Bharatarishabha, the aged minister tells Devavrata about the fisherman's condition, for which he would give his daughter Gandhavati to Shantanu. Immediately, taking many venerable old Kshatriya lords with him, Devavrata goes to the home of the fisherman and begs him for his daughter's hand for Shantanu.

The fisherman receives him respectfully in his court of fishermen. When Devavrata sits comfortably, the fisherman says, 'Bharatarishabha, you are Shantanu's only son and the greatest warrior on Earth. Your prowess is great indeed. Let me say this to you: if Shantanu asks for the hand of the daughter of Indra himself, Indra could not dream of rejecting the proposal.

Satyavati is not my natural daughter. The Rajarishi from whose seed she was born is your equal in birth and dharma. He has often told me about your father Shantanu and that only he is worthy of marrying my child.

Why, the Brahmarishi Asita has asked me for her hand more than once, and I have refused him because I have believed that your father is destined to be her husband. However, there is one great fear I have in giving her to your father: that he already has a son and that son is you. If my daughter's sons have you for a rival, how will they fare?

Parantapa, scourge of your enemies, even if he was a great Asura or Gandharva no enemy could hope to prevail against you, mightiest of all Kshatriyas. Be blessed, great Devavrata. But understand clearly what I am saying, and that the decision of whether or not my daughter will marry your father does not rest with me.'

O Bhaarata, hearing this, Devavrata says in that rustic court of fisher-chieftains and Kshatriyas, 'Honest friends, then listen to the vow that I swear. I agree to your condition, fisherman: your daughter's son shall be king of Hastinapura. I renounce my right to the throne forever. No other man in this world, I tell you, would swear such an oath. But for my father's sake, I will not break it!'

The fisherman's eyes shine. This is good fortune that he could hardly credit. But that shrewd man now says, 'Prince of dharma, you have come here on behalf of your father Shantanu, whose glory is beyond measuring. I ask you now to also represent my interest—you and you alone—in this matter of my Satyavati marrying the king.

Most excellent Kshatriya, I have something to add, something else that you must consider. Parantapa, any father who has a care for his daughter would say what I am about to. You are certainly a man of dharma, Mahabaho, Mighty-armed, and I have no doubt that you will honour the solemn word you have just sworn before all these worthy ones. But what about your sons after you? How can I trust them?'

O King, Ganga's son says, 'O Fisherking, most worthy friends, listen to what I now swear in the presence of all of you. Kshatriyas, I have already relinquished the throne of my ancestors. I will now settle the question about my sons. Fisherman, from this day, I swear to remain a Brahmachari, a celibate all my life. Even if I die without having a son, I will find the highest heaven for myself, realms of eternal bliss.'

The hairs on the fisherman's body stand on end in unbridled delight, he can hardly believe this great fortune. His eyes shining, he says, 'I give my daughter to be your father's wife!'

The Devas, Apsaras and myriad tribes of Rishis pour down a rain of flowers from the sky, over Devavrata's head, and heavenly voices cry in awe, 'Bhishma! Bhishma!' , because his vow is so terrible.

Bhishma, as we shall call him from now, bows to Satyavati, and says, 'Mother, come, climb into my chariot and let us go home to Hastinapura.'

Bhishma helps the beautiful and fragrant one into his chariot. Coming to Hastinapura he brings her straight to Shantanu and tells him everything. The great Kshatriyas who had gone with him say, 'Truly he is Bhishma!'

When Shantanu hears what his son has done for his sake, he blesses him, saying, 'Death will come to you only when you call him; otherwise no power of Heaven or Earth will end your life.'"

CANTO 101

SAMBHAVA PARVA CONTINUED

Vaisampayana continued, "O King, Shantanu marries Satyavati with all the prescribed and proper rituals. Then he takes her to himself with great delight.

Soon, Satyavati bears an intelligent and heroic son and he is called Chitrangada. He is endowed with terrific vitality and strength and becomes a great man. Shantanu of untold prowess also begets on Satyavati another son: Vichitravirya, who becomes a mighty bowman and the king after his father. But before Vichitravirya grows to manhood, Shantanu the Great yields to Time.

When Shantanu passes on to Swarga, Bhishma, with the support of Satyavati, installs Chitrangada on the throne. At an early age, Chitrangada, with Bhishma for his master, proves himself a matchless warrior, indeed no man other than his elder brother is his equal at arms.

He vanquishes every king of the Earth, and when his namesake, the Gandharva king Chitrangada, sees that the prince of the world could easily subdue men, Asuras and even the Devas, the celestial challenges the Kuru prince before his power grows beyond controlling.

They meet on the hallowed field of the Kurus, Kurukshetra, and the battle between them lasts a full three years, on the banks of the golden Saraswati. Fierce and dreadful is that battle and the sky is thick with banks of arrows and spears, and lusty mace blows ring out; but finally, with superior strategy, indeed with subtle deception, the Gandharva kills the human Chitrangada and flies up into heaven.

When Chitrangada, tiger among men, of strength beyond all measure, is killed, Bhishma, son of Shantanu, performs his last rites. Then he crowns the young boy Vichitravirya as king, while he himself rules as regent in his younger brother's name. Vichitravirya, for his part, worships his older brother, and Bhishma loves him like a son, that fine prince of dharma."

CANTO 102

SAMBHAVA PARVA CONTINUED

Vaisampayana said, "O Scion of the House of Kuru, thus Bhishma rules the kingdom with the support of Satyavati, when Vichitravirya is a boy. When his brother grows into a young man, the wise Bhishma decides to get him married.

He hears that the king of Kasi is to hold a combined swayamvara for his three daughters, all said to be as beautiful as Apsaras. With Satyavati's approval, Bhishma Maharatha, Parantapa, rides to Kasi in a single chariot.

Shantanu's son sees all the kings come from across the land, from every direction in the hope of winning one of the princesses' favour; he sees the three exquisite Rajakumaris, each of whom would choose her own husband.

As the names of the gathered kings are being recited, Bhishma declares that he chooses the three princesses to be his brother's wives. In a flash, Ganga's awesome son has the amazed young women in his chariot. He speaks to the assembled kings in a voice like the rumbling of thunderclouds.

'The Rishis have said a maiden may be given to an accomplished groom, by inviting him to the girl's house and giving her away, decked in fine jewellery and with valuable dowry besides.

Others might give their daughters away by accepting a pair of cows or bulls as brideprice. Yet others take gold for giving their daughters in marriage, while some men carry away their brides by force.

Some men marry young women with their consent; others drug them into giving their consent; and still others by getting the permission of the girl's parents. Some men marry wives for having sat or helped at yagnas.

Of these, the Sages always laud the eighth form of marriage for Brahmanas. Kshatriyas however, approve of the fifth, swayamvara, where the girl consents herself and chooses her own groom. Kings marry by this custom.

But the Rishis say that the wife taken by force, from a conclave of Kshatriyas invited to a swayamvara, after a battle, after slaying adversaries, is the most prized. Therefore, O Kshatriyas, look, I am taking these three by force for my brother. Do your best to stop me, if you dare; come, defeat me or be vanquished!'

With that the invincible Kuru prince Bhishma thunders away in his chariot with the three princesses. The challenged kings jump up, slapping their arms and their thighs in anger. Such a din they make, throwing down their fine ornaments in haste, and pulling on their armour.

O Janamejaya, jewellery and armour being flung down and pulled on flashes like meteors in the night sky. Their great brows knit and eyes red with fury, the Kshatriyas rush towards the fine chariots that their sarathys bring, yoked to steeds of lofty pedigree.

Weapons raised, and roaring, the magnificent Kshatriyas give hot chase to the great Kuru lord. Then, O Bhaarata, ensues the dreadful battle between all those warriors on one side and Bhishma on the other. Ten thousand arrows they shoot at him, at once, and he cuts them down with an incredible volley of shafts as numerous as the down on one's body.

The kings surround him and rain arrows on him like thunderclouds do upon the crest of a mountain. Bhishma not only stops that downpour of barbs, he pierces every king surrounding him with three arrows, in a flash. They strike him back with five arrows each. But the shafts fall off his mighty body like straws, Rajan, and he shoots each Kshatriya again with two arrows.

The encounter swells and arrows stream around Bhishma's chariot so that it becomes like the Devasura yuddha of old. Men that do not fight but only watch, brave men tremble. Bhishma breaks bows with his fusillades, cuts down flagstaffs, severs coats of armours and sloughs off human heads, in thousands.

So light, swift and sure is his hand, so awesome his prowess and skill as he keeps them at bay, that soon the kings around him, their breath taken away, put down their weapons and begin to applaud him. With a quick bow, he turns his chariot and flashes away towards Hastinapura, capital of the Bhaaratas, taking the princesses with him.

Suddenly, the Maharatha Salva roars out a challenge to Bhishma. He thunders towards Bhishma like a great tusker rushing at another and goring it with his tusks for the sake of a cow elephant in heat. Salva wants the princesses for himself and cries, 'Stop and fight!' to Bhishma.

Bhishma, tiger among men, desiccator of enemy armies, blazes up in anger. He knits his great brow, reins in his chariot and, bow in hand, turns to face Salva: for this is Kshatriya dharma. The other kings grow still to watch this duel.

The fight begins, and their roars are like the trumpeting of bull elephants that fight over a cow elephant in season. Salva shoots a hundred thousand arrows at Bhishma, quick as thinking. The other kings are wonderstruck by his archery and shout out their praise.

Infuriated by the yells of the crowd of kings, Bhishma cries to his sarathy, 'Ride at Salva! I will kill him as Garuda does a snake.'

Warding off Salva's cloud of shafts, the peerless Kuru fits the Varunastra to his bowstring, and harries Salva's four horses. And, O tiger among kings, in a flash Bhishma kills Salva's charioteer, while he keeps his enemy's fire at bay. Next moment, Shantanu's son, fighting for the princesses, kills Salva's pedigreed horses with the Aindrastra, Indra's weapon.

He shoots the bow out of Salva's hands and has him in the eye of his arrow, but spares his life. Bhishma turns his chariot round and rides back towards Hastinapura.

Bharatarishabha, the humiliated Salva returns to his kingdom, and rules again, justly. The other Kshatriyas who have come to the swayamvara do the same; they all go home empty-handed, and routed: those that do not die.

Bhishma rides back like the wind, with his three prizes, towards Hastinapura, from where Vichitravirya, prince of dharma, rules the Earth as righteously as his father Shantanu had. Rajan, through many forests rides Bhishma; he fords many rivers, and arrives swiftly.

The son of Ganga who flows into the Ocean, invincible Bhishma comes home to Hastinapura, having killed countless Kshatriyas; and not a scratch on him. He brings the daughters of the king of Kasi to the home of the Kurus, tenderly, as if they are his daughters-in-law, younger sisters, or his own daughters. Bhishma Mahabaho brings the lovely and accomplished princesses to Vichitravirya and offers them to his brother.

Bhishma, knower of dharma, immediately begins to make preparations for a royal wedding. When all is ready and the arrangements have been made by Satyavati and Bhishma, the eldest princess from Kasi, Amba, says smiling shyly, 'Long ago, I gave my heart to Salva, Lord of Saubha, and he too loved me. My father approved of our love and I would have chosen him at the swayamvara. Mighty Bhishma, you know dharma better than anyone. You decide what you must do.'

Bhishma falls thoughtful; he consults the Brahmanas present there, all knowers of the Veda; then he says to Amba, 'Princess, you may do as you please.'

But he marries Ambika and Ambalika to Vichitravirya with every proper ritual. The handsome and youthful Vichitravirya is a virgin, a brahmacharin so far. But when he marries the exquisite princesses of Kasi desire seizes him powerfully.

They are tall, these girls, their soft skin like liquid gold, their tresses thick and curly, their fingernails raised and red, their hips ample and rounded, and their breasts full and their cleavage deep. They bear every auspicious mark upon their ravishing bodies, and those young women of one of the oldest and noblest royal houses see the handsome Vichitravirya as being worthy of themselves in every way, and they love him passionately. For, indeed, he is as strong as a Deva and as handsome as the Aswin twins, and he could steal the heart of any woman.

Seven rapturous years Vichitravirya spends with his two wives. Then, in the prime of his youth, he catches a galloping consumption. Those around him do everything in their power to effect a cure, but the Kuru prince dies, like the sun setting.

Bhishma is stricken. Satyavati and he perform the last rites for the dead prince, solemnly, with many learned priests and all the great Kurus present, all of them shocked."

CANTO 103

SAMBHAVA PARVA CONTINUED

Vaisampayana said, "Grief-stricken herself, having lost her second son, Satyavati performs the funeral rites for Vichitravirya, with her weeping daughters-in-law and the broken-hearted Bhishma, greatest of Kshatriyas. Then, summoning her great woman's strength, she consoles them as best as she can.

When the formal mourning is over, Satyavati thinks of dharma, she recalls the great ancestry of the Kuru line. She calls Bhishma and says, 'Now the pinda, the glory and the future of the line of the great Shantanu of the house of Kuru all depend on you. Just as Swarga and punya are inseparable, as longevity is inseparable from truth and faith, Bhishma and dharma are inseparable.

Virtuous son, you know dharma in theory and in every detail of practice; you know all the Srutis, the Vedas and Vedangas. You are equal to Shukra and Angiras in steadfastness in dharma, in the knowledge of family tradition and customs, and you know that crises require unusual solutions. Therefore, O best of good men, I am relying on you to find a solution to our crisis. You must listen to me and then do as I say. Manavarishabha, your brother Vichitravirya, my son who you loved so much, has left us and gone childless to Swarga, when hardly more than a boy himself.

Your brother's wives, the young and lovely daughters of Kasiraja, want to become mothers. Mahabaho, mighty-armed, I command you to father children in your brother's widows, so that the line of Kuru might have heirs. You must protect dharma from being lost. Crown yourself king now and rule the kingdom of the Bhaaratas. Take a wife and beget sons. Do not let your ancestors' spirits fall into hell.'

Indeed, not only Satyavati but others in the palace, friends and kinsmen, say the same thing to Bhishma Parantapa.

Bhishma replies, 'Mother, what you are asking of me is certainly dharma. But don't you know my vow that I will never beget children? Surely, you have not forgotten the brideprice that your father asked and which I readily gave: my solemn vow.

Satyavati, I will renounce the three worlds, the empire of Swarga, anything that might exceed these, but I will never break my oath, or renounce the truth. The Earth may cease to be fragrant, Water might no longer be wet, Light may not illumine forms anymore, Air might relinquish its nature of touch, the Sun might cease to be glorious, the Moon might stop being cool, Agni might not burn anymore, Akasa might not create sruti, sound, Indra, who slew Vritra, might cease to be strong, Dharma may lose his impartiality, but I cannot abandon the truth or break my vow.'

Satyavati says to Bhishma, 'Bhishma whose strength is dharma, I know that you never swerve from the truth. Why, with your dharma you can create another Swarga, Bhumi and Patala.

Bhishma, I know that you swore your oath on my account. But now you must think of our crisis, and the dharma that you owe your ancestors. Parantapa, scourge of your enemies, you must ensure that the House of Kuru has an heir, that the line of father and son that has come down the ages since the dawn of time is not now broken. You must ensure that our well-wishers and kinsmen do not grieve, that our people do not grieve.'

Desperately, sobbing, she speaks, still pierced through by grief at the loss of her son, and it seems that she urges him to break his vow and dharma, too.

Bhishma says, 'O Queen, do not turn your face from dharma. Do not destroy us all. No Shastra ever tells a Kshatriya to break his solemn oath. Yet, I will tell you what Kshatriya dharma prescribes so that Shantanu's bloodline does not become extinct.

Listen to what I have to say, then consult with your learned and devout Brahmanas, and others who know the remedies that are allowed to alleviate a crisis, and also consider honourable social mores, before deciding what you will do.'"

CANTO 104

SAMBHAVA PARVA CONTINUED

"Bhishma continues, 'In ancient days, wrathful at the death of his father, Jamadagni's son Rama killed the Haihaya king Arjuna with his Parasu, his battle axe. Rama cut off the Haihaya's thousand arms, which no one else could have hoped to do. Not content, he set out in his chariot to conquer the world. Bow in hand, spewing awesome astras, he ranged the Earth to raze the very race of Kshatriyas.

Twenty-one times, single-handedly, he annihilated Kshatriya armies mustered to quell him, that illustrious Bhargava. And when he had indeed killed the last Kshatriya, Kshatriya women across the world resorted to Brahmanas, knowers of the Veda, to have children.

The Vedas say that a son so begotten belongs to the man who marries the woman. The Kshatriya women went to the Brahmanas not from lust but for the sake of dharma. Indeed, the very Kshatriya race was thus revived.

On this subject there is another olden tale, which I will tell you.

In the most antique times, there was a great Rishi called Utathya. His wife was Mamata and he loved her dearly. One day, Utathya's younger brother Tejasvin Brihaspati, Guru to the Devas, importuned Mamata. But she told that most eloquent of the great that she was pregnant by her husband, Brihaspati's elder brother, and that he should not seek to lie with her.

Mamata said, "Illustrious Brihaspati, the child in me has already imbibed the Vedas with their six Angas. How can my womb make space for another child? It does not become you to ask to satisfy your desire in me at this time."

But even the wise Brihaspati could not help himself and sought to thrust himself upon her.

Then the child in her womb spoke to him, "Sire, stop! There is no room here for two, and I am already here. Wise one, do not make me suffer."

Brihaspati would not listen and still sought to have intercourse with Mamata of the most beautiful eyes. He grew enraged to hear what the child said, and cursed his brother's Utathya's son, "You dare speak to me from there at this moment of a pleasure that all creatures crave? I curse you to remain in darkness forever!"

Because of Brihaspati's curse Utathya's child, whose tejas equalled Brihaspati's own, was born blind. He was called Dirghatamas, enveloped in long darkness. Dirghatamas knew the Vedas, and was a true Sage, and though he was blind he married a beautiful Brahmana girl, Pradweshi. He fathered many children upon her, Gautama the eldest. But they were covetous and sinful.

Dirghatamas, master of the Vedas, studied under Saurabhi's son, and began to practise the rituals of that Tantrik order, fearlessly and reverently. The other Munis who lived in the asrama were outraged, seeing sin where none was, for Dirghatamas' heart was pure, as were his intentions.

Those Sages said, "This man has broken every law of dharma. He does not deserve to live among us anymore. Let us cast the sinner out!"

They said worse about Dirghatamas, and then his wife turned on him as well.

Dirghatamas said to Pradweshi, "Why do you also turn against me?"

She replied hotly, "A husband is called the Bhartri because he supports his wife. He is called Pali because he protects her. But you neither support nor protect me, for despite all your tapasya, you are blind and it is I that support and protect you and your children. But from now I will not."

Dirghatamas was annoyed and said to her and her children, "Take me to the Kshatriyas and I will get you wealth."

His wife replied, "I do not want any riches that you get, for that will never make me happy. Brahmana, do what you like; I cannot look after you anymore."

Dirghatamas cried in rage, "I declare that from today all women shall have only one husband for life. Even if he dies, it shall be unlawful for her to take another man. The woman that breaks this law shall be a fallen woman. A woman without a husband shall always be inclined to sin. And even if she is wealthy she will not enjoy her wealth. Calumny and disrepute will darken her life."

Pradweshi screamed to her sons, "Throw him into the Ganga!"

The evil Gautama and his brothers, slaves of greed and folly, said, "Why should we support this old fool?"

They bound the Muni to a raft, cast him to the mercy of the river, and came home with no twinge of conscience. The blind old man floated through the lands of many kings. One day, a king called Bali, a knower of dharma, went to the Ganga to perform his ablutions, when the raft bearing Dirghatamas floated up to him. Bali drew the raft ashore and untied the Sage.

When he learnt who this Rishi was, the virtuous Bali said to him, "Maharishi, I am childless and I beg you to father some children of dharma and wisdom on my queen."

Dirghatamas of great tejas agreed. Bali built an asrama for the Rishi, installed him there and asked his queen Sudeshna to go to him. But when Sudeshna learnt that the Sage was old and blind, she did not go to him herself but sent her sakhi, a maidservant, in her place.

Dirghatamas begot eleven children on that Sudra woman, Kakshivat the eldest. All eleven became masters of the Veda and chanters of the Brahman; all of them possessed great spiritual powers.

One day, King Bali asked Dirghatamas, "Are these my children?"

The Muni replied coldly, "No, they are mine. Your queen Sudeshna saw that I was old and blind and she insulted me by sending me her Sudra maidservant rather than coming to me herself. Kakshivat and his brothers are my sons begotten on the sakhi."

The king pacified Dirghatamas, begging his forgiveness. He sent his queen to the Sage. The Rishi only touched her with his fingers and said, "You will have five sons as glorious as Surya Deva. Call them Anga, Vanga, Kalinga, Pundra and Suhma. The kingdoms they found shall be known by their names."

Thus Bali's lineage was continued by a Maharishi. So, indeed, many great warriors and Maharathas have been born to Kshatriya women by Brahmana fathers.

You know my opinion now, mother; do as you see fit,' says Bhishma to Satyavati."

CANTO 105

SAMBHAVA PARVA CONTINUED

"Bhishma continues, 'Mother, this is how we can continue the royal line of Bhaarata. Let us offer substantial wealth to a great Brahmana Sage and have him father children upon Vichitravirya's wives.'

Now smiling shyly, blushing, Satyavati says, 'Bhaarata, Mahabaho, what you say is true. I, too, have something to tell you in confidence. You are the punya of our House and its dharma, too; you will not refuse what I am going to ask you, when I have told you my secret, which no one else knows.

My father was a man of dharma. For dharma he plied a ferry on the river, to help wayfarers make the crossing. One day, when I was in my early youth, the Maharishi Parasara wanted to cross the river and I was rowing him across.

As we went, suddenly desire seized the Sage and he importuned me, softly. I was afraid of my father, but feared the Rishi's curse more, if I refused him. He blessed me with a rare boon and then I could not refuse him. Parasara covered the river in thick fog, so that my father could not see us anymore and he took his pleasure of me in the boat.

Until that day, my body had always smelled pungently of fish, but Parasara removed the stink and instead gave me the fragrance of heaven spreading on every side for a yojana. He also blessed me that though I would immediately give birth to his son upon an island in the stream, I would have my virginity restored to me.

Bhishma, my son by Parasara Muni has become a great Sage of profound tapasya. For where he was born, he is called Dwaipayana. He has divided the Veda in four to suit our times; he is also called Vyasa, the arranger, or divider. He is dark of complexion and is also known as Krishna.

He is perfectly truthful, free from passion, a mighty Yogin, who has made ashes of all his sins with tapasya. For, he went away with his father as soon as he was born.

If I summon him here, and we both ask him to beget children on Ambika and Ambalika, he will not refuse us. He is a glorious one himself and will sire wonderful sons.

When he left, that day, and he was full-grown as soon as he was born, he said to me, "Mother, think of me if you need me and I will come to you."

If you wish, O Bhishma, I will summon Dwaipayana even now. If you agree, Mahabaho, he will certainly sow his seed in Vichitravirya's field.'

When he hears the Maharishi's name, Bhishma joins his palms together and says, 'The intelligent man regards dharma, artha and kama judiciously. He considers these patiently and carefully, then acts in a manner so that dharma leads to more dharma, artha to further artha, and kama to future kama: virtue, profit and pleasure.

Mother, what you have suggested conforms to dharma and must lead to artha and kama. It is the best course, and you have my complete consent.'

O Kuru, Satyavati now thinks of her son Dwaipayana. The Muni has engaged himself in interpreting the Vedas, but as soon as he senses his mother summoning him, he appears before her in a moment. Satyavati greets her son, embraces him, bathing him in her tears, for the fisherman's daughter has not seen him since he was born.

Maharishi Vyasa sees his mother crying and tenderly washes her tears with cool water. Then, bowing to her, he says, 'I have come, mother, to do your bidding. Tell me what you want that I may satisfy your wish.'

The family priest of the Bhaaratas now worships the Maharishi formally, and Vyasa accepts his offerings, chanting the apposite mantras. Gratified by that adoration, he sits in the high chair offered him.

When he sits, Satyavati makes the customary inquiries about his well-being and his life, then says, 'Most learned one, sons are born through both their mother and their father; they belong equally to both parents. The mother wields as much right and power over her son as his father does.

By law, O Brahmarishi, you are my firstborn, my eldest son; and Vichitravirya is my youngest. Just as Bhishma is Vichitrvirya's brother on his father's side, you are Vichitravirya's brother on his mother's side, and yours.

I am not certain what you will think or say but I am going to tell you what I think and want from you. Shantanu's son Bhishma refuses, because of dharma and his vow that he once swore, either to become king or to beget children. So, out of love for your brother Vichitravirya, in order to continue this royal line come down from Bharata himself, because Bhishma asks you and because I command you as your mother, out of compassion for all the living, for the protection of the people and from the generosity of your heart, sinless one, you must do what I ask.

Your younger brother has left behind two widows of youth, beauty and grace which compare with those of the Devastris. For the sake of dharma and moksha, they want to have children. You are the ideal person to make mothers of them. So, my child, beget sons on Ambika and

Ambalika, sons worthy of this House and worthy to continue the royal lineage of Bhaarata.'

Vyasa listens to this quietly, then says, 'Satyavati, you know what dharma is both in this life and the next. Also, you are devoted to dharma. So, at your command, with dharma as my motive, as well, I will do what you ask.

Indeed, what you ask conforms to Sanatana Dharma, and I will beget sons on my brother's wives, sons who shall be like Mitra and Varuna. I will give them a stern vrata to keep for a year, and then they shall be purified. For no woman who is not pure can come near me, let alone bear my sons.'

Satyavati says, 'Anagha, sinless, do what is needed for the princesses to conceive immediately, for danger threatens. In a kingdom that has no king, the people are destroyed without protection; sacrifices no longer take place; evil holds sway; the clouds send down no rain and the gods vanish. A kingdom without a king is quickly destroyed.

No, my daughters-in-law must conceive at once. Bhishma will watch over the children while they are in their mother's wombs.'

Vyasa says, 'If I am to impregnate my brother's wives unseasonably, then let them bear my ugliness, and that shall be the sorest penance for them. Let the Kosala princess bear my smell, my grim and ugly face, my filthy clothes and my black body, and she will conceive an excellent child.'

Vyasa then says to Satyavati, 'Let her wear clean clothes, put on her ornaments and wait for me in her bedchamber,' and he vanishes before her eyes.

Satyavati goes to her daughter-in-law Ambika, privately, and says to her, 'O Kosala princess, listen to me for what I have to say is dharma. From my ill fortune the race of Bharata has become extinct. Seeing me grieve and faced with the end of his father's line, Bhishma has suggested a solution, which, however, depends on you.

Do this for dharma, my daughter, and resurrect the lost lineage of Bharata. O child of the fair hips, bring forth a child as resplendent as the king of the Devas. Let him inherit the kingdom and bear its heavy burden.'

Ambika demurs at first, when she hears what is being asked of her, but Satyavati insists and finally, with great reluctance and anxiety, the chaste Ambika is persuaded that what she is being asked to do is no violation of dharma. To celebrate, Satyavati feeds Brahmanas, Rishis and numerous other Sadasyas who arrive for the occasion; she feeds them a banquet."

CANTO 106

Sambhava Parva Continued

"Then, Ambika's next period is over. Satyavati bathes her and takes her to the bedchamber. Making her sit upon the luxurious bed, Satyavati says to her daughter-in-law, 'Kosala princess, your husband has an elder brother, my firstborn son. He will come to you tonight and enter your womb as seed. Do not sleep, but wait for him.'

Satyavati leaves and the beautiful princess lies back on the bed. In her mind, she prays to Bhishma and the other elders of the Kuru House. Then Dwaipayana enters that room in which a taper burns. Ambika sees him, dark as a moonless night, with coppery matted jata hanging down to his shoulders, his beard thick and unkempt, his eyes like fire, and with a shiver and a moan of terror Ambika shuts her eyes tightly.

But having given his word to his mother, Dwaipayana takes her, while she lies beneath him trembling and never once opens her eyes. When he has finished he emerges from that chamber and immediately Satyavati accosts him.

Excitedly she demands, 'Will the princess have a great son?'

Vyasa replies, 'He will be as strong as ten thousand elephants. He will be a Rajarishi, of great learning, intellect and energy. He will beget a hundred sons. But because of his mother's sin against me, that she never opened her eyes when I was with her, he will be born blind.'

Dismayed, Satyavati says, 'Muni, how can a blind man become a worthy king of the Kurus? How will he protect his clan and uphold the ancient glory of his father's race? You must give the Kurus another prince, who can be king.'

Vyasa says, 'So be it,' and vanishes. In due time, Ambika gives birth to a blind son, a mighty boy.

Now Satyavati goes to Ambalika, her younger daughter-in-law, and once more tells her what she wants from her – to conceive a child by Vyasa. Securing her consent, Satyavati summons Vyasa again.

Dwaipayana comes again and goes in to Ambalika, who sees him and turns white as a sheet from fright and remains thus. O Bhaarata, Vyasa keeps his word to his mother and sows his seed in Ambalika, too.

But as he is leaving, he says to her, 'Because you turned pale to see my face, your son shall be born pale, an albino with no pigment in his skin. Beautiful princess, your son shall be called Pandu, the pale one.'

With that, he leaves the chamber, that best of Rishis. His mother is waiting for him in the corridor to ask about this child he has fathered. Dwaipayana tells her that he would be white and named Pandu.

Satyavati begs him to father one more son, on Ambika again.

'So be it,' Vyasa Muni gives her his word.

Nine months pass and Ambalika gives birth to a son who is indeed without colour in his skin, a pale child, an albino. Yet he is radiantly handsome and bears every auspicious mark upon his body. Later, he, Pandu, would become the father of those five matchless bowmen, the Pandavas.

Again, when Ambika has just finished her period and is in her fertile time, Sayavati goes to her and says that she must receive Vyasa once more. Ambika, as lovely as a Deva's daughter, remembers how grim and fierce

Vyasa had been; she remembers the strong smell of his body.

She does not go to Vyasa herself, but sends a maid of hers instead. This woman is as beautiful herself as an Apsara and she waits for the Rishi, wearing her mistress' ornaments.

When Vyasa comes in, the maid rises and greets him reverently. She welcomes him and waits on him respectfully and when he calls her to him she does not demur but goes gladly. O King, that stern Rishi is well pleased with her.

When he rises to leave, he says, 'Beautiful, humble one, you will no longer be a slave. Your son will be the most intelligent of men, fortunate, wise, and of unswerving dharma. I, Vyasa, bless you.'

Rajan, that son of Krishna Dwaipayana begotten on a maidservant is Vidura. He is the brother of Dhritarashtra, the eldest, and the illustrious Pandu.

Vidura is free from the bonds of desire and passion; he is a master of the laws of kingship and governance; why, he is Dharma Deva, God of Truth, born on Earth through the curse of the Rishi Mandavya. Emerging from his encounter with Ambika's maid, Vyasa meets Satyavati again and tells her how her daughter-in-law has deceived her, and that he has begotten a son in the Sudra woman whom the princess sent to him.

Then Vyasa vanishes before her eyes, just as he had come. Thus, in Vichitravirya's field, his elder brother Dwaipayana sows his seed, and from him are born sons as splendid as children of Heaven, to continue the race of Kuru."

CANTO 107

Sambhava Parva Continued

Janamejaya asked, "What did Dharma Deva do that he was cursed? Who is the Rishi who cursed him to be born a Sudra?"

Vaisampayana said, "There was a Brahmana calls Mandavya. He knew dharma and devoted himself to truth and tapasya. The Maharishi sat under a tree just outside his asrama, his arms raised skyward and keeping a vow of silence.

For years he sat thus, when one day a band of thieves, laden with booty, arrived in his hermitage. Bharatarishabha, some of the king's soldiers were hot on the heels of those thieves and in panic they ran into Mandavya's asrama and hid there.

Almost immediately, the pursuers arrived and saw the Rishi under his tree.

They asked him, 'O Muni, which way did the thieves go? Show us before they escape.'

Rajan, the Rishi made no response at all. The soldiers entered the asrama and discovered the robbers with their plunder. Now the king's men suspected the Sage as well, and seized him and brought Mandavya before the king. The king sentenced him to be executed with the thieves.

The king's men impaled the renowned Muni with the bandits, and gave the king the gold they had recovered. Though impaled on a stake, and given neither food nor drink, the Rishi Mandavya did not die.

With his tapasya shakti, his ascetic power, he summoned other Rishis to him. They came at night as birds, and saw him impaled but deep in dhyana. The Sages were grief-stricken.

They spoke to Mandavya, telling him who they were. They asked, 'Brahmana, tell us what sin you committed that you are suffering this dreadful torture.'"

CANTO 108

Sambhava Parva Continued

Vaisampayana said, "That tiger among Munis answered those Rishis rich in tapasya, 'Who shall I blame for this? Only myself.'

Hearing him speak after being impaled for so long, the king's soldiers rushed to tell the king about the miracle. Now the king consulted his ministers and realised his folly: that he had impaled a true Sage. He ran to where the stake was planted and began to pacify the Rishi who hung on it.

The king said, 'O Mahamuni, I have done you great harm in my ignorance. I beg you, forgive me. I beg you do not be angry.'

Mandavya was pacified. When the king saw anger ebb from the Sage's face, he had the stake taken down and attempted to remove it from the Rishi's body. But he could not, so he cut it off where it entered the Sage's person; and that greatest of Rishis continued his life with a portion of the stake inside him. He walked, performed the most rigorous tapasya, and attained countless lofty realms that others could not dream of.

For the portion of the stake that remained inside his body, he became known through the three worlds as Ani Mandavya: Mandavya with the stake within.

One day, that Brahmana who knew the highest dharma went to the home of Dharma Deva, God of Justice. Seeing Dharma upon his lofty throne, the Rishi asked reproachfully, 'Tell me what sin I have committed that I am punished like this. Tell me now, and behold my tapasya shakti!'

Dharma Deva replied, 'Once you impaled a little insect on a blade of grass; this is your payment for that sin. O Rishi, just as daana, charity, however small, bears great fruit, multiplied many times over, so does paapa, sin, bring pain in its wake, inexorably.'

Ani Mandavya asked, 'Tell me when I committed this sin because I cannot remember.'

Said Dharma, 'When you were a child.'

The Rishi said, 'The Shastras do not recognise any sin done by a child until his twelfth year. The punishment you have inflicted on me is unjust, out of all proportion.

Dharma Deva, Brahmahatya, killing a Brahmana, is a sin greater than killing any other living being. You have committed Brahmahatya, O God of Justice, and for that you shall be born as a Sudra in the world!

Also, from today I declare that no sin committed by a child below fourteen years shall be any sin or punishable, but only by those above fourteen.'

Cursed by that illumined Rishi, Dharma Deva is born as Vidura to a Sudra mother. Vidura is learned indeed, with an uncanny knowledge of dharma, of politics, and of artha too. He is absolutely without greed and anger. Having deep foresight and an imperturbable mind, he is always selflessly devoted to the welfare of the House of Kuru."

CANTO 109

Sambhava Parva Continued

Vaisampayana said, "When those three children are born, Kurujungala, Kurukshetra, knows untold prosperity. The Earth yields unprecedented harvests, and the bountiful crops are all uncommonly flavoursome. The clouds bring rains in season, and the trees bring forth flowers and fruit. Draught cattle are contented and the wild birds and beasts, too, are full of delight.

Flowers are fragrant and fruit sweet; merchants, artisans, traders and artists of every kind teem in towns and cities, and thrive. The people are all brave, learned, honest and happy. There are no robbers then, nor does anyone sin. It seems as if a Satya Yuga, a golden age, permeates every corner of the kingdom.

The people are devout, truthful, follow dharma, perform yagnas, are generous and charitable, and full of love for one another; and they prosper. They are free from pride, anger and greed; they are pure-hearted and find delight in natural and innocent things.

Hastinapura, capital of the Kurus, is another Amaravati, as full of beauty and joy as the sea is with water. Hundreds of great palaces and mansions line its wide avenues and highways; its lofty gates and archways are dark as clouds.

Elsewhere in the kingdom, the people swim and frolic in rivers, lakes and tanks; they roam and sport in charmed forests and airy woods. The southern Kurus, in virtuous rivalry with their northern kinsmen, keep company with Siddhas, Charanas and Rishis.

Throughout the blessed kingdom, no Kuru man is miserly and no woman a widow. The wells and lakes are always full of sweet water; the forests are rich with wonderful trees; the homes of Brahmanas are full of riches, and life is a constant and joyful celebration.

O King, Bhishma rules the kingdom with dharma and he covers it with hundreds of yupastambas, sacrificial posts. Indeed Bhishma's rule brings such contentment to the Kuru kingdom that people from other kingdoms migrate to Kuru lands, swelling the population.

And the people all watch the three splendid young Kuru princes grow and are full of hope for the future, as well. O Rajan, in the homes of the Kuru nobility you could always hear the words *give* and *come eat with us*.

From their very births, Bhishma raises Dhritarashtra, Pandu and the exceptionally intelligent Vidura like his own sons. With every prescribed and successive ritual of their varna being performed timely for them, the princes devote themselves to vratas and study.

They grow into truly exceptional youths, versed in the Vedas and skilled at all sports. They become excellent bowmen, horsemen, mace-fighters, swordsmen, elephant warriors, and deep scholars of dharma. They know Itihasa, the Puranas and all the arts and sciences. They know the great truths and wisdom enshrined in the Vedas and the Vedangas; their education is profound and extensive.

Pandu is soon the best of all archers, while Dhritarashtra is the strongest man; and no one is Vidura's equal in his knowledge of and devotion to dharma, to virtue and morality. Seeing the extinct line of Shantanu restored, people the world over begin to say that, among mothers of Kshatriyas, the princesses of Kasi are foremost; of kingdoms Kurujungala is the best; of men of dharma Vidura is the finest; and of cities Hastinapura has no rival.

Dhritarashtra is blind and Vidura is the son of a Sudra woman, so Pandu becomes king. One day Bhishma, first among those that know the Rajaneeti, the code of kings, as well as the laws of dharma, calls Vidura, wise in matters of the spirit himself."

CANTO 110

SAMBHAVA PARVA CONTINUED

"Bhishma says, 'Ours is an ancient and glorious royal line, shining through the ages with the lustre of countless magnificent kings of dharma. The enlightened Krishna Dwaipayana, Satyavati and I myself have raised you three princes, so that the royal lineage of Kuru does not become extinct.

You and I must see to it, my wise Vidura, that our dynasty grows again and expands like the very sea. I have heard that there are three princesses worthy of being married into our house. The first is the daughter of Surasena of the Yadavas; the second is Subala's daughter, the Gandhara princess; and the third is the princess of Madra.

My son, all three are of the purest descent, beautiful and accomplished as well; truly, they are fit to marry into our royal house. Most intelligent child, I feel that we should make these princesses and no others our daughters-in-law, to continue our race. But tell me what you think, Vidura.'

Vidura replies, 'You are our father and our mother, as well. You are our Guru. Do whatever you think is best for us.'

Soon after this, Bhishma hears from some Brahmanas that Subala's lovely daughter Gandhari has worshipped Lord Siva, and Hara has granted her a boon that she would have a hundred sons. Bhishma, the Kuru patriarch, immediately sends his messengers to the Gandhara king, asking for his daughter's hand for Dhritarashtra.

At first, King Subala is reluctant because Dhritarashtra is blind. However, when he thinks of the prince's ancestry, and the majesty and dharma of the House of Kuru, he agrees to give his devout daughter to become Dhritarashtra's wife.

When the chaste and deeply religious Gandhari hears that her husband to be is blind, she puts on a blindfold to share her husband's disability, which she would never remove until the very end of her life.

Subala's son Shakuni brings his beautiful sister, in the flower of her youth, to Hastinapura and formally gives her away to Dhritarashtra. Under Bhishma's watchful and loving eye, Gandhari is received with great honour, and the wedding ceremony is conducted with great pomp and celebration.

The valiant Shakuni brings a fine dowry for his sister, and many costly garments and ornaments, and Bhishma welcomes him with respect. When the marriage has been solemnised, he returns to his own city.

O Scion of the Bharatas, the beautiful Gandhari pleases all the Kurus with her demeanour, her affection and her reverent attention to her elders. She is a perfectly devoted wife, so chaste that she never so much as speaks another man's name or refers to an elder by their name."

CANTO 111

SAMBHAVA PARVA CONTINUED

Vaisampayana continued, "There is a Yadava chieftain called Sura; he is Vasudeva's father. He has a daughter called Pritha who is the most beautiful young woman on Earth. O Bhaarata, the honest Sura gives this firstborn child of his to his childless cousin, his father's sister's son Kuntibhoja, whom he loves and to whom he has promised his first child.

In the palace of her foster-father, where she is called Kunti because Kuntibhoja so dotes on her, Pritha has charge of the household, especially of looking after visiting Brahmanas and other guests.

Once, the dreaded Durvasa Muni, famed as much for his quick and fierce temper as his spiritual greatness and profound knowledge of the recondite aspects of dharma, comes to visit Kuntibhoja. Pritha looks after him so well and worshipfully that the great Sage, who indeed has clear foreknowledge of the curse that Pandu would one day incur in the forest, teaches her a mantra by which she can summon any Deva she chooses to give her children.

Durvasa says, 'Any Deva you summon shall come and give you children.'

After the Rishi leaves, curiosity gets the better of Kunti. One day, she says the mantra thinking of Arka: Surya Deva, the Sun God. As soon as she says the secret words, the refulgent deity, witness of the world, appears before her.

That exquisite princess, no flaw in her features, is awe-stricken. The Sun God Vivaswat comes near her and says, 'Black eyes, here I am, now say what you want from me.'

Trembling, Kunti says, 'O bane of your enemies, a Rishi taught me this mantra as a boon. Lord, I was curious and said it only to see if it actually worked. I beg your forgiveness; my lord, whatever her offence a woman must always be forgiven.'

Surya replies, 'I know that Durvasa gave you this boon. But sweet, shy girl, do not be afraid and come to me. Lovely woman, you cannot summon a Deva in vain; my coming must bear fruit. You have called me and if it is for nothing, you shall incur sin for sure.'

Vivaswat says many sweet things to her, but, O Bhaarata, she would not go to him out of modesty and fear of her family.

Bharatarishabha, blazing Akra says again, 'Princess you will not sin if you come to me, for I desire you.'

Then he would not be resisted anymore, and the irradiant Tapana, who illumines the Universe, has his way with Kuntibhoja's delicate daughter. From their union, immediately, is born a splendorous son, clad in natural golden armour and earrings, who would become renowned throughout the world as Karna.

Karna is to be the greatest of all warriors, blessed with fortune and as handsome as a Deva child. As soon as he is born, the lustrous Tapana restores her virginity to Pritha and vanishes back into Devaloka.

Now the Vrishni princess despairs that she has borne an illegitimate son and begins to think feverishly about what she should do. Out of her fear of her relatives and her father, and the censure of the world, she decides to keep her folly secret. She floats her divine child of supernatural prowess down the river in a wooden box.

A famous Suta, whose wife is Radha, sees the shining infant floating upon the current and brings him home to his wife. The couple looks at his golden kavacha and kundala in wonderment, and names him Vasusena: he who is born with wealth.

Blessed with prodigious strength and genius, as he grows, he becomes expert at wielding weapons of every kind. Owning terrific energy, he would worship the Sun from dawn to high noon, until his back is hot from the rays of Arka. During the hours of his worship, there is nothing on Earth that the valiant and brilliant Vasusena would not grant as a boon to any Brahmana who asks him for one.

One day, knowing that this magnificent warrior could kill his son Arjuna, Phalguni, Indra comes to Vasusena during his time of worship. Indra comes as a Brahmana and asks for Vasusena's kavacha, the golden armour with which he has been born: as alms. Vasusena folds his hands reverently, cuts the armour from his body and gives it to Indra. The king of the Devas is so moved by the generosity and the truth of Karna that he, in turn, gives Vasusena an irresistible weapon, a shakti.

Indra says, 'This shakti of mine will kill any Deva, Asura, Manava, Gandharva, Naga or Rakshasa, anyone at all that you use it against. But it will kill just one enemy and then return to me forever.'

Until that day, Surya's son has been called only Vasusena, but when he cuts the natural kavacha from his body and gives it to Indra, he becomes Karna, he who cut the armour from himself."

CANTO 112

SAMBHAVA PARVA CONTINUED

Vaisampayana said, "Kuntibhoja's daughter, Pritha of the large eyes, is not only exquisite, she is a most accomplished and capable young woman. She is virtuous, youthful, and possesses every desirable feminine quality. Yet, strangely, no Kshatriya comes to ask for her hand.

Kuntibhoja arranges a swayamvara for his princess, and invites kings and princes from across the length and breadth of Bharatavarsha to attend it. As soon as she enters the arena where her hopeful suitors have gathered, her eyes sees just one of them – Pandu, king of the Bhaaratas, tiger among kings.

She sees him regal as a lion, his chest wide, eyes like a bull's, rippling with tremendous strength, making all the other kings seem plain beside him, for he is as magnificent as Indra. Kuntibhoja's lovely daughter, no trace of any flaw among her features, trembles to look at Pandu. It is as if the sight of him pierces her through.

Going forward shyly, her head bent, her hands quivering with powerful emotion, she drapes the garland of flowers in her hand around Pandu's neck. When the other kings see Kunti choose Pandu, they return to their kingdoms as they had come, on elephants, horses, and in chariots. When the others have gone, Kuntibhoja has the wedding ceremony performed. O King, the Kuru prince blessed with great fortune and the daughter of Kuntibhoja are as radiant a couple as Maghavat and Paulomi, Indra and his queen Sachi.

Best of Kuru kings, when the wedding ceremonies are over, Kuntibhoja gives his son-in-law great wealth and sends the couple back to Hastinapura. The Kuru prince Pandu returns triumphantly to his capital, with his vast army holding aloft and waving bright and colourful flags and banners, with Brahmanas singing his praises, and Maharishis chanting benedictions.

Entering his palace, Pandu ensconces his queen therein."

CANTO 113

SAMBHAVA PARVA CONTINUED

Vaisampayana continued, "A while later, Bhishma wants Pandu to marry a second wife. Taking an army, with elephants, horses, chariots and footsoldiers, taking court elders, Brahmanas and great Rishis with him, he goes to the capital of the king of Madra.

When the bull of the Balhikas, the Madra king, hears of Bhishma's arrival, he comes out of his city gates to receive him. Welcoming him reverentially, he brings the great Kuru into his palace, where he offers him a chaste white carpet to sit upon, padya, water to wash his feet, arghya; and he pays him every customary and formal homage.

Later, when they sit together at their ease, the king asks Bhishma why he has come. Bhishma, supporter of the honour of the Kurus, says to that king, 'Parantapa, I have come seeking the hand of a princess. We have heard that you have a sister called Madri, blessed with great beauty and every virtue, as well. I want my brother Pandu to marry her.

O King, you are perfectly worthy of an alliance with us, as are we with you. Consider this, and accept my proposal.'

The sovereign of Madra replies, 'To my mind, there is no other royal family on Earth with whom I can enter into an alliance. But in our family we have a custom, which all my ancestors observed, for good or bad. I cannot break the tradition, which is a well-known one and no doubt you are familiar with it. Bhishma, it is not apposite that you just say to me, *Give me your sister.*

You know the custom of which I speak, and that is our family tradition. For us that is dharma, and we must preserve it. This is the only reason why, Parantapa, I cannot accede unconditionally to your request.'

Bhishma says, 'The custom to which you allude is certainly dharma. Why, Brahma himself has said so. Your ancestors upheld the tradition, and no fault can be found with it. It is established, O Salya, that the tradition relating to family honour finds approval with the Sages and all the virtuous.'

And Bhishma, of blazing tejas, gives Salya gold beyond count, coined and uncoined, jewels of every hue in thousands, numberless elephants, horses and chariots, rich cloths and incomparable ornaments, yes, great pearls and resonant corals from the sea as well.

Salya receives these priceless gifts joyfully, and then gives his sister, wearing rich silk and jewellery past compare, to that bull of the House of Kuru. The sage Bhishma, son of the ocean-going Ganga, delightedly takes Madri back to Hastinapura, the city named for the elephant.

There, on an auspicious day and time, chosen by the Brahmana astrologers, King Pandu marries the princess Madri. When the wedding ceremony is concluded, the Kuru king installs his second wife in regal apartments.

Rajadhiraja, Pandu then enjoys his two lovely wives, why, unto the very limits of his desire. When thirty days have passed, Pandu goes forth from Hastinapura to conquer the world.

He prostrates himself before Bhishma and the other elders of the Kuru clan, bids fond farewell to Dhritarashtra and to every other member of the family. With their blessings and leave, he sets out on his grand campaign, taking with him an immense force of elephants, horses and chariots. He goes well pleased by the blessings chanted over him and the auspicious rituals performed for his success by the priests and the people.

Taking an awesome army with him, Pandu goes forth against myriad enemies. That tiger among men, who is to spread the fame of the Kurus across the world, first subdues the bandit tribes of Asarna. He next turns his army of countless elephants, horsemen, footsoldiers and charioteers, flying standards of many brilliant colours, against Dhirga, haughty king of Magadha, who has given offence to more kings than a few.

Pandu attacks his capital and slays him. The Kuru empties Dhirga's treasury, takes all his chariots and other vehicles, and his numberless beasts of burden.

Pandu next marches to Mithila and subjugates the Videhas. Then, Manavarishabha, he leads his army against Kasi, Sumbha, and Pundra, and by his prowess spreads the fame and empire of the Kurus.

Indeed, Pandu Parantapa is like some great conflagration sweeping across the Earth, its flames his arrows, its lustre the weapons of his legions, and consuming every king and Kshatriya who dares stand against him. Those whom he vanquishes, along with their armies, become vassals of the Kurus.

Finally, every king is subdued and they all look upon Pandu as the Devas do Indra in Heaven. With folded hands, they pay him homage and bring him tribute of every rare kind: jewels and gold, pearls and corals from ocean deeps, silver and superior kine, exceptional steeds, chariots and great war elephants, donkeys, camels and buffaloes, goats and sheep, beautiful blankets and hides, and furs.

The king of Hastinapura takes these offerings and returns to his capital, to the delight of his people. Joyfully, the citizens and the noblemen all now say, 'The fame and achievements of the great Shantanu, tiger among kings, and indeed of Rajarishi Bharata were about to be extinguished. But Pandu has restored them; indeed, he has swelled the glory of the House of Kuru. He has crushed those that steal land and wealth from us, and they now pay him tribute.'

When Pandu returns from his expedition, Bhishma and all the people of Hastinapura come out of the city to receive him. They have not gone far, when they see the king's servitors laden with the extravagant spoils of war—a train of every kind of conveyance, bearing wealth of every sort, elephants, horses, bullocks, camels and other beasts of burden—a train so long that they cannot see its end.

Then Pandu sees Bhishma and comes to prostrate himself at the patriarch's feet; he greets every other elder and citizen according to their status. Bhishma embraces Pandu, who is like a son to him, in great joy, for has he not ground the enemies of the Kurus underfoot? Bhishma weeps for joy.

Finally, borne upon a veritable tide of joy, Pandu enters Hastinapura triumphantly, to a resounding flourish of trumpets, conches and kettle-drums."

CANTO 114

Sambhava Parva Continued

Vaisampayana said, "Then, at Dhritarashtra's command, Pandu offers the spoils of his conquests to Bhishma, to Satyavati, and to Ambika and Ambalika. He gives some of the wealth to Vidura, as well as his other kinsmen. All these are well pleased with him, and his great prowess. Especially his mother Ambalika is beside herself for joy, and embraces her peerless son, with delight equal to that of Sachi when she embraced Jayanta. Using the wealth that Pandu won, Dhritarashtra[6]* performs five Mahayagnas that are like a hundred great Aswamedhas; the offerings made to the Brahmanas during these sacrifices are counted in hundreds and thousands, be it gold, jewels or sacred cows.

Soon after, O Bharatarishabha, the triumphant Pandu goes into the forest with his wives Kunti and Madri. He leaves the luxury of his palace, with its soft beds, and devotes himself assiduously to the hunt. He begins living in a charmed jungle of great sala trees, on the

---

[6]There seems to be some ambiguity about who was, in fact, the king, Pandu or Dhritarashtra.

southern foothills of the Himalaya, and ranges that forest in complete abandon.

The handsome Pandu roams those pristine jungles with his two wives quite like Airavata with two she-elephants, grandly. The forest-dwellers see the magnificent Bhaarata prince, with his sword, his bow and arrows, his gleaming armour, with Kunti and Madri, and they feel certain that he is a Deva come amongst them.

At Dhritarashtra's command, his servants keep busy seeing that Pandu is supplied with everything he needs for his pleasure in the wilderness.

Meanwhile, Bhishma hears that King Devaka has a young and exquisite daughter by a Sudra wife. Bhishma fetches her from her father's home and marries her to the wise Vidura. Vidura begets many children upon her, all as virtuous and accomplished as himself."

CANTO 115

SAMBHAVA PARVA CONTINUED

Vaisampayana said, "O Janamejaya, Dhritarashtra fathers a hundred sons on Gandhari, and another son upon a Vaisya wife. Pandu has five sons by Kunti and Madri, all of them Maharathas, their natural fathers being Devas, invoked by Kunti to continue the Kuru lineage."

Janamejaya said, "Dvijottama, how did Gandhari give birth to a hundred sons? How many years did this take her? How long were they destined to live? Tell us how Dhritarashtra begot his son upon a Vaisya woman. How did Dhritarashtra treat his loving, always obedient, and chaste queen Gandhari?

Tell us in detail how Pandu had five sons, the Maharathas, even after the Maharishi, whom he kills, cursed him. Ah, I am still athirst to hear everything about my sires."

Vaisampayana said, "One day, Dwaipayana comes to Hastinapura, tired and hungry. Gandhari lavishes her reverential hospitality upon him, and well pleased, the Rishi grants her the boon she wants from him:

that she will bear a hundred sons, each one as strong and accomplished as Dhritarashtra.

Soon after, Gandhari conceives and she carries the great burden in her womb for two years, but does not deliver. She is in anguish and pain, when she hears that Kunti has borne a son who is as radiant as the morning Sun.

Demented by the news, especially after her long discomfort, Gandhari strikes herself in the belly, violently, without Dhritarashtra knowing. At once, she is delivered of a single mass of flesh, hard as a ball of iron. She is about to have it cast away, when Dwaipayana arrives there, having intuited what has happened.

That Maharishi sees the solid ball of flesh and cries to Subala's daughter, 'What did you do?'

Gandhari does not lie, but says, 'I heard that Kunti has borne a son as splendid as Surya Deva, and struck my womb in grief. O Muni, you said that I would have a hundred sons but all I have is this lump of flesh.'

Vyasa says, 'Gandhari, my words shall never prove false; no falsehood has ever left my lips, even in jest. Have a hundred pots full of ghee fetched at once. Meanwhile, let the lump of flesh be sprinkled with cool water.'

When the lump of flesh is sprinkled with cool water, Vyasa divides it into a hundred shreds and one, each about the size of a thumb. The Rishi has each bit placed in a separate pot of ghee, in a secret chamber, tightly sealed and carefully guarded. Vyasa says to Gandhari that the seals should be broken only after a full two years.

With that, the enlightened Dwaipayana goes away to the Himalaya, to perform tapasya.

When the time comes, first of all, Duryodhana is born from a piece of flesh slightly larger than the others in the hundred pots of ghee. Thus, Yudhishtira is the eldest in his generation. News of the haughty Duryodhana's birth comes to Bhishma and Vidura. It is on the same day that, in the forest, Bhima Mahabaho of immeasurable strength is born.

As soon as Duryodhana is born, he begins to cry horribly: he brays like a donkey. At these unnatural sounds, every donkey, vulture, jackal and crow for yojanas around, answer his weird cries in evil cacophony. Violent winds blow everywhere, crookedly, and dreadful fires spume up from the very Earth all across the land.

Terrified, King Dhritarashtra summons Bhishma, Vidura and other friends and ministers. He calls all the great Kurus and their countless Brahmanas and says to them, 'Pandu's eldest son Yudhishtira is the heir to our line, for he is born first. I have no argument with this, but will my son Duryodhana, born next, succeed Yudhishtira as king? I want to know what is dharma in this matter.'

No sooner has he spoken, O Bhaarata, than the wild cacophony of hideous cries by jackals and other predators and scavengers, every fell creature of night, resounds all around; ominously they howl.

Hearing and seeing the macabre omens, the Brahmanas and the wise Vidura say, 'Rajan, Narapumgava, the omens at his birth all cry aloud that your eldest son shall be the nemesis of your race. If we are to prosper, no, even survive, you must kill him now. You will still have ninety-nine sons after his death.

But if you let him live, calamity will strike the House of Kuru, why, the very Earth. O Bhaarata, if you wish for the welfare of your ancient race and the world, abandon this child, do away with him.

O King, it has been said that an individual should be sacrificed for the sake of a family; a family for the sake of a village; a village for the sake of a country; and the very Earth for the sake of the Atman, the Soul.'

But from his love for his firstborn son, Dhritarashtra cannot bring himself to do what Vidura and the Brahmanas ask of him. In a month's time, a hundred sons are born to Dhritarashtra from the hundred pots of ghee; and the hundred and first is a daughter.

During the second year of Gandhari's long pregnancy a Vaisya maidservant of hers would attend on Dhritarashtra. Dhritarashtra sires a son on her, a boy of great intelligence called Yuyutsu.

Thus the wise Dhritarashtra has a hundred sons, all heroic Maharathas, and a daughter, all by Gandhari, and Yuyutsu, tejasvin, by a Vaisya woman."

CANTO 116

SAMBHAVA PARVA CONTINUED

Janamejaya said, 'Sinless, you have told me in some detail about the Rishi's boon, which led to the birth of the hundred sons of Dhritarashtra. But you have not said anything about how his daughter comes to be born, saying only that beyond the hundred, he has Yuyutsu by a Vaisya woman and a daughter. Maharishi Vyasa, of measureless energy, said to the Gandhara king's daughter that she would have a hundred sons; illumined one, now you say that she also has another child, a daughter. If the lump of flesh was divided only into a hundred parts, and if Gandhari did not conceive again, how was Duhsala born? O Rishi, I am curious, tell me how this happened."

Vaisampayana said, 'O Scion of the Pandavas, your question is well asked and I will answer it. The illustrious Dwaipayana sprinkles cool water over the hard lump of flesh and begins to divide it in a hundred pieces; as he does this, the midwife takes each portion and places it in a pot of ghee.

Even as this is being done, Gandhari feels the desire for a daughter and thinks, 'I will surely have a hundred sons from the Rishi's boon, but how wonderful if I also had a daughter younger than the hundred. Why, then my husband would attain to the realms that are conferred by the birth of a daughter's sons. Besides, a mother-in-law has a special love for her son-in-law. Ah, if I have one daughter after my hundred sons, my joy will be complete.'

She made a fervent wish, 'If I have ever done tapasya, if I have given charity, if I have performed homa through Brahmanas, if I have revered and served my elders, then let me have a daughter as well!'

Meanwhile, Dwaipayana continues dividing the lump of flesh. Finally, finishing, he says to Gandhari, 'Here are your hundred sons; I, Vyasa, did not lie to you. However, there is a hundred and first part, smaller than the others, which shall bless you with a daughter and her sons. Yes, she will be a charming and fortunate girl.'

The Sage has a hundred and first pot of ghee fetched and immerses the last shred of flesh in his hands in it. From it, O Bhaarata, in time, Duhsala is born. Now tell me what you want to hear next."

CANTO 117

Sambhava Parva Continued

Janamejaya said, "I beg you, recite the names of Dhritarashtra's sons in the order of their birth."

Vaisampayana said, "Duryodhana, Yuyutsu, Dushasana, Duhsaha, Duhssala, Jalasandha, Sama, Saha, Vinda, Anuvinda, Durdharsha, Subahu, Dushpradharshana, Durmarshana, Durmukha, Dushkarna, Karna, Vivimsati, Vikarna, Sala, Satwa, Sulochana, Chitra, Upachitra, Chitraksha, Charuchitra, Sarasana, Durmada, Durvigaha, Vivitsu, Vilatanana, Urnanabha, Sunabha, Nandaka, Upanandaka, Chitravana, Chitravarman, Suvarman, Durvimochana, Ayobahu, Mahabahu, Chitranga, Chitrakundala, Bhimavega, Bhimabala, Balaki, Balavardhana, Ugrayudha, Bhima, Kanakaya, Dridhayudha, Dridhavarman, Dridhakshatra, Somakitri, Anudara, Dridhasandha, Jarasandha, Satyasandha, Sada, Suvak, Ugrasravas, Ugrasena, Senani, Dushparajaya, Aparajita, Kundasayin, Visalaksha, Duradhara, Dridhahasta, Suhasta, Vatavega, Suvarchas, Adityaketu, Vahvashin, Nagadatta, Agrayayin, Kavachin, Krathana, Kunda, Kundadhara, Dhanurdhara, Ugra,

Bhimaratha, Virabahu, Alolupa, Abhaya, Raudrakarman, Dridharatha, Anadhrishya, Kundabhedin, Viravi, Dhirghalochana, Pramatha, Pramathi, Dhirgharoma, Dirghabahu, Vyudhoru, Kanakadhvaja, Kundasi and Virajas.

And then there is the daughter Duhsala. All hundred are heroes, Atirathas, and great warriors. All of them know the Vedas, and are masters of astras and every other kind of weapon.

Rajan, in due course, suitable wives are chosen for them, with the utmost care. And when his daughter Duhsala comes of age, Dhritarashtra gives her to be the wife of Jayadratha, the king of Sindhu."

CANTO 118

Sambhava Parva Continued

Janamejaya said, "O Chanter of Brahman, you have told us all about the exceptional births of Dhritarashtra's sons, through the boon of Dwaipayana. You have also told us their names, in the order of their births. Indeed, Brahmana, all this we have heard, but now tell me about the sons of Pandu.

When you narrated the incarnations of the Devas, the Asuras and other unearthly beings into the world, you said that the Pandavas were the most illustrious, powerful as the Devas, and indeed amsas of the gods themselves. I want to hear everything about these extraordinary princes, from the beginning, the moments of their births. O Vaisampayana, tell us about their glorious achievements."

Vaisampayana said, "O King, one day Pandu ranges through the forests on the southern slopes of Himavat, which teem with both deer and predators, when he sees a great stag, seemingly the leader of his herd, in the act of mounting his hind. As soon as he sees them the Kshatriya strikes them with five arrows, plumed with golden feathers.

Rajan, of course it is no stag but the son of a Rishi of profound tapasya, who assumed the form of a deer to enjoy his wife. Shot through by Pandu in the very act of coition, he falls onto the ground crying out in a human voice; bitterly he laments and sobs.

The deer says to Pandu, 'Kshatriya, even men that are slaves to lust and anger, and always sinning, do not commit such a savage crime. You, O Bhaarata, are the scion of a great house of dharma. How have you allowed passion and wrath to sway you, and make you lose your reason that you have done this dreadful thing?'

Pandu replies, 'Mriga, O Deer, Kshatriyas are ruled by the same impulse when they slay deer that rules them when they kill their enemies. You must not blame me for what I did; it is my innate nature. We kill animals of your species openly or from hiding; and this is the way of kings, of yore.

Of old, when he performed a Mahayagna, the Rishi Agastya hunted every deer in the forest and offered them to the Devas as part of his sacrifice. It is he that sanctioned the slaying of your kind; then why do you blame me now? For his most special sacrifices Agastya always uses the fat of deer, to perform the homa.'

The deer says, 'King, men do not loose their arrows at unprepared enemies, but only after declaring themselves. Such killing is not censured.'

Pandu says, 'But deer are killed openly or by stealth. Why do you blame me for what I did?'

The deer says, 'Shura, I do not blame you for killing a deer, nor even for the pain you have caused me. But you killed me while I was mating; you should have waited until I had finished. Which wise man of dharma will kill a deer while it mates? Coition is an intense pleasure for every species, and brings goodness to all.

Kshatriya, I was in the very act of satisfying my desire with my mate, and you have killed me before I finished. O King of the Kurus, you are a scion in the line of Pururavas, a house known for its dharma; what you have done is unworthy of you and your race.

Bhaarata, what you have done is despicable, vile, cruel and sinful in the extreme, and deserves to be punished with hell. You know the pleasures of sexual intercourse; you know the dictates of dharma. Why, you are like a Deva, and this does not become you.

Best of kings, it is your Kshatriya dharma to punish anyone who is cruel and sinful, anyone who abandons dharma, artha and kama, as they are laid down in the Shastras. Manavottama, what have you done by killing me, who gave you no offence? Raja, I am a Muni living on roots and fruit, though I have assumed this form of a deer. I lived peacefully in this forest, giving no offence to any living creature, rather, in harmony with all.

Yet you have killed me and I will curse you for it. I curse you Kshatriya, that for your savagery towards a mating couple, you will die as soon as you indulge your own desire. I am the Muni Kindama of great tapasya. I was mating as a deer because I felt bashful to have intercourse in human form in this forest where other Rishis abound. I often roam deep in this forest in the company of other deer.

You slew me without knowing that I am a Brahmana, so the sin of Brahmahatya shall not cling to you. But, O witless man, because you have killed me while I mated with my wife your fate shall be the same. When desire next takes you to your wife and you join with her, as I have with mine, you will leave your body and enter the world of spirits. And your wife, with whom you are having intercourse, will follow you out of this world, out of her love and adoration, to the realm of Yama.

You brought me anguish when I was in transport; grief will visit you when you are in ecstasy.'

With this curse, the deer breathes its last, and Pandu stands stricken, staring at the corpses."

CANTO 119

SAMBHAVA PARVA CONTINUED

Vaisampayana said, "Long and bitterly Pandu and his wives grieve over the deer.

Pandu cries, 'Ah, even if they are born into pure and noble families evil men are quickly brought to grief by their own sins, for their passions delude them into sinning violently. I have heard that, though he was the son of the noble Shantanu, Vichitravirya died young because he had become a slave to his lust.

In the soil of the lustful Vichitravirya the enlightened Muni Krishna Dwaipayana, who has never told a lie, begot me. Though I am the natural son of such a Mahatman, my heart is evil: look at me, ranging the forest, daily killing innocent deer. Oh, the gods have forsaken me, and I mean to seek my redemption, mukti.

The great obstacles on the path to salvation are the desire to father children, as well as other mundane attachments and concerns. I mean to swear a vow of brahmacharya and follow in my natural father's immortal footsteps. I will perform stern tapasya and bring my lust and every other passion under control.

I will abandon my wives and the rest of my kin, shave my head, and wander the Earth alone as a Bhikshu, begging fruit as alms from the trees I find. I will cover my body with dust, forsake every object of attraction or distaste, and shelter under trees or in deserted huts that I find. No joy or sorrow will move me; I will look upon blame and praise equally. I will not seek blessings or adoration.

I shall be at peace with everything, and accept no gifts. I will never mock anyone, or frown at anyone, but always be cheerful and devote myself to the welfare of all creatures. I will do no injury to any of the four forms of life, mobile or unmoving, but treat them all as if they are my own children.

Once a day I will visit five or ten families, at most, and beg for alms. If I receive none I will not eat. I will never beg from the same person twice. I will not go to more than ten homes, and shall remain as unmoved as a Rishi whether I get food or not. I will look equally upon someone who hacks away my arm with an axe and another who smears it with sandalwood paste. I will not curse the first or bless the second.

I will not be pleased to remain alive or grieve if I am to die; I will look equally upon life and death. Cleansing my heart of every sin, I will rise above the sacred rituals that men perform, during auspicious times, in order to attain happiness. I will relinquish all dharma and artha, as well as rituals that gratify the senses.

I will become as free as the wind, going where I please with no sin or attachment to bind me. Fearlessly shall I tread the path of Sannyasa, until the day of my death arrives. Now that I cannot father children, I shall walk in dharma, never leaving the golden path to walk the vile alleyways of the world, all of which lead to sorrow.

Whether the world honours him or not, the man who begs from greed is certainly like a dog. I cannot have children and I must never ask another to give me sons.'

Wiping his tears, Pandu fetches a deep sigh and says to Kunti and Madri, 'Let my mother, my uncle Vidura, King Dhritarashtra, all our friends, the Devi Satyavati, Pitama Bhishma, our family priests, the

Brahmanas who keep stern vratas and drink Soma rasa, and all the elders in our city be told that Pandu has taken Vanavasa and will lead the life of a Sannyasi.'

Kunti and Madri say, 'O Bharatarishabha, there are other paths of Sannyasa that you can follow, and perform the sternest tapasya, in which we can join and serve you: paths that also lead to moksha and liberation from rebirth. We, too, shall control our passions, forsake every luxury, and be austere in all things. But, O king of great wisdom, if you abandon us, we will take our own lives this very day.'

Pandu replies, 'If what you say is dharma, then I will tread the immortal way of my ancestors with both of you. I will renounce the comforts of towns and cities, wear valkala, eat only fruit and roots, and wander in the deepest jungles, performing tapasya.

Bathing morning and evening, I will perform homa. I will wear animal hide, or rags, jata on my head, and emaciate my body by hardly eating. I will ignore hunger and thirst and expose myself to extremes of heat and cold; living in solitude, I will abandon myself to dhyana, a life of meditation.

I will eat such fruit as I find, raw or ripe; I will make offerings to the Pitrs and the Devas, of mantras, holy water and the fruit of the jungle. I will not see any of the creatures of the wild, much less harm them; I will never again see any of my friends or kinsmen, or any that live in towns or cities.

Until I leave this body, I will keep the most extreme observances of the Vanaprastha Shastras, always seeking out the most difficult and harsh ones.'

Pandu now gives away the large jewel in his crown to Brahmanas, as also his golden necklace, his bracelets, his heavy earrings, his opulent robes, along with all the jewellery of his wives.

Calling his servants, he says, 'Go back to Hastinapura and tell everyone there that Pandu has renounced wealth, every desire, pleasure, even his sexual life, and has become a Sannyasi in the forest.'

He speaks quietly, but when they hear him, his attendants set up a loud lament, crying, 'Ah, we are ruined!'

Hot tears streaming down their faces, they leave their prince and, taking the gold and ornaments he has given them to be distributed as charity, return to the city of elephants. When Dhritarashtra, best among men, hears the news that those servitors bring, he weeps for his brother. He is plunged in gloom, and, now, hardly takes any delight in the pleasures of his palace, with its soft beds and seats, its exquisite cuisine.

Pandu goes to the mountains called Nagasata, with Kunti and Madri. Eating fruit and roots, they cross the Chaitraratha, the Kalakuta, and finally crossing the Himalaya, they arrive on fragrant Gandhamadana. Watched over by Mahabhutas, Siddhas and Maharishis, Pandu lives at times in the plains and at others on mountains.

He journeys to Lake Indradyumna, and then crossing the Hansakuta Mountains, arrives at the range of a hundred peaks, Satasringa, where he lives in tapasya."

CANTO 120

SAMBHAVA PARVA CONTINUED

Vaisampayana said, 'Pandu devotes himself to his austerities. Quickly, he becomes a favourite with all the great Siddhas and Charanas who live on that mountain. O Bhaarata, he serves his spiritual masters, with his mind perfectly controlled, with complete humility, and gains enormous ascetic powers. Some of the Rishis would call him their brother, others their friend, while others love him like a son.

Bharatarishabha, pursuing his tapasya with intense devotion and singlemindedness, Pandu, though he is born a Kshatriya, soon becomes even like a Brahmarishi.

On a day of the new moon, amavasya, some awesome Rishis gather to set out to see Brahma, in his lofty realm. Pandu asks them, 'Great ones, where are you going?'

The Rishis reply, 'There will be a great Satsangha today in the court of Brahma, of Devas, Pitrs and Maharishis. We want to see the Svayambhuva, the Self-Created Lord, and are going to the sacred conclave.'

Pandu jumps up in excitement; he wants to go as well. But as he is about to follow them with his two wives, the Munis who are travelling north of Satasringa say, 'As we journeyed north, gradually climbing the King of Mountains, we have seen many marvellous realms, which are inaccessible to ordinary men.

We have seen the worlds of Devas, Gandharvas and Apsaras, with hundreds of palaces, wondrous past describing, echoing softly with heavenly music; we have seen the enchanted gardens of Kubera, spread across plains and rising into mountain slopes, with mighty rivers flowing through, and deep and secret caves.

Many of those heights are covered in perennial snow and ice, places where no animals live or plants grow. Other realms are uninhabitable, indeed inaccessible, for the torrential rains that pour down upon them. Why, other beasts, even birds do not venture into these. Only the air dares go freely through those glacial realms, as do Siddhas and Rishis with great powers.

O Pandu, how will your wives, these tender princesses, climb those pinnacles of the Lord of mountains? They are not used either to the hardship or the inevitable pain; they will not survive. Therefore, O Bharatarishabha, you must not come with us.'

Pandu replies, 'Most fortunate ones, it is told that the sonless can never enter Swarga. I have no son! I speak to you in great grief for I have not been able to repay the debt I owe my manes. Ah, I feel certain that when this body of mine dissolves into its constituent elements, my ancestors, my Pitrs on high, shall fall into hell.

Men are born into this world with four debts: those due to the Pitrs, the Devas, the Rishis, and to other men. In dharma these must be paid. The wise all agree that no blissful realms await those that do not discharge these debts.

The Devas are paid with yagnas; the Rishis are paid by gyana, dhyana and tapasya; the Pitrs are paid by begetting children and by offering tarpana and pinda; and one's fellow men by leading a blameless life that gives no injury.

I have done my dharma by the Devas, the Rishis and toward my fellow men. But ah, my sires, my Pitrs will surely perish because I have not paid my dues to them; I have not fathered any children. O Munis, I am still in debt to my ancestors. The best men are born into this world to father children, so their ancestors are liberated. Wise ones, I ask you now, should children be begotten in my field, even as I was in my father's, by the great Dwaipayana?'

The Rishis say, 'Virtuous Kshatriya, you shall indeed have sons, sinless princes, blessed with fortune and brilliant like the Devas. We see this clearly with our eyes of prophecy. So, Purushavyaghra, O tiger among men, accomplish destiny's purpose, for intelligent men act after clear and careful thought and invariably find great punya. We see the shining fruit that shall be your sons. Pandu, that is your direction.'

But Pandu remembers the curse of the stag and his enforced celibacy. He thinks hard and deep about what the Sages said to him before they departed towards the north. Then he calls the chaste Kunti and says to her privately, 'In this time of our distress you must try to bear children. Rishis who expound the Sanatana Dharma say that having a son fetches a man virtue and fame in the three worlds.

No sacrifices, charity, penance, or the sternest vows can bestow punya on a man who has no son. O my Kunti of the sweet smile, I fear that I will never attain Heaven because I have no son. Ah, a vile and wretched sinner I was, addicted to violence and savagery, so the deer cursed me that I can never have children.

The Shastras speak of six kinds of sons that are both kin and heirs, and six more that are not heirs but only kin. Pritha, the first of these is a son that a man begets upon his wife; the second is a son fathered by another sage and accomplished man upon one's wife, out of kindness; the third is a son begotten by another upon one's wife for money; the fourth a son begotten upon a wife after her husband's death; the fifth a son born to an unwed mother; the sixth a son born to an unfaithful wife; the seventh is a son given as a gift; the eight is a son bought for money; the ninth is a son adopted; the tenth is a son that comes with an already pregnant bride; the eleventh is a brother's son; and the twelfth a son begotten upon a woman of a lower caste.

If a woman cannot conceive by her husband of her own varna, she must try to conceive with a man of the next varna. If a man cannot father a child, he may ask his younger brothers to father children for him. Manu himself has said that when a man cannot beget a son, he can have another good man father a son on his wife, because having a son is the highest punya.

Kunti, I cannot sire a child in you, and I command you to conceive a child with a man who is either my equal or my superior. Let me tell you the story of the daughter of Saradandayana, whose husband asks her to bear him children by another man.

When her period ended and she came into her fertile time, that Kshatriya woman bathed in the evening and went out at night to a crossroads. Soon enough, a Brahmana of tapasya came along and Saradandayana's daughter asked him for children. He poured ghee as offering into a sacred fire, in the ritual called Pumsavana, and then sired three mighty Maharathas in her, Durjaya being the eldest.

My precious and fortunate Kunti, I want you to follow that Kshatriya princess' example. I want you to bear me a son by the seed of a Brahmana of lofty Sannyasa.'"

CANTO 121

Sambhava Parva Continued

Vaisampayana said, "Kunti says to her husband, that bull among the Kurus, 'O my lord, do not say this to me! Lotus eyed Pandu, I am your wife and I love you. Bhaarata Mahabaho, come and beget your children in me yourself, sons of great tejas! When they are born, I will follow you out of this world into Swarga. But not even in my imagination or dreams can I let myself be embraced by another man.

Besides, which man in this world is your equal, let alone your superior? My husband of dharma, let me tell you a story from the Purana, O Pandu of the large eyes.

Long ago, in ancient times, there was a Puru king calls Vyushitaswa. He was devout, truthful and a man of dharma. Once, while the mighty and pure Vyushitaswa was performing a sacrifice, Indra, the Devas and the Devarishis came to his yagna. Indra and the Devas were so drunk with the Soma rasa that the king offered them, the Brahmanas so delighted with the munificent gifts he gave them, that the Gods and the Sages began to perform the rituals at that Rajarishi's yagna.

Vyushitaswa shone as brightly as the Sun when he appears after the winter of snow; he was twice as splendid as before, more splendid than any other man. Soon, O best of kings, the magnificent Vyushitaswa, as strong as ten elephants, performed the Aswamedha yagna, vanquishing every other ruler of the East, the North, the West and the South, and received tribute from them all.

Kurushreshta, all the Pauranikas sing a tale about that Manavottama, the brilliant Vyushitaswa. When he had conquered all the Earth, from Sea to Sea, that king protected his people, all the varnas, just like a father would his own children. He performed great yagnas, at which he gave away untold wealth to Brahmanas.

When he gathered precious jewels past counting, he arranged to perform still greater sacrifices. He also performed the Agnishtoma, and other arcane Vedic sacrifices, extracting copious quantities of Soma rasa.

Rajan, Vyushitaswa's wife was the daughter of Kakshivat, Bhadra, whose beauty was unrivalled on Earth, and the two of them loved each other deeply. King Vyushitaswa seldom left his wife for any length of time, but united with her always, as frequently as he might. However, this excessive sexual indulgence caused a galloping consumption, which killed the king in a matter of days. He died like the Sun setting, in glory.

The beautiful Queen Bhadra had no son and she was plunged in grief; day and night she wept. With tears streaming down her face, Bhadra said, "Women serve no purpose when their husbands are dead; she is a dead woman that survives her lord, dragging on a wretched misery that is no life, but a terrible death. Ah Bharatarishabha, my Lord Vyushitaswa, I have no wish to live without you. I beg you be merciful and call me to you.

Every moment I live without you is a lifetime in hell. Oh, be kind, beloved King, call me to you quickly. O tiger among kings, I will follow you wherever you go, through rough and smooth. You have gone and will never return; let me come to you as your shadow. O I will be your slave, and do everything you want, whatever pleases you.

O my lotus eyed husband, without you, day by day, anguish will overwhelm me; grief will consume my heart. Oh, I am a wretched sinner and must have been the cause of separating some loving couple in another life that I have to suffer being apart from you in this one. Rajan, Rajan, the woman who lives for even a moment after her husband's death lives only in Naraka. My Lord, do you not see the torment I am in?

I shall lay myself down on a bed of kusa grass, and neither eat nor drink, so that I might see you again soon. O tiger among men, show yourself to me! O my sweet lord, let me hear your voice again, commanding your wretched, grief-stricken wife!"'

Kunti continues, 'Pandu, thus the lovely Bhadra wept when her husband died. She clasped his corpse in her arms and sobbed. Suddenly, an asariri, a disembodied voice spoke to her, "Rise O Bhadra and leave this chamber of death. Woman of the sweet smiles, I grant you a boon: I will beget children in you. Bathe after your period on the eighth or fourteenth night of the waxing moon and wait for me in your bed, and I will come to you."

Bhadra did as the voice asked, so that she might have sons. The chaste Bhadra did as the voice said, and her husband's corpse begot seven children upon her, three Salvas and four Madras.

Bharatarishabha, you can do the same as Vyushitaswa, by using your occult siddhis, your mystical powers.'"

CANTO 122

SAMBHAVA PARVA CONTINUED

Vaisampayana said, "Pandu says to Kunti, 'Vyushitaswa of yore did indeed do what you say; why, he was like a Deva. But let me tell you about a custom of old, of which the Rishis who know every nuance of dharma approve.

Lovely Kunti of the sweet smile, in ancient times, women were not confined to their houses, nor did they depend upon their husbands or other male relatives; they were free, and indeed they took their pleasure where they pleased and were not faithful to a single man. And this was not considered sinful, but was perfectly lawful and sanctioned, of old.

As the birds and beasts of the wilds do today, with no jealousy or possessiveness, the women of antiquity did, and the greatest Sages approved heartily. Why, even today, the Northern Kuru women live in the same manner and meet with no reproval. The very idea of a woman being bound for life to a single husband is a very recent one, and I will tell you how it came about, who is responsible for it and why.

There was a great Sage, Uddalaka, whose son was the Rishi Swetaketu, who was also a Sannyasi of great punya. My lotus eyed Kunti, monogamy for women was first established by Swetaketu and he did it from wrath.

Listen to the reason. One day, in the presence of Uddalaka, another Brahmana seized Swetaketu's mother's hand, and said, 'Come with me!' and she went with him. Thinking his mother had been taken by force, Swetaketu was furious.

Seeing his son's anger, Uddalaka said gently, 'Do not be angry, my child. The women of every varna are entirely free, and their freedom is accepted since time out of mind. In sexual matters, they behave even like cows, and it is lawful and just.'

But Swetaketu would not listen to his father and pronounced that, from that day, women shall be faithful to their husbands and be considered sinners if they strayed. His law bound only human beings and not the other creatures of the Earth. From that time, women who were not chaste would be guilty of the sin of foeticide; and men who violated the chaste wife of another man would be condemned for the same sin.

However, the woman who does not give her husband children, though he commands her, is also guilty of the same crime, O my Kunti of the tapering thighs.

My timid wife, it was Uddalaka's son Swetaketu who imposed monogamy on humans, in defiance of the freedom that women enjoyed since the dawn of time. I have also heard, my wife of the softest thighs, that when her husband Sadasa commanded her, his chaste wife Madayanti gave him a son called Asmaka, by the Rishi Vasishta. She did this out of her love for her husband.

Why, lotus eyes, you know very well how my brothers and I were begotten by Krishna Dwaipayana to continue the Kuru line. Chaste Princess, consider these precedents, which do not violate dharma, and do what I ask.

Of old it has been said that a devoted wife always seeks her husband during her fertile time, while at others she has her liberty. The Rishis say that this is the ancient way of dharma. Also, whatever a husband asks his wife to do, sin or not, the Veda says that she must obey him.

Most of all, beautiful Kunti, I who cannot father children, long to see sons before me; you must not refuse to do what I ask. Look, sweet Kunti, I fold my red-fingered hands into a lotus-cup, and place them on my head to implore you. Beloved Kunti, I beg you, beget children for me by some lofty Brahmana. For only then, because of you, I will find my way into the Swarga meant for men that have sons!'

Having heard him out in silence, attentively, now Kunti says, 'When I was a young girl, it fell to me to look after the most honoured guests who visited my father's palace. Reverently I waited upon Rishis of vast tapasya. Once, I served the great Brahmana Durvasa, whose mind is perfectly controlled and who is a master of the deepest secrets of religion.

He was pleased with my devotion and Durvasa Muni taught me a mantra with which I could summon any Deva I chose.

The Rishi said, 'Any Deva that you summon with this mantra shall perforce come to you and give you children.'

O Bhaarata, the Brahmana said this to me when I was a maiden in my father's house, and surely Durvasa Muni could never tell a lie. It seems that the time has come when the Rishi's boon might bear fruit. Rajarishi, if you command it I can summon any Deva and bear his children for you. Tell me, my lord, which god shall I call? I will do what you say.'

Pandu replies excitedly, 'Exquisite Kunti, use the mantra even today! Woman of great fortune, summon Dharma Deva, who is the most virtuous of all the gods and can never stain us with any sin, the God of Truth. Also, then, the world shall never point a finger at us that we strayed from dharma.

Besides, the son he gives us shall be a paragon of virtue, certainly the best of the Kurus. Dharma Deva being his natural father, his heart will never turn to the least sin. Sweet woman, keep dharma before your mind's eye, purify yourself with the proper vratas, and waste no time in summoning the God of Justice with both your beauty and your mantra!'

Says Kunti, best among women, 'So be it.' She bows deeply to touch his feet, walks around him in pradakshina, and resolves to do what her husband asks.'"

CANTO 123

SAMBHAVA PARVA CONTINUED

Vaisampayana said, "O Janamejaya, Gandhari has already been pregnant for a full year with her torpid conception, when on Satasringa, Kunti invokes the Deva Dharma, to have a son by that God. She makes various offerings to the God, and begins to chant the mantra that Durvasa had taught her.

Compelled by her incantation, Dharma Deva flies down to Kunti in a vimana bright as the Sun. Smiling, he asks, 'O Kunti, what would you have from me?'

Smiling, bashful, overwhelmed, she replies, 'Give me a son.'

The beautiful Kunti and the God of Truth have intercourse between them, and in time Kunti gives birth to a shining son, who would be devout and devoted to the welfare of every living creature. This radiant child, who would acquire fame that would spread across the worlds, is born at the eighth muhurta, Abhijit, at high noon of a most auspicious day, the fifth of the bright fortnight, during Kartika, the seventh month, on that very auspicious day of the seventh month when the asterism Jyeshta is conjoined with the waxing Moon.

As soon as he is born an asariri pronounces from the sky, 'This child shall be the most virtuous of all men. He will have great strength, and perfect truthfulness, and he will surely rule the Earth. Let this first son of Pandu be called Yudhishtira, and his fame shall spread through the three worlds!'

Then Pandu goes to Kunti again, and says, 'The Rishis have said that a Kshatriya must possess great physical strength or he is no Kshatriya. Beget another son, of immense strength, who can be Yudhishtira's support.'

Kunti invokes Vayu, the Wind God, strongest of the Devas. He comes to her riding upon a deer, and says, 'O Kunti, what is in your heart that you have called me. What would you have of me?'

Smiling bashfully, she says, 'O best of Devas, give me a son endowed with great strength, great limbs, a great heart, and one that can humble the pride of anyone at all.'

The God of winds sires a child of untold strength and great arms upon her, who would be known as Bhima. As before, O Bhaarata, when Bhima is born, a disembodied voice speaks in thunder from the sky, 'This child shall be the strongest of all men.'

O Janamejaya, I must tell you about something else very wonderful that happens after Vrikodara Bhima's, birth. One day, he falls out of his mother's lap onto the slope of the mountain, and the crag he falls upon far below is smashed to pieces, while his child's body has no scratch or bruise, and he does not even cry. The reason he falls is that a tiger suddenly appears before Kunti, sitting at the edge of a sheer drop, with Bhima asleep in her lap. She jumps up in alarm and Bhima falls over the edge, onto a large rock many hands below.

When Pandu sees how Bhima's body, hard as adamant, crushes the rock and suffers no harm, he marvels.

Also, it is on the same day that Bhima is born on Satasringa that far away, in Hastinapura, Duryodhana is also born, Duryodhana, who too, would one day rule the Earth.

After the birth of Vrikodara, a persistent ambition begins to haunt Pandu: 'How shall I have a truly exceptional son, superior to every other man, and who will achieve everlasting fame? Everything in this world depends on both destiny and effort; but destiny by itself is fruitless without timely effort.

'Indra is the King of all the Devas; immeasurable is his strength, his power, his energy and his glory. I must worship him and persuade him to give me a son of matchless prowess. The son that he gives me must become the greatest Kshatriya on Earth, with no rival, and one who can vanquish every other man and every creature in this world. Yes, I will perform a stern tapasya, and be perfectly austere in thought, speech and deed.'

Pandu seeks the advice and guidance of the Maharishis of that forest, and then tells Kunti that she must observe a vrata of austerity for a full year. Then Pandu, O Bhaarata, begins to stand upon one leg, from dawn to dusk, his mind withdrawn in dhyana and worshipping the Lord Indra. Other rituals also he performs to please the Deva King.

In some months, Indra becomes gratified with Pandu's adorations and appears before him.

Indra says, 'O King, I will give you a son who will be the best of all men. Invincible in battle, he will be celebrated across the Earth. He will uphold dharma, be a guardian of Brahmanas, cows and all good men. He will be a Parantapa, the scourge of the evil, the joy of his friends and kin. He will become an inexorable slayer of his enemies.'

Overjoyed at what Indra says, Pandu goes to Kunti and cries, 'Your vrata has borne fruit! The King of the Devas is pleased and has agreed to give us the son we want. Our child will be wise past compare, his achievements superhuman and his fame unequalled.

'He will be a Mahatman, the bane of his enemies and of the forces of evil. His splendour will be as the Sun's, and he will be as handsome as a God. O Kunti of the swaying, fair hips, Kunti of the sweetest smile, the Lord of the Devas has become pleased with you! Call him to you with your mantra, and bear a son who will be the very embodiment of every Kshatriya virtue.'

Kunti invokes Sakra, Indra the Deva king, who comes to her and sires in her the one who would be known throughout the world as Arjuna. As soon as Arjuna is born, an asariri like the rumbling of thunderheads fills the sky with its echoing tones.

The disembodied voice says to Kunti, and every creature in that forest hears it clear, 'O Kunti, this son of yours will be as strong as Kartavirya and as powerful as Siva. Invincible like Indra himself, he will spread your fame across the Earth. Even as Vishnu, her youngest son, causes the joy of his mother Aditi to swell, so will this boy swell yours.

He will subdue the Madras, the Kurus, the Somakas, the Chedis, Kasi and Karusha, and he will preserve the glory and prosperity of the House of Kuru. Agni will feast upon the fat of the fell creatures of the Khandava vana, by the might of your son's arms, when your prince burns that forest.

This mighty Kshatriya will vanquish all the kings of the Earth, effeminate before him, enabling himself and his brothers to perform three Mahayagnas. O Kunti, his prowess shall be no less than that of Jamadagni's son Parasurama or Vishnu. By his extraordinary archery, he will find unparalleled fame.

Why, he will delight the Lord Siva by having a battle with him, and the Lord Sankara Mahadeva will give him his own Pasupatastra, the greatest of all weapons. This mighty son of yours will also kill the Nivatakavacha Daityas, the enemies of the Devas. He will acquire every kind of Devastra and this Purusharishabha, this bull among men, will restore the very fortunes of his clan!'

Kunti lies in the room where she has given birth to Arjuna, and listens to these awesome prophecies. Hearing the divine asariri speak in thunder from the sky, the Rishis who live on the mountain of a hundred peaks, and all the Devas and Indra in their vimanas in the firmament are overjoyed.

Celestial drumrolls fill the sky, as do divine cries of joy; all of Satasringa is covered by a deluge of unearthly flowers flung down by unseen hands. Many divine beings arrive on the mountain of a thousand peaks to adore the son of Pritha – the sons of Kadru, the sons of Vinata, the Prajapatis, the Lokapalas, the Saptarishis, Bharadwaja, Kashyapa, Gautama, Viswamitra, Jamadagni, Vasistha, and the irradiant Atri who lit up the world when once the Sun was lost.

Marichi, Angiras, Pulastya, Pulaha, Kratu, Daksha Prajapati, the Gandharvas and Apsaras come there as well. The many tribes of Apsaras, wearing unworldly ornaments and garlands, raiment past describing, arrive in the forest asrama and dance for joy, while they sing the praises of little Arjuna.

All around, Rishis chant mantras of blessing, while Tumburu and his Gandharvas sing in their superlative voices. Among the celestial minstrels are Bhimasena, Ugrasena, Urnayus, Anagha, Gopati, Dhritarashtra, Suryavarchas, Yugapa, Trinapa, Karshni, Nandi, Chitraratha, Salisirah, Parjannya, Kali, Narada, Brihatta, Brihaka, Karala Mahatman, Brahmacharin, Bahuguna, Suvarna the famed, Viswavasu, Bhumanyu, Suchandra, Saru and the renowned people of Haha and Huhu – all come and sing in abandon, in divine voices.

Among the Apsaras that dance to the music of the Gandharvas, O Rajan, are Anchana, Anavadya, Gunamukhya, Gunavara, Adrika, Soma, Misrakesi, Alambusha, Marichi, Suchika, Vidyutparna, Tilottama, Ambika, Lakshmana, Kshema Devi, Rambha, Manorama, Asita, Subahu, Supriya, Subapuh, Pundarika, Sugandha, Surasa, Pramathini, Kamya and Saradwati.

Menaka, Sahajanya, Karnika, Punjikasthala, Ritusthala, Ghritachi, Viswachi, Purvachiti, Umlocha, Pramlocha and Urvasi, all with large and lustrous eyes, the nymphs of heaven, also come there and sing in their voices past all compare: *choros nympharum*.

Dhatri, Aryaman, Mitra, Varuna, Bhaga, Indra, Vivaswat, Pushan, Tvastri, Parjanya and Vishnu: the twelve Adityas come to that hermitage to bless Pandu's son. And, O King, Mrigavyadha, Sarpa, Niriti, Ajaikapada, Ahivradhna, Pinakin, Dahana, Iswara, Kapalin, Sthanu, Bhaga: these eleven Rudras also come to see and bless the glorious child.

The Aswin twins, the eight Vasus, the mighty Maruts, the Viswedevas, and the Sadhyas come to Satasringa, too; as do Karkotaka, Vasuki, Kachchhapa, Kunda and the great Takshaka – mighty and fierce Nagas of immense tapasya. Tarkshya, Arishtanemi, Garuda, Asitadvaja, many other Nagas arrive upon the blessed mountain, as do Aruna and Aruni of Vinata's race.

Only the Maharishis of lofty spiritual evolution see all these divine beings who either walk upon the mountain or look down from their vimanas in the sky. Those great Munis see the Gods and the rest of the unworldly ones and are amazed, and their love for the sons of Pandu grows in tide.

Some time passes, then Pandu wants to have more children. He asks Kunti to conceive again, but she says, 'The Sages have not given their sanction to have a fourth child, not even in a crisis. The woman who sleeps with four men is a swairini, while she that has five is a whore.

My most learned lord, you know very well what the Shastras say about this, then why do you allow your greed for children to make you forget dharma?'"

CANTO 124

SAMBHAVA PARVA CONTINUED

Vaisampayana said, 'After the birth of Kunti's sons and the hundred sons of Dhritarashtra, Madri comes privately to Pandu one day.

She says, 'Shatrughana, scorcher of your enemies, I never complain though you pay me scant attention. I do not mind that though I am higher born than Kunti her position is higher than mine. I do not grieve, O Kurusthama, that Gandhari has a hundred sons. However, I am terribly sad that while Kunti and I are both your wives, she has three sons and I have none for you.

If Kuntibhoja's daughter can help me also become a mother I would be beholden to her forever, and she would also be giving you more sons, as you want. She is my rival for your love, and I cannot ask her this myself. But if you want to be kind to me, O Purushavyaghra, tell her to grant me this boon.'

Pandu says eagerly, 'Madri, I have often thought of exactly what you are saying. But I never mentioned it lest I offend you. Now that you say you want the very same thing, I will certainly speak to Kunti and she will not refuse me.'

Pandu speaks alone to Kunti, 'O Kunti, give me more sons to increase my clan and to benefit the world. Sweet wife, let us make sure that my Pitrs and I, and your manes, too, always have pinda offered them. Be kind to me, Kunti, and in that be most kindly towards the very Earth. Let your heart be moved to find immortal fame, and do what you might find difficult to do.

Though he is King of the Devas, Indra still performs yagnas: only to enhance his fame. O lovely Kunti, Brahmanas who know the Veda and have acquired lofty punya still approach their Gurus reverently: only for their fame. All the Rajarishis and Brahmarishis achieved their most strenuous accomplishments only out of a desire to have fame.

I ask you, chaste Kunti, to help make Madri a mother, too, and save her like a raft from the sea of grief in which she is drowning, and so acquire undying fame for yourself!'

Kunti agrees readily, and calls Madri and says to her, 'Think of any Deva you like and you shall have a child by him.'

Madri considers a few moments then thinks of the Aswini twins in her heart, as Kunti softly chants Durvasa's irresistible mantra. As soon as Madri is alone the splendid Aswini Kumaras come to her and beget two incomparably handsome sons on her, also twins, who come to be called Nakula and Sahadeva.

As soon as they are born, a disembodied voice speaks, 'These children will surpass the Aswins themselves in tejas and beauty.' And truly, the infants are so lustrous that they light up the mountain.

Rajan, when these five children are born, the Rishis of Satasringa come to bless them, and lovingly perform their birth rites and name them. Kunti's eldest son is named Yudhishtira, her second Bhimasena, her third Arjuna; Madri's older child is called Nakula and the second Sahadeva.

Those magnificent sons, born a year apart, look even like five years embodied. Pandu would look at his sons of divine handsomeness and boundless energy, of incalculable strength, of great generosity, and be overwhelmed with joy. Of course, those five become the favourites of all the Rishis of the mountain of a hundred peaks, and of their wives, all of whom dote on them.

Some time passes, when Pandu asks Kunti to enable Madri to have another child. But Kunti says, 'I chanted the mantra for her once and she deceived me by having two sons. If I say it for her again, I cannot tell who she will invoke but she will have more sons than me. She is always envious and this is the way of women like her.

As for me, I am naïve that I did not think to invoke the Aswins myself so that I could have had two sons. My lord, I beg you do not ask me to use the mantra for Madri again.'

Thus, Rajan, Pandu has five sons begotten by Devas: princes of immense strength, who achieve great fame and increase the glory of the House of Kuru. Each of them bears every auspicious mark upon their bodies; each is as handsome as Soma. As they grow, they are majestic as the lion – in gait, in the broadness of their chests, in the largeness of their hearts and their eyes, their powerful necks and vast strength; each becomes a master archer, and they are, all five, truly like Devas themselves.

Watching them grow, seeing their virtues grow with them, the great Munis who live on that snowcapped and holy mountain are wonder-stricken. Swiftly they grow, the five sons of Pandu on Satasringa and the hundred sons of Dhritarashtra in Hastinapura, as swiftly as a bank of lotuses in a lake."

CANTO 125

SAMBHAVA PARVA CONTINUED

Vaisampayana said, "Watching his sons grow in the great vana upon the charmed mountain, Pandu feels the final strength in his body assert itself again.

One day in spring, which maddens every creature with desire, Pandu is out walking with Madri in the forest, where every tree is decked in fresh new blooms. He sees Palasas, Tilakas, Mango trees, Champakas, Parihadrakas, Karnikaras, Asokas, Kesaras, Atimuktas and Kuruvakas, all with swarms of inebriated bees humming over their blossoms. Parijatas are in full heady bloom, and the Koyals sing their hearts out, ah so sweetly, against their sruti of the humming of the black bees.

Pandu sees other trees, branches bent with the weight of their abundant flowers and fruit. He sees crystalline pools brimming with delicately fragrant lotuses. Pandu looks at all this, he feels spring in his blood; he feels his blood quicken with soft desire. As Pandu ranges through that enchanted realm, like a god, the still youthful Madri beside him wears a single diaphanous garment. Pandu looks at her and suddenly the long suppressed desire of all the years of enforced celibacy flares up and overwhelms Pandu.

She sees the look in his eye and cries out, but he seizes her roughly, her of the eyes like lotus petals. She does everything she can to resist him, for she has not forgotten the curse of the deer. O Kurusthama, compelled by fate, overpowered by lust, Pandu forces himself on Madri, just as if he wants to end his life. Her strength is as nothing before his, and he thrusts himself into her, and immediately becomes senseless. Pandu of dharma dies even as he is joined with Madri.

Madri clasps her dead husband's body and sets up a loud wailing. Kunti, her sons and Madri's twins hear her cries and come running to the place. When Madri sees them some way off, she cries to Kunti, 'Leave the children and come alone!'

Telling the princes to stay where they are, Kunti runs to Madri and sees what has happened. She sees Madri and Pandu as they are, and her husband dead. Dementedly, she cries, 'Madri, what have you done? I watched over him all these years, my own passion controlled, so that he would be protected. How did he forget the Rishi's curse, O how did you? How did you let him near you thus aroused? He always grieved over the curse, then how did he forget it? How did you allow him, how could you tempt him in solitude?

Ah daughter of Bahlika, finally you have prevailed over me and proved yourself the more fortunate one, for you saw desire on his face and joy as he united with you!'

Madri sobs, 'O my sister, I tried to stop him, but he could not control himself. It was as if he was determined to fulfil the Rishi's curse.'

Kunti is quiet, then says, 'I am the older of his wives; the first karma must belong to me. Madri, you must not try to stop me from doing what must be done. I must follow our husband to the land of the dead.

Get up Madri, and let me have his corpse; and from now, you raise these children.'

Madri replies, 'I still hold him within my body. My desire is unslaked, so I must be the one to follow him. You are my elder sister; I beg you, let me have this one boon from you. This Bharatottama was joined with me in intercourse when his spirit left his body. He died without having his desire satisfied; must I not follow him, as we are, to Yama's realm so that he can satiate himself on me?

Besides, O my adored sister, if I am the one to live and you die I shall not be able to treat your sons and mine equally, and you know that is true. I will sin and in all likelihood divide the princes among themselves. But you, Kunti, will raise my sons as your own, making no difference between them.

Our lord Pandu sought me out and he remains within me. He has gone to the realm of the spirits; it is right in every way that my body is not separated at this time from his but that I am burnt with him. Kunti, my sweet sister, you were always his first wife in this world; let me be the one to go with him out of it. Do not deny me this, I beg you!

I know that you will be the best of mothers to all the children; I have no other wish or request to make of you.'

So, indeed, the daughter of the king of the Madras is burnt upon the funeral pyre of her husband Pandu, that Purusharishabha, that bull among men, while he still lay in her arms."

CANTO 126

SAMBHAVA PARVA CONTINUED

Vaisampayana said, "Now the godlike Rishis see Pandu dead, consult together, and declare, 'Pandu relinquished power and throne to come among us to live in tapasya upon this mountain. He has left us and gone to Swarga, leaving his wife and sons as a sacred trust in our hands. It is our dharma now to take them to Hastinapura.'

The Maharishis decide to take Kunti and the sons of Pandu to the kingdom of elephants and deliver them into the custody of Bhishma and Dhritarashtra. They set out immediately, taking the woman and the children with them, as well as the unburnt remains of Pandu and Madri, which they wrap tightly and carefully so no portion of them is visible.

She has always lived a life of comfort, yet now Kunti sees the long and arduous journey as a short and almost happy one.

Arriving in Kurujangala, Kunti comes to the main gate of the great city and presents herself there. The Rishis command the dwarapalakas to inform the king within the city of their arrival. The excited guardsmen run into the court with their amazing message. When the citizens of Hastinapura hear about the arrival at their gates of thousands of Munis and Charanas they are wonderstruck, and soon after dawn begin to throng to those portals in crowds, with their wives and children.

In chariots and other regal vahanas, in thousands, come the Kshatriyas with their wives; the Brahmanas arrive with their women; as do the Vaisyas and Sudras with theirs. It is a calm crowd, for the people of Hastinapura are all given to dharma; they are a pious people.

Bhishma, son of Shantanu, comes to the city gates, as do Somadatta, Bahlika, Rajarishi Dhritarashtra whose vision is his wisdom, Vidura the sage, the venerable Satyavati, the princesses of Kosala, Ambika and Ambalika, Gandhari, and other noble women of the royal household.

The hundred sons of Dhritarashtra, decked in lavish ornaments, also emerge from the gates of the ancient city.

The Kauravas and their Kulaguru, the family priest, worship the Rishis from Satasringi by bowing low to them, and then they sit before the Sages. The citizens also bow to the hermits, touch the ground with their hands in reverence, and then they also sit down.

When the great gathering is perfectly still and silent, Bhishma worships the Rishis, offering them padya, water to wash their feet, and arghya. He then speaks to them about the kingdom and the kingship.

Then the eldest Rishi, jata piled on his head and animal hide covering his loins, stands up and speaks for all the Sages. 'You all know that Pandu, sovereign of the Kurus, renounced the pleasures of this world and became a Sannyasi on Satasringa of a hundred peaks. He became a brahmachari, yet for some inscrutable reason of the Gods, Pandu's eldest son Yudhishtira was born upon the mountain and he was begotten by Dharma Deva.

Pandu's second son, this Bhima, strongest among all men, is the son of Vayu, the Wind God. This third prince, begotten upon Kunti by Indra, is Arjuna who will one day be the greatest of all bowmen on Earth.

Now look at these young vyaghras, tigerish twins, whose mother is

Madri and their fathers the Aswins of heaven. They, too, are great archers. Living in dharma as a Vanaprastha in the forest, Pandu did thus revive the illustrious lineage of his grandsire, a line threatened with extinction.

You will no doubt be delighted to learn of the birth, the growth and the Vedic education of these sons of Pandu. After cleaving unwaveringly to dharma, seventeen days ago, Pandu left this world, leaving these children behind.

His wife Madri burnt herself with him on his funeral pyre; she too has gone with her lord to the realm of chaste wives. You must now perform whatever rites need to be done for the two of them. Here are their remains.

Here also are their children, these Parantapas, and their mother Kunti. Welcome them now with honour.

When the first funeral rites have been completed let the first annual sraddha, the sapindakarana, be performed for Pandu of dharma, who always defended and spread the honour and glory of the Kurus; let him thus find his formal place among the Pitrs of your royal clan.'

When the eldest Rishi has spoken, all those Rishis and Guhyakas vanish before the very eyes of the people of Hastinapura. Astonished to see the Munis and Siddhas dissolve even like wisps of cloud, which come and go in the sky, the people slowly return to their homes."

CANTO 127

SAMBHAVA PARVA CONTINUED

Vaisampayana continued, "Now Dhritarashtra says, 'Vidura, arrange for great royal funerals for my brother, the Rajasimha Pandu, and his wife Madri. Spare no expense, for these rituals are for the souls of our beloved departed. Let everyone that asks be given as much as they ask for – cattle, clothes, jewels, gold and every kind of wealth.

Let Kunti arrange for the last rites for Madri, in whatever fashion pleases her. Let Madri's remains be so closely wrapped that not Surya Deva or Vayu sees them. Do not mourn for Pandu; he was a great Kshatriya and has left behind five sons as magnificent as Devas.'

O Bhaarata, Vidura says, 'Tathaastu, so be it,' and consulting with Bhishma finds a sacred and auspicious place to perform the funeral rites for Pandu. Without delay the family priests go there, carrying the sacred agni from the palace, fragrant with the ghee they fed it.

Now friends, kinsmen and followers bathe Pandu's body, wrap it in cerement, sprinkle it with fine perfumes and strew flowers over it.[7*] They set Pandu upon a hearse, which also they adorn with garlands and rich hangings. Madri's body is placed beside Pandu's and the colourful bier is lifted onto sturdy shoulders.

The white parasol of state is unfurled over that hearse, yak-tail whisks waved over it, and hundreds of musicians play as the funeral procession makes its way through the streets, looking bright and festive: for death, after all, is a release.

Hundreds of palace servitors give out precious jewels to the people who line the streets in crowds. Later, more beautiful robes, more sovereign white parasols, and larger yak-tail chamaras are fetched for the great ceremony.

The priests, wearing white, walk at the head of the procession, ladling libations of clarified butter into the sacred fire burning in an ornamental vessel. Brahmanas, Kshatriyas, Vaisyas and Sudras, in their thousands, follow the dead Pandu.

They lament loudly, sobbing, 'O Prince, where did you go, leaving us behind, wretched forever?'

Bhishma, Vidura and the Pandavas all weep. Finally, they come to a charmed glade in the forest on the banks of the Ganga. They set down the bier on which the lion-hearted Pandu and Madri lie. They bring sacred water in golden vessels, wash the Kshatriya's body, which has been smeared with many kinds of fragrant unguents; they smear it again, all over, with sandalwood paste.

They cover him in white homespun cloth, and now Pandu seems as if he is alive and asleep upon a luxurious bed.

Guided by the priests, they proceed to perform the last rites meticulously. When these are over, the Kauravas touch the bodies of Pandu and Madri alight, and fetch lotuses, sandalwood paste and other fragrant substances to the blazing pyre.

7* It is not clear how much of the bodies the fire in Satasringa consumed, since definitely Madri also comes as a corpse to Hastinapura.

Seeing the bodies burning, Ambalika wails, 'My son! My son!' and faints. Seeing her fall, the people of Hastinapura and also the rustic people from the provinces set up a great lament. Why, even the beasts of the field and the birds of the air are moved to grief hearing the lamentation of Kunti. Bhishma, son of Shantanu, the sagacious Vidura – they too grieve.

Weeping, Bhishma, Vidura, Dhritarashtra, the Pandavas and the Kuru women together perform tarpana for the departed Pandu. When this is done, the people, sorrowing, come up and, with touch, kind words, with embraces and their love, console the sons of Pandu.

The Pandavas mourn and sleep on bare ground. Seeing this, the Brahmanas and indeed all the other citizens of the city of elephants do the same, giving up their beds. Young and old, they mourn the dead Kshatriya with his sons who weep ceaselessly for twelve days."

CANTO 128

Sambhava Parva Continued

Vaisampayana said, "At the end of twelve days, Bhishma and Kunti with their kinsfolk and friends, perform the sraddha for the dead prince and offer the pinda for his soul. After this, they arrange for great feasts and give away vast pieces of land and great gemstones as gifts.

The people return to Hastinapura with the sons of Pandu, now cleansed of the impurity that attends a father's death. Again, the citizens weep for the departed Pandu, as if they have lost one of their kin.

When the sraddha has been performed, Vyasa Muni sees how all the people are plunged in despair, and says quietly one day to Satyavati, 'Mother, the days of joy have left the world and those of danger and calamity have begun. The power of sin increases, day by day, for the world has become old. Because of the swelling force of evil, the Kuru empire will crumble.

It is best that you retire to the forest and embark upon a life of dhyana and yoga. From now, human society will be full of deceit and treachery. Evil will have sway, and all goodness and dharma will cease to be. Do not stay here anymore, to watch the destruction of your clan.'

He prophesies more, and she sees her son, the Sage, means what he says, and Satyavati goes into the antahpura and says to her elder daughter-in-law, 'Ambika, your grandsons shall cause the ruin of the House of Kuru; the very race of Bhaarata and all its people will perish because of what they do. If you agree, I mean to take sannyasa in the jungle with Ambalika, who is heartbroken at the death of Pandu.'

Unexpectedly, Ambika says that she will also accompany the other women. In the vana, Satyavati practises rigorous penance and profound dhyana, and in time leaves her body and finds Swarga for herself, as do her daughters-in-law, later.'

Now, the sons of Pandu undergo the purificatory and initiatory rites prescribed in the Veda, and for the first time, begin to live as princes in their dead father's house.

Quickly, while the youngsters play together, it is obvious that the Pandavas are stronger than their cousins, the Kauravas. The ebullient Bhima by himself is more than a match for Dhritarashtra's sons – he is faster and stronger than they are; his aim is truer, more unerring, his appetite grander. Vayu's son pulls the Kauravas' hair and drags them roughly on the ground; he mischievously makes them fight with one another, and kicks dust into their faces. The gardens of the palace ring with his loud laughter as he does all this.

Vrikodara easily beats up the hundred and one sons of his uncle, as if they are not a hundred and one but just one. When he seizes their hair, flings them down and hauls them over the rough earth, he cuts open some knees, some heads, and dislocates some shoulders.

At times, he holds ten Kauravas together under water, until they nearly drown. When Dhritarashtra's sons climb a tree to pluck its fruit, Bhima delivers a tremendous kick to the tree and brings fruit-pluckers and fruit raining down from the branches.

Yes, the king's sons are no match at all for the son of the Wind, not in strength, speed or skill. However, Bhima is innocent and all the mischief he wreaks is out of a huge sense of playfulness and fun, and never seriously malicious. His heart is truly a child's.

But the king's eldest son, the mighty Duryodhana, hitherto unchallenged in the palace, sees these marvellous feats of strength and swiftness from Bhima and begins to hate his cousin to distraction, seeing clearly and astutely that the young giant is the greatest threat to him in the future. And being neither innocent nor childlike in his heart, but already evil, the ambitious and ruthless Duryodhana conceives a sinister plot.

He says to himself, 'No one else is nearly as strong as Pandu's second son Bhima. He is the main threat to me, so I will have to kill him with cunning. Perhaps I will push him into the Ganga and drown him. Later, I will imprison Yudhishtira and Arjuna, who are nothing without their brother's strength, and rule as the only king of the Kurus, unopposed.'

Having decided on his course, Duryodhana is always on the lookout for an opportunity to do away with Bhima. O Bhaarata, the devious Duryodhana has a palace built in beautiful Pramanakoti on the banks of the Ganga. He has it furnished with fine tapestries and every other lavish embellishment. He has the palace provided with every manner of entertainment, the finest food, and of course it is ostensibly a place for the Kuru princes to visit so they can swim in the river, a retreat for water sport.

Bright flags wave on this mansion, which is called the House of Water Sport. Master cooks prepare every kind of delicacy. When the preparations are complete, his men tell Duryodhana that everything is ready. That evil prince says to the Pandavas, 'Let us all go to the banks of the Ganga, and swim and play in the water.'

Yudhishtira agrees, and the sons of Dhritarashtra set out from Hastinapura with the sons of Pandu, mounted on massive elephants born in the jungle and in chariots as big as towns.

Arriving at the House of Water Sport, they dismiss their attendants, admire the fine gardens and groves of trees, created for their pleasure and their games, and enter the great mansion as a pride of young lions does a mountain cave.

With perfect skill, the architects have designed the palace, and masons plastered and painted the walls and the ceiling. The windows are gracious and large, and the artificial fountains elegant, splashing softly.

Both inside and out are tanks of clear water, in which banks of lotuses bloom, in regal profusion. Upon their banks grow numberless other flowers, whose scents fill the air headily.

The Kauravas and the Pandavas begin to sport there and to enjoy themselves. As they play, in some delight, they feed each other small portions of the fine fare laid out for them by the cooks and servants. Meanwhile, Duryodhana mixes a potent poison into some food, to kill Bhima. Honey on his tongue and a razor in his heart, he is absolutely friendly towards his cousin today, and soon manages to feed him a goodly quantity of the poisoned food. Certain that he has achieved his purpose, he is glad.

Soon the Pandavas and the Kauravas begin to swim and play in the river. When they finish, they put on white robes and fine jewellery. A little tired, they decide to rest in the pleasure-house in the garden.

Bhima, who has exerted himself the most, swum the fastest and longest, feels most tired of all. He comes out of the river and flops down on its bank. The poison is taking effect and great exhaustion sweeps over the second Pandava. The cool evening breeze seems to enhance the effect of the poison, and Bhima immediately loses consciousness.

Now Duryodhana, who has not gone with the others, quickly binds Bhima with some strong vines and creepers, and rolls him into the water. The unconscious Pandava sinks down into Nagaloka, the realm of the Nagas. Alarmed by the sinking titan, thousands of serpents, their venom virulent, bite him.

The snake venom acts as an antidote to the vegetable poison in the blood of Vayu's son. The serpents bite him all over his body, except for his chest, which their needle sharp fangs cannot pierce, so tough is its skin.

Bhima awakes, and easily snapping the green thongs that hold him, falls upon the snakes, trampling hundreds of them. The rest flee to their King Vasuki, and cry, 'Nagaraja, a human sank into the river, his arms bound with cords of vines and creepers. It seems he drank poison before he fell into the water, because he was unconscious when he fell among us. But when we bit him he awoke, broke his bonds and fell on us dreadfully. Lord, you must find out who he is.'

Vasuki goes to where Bhima is; with him is an aged Naga, Aryaka. Aryaka is Kunti's great grandfather. Seeing Bhima, Aryaka knows him at once and embraces him fondly.

When Vasuki realises who this magnificent youth is, he says to Aryaka, 'We must please him. Let us give him vast gold and jewels.'

Aryaka says, 'Nagaraja, he does not need wealth as long as you are pleased with him. Let him drink from the rasakunda, the chalices of nagamrita, and acquire immense strength. Each chalice contains the might of a thousand elephants. Let this prince drink as much as he can bear.'

Vasuki agrees, and the Nagas perform auspicious initiatory rituals for the nectar drinking. Purifying himself with care, Bhimasena faces the east and begins to drink the amrita of the snakes. In one gulp he drains the first chalice; in another, the next; and so on, until he drinks eight full chalices of nagamrita.

Now, at last, he can drink no more and feels drowsy. The Nagas make a soft bed for him and he lies upon it and falls asleep."

CANTO 129

SAMBHAVA PARVA CONTINUED

Vaisampayana said, "Meanwhile, the Kauravas and the Pandavas finish their games and swimming, and set out home for Hastinapura, without Bhima. Some princes ride horses, others elephants, while still others go in chariots.

On the way, Bhima's brothers and some others say, 'Bhima must have gone alone before us.'

Duryodhana is the only one who knows the truth, and his heart is bursting for joy as he enters Hastinapura, but he says nothing, nor does he show what he feels. Of course, Yudhishtira is so virtuous that he thinks of everyone else as being as good-hearted as he is; he does not yet know what vice and evil are.

Kunti's eldest son goes straight to her, and after bowing to her, asks, 'Mother, has Bhima come home? I do not see him here. We searched for him on the banks of the river, in the garden and in the woods there, but he is nowhere to be found. We decided that he must have returned alone, before the rest of us.

But mother, I do not see him here. Have you sent him on an errand? Ah, I am sick with worry. My mighty brother was asleep beside the river and now he has vanished. I fear for his life.'

Kunti gives a small scream, and says, 'My son, I have not seen Bhima. He did not come to me. You must go back to Pramanakoti and look for him again. Go with your brothers, hurry!'

In great distress, she summons Vidura, and says, 'Illustrious Kshattri, Bhima is missing. All his other brothers have returned from the pleasure house by the river, but not my Bhima. Where has he gone?

O Vidura, Duryodhana hates my child. The Kaurava prince is evil and rash; he openly covets the throne. Oh, I am terrified that he has killed my Bhima out of his ambition. Vidura, my heart feels as if it is on fire.'

Vidura replies, 'Say nothing Kunti, think of your other sons. You must protect them. If you accuse Duryodhana, he might kill your other boys as well. The great Dwaipayana has foretold that all your sons shall live long lives. The Sage's words shall not be proved false. Bhima will come back safely to you.'

Vidura returns to his own palace, not wanting to arouse any suspicions, while Kunti remains in hers, in terrible anxiety, with her sons.

Eight nightmarish days pass for Kunti and her sons in Hastinapura. On the eighth, Bhima awakes from his deep slumber after drinking the nagamrita. He feels awesome new strength in his body – strength past measure.

Seeing him awake, the Nagas set up a cheer, crying, 'Bhimasena, the nagamrita you have drunk has given you the strength of ten thousand elephants! No one will ever be able to vanquish you in battle now. Kururishabha, now bathe in this sacred water, and go back home. Your brothers are full of anxiety for you.'

Bhima bathes in those sacral waters, puts on white robes and garlands of white flowers. He eats the paramanna, of rice and sugar, which the Nagas give him. Wearing unearthly ornaments, he receives worship and blessings from the serpents, and saluting them, thanking them, he rises up from Nagaloka in Patala.

The Nagas brings the lotus-eyed Bhima up from under the river and set him back in the same garden, on the bank where he had fallen asleep eight days ago. Then they vanish before his eyes.

Great Bhimasena now runs back to his mother, as quickly as his father Vayu flies. He bows to her and to his eldest brother Yudhishtira, and sniffs the heads of his younger brothers. She, in turn, and those other rishabhas, his brothers, embrace him, the scourge of all his enemies.

With boundless love, they cry repeatedly, 'Ah, what joy today, what wondrous joy!'

Now Bhima, the mighty, tells his brothers about the murderous treachery of Duryodhana, and also everything that happened in the realm of the Nagas.

Then Yudhishtira says, 'Do not speak of this to anyone but be silent. But from today be vigilant and all of you watch over one another closely.'

And vigilant indeed they are from then. Lest they lapse into carelessness, Vidura is always cautioning the sons of Kunti.

Some time passes, then again Duryodhana mixes some deadly poison in Bhima's food. But Yuyutsu, Dhritarashtra's son by a Vaisya woman, who loves the Pandavas, warns them. However, Bhima eats the food that Duryodhana gives him, and digests it, poison and all, with no ill effect at all.

The poison failing to do its work, Duryodhana, Karna and Shakuni hatch many other plots to kill the second Pandava. The sons of Pandu know about every one of these, but having been warned by Vidura, they never let on that they do, and never show their anger in the least way.

Meanwhile, Dhritarashtra sees the Kuru princes becoming idlers, and turning to mischief to pass their time, and appoints Kripa as their Guru, and sends them to him for instruction. Born in a bank of reeds, Kripa is a knower of the Vedas, and he becomes the Kuru princes' first master at arms."

CANTO 130

SAMBHAVA PARVA CONTINUED

Janamejaya said, "Brahmana, tell me everything about the birth of Kripa. How was he born in a bank of reeds, and where did he get his weapons from?"

Vaisampayana said, "Rajan, Maharishi Gautama had a son called Saradwat, who was born holding some arrows in his hand. Parantapa, Saradwat showed an exceptional gift for mastering the use of weapons but no special genius for any other branch of learning. He acquired all his astras with the rigours with which other Brahmanas study the Vedas.

Indra became afraid of the astras, the might and the tapasya of Saradwat. Kurusthama, the king of the Devas summoned an Apsara calls Janapadi and said to her, 'Go and distract Saradwat from his tapasya.'

Janapadi went to Saradwat's enchanting asrama, and proceeded to tempt the hermit armed with bow and arrows. Saradwat saw the nymph, who wore a single diaphanous robe over her peerless and unearthly body, and his eyes widened. His bow and arrows slipped from his hands, and his body shook with powerful emotion.

Somehow, he summoned the strength to resist her temptation, but the initial surge of excitement that seized him at the sight of her made him ejaculate involuntarily. He sprang up, left his bow and arrows and his deerskin, and fled from Janapadi as if for his life. His seed, though, had fallen into a clump of reeds, where it was divided in two. From the two portions of semen, twin children, a boy and girl, were born.

At that time, King Shantanu was out hunting in the same forest, and one of his soldiers came upon the magically born twins. The man saw the abandoned bow, quiver and deerskin, and felt the children might belong to a Brahmana who was a master at arms.

He picked up the bow and arrows, and the twins, and brought them to Shantanu. Moved to pity, Shantanu said, 'Let them be as my own children,' and took them to his palace.

Purushottama Shantanu, son of Prateepa, had the ritual karma performed for Saradwat's twins. Because he had adopted them out of pity, and because he considered them to be God's gifts of kindness to him, he called them Kripa and Kripi.

Meanwhile, having left his old asrama, Saradwat continued earnestly with his study of the science of weapons. With occult vision, he learnt that his twins were growing in the palace of Shantanu. He went to the king and told him who he was, and then he taught his son Kripa the four branches of the science of arms, and also the Vedas and other secret and hermetic mysteries.

In short time Kripa also became a master of the astra shastra. Later, Dhritarashtra's hundred sons, the Pandavas, the Yadava princes, the Vrishnis, and indeed young Kshatriyas from many other kingdoms all learnt the arts of weapons and warfare from Kripa Acharya."

CANTO 131

SAMBHAVA PARVA CONTINUED

Vaisampayana said, "Then, Bhishma thinks it is time that his grandsons receive a higher education than what Kripa can give them, and he begins to seek a Guru for his wards, a master of exceptional tejas and an even greater master of astras than Kripa.

Deciding, Bharatottama, that only he is sufficiently intelligent, illustrious, a great enough master at arms and truly one that himself possesses godlike prowess, Ganga's son, O Purushavyaghra, appoints Bharadwaja's son Drona, who knows the Vedas deeply, to be the preceptor of Kuru princes. Drona, famed throughout the world as being the greatest master of weapons, is pleased by the warm welcome and the honour accorded him by Bhishma, and he accepts charge of the Kuru princes.

He teaches them all the skills of weapons and warfare, and in quick time, the Kauravas and the Pandavas, all endowed with great strength and talent, become highly proficient in the use of every kind of weapon."'

'Janamejaya asked, "Brahmana, how was Drona born? How and where did he acquire his astras? Why did he come to the Kurus? Whose son was he, that he possessed such tejas? Also, tell us about Drona's son Aswatthama, who was also a great warrior, and how he was born.

All this I want to hear in detail, O Muni. I beg you tell me about it all."

Vaisampayana said, "At the source of the Ganga, there lived a Maharishi called Bharadwaja, always at stern and ceaseless tapa. One day, long ago, he went with many other great Rishis to the river to bathe before performing the Agnihotra. Arriving on the banks of the river, he saw the beautiful and youthful Apsara Ghritachi in the water, bathing.

Her lovely face was haughty, and now suffused with the languor of her bath, as, finishing, she rose from the water. As she stepped softly onto the bank, the single garment she wore parted, showing her shining nakedness. Seeing her like that the Rishi Bharadwaja was stricken by such desire that in a moment he ejaculated.

Hastily the Sage caught his emission in the waterpot he carried, his drana. Later, a splendid son was born from his seed, and Bharadwaja called him Drona for the vessel from which he was born.

Drona mastered the Vedas and all their angas. In the past, Bharadwaja, master of astras, had taught the secret of the fiery Agneyastra to the Rishi Agnivesha; now Agnivesha, the fireborn Sage, imparted the secret to Drona, the son of his Guru.

King Prishata of the Panchalas was a great friend of Bharadwaja. Prishata had a son, whom he named Drupada. Every day that Kshatriyarishabha, Drupada, came to Bharadwaja's asrama, to play with Drona and study with him.

Rajan, when Prishata died, the mighty-armed Drupada became king of the northern Panchalas. About this time, the illumined Bharadwaja also left his body and rose into Swarga.

Drona continued living in his father's asrama and performing tapasya. He mastered the Vedas and Vedangas, made ashes of his sins with penance, and then married Saradwata's daughter Kripi. She was chaste, always performing tapa and the agnihotra, and she gave birth to a son. As soon as he was born, he neighed delightfully, even like a small Uchhaisravas.

An invisible being spoke from the sky, 'Let the child whose cry has echoed everywhere be named Aswatthama,' which, of course, means horse-voiced.

Drona's joy knew no bounds when little Aswatthama was born; the child was the very vision of his eye. He continued living in his father's hermitage and devoted himself to the study of astra shastra, the science of weapons.

Rajan, around this time, Drona heared that the great Brahmana Parasurama Jamadagnya, son of Jamadagni, slayer of his foes, greatest of all warriors, of incalculable learning of every kind, had declared that he meant to give away all his wealth to deserving Brahmanas.

Drona had heard all about Rama's unrivalled knowledge of arms and especially the Devastras, as well as his knowledge of dharma. Drona wished fervently for both, and set out with his disciples for the Mahendra Mountain. Arriving there, he saw the Bhargava, the radiant son of Bhrigu, sitting in dhyana with his mind perfectly controlled.

Drona and his sishyas approached Rama, and Drona told the Avatara his name and that he was born into the line of Angiras. He laid his head on the ground at Parasurama's feet in worship.

Drona said, 'I am the son of Bharadwaja, but I am not born of any woman. I am a highborn Brahmana, called Drona, and I have come to you for the wealth you want to give away.'

The illumined savager of the Kshatriyas replied, 'You are welcome, Dvija! Tell me what you want from me.'

Drona replied, 'I want your immortal wealth, O you of vratas beyond count!'

'Tapasvin,' replied Rama, 'All my gold and other wealth I have already given away to various Brahmanas. This Earth also, adorned with towns and cities as with a garland, down to the very Sea, I have given to Kashyapa. I now have only this body and my astras. I can give you either of these. Say which you want, quickly!'

Drona replied, 'O Bhargava, I beg you, give me all your astras, and the mantras to cast and recall them.'

Parasurama said, 'So be it' and gave all his astras to Drona; he made a gift to him of the very astra shastra, the science of weapons, with all its mysteries and laws. Drona received this greatest gift in joy, and prostrating gratefully at Bhargava's feet, set out for the city of his childhood friend Drupada."

CANTO 132

SAMBHAVA PARVA CONTINUED

Vaisampayana said, "O King, Bharadwaja's mighty son presents himself before King Drupada, and says joyfully, 'I am your friend Drona!'

But the lord of the Panchalas does not like what he hears. Deluded by power and wealth, he knits his brows in anger, and his eyes turn red.

Drupada replies, 'Brahmana, surely you are dimwitted that you suddenly claim to be my friend! Fool, how can a great king like me and a pauper like you be friends? Yes, once we were both students in your father's asrama and then we were equals and also friends.

Time wears away all things and friendship as well. In this world, no friendship endures in any heart, for time gnaws at it and anger destroys it. Forget, Brahmanashreshta, that we were ever friends. That old friendship I had with you was for a specific purpose: you were my Guru's son.

Between a rich man and a poor one, between a learned man and an unlettered one, between a hero and a coward, how can there ever be friendship? Why do you want to be my friend? There can be friendship or even enmity between equals in wealth or in strength. A beggar and a king can neither have friendship nor enmity between them, for they are not equals but a superior and an inferior.

A pure born man can never have friendship with a lowborn one. A man who is a Maharatha cannot be the friend of a man who is not a Maharatha; and a king cannot be the friend of one who is not a king! Tell me, foolish Drona, why do you invoke our old friendship and dream of renewing it?'

Drona trembles with wrath. He says nothing, but considers for a moment what he would do to Drupada, to humble the Panchala king. Turning on his heel, he strides out from Drupada's court and makes his way towards the capital of the Kurus, named after the elephant."

CANTO 133

SAMBHAVA PARVA CONTINUED

Vaisampayana said, "Drona comes to Hastinapura and, without disclosing his presence in the city, begins living in the house of his brother-in-law, Kripa. During the intervals between Kripa's classes to the Kuru princes, Drona's son Aswatthama gives Kunti's sons some casual hints about the use of arms. But he does not reveal his true skills even to them, or how mighty he is.

Drona has been living secretly in Kripa's house for some time, when, one day, all the Kuru princes come out of the city together. They begin to roam about, in freedom, and to play with a ball, which soon enough falls down a well. The young Kshatriyas do their best to retrieve the ball, but in vain; they cannot fetch it out.

They feel ashamed and begin to look at one another with some anxiety: Imagine, the great scions of the House of Kuru not being able to get a ball out of a well! Suddenly, they see a rather dark-skinned, lean Brahmana quite close to them; he has obviously just performed the Agnihotra and sanctified himself with it, and finished his nitya, his daily worship.

The princes are drawn to the stranger and surround him. Smiling slightly, Drona says, 'Well, Princes, a shame upon your Kshatriya prowess, and a shame also upon your skill at arms. To think that you are born in the race of Bhaarata and cannot retrieve a ball from a well. Promise to feed me tonight and I will fetch out your ball for you with these blades of grass. Look, I will throw my ring after your ball and fetch that as well.'

Drona pulls a valuable ring from his finger and throws it into the well.

Yudhishtira says, 'Brahmana, you ask for a trifle. With Acharya Kripa's leave, ask us for something that will last you a lifetime.'

His smile widening, Drona says, 'With mantras I will make astras of these long blades of grass. This grass will have powers that other weapons do not. One blade will pierce your ball, another my ring, and the rest shall form a chain and fetch both out of the well.'

Without a moment's hesitation, Drona does exactly as he says. The princes goggle; they feel their chests will burst with wonder and disbelief.

They whisper, 'We bow to you, O Brahmana, no one on Earth has your skills. Tell us who you are, tell us whose son you are. Tell us what we can do for you.'

Drona replies, 'Go to Bhishma, describe me to him and tell him what I did. He will know who I am.'

The princes cry, 'We will!' and run to their grandsire, and tell him about the extraordinary Brahmana's feat. Bhishma knows at once that this is Drona they describe. He knows that this is the Guru he has been seeking for his grandsons, and goes out himself to welcome the Brahmana reverently, and brings him into the palace.

Bhishma, greatest of warriors, asks Drona, 'What brings a Mahapurusha like you to Hastinapura?'

Drona tells him his story. 'Mighty Bhishma, I once went to the Rishi Agnivesha to learn the use of weapons and the astra shastra from him. I lived as a brahmacharin, with jata on my head, and served my Guru humbly for many years.

At that time, the Panchala prince Drupada Yagnasena also lived in the same asrama, serving Agnivesha as I did for the same reason that I did. He and I became friends; he always looked after me and we grew close as brothers, loving each other dearly. As I said, many years we spent together.

O Kurusthama, we were together from our early boyhood, studying together, and Drupada always did and said whatever he felt would please me. Once, O Bhishma, he said to me, "Drona, I am my great father's favourite son. When I become king of the Panchalas, my kingdom shall be yours. My precious friend, this I swear. My kingship, my wealth and my happiness will all depend on you, O Drona."

Finally, we finished our tutelage, and he left for home. We parted warmly; he repeated what he had said to me, and ever since I have kept it in my heart.

A while later, my father wanted me to marry and since I also wanted to have a son, I married Kripi of the short hair, of great intelligence, who kept many stern vratas and always performed the agnihotra and other austere rituals.

In time, she gave birth to our son Aswatthama, who is as splendid as the Sun and as powerful. I was as delighted when my son was born as my father had been when I was born. I doted on him.

One day, Aswatthama saw some rich men's sons drinking milk, which we could not afford, and began crying. I felt so stricken that I lost my very reason, why, I could not have told east from west, or north from south, so sad did I feel. I could have begged for a cow, but it would have been of someone who had only a few cows himself and would have perhaps had to stop performing his sacrifices and lost punya because of that.

Instead, I decided I would beg a cow from someone who had many cows and would not feel the loss of one. I wandered from country to country, kingdom to kingdom, but I could not get myself a milch cow.

When I returned home, disappointed, I saw something that truly broke my heart. Some of my son's playmates mixed powdered rice in water and gave it to my little Aswatthama, telling him that it was milk. My poor child drank it eagerly, and began to dance for joy, crying, 'I have drunk milk! I have drunk milk today!'

His friends grinned at his naïveté. Then there were those that whispered, but within my hearing, 'Drona claims to be the greatest master of weapons on earth. But he makes no effort to earn a livelihood and his son drinks rice powder mixed in water and dances for joy thinking that it is milk.'

I was desperate, but I still decided that even if I had to live as an outcast, I would not become anyone's servant for the sake of wealth. Then I heard that Drupada, my old friend, had become king of the Somaka Panchalas. In great joy, the words he had once said to me ringing in my mind, fondly remembering our old friendship, I took my wife and my child and went in great hope to Drupada's kingdom.

He made me wait a day before he even allowed me into his court, but I never doubted him for a moment. Entering his grand sabha, I cried, 'Purushavyaghra, tiger among men, I am your friend Drona, to whom you promised your kingdom!'

I approached him confidently, as a friend should. But Drupada laughed in my face; he mocked me, saying, 'Brahmana, surely you are dimwitted that you suddenly claim to be my friend. Fool, how can a great king like me and a pauper like you be friends? Yes, once we were both students in your father's asrama and then we were equals and also friends.

Time wears all things away and friendship as well. In this world, no friendship endures in any heart, for time gnaws at it and anger destroys it. Forget, Brahmanottama, that we were ever friends. The old friendship that I had with you was for a specific purpose.

Between a rich man and a poor one, between a learned man and an unlettered one, between a hero and a coward, how can there ever be friendship? Why do you want to be my friend? There can be friendship or even enmity between equals in wealth or in strength. A beggar and a king can neither have friendship nor enmity between them, for they are not equals but a superior and an inferior.

A pure born man can never have friendship with a lowborn one. A man who is a Maharatha cannot be the friend of a man who is not a Maharatha; and a king cannot be the friend of one who is not a king. Tell me, foolish Drona, why do you invoke our old friendship and dream of renewing it?

I do not remember ever having promised you my kingdom, but Brahmana I will certainly give you shelter for a night, and food.'

With my wife and child, I left his palace and his city immediately, vowing in my heart to do what I certainly will, and soon. Anger seethes in me, O Bhishma, ever since Drupada humiliated me. His mockery rings in my ears. I have come to the Kurus to find gifted and obedient pupils; I have come to fulfil your wishes. Tell me what I should do now.'

Bhishma says to Bharadwaja's son, 'String your bow, Brahmana, and make the Kuru princes master warriors. You shall have honour and worship in Hastinapura, and a fine home filled with every luxury, which you must enjoy to your heart's content. Drona, from now you are the lord of whatever wealth the Kurus own, and of their kingdom and sovereignty.

From today, the Kurus belong to you, so whatever the wish that burns your heart: consider it already accomplished. You, O Brahmana are the fruit of our greatest punya and fortune. By coming here you confer the greatest favour upon me.'"

CANTO 134

SAMBHAVA PARVA CONTINUED

Vaisampayana said, "Honoured by Bhishma, that Manavottama Drona, tejasvin, now begins living openly among the Kurus, who duly revere him. When he has rested, Bhishma brings his grandsons to the Brahmana, and also many precious gifts. The mighty Bhishma joyfully gives Bharadwaja's son a fine house in which to live, stocked with rice and furnished with every comfort and all manner of wealth.

Drona, best of archers, now accepts the sons of Pandu and the sons of Dhritarashtra to be his sishyas. He takes them apart, makes them touch his feet, and then says to them with some emotion, 'There is something that I want you to do for me when I have made you master warriors. Tell me, princes, that you will do what I want.'

All the other Kuru princes remain silent, but without a moment's hesitation Arjuna says, 'I will do whatever you want.'

Drona clasps Arjuna in an embrace, sniffs the top of the prince's head repeatedly in affection, and tears roll down his cheeks. The princes' tutelage begins, and he teaches them the use of weapons both mundane and unearthly. Bharatarishabha, apart from the young Kurus, many other Kshatriyas princes from other lands come to Drona for instruction, including the Suta's son Karna.[8*]

Karna is envious of Arjuna and frequently taunts the Pandava; Duryodhana befriends him and together they always mock all the sons of Pandu. But Arjuna is entirely devoted to the study of the astra shastra, and becomes like his master's shadow. He excels all the rest in his natural gifts, his prowess especially with the longbow, and his dedication and perseverance.

Drona teaches them all equally, but quickly Arjuna outstrips the others, and the master is soon convinced that none of the rest could ever hope to match the skills of this pupil, the son of Indra.

Drona's lessons continue, and one day he gives all his pupils earthen pots to fill with water from the river and bring back. To his own son Aswatthama he gives a pot with a larger mouth than all the rest. He says that the lesson would begin as soon as the first student arrives in his presence with a full waterpot. Of course, Aswatthama arrives earlier than the princes and his father imparts some choice secrets of the astra shastra to him.

Arjuna chafes at this for some days, then, one morning, he arrives with a filled waterpot long before even Aswatthama, and in honour now, Drona teaches this exceptional pupil before the others; he shares his special secrets with Arjuna, who has used the Varunastra to fill his vessel.

So, Aswatthama loses his advantage and Arjuna serves his Guru so diligently and lovingly that he becomes Drona's favourite sishya, yes, as dear to him, at least, as his own son.

One day, Drona summons the palace cook and says to him, 'Never serve Arjuna his meal in the dark, and do not tell him that I said anything to you.'

---

[8] There is some doubt about Karna appearing here. It seems likely that he enters the picture only later, during the exhibition of arms.

However, just a few days later, while Arjuna is eating his night meal a sudden gust of wind blows out the lamp upon his table. Arjuna continues eating in the dark, by force of habit his hand taking the food to his mouth without the help of his eyes. That brilliant prince does not fail to notice this. It means that now he can continue to practise his archery at night!

The same night, Drona hears the lone twang of a bowstring, and coming out embraces his favourite sishya. The Acharya cries, 'I swear that you will be the greatest archer in the world, and no one shall be your equal.'

Now Drona teaches Arjuna the art of fighting from horseback, from the back of an elephant, from a chariot, and on the ground. He teaches Arjuna all about the mace, the sword, the lance, the spear and the dart; he teaches him how to fight many opponents simultaneously.

Drona's fame as an unrivalled master spreads across the land, and princes and even kings arrive in Hastinapura from the most far-flung places, in thousands, to have some instructions from the Acharya. Among those that come, in hope, O Rajan, is Ekalavya, son of Hiranyadhanush, king of the Nishadas. Drona senses the boy's genius at once and refuses to take him as his pupil, saying that he is a Nishada. The master fears this youth might surpass all his highborn sishyas.

But, O Parantapa, Ekalavya lays his head at Drona's feet, makes his way into the deep jungle, where he fashions a lifelike image in clay of Drona, and begins to worship the statue as if this is Drona himself, whom the youth has taken in his heart for his Guru.

Before that clay image Ekalavya ceaselessly practises with his bow and arrows. Such is his devotion to his master, his extraordinary talent, and the rigour of his discipline that he quickly becomes an exceptional archer. Effortlessly he fits arrows to his bowstring, aims and looses them with unerring accuracy: the three parts of archery. His skill is prodigious, matchless.

One day, with Drona's leave, the Kuru and Pandava princes go hunting in their chariots. A servant follows them, with a hunting dog and carrying whatever the princes might need in the wilderness.

Arriving in the forest, the young Kshatriyas earnestly begin their hunt. The dog wanders off on its own and comes upon Ekalavya. It sees the black Nishada, covered in dirt, wearing a black hide, his hair tangled in wild jata, and barks at him.

Quick as thinking, Ekalvya turns and shoots seven arrows into the dog's mouth, silencing it. Whimpering, the dog runs back to its masters, the princes. They gape in wonder and disbelief at the beast. They feel humbled, for certainly none of them could have shot seven arrows into the dog's mouth so swiftly and unerringly, when it must have turned to run after receiving the first one.

The princes comb the forest for the hidden archer. Soon enough, they find him, shooting arrows from his bow in an incredible, endless stream. Seeing the grim faced stranger, they ask, 'Whose son are you?'

He replies, 'Kshatriyas, I am the son of Hiranyadhanush, king of the Nishadas. Know that I am the sishya of Drona, and I toil to become a master of the longbow.'

The Kuru princes learn all there is to know about Ekalavya, ride back to Hastinapura and go straight to Drona, to whom they describe the miraculous archery that the young Nishada in the forest displayed.

Arjuna is terribly distressed, trembling with envy. He draws Drona aside privately and says accusingly, 'Master, you clasped me in your arms with love and told me that no other pupil of yours would be my equal, and that I would be the greatest archer in the world. How, then, is the Nishada king's son clearly better than I am?'

Drona thinks for a moment, and quickly decides what he must do. Taking only Arjuna with him, he goes into the jungle to where Ekalavya was. He sees the Nishada prince, wearing filthy rags, matted jata on his head, his body covered in dirt, with a bow in his hands from which the arrows flare in a ceaseless, effortless tide.

When Ekalavya sees Drona, he runs to him, touches his feet and prostrates himself before the Brahmana. Worshipping Drona, the Nishada tells him that he is his sishya and then stands with folded hands, awaiting his Guru's command.

Rajan, now Drona says to Ekalavya, 'If, O Archer, you are truly my sishya, then you must give me dakshina.'

Beaming to hear this, Ekalavya cries, 'O my Guru, tell me what you want as dakshina, for there is nothing that I will not give my master.'

Drona says, 'Ekalavya, give me the thumb of your right hand.'

Never pausing, the smile of joy still on his face, Ekalavya slices off his right thumb with a sharp arrow and hands it to Drona. When his wound heals, and he begins to shoot again without his thumb, he is not the archer he has been; he has lost his lightlike swiftness and sureness of hand. Arjuna's feverish jealousy leaves him.

Two of Drona's pupils are masters of the mace: Duryodhana and Bhima, who, of course, are inveterate rivals, as well. Aswatthama excels all the others at the secrets of the most mysterious astras; Nakula and Sahadeva are the finest swordsmen; Yudhishtira is the best rathika, chariot warrior. However, as a complete warrior, Arjuna has no equal by a long way: he is the most intelligent, resourceful, tireless and persevering prince.

A great master of every weapon, he outstrips the greatest of Maharathas, and his renown spreads across the world, from sea to sea. Though all the princes receive the same instruction, none can approach Arjuna at archery, or, indeed, in the devotion he bears to his Guru.

Amongst all the princes, Arjuna alone becomes an Atiratha, a chariot warrior who can face sixty thousand enemies at once! Dhritarashtra's fell sons see the awesome strength of Bhima and the matchless archery of Arjuna, and envy roils their very entrails.

Narapumgava, one day, when their tutelage is complete, Drona wants to test the skills of his disciples, and gathers them together. Before this, he has a wooden bird, a vulture, made and perched on the highest branch of a lofty tree, to be a target.

When the princes stand before him, Drona says crisply, 'Pick up your bows and aim at the bird in the tree. As soon as I tell you, shoot to cut its head off. You will each have one shot, turn by turn.'

Drona, best among all Angira's descendants, says first to Yudhishtira, 'Yudhishtira, you will have the first chance.'

Yudhishitra picks up his bow and aims at the faraway wooden bird. Bharatarishabha, now Drona asks Yudhishtira, 'Prince, do you see the bird on the treetop?'

Yudhishtira replies to his Guru, 'I do.'

Drona now asks, 'What else do you see? Do you see the tree, your brothers, and me?'

Yudhishtira says, 'I see the tree, yourself, my brothers and the bird.'

Drona repeats his question, and Yudhishtira's reply is the same. Apparently annoyed, Drona says, 'Stand back, Yudhishtira; you will not strike the bird.'

Now Drona calls, one by one, the other princes, Duryodhana and his brothers, Bhima and also the princes from other lands who are his disciples. He asks each one the same question, and from each he has the same answer that Yudhishtira gives him: 'I see the tree, yourself, my fellow sishyas, and the bird.'

Drona does not give any of them a chance to shoot at the wooden bird but reproachfully tells them all to stand down."

CANTO 135

SAMBHAVA PARVA CONTINUED

Vaisampayana said, "When all the other princes have failed his test, Drona, with a smile, calls on Arjuna. He says, 'It seems you are the one to bring the bird down. Raise your bow and aim, my son.'

Arjuna raises his bow, bends it and takes aim. He stands very still, then Drona asks softly, 'Arjuna, do you see the bird, the tree and me?'

Arjuna replies, 'I only see the bird, master, not the tree or you.'

Drona seems pleased with Arjuna's answer. He asks that Pandava Maharatha, 'If you see only the vulture, describe it to me.'

Arjuna says, 'I see only the head of the vulture, not its body.'

The hair on Drona's body stands on end in delight. He says to Partha, 'Shoot it.' Arjuna looses his arrow and neatly severs the wooden vulture's head, bringing it down. Drona clasps Arjuna in his arms; he feels certain that Drupada and his allies are as good as vanquished.

Some days after this, Bharatarishabha, Drona goes to bathe in the holy Ganga, taking all his pupils with him. As soon as Drona enters the water an enormous crocodile, which seems to have been sent by Yama himself, seizes him by the thigh. Now, the Brahmana is quite capable of killing the beast and saving himself. Instead, pretending to be helpless, he cries as if in a panic to his sishyas on the shore, 'Save me! Save me!'

The words hardly leave his mouth, when Arjuna has shot the monstrous crocodile with five terrific arrows, cutting it in five pieces so it releases Drona's leg and dies, while the others still stand dazed on the riverbank. Once again, seeing how vigilant Arjuna is, how quick his reflexes are, Drona is pleased no end.

Bharadwaja's illustrious son says to the irresistible rathika Arjuna, 'Powerful one, receive this ineluctable astra from me, and the mantras for discharging and recalling it. It is the Brahmasirsa, the weapon formed like the heads of Brahma. You must never cast it at any human adversary, for if invoked against an inferior enemy it can consume the very universe.

Child, they say that this astra has no equal in the three worlds. Keep it with the utmost care. If ever a superhuman enemy threatens you, you can use the Brahmasirsa to kill him, and only then.'

Arjuna swears that he will do as Drona says, and then, folding his hands to his Guru, receives that Mahastra.

Drona says to him, 'No one on Earth shall become a better archer than you. No enemy shall ever vanquish you, and your achievements shall be unparalleled.'"

CANTO 136

SAMBHAVA PARVA CONTINUED

Vaisampayana said, "O Bhaarata, when Drona sees that his pupils, the sons of Dhritarashtra and Pandu, are masters at arms, he goes to the blind king and speaks to him in the presence of Kripa, Somadatta, Bahlika, the sage Bhishma, Vyasa and Vidura.

Drona says, 'Greatest of the Kuru kings, your children's tutelage is complete. I crave your leave for them to show their skills to the people, at an exhibition of arms.'

Dhritarashtra says in joy, 'Brahmana, you have accomplished a great task. You decide the time, the place and the nature of the exhibition. Ah, today sorrow overwhelms me that I am blind and I envy those blessed with sight who can watch my children perform. Vidura, my brother, give Drona all the help he needs; nothing will make me happier.'

Vidura assures the king that he will, and goes with Drona. Drona selects a plot of land where no trees or bushes grow, but which has a good number of wells and small springs. Upon that land, he worships and offers a sacrifice to the Gods, on a day of an auspicious nakshatra, in the presence of the people. Bharatarishabha, the king's artisans build a large and elegant arena and dais on that land, by the rules for such a construction laid down in the Shastras. They bring every kind of weapon to the dais.

They build a separate, fine enclosure for the women, while the common citizens build themselves tiered stands from where to watch the princes' display, while the richer ones pitch bright and luxurious tents for themselves around the arena.

Comes the day of the tournament and Dhritarashtra arrives at the royal enclosure, of almost unearthly beauty, made from gold, adorned with strings of pearls, and with lapis lazuli. Bhishma and the great Kripa walk before Dhritarashtra, and his ministers come with him.

Wearing rich finery, accompanied by their sakhis, Gandhari, of great fortune, Kunti and the other ladies of the royal household climb the steps to their platforms, even as the Devastris do the Sumeru Mountain, in joy.

People of the four varnas throng the arena, to watch the princes show their skills. So impatient are they that the teeming crowd assembles there in what seems like a single moment. Trumpets blare, drums sound on every side, and the voices of the people echo as a single great voice. The arena is like a disturbed sea.

Finally, Drona, wearing white, the sacred thread around his body white, his hair all white, and his beard, as also the garland he wears, and his body smeared with white sandalwood paste, enters the arena, with Aswatthama at his side. They appear like the full Moon in a clear sky with Mangala, Mars, beside him.

Entering, the son of Bharadwaja performs the apposite worship, and other Brahmans, all knowers of mantras, perform every auspicious and solemn ritual. Melodious music is played on stringed and wind instruments, then some servitors enter, bearing armfuls of shining weapons, which they set down upon the dais.

Now the Bhaarata princes, mighty Kshatriyas, file in, led by the eldest prince, Yudhishtira. They wear gauntlets, and carry bows and quivers, and march in, in order of their age, and begin a breathtaking display of their skills at arms.

So powerful and swift is that exhibition that some of the people lower or cover their heads in fright, that arrows might fall upon them from the sky, while others watch calmly, but wonder-stricken.

Targets are set up, each bearing one prince's name. Flying around the arena on horseback every prince finds his own target, unerringly, with a clutch of arrows. So magnificent are they that the people feel they have been transported to a city of Gandharvas.

And, O Bhaarata, suddenly hundreds of thousands of voices are raised, crying, 'O well done! Well done!' The people gape in wonder.

Repeatedly, the princes show their mastery at the longbow, their stunning skills as charioteers. Then they pick up their swords and small shields, and begin to circle the arena, like a pride of young lions. The people stare unwinkingly at their magnificent physiques, their agility, grace and lightning-swift control over their weapons, with which they hew and strike at one another, but never once so much as nick their adversaries' skin.

Next, like two mountains Bhima and Suyodhana enter the arena, maces in hand, both of them inwardly delighted at the prospect of this duel. They gird their loins and, drawing deep breaths, roar like two elephants trumpeting against each other for the favours of a cow-elephant.

Like two enraged elephants, the two awesome Kshatriyas circle each other, right and then left, and then they strike out like thunder and lightning at one another, while Vidura describes their duel to the blind Dhritarashtra and Kunti does the same for Gandhari, whose eyes are bound."

CANTO 137

SAMBHAVA PARVA CONTINUED

Vaisampayana continued, "When Duryodhana and Bhima, strongest of all Kshatriyas, fight in the arena, they immediately divide the spectators between them.

Some of the people cry, 'Look at the mighty Suyodhana!'

Others shout, 'Bhima! The invincible Bhima!'

There is great uproar, and seeing the crowd like an agitated sea, Drona immediately calls his son and says, 'Stop them! They must not divide the people like this and provoke the fury of the crowd.'

Aswatthama comes between the combatants, who have their maces in the air and are like two swollen oceans agitated by the winds of the Pralaya. Reluctantly they stand apart.

Now Drona walks into the arena himself and holds his hand up so the musicians stop playing and silence falls. Drona speaks in a voice like rumbling clouds, 'Now you will see the skills of Arjuna, dearer to me than my own son. Partha is the son of Indra and a master of every weapon, like Vishnu's younger brother himself!'

The young Arjuna performs the rites of propitiation, and walks into the arena wearing his finger-guards, carrying his bow and his quiver full of arrows, clad in golden mail. He appears like an evening cloud that reflects the sun's last rays, and is lit by the colours of a rainbow, and also by streaks of lightning.

The crowd is beside itself to see this prince, and conches resound all around the stadium, and the musicians take up again in celebration. There is a great roar in that place, for thousands of voices are raised at once in praise of Arjuna.

'Here is Kunti's son, so full of grace!'

'This is the third Pandava, the middle one!'

'He is the son of Indra!'

'The protector of the Kurus!'

'The greatest warrior!'

'The greatest man of dharma!'

'No one is as dignified, respectful and well behaved as Arjuna!'

When Kunti hears all this, her breasts well with milk, and the tears of joy that stream from her eyes mingle with the milk.

Dhritarashtra hears the uproar of affection for Arjuna, and in some delight asks Vidura, 'Kshatri, what is this din, like an ocean suddenly risen to tear open the sky?'

Vidura replies, 'Rajan, Arjuna, the son of Pandu and Pritha, has entered the arena wearing his kavacha. The crowd is shouting for him!'

Dhritarashtra says, 'Mahatman, I am blessed, favoured and protected by the three fires that have sprung from the sacred fuel which is Kunti!'

When the excited people are somewhat calm again, Arjuna begins an amazing display of his skills at arms. He makes fire with the Agneyastra, creates water with the Varunastra, winds with the Vayavyastra, and clouds in the sky with the Parjannyastra.

With the Bhaumastra he creates land, earth, and with the Parvatyastra he makes mountains; then, with the Antardhana, he makes all these vanish in a wink. With other weapons, he makes himself great and minuscule; one moment, he appears at his chariothead; the next, he rides in the chariot; and the next instant he stands upon the ground.

He strikes targets set up for him with dazzling volleys of different shafts, some soft, some slender and others thick. An iron boar flies, swift as time, around the arena, and the peerless bowman shoots five arrows, like a single shaft into its mouth, all five together from his bowstring. He looses twenty-one shafts into a hollow cow's horn hung from a rope swaying wide.

Sinless one, Arjuna shows his magical skills at the longbow, the sword and the mace, as he walks around the arena.

Bhaarata, when Arjuna has almost finished his stunning display, when the crowd has fallen hushed by it, and the music, too, has stopped, suddenly, from the main gate to the arena comes a sound of someone slapping his arms against his shoulders and chest, like thunder, announcing himself and his might.

O King, the people cower at that sound, thinking, 'Are the mountains being riven, is the Earth herself cracking open, or are thunderheads roaring from a clear sky?'

Every eye is turned to the gate. Drona stands very still, with the five Pandavas around him, looking like the Moon surrounded by the five stars of the constellation Hasta. Duryodhana jumps up, surrounded by his hundred brothers and Aswatthama with them. The Kaurava prince and his brothers with their weapons raised looks like Indra, in the eldest days, surrounded by his celestial warriors just before the war against the Danavas."

CANTO 138

SAMBHAVA PARVA CONTINUED

Vaisampayana continued, "Slowly, wide-eyed, the people make way for that Purandara, and Karna enters the arena majestically, a walking mountain of presence, with his natural golden armour, his golden earrings that he is born with, his sword at his waist and his bow in his hand.

The great-eyed hero, who would become a razer of enemy armies, is Kunti's son, born when she is a virgin in her father's house. He is an amsa of the livid Sun, and his strength and his energy are those of a lion, a bull or of a tusker that leads his herd. He is as splendid as Surya, as handsome as Soma, and he blazes like Agni Deva. He is tall, like a golden palm tree, bursting with vital youth, and he can kill a lion with his bare hands, that son of Surya.

Handsome is Karna, and beyond counting his gifts and accomplishments. He walks haughtily into the arena and bows cursorily to Drona and Kripa, barely inclining his head. No one in the crowd can take their eyes off him for a moment and a single impatient thought is in everyone's mind: 'Who is he, this godlike warrior?'

The Suryaputra says to Arjuna, his brother he does not know, in a voice deep as rumbling thunderheads, 'I will better your every feat, O Partha, before this staring crowd, and you will be astonished.'

In a moment, that crowd is on its feet, as if compelled to rise by an unseen and irresistible force. O Purushavyaghra, suddenly Duryodhana feels a tide of joy in his blood, while Arjuna feels a rush of shame and anger.

Taking Drona's permission, formally, Karna proceeds calmly to perform every feat that Arjuna has; only he excels the Pandava's exhibition, effortlessly. Duryodhana and his brothers run to embrace the golden warrior.

Duryodhana cries in joy, 'Welcome, O Mahabaho, great hero! It is my great fortune that has brought you here today. Live among us as long as you please, for I am yours to command, as is this kingdom of the Kurus.'

Karna replies, 'When you say it, I think of it as being already done. But, Suyodhana, I want only your friendship and your love. Also, my lord, I now challenge Arjuna to single combat, a duel.'

Duryodhana says, 'Enjoy the best that life has to offer with me. Be my friend and my benefactor. O Parantapa, grind the heads of your enemies beneath your feet.'

Feeling humiliated, Arjuna says to Karna, who stands among the Kauravas like some shining cliff, 'Karna, you shall find the fate of the unwelcome intruder and the uninvited speaker, for I will kill you.'

Karna replies, 'This arena is not your private preserve, Arjuna, but meant for everyone to show their skills. The Kshatriya regards deeds not words. Argument is for the weak. Bhaarata, talk to me with arrows and I will strike your head off with arrows, why, in the very presence of your Guru.'

His brothers embrace Arjuna, one by one, and bowing to Drona, Partha stands forth, ready for the duel. On the other side, Duryodhana and his brothers embrace Karna, and he also stands forth with his bow and arrows. Suddenly the sky fills with dark clouds, gashed by lightning, and Indra's bow, the rainbow, the Indradhanush, flashes its colours across the stadium and the arena. A flight of white cranes wings its way across the clouds, which seem to rumble with laughter at the pale birds.

Seeing Indra looking down upon the arena of the Kurus, out of love for his son, Surya dispels the clouds above his son, bathing Karna in golden light. Arjuna is hidden by the darkness of clouds, while Karna shines in the rays of the Sun.

Dhritarashtra's sons stand with Karna, while Drona, Kripa and Bhishma stand behind Arjuna. The crowd is also divided in its loyalty, as are the women in their enclosure. Realising who the golden warrior is, Kunti faints. Helped by the women of the palace, Vidura revives her by sprinkling sandalwood paste mixed with water over her.

Waking, Kunti sees her two sons, wearing armour, facing each other, and fear grips her. But she is helpless to do anything. Saradwat's son Kripa sees the two warriors with their bows in their hands, strung, ready for the duel. He knows the rules for such an encounter and speaks to Karna.

Kripa says, 'This Pandava of the House of Kuru is the youngest son of Kunti, and stands ready to battle with you. Mahabaho, you must also declare yourself. Tell us your lineage, the names of your father and your mother, and of the royal line of which you are the jewel. When you have declared your ancestry, Arjuna will decide if he will fight you or not. For the sons of kings never engage lowborn men.'

Suddenly Karna's face falls; he is like a brilliant lotus turned pale and its petals shredded by lashing rain.

But now Duryodhana speaks. 'Acharya, the Shastras clearly say that three kinds of men can claim royalty for themselves: those that are born royal, great heroes and men that lead armies. If Arjuna will not fight anyone that is less than a king, I say to you I will crown Karna king of Anga!'

Immediately calling for a golden throne to be fetched, with dry rice grains, flowers, urns with holy water, gold for daana, Duryodhana has his Brahmanas formally crown Karna king of Anga, which is part of the

Kuru kingdom but has no ruler. The white sovereign parasol is unfurled over Karna's head, and yak-tail chamaras waved around that most graceful and tremendous warrior.

When the lusty cheering of the section of the crowd loyal to Duryodhana subsides, Karna, now a king, says to the Kaurava prince, 'Tiger among princes, what can I give you in return for this gift of a kingdom? I will give you anything at all.'

Suyodhana says to him, 'I want your friendship.'

Karna replies, 'That is already yours.'

They embrace in joy, and feel untold delight."

CANTO 139

SAMBHAVA PARVA CONTINUED

Vaisampayana said, 'Now Adhiratha walks into the arena, sweating, trembling, and supporting himself with a staff.'

Karna sees his adoptive father, puts down his bow and bows his head still dripping with the waters of the abhisheka that has made him a king. The Suta charioteer quickly covers his feet with his cloth and clasps Karna in his arms, his son who has become a king! His tears of love and joy fall onto Karna's head, mingling with the water of the coronation.

Bhima sees Adhiratha and mocks Karna, 'Suta putra, son of a charioteer, you do not deserve to die at Arjuna's hands. Throw away your bow and take up a horsewhip; it better suits your birth and your station. Lowborn fellow, surely you deserve to be king of Anga as much as a dog deserves to feed on the ghee from a yagna fire!'

Karna fetches a resounding sigh and looks up in despair at the Sun God in the sky, for he cannot respond to Bhima's taunts. But now, like a maddened elephant rising from a bank of lotuses, Duryodhana rises in wrath from amongst his brothers.

He says to the mighty Bhima, 'Vrikodara, your words demean you. A Kshatriya is always judged by just his prowess, and a Kshatriya even if he is a lowborn, deserves a fight if he is powerful. The origin of the greatest heroes is like the spring of a great river: unknown, hidden.

The Badava that consumes the world in flames rises from the Sea; the Vajra that burns the Danavas is made from a bone of a mortal man: Dadhichi. The lineage of the lustrous God Kartikeya, who is an amsa of every other Deva, the deity Guha, remains a mystery. Some say he is the son of Agni; some say he is Krittika's son; others say he is the child of Rudra, and yet others say he is Ganga's son.

We have all heard of men born as Kshatriyas becoming Brahmanas. Viswamitra and other Rajarishis, too, attained the Parabrahman. Our peerless Acharya Drona is born from a waterpot, and Kripa of the race of Gautama in a clump of reeds. O Pandavas, consider your own births!

I ask you, can a doe bring forth a tiger like this Karna, as splendid as the Sun, and bearing every auspicious mark upon his body, and born with natural kavacha and kundala? I tell you this prince among men deserves to be not merely king of Anga but of the world! For he is so mighty, and I have sworn to obey him in all things. If there is anyone here who disagrees with what I have done for Karna, let him climb into his chariot and bend his bow with his feet!'

There is a loud and somewhat confused murmur among the crowd at what Duryodhana says. But now the Sun sets and Duryodhana takes Karna's hand and leads him out of the arena, now being lit with countless lamps. Rajan, the Pandavas, with Drona, Bhishma and Kripa, also return to the palace. The people also go to their homes, some with Arjuna's name on their lips, others with Karna's and others praising Duryodhana's deed.

Kunti, who recognises her firstborn son from all the auspicious marks upon his body, is delighted to see him made king of Anga. As for Duryodhana, having made a friend of Karna, he banishes the fear of

Arjuna's stellar archery from his heart. Karna, great warrior, gives his wholehearted friendship and loyalty, and speaks sweetly and gently to the Kaurava prince, pleasing him in every way.

Yudhishtira is certain that there is no warrior on Earth like Karna."

CANTO 140

SAMBHAVA PARVA CONTINUED

Vaisampayana continued, "Now that their education is complete and the sons of Dhritarashtra and Pandu are proficient at arms, Drona feels the time has come to ask them for Guru dakshina. He calls them together one day and says, 'It is time you gives me my dakshina for what I have taught you. I want you to vanquish the Panchala king Drupada in battle, bind him and bring him before me as a captive.'

Without hesitation, the young Kshatriyas reply, 'We shall!' They climb into their chariots and ride out of Hastinapura, taking Drona with them, to give their Guru the fee he wants. Those Purusharishabhas, bulls among men, sweep through Panchala lands, disdainfully razing any resistance they meet, and lay siege to Drupada's capital.

Duryodhana, Karna, mighty Yuyutsu, Dushasana, Vikarna, Jalasandha, Sulochana and so many other tremendous Kshatriya princes are now keen to lead the attack on the city. Riding in fine chariots, the princes follow the first charge of their cavalry, burst into the Panchala capital and thunder down the city streets.

Drupada, meanwhile, sees the attacking force; he hears the din it makes as it breaches his city gates and emerges from his palace with his brothers to face the intruders. The great Drupada Yagnasena is mighty indeed, but the Kurus roar all together and cover him with their arrows. But Drupada is a quenchless Kshatriya, with hardly an equal on Earth at arms; he flies at the enemy in his flashing white chariot, flitting here and there, and assailing them with a veritable gale of arrows from his wizardly bow.

Before this battle begins, and while the Kauravas are beating their chests to be at the city and its king, Arjuna does not string his bow but says quietly to his master, the great Brahmana, 'None of these can ever hope to take captive Drupada in battle. Let him exhaust them and then we will ride.'

Thus, the Pandavas wait a yojana outside the city, while the Kauravas attack it. Inside Drupada's capital, in the main city-square outside the palace, Drupada by now has the measure of the Kuru princes; his arrow storms steadily beat the marauders back, injuring almost every prince. So swiftly and adroitly does he manoeuvre his chariot that the Kurus feel that not one but a hundred terrible Drupadas harry them.

From every side, that dauntless king's shafts fly at the Kuru force, and then everywhere conches boom and drums are heard, in thousands and thousands, sounding the general alarm for the Panchalas to rouse themselves, for danger threatens. Quickly, a great Panchala force gathers and faces the enemy; from that teeming host there arises a roar like some mythic lion's; the twanging of their bowstrings threatens to tear open the sky.

This only enrages the dauntless Duryodhana, Vikarna, Subahu, Dirghalochana, Dushasana and their brothers. They loose fierce volleys of arrows at the Panchalas, wounding even their king.

But Prishata's son, O Bhaarata, the invincible Drupada raises his own archery to another realm. He whirls across the field like a wheel of fire, and in the twinkling of an eye strikes Duryodhana, Vikarna and even Karna, as well as countless other enemy warriors, with his fierce barbs, as if to quench those shafts' thirst for blood.

And now the people of the Panchala capital attack the Kurus from every side, with any kind of weapon on which they can lay their hands. Young and old rush into the fray, hurling spears and staffs and pestles at the enemy like clouds pour raindrops upon the Earth. The Kauravas are overwhelmed; they panic, and flee howling back out of the city and to where Drona waits with the Pandavas.

The Pandavas hear the wails and screams of their cousins, as they turn tail, and now the sons of Pandu calmly climb into their chariots. Arjuna quickly tells Yudhishtira that, as the heir to the throne of Hastinapura, he must not take part in this skirmish. Drona endorses the view, and Yudhishtira remains with his Guru.

Bhima, mace in hand, leads the charge of four brothers, while Nakula and Sahadeva ride beside the chariot wheels of Arjuna following his titanic brother, whose roars shake the Earth and the Sky. The Panchalas roar back, but their yells are drowned by the thunder of the chariot wheels of Atiratha Arjuna.

Like a great makara entering the Sea, Bhima Mahabaho rushes eagerly into the Panchala ranks, mace in hand, and he is like another Yama. His roars are like a tempest raging upon an ocean. Bhima first goes among the Panchala war elephants and smites them with his dreadful gada, like Death himself.

The mountainous beasts fall all around him, their heads smashed like melons. Their blood spraying everywhere, running in streams down their own bodies the mastodons collapse like cliffs struck by thunder and crumbling.

Meanwhile, the carnage Arjuna brings to the elephants is as savage as his mace-wielding brother's: he fells them at will with searing fusillades of arrows. Nakula and Sahadeva are not far behind in the havoc they fetch. The Pandavas fell thousands of elephants and horses, shatter chariots beyond count, and kill as many footsoldiers and rathikas.

Bhima drives the Panchalas before him, on pachyderms, horses or in chariots, as a herdsman in the forest does his cattle!

Remembering the purpose of their mission, remembering the word he has given Drona, Arjuna shoots Drupada down from the back of the elephant that king now rides. Again, he turns his attentions to the rest of the Panchala army, and once more consumes them all around him, even like the fire at the end of the Yuga. In thousands upon thousands he razes the enemy.

Roused, the Panchalas and the Srinjayas loose a gale of every manner of weapon at Arjuna. Roaring to shake the ground beneath their feet and chariot wheels, they fight frantically against the Pandava. A pitched, brutal battle breaks out.

Hearing the enemy roar at him, the eyes of Indra's son turn red and he charges at them, covering them with a dense swarm of deadly arrows, falling on them with renewed ferocity. Those that watch Arjuna, his body bright, see his hands as a blur; they see no pause in his archery: it is a single, constant stream, a thing of marvel. The screams of those that Arjuna slays mingle with the helpless cries of admiration that he draws from his enemies at his unearthly archery.

Drupada, king of the Panchalas, with his Senapati Satyajit at his side, rushes at Arjuna, rather as the Asura Sambara did at Indra during their contention in time out of mind. Arjuna covers him in a cloak of brilliant arrows. A dismal cry erupts from the Panchala host, like that of a herd of elephants when a lion springs at the leader of the herd.

Satyajit sees Arjuna bearing down on Drupada to seize him, and the mighty Panchala Senapati flies at the Pandava. They fight, circling in their chariots, like Indra and Virochana's son Mahabali did of yore. Suddenly, Arjuna shatters Satyajit's defences and strikes him with ten arrows, drawing a gasp from the watching army.

But the doughty Satyajit looses a hundred shafts in reply at Arjuna. Quick as thinking, Maharatha Arjuna tightens his bowstring and raises his archery. He breaks the bow in Satyajit's hand and speeds towards Drupada again. But Satyajit seizes up a stronger bow and, in a flash, strikes Arjuna, his chariot, his horses and his sarathy with a cluster of arrows.

Arjuna is not forgiving, but retorts with a rash of shafts that find Satyajit's horses, charioteer, shred his banner, break his bow, pierce agony through his left hand that loosed fire, and shoots the warrior who guards his back. Finding his bows repeatedly cut in twain and his horses slain, Satyajit gives up the unequal fight and retreats.

Drupada sees his Senapati beaten and looses a flurry of arrows at Arjuna, who breaks the Panchala king's bow, also his flagstaff, and strikes his horses and his sarathy, all with five shafts each. Suddenly, with a roar, Arjuna throws down his bow and quiver, seizes up a curved sword, and leaps from his chariot into his adversary's ratha.

In a wink, he sets the sword to Drupada's throat and seizes him, as Garuda does a great sea serpent after stirring the waves with his wings. The Panchala soldiers flee in every direction.

Roaring still, triumphantly at having shown his prowess in his first actual battle, Arjuna issues from the Panchala army and the city gates, with his captive now in his own chariot. Seeing him, Bhima roars like ten lions and falls even more ferociously upon the hapless Panchala troops, while Nakula and Sahadeva also begin to raze the city.

Arjuna cries to them, 'This best of kings is related to the Kurus. Spare his men, Bhima. We come only to give our Acharya his dakshina, and that we have now.'

Reluctantly, for he has not had his fill of bloodshed, Bhima stops his slaughtering. The Pandava princes ride back to Drona with Drupada, whom they offer to their master for his fee.

Drona sees Drupada his captive, to do with as he pleases; he sees the Panchala king humbled and helpless, and he remembers how his childhood friend had humiliated him.

Says Drona, 'I have laid waste your kingdom and your capital. But do not fear for your life, though it is now in your enemy's hands. Tell me Drupada, do you now want to be my friend again?' Drona smiles, 'No, have no fear for your life, because we Brahmanas are forgiving by nature. Kshatriyarishabha, I have not forgotten our old friendship and love, from when we were boys together in our Guru's asrama.

And so, O King, I ask you once again for your friendship, and in return, as my gift to you, I will give you back half your kingdom, which is now mine. You once told me that only one king could befriend another; so, O Yagnasena, I will keep half your kingdom.

You will be king of all the Panchala lands south of the Ganga, while I become king of those north of the river. Panchala, if it pleases you, be my friend again.'

Drupada replies, 'You are a noble soul and mighty indeed, O Drona, and I am not surprised by your generosity. I wish for eternal friendship with you.'

Drona releases the Panchala king, O Bhaarata, and formally returns half his kingdom to him, believing innocently that the past is forgotten and they are both pleased. Thereafter, Drupada begins to live, in some sorrow, in the city of Kampilya in the province of Makandi on the banks of the Ganga. He still rules over many towns and cities.

After Drona vanquishes him, Drupada also rules the southern Panchalas up to the bank of the Charmanwati, and he is utterly convinced that he can never hope to defeat the Brahmana in battle because Drona is immeasurably more powerful than he is: in Brahma shakti.

But being a Kshatriya, Drupada is determined to have his revenge. He ranges the world, wishing for a son who will one day kill Drona.

Meanwhile, Drona lives in Ahicchatra, ruling over the northern Panchalas. Thus, indeed, is the land of Ahicchatra, full of towns and cities, won in battle by Arjuna and given to Drona for his Guru dakshina."

CANTO 141

SAMBHAVA PARVA CONTINUED

Vaisampayana continued, "A year passes, then Dhritarashtra makes Pandu's son Yudhishtira the Yuvaraja, the heir apparent. It is the wish of the people and the eldest Pandava is an embodiment of dharma: in his rectitude, his firmness, fortitude, patience, kindness, frankness and perfect honesty.

Very quickly, Kunti's son overshadows even his father Pandu's great deeds. So punctilious and righteous is Yudhishtira, so devoted to the kingdom and his people.

At about the same time, Bhima Vrikodara receives further lessons from Balarama at mace fighting, and fighting with a sword and from a chariot. When he completes his tutelage, Bhima is as mighty as Balarama himself, and he is as devoted as ever to his brothers.

Arjuna, of course, wins great renown for his archery: his swiftness of hand, the firmness of his grip, his incredible accuracy. Besides, he is a master of the kshura, the naracha, the bala and the vipatha; why, he is an expert at every weapon, be it straight or crooked, heavy or light.

Drona openly endorses the belief that there is no archer, no complete warrior on Earth to rival Arjuna.

One day, in the presence of all the Kuru princes, Drona says to Arjuna, 'Agastya Muni has a disciple in the astra shastra, and his name is Agnivesa. Agnivesa was my Guru, and I was his sishya. I performed tapasya and served my master diligently, so he gave me the Brahmasirsa, which never fails, which is like thunder, and which can consume the very Earth.

O Bhaarata, that astra can now pass from one sishya to another. When he gave it to me, my Guru said, "O son of Bharadwaja, you must never cast this astra at any Manava, especially not at one who is not himself a great warrior." Kshatriya, you and you alone have received that weapon from me, and no one else deserves to have it. But you must honour the command of the Rishi Agnivesha. Also, Arjuna, now swear in the presence of your brothers and cousins, and other kin, that you will give me whatever dakshina I demand from you.'

Arjuna says, simply, 'I swear, Acharya.'

Drona says, 'Sinless, if you ever meet me in battle, you must fight without giving me any quarter.'

Arjuna is startled, but he bows his head, swearing to do what his master asks. He then touches Drona's feet for his blessing, and taking it, goes away to the north.

Soon, a cry ranges through the world, a great shout that covers the Earth and her girdle of seas: that there is no bowman anywhere like Arjuna the Pandava. It is true; no one can face him in battle, with the mace, the sword, in a chariot, and especially with a bow. His skills and his prowess are unearthly.

Sahadeva learns dharma, all the laws of morality and duty, from Brihaspati, and he continues living under the control of his elder brothers. Nakula, the favourite of his brothers, becomes a Maharatha, a master of chariot warfare, and his guru is Drona.

Arjuna and the other Pandavas become so powerful that they kill the great Sauvira in battle, Sauvira who has performed a yagna that lasted three years, easily repulsing the constant raids of marauding Gandharvas.

Arjuna subdues the king of the Yavanas, whom even Pandu had failed to conquer. The brilliant Arjuna makes Vipula, a Sauvira king, of great might, who had always shown disregard for the Kurus, feel the keen edge of his power. He humbles King Sumitra of the same race, who is also called Dattamitra, who had challenged him contemptuously.

Bhima and Arjuna, by themselves, in a single chariot, subdue all the kings of the East, who have ten thousand chariots. Arjuna by himself conquers the entire South, and sends back vast wealth to Hastinapura; he is then called Dhananjaya, winner of wealth.

Thus, the Pandavas extend the Kuru kingdom in every direction, with their unearthly, irresistible prowess. Seeing their astonishing achievements, suddenly Dhritarashtra is stricken by envy, which enters his heart like poison. Dreadful anxiety seizes the king in green talons and he can hardly sleep."

CANTO 142

SAMBHAVA PARVA CONTINUED

Vaisampayana continued, "The wretched Dhritarashtra sees his nephews become more powerful than he likes, and he calls his wily minister Kanika to him. This man is an expert politician and a trusted advisor.

Dhritarashtra says, 'Brahmanashreshta, daily the Pandavas increase their power over the Earth, and envy stings my heart like a serpent. Shall I live in peace with them or become their enemy? Kanika advise me well, for I will do what you say.'

Kanika replies, 'Listen carefully, sinless king, and, Kurusthama, do not be angry when you hear what I say.

Kings should always increase their own power, and keep their maces raised always to crush anyone who threatens them. A king must be most discreet himself, and ever watchful of the indiscretions of his enemies. If a king is always prepared to strike, everyone fears him. So, a king must be ever ready to punish those that transgress his will, or threaten his power.

He must conduct himself so he shows no weakness, ever, while he finds any chink in his enemy's armour and then hunts him down and kills him. A king keeps his own weaknesses hidden, like the tortoise hides its soft body in its shell, as also his purposes and his means to achieve them.

Once he sets a course for himself, he does not rest until his end is achieved; he never turns back. My lord, if you do not remove a thorn completely from your flesh, it festers and creates a sore. So, too, if a king has an enemy, he must not let him live, but kill him. If his enemy is powerful, he must watch and wait for his evil hour, his enemy's time of misfortune, and then strike him down ruthlessly.

Sire, you must never underestimate an enemy, however contemptible he might be; you must never mock him openly or show your enmity towards him. A small spark can consume a great forest, if it can leap from one tree to the next.

Kings must sometimes pretend to be deaf and blind to faults they most want to punish, enemies they most want to crush, especially when they are powerless to effect the killing they wish for in their hearts. When powerless, they must think that their bows are made of straw, while being always as vigilant as a herd of deer sleeping in a jungle.

When the enemy is in your power strike and destroy him without mercy, openly or secretly, by fair means or foul. Why, he might seek your protection, but your heart must be like a stone, and you must not spare him, for then later he will surely take revenge on you. Spare no expense to kill your enemy, and then you will have peace, for the dead can never be a threat to you.

You must destroy your enemy's resources: the three, the five and the seven. You must destroy your enemies, root and branch. Then you must destroy their friends and allies, who cannot flourish anymore once their leader dies. If you tear up the root of the tree, the branches and twigs will wither and die of themselves.

Keep your own purpose secret and hidden, and watch your enemy like an eagle, always watching for his weakness. A king must always be vigilant and watch his enemies anxiously.

First win the confidence of your enemy by keeping the fire of sacrifice lit, by wearing valkala and jata, and sleeping on animal hide. And when he lets you near him, spring on him like a wolf! It has been well said that to acquire wealth and kingdom even a guise of holiness can be adopted, as a hooked staff to draw the branch down to you so you can pluck the ripe fruit from it.

So, too, should you select the enemy that is ripe for killing. Support your enemy, carry him upon your shoulders, until the right moment arrives to fling him down and break him in pieces like an earthen pot hurled down on a rock. Let your enemy beg piteously for his life; you must not spare him.

An enemy can be destroyed by artful conciliation, by lavishing money on him. Cause dissension among his friends and allies; poison their minds subtly against him. Yes, use whatever means you need to, that is in your power, do anything that you must to kill the enemy who is dangerous to you.'

Dhritarashtra says, 'Tell me truly how an enemy can be destroyed by conciliation or gifts, by dissension and finally by the use of force.'

Kanika replies, 'Listen, O King, to the story of the jackal who lived once in the forest and was a shrewd master of politics. Yes, he was a wise jackal, who lived with four friends in the jungle: a tiger, a mouse, a wolf and a mongoose.

One day the five friends saw a powerful, well-fleshed stag in the forest, a leader of his herd, but they could not catch or kill him, so strong and so swift was he. They called a council to discuss how the stag could be hunted.

The jackal said, "Tiger, many times you have tried to stalk and kill the stag, but you haven't succeeded because he is young, quick and intelligent. Let the mouse go and gnaw his hooves while he sleeps, and when this is done, you, Tiger, will be able to seize him. Then all of us can feast on him."

They agreed with him, and the mouse ate into the deer's hooves while it slept, weakening them, and then the tiger easily killed the stag.

When the tiger had broken his neck and the stag lay motionless on the ground, the jackal said to his companions, "We are blessed today! Go now and bathe in the stream before we begin our feast. I will watch over the carcass until you return."

The others promptly went off to bathe and the jackal sat with the fat carcass of the stag, lost in thought about what he should do next. The mighty tiger returned first after bathing. He saw the jackal plunged in thought.

The tiger said, "Wise one, why do you seem so sad? Most intelligent Jackal, let us feast on the stag."

The jackal said, "Mahabaho, listen to what the mouse said. He said, 'Fie upon the strength of the king of beasts! I killed the deer, and because of me the tiger will eat his fill today.'

After hearing his brag, I have no wish to eat today."

The tiger said, "If this is what the mouse said, from today I will kill any creature I find in the jungle by myself and eat alone." With that, the tiger left.

Soon, the mouse arrived, and seeing him the jackal said, "Blessings, O Mouse, but have you heard what the mongoose said? He said, 'The carcass of this stag is poisoned by the claws of the tiger and I will not eat it.' But, if you allow me, O Jackal, I will kill the mouse and feed on his flesh."

The mouse heard this and fled down into his hole in the ground. And after the mouse had gone, O King, the wolf arrived there after his ablutions.

The jackal said to him, "The king of beasts is angry with you, and I fear evil will overtake you. He is on his way here with his mate, and you must do as you please."

The wolf, of course, slunk away and, immediately after, the mongoose arrived. The jackal said, "I have vanquished the others who want to eat the stag, and they fled. You, too, must fight me first if you want to eat."

The mongoose replied, "When you have beaten the tiger, the wolf and the intelligent mouse, all heroes in their way, you must be truly strong. I do not want to fight you."

The mongoose also left. When the others had all gone, the jackal feasted alone on the stag. My lord, if kings would be as wily as that clever jackal, they would always prevail over their enemies, and always be happy.

You must defeat the timid by playing on their fears, the brave and the strong by conciliation, the greedy by gifts, and your equals and your inferiors by an open show of strength.'

Kanika pauses before continuing, 'Listen, O King, to something else. If your son, friend, brother, father, your Guru or anyone at all becomes your enemy, you must never hesitate to kill him, if you wish your own happiness. Never disdain to kill an enemy, whoever he might be.

If two enemies are equally strong, and uncertain of success in an open encounter, the diligent one will prosper. If your Guru himself is vain, lacks discrimination about what needs to be done and what needs to be left alone, if he is cruel, even he must be punished.

Even if rage burns your heart, never show your anger but always speak with a smile. Never reprove anyone angrily. O Bhaarata, instead speak most sweetly to the one you mean to strike down, why, even as you kill him! Once the killing has been done, then grieve loudly for the victim, shed copious tears in public.

Lull your enemy into false security with conciliation and gifts, sweet words; the moment his guard is down, strike without scruple or mercy. As king, you must always strike down the sinner who dons a disguise of virtue, for being outwardly virtuous only hides his true nature, his sins, as dark clouds do a mountain.

When you have killed an enemy, be sure you burn his house down, and his kin. Never let beggars, atheists and thieves live in your kingdom. Kill your enemy by a surprise attack, an ambush, by corrupting his allies with gifts and wealth; kill him secretly with poison. You can be as ruthless as you like, my lord; sharpen your teeth to deliver a fatal bite.

And when you strike, be certain that you do so with finality, so that the one you strike can never raise his head again. Be ever vigilant; suspect even those from whom you apparently have nothing to fear, let alone those that are a known threat to you. For the one who apparently poses no threat can be the most dangerous enemy, especially if he is powerful and decides to strike at you, when you least expect it from him.

Never trust those that are disloyal, and do not overly trust even those that are loyal. For, if a faithful one turns against you, you are certain to be destroyed. Employ spies, after making sure of their loyalty. Use them within your kingdom and in other kingdoms, in the courts of other kings. Your spies abroad must be masters of deception, preferably men that roam the Earth as Rishis.

Deploy your secret agents in public gardens, places of amusement, temples and other holy places, drinking halls, in the streets, and close to the eighteen tirthas of your kingdom: your Prime Minister, the Chief Priest, the Yuvaraja, the Senapati, the Dwarapalakas of the court, those that work in your inner apartments, your Jailor, your Surveyor, your Treasurer, the General Executor of all your ordinances, the Head of your own Police, the Chief Architect, the Chief Justice, the President of your Council, the Chief of the Department of Punishment, the Commander of the Fort, the Chief of the Arsenal, the Commander of the Frontier Guards, and the Keeper of the Forests.

Deploy your spies in places of sacrifice, near public wells, on mountains and at river ferries, in forests, and in every place where people congregate. Speak sweetly and humbly, my lord, but let your heart be sharp as a razor.

Even while you do the most savage and vicious deed, wear a smile on your lips, while speaking. If you desire lasting prosperity, you must cultivate the arts of humility, of swearing falsely when required, of conciliation, of creating hope, why even of worshipping your enemies by bowing your head at their feet.

A man who knows how to conduct himself politically is like a tree always adorned with flowers but never bearing fruit. If indeed there are any fruit they grow only from the loftiest branches, and if any of these do ripen, make sure that they look raw.

A king who learns how to conduct himself thus will never wane. Dharma, artha and kama all bear fruit, both good and evil. The wise man knows how to take the good fruit and avoid the evil.

Men that follow only dharma become unhappy for want of artha and kama, wealth and pleasure. Men who only pursue wealth become afflicted for want of dharma and kama. Those who chase only after pleasure suffer from not having virtue and wealth.

You must pursue all three in a balanced fashion, never neglecting any of them, so that the lack of none afflicts you. Consult your Brahmanas, O King, but those that have humility and attention, no envy, and the utmost sincerity, if you wish to accomplish your most secret purpose.

If you fall, raise yourself up again, by any means – fair or foul, gentle or violent; when you have resurrected your fortunes, then by all means practise dharma. One who has not suffered or experienced some calamity can ever hope to prosper. You can see this from the life of anyone who survives misfortune.

If a man be grief-stricken, in dire straits, you should comfort him by narrating the olden legends to him, of others that suffered and then recovered good fortune: the tales of Nala and of Rama. He whose heart has been riven by sorrow should be consoled with hope of future prosperity.

Comfort the learned and the wise with gifts and pleasing responsibilities. But remember that a man who makes peace with an enemy and then allows his guard to drop, as if the enmity itself is finished, is like one that chooses to fall asleep on the highest branch of a tree: he will surely fall!

A king should always keep his own counsel. His scrutiny must always be on his enemies, gazing upon them through the eyes of his spies; and he must be careful to keep his own feelings hidden from the spies of his enemies. Even as a fisherman cannot prosper without killing and gutting his catch, a king cannot hope to prosper without ripping out the innards of his enemies, without committing some violence.

You must raze the armies of your enemies, destroying them directly, or setting the scourges of disease, hunger and thirst upon them, mowing them down like weeds. A needy man never goes to a rich man out of love, but to gain from him; and when he has what he wants he will turn his back on the one whose help he sought when he was needy.

So, when you help someone, never give him everything that he wants but leave something that he still desires, so that he will continue to serve you.

The king who wishes to prosper must diligently seek out allies, and conduct his wars with their help, with the utmost care and careful preparation. He must be unwaveringly prudent, so that neither his friends nor his enemies know his true motives and purposes, before he actually acts.

Only when the deed has begun or ended, must they discover your purpose. Until danger shows itself, you must behave as if you are afraid. But when it comes, you must face it fearlessly and only then reveal that you were always well prepared for it. He that trusts an enemy whom he has once subdued by force is like the she crab that calls her death to her when she conceives.

You must always think of danger as having already arrived, and threatening you, otherwise you will not have the calm and perfect preparedness required for facing it when mortal peril actually does come. Prudence, O King, grave caution at all times, and the correct choice of time and place for action: these lead to prosperity.

A king must know that destiny can be moderated by mantras and yagnas; the king must always have his eye on the proper balance of dharma, artha and kama. Time and place must always be carefully considered to reap the greatest benefit from one's deeds.

Even if an enemy is slight, you must not scorn or ignore him; he might grow swiftly to become dangerous, like the palm tree plunging its roots down with great speed and growing, or the spark in the forest that blazes up to become the devouring conflagration. Just as a small fire fed with faggots soon becomes great enough to devour the biggest blocks of wood, so does the power of the enemy that forms alliances and friendships grow apace, and he becomes a formidable adversary.

Give hope to your enemy of great favour, but keep him hoping and postpone satisfying his wish; when the time comes to keep your word to him, defer its fulfilment again, find or create some excuse. Let that excuse appear to be founded upon some real reason, and that reason again upon another.

In the matter of destroying their enemies, kings must be like razors, in every detail and particular: as ruthless as they are sharp and keen. They must keep their intentions hidden as blades in sheaths of leather, and strike when opportunity presents itself, razing their enemies with all their friends and families in a fell sweep – just as a fine razor blade will shave a face without leaving a single hair.

O you who support the honour of the Kurus, you must behave with the Pandavas and others, too, in a manner that is politic, so you do not later regret what you do. You are blessed with every auspicious sign of fortune and grace. I say to you, O King, guard yourself against the Pandavas!

The sons of Pandu are more powerful than your sons. So Parantapa, let me tell you plainly what you must do. Hear what I say, and let your sons listen to me as well, and having done so, move to achieve your purpose. Rajan, you must make sure that you have nothing to fear from the Pandavas. Yes, you must act in such a manner, which is perfectly politic, so that you do not grieve in the future.'

Having said so much, Kanika leaves the presence of Dhritarashtra and returns to his home, while the king is plunged in melancholy and dark brooding."

CANTO 143

JATUGRIHA PARVA

Vaisampayana said, "Meanwhile, Subala's son Shakuni, Duryodhana, Dushasana and Karna are already conspiring in evil to do away with Kunti and her sons. They seek Dhritarashtra's leave and hatch a plot to immolate the Pandavas and their mother, burn them to death.

However, the wise and gifted Vidura, who can read men's inmost thoughts and intentions by looking at their faces, sees what is afoot. Sinless Vidura, illumined by true knowledge, devoted to the sons of Pandu, decides that Kunti and her sons should fly from their deadly enemies.

Arranging for a boat that can withstand wind and wave, he says to Kunti and her princes, 'Dhritarashtra has been born to ruin the honour and the sons of the race of Kuru. His heart is evil, and he is about to abandon dharma.

Dear Kunti, I have readied for you and your sons a boat that shall be stable in wind and against wave; escape in it from the net of death that is tightening around you.'

Kunti is stricken to hear what Vidura says, and she boards the boat with her sons and crosses the Ganga. Leaving the boat, as Vidura advised, taking the wealth their enemies had given them in Varanavrata, the Pandavas enter the deep emerald jungle on the other side.

Meanwhile, in the house of lac, which the Kauravas built to immolate the Pandavas, a Nishada woman and her five sons are burnt to death, as is that vilest of mlechchas, Purochana, who has actually built the house of lac for Duryodhana.

Believing the Nishada woman and her sons' corpses to be Kunti and the Pandavas, the sons of Dhritarashtra and their conspirators are deceived. Thus, Vidura saves the lives of his nephews and their mother. But the people of Varanavrata also do not know that the Pandavas have escaped secretly, and when they see the lacquer palace burn down, they are grief-stricken.

They send messengers to Dhritarashtra, saying, 'Evil King, your vile ambition has been achieved. The Pandavas have been burnt to death. Your wish has come true, and you and your murderous sons can now enjoy the kingdom.'

Hearing the message, Dhritarashtra and his sons make a great show of grief. With the Kshattri Vidura, Bhishma the Kuru patriarch, and the rest of the family, the blind king performs the last rites for the Pandavas and their mother, but, unknowingly, with the remains of the Nishada woman and her sons."

Janamejaya said, "Brahmanottama, I want to hear in full this story of the burning of the house of lac and how the Pandavas escaped the fire. Ah, that was a dire thing that the Kauravas tried to do, at the dark counsel of the evil Kanika. Tell me every detail of it, O Suta, for I burn with curiosity to hear that story from you."

Vaisampayana said, "Parantapa, O King, listen then to the tale of the burning of the house of lac and the escape of the sons of Pandu.

The malignant Duryodhana sees that Bhima is stronger than everyone else; he sees Arjuna excel at arms, and he is envious and dejected. Karna Suryaputra and Subala's son Shakuni try, in many ways, to kill the sons of Pandu. But the Pandavas escape every time, and, obeying Vidura's counsel, avoid ever making these attempts on their lives public or accusing Duryodhana of trying to kill them.

The people see how noble the Pandavas are and how accomplished, and they become the topic of conversation and praise at every street corner and public gathering. In open courtyards and other places where the citizens assemble all the talk is about how Yudhishtira should become king.

The people say, 'Dhritarashtra might have the eye of knowledge, but being born blind he is never truly a king. How can he rule now? Shantanu's son Bhishma will never accept the kingship because of his solemn oath. Yudhishtira is young, a great warrior, versed in the Veda, honest and kind. It is time that the eldest Pandava becomes our king, and is crowned with every proper ritual and ceremony.

He worships Shantanu's son Bhishma, as well as Dhritarashtra; knowing dharma, Yudhishtira will care well for both these, as well as the sons of Dhritarashtra, and keep them in every luxury.'

When Duryodhana hears what the people are saying, he cannot bear it. Beside himself with jealousy, he comes to Dhritarashtra, alone. Greeting his father reverently, the evil prince says to the king, 'Father, I hear fell words being spoken by the people. They want Yudhishtira to be king, not you anymore, or even Bhishma. Bhishma will agree because of his oath.

The people wish to do us grave harm. Pandu ruled by his deeds and not you, because you are blind. If Pandu's son inherits the kingdom, after him his son will rule, then his son, and so on, and theirs shall become the royal line, while we and our children will be inconsequential, minions at best, with neither power nor honour.

We shall be dependants for our very food, and lowliness and distress be our lot. Rajan, you must prevent this from happening. You are the king and your son must rule after you, regardless of what the people say.'"

CANTO 144

JATUGRIHA PARVA CONTINUED

Vaisampayana continued, "Dhritarashtra, whose eyes are his gyana, remembers all that Kanika has said to him. Sorrow grips his heart and his mind falters.

Duryodhana, Karna, Subala's son Shakuni, and Dushasana have already plotted secretly before Duryodhana goes to the king.

Duryodhana now says, 'Father, somehow contrive to send the Pandavas to Varanavrata and we shall never have anything to fear from them again.'

Dhritarashtra falls thoughtful, then, says, 'Pandu always walked the way of dharma and was dutiful to all our kinsmen, and most of all to me. He cared little for the pleasures of this world, but rather gave everything that was his to me, including the kingdom.

Yudhishtira is as devoted to dharma as his father was; he is as gifted and accomplished as Pandu. His fame has spread across the world and the people all love him. He has powerful allies; how can we ever hope to banish him from his father's kingdom?

Pandu nurtured all the counsellors of the sabha, as well as the commanders of the army, and their sons and grandsons, too. The people loved him dearly. My son, will all these not kill us now for the sake of Pandu's son?'

Duryodhana replies, 'What you say my father is true. But take thought for the evil that looms for you and yours. Let us win the people over with lavish gifts and wealth, and being what they are they will stand with us. My lord, the treasury and the ministers of state are already under our control.

Send the sons of Pandu away to Varanavrata, gently. And when, O Bhaarata, I have taken the reins of power firmly into my hands, let Kunti and her sons return.'

Dhritarashtra replies, 'Duryodhana, you speak my very mind, but I dared not give in to this thought for its sinfulness. Also, Bhishma, Drona, Kshattri and Gautama Kripa would never countenance the Pandavas being exiled. My child, the wise ones see the Pandavas and ourselves as being equals in the House of Kuru.

If we exile the sons of Pandu shall they not say that we deserve to die at the hands of the Kurus for our sin, why, to die by their very hands? Shall the whole world not say the same?'

Duryodhana says, 'Bhishma has no partiality and will take no side in any dispute between the Pandavas and us. Aswatthama is on my side, and where the son is so shall the doting father be. Saradwat's son Kripa will not oppose Drona and Aswatthama; he will never go against his sister's husband and son.

As for Kshattri Vidura, he is indeed our secret enemy, but he depends on us for his livelihood. Besides, even if he sides with the Pandavas, by himself he can do us no harm.

So, my lord, banish the Pandavas to Varanavrata without fear. Indeed, I say to you, do it today and by this put out the grief that burns my heart like fire, pierces it through like an arrow, robs me of my sleep.'"

CANTO 145

Jatugriha Parva Continued

Vaisampayana said, "Duryodhana and his brothers begin working assiduously to win over the people with liberal gifts of land and wealth. Honours and encomiums are bestowed, cannily.

Then, instigated by Dhritarashtra, some of his chosen ministers one day begin to eulogise the town of Varanavrata in the royal sabha of Hastinapura. They say that the festival of Pasupati Siva has just begun in Kasi, and that it is indeed the most wonderful gathering of worshippers on Earth. It enchants all that are fortunate enough to witness it, for the people come wearing their finest attire and most precious ornaments.

Listening to the fulsome and cunning praise of Kasi, the Pandavas feel stirred to visit the sacred city of Siva. When Dhritarashtra senses that his nephews' curiosity and interest have been aroused, Ambika's son, the blind king, says to them, 'Ah, these men of mine always speak of Varanavata as being the most delightful town in the world.

Children, if you feel the desire to attend the festival of Pasupati. with your friends and followers, by all means go and enjoy yourselves like the very Devas, to your hearts' content. Take pearls and other jewels with you to give to the Brahmanas and the bards and musicians you find in Kasi.

And when you have sported there like the gods, and satisfied yourselves with every pleasure, return to us in Hastinapura, in your own time, at your leisure.'

Yudhishtira immediately understands Dhritarashtra's intention. Yet, he knows the king is powerful and he himself relatively weak. He says quietly, 'So be it.'

Turning to Shantanu's son Bhishma, the sage Vidura, Drona, the Kuru Bahlika, Somadatta, Kripa, Aswatthama, Bhurisravas, the other ministers, Brahmanas and Rishis, the priests and the people and the regal Gandhari, he says slowly and humbly, 'At my uncle's command we will go to sacred Varanavrata with our friends and followers. I beg you, bless us that we go happily and incur no sin in Kasi.'

The Kaurava chieftains all cheerfully bless them, saying, 'Pandavas let the Panchamahabhutas themselves bless you on your way, and not the least evil befall you.'

The Pandavas perform the rituals so they will inherit their due share in the kingdom when they return, make their preparations, and set out for Varanasi."

CANTO 146

JATUGRIHA PARVA CONTINUED

Vaisampayana said, "Duryodhana, O Bhaarata, is delighted. Bharatarishabha, he calls his trusted man Purochana, privately, seizes his right hand and says to him, 'Purochana, this world, replete with wealth, belongs to me; and you share in it equally. So you must protect the world from our enemies.

There is no one I trust more than you, my lord, and I rely on you to kill my enemies for me, cunningly. Dhritarashtra has sent the Pandavas to Varanavrata, to enjoy the festival of Pasupati.

Take a cart drawn by our swiftest mules; fly to Kasi, and there build a square palace near the arsenal. Furnish it lavishly, watch over it keenly, and, Purochana, make it with hemp and resin and every flammable material you can find. Mix earth with ghee, lard, oil and fat, and all the lac on which you can lay your hands. With this deadly mixture plaster the walls of the palace.

Strew and grease the precincts and the insides of the palace with more hemp, ghee, lacquer and wood, but so craftily that neither the Pandavas nor anyone else suspects a thing, for even a moment.

When you have built the mansion, Purochana, go to the Pandavas, offer them every reverence and invite Kunti and her sons and all their company to come to stay in the palace of lac.

Let the chairs and thrones, the beds and all the furniture be of the finest craftsmanship, things of beauty, so the Pandavas shall be well content, and Dhritarashtra receive no complaint from them. You must manage all this without anyone in Varanavrata suspecting anything until our aim is accomplished.

When you are certain that the Pandavas sleep fearlessly, unsuspiciously, in the lacquer palace, Purochana, apply a torch to the outer door. When the palace burns and the sons of Pandu are immolated inside, the people will say that a terrible accident killed them.'

Purochana does not hesitate to say 'So be it' to his evil prince, and leaves immediately for Varanavrata in a swift mule cart laden with all the incendiary materials he will need for his dastardly mission. Arriving in the sacred city, he loses no time in doing what Duryodhana has asked of him."

CANTO 147

Jatugriha Parva Continued

Vaisampayana said, "Meanwhile, the Pandavas are about to climb into their chariots, yoked to horses as fleet as the wind. They touch Bhishma's feet, in sorrow, Dhritarashtra's, their Acharya Drona's, Kripa's, Vidura's and those of all the elders of the House of Kuru.

Reverently saluting their elders and embracing their equals fondly, being hugged in farewell by the little children of the clan, and bidding sad farewell to the royal ladies of the palace, walking around them in pradakshina, taking loving leave of the people of Hastinapura, the sons of Pandu, men of dharma, set out for Varanasi.

Vidura of untold wisdom, along with other bulls among the Kurus and the citizens, as well, all grieving, follow the Pandavas some way.

In that grief, seeing the Pandavas full of sorrow, some of the citizens and the people from the countryside, too, begin to say aloud, 'Dhritarashtra is evil and turns away from dharma. Not sinless Yudhishtira, not Bhima mightiest among men, not Kunti's youngest son Arjuna will ever sin by revolting against this crime against them. Then how will the sons of Madri go against their older brothers' wishes?'

'Dhritarashtra inherited the kingdom from Pandu, and he could not bear his brother's sons. But how does Bhishma sanction this crime and allow the Pandavas to be exiled to that wretched town? Shantanu's son Vichitravirya and Rajarishi Pandu cared for us like their own children. But now that Purushavyaghra Pandu has left this world, Dhritarashtra cannot bear to see his sons beside his own vile princes. But we the people cannot tolerate this adharma and we will leave our homes and this great city and come with you, Yudhishtira Dharmaputra, wherever you go.'

Yudhishtira grows sad and thoughtful, then speaks to the distraught people. 'The king is our father, worthy of worship. He is our Guru and our superior. It is our dharma to do his bidding, never suspecting his motives. You are all our friends. I beg you, walk around us in pradakshina, then give us your blessing and turn back to your homes.

When the time comes for you to go with us or help our cause otherwise, we shall surely be grateful for your support. This is not that time.'

Gently he spoke, and his resolve they see is firm. The people do as he asks. They make a pradakshina around the sons of Pandu, bless them and then return to their homes.

When the people no longer follow the Pandavas, Vidura, knower of dharma's every nuance, speaks to Yudhishtira to make him sensible of the peril he is in. The learned Vidura speaks to Yudhishtira in the dialect of the mlechchas, which only they two understand.

Vidura says, 'He who knows that his enemies are plotting against him must take care to guard himself against danger. He who knows that there are weapons other than blades of steel, which can kill the body, and who knows how these can be rendered harmless, shall always be safe from his enemies.

The wise man protects himself with the knowledge that neither the consumer of straw nor the drier of dew burns those that live in a hole in the heart of a jungle. The blind man does not see into the future;

he has no sense of direction. He whose purpose is not firm, never finds prosperity.

Remember this, and be vigilant. He who accepts the perfidious offering of a deadly weapon, not made of steel, from his enemy, to dwell in, escapes death by fire by burrowing like a jackal underground: a tunnel with many exits. Ranging over the world a man acquires knowledge of its ways; by the stars he finds his direction; and he that controls the five senses remains safe from his enemies.'

Yudhishtira says to Vidura, 'I have understood you.'

Now Vidura walks around them in pradakshina, bids farewell to them and turns back into the city. When the people, Bhishma and Vidura have all gone back, Kunti goes up to Yudhishtira alone, and asks, 'Kshattri spoke to you strangely and softly, and you replied in the same tongue which none of us understood. If I can know what he says, tell me.'

Yudhishtira replies, 'The virtuous Vidura said to me that we should be warned that the mansion built to house us in Varanavrata has been built with incendiary materials. He said, "The path to escape will be revealed to you," and also "Those that can control their five senses shall gain sovereignty over the whole world." What I said to the good Vidura is "I have understood you."'

The Pandavas set out on the eighth day of the month of Phalguna, when the Rohini nakshatram is rising. Arriving in Varanavrata, they see the sacred town and its people."

CANTO 148

JATUGRIHA PARVA CONTINUED

Vaisampayana continued, "Full of joy, the people of Kasi come out to greet the sons of Pandu, in crowds. They come on foot and in myriad vehicles, bringing everything auspicious that the Shastras recommend with them, to welcome those greatest among men.

They approach Kunti's sons, bless them, cry *Jaya!* and crowd lovingly around their chariots. Purushavyaghra Yudhishtira looks like Indra among the Devas, with the Vajra in his hands.

Being adored and adoring in return, the Pandavas enter the town of Kasi that has been decked out for the great festival. The Kshatriyas first go to the homes of the Brahmanas of Kasi, who live by their svadharma. They go next to the homes of the officers of the town, then to the homes of the Sutas and the Vaishyas, and then also to the houses of the Sudras.

Bharatarishabha, with Purochana leading the way, the Pandavas finally go to the old palace of the city. They see the fine seats, beds and carpets, the airy rooms full of light; they eat the delectable royal fare that Purochana serves them and drink the excellent wine. Thus arriving in Varanasi, clad in royal finery, the Pandavas live in that ancient palace, being served and adored by Purochana and the people of Kasi.

When ten days pass, Purochana tells them about the 'Blessed House' that he has built for them. Wearing royal silks, those tigers among men go with Duryodhana's man to the treacherous house of lac. They enter like Guhyakas entering Lord Siva's palace on Mount Kailasa.

Yudhishitra looks around the edifice, and drawing Bhima aside tells him that it has been built with every possible incendiary material. The eldest Pandava smells the fat mixed liberally with ghee and lac, and says to his brother, 'Parantapa, our enemies have used clever artisans to create this palace. They have built it with hemp, resin, heath, straw and bamboos, all soaked in ghee.

The villainous Purochana is Duryodhana's man and he stays close to us because he wants to immolate me in this murderous palace. But, my brother, the keen Vidura knew about the danger and warned me of it. He warned me that Duryodhana has plotted to kill us all.'

Bhima says, 'We must return to the old palace.'

Yudhishtira replies, 'No. We must continue living here otherwise Purochana will know that we suspect him. They might kill us suddenly then, for surely Purochana has no conscience, and is his murderous master Duryodhana's man. Yet, we must be constantly vigilant.

If we die by fire, will our Pitama Bhishma be enraged? No, for what use will it be then to show his wrath to the Kauravas, and risk their anger in return? But, perhaps, he will be angry, outraged by such a sin.

It will matter little if we are dead. If we flee this palace of lac, Duryodhana will certainly have us murdered by other agents, other assassins, for he wants to be king.

Moreover, being the king's son he has both influence and power today, while ours are small by comparison. He has allies and wealth, a full treasury; we have neither. Will he not easily manage to have us slain, by any means?

Our way ahead is that of secrecy and stealth. We must escape from here without their knowing that we have fled; then, we must go disguised, living as nomadic hunters in the hearts of jungles, in remote places, while our enemies believe us to be dead.

Only thus shall we effectively escape our enemies and become familiar with these parts of the world. Even today, we shall, in utmost secrecy, have an underground tunnel excavated out of our chamber, and this house of death, and when the time comes escape through that passage.

Thus, no fire shall burn us and our enemies will remain in the dark. So, my brother, we must continue to live here and plan to make our way out in such privacy that not Purochana or indeed anyone in Varanavrata suspects anything of our intentions.'"

CANTO 149

Jatugriha Parva Continued

Vaisampayana continued, "The same day, a miner, a friend of Vidura's, comes to the Pandavas and says to them in private, 'I am a master tunneller, and your uncle Vidura sent me to you. Tell me what you want me to do. Vidura, who trusts me, said, "Go to the Pandavas and help them."'

'Tell me what I can do for you.'

'I have learnt that Purochana means to torch this house of lac on the fourteenth night of this dark fortnight. He will fire the front door and immolate the Purushavyaghras, the Pandavas, and their mother Kunti while they sleep."

The vile Duryodhana has plotted your murder, my lords. So that you believe me Vidura said these words to me in the mlechcha bhasha, the very ones he spoke to you as you left Hastinapura, and also the reply you made to him in the same tongue.'

The miner repeats Vidura's conversation with Yudhishtira in the rare dialect. Hearing those words, Yudhishtira is satisfied. He says to the miner, 'Welcome friend! I know now that you are indeed a true and trusted friend, devoted to my loving uncle Vidura, and that he has sent you.

There is little the wise Vidura does not know. Make no difference between him and us: as you are to him, from now you are to us. We are as much yours as he is. Friend, protect us as our loving uncle always has and still does.

I know that Purochana has built this deadly mansion at the command of Dhritarashtra's son. Strong with allies and confident with wealth he hunts us relentlessly. Friend, save us from the fire that Duryodhana has planned, for if we die here his most cherished purpose will be fulfilled.

Look how cunningly Purochana has built this great house of lac. It is slick against the arsenal of Varanavrata, with its lofty ramparts and no escape on any side when the fire breaks out. Thus Vidura guessed at the murderous intention of Duryodhana; the mortal peril the Kshattri sensed is at our very door. You must save us, good friend, without Purochana suspecting a thing.'

The miner replies, 'So be it,' and immediately and carefully begins his excavation, to create a large subterranean tunnel leading out of the palace. The mouth of the tunnel is in the very heart of the palace, level with the floor, covered over by planks of wood and a carpet, so Purochana who is always at the front door never suspects a thing.

The Pandavas sleep at night in their bedchambers with their weapons beside them, ready for use. During the day, taking Purochana with them, they go hunting afar, from forest to forest, to have some fair idea of the lie of the surrounding lands. O King, they live vigilantly in the palace of lac, with every show of friendship and trust in Purochana, while in fact they are anxious and intensely sensible of danger.

The citizens of Varanavata never know anything, either, about the Pandavas' plans. Indeed, apart from themselves, only Vidura's trusted friend, the miner, has any inkling of what is afoot."

CANTO 150

JATUGRIHA PARVA CONTINUED

Vaisampayana said, "Purochana sees the Pandavas apparently comfortable and unsuspicious in the house of lac, and he is glad. Seeing him relaxed, Yudhishtira says to Bhima, Arjuna and the twins, 'We have deceived this ruthless fellow and his guard is down. I believe the time has come to escape. We must torch this deadly palace ourselves, with Purochana inside it, and flee through the tunnel. No one must know that we have gone, but believe us dead, too.'

On the day of an almsgiving, Kunti has a feast for Brahmanas, and a poor-feeding, as well. It is an extravagant feast, to which a large number of women come, and drink and eat to their hearts' content and more, and finally leave, with Kunti's permission.

Among those that come, as if fetched by fate, are a Nishada woman and her five sons. Rajan, this woman and her youths drink so much wine that they fall asleep or unconscious inside the house of lac.

A sharp wind blows through the night, and while Purochana also sleeps from a surfeit of wine with which Bhima plies him, Bhima sets fire to the room where Duryodhana's man lies. He then sets his brand to the front door and to other parts of the deadly house, which blazes up fiercely, as it has been built to do.

The Pandavas and their mother go down into the miner's tunnel. As the palace burns, the heat and the roar of the towering flames awaken the people of Varanavrata, who come running out of their homes.

Their hearts breaking to see the inferno, they cry, 'Ah, Duryodhana's evil man built the palace with incendiary materials under our very noses. And now he has murdered the sinless sons of Pandu, as if they are enemies. A curse be upon Dhritarashtra, who allowed this. Purochana has already paid with his life for his sin; one day the king and his demonic son will also pay.'

And they weep, helplessly, for by now the fire has all but consumed the great edifice. All night, the people stand around the blazing mansion, and lament.

Meanwhile, Kunti and her sons emerge from the mouth of the tunnel, some way from the palace and melt away into the night, unobserved. But they are full of sleep and fear, and they cannot go as quickly as they want, since Kunti is with them. The others, too, are faint from exhaustion, all but one of them.

Then, Rajan, Bhima of untold strength and the fleetness of his airy father picks up all his brothers and his mother, and carrying them easily, plunges along through the night. He sets Kunti upon his shoulders, the twins on his hips, and carries Yudhishtira and Arjuna in either arm. Vrikodara, son of the Wind, goes along like a strange gale, thrusting down trees that loom in his path with his brawny chest. His footmarks fall deeply upon the Earth."

CANTO 151

Jatugriha Parva Continued

Vaisampayana said, "At this same time, Vidura has sent another man he trusted, a pure soul, into the forest surrounding Varanavrata. This man sees the Pandavas making their way through the trees with their mother. He sees them trying to measure the depth of the river in a certain place, obviously wanting to ford the water to safety on the other side.

Vidura knows well how deep Duryodhana's hatred runs and how murderous his agents are. He sends his trusted agent to the Pandavas to help them, and this man now brings the sons of Pandu to a boat tethered to the riverbank, an extraordinary craft with engines and sails, made by the finest shipwrights, one that is proof against wave and wind, a boat that flies across any current as swiftly as a thought.

The man now says to the Pandavas, 'O Yudhishtira, listen to what I have to say, so that you know that I am indeed sent by your uncle Vidura. "The wise man protects himself with the knowledge that neither the consumer of straw nor the drier of dew burns those that live in a hole in the heart of a jungle."

These are the very words Vidura said to you and by these know that I am his trusted man and his agent. Vidura, who knows all things, says to you, "Kuntiputra, you will one day surely prevail over Karna, Duryodhana and his brothers, and the evil Shakuni in battle."

My boat is ready to bear you away, far from these places of danger. It is a marvellous boat and goes softly and smoothly over the river.'

Then, seeing Kunti and her sons apprehensive and forlorn, the tall man goes on the boat with them himself.

He says again to them, 'Vidura, who sniffed your heads in love and embraced you fondly, says that you must be ever vigilant, for the peril to your lives is very real.'

With that, he takes the Narapumgavas and their gracious mother across the Ganga. He helps them ashore there and softly cries *Jaya!* Then he leaves them, that good man, who is yet so mysterious, and melts back to wherever he comes from.

The Pandavas send a secret message through him back to Vidura, and then enter the great jungle that lies ahead of them on the far shore of the sacred river. They go quickly and stealthily."

CANTO 152

Jatugriha Parva Continued

Vaisampayana said, "When day breaks, a great crowd of townspeople converge at the house of lac. When they have put out the last flames, they see the edifice has indeed been built with hemp and lacquer. They find the corpse of Purochana.

The people begin to wail loudly, 'It is certain that Duryodhana had this treacherous palace built to murder the sons of Pandu. Surely, his father knew of the plot and acquiesced in it, or he would have prevented this dire crime.'

'There is little doubt that even Shantanu's son Bhishma, Drona, Vidura, Kripa and the other Kauravas did not follow dharma by sending the Pandavas here to die.'

'Let us send word to Dhritarashtra saying, "You have achieved your heart's great desire. You have immolated the noble sons of your brother Pandu in the house of lac."'

They fetch water and put out the embers that still burn, and begin a search for the bodies of Kunti and her sons. They find the charred corpses of the poor Nishada woman and her five sons. Vidura's miner, the tunneller, goes with the people and cunningly covers the mouth of the underground passage, which he has dug, with debris and ashes, so that no one discovers it.

The people of Varanavrata send a message to Dhritarashtra that the Pandavas, Kunti and Purochana have perished in the fire in the palace. Dhritarashtra hears the message and begins to sob loudly.

He says, 'Today my magnificent brother has died in the persons of his wife and sons! O, go at once to Varanavrata and perform the funeral rites for the daughter of Kuntiraja and her great Kshatriya sons. Sanctify the bones of the dead with the proper rituals, and give alms, and do everything that is proper and sacred at such a grave occasion.

Let all the relatives and friends of the dead go to Kasi. Let no expense be spared so that their spirits find peace.'

Surrounded by his kinsmen, Ambika's son Dhritarashtra offers tarpana for his nephews.

The Kurus weep, crying out the names of the princes whom they believe dead.

Some cry, 'Ah Yudhishitra, Yuvaraja, you have left us!'

Others sob, 'Oh, magnificent Bhima!'

Yet others cry, 'Phalguna, you have gone, and the Earth is dim!'

'Ah, the twin sons of the Aswins, Nakula and Sahadeva, the young ones handsome as Devas!'

'Oh Kunti, you have also gone!'

Thus they lament and offer tarpana, oblations of water to allay the thirst of the dead on their final journey. The people weep as well, only Vidura seems strangely composed, though he does shed some tears to show that he grieves. But then, he knows that the Pandavas are not dead.

Meanwhile, Kunti and the Pandavas cross the Ganga swiftly, helped by the strength of the boatman's sinews, the river's rapid current and a timely wind that favours them. Leaving the boat, they go south, making their way through the moonless night by the light of the stars that fill the sky.

They enter a deep and dense jungle. They are overcome by exhaustion and thirst; they can hardly keep their eyes open, for sleep comes strongly over them.

Yudhishtira turns to Bhima in some despair, 'My brother, this is terrible; we are in the deep jungle and cannot tell which way to turn. And fatigue numbs us. Ah, are we certain that the vile Purochana is dead? How shall we ever be safe again? Danger is still near us, my brother. Bhaarata, you are the only one among us that is not tired, for you are as strong and swift as the wind. Take us up again, Bhima, and fly through the forest.'

The mighty Bhimasena picks up Kunti and his brothers again, and once more, speeds through the trees."

CANTO 153

Jatugriha Parva Continued

Vaisampayana said, "As the tremendous Bhima hurtles along, the entire forest seems to tremble at his footfalls; the trees that strike or brush his great chest shake and sway. His thighs churning the air raise a wind like the ones that blow during the months of Jyeshta and Ashadha.

Bhima brings trees that stand in his path crashing down and tramples on them, rending the creepers and vines which clung to their branches, crushing their flowers and fruit. He goes through that jungle like the king bull of a great elephant herd, a musth maddened angry tusker of sixty years, in his prime and in rut, when the ichor bursts forth from his temples and trickles down his body.

Indeed, so vigorously does Bhima, as swift as Garuda or Vayu, go, that his brothers swoon at his speed. Often he plunges headlong and easily across deep and swirling streams and rivers, difficult to cross.

The Pandavas have cast away their royal finery and disguised themselves as hunters, for fear of the ubiquitous spies of the sons of

Dhritarashtra. Bhima now carries just his delicate mother upon his shoulders across the undulating banks of rivers.

O Bharatarishabha, towards evening, still carrying his mother, and now also his brothers, Bhima arrives in a dreadful jungle, where there seem to be no fruit, roots or even water, and where the cries of the birds and beasts are eerie and threatening. As twilight grows into night, these cries and roars grow fiercer and more ominous.

Soon, the darkness is complete, and a howling gale blows out of nowhere, felling trees, big or small, in its path like straws. Exhausted beyond all measure and with raging thirst having its way with them, the princes collapse onto the jungle floor. They sit there panting, parched and also not having eaten.

Kunti, who cannot bear her searing thirst anymore, cries weakly, 'I am the mother of the five Pandavas, and I am with all five of them. Yet, I burn with thirst.' Again and again, as if demented, she repeats this.

Bhima cannot bear it. Springing up, picking up his brothers and mother again, he charges once more through that fearful jungle, out of love for them, in quest of water. No living soul does he see anywhere, indeed few beasts, which slink away through the undergrowth and vanish; until suddenly he arrives in a clearing and sees before him a great and beautiful pipal tree, with spreading branches.

Gently he sets his family down beneath that tree, Bharatarishabha, and says softly to them, 'Rest, while I go to search for water. I hear the sweet cries of waterbirds not far from here. There must be a lake or at least a large pool at hand.'

Yudhishtira whispers through arid lips, 'Go.'

Bhima runs towards the dim squawking of the waterfowl, and soon enough comes upon a lovely lake into which he plunges, bathing and slaking his thirst. Quickly, then, he soaks his upper cloth with water and speeds back to Kunti and his brothers, half a yojana away. Tenderly he squeezes the precious life-giving water through their lips. They sigh to drink it and then sleep again.

Bhima sits in vigil over them. He sees Kunti swooned, where she sits, and wilted, and seized by terrible grief, Bhima begins to sigh like a snake. His gaze roves over his regal mother and brothers asleep on bare ground in the midst of this wilderness, and tears trickle down the mighty Vrikodara's great face.

'Ah, miserbale wretch I am that I have to see this sight today of my mother and my brothers asleep on bare forest ground. What can be more painful than this? In Hastinapura and even Varanavrata, they slept on the softest, costliest beds of down.

I am a sinner that today my eyes see Kunti, Vasudeva's sister, daughter of the formidable Kuntiraja, she who bears every auspicious mark upon her regal person, the daughter-in-law of Vichitravirya, wife of the incomparable Pandu, mother of the five Pandavas, she who is radiant as the filaments of a lotus, as tender and delicate, her body only fit to sleep on the softest bed. But today that Kunti lies on rough earth.

She who has borne the sons of Dharma, Indra and Vayu, who has always slept in palaces, now lies exhausted, in a swoon, on the ground under a tree.

Ah, what more terrible sight shall my eyes ever see than these Purushavyaghras, my noble brothers, asleep beside our mother? Yudhishtira Dharmaputra, who deserves to have sovereignty over the three worlds, lies on the crude ground. Arjuna, his skin the hue of thunderheads, who has no equal among men, lies like any common man on the ground.

Oh, what can be more painful than this? And the young twins, handsome as their sires, the Aswins, also lie like ordinary men upon rough earth.

Truly, truly, he that has no envious, evil kinsmen lives in this world like a lone tree in a village, happily. The tree that stands alone in a village, fruit and leaves, is worshipped by everyone. Yet, there are those that have noble and righteous kinsmen and live joyfully in their midst, depending on one another, giving each other strength and support. These grow day by day in prosperity and strength, like great trees growing together, in a stand, inside a jungle.

But as for us, we are banished by the evil Dhritarashtra and his murderous sons, and narrowly escaped death by fire. Now here we are under this tree in the heart of a forest. After everything we have suffered, where do we go next?

Ah, evil cousins, enjoy your success, for it will be short-lived! For now the gods certainly favour you, but I swear you still live only because Yudhishtira does not tell me to have done with you. Otherwise, Duryodhana, I would already have sent you to Yamaloka, with your brothers, your sons and your friends, with Karna and Shakuni.

But I am helpless because my elder brother is a man of such dharma that his rage has not yet been roused.'

Full of grief and wrath, Bhima clenches his great fists and sighs. Vrikodara looks at his sleeping mother and brothers again, and his fury flames up like a fire fed with ghee.

Then, calming himself with an effort, he says, 'There is sure to be some town not far from here. Let them awake and we will slake our thirst together, and be refreshed. Afterwards, we can consider what to do next. Until then I must stay awake and watch over them.'

Bhima sits in vigil over his sleeping family."

CANTO 154

HIDIMBAVADHA PARVA

Vaisampayana continued, "Not far from the place where the Pandavas sleep is a Rakshasa called Hidimba who lives in a lofty sala tree. Feral and ugly, his fangs are as long and sharp as daggers.

Hidimba is hungry; he is filled with the yearning today to feast on some human flesh. Long are his legs, great and distended his belly, and his wild hair and beard are red.

His shoulders are as wide tree boles; his ears are pointed like arrows; altogether, his face is savage and dreadful. Waking from a slumber in his branch, casting his crimson eyes around, the ravenous Hidimba sees the sons of Pandu sleeping in that jungle, some way off.

He shakes his horrid head, scratches his tangled hair, with his talons pointing up, yawns, looks at the Pandavas, looks away, and back again at them. His skin is as dark as thunderclouds; he is quite enormous, and his body gives off a dull sheen.

More than any other meat, Hidimba loves human flesh. He dilates his nostrils and sniffs the delectable scent upon the air: of the sons of Pandu.

He turns to his sister Hidimbi and says languidly, 'Ah, so long since I smelt sweet human meat. My mouth is watering. How long it is since I sank my eight fangs into the finest flesh of all. What can match sinking my fangs into a human throat, and drinking the blood as it sprays? Fresh, frothy human blood; and it seems that today I will drink to my heart's content.

Go and see, my sister, who these humans are. Oh, the scent of them invades me; it conquers me! Go, Hidimbi, kill all of them and bring them here. They are asleep in my jungle, in Hidimbavana.

Have no fear but go quickly. Do what I say and we shall feast on them, tearing the meat from their bones as we please. And my sweet sister, when we have had our fill, we shall dance together to various songs!'

Bharatarishabha, Hidimbi the Rakshasi flies to where the Pandavas are under the tall and graceful pipal tree. Arriving near them, she sees four Pandavas sound asleep under the nyagrodha; she sees Kunti, also sleeping beside her sons, and then her eyes fall upon the mighty Bhima, awake and keeping watch over his family.

Hidimbi sees Bhima, rugged and handsome, like a sala tree himself, full of raw vigour, and she falls immediately and hopelessly in love with him.

The Rakshasi sighs. She tells herself, 'Oh, look at him, his skin like molten gold, his arms like tree branches, his shoulders like a lion's, his throat marked with three auspicious lines like a conch shell, his eyes like lotus petals, and altogether splendid.

I want him for my husband. I will not kill him as Hidimba wants. A woman's love for her husband is stronger than her fondness for her brother. If I do kill him, Hidimba and I will enjoy him briefly, momentarily. But if I marry him instead, I can enjoy him forever.'

The Rakshasi can assume any form she wishes, and now she turns herself into a stunning human beauty and walks slowly towards Bhima

Mahabaho. She wears unworldly ornaments, a smile on her full lips; her gait is modest and she comes up to him and says, 'Who are you, Narapumgava, and how did you come here?

Who are these warriors of heavenly beauty that sleep beneath the tree? Who, Sinless, is this woman, her loveliness also unearthly, who sleeps here in this jungle as trustfully as she might in her own bedchamber?

Do you not know that this jungle belongs to a terrible Rakshasa whose name is Hidimba? He is my brother and he sent me to kill you for his meal. But then I saw you, magnificent as a Deva, and I knew that I would have no one else for my husband.

I love you, Manava; you surely know dharma and, knowing that I have given my heart to you, do as you see fit. Oh, Kama's arrows have pierced my heart and my body. I want you for myself; I beg you, make me yours.

Mahabaho, I will rescue you from my brother; Anagha, only become my husband. We will fly far from here and live together upon the breasts of great mountains where no ordinary men ever set foot: for I can fly through the sky at will. Mighty one, you will enjoy me in those secret realms, I will give you great joy and pleasure.'

Bhima replies, 'Rakshasi, perhaps a Muni, who has all his passions controlled and no attachments whatever, could abandon his sleeping mother and brothers. But I certainly cannot go with you to satisfy my desire, leaving my brothers and my mother as food for a Rakshasa.'

Hidimbi says, 'Then wake them up and I will bear you all away from danger.'

But Bhima says, 'Rakshasi, I am not afraid of your vile brother that I will awaken my family that sleeps so peacefully under the tree. Timid one, no Rakshasa has ever resisted the strength of these arms. Beautiful-eyes, no Manava, Gandharva or Yaksha can withstand my might. Sweet one, ah your form so fine, stay or leave as you please. Or even send your brother here, I do not care.'"

CANTO 155

HIDIMBAVADHA PARVA CONTINUED

Vaisampayana said, "Hidimba Rakshasa finds that his sister has not returned. He clambers down from his tree, and stalks towards where the Pandavas lie asleep.

His eyes are red, his arms powerful, the wiry hair on his head sticks out, his slavering mouth hangs open, his body is like a mass of dark clouds, his fangs are like great needles, and he is a terrifying sight.

Hidimbi sees her brother climb down from his sala tree. She sees the anger on his face and trembles. She says to Bhima, 'My evil brother comes in wrath. I beg you awaken your brothers and mother and we must fly. I am as strong as any Rakshasa, O Fearless, and I can go wherever I like. Climb onto my back and I will carry all of you away from here.

Parantapa, wake them up quickly and let us fly!'

Bhima says, 'O fair hips, fear nothing. As long as I am here no Rakshasa can harm any of us, slender waist. I will kill your brother in front of you. I tell you this scourge of the jungle is no match for me, why, not all the Rakshasas of this world together can stand the strength of these arms.

Look at my arms, sweet one, each is like an elephant's trunk! Look at my thighs, like iron maces; look at my chest, how wide it is, and hard like adamant. My beautiful one, today you shall see my strength like Indra's. Fair hips, do not imagine that I am just an ordinary man. I beg you do not look upon me with contempt or dislike.'

Hidimbi says, 'Purushavyaghra, who are as handsome as a Deva, I have no contempt or dislike for you, but only love. But I have seen what Rakshasas do to Manavas, how much stronger they are than men.'

Bhaarata, now that he is closer, Hidimba hears their conversation. He sees his sister has assumed a human form, her hair woven with jasmine garlands, her face like the full moon, her nose, her eyes and brows exquisite, her complexion fair and her skin soft, her nails of lovely hue, her ornaments beautiful, and wearing a flowing diaphanous robe.

The Rakshasa suspects at once that she desires the human, and his eyes blaze. Glaring at his sister, he growls at her, 'When I am so hungry what witless creature dares keep me from eating? Have you lost your mind, Hidimbi, that you do not fear my anger? Fie on you, disloyal Rakshasi.

You are flushed with lust and do not think twice about hurting me. Why, you are ready to dishonour our very race and all your ancestors. I will kill you, wretched woman, and all these that are with you.'

Eyes smouldering, fang grinding against fang, Hidimba runs roaring at his sister to have done with her. But great Bhima jumps up in his way and cries, 'Stop!'

Bhima smiles contemptuously at the Rakshasa. He says to him, 'Hidimba, why do you want to wake my brothers and mother, who sleep so peacefully? Evil one, you should not kill a woman, especially one that has not sinned.

Rakshasa, fight me first. This young woman has not sinned that she desires me, for it is Kama Deva, the God of Love, who inflames her as he does all the living. Wretch, your sister came here at your command; she saw me and lusted after me.

What harm has she done to you by desiring me? It is Kama that offends you, Rakshasa, and you will not hurt her while I am here; you will not kill a woman. Come, let us go some way off and fight, for, vilest of Rakshasas, today I mean to send you to Yamaloka.

Rakshasa, I will crush your head today as if an elephant stamped it. When I have killed you, herons, jackals and kites will gleefully tear the flesh from your limbs and feast on your carcass.

For too long you have ruled this jungle with terror, and it shall be rid of you in a few moments. Hidimba, you are as big as a hill but your sister will soon see you being dragged about like a fallen elephant by a great lion. Vilest of Rakshasas, when I have killed you, men shall pass in safety through this vana again, and without fear.'

Hidimba replies, 'Manava, grand boasts indeed. But do what you say you will and then perhaps you might surely boast. Come, let us not waste a moment. You are strong indeed but today test your strength against me.

I swear that I will not kill your brothers until I have killed you. Till then, let them sleep in peace. But when I have killed you, O fool and braggart, I will drink your blood and then kill your family, and finally my sister, as well, for she has betrayed me.'

Hidimba stretches out his huge arms and rushes at Bhima Parantapa. In a flash, almost playfully, terrible Bhimasena seizes the Rakshasa's arms. Roughly, as easily as a lion might some small creature of the jungle, the Pandava drags Hidimba some krosas from that place where his brothers and mother sleep.

Outraged, enraged, startled to feel the strength of the human, the Rakshasa gives an earthshaking roar. Bhima drags him farther away lest his roars and curses awaken Kunti and his brothers.

Now they lock together, the Manava and the Rakshasa, and fight like two grown tuskers mad with rage. They uproot the trees that grow around them and strike each other with their trunks. Such a noise do they make that the other Pandavas and Kunti awake, and see Hidimbi sitting before them, disconsolately."

CANTO 156

HIDIMBAVADHA PARVA CONTINUED

Vaisampayana continued, "Waking and seeing the extraordinary beauty of Hidimbi, Kunti and her sons are full of wonder. Kunti speaks to her sweetly.

'Who are you that are as beautiful and radiant as a child of the Devas? Fair one, whose daughter are you, where have you come from? If you are the Devi of this vana or an Apsara, tell me about yourself and why you are here.'

Hidimbi replies, 'This great jungle, of the colour of a blue cloud, is the domain of a Rakshasa called Hidimba. Most beautiful and gracious lady, I am his sister and he, O blessed one, sent me to kill you and your sons.

But when I arrived here I saw your mighty son who sat awake. Gracious lady, Kama, who pervades the nature of all the living, struck me with his flowery arrows, and I fell in love with your great son and chose him in my heart for my husband.

I told your son that I would carry all of you away from this place, but he would not allow me. When I did not return to Hidimba, my brother came here and your son hauled him away. Now they fight, the Manava and the Rakshasa, both of them endowed with untold strength, and make the vana tremble with their dreadful roars and blows.'

Yudhishtira jumps up, as do Arjuna, Nakula and tejasvin Sahadeva, and they see that Bhima and the Rakshasa do indeed fight some way off, like two lions. The dust they raise with their flying heavy feet seems like the smoke from a forest fire. Covered by that dust, their massive bodies are like two cliffs shrouded in mist.

Arjuna sees Bhima a little beleaguered by Hidimba, for the Vayuputra has not rested at all. With a smile, Arjuna says to his brother, 'You are tired, Bhima. Let Nakula and Sahadeva watch over our mother, and you must rest. I am here now, I will kill the Rakshasa.'

Bhima retorts, 'Look upon this fight as a spectator, Arjuna. For he has come within reach of my hands and he will not escape with his life.'

Arjuna says, 'Then why, O Bhima, do you let him live so long? Parantapa, we must be on our way. He will become stronger with dawn, as his kind always do, during the three sandhyas. He will also use his maya shakti then. Do not toy with him any longer, but use all your strength now and kill him, my brother.'

Blazing up, Bhima summons the awesome strength that his father Vayu employs during the Pralaya. With a roar, he seizes Hidimba and lifts him easily into the air. He spins the Rakshasa's great body, blue as thunderheads, around, a hundred times in a moment.

Bhima says, 'Rakshasa, you are blessed with intelligence in vain. You have fed for too long on unsanctified meat. You deserve an unholy death. I will rid this vana of you today, and make it a jungle without thorns. No more, Hidimba, will you feast on human flesh.'

Arjuna says again, impatiently, 'Bhima, if you are finding it difficult to kill the Rakshasa, let me help you. Kill him quickly or let me do it. You are tired and must rest.'

Bhima flings Hidimba Rakshasa down savagely onto the ground. He plants his foot on the Rakshasa's back and breaks his body in two like some twig. Hidimba lets out a dying cry that echoes through that vana, deep as the sound of a wet drum.

His brothers crowd around Bhima, slayer of all his enemies, and embrace him.

Then Arjuna says, 'Jyeshta, I believe there is a town not far from this vana. Let us go and hide there, so Duryodhana's spies do not find us here.'

His brothers, those Maharathas, those tigers among men, agree, 'So be it.'

They set out, with Kunti, and Hidimbi the Rakshasi following them."

CANTO 157

Hidimbavadha Parva Continued

Vaisampayana said, "Bhima sees Hidimbi following them and turns on her with a soft growl.

He says, 'Rakshasas avenge themselves on their enemies with impenetrable deception. So, Hidimbi, you must also go after your brother.'

He would have killed her, but Yudhishtira intervenes. 'Bhima, Purushavyaghra, however angry you are you must never kill a woman. Pandava, dharma is more important than protecting one's life.

You have killed Hidimba who came to kill us. This woman is surely his sister, but what harm can she do us even if she wants to?'

Hidimbi folds her hands before Kunti and Yudhishtira as well. She says, 'Gracious lady, you know the pangs that Kama makes a woman feel. He torments me now with them, with love for your son Bhimasena. I live only for the moment when your son will soothe the fever that consumes me. The time has come, sweet lady, and I hope that he will make me glad.

I abandoned my brother and my people only to have Bhimasena for my husband. Most illustrious lady, if he will not have me I will kill myself. Fair one, gracious, beautiful one, be merciful to me. Think of me as being either a fool or your slave, but let your son Bhima, handsome as a Deva, marry me now and let me take him with me, where I go, where I will.

Noble lady, trust me, I will bring him safely back to you. Also, think of me at any time and I will come to you immediately and take you wherever you wish to go. I will protect you from every danger, and carry you over the most inaccessible and remote places, upon my back, through the sky.

Ah, be merciful and tell your son to make me his wife. The Rishis have said that in times of peril one should protect one's life by any means at all, without considering scruples. Yet, he that keeps to dharma in times of duress and trial is the best of men, for distress is the greatest threat to men of dharma.

Dharma protects life; indeed, dharma is called the giver of life. Thus, nothing one does to keep dharma and save one's life can be censured. I am the means to your safety; tell your son to make me his.'

Yudhishtira now says, 'Hidimbi you speak truly. But slender-waisted one, you must keep your word. After his morning ablutions, his prayers and dawn rituals, Bhima shall be yours during the days, until the sun sets. Enjoy the days with him as you please and wherever you like. But Hidimbi, who can fly as swiftly as the mind, you must bring him back to us at nightfall of every day.'

Bhima bows his head to what Yudhishtira says, for he does indeed desire Hidimbi. He says, 'Slim-waisted Rakshasi, I promise to remain with you and to be yours until you have a son.'

Joyfully Hidimbi cries, 'So be it!' She then picks Bhima up effortlessly, rises up into the sky with him and flashes away. She flies with him to lofty mountains, sacred to the Devas, of unearthly beauty, where nameless and rare birds sing as they do nowhere else in the world.

Upon their peaks, on their sides where magnificent trees grow, great sires of their kind, and in their secret valleys, Hidimbi makes love with Bhima all day long. She assumes the most beautiful form for him, wears ornaments past compare, and often breaks into fine song herself, singing more sweetly than the birds.

They take their deep pleasure of each other in the hearts of impenetrable forests, beside lakes like great jewels upon the Earth, fragrant and laden with lotus and lily, on exquisite islands that stand in the flow of great rivers, on soft sands and smooth pebbles, in caves hidden behind towering waterfalls, upon the sylvan Himalaya, in crystalline pools at the foot of these cascades, upon which, also, resplendent lotuses shine, on seashores, great and empty beaches where no man has ever set foot, where gold dust and nuggets sparkle and pearls shine like small moons, in great towns and cities, in sprawling gardens, in sacred tapovanas, upon myriad hills, in the hidden domains of the Guhyakas and Siddhas, on the banks of the Manasarovara, where flowers and fruit festoon the radiant giant trees perennially.

Indeed, Hidimbi flies swiftly as the mind, and she makes love with Bhima in all these places, until she becomes pregnant and in her time delivers a mighty son. His eyes are fierce, his mouth wide, his ears long and pointed like arrows; he is altogether ferocious to behold.

His lips are coppery, his teeth sharp fangs, his arms great, his strength greater, and that child quickly becomes a master archer. His nose is long and sharp, his chest wide as houses, his calves are tremendous, his swiftness incredible, and there is nothing human about his face or appearance though he is indeed the son of a man.

As soon as that child is born, within an hour, he grows into a youth. He is stronger than any Pisacha, of any tribe, and any Rakshasa, too.

Quickly, taught by his great uncles, he becomes a master of every weapon. Rakshasa women give birth the very day they conceive; it is an ancient blessing given them by the Devi Durga, so they do not have to forgo sexual pleasure for any length of time. Of course, they can assume any form they choose, terrible or beautiful.

Bhima and Hidimbi's son has no hair on his head. When he is born, he bends to touch the feet of his mother and his father. Hidimbi remarks that his head is as smooth as a Ghata, a waterpot, and his parents name him Ghatotkacha, the pot-headed.

Ghatotkacha is devoted to his father and his uncles, and he is soon their favourite. But now Hidimbi knows that her time with Bhima has come to an end. She takes sad leave of them and goes away, to range the world as she pleases.

Ghatotkacha, greatest among Rakshasas, takes their blessing, as well, and, promising to appear before them whenever they need him and summon him with a thought, also leaves them and journeys north.

It is told that Indra gives an amsa of himself to create Maharatha Ghatotkacha. His reason for this is to create a worthy adversary for Karna, sadly one that he could finally kill with the deadly shakti, inexorable weapon which Indra himself gives that matchless warrior."

CANTO 158

Hidimbavadha Parva Continued

Vaisampayana said, "The Pandava Maharathas wander from jungle to jungle, hunting deer and other animals for their food. Their travels take them through the kingdoms and lands of the Matsyas, the Trigartas, the Panchalas and the Kichakas, with their emerald forests jewelled with lakes like the faces of the purest diamonds.

The brothers all wear their hair in matted jata, and valkala for garments, or animal hides: those redoubtable Kshatriyas wear the garb of wandering Sannyasis; and Kunti goes with them, their mother. At times, the Maharathas carry her upon their backs, and hurry along their way when they fear that they might be discovered. They go in disguise across the world's wild places.

They study the Rik and the other Vedas, as well as the Vedangas, and the other Shastras that deal with dharma and politics, too. During their wandering, they meet their grandsire Krishna Dwaipayana, the Maharishi Vyasa. They prostrate at his feet, then stand before him with folded hands, the Pandavas and Kunti.

Vyasa says, 'Bharatarishabhas, I know everything that has happened, indeed I had foreknowledge of it during my dhyana. I have come to bless you and to tell you that all that has transpired, your suffering and exile, will finally turn out for the best, and you will benefit from it. Do not grieve over any of this; it is all for your final happiness.

It is true that Dhritarashtra's sons and you are all the same to me. Yet, I must be partial to those that have suffered during their tender years; so, certainly, my affection for you is now greater, and because of that love I want to bless you and do some great good to you.

Not far from this place is a fine little town, where you will be perfectly safe. Take yourselves there, disguised, and wait for me to come to you again.'

Satyavati's son Dwaipayana comforts the sons of Pandu and leads them to the township of Ekachakra.

The Muni also consoles Kunti, 'Live long, daughter! For your son Yudhishtira, devoted as he is to truth, this radiant Purusharishabha who has conquered the world with his dharma, will soon rule over all the rulers of the Earth and be a king of kings.

Arjuna and Bhima will subdue the world in their brother's name, the Earth with her girdle of seas, and Yudhishtira will rule as emperor. Your sons and Madri's Maharathas, as well, will enjoy all power and every luxury and pleasure.

These Purushvyaghras will perform many great sacrifices, including the imperial Rajasuya yagna and the Aswamedha yagna, and munificent shall be the gifts they bestow upon the Brahmanas of the world.

Your sons will one day also rule over the kingdom of their ancestors, the Kuru kingdom, and they will keep their friends and kinsmen in great comfort, wealth and joy.'

Vyasa brings them into the home of a Brahmana in Ekachakra. Then the island-born Rishi says to Yudhishtira, 'Live here and wait for my return. Adapt yourself to the place and your situation, and I, Vyasa, say to you that happiness waits for you around the corner of the days.'

The Pandavas fold their hands humbly to him, and say, 'So be it.' The illumined Dwaipayana then leaves them and returns to his asrama, from where he has come."

CANTO 159

BAKAVADHA PARVA

King Janamejaya asked, "Dvijottama, best of Brahmanas, what did those mighty Maharathas, those Kuntiputras, do in Ekachakra?"

Vaisampayana said, "They live for a time in the home of a Brahmana, disguising themselves as Brahmanas, too. During the day they go begging for alms, and return at dusk with whatever they have received and give it all to Kunti, who divides the alms in two equal portions. Bhima eats one portion, while the other is shared by Kunti and her other sons.

They range far, the sons of Pandu, wandering through enchanting forests, past crystalline lakes and frothing, clear rivers, and they become great favourites with the people of Ekachakra for the manner in which they deport themselves. Thus, O Bharatarishabha, some time passes.

One day, while four of her sons are out begging alms, Bhima is in the room in the home of the Brahmana, their host, with his mother Pritha. Suddenly, Kunti hears piteous sobs echoing from within the Brahmana's house. She hears the man, his wife and children all crying in the most heartbroken manner.

Kunti cannot bear it and says to Bhima, 'My son, we are living peacefully and happily in the house of this Brahmana, who shows us such kindness and respect. Duryodhana has no idea where we are, but believes us to be dead.

My child, I am always blessing this Brahmana in my heart and wondering what great good I should do to him. The true man, my Bhima, always pays back more than he receives. Some terrible tragedy has overtaken our host. If we can be of any help at all to him, we must requite his generous hospitality.'

Bhima says at once, 'Mother, find out what ails the Brahmana. Whatever it might be, I will do everything I can to remove his distress, however difficult that might prove.'

They hear more anguished cries from the Brahmana and his wife. Kunti rises and runs towards the inner chambers of the house of their host, even like a cow does to her tethered calf. She pauses at the door and sees the Brahmana, his wife, their son and daughter all sitting in utmost dejection, with tears streaming down their faces.

The Brahmana says, 'Oh, curse this worldly life! It is as hollow as a reed, pointless, and founded just on sorrow. It begins and ends in grief and knows no freedom. Life is a disease, a tale of misery.

The Atman is one, but it must pursue dharma, artha and kama. And because it does so, and all at the same time, discord arises, and then untold grief. Some say that moksha is our final desire and goal, but I am certain that it can never be attained.

The acquisition of wealth is hell; the pursuit of it attended by misery; and when one finally does acquire wealth one is even more miserable for one has grown attached to one's hard-earned possessions and lives in constant anxiety of losing them.

And today mortal danger has entered my life, and I cannot see how to escape it. Wife of mine, how often I told you let us leave this town and go somewhere else, where we would be happy. But you would not listen.

You always replied, simple woman, "I was born here and have grown old here. This is my home, the place of my ancestors."

But your mother and father left this world a long time ago; all your relatives are also dead. Then why did you want to go on living in this wretched place? No, you would not listen to me, and now that terrible time has come for you to lose one member of your family.

What could be more terrible for me? But no, it is I that will offer myself to death because I could never sacrifice any of you, while keeping myself alive. You have been such a good wife to me, a helpmeet in any punya that I undertook, always self-effacing, and always as loving as a mother.

The Gods gave you to me as a true companion and you are my mainstay, my greatest support. My parents got us married. Your lineage is as pure as your nature is sweet. You are the mother of my children, devoted, chaste and innocent. I married you with every holy rite and I will not abandon you now, who have been so constant in your vratas. I will not sacrifice your life to save mine.

Ah, how will I sacrifice my son who has not yet attained puberty? How will I sacrifice my daughter, my own child given to me by God to become the mother, one day, of my grandchildren, through whom my ancestors and I will attain those realms that only a daughter's sons can bestow upon our souls?

There are those that say that a father loves his son best, while others insist that a daughter is a father's favourite. But for me both my children have always been equal and equally loved.

It is plain that I cannot sacrifice the life of any of you, yet if I die myself who will look after you when I am gone? What peace will my spirit have even in the next world? You will certainly perish, as well, without me.

Oh, there is no cure for the horrible tragedy that has overtaken us, no escape. I do not know what to do. It seems the only course is for all four of us to go and die together. Yes, that seems the only way.'"

CANTO 160

BAKAVADHA PARVA CONTINUED

Vaisampayana continued, "Hearing the Brahmana's stricken words, his wife says, 'O Brahmana, you must not grieve like an ordinary man. This is no time for lamenting. You are learned and you know that all who are born must surely die; you must not grieve over the inevitable.

A man seeks a wife, a son or daughter, all for his self. You are a wise man; kill your grief. I will go in your place, for it is the highest dharma of a woman to save her husband's life by sacrificing her own. I could hope for no greater fortune. By doing this I will find joy and great fame in this world, and eternal bliss in the next.

I tell you, my husband, this is a woman's highest dharma, and by this we shall both find both punya and sukha. I have fulfilled my womanhood by bearing you our children; I owe you no further debt. You are able and can support and nurture our son and daughter; but not I.

You are my life, my wealth, and my lord; without you, how will I feed or care for these young ones, why, how will I support myself? If I am a widow and without a lord, how will I keep the three of us alive and still lead a chaste and honest life?

If arrogant or otherwise unworthy suitors come for your daughter's hand, how will I protect her? My lord, even as birds fly hungrily at discarded meat, so do men seek out a woman who has lost her husband.

Brahmanottama, my virtue might well falter if evil men repeatedly importune me. Then how will I be able to set this innocent daughter of yours upon the pure path which all her ancestors have walked?

As for your son, how will I, as a widow, teach him everything that he should know, so that he becomes as accomplished and virtuous as yourself? Like Sudras that demand to hear the Veda, base men will come for your daughter's hand, and how will I resist them? Even if I refuse, they might well take her by force, like crows stealing sacrificial ghee, this pure child blessed with all your qualities.

And when the world sees your son become so unlike his father, and your daughter married to some low man, it will despise and dishonour me, even the worst in it, and I will certainly die. And when the both of us are dead, these children will also perish like fish when they have no water in which to live.

So, O Brahmana, you must allow me to sacrifice myself. Also, those that know dharma always say that for a woman who has borne children to die before her husband is the greatest punya. Ah, I am more than ready to abandon my son and my daughter, all my kin, and life itself for your sake.

For a woman to serve her husband is her highest dharma, loftier than yagnas, vratas, sannyasa or any kind of daana. So what I mean to do is the purest dharma and punya for you and your race.

The Rishis say that a man treasures his wife, children, relatives and all his possessions to save himself from danger and sorrow. He watches over his wealth to keep danger away and with this wealth he supports and protects his wife. And himself he protects through both his wealth and his wife.

The Sages truly say that a man acquires a wife, a son, wealth and a house in order to safeguard himself against any misfortune, expected or unforeseen. The ancients have also declared that all one's relatives together are not equal to oneself. So, my lord, you must sacrifice me to save yourself. I beg you let me sacrifice myself so that you can care for these young ones of mine.

Besides, those who know dharma always say that a woman must never be killed. Rakshasas also know the laws of dharma. It is certain that the Rakshasa will kill a man but not so that he will dare kill a woman. This is another reason for you to send me to the Rakshasa.

My lord, I have enjoyed great happiness, so much joy and pleasure, and I have also acquired a good deal of spiritual punya. I have borne you these two children who are so precious to me. All my womanly wants and needs have been fulfilled, and I have lived a long life. I am not afraid to die.

I am always eager to serve and please you, that is my nature; keeping all this in mind, I have arrived at my resolve. When I am gone, you can marry another wife, and through her find more religious merit. There is no sin in it. For a man to take a second wife is punya, while for a woman it is a sin to marry a second husband. Remember all this, my lord, and also that for you to sacrifice your life is sinful.

And so, do not delay, but set us all free from our burden of grief: yourself, your family, and these children of ours.'

Bhaarata, the Brahmana embraces her emotionally, and tears stream down their faces, while grief and silence fill the room."

CANTO 161

BAKAVADHA PARVA CONTINUED

Vaisampayana continued, "Listening to her parents, the daughter is stricken and cries, 'Why do you lament and cry like this, as if you have no one to care for you? Hear what I have to say, O my father and mother, before deciding what you are going to do.

Is it not true that one day you will have to send me away, give me to someone to be his wife? Since you must sacrifice me one day, let it be today, and so save three lives for the price of one.

Men wish for children, believing that they will save them in this world and the next. So, today, ford the river of your misfortunes by making a raft of me, your child. The Sages call a child a Putra, a saviour, because a child does indeed save its parents both in this world and the next.

The Pitrs wish for grandchildren from me, to become their special saviours. But by saving my father's life today, I will become a saviour to them myself. My brother, this little one is young and tender. There is no doubt that he will not survive if you die. If both my father and my brother perish, there will be no one left to offer the pinda and tarpana for the spirits of our manes. Nothing could be more terrible.

And if you both leave me, and my mother will certainly not survive your deaths, I will sink into the deepest despair, and die myself, a heartbroken death. However, if you, my mother and father, and this little one continue to live, our family will continue and the ancestral pinda will also continue to be offered.

A son is a man's very soul; his wife is his dearest friend; but a daughter is only a burden. Rid yourself of this burden, father, and let me tread the high path of dharma. I am a girl; if you die, I will become helpless and certainly come to grief, one way or another.

That is why I have decided to save our clan and gain the punya of this fearful sacrifice. Dvijottama, if you leave me and go to the Rakshasa yourself, I will never recover from the grief of it. Be merciful to me, Purushottama, for all our sakes, for the sake of dharma, and for our clan. You must sacrifice my life and live on. You must send me away one day soon, it is inevitable; let this be that day.

What could be more terrible than if you are to die and we are forced to live on, begging for our food like dogs, at the mercy of any stranger who wants to take advantage of us? But if you live on, I will surely find great joy in Devaloka.

I have heard that if a man sacrifices his daughter, offering her like an oblation to the Devas and the Pitrs, he and his shall find prosperity.'

Tears roll ceaselessly down her face as she speaks, and her parents are plunged deeper into despair. The three of them hug one another and sob.

Seeing them, the son of the house, the little innocent, says in the sweetest lisp, and his eyed wide and shining, 'Don't cry, my mother, my father, my sister.'

He goes up to them smiling and brandishing a blade of grass in his small hand. Screwing up his face into a delightful snarl, he cries, 'I will slay the Rakshasa who eats people!'

At which, despite their predicament and their terror, the other three burst out laughing. Kunti sees her moment and enters the room. She speaks to them and truly what she says revives their spirits as amrita does a dying man."

CANTO 162

BAKAVADHA PARVA CONTINUED

"Kunti says, 'Tell me the cause of your grief and I will remove it if I can.'

The Brahmana replies, 'Sannyasini, I thank you for your noble intention, but our grief cannot be removed by any human agency.

Not far from our town there lives a Rakshasa calls Baka, and he is the lord and master of all these lands. He is inordinately strong and rules our country. He is also the lord of all the Rakshasas and thus he protects our town from the rest of them, and we fear no enemy at all.

However, in return for his protection we must send him a regular offering of food: a cartload of rice, drawn by two buffaloes, and the human that drives the cart. Every family's turn comes to send the Rakshasa his offering, and there being so many homes in our country, each one's turn comes after many years.

If any household tries to escape their turn when it comes, Baka descends on them and kills the entire family, men, women and children, and eats them.

The king of this country lives in a city called Vetrakiya. He is a wanton and an imbecile, and does nothing to protect us. And continuing to live in the kingdom of such a weak and impotent monarch, we surely deserve our fate.

No one can force a Brahmana to dwell permanently in any place, and they are like birds that migrate from kingdom to kingdom, in complete freedom. The Rishis have always maintained that one must first find a good king, then a good wife, and then seek wealth. Acquiring these three one becomes capable of saving oneself and one's clan.

But I have been foolish in my pursuit of the three, and today I find myself plunged in a sea of mortal danger and misery, for today it is my turn to send Bakasura his offering of food, which will destroy my family.

I do not have the money with which I might buy a man willing to sell his life and take Baka his cartload of rice. I cannot think of sacrificing my wife or my children. I see no ray of hope or escape, and am sinking in the sea of dread.

I have decided that the only course for us is to go all together to the monster and let him devour us all.'"

CANTO 163

BAKAVADHA PARVA CONTINUED

"Kunti says with a smile, 'Do not grieve anymore, good Brahmana, for I have a way to save you from the Rakshasa. You have just one son, and besides he is a young child, and only one daughter, as well, also a tender girl. I see no reason why either of them, your wife or even you should sacrifice yourselves to satisfy the Rakshasa.

Brahmana, I have five sons. Let one of them take the cart of rice to Baka.'

But the Brahmana is aghast at the idea, 'I can never allow someone else to sacrifice his life for me! You are Brahmanas and my guests. Why, even a lowborn man would not accept your offer. It has always been said that one should sacrifice oneself and one's children for the sake of a Brahmana, and certainly not the reverse. I believe this, and if I have to choose between the death of a Brahmana and my own, I will always choose to die myself.

Brahmahatya is the most heinous sin of all, and there is no expiation for it. It is better to sacrifice one's own life, however sadly, than a

Brahmana's. Noble, blessed lady, I will not be committing suicide if I go to the Rakshasa, and no sin will cling to me in my next life. But if I countenance a Brahmana giving his life for mine, I would sin grievously and would never escape the consequences.

The Rishis have said that abandoning or betraying someone who comes to your home for protection, as well as participating in the death of one that seeks death at your hands are both dreadful sins. The Sages say this in the context of what is permissible in grave danger and distress.

So, dear lady, it is far better for me that I die with my wife and children today than that I sacrifice a Brahmana's life so that I can continue living.'

Kunti replies, 'Brahmana, I also believe firmly that a Brahmana should never be sacrificed. And as for me, even if I had a hundred sons instead of the five that I do, none of them would be any less dear to me than the others. But the Rakshasa will not kill my son because this son of mine is blessed with strength beyond your imagination. He is also a master of occult mantras.

He will deliver the offering of food to the Rakshasa, but will escape with his life. It will not be the first time, either; I have seen, more than once, my son killing the most powerful Rakshasas, fiends big as hillocks.

But Brahmana, you must not tell anyone this secret, for then those that want this secret power for themselves will never leave my sons in peace. The Rishis have said that if my son teaches his secret knowledge to anyone without his Guru's leave, he himself will lose his strength.'

Hearing what Pritha says, incredulous joy fills the Brahmana and his wife, for surely her words are like amrita to them. Kunti takes the Brahmana to Bhimasena Vayuputra, and tells him about the Rakshasa and what she wants him to do.

Bhima replies casually, as if this is nothing, 'So be it.'"

CANTO 164

Bakavadha Parva Continued

Vaisampayana said, "After Bhima gives his word, O Bhaarata, saying 'I will', the other Pandavas return with the alms they have begged during the day. Yudhishtira takes one look at Bhima's delighted expression and guesses at what has transpired while he is out.

Yudhishtira sits beside his mother and says quietly, 'What task has Bhima undertaken? Did you command him or did he take it upon himself?'

Kunti replies calmly, 'I told Bhima Parantapa to do this great thing for the sake of the good Brahmana and to liberate this lovely township from fear.'

Yudhishtira says sharply, 'What rashness, mother. You do not know what you have done. This is like telling Bhima to commit suicide. The Sages never approve of abandoning one's child.

O my mother, why do you want to sacrifice your own son to save another's life? This is not only unnatural for humans but against everything that the Veda teaches.

We sleep peacefully at nights because of Bhima's strength. We have some hope of recovering our kingdom from the envious sons of Dhritarashtra because we rely on Bhima's strength. Duryodhana and Shakuni do not sleep at night because the thought of Bhima's strength haunts them.

We escaped from the house of lac because of Bhima's strength; countless other perils he has saved us from. Bhima killed Purochana. Because of him we already think of ourselves as killing Dhritarashtra's sons and ruling the Earth again very soon, and over all the wealth that is in her.

Mother, what were you thinking when you decided to sacrifice Bhima to the Rakshasa today? Have you lost your reason Kunti, or have our recent trials clouded your mind?'

Kunti says, 'I have not lost my reason, neither is my mind clouded, Yudhishtira, and you need have no fear for Bhima. We have been living safely in this Brahmana's house, undiscovered by Duryodhana, and our host has shown us great respect and affection.

We are in his debt, and gratitude is the mark of a noble man; indeed, the true man returns more than he receives. And it is to repay our debt to the good Brahmana that I decided to send Bhima to the Rakshasa.

I have now seen Bhima's strength, when we escaped from the house of lac, when he killed Hidimba, and I have complete faith in him. My son is as strong as ten thousand elephants; that is how he carried five of us, each one weighty as an elephant, from Varanavrata.

No one on Earth is as strong as Bhima, why, I venture that he may well defeat Indra, who wields the Vajra and is the greatest warrior. Soon after he was born, he fell from my lap down onto the mountain below. The fall left no scratch on him, but the rock onto which he fell was shattered. Pandava, even then I knew my son's matchless strength.

No, neither rashness nor foolishness made me decide to send Bhima against the Rakshasa, or any ulterior motive. Deliberately, and after careful thought, I decided to do this thing.

Yudhishtira, we shall repay our deep debt to our host by this deed as well as gain great punya by it. A Kshatriya who serves a Brahmana in any manner acquires many lofty realms of bliss in the hereafter. A Kshatriya who saves a Brahmana's very life certainly finds great fame in this world and the next.

A Kshatriya who helps a Vaisya becomes very popular, and a warrior must not hesitate to help even a Sudra who comes to him for refuge, for then he shall be born into the noblest of royal houses in his next life, and be prosperous and have great honour from other kings.

O Scion of the House of Puru, the illustrious Dwaipayana himself told me all this once. Remembering what he said, I made my decision.'"

CANTO 165

Bakavadha Parva Continued

"Now, Yudhishtira is contrite. He says, 'Mother, what you have done is wise and excellent. Our Bhima will certainly kill the Rakshasa and come back alive, not only for his indomitable strength but for our mother's unfaltering kindness towards Brahmanas.

But, mother, you must get the Brahmana's solemn pledge that he will say nothing of this to anyone else.'"

Vaisampayana continued, "At dawn the next day, Bhimasena sets out for the Rakshasa's lair, with the cartload of fine food which the Brahmana's wife has prepared. As he goes towards the forest where the Rakshasa lives, Bhima himself begins to eat, and how he relishes the Brahmana woman's cooking!

As he eats, the great Pandava begins to roar out the Rakshasa's name, to taunt him. Baka hears him, and flies out in a rage from his cave towards the impertinent cartman. He is immense, as is his strength; his eyes are red, and so are his hair and beard; he is altogether terrible as he strides along, his footmarks deep upon the earth.

His maw stretches from one ear to the other, and his ears are sharp, pointed like arrowheads. Three deep furrows mark his thick brow. The Rakshasa arrives where Bhima sits contentedly eating the food; Baka bites his lip and glowers.

Softly, in a voice full of menace, he says, 'Who is this fool that dares eat my food before my very eyes? Who is this fool that wants to see Yamaloka at once?'

Bhima only smiles in contempt, and continues eating; he does not so much as turn to look at the Rakshasa. Baka gives the most dreadful roar, thrusts out his long hirsute arms and rushes at Bhima.

Bhima Parantapa gives him just one brief glance, then goes back to eating the Rakshasa's food with undimmed relish. Baka strikes Vrikodara a tremendous blow from behind, smiting him with two clenched fists. Kunti's son does not stir; he still does not look at the Rakshasa, only continues to eat.

Beside himself, Baka tears up a tree and advances upon Bhima again. Meanwhile, Vrikodara finishes the last of the great meal. He washes his hands and now turns with a smile to face the Rakshasa, ready at last to fight him. Baka casts the tree like a javelin at Bhima, who catches it in his left hand.

More trees Baka tears up and casts them in a fair blizzard at the Pandava. Bhima also now pulls up trees and hurls them at the monster. Soon, the entire forest around the dreadful two is denuded of trees.

Baka roars, 'I am Baka!' and he springs at Bhima and seizes him with his hands. Bhima seizes the Rakshasa, too, and they begin to drag each other about violently. The ground shakes beneath their great feet, and the trees they cast at each other snap in pieces and are crushed.

Baka tires quickly, and Bhima flings him down on the ground, holds him down with his knees and begins to rain awesome blows on the supine Rakshasa. Then, in a flash, he turns Baka on his face, plants one knee on his spine and, seizing the Rakshasa's neck in one hand and his waistcloth in the other, begins to bend him back in two.

Baka's screams and roars shake that place. Rajan, he vomits blood as Bhima inexorably breaks his back."

CANTO 166

BAKAVADHA PARVA CONTINUED

Vaisampayana said, "Finally, with a resounding crack, Baka's back breaks and, with a last scream, the Rakshasa, big as a hill, dies.

Terrified by the sounds of that battle, Baka's kinsmen run out, Rajan; they come with their servants to see what the matter is, and find their lord broken upon the ground and his slayer standing over him.

Seeing them terror-stricken, trembling and grieving, Bhima comforts them. But he says, 'Never again kill a Manava, for if you do, you will also die as Baka has died.'

Those Rakshasas say, 'So be it,' giving their solemn word. And indeed, from that day on, the people of Ekachakra and that entire region find those Rakshasas gentle towards humankind, those of the fiends that do not fly that country after they see Baka killed by the mighty Bhima.

Bhima brings Baka's corpse back to Ekachakra. Unobserved, he leaves the great carcass at one of the town gates, by dark, and returns to the house of the Brahmana, where he tells Yudhishtira what has happened.

Next morning, some people of Ekachakra come out and see the hilly Rakshasa, covered in blood and dead. Seeing how he has been mangled by whoever killed him, their hair stands on end.

They run back into the town and the news spreads like wildfire. Now the people come out in thousands, men, women and children, to the gate where the Rakshasa lies like a fallen cliff. They stand stunned by the sight, and at the thought of who could have done this thing.

Rajan, those people give fervent thanks to all their gods, and then they begin to think whose turn it was to take the cart of food the previous day to Baka. Soon they arrive in the house of the good Brahmana, and demand to know what has happened.

At first, he will say nothing. But when they press him repeatedly, that Brahmanarishabha says, 'Yesterday, a Brahmana, a master of mantras, saw me crying with my family at the fate that had overtaken us. He asked why we wept and when I told him, he consoled me, smilingly, and said, "Fear nothing, for I will take his food to the Rakshasa."

At first I would not allow him, but he assured me that he would come to no harm. Surely, he slew Baka and has done us all a great service.'

All the Brahmanas and Kshatriyas of Ekachakra are wonderstruck, and the Vaisyas and the Sudras also rejoice. Indeed, they decide to mark that day with a festival to worship the Brahmana stranger who had freed them from the terror of Baka."

CANTO 167

CHAITRARATHA PARVA

Vaisampayana continued, "After the slaying of Baka, and the ceremony they hold to celebrate the amazing feat by the unknown Brahmana, the people of Ekachakra go back to their homes and resume their daily lives."

Janamejaya asked, "Brahmana, what did the Pandavas, those Purushavyaghras, do after they kill Baka Rakshasa?"

Vaisampayana said, "Rajan, they continue to live in the house of the good Brahmana, who constantly studies the Veda. A few days later, yet another austere Brahmana arrives in the home of the Pandavas' host. Always generous to a fault, the Ekachakra Brahmanarishabha welcomes the visitor and makes him stay in his own home.

Hearing from their host that the newcomer is a gifted raconteur, one evening Kunti and her sons ask him to tell them about his wanderings and experiences. The Brahmana begins by telling them about his journeys and pilgrimages through various lands, their holy shrines and tirthas and rivers. Of great kings that he has met he speaks, and describes many wonderful kingdoms and cities.

When he has done this, O Janamejaya, the Brahmana begins to tell them about the forthcoming swayamvara of the daughter of Drupada Yagnasena of the Panchalas. He describes the unusual births of Dhrishtadyumna and Sikhandi, and of the princess Krishnaa Draupadi, who also is born not from a woman but from a holy fire during a great yagna that Drupada performs.

Their curiosity aroused to hear about the extraordinary events in Drupada's life, the Pandava Purusharishabhas ask the Brahmana, 'Brahmana, how was Dhrishtadyumna born from a yagna fire? How was his sister Krishnaa born from the heart of the yagnashala? How did Dhrishtadyumna acquire all the astras from the peerless Acharya Drona? And, O Brahmana, how did Drupada and Drona become enemies?'

And the itinerant Brahmana tells them about the exceptional birth of Draupadi."

CANTO 168

Chaitraratha Parva Continued

"The Brahmana says, 'Where the Ganga flows down into the plains, there lived a Maharishi called Bharadwaja, a great brahmacharin, who practised the most severe austerities. Stern were his vratas and profound his wisdom.

One day, he came to the river to perform his daily ablutions and saw the Apsara Ghritachi, who had finished bathing and stood on the river's bank, gazing across its flow.

Just then a gust of wind blew her single garment from the Apsara and she stood entirely naked, and ravishing. Seeing her like that, Bharadwaja was stricken with lust. He was a brahmacharin, continent from puberty, but now he helplessly ejaculated.

As soon as his semen spurted from him, Bharadwaja caught it in his drana, his waterpot. From the Sage's seed in the pot there emerged a lustrous son, whom the Rishi named Drona, the one born from the pot. Drona mastered all the Vedas and Vedangas.

Bharadwaja had a friend called Prihasta, who was king of the Panchalas. At almost the same time that Drona was born, Prihasta also had a son, whom he called Drupada. The Kshatriyarishabha Draupada would go daily to Bharadwaja's asrama, to study and play with Drona.

When Prihasta died, Drupada became king of the Panchalas. At this same time, Drona heard that the mighty Parasurama had decided to take final Sannyasa and had decided to give away all his wealth before doing so.

Drona went to Parasurama and said, "Brahmanottama, I am Bharadwaja's son Drona who has come to receive your wealth from you."

Rama replied, "I have already given away all my wealth. All that I now have are my body and my astras. Brahmana, ask me for either of these and I will give it to you."

Drona said, "I beg you, Lord, give me all the astras you have, and teach me how to loose and to recall them."

Parasurama Bhargava said, "So be it," and bestowed all his astras upon Drona, including the great Brahmastra, loftiest among weapons. Drona thought of himself as being the most fortunate man alive, and indeed, having the Brahmastra did render him superior to almost every man.

A master of untold prowess now, Bharadwaja's son, tiger among men, went to Drupada and said to him, "I am your friend Drona."

But Drupada replied scornfully, "A lowborn man can never be the equal or friend of a king of pure lineage. A man who is not a Maharatha can never become the friend of a Maharatha. So, too, though once we might have been friends, Drona, a commoner can never hope to be the friend of a king. Our friendship is a thing of the past."

Shaken and humiliated, Drona, blessed with great intelligence, left the Panchala kingdom and came to the capital of the Kurus, the city named after the elephant. His heart was set on taking revenge on Drupada.

In Hastinapura, Bhishma welcomed Bharadwaja's mighty son, appointed him as Guru to his grandsons, the Kuru scions, and gave the Brahmana much wealth, as well. Drona called his disciples and said to them, "Sinless princes, when I have taught you the use of weapons, made master warriors out of you, you must give me the dakshina that I will ask for, for it is something I hold very dear."

Arjuna and others said to their Acharya, "We shall."

And when they did become proficient at arms, and their aim was true, Drona asked for his dakshina, "Prihasta's son Drupada is king in Chatravati. Take his kingdom from him and give it to me!"

The Pandavas defeated Drupada in battle, took him captive, and brought him with his ministers to Drona; they offered him to their master as dakshina. Drona looked at the humbled king and said, "Drupada, I still want your friendship. But you say that no man who is not a king can be the friend of a king. So, Yagnasena, I will divide your kingdom, which now is mine, in two. You shall rule the Panchala lands south of the Bhagirathi, while I will be king of the northern lands."

Drupada said to that best among Brahmanas and foremost among masters of astras, "Noble son of Bharadwaja, let us be friends forever!"

With that they embraced and went to their separate abodes. However, while Drona naïvely believed that he had struck peace and friendship with Drupada, that Kshatriya never forgave him, and his every moment was full of the rancour of his humiliation. He wasted away, thinking of it ceaselessly,' says the Brahmana at Ekachakra."

CANTO 169

Chaitraratha Parva Continued

Vaisampayana said, "The Brahmana continues, 'Drupada began to roam the jungles in quest of Brahmanas that were masters of yagnas, who could relieve his terrible distress. He was grief-stricken and he had no children who were superior enough to avenge what Drona had done.

Over and over Drupada would say, "Fie on my weakling children, none of them can avenge me. Fie on my kinsmen, weaklings all," and he would hiss and sigh like a serpent, from dejection.

O Bhaarata, that mightiest of kings never stopped thinking about it, but he saw no way by which he could, with all his Kshatriya might, defeat the discipline, prowess and the accomplishments of Drona.

One day, as he ranged the banks of the Yamuna and the Ganga, Drupada came upon a sacred asrama of some Brahmanas, all of them Snatakas, of stern vratas and tapasya, and of deep dharma and lofty punya. There he saw two Rishis called Yaja and Upayaja, masters of the spirit, most evolved and powerful of Sages.

They belonged to the race of Kashyapa and had devoted themselves to the study of the most ancient and arcane scriptures, arts and sciences. Drupada knew at once that, if anyone, those Brahamanashreshtas could help him. Assiduously, singlemindedly, he began to worship and to cultivate them.

He found the austere Upayaja, the younger of the Rishis, possessed of great wisdom and power, and he offered him measureless wealth, privately. He served that Rishi like a common acolyte, always speaking the most flattering and sweet words to him, prostrating at his feet, and offering him everything that any man might desire.

One day, after offering his usual worship, Drupada said to Upayaja, "O Brahmana, if you perform a putrakama yagna for me through which I have a son who will kill Drona, I will give you ten thousand cows, or whatever else you want from me."

But the Sage replied, "I cannot."

However, Drupada would not give up and continued to serve and worship the Rishi diligently. When a year passed, one day Upayaja said sweetly to Drupada, "One day, as he roamed in the heart of the forest, I saw my elder brother Yaja pick up a fruit which had fallen from a tree. He did not care to examine the purity of the ground on to which it had fallen. Why, he has no scruples about accepting impure gifts. He that can be impure in one instance can well be the same in others.

While we were students in the home of our Guru, studying the Shastras, my brother had no compunction about eating the unclean leavings from feasts. He always delighted in food, and has no distaste for any kind of food. I would surmise from this that my brother Yaja would in general be fond of mundane acquisitions.

O King, I suggest that you approach my brother; he will perform the yagna you desire."

Drupada heard this and surely had no great esteem for Yaja, but went to him nonetheless. He worshipped Yaja, and said, 'Master, perform a putrakama yagna for me and I will give you ten thousand cows. Hatred for Drona consumes me; only his death can put out the fire that burns my heart.

Greatest among those that know the Veda, Drona has the Brahmastara and I cannot vanquish him in battle. Bharadwaja's son is a great genius and he is Guru now to the Kuru princes. No Kshatriya in the world is his equal.

His formidable bow is twelve feet long and his arrows can kill every living thing. Bharadwaja's son, awesome bowman born as a Brahmana, denudes the power of the Kshatriya the world over. Why, he is like another Parasurama, born to destroy the very race of kings.

No man on Earth can withstand the ferocity of the astras of Drona. He is like a fire fed with ghee; he combines the power of the Brahmana with the prowess of a Kshatriya, and razes his adversaries.

But, O Yaja, your Brahma shakti, by itself, is greater that Drona's Brahma shakti and his Kshatriya shakti. As for me, I have only my Kshatriya shakti and I am no match for Bharadwaja's son. I have come to beg for your help, using your Brahma gyana that is far superior to Drona's.

Great Yaja, perform a yagna for me by which I might have an invincible son who will kill Drona. I will give you ten thousand cows for this, or any wealth you wish."

Yaja said, "So be it," and he turned his mind to remembering all the rituals for such a sacrifice. Realising that it was a weighty undertaking, he sought the help of his brother Upayaja, who had no desire for any worldly possessions.

When Upayaja agreed to help, Yaja began the yagna that would one day kill Drona. Upayaja detailed everything that they would need for the fire sacrifice, by which the king would have a son.

The Sage said, "Rajan, you will have a son such as you want, of matchless strength, vitality and valour."

Drupada began to make preparations for the great yagna. When everything was ready, Yaja poured libations of ghee into the sacred agni, and called Drupada's queen, "Come here, O daughter-in-law of great Prihasta, for, look, a son and a daughter have arrived for you."

The queen said, "Great Brahmana, my mouth is still full of saffron and other sweet things. My body is still daubed with perfume; I am not pure or fit to accept your offering of ghee that will give me children. O Yaja, I beg you, wait a little for me."

But Yaja replied, "Queen, it matters little whether you come or no. I have the oblation ready and Upayaja has sanctified it with his mantras. Let the object of the yagna be fulfilled!"

With that, Yaja poured the sanctified libation into the fire, and immediately a resplendent and fierce looking prince arose from the flames, a youth who looked like a Deva and shone like fire himself. He wore a crown upon his head, and excellent armour upon his body, carried a bow and arrows, and let out resounding roars from time to time.

As soon as he was born he climbed into a fulvid chariot, which also arose from the yagna flames, and dashed about in it for a while; and the overjoyed Panchalas shouted, "Jaya! Jaya!" They were so full of joy that it seemed the Earth at that moment could hardly contain them or bear them.

Then, an asariri spoke from the sky, "This prince has been born to kill Drona. He will remove all the fear of the Panchalas, and spread their fame across the world. He shall dispel the anxiety of his father, the king."

As soon as the voice has spoken, from the heart of the yagnashala there arose a princess of unearthly beauty and great fortune, and she would be called Panchali. Her skin was dark, her eyes were black and long as lotus petals, and her hair was deep blue, a glossy cascade of curls. Her nails were curved, as brilliant as burnished copper, her eyebrows were fair, and her bosom was deep. She was like the daughter of a Deva born into the world of men.

Her body was fragrant like a blue lotus, and this exquisite scent of her spread a full two miles. Her beauty had no equal on Earth. She was like a Goddess herself, and any Deva, Danava or Yaksha would gladly choose her for his wife.

When this incomparable princess, her hips wide and delicate, was born, again a disembodied voice spoke out of the sky. "This dark girl will be the best of all women and she shall cause the destruction of Kshatriya kind. This slender-waisted one will fulfil the deep purpose of the Gods, and with her advent all danger shall overtake the House of Kuru."

All together, the mighty Panchalas gave a great lion's roar, and the Earth trembled at that sound as if she would be cloven. Then, looking at the two fireborn children, Drupada's wife wanted them for her own, and she said to Yaja, "Let these two never know any other mother except me."

Yaja said, "Tathastu. So be it."

Then the Brahmanas who were present named the two children, with whom they were absolutely gratified. "Let Drupada's son be called Drishtadyumna for his terrific valour and because, like Dyumna, he has been born wearing armour and carrying weapons."

"Because the princess of matchless beauty is dark, let her be called Krishnaa."

Thus, from Drupada's great yagna those splendorous twins were born. And when Drona heard the news, he brought Drishtadyumna to his own kingdom in northern Panchala and taught him all the astras: to pay, as it were, for half the kingdom that he had taken from Drupada.

Bharadwaja's son was a Mahatman enough to know that fate is ineluctable, and by what he did he swelled his fame,' says the Brahmana at Ekachakra."

CANTO 170

CHAITRARATHA PARVA CONTINUED

Vaisampayana said, "Kunti's sons listen to what the Brahmana says, and it seems as if their hearts are pierced by subtle arrows; gone is their peace of mind.

Honest Kunti sees her sons distracted and says to Yudhishtira, 'Many days and nights we have lived here in Ekachakra and our time has passed pleasantly, living off alms that these good people have given us.

Parantapa, we have ranged through all the fine woods and forests in this region of the Earth, and they hold no freshness for us anymore. Also, Scion of the House of Kuru, alms are not as easy to find as before. If you wish, I think we should now go to Panchala. We have never seen that country and, Kshatriya, we should find some delight in it.

I have heard, O scourge of your enemies, that alms are not difficult to find in Panchala, and that King Drupada himself is a great patron of Brahmanas. I feel that it is never good to live too long in one place. So, my son, if you also agree let us leave for the Panchala country.'

Yudhishtira agrees immediately, 'It is our dharma to do whatever you wish, mother. I am willing to leave at once, but I do not know what my brothers will say.'"

CANTO 171

CHAITRARATHA PARVA CONTINUED

Vaisampayana continued, "Kunti speaks to Bhimasena, Arjuna and the twins about going to the Panchala kingdom. Immediately, they agree, 'Tathastu, so be it!'

Rajan, now Kunti and her sons bid farewell to their host, the Brahmana, and set out for Drupada's wonderful city.

While the Pandavas live disguised in the home of the Ekachakra Brahmana, Satyavati's son Vyasa comes to see them one day. Those Kshatriyas see him coming and come out to receive him. They worship him with folded hands, and stand thus silently before him.

The Maharishi is pleased by their welcome and asks them to sit down around him. When they do so, he speaks to them cheerfully, 'Slayers of your enemies, are you living in dharma and the way of the Shastras? Do you worship the Brahmanas? I do hope that those that deserve your adoration duly receive it.'

He continues genially, but speaking of matters of great depth and import, words of dharma, and which dwell upon many a fascinating theme.

Then Dwaipayana says, 'Once, an illumined Rishi, who lived in his asrama, had a tender-waisted daughter, a girl of lovely lips, fine eyebrows, who was accomplished in every way. However, as a result of her karma from a past life, this maiden was taken by misfortune: she was chaste and she was beautiful, but she could not find a husband.

In sorrow she began to perform tapasya so that she would find a man to marry her. So excellent was her penance that she quickly pleased the Lord Siva, who appeared before her and said, "Ask for the boon you want, for I am Sankara who will give you whatever your heart wishes for."

In transport she cried, "Lord, give me a husband. Give me a husband blessed with every quality and virtue!" Indeed, five times she repeated this.

The Lord Isana said, "Blessed child, you will have five husbands from among the Bhaarata princes, and they shall be the best of men."

She was taken aback, "Lord, I want just one husband through your grace."

Siva said to her, "Five times, young woman, you asked me for a husband; so, in another life, five husbands you shall have."

Bharatarishabhas, that young woman of unworldly beauty has been born as the daughter of Drupada, and she, the flawless Krishnaa of the line of Prihasta, is destined to become the wife of all five of you. Mighty Kshatriyas, go to the capital of the Panchalas and live there, and when you have made Panchali your wife you will find untold joy.'

Saying this to the Pandavas, their august and illustrious grandsire bids them farewell, and the Maharishi returns to his asrama from where he had come."

CANTO 172

CHAITRARATHA PARVA CONTINUED

Vaisampayana said, "After Dwaipayana leaves, the Pandavas bid their host the Brahmana a warm farewell, and set out for the Panchala kingdom, with Kunti walking at their head and joy brimming in their hearts. Those slayers of all foes go north towards their destination, walking by night and day, and arrive at a holy temple to the Lord Siva, with the crescent Moon upon his brow.

Then the Pandava Purushavyaghras arrive on the banks of the Ganga. Maharatha Arjuna Dhananjaya now walks before them with a brand lit in his hand to show the way, and to protect them from wild animals.

A haughty Gandharva king is in the river with his wives, at pleasure in that secluded place. The Gandharva hears the footfalls of the Pandavas as they near the river. He flares up in anger to see Kunti and her sons approach.

Bending his terrible bow in a circle, he cries, 'Apart from its first forty instants, it is known that the grey twilight which comes before nightfall has been kept for Yakshas, Gandharvas and Rakshasas to range the Earth; and all of these can go anywhere they wish. Manavas have been given the rest of the day for their work, but if mortal men dare approach us during the third sandhya, roaming the world for gain, both the Rakshasas and we Gandharvas kill the fools.

No one who knows the Veda will ever approve of any human, be he not a king leading his army, daring to approach a pool or a river during this hour. Stay away, mortals; stay far and do not come near me. Can't you see that I am bathing in the Bhagirathi?

I am the Gandharva Angaraparna. Mighty I am, proud, and a friend to Lokapala Kubera. This forest on the banks of the Ganga, where I sport to please all my senses, belongs to me; it is calls Anagaraparna after me. Not Devas, Kapalikas, Yakshas, Gandharvas or Rakshasas dare come to this vana of mine, for I am the brightest jewel on the crown of Kubera. How dare you paltry Manavas approach me?'

Annoyed by the Gandharva's arrogant tone, Arjuna replies, 'Fool, be it day or night, dawn or dusk, who can prevent anyone from going to the Ocean, the Himalaya or to the banks of this holy river? Sky ranger, be one's belly empty or full, be it day or night, there is no prescribed time when one might or not come to the Ganga, greatest of rivers.

As for us, we are powerful and do not care that we disturb you. Vain Gandharva, only those that are weak will have any regard for you. This Ganga springs from the golden peaks of Himavan, and she flows into the Ocean in seven sacred streams. They that drink the waters of Ganga, Yamuna, Saraswati, Vitashtha, Sarayu, Gomati, and Gandaki are washed of all their sins.

Gandharva, this most holy Ganga when she flows through the heavens is called Alakananda; in Pitriloka, realm of the manes, she is Vaitarani that no sinner can cross, Krishna Dwaipayana himself has said so. She is auspicious and blessed; there is no danger in her, and she can lead those that touch her waters to Swarga. Why do you want to keep us away from her? It is not dharma that you do.

We will not obey you, Gandharva, but touch the holy waters of the Bhagirathi. No one shall prevent us.'

Angaraparna replies with a flurry of lightlike arrows, narachas like serpents. But, Arjuna easily strikes them aside with a shield in one hand and with the brand he carries in the other.

Says Dhananjaya again to the raging Gandharva, 'Gandharva, you cannot frighten those that know arms, for your weapons dissolve before me like wavefroth. Yet, I feel that you are a better archer than mortal men, and I will fight you, using astras and with no maaya or deceit.

Look, this Agneyastra that I cast at you was given to Bharadwaja by Indra's Guru Brihaspati. Bharadwaja taught it to Agnivesya, from whom my Guru had it. Drona gave this astra to me.'

With a roar, and in some fury, Arjuna casts the Agneyastra, weapon of fire, at Angaraparna. The astra burns the Gandharva's chariot to ashes and flings him unconscious on to the ground. In a flash, Arjuna seizes his long hair, wreathed with fine garlands, and drags him toward his brothers.

The Gandharva's wife Kumbhinasi runs to Yudhishtira, wailing, 'Noble one, I am Kumbhinasi and I am this Gandharva's wife. I seek your protection, great one. I beg you spare my husband's life!'

Seeing her terrified, Yudhishtira says to Arjuna, 'Parantapa, child, who will kill a beaten enemy, whose honour is lost that a woman begs for his life, for he himself cannot defend himself anymore?'

At once, Arjuna says, 'Keep your life, Gandharva. Leave us and go in peace, for Yudhishtira, lord of the Kurus, commands me to show you mercy.'

The Gandharva says, 'You have vanquished me and consumed my chariot. I will give up my name Angaraparna, Blazing Chariot, for, O friend, I have no right left to it when you have humbled me. From now I shall call myself Burnt Chariot for what you did to my ratha.

I am fortunate to have found you, O mighty Arjuna, for you have spared my life and there is no greater gift. In return, I would give you, O Astradhari, a power that only the Gandharvas possess. It is calls the Chakshushi, the art of creating illusions, and I acquired it through tapasya of old.

Manu taught Soma the Chakshushi; Soma Deva taught it to Viswavasu, who gave it to me. Though my Guru gave me this potent gift, it withers now with me, who have been defeated in battle and have lost my tejas.

I have told you only about some of the powers of the Chakshushi; he who owns it can see whatever he wishes to, anywhere, in any time, and in any manner that he chooses. Usually, the occult power can be had only after standing on one leg in tapasya for six months. But I shall give it to you freely, without your having to keep any vrata or perform any penance.

Kshatriya, it is for this power that we Gandharvas are superior to Manavas: for using the Chakshushi, we see all things with spiritual sight and are equal to the Devas.

Purushottama, I also mean to give each of your great brothers a hundred horses born in the realm of the Gandharvas. Their colouring is unworldly and their speed that of the mind. The Devas ride them and the Gandharvas. They are lean but they never tire or slow.

In the olden days, the original thunderbolt was made for Indra to kill Vritrasura. But when he cast it at Vritra, it shattered in a thousand pieces. The Devas still worship those fragments of the thunderbolt. What is called glory in this world of men is just one fragment. The Brahmana's hand, with which he pours libations into the holy fire, the Kshatriya's chariot, the Vaisya's charity, the Sudra's service to the higher varnas, all these are fragments of the thunderbolt.

Horses are a part of the chariot of the Kshatriya; for this, they are called immortal. Also, they are the children of Badava, the fire of the Pralaya which dwells beneath the Ocean, as a mare of flames. The steeds that are foaled in the land of the Gandharvas can go anywhere, at any speed their owners will, and assume any colour their masters choose.

My horses will always obey your every wish.'

Arjuna says, 'Gandharva, if you want to give me your mystic power and your horses because I spared your life, I will not accept your gifts.'

The Gandharva replies, 'To meet a great man is always an honour and joy, and you have also given me the gift of my life. For this I will give you the Chakshushi. However, so that the obligation is not one-sided, I will also take something in return from you, O Arjuna: Bharatarishabha, give me your unearthly Agneyastra.'

Arjuna says, 'I will accept your horses in return for my astra, and may we be friends forever. But friend, tell me why we Manavas must go in fear of the Gandharvas. We are virtuous, the terrors of our enemies and knowers of the Veda. Yet, Gandharva, by twilight, you censured and challenged us.'

Says the Gandharva, 'You have no wives or asrama of life, though you have completed your tutelage. Pandavas, no Brahmana walks before you as your priest and mentor, and that is why I challenged you.

The Yakshas, Rakshasas, Gandharvas, Pisachas, Uragas and Danavas are all wise and well acquainted with the history of the race of Kuru. Kshatriya, I myself have heard about the great dharma of your illumined ancestors, from Narada and other Devarishis. Why, while I ranged over the Earth, girdled by her oceans, I have seen with my own eyes the might and power of your great race of kings.

Arjuna, I know Bharadwaja's son, your Guru, who is renowned throughout the three worlds for his knowledge of the Vedas and for his mastery over the science of weapons.

Kuruvyaghra, Prithaputra, I also know Dharma, Vayu, Sakra, the Aswins and Pandu, as well: your sires, divine and human. I know that you five brothers are learned and noble, greatest among warriors, brave, virtuous and keepers of your vratas.

Knowing that your hearts and minds are pure and wise, and your conduct faultless, still I have censured you – because, O Kurus, no man who is honourable and a warrior will endure being slighted in the presence of his wife. Kuntiputra, the prowess of the Gandharvas increases during the hours of darkness, and for this reason also I challenged you, for my wife is with me and I was inflamed.

Yet you vanquished me, O Pandava, and I will tell you why. Your brahmacharya, your continence, gives you great power; and with that strength you have defeated me. Parantapa, let any Kshatriya who is married fight a Gandharva by night, and he will not escape with his life. Yet, it is also true that a Kshatriya, be he married or not, who has been blessed by Brahman and who has given the burden of his kingdom into the hands of a Brahmana – such a one might indeed humble any ranger of the night.

O Tapatya, son of Tapati, wise Kshatriyas should always have learned and self-controlled Brahmanas in their employ, so that fortune favours them and they acquire everything that their hearts wish for.

The Brahmana who knows the Vedas and their six Angas, who is pure and honest, who is virtuous and restrained, is worthy of being the priest of a king. The king whose priest is a good Brahmana, who knows the laws of dharma, who is eloquent, pure and of taintless conduct: that king is always victorious and finally finds Swarga.

A king must choose an accomplished Brahmana to gain what he does not possess and to protect what he does. The Kshatriya who wants to prosper must submit himself to the guidance of his priest, and then he can become lord of the sea-girt Earth.

Tapatya, not through the noblest birth or by the most valiant or glorious deeds alone can a Kshatriya ever hope to gain a kingdom. He must have a Brahmana priest to guide him. For, O Scion of Kuru, the kingdom in which Brahmanas wield influence lasts forever.'"

CANTO 173

Chaitraratha Parva Continued

"Arjuna says, 'More than once you have called me Tapatya. Why, good Gandharva? As sons of Kunti, Kaunteyas we surely are, but who is Tapati that we should be called Tapatyas?'"

Vaisampayana continued, "Then the Gandharva tells Arjuna a tale known through the three worlds.

'Pandava, most intelligent of men, listen to the reason in full, for it is a charming story: the reason why I call you Tapatya. He in the sky who bathes this world in his light, had a daughter called Tapati, who was his very equal. Vivaswat's daughter Tapati was the younger sister of Savitri, the Sannyasini renowned throughout the Trilokas and famed for her tapasya.

No Asuri, Yakshi, Rakshasi or Gandharvi was as beautiful as Tapati. Flawless were her features, her black eyes large and lustrous, most elegantly attired, she was chaste, and immaculate were her deportment and character.

When the Sun looked at his daughter Tapati, he thought that there was no one in Swarga, Bhumi or Patala fit to become her husband.

She came to puberty and the Sun God had no peace for he was always thinking about who in the three worlds could be a suitable husband for his daughter.

At this very time, O Kaunteya, the Kururishabha, mighty King Samvarana, son of Riksha, worshipped Surya Deva with arghya, vanamalas, fine perfumes, and vratas and tapasya of every kind. Indeed, Samvarana worshipped the glorious Sun constantly, with deep and humble bhakti.

Surya saw Samvarana, unequalled for his beauty and his dharma, and felt he was the only man fit to marry Tapati. Vivaswat decided that he would give his precious daughter to King Samvarana to be his wife, for just as Surya himself filled the sky with his lustre, so too did Samvarana pervade every part of the Earth with the light of his dharma.

Partha, all men, other than Brahmanas, worshipped Samvarana. He was blessed with great fortune and surpassed Soma the Moon in soothing the hearts of his friends, and Surya in searing the minds of his enemies. Kaurava, Tapana Surya did indeed decide to give his peerless daughter Tapati in marriage to Samvarana of matchless virtue and deeds.

One day, Samvarana went hunting in the jungles on the foothills of the mountains. As he rode in quest of deer, his pedigreed steed fell and died under him, from hunger, thirst and exhaustion. Leaving the dead horse, Arjuna, Samvarana roamed the mountain, and he saw a young woman more beautiful than any other, and her eyes large.

That Parantapa, Rajavyaghra Samvarana, was by himself, as was she; they stood transfixed, gazing at each other. She was so beautiful that the king felt sure that she was the Devi Sri Lakshmi. Then he thought of her as being the rays of Surya Deva, embodied.

She was a brilliant flame, yet also soft and lovely as a clear digit of Soma. Black-eyed, she stood upon the mountain like a shining golden statue; why, the very mountain, with all its plants and vines and trees, seemed to be made of gold because of the beauty and raiment of Tapati.

Samvarana looked at her and he felt contempt for every other woman he had seen before; seeing her he thought that the vision of his eyes had at last been blessed. Nothing he had ever seen, from the day he was born, could compare with the beauty of this young woman.

His eyes were riveted to her, as was his heart, as if an unseen rope bound them to her; he stood transfixed, gazing, seeing nothing but her. Samvarana thought that he that had created such beauty could have done so only after he churned all the worlds of the Devas, Asuras and Manavas.

His own mind churning within him, that king felt certain that no woman in any of the three worlds could rival this one for her abundance of beauty.

The highborn Samvarana looked at Tapati and Kama Deva's arrows pierced his heart and the king's peace of mind left him. Burning with desire's scorching flame, Samvarana asked that full-grown yet innocent young woman, "Who are you and to whom do you belong? Why are you here, sweet smiles, wandering in this lonely vana by yourself?

Ah, you are flawlessly beautiful, in every feature, as are all the ornaments that you wear, which seem to covet you for their ornament. You do not seem to me to be a Devastri, an Asuri, a Yakshi, a Rakshasi, Nagini or a Gandharvi or a Manushi but from a race of your own, for none of the loveliest women that I have ever seen could remotely rival you for beauty.

Ah, exquisite one, I look at you more beautiful than the Moon, your eyes like lotus petals, and Kama Deva has his way with me. Ah, he burns me with desire for you."

Samvarana's voice quivered with desire, but the young woman made no reply to his ardent speech. Instead, like lightning in clouds, she of the great eyes vanished before the king.

Samvarana staggered through that forest like a mad man, seeking her of the lotus eyes, desperately. He did not find her and his heartbroken cries echoed against the mountainside; he sobbed and fell unconscious.'"

CANTO 174

CHAITRARATHA PARVA CONTINUED

Vaisampayana said, "The Gandharva continues, 'When that young woman vanished, Samvarana, razer of enemy armies, fell onto the ground, stricken by Kama. As he lay in a swoon, she of the wide round hips stood before him again.

Favouring the king with her sweet smile, she said to the scion of the House of Kuru in her voice like honey, "Arise, arise Parantapa! Rajavyaghra, tiger among kings, it does not become a world renowned personage like you to faint."

Samvarana opened his eyes and saw her again, she of the full hips and breasts. Still blazing with desire, he spoke to her of the black eyes in a voice tremulous with emotion, "Be blessed, O most beautiful among all women. I burn for you, why my very life leaves me for what I feel for you. Black eyes, you who are as radiant as the filaments of a lotus, Kama strikes me with his arrows, mercilessly, every moment, one after the other, for your sake. He sinks a viper's fangs into me.

Lovely one, O you of the flaring hips, you of perfect features, you who are as lovely as the moon, soft as a lotus petal, whose voice is as sweet as a singing Kinnari's, my life depends on you. I cannot live without you, O timid, bashful one.

Ah, Kama strikes me relentlessly. Take pity on me, young woman whose eyes are like lotus petals. Big eyes, black eyes, it does not become you to abandon me, to cast me aside. Instead, save me. Grant me your love and soothe my anguish.

You have taken my heart captive at first glance. My mind wanders wildly, madly. I look at you and never want to see another woman. O be merciful, for I am your slave, your ardent servant.

Accept me, peerless one, put out Kama's terrible fire with the waters of your love. Be mine, O you beauty, and appease the God of Love who is here with his sugarcane bow and his flowery arrows, sharp as daggers. Marry me by Gandharva vivaha, O fair one with swaying hips, for it is said to be the finest form of marriage."

Tapati said, "I am not my own mistress, but a maiden commanded by her father. If you truly want to marry me, ask my father for my hand. O King, you say that I have stolen your heart, and I say to you that I have also fallen in love with you at first sight.

But no woman is mistress of herself, and that is why I dare not make love to you. Ah, which woman in the three lokas would not want you for her husband, for not only are you most nobly born but you are like a father and kindly to all your people.

So, Rajan, when opportunity presents itself, ask my father Aditya for my hand; worship him, perform tapasya and keep vratas so that I become yours. For if my father gives me to you I shall be your loving and obedient wife forever.

I am Savitri's younger sister and my name is Tapati. O Kshatriyarishabha, I am the daughter of Surya who illumines Earth and Sky," said she,' says the Gandharva."

CANTO 175

CHAITRARATHA PARVA CONTINUED

Vaisampayana said, "The Gandharva continues, 'Saying this much to Samvarana, Tapati rose straight up into the sky and disappeared. The king fell unconscious on the ground once more.

Meanwhile, his ministers and soldiers combed the forest for him, and finally found him supine in that lonely place, that magnificent king, great archer, lying like a rainbow fallen on to the Earth. His chief minister was like a man scalded by fire. He rushed to his sovereign's side, Samvarana who had fainted from desire.

This minister was a man as advanced in age as wisdom, in achievements as in policy, and he gently roused his unconscious lord, and became reassured that he lived.

Thinking that the mighty Samvarana had been felled by hunger, thirst and exhaustion, the minister said kindly, "Be blessed, sinless one. Rajavyaghra, tiger among kings, fear nothing."

The old man sprinkled cold water, made fragrant by lotus petals over his monarch's crownless head. Slowly, Samvarana awoke and ordered all his men and companions away, keeping only the old minister with him.

When they had all gone, the king rose and purified himself with a bath. He then sat upon that Lord of all Mountains, with his hands folded and his face turned heavenward. He sat worshipping Surya Deva. Samvarana, scourge of his enemies, also thought of his Kulaguru Vasishta, Brahmanottama. Night and day, Samvarana sat thus in dhyana, unmoving.

On the twelfth day, Brahmarishi Vasishta, priest to the Kuruvamsa, arrived on the mountain, and with mystic intuition he knew at once that Tapati was the cause of Samvarana's condition, the cause for his tapasya. He comforted the king of unswerving vratas.

Then, before Samvarana's eyes, the illumined Sage rose up into the sky to meet Surya Deva; the Rishi was like a luminary himself. With folded hands, the Brahmana approached the God of a thousand rays, and said, "I am Vasishta."

Vivaswat of terrific tejas said, "Maharishi, be welcome! Tell me what brings you here, for, most blessed and eloquent one, I will give you whatever you ask of me, however hard I might find it to give."

Vasishta bowed to the splendid Deva and said, "Vibhavasu, I have come to ask for the hand of Savitri's younger sister, your daughter Tapati's hand, for Samvarana. Great are the dharma and the achievements of that king, he is a Mahatman. Sky crosser, he will make a worthy husband to your daughter."

Vibhakara Surya, who had already decided to give Tapati to Samvarana, says to Vasishta, "You are the greatest of Munis, Samvarana is the greatest of kings and Tapati the best of women. How can I refuse to give my daughter to him?"

So saying, the Deva Tapana gave his blemishless Tapati into the hands of the Rishi, to convey her to Samvarana to be his bride. Accepting her formally, the Brahmarishi brought her back to the Earth, to the place where the Kururishabha, his accomplishments godly, sat in worship, waiting anxiously.

The king saw Vasishta bring the unearthly Tapati to him and felt as if his heart would burst for joy. She came down from the sky like lightning from clouds, dazzling the ten cardinal points of the firmament. The twelve nights of King Samvarana's vrata and tapasya had ended when the Rishi Vasishta brought Tapati to him.

Samvarana, that Narapumgava, bull among men, took Tapati's hand upon that mountain, where Devas and Gandharvas roamed. He sought Vasishta's leave to be with his new wife in the wilderness, and he proclaimed Brahmarishi Vasishta to be regent of all of his kingdom, his capital and all his forests, mountains and plains.

Vasishta blessed Samvarana and left him. For twelve years, that king then sported and made love with Tapati in the forests and foothills of the Himalaya. But Bharatottama, the thousand-eyed Indra sent no rain down on Samvarana's kingdom for twelve years.

Men perished in that drought, as did animals, trees and plants. No drop even of dew moistened the arid Earth and no ear of corn grew during that time. The people fled the kingdom to all parts. Men abandoned their wives and children, and lawlessness reigned. Those that survived were reduced to skin and bones, hardly more than skeletons, and Samvarana's great capital resembled the city of Yama, full of ghosts.

Vasishta saw the piteous condition of the people and fetched Samvarana back to his city, with Tapati, after twelve long years. As soon as the king returned, the thousand-eyed Deva, destroyer of Asuras, sent down copious rains. Corn sprouted everywhere, and with the drought and the famine ending, joy returned to the kingdom.

Samvarana and his queen Tapati performed great yagnas for twelve years, sacrifices such as Indra and Sachi perform in Devaloka. Partha, such was the story of Tapati, the daughter of Vivaswat. Samvarana begot a son upon his beautiful queen. That prince was Kuru, greatest among Rajarishis. You have been born into the race of Tapati's son Kuru, O Arjuna, and that is why I called you Tapatyas. And it was with the help of the Brahmarishi Vasishta that Samvarana gained his wife and continued his royal line,' says the Gandharva to the Pandavas.

Arjuna, mighty bowman, Kurusthama, best among all the Kurus, is deeply moved and stands with folded hands before the Gandharva.

The Pandava is curious indeed about the Sage Vasishta. He says, 'O greatest of Gandharvas, tell me everything about the Maharishi Vasishta, who was the priest of our ancestors.'

The Gandharva says, 'Vasishta is Brahma's son, born immaculately from his spirit. The Rishi was the husband of the chaste Arundhati. He has vanquished desire and wrath, kama and krodha, which hardly any man ever subdues; why, lust and rage washed Vaishta's feet, for they were his servants.

Once Viswamitra tempted Vasishta's anger, but Muni Vasishta did not raze the race of Kaushikas to which Viswamitra belonged. His sons perished at Viswamitra's hands, but Vasishta behaved like a powerless one, though truly he is far from that. Even as the Ocean does not transgress the shores of his continents, Vasishta did not bring his dead sons back from Yama's realm, though he well could have with power such as his.

Ikshvaku of yore and other awesome kings had Vasishta for their Kulaguru when they conquered all the Earth. Scion of Kuru, with Vasishta as their Ritvik, their chief priest, those kings performed many Mahayagnas. Pandavottma, he enabled those kings to perform their sacrifices even as Brihaspati does for the Devas.

And that is why I say to you, Pandavas, find a lofty and accomplished Brahmana to become your priest, a man who knows the Veda, and whose heart is replete with dharma. For, O Partha, the Kshatriya who wants to conquer the world and have great kingdom must first have a fine and great Brahmana to be his spiritual guide. Arjuna, I say again to you, seek out a learned Brahmana, whose senses are under perfect control, who knows all about dharma, artha and kama, and set him before you as your priest.'"

CANTO 177

CHAITRARATHA PARVA CONTINUED

Vaisampayana continued, "Arjuna asks, 'Gandharva, both Viswamitra and Vasishta dwell in unearthly asramas. Tell us, how was there hostility between these two?'

The Gandharva says, 'Partha, the legend of Vasishta is thought of as being a Purana throughout the three realms. Listen and I will narrate it in full.

Bharatarishabha, in Kanyakubja, there once was a king whose fame echoed throughout the world. He was Gadhi, the son of Kusika. Gadhi of dharma had a son called Viswamitra, who became king after his father. Viswamitra, bane of his enemies, lord of a great army comprising countless men, beasts and chariots, would range over the Earth with his ministers, through deep jungles in quest of deer and wild boar, killing them wherever he saw them.

One day, while thus out hunting, the king was tired and thirsty and he came upon the asrama of Vasishta. The Brahmarishi saw him and welcomed him with great respect, offering him padya, water to wash his face and feet, and arghya, wild fruit and ghee.

The Rishi had a cow of wishes, Nandini, who yielded anything that he asked of her. He would merely ask and she would give him whatever he wanted. Fruit and grain she gave, wild, or as are grown by men in orchards and fields. She gave milk like amrita, and every kind of unworldly delicacy to gratify the six tastes, by way of food and drink, ambrosial, and she gave incomparable ornaments, gemstones and raiment also, not of this world.

Arjuna, Maharishi Vasishta made offerings of all these wonderful things to King Viswamitra and his men; and they were delighted and amazed. The king gazed in wonder upon the wondrous cow, with six long legs, her flanks glossy, her eyes bulging and utterly beautiful, her udders and teats full, high and perfect, her ears straight and erect, her horns beautiful, as also her head and her neck.

Kshatriya, well pleased and praising the cow Nandini, Gadhi's son said to the Rishi, "Brahmana, Mahamuni, I will give you ten thousand fine milch cows or my kingdom for your Nandini."

Vasishta replied, "Sinless one, I keep Nandini for the sake of the Devas, for honoured guests like you, and for the Pitrs, as well as for my yagnas. I cannot give her to you and take your kingdom."

Viswamitra said, "I am a Kshatriya, while you are a Brahmana, an ascetic devoted to meditation and study. You are a man of peace, with your senses and your mind perfectly controlled. If you do not give me what I want when I offer you ten thousand cows in exchange for her, why I will even take your Nandini from you by force, for that is the way of the Kshatriya, and you can do nothing to stop me, Brahmana."

Vasishta smiled. "You are indeed a mighty Kshatriya king. Why wait? Do what you will, but remember that you are not pausing to think of dharma."

Partha, Viswamitra had his men seize Nandini, white as the moon or a swan; they began to drag her away, injuring her smooth flanks, marking her with stripes of violence. Lowing piteously, Nandini broke free of her captors and ran to Vasishta and stood before him with her face raised and tears flowing down her cheeks. She would not leave the Sage's hermitage.

Vasishta saw her and said sadly, "O Susheela, sweet one. You cry, my Nandini, and I hear you. But I am a Brahmana, sworn to forgiveness and peace. How can I prevent Viswamitra from taking you from here forcibly?"

Terrified by the threatening Viswamitra and his fierce soldiers, Nandini came still closer to the Rishi and said, "O illustrious one, are you not my master, do you not love me, that you can be so unmoved when Viswamitra's cruel men beat me so savagely, marking me with their lashes, and when you hear me crying?"

Still Vasishta did not lose either his patience or turn away from his sworn vow of non-violence. He said, "The Kshatriya's strength lies in his might, the Brahmana's in his kshama, his forgiveness and patience. I cannot renounce my kshama; so Nandini go with the king."

Nandini sobbed, "Do you then abandon me and cast me out, Illustrious? For, if you do not, O Brahmana, no one can take me from you, not with any force on Earth."

Vasishta said, "Blessed, I do not cast you out or abandon you. If you can, stay. But look, they have your calf tied with a thick rope and it is already weak by struggling against the noose around its neck."

Hearing the word "stay" from Vasishta's lips, Nandini raised her head higher, tossed her horns and suddenly she was terrible. Her eyes crimson, lowing as if she roared, deafeningly, she flew at Viswamitra's men on every side, a dreadful storm of wrath.

They ran and they struck her again and again, and her anger grew, until she blazed with fury and was like the Sun at high noon, her eyes turning redder by the moment. From her rear she sprayed a shower of burning coals over Viswamitra's soldiers.

Next moment, she brought forth an army of Pallavas from her tail, and from her teats another of ferocious Dravidas and Sakas; and from her womb there issued a great force of Yavanas. She dropped dung and from that there sprang up an aksauhini of Savaras, while from her urine a legion of Kanchis arose and another army of Savaras from her flanks.

Paundras, Kiratas, Yavanas and Sinhalas, and the barbarian tribes of Khasas, Chivukas, Pulindas, Chinas, Hunas, Keralas, and numberless other Mlechchas sprang forth from the foam of her mouth. The teeming host of Mlechchas wore motley garb, carried diverse and strange weapons, and as soon as they materialised they were deployed in battle formation and attacked Viswamitra's legions with savage yells and roars.

That king's men were outnumbered by six and seven to one. Assaulted by a storm of weapons, Viswamitra's men broke rank and fled, even as he watched in dismay. However, Bharatarishabha, Nandini only chased away the enemy troops; her Mlechchas did not kill a single man.

Indeed, the wild horde chased the king's men for a full three yojanas, and Viswamitra's men fled shrieking and no one could help them.

Viswamitra saw what happened, hung his head and raged, "O fie on the power of the Kshatriya, it is as nothing compared to Brahmana bala! The power of tapasya is the only true strength."

That king renounced his vast kingdom, all his regal glory, turned his back on every mundane pleasure, and sat in a searing tapasya. After a long time and many trials, his dhyana grew so awesome that it began to burn the three worlds with its heat, scorching every creature in them. Brahma appeared before the Kshatriya at his penance and declared him to be a Brahmana, a Brahmarishi and the equal of Vasishta.

Finally, Kusika's son drank Soma rasa with Indra himself in Swarga,' the Gandharva says."

CANTO 178

CHAITRARATHA PARVA CONTINUED

Vaisampayana continued, "The Gandharva continues, 'Partha, once there was a king called Kalmashapada, of the race of Ikshvaku, and he had no equal for strength or power on Earth.

One day, he went hunting in the forest and killed many deer and boar with his arrows; in open glades in the heart of the jungle, he killed many a great rhinoceros. Finally, tiring after a long hunt, the king decided that he would rest for a while.

Some time ago, the great Viswamitra, of tremendous splendour, had wanted to make this king his disciple. Now, as Kalmashapada went weakly along a trail through that vana, hungry and thirsty too, he encountered Vasishta's lustrous son Saktri, his firstborn of a hundred sons, upon that path.

The invincible king saw the Muni coming towards him and cried haughtily, "Get out of my way!"

The Rishi replied gently, in the sweetest tone, "Rajan, by dharma the right of way is mine. Every Shastra says that a Kshatriya must always make way for a Brahmana."

But Kalmashapada cried again, "Out of my way!" Vasishta's son replied in the same words, but softly.

The Rishi was in the right and so he would not give in; the king would not yield out of pride and anger. Suddenly, Kalmashapada lost control and, growling like a Rakshasa, lashed out at the Sage with his whip.

At the lash, Saktri Muni also lost his temper and lashed out at the king with a curse. "Basest of kings, dare you strike a Brahmana! You have behaved like a Rakshasa, so become a Rakshasa from this moment and wander the Earth in a demon's form, living on human flesh."

At this moment, Viswamitra arrived in that place. There was dispute between Vasishta and him about whose sishya Kalmashapada would be. Partha, Viswamitra knew with mystic insight that Vasishta's son had cursed the king; he knew that Saktri was his father's equal in spiritual power.

Viswamitra made himself invisible.

As soon as the Sage cursed him, the king began to beg Saktri for mercy. Kurusthama, Viswamitra feared that the two might make peace between them, and he sent a Rakshasa to enter Kalmashapada's body. The Rakshasa Kinkara possessed the king, at Saktri Muni's curse and Viswamitra's command. Viswamitra melted away from the forest path. Saktri also left.

Upon being possessed, Kalmashapada was no longer himself and another Brahmana came upon him in that condition. This Brahmana was tired and hungry and begged the king for some food, cooked with meat.

The Rajarishi Kalmashapada, known for his generosity and kindness, said, "Brahmana, stay here for a while. I will go and bring you the food that you want."

Leaving the Brahmana in the vana, Kalmashapada returned to his palace and his royal chambers, but only after he had roamed the forest for some hours. Tired himself, he fell asleep. At midnight, he suddenly awoke and remembered his promise to the Brahmana. He summoned the palace cook.

Said the king, "A Brahmana is waiting for me in the forest. He is hungry and wants some meat to eat. Hurry, cook some meat and take it to him."

The cook went looking for meat but could find none at that hour. He went back to the king, and said with some trepidation that he had not been able to find any meat.

Now it was the Rakshasa Kinkara who spoke from the king's mouth, "Feed him human flesh."

Trembling, the cook said, "Tathastu, so be it."

He went to the king's execution chamber, cut some flesh from a corpse there, washed it, cooked it, covered it with fragrant rice and ran to the waiting Brahmana with that meal.

But the Brahmana, who had occult sight, immediately saw that the food was unclean. His eyes turning red, he cried, "This worst of kings sends me unholy food, so let him crave human flesh himself! Let the Rishi Saktri's curse come true and let Kalmashapada wander the Earth as a fiend."

When the curse was repeated, it became twice as powerful. The Rakshasa within him gained complete control. A while later, Kalmashapada saw Saktri again, who had first cursed him and screamed, "You first cursed me to become a cannibal, so let me begin by eating you!"

He pounced on Saktri Muni and devoured him like a tiger does its prey. Seeing Saktri killed, Viswamitra began to repeatedly instigate Kinkara to eat Vasishta's other sons as well. Like an angry lion swallowing small animals, the Rakshasa quickly killed and ate all of Vasishta's hundred sons.

Vasishta knew that Viswamitra was responsible for the death of his sons, but he did nothing; only bore his grief as the Great Mountain does the Earth. He would rather sacrifice his own life than yield to anger and commit any violence against the race of Kusikas. That illumined Sage threw himself down from the summit of Meru but he fell on hard rock thousands of feet below as if onto a bed of cotton-wool.

Pandava, when he did not die from his leap, Vasishta lit a forest fire, a blazing conflagration, with his power of yoga and walked into it. But the flames did not even singe him but were like cool water upon his skin.

Next the grief-stricken Sage looked at the Sea, tied a heavy stone around his neck, and flung himself into the water. But the waves washed him gently ashore. Distraught that he could not even do away with himself, Vasishta returned to his asrama,' says the Gandharva."

CANTO 179

CHAITRARATHA PARVA CONTINUED

Vaisampayana continued, "The Gandharva goes on, 'The Rishi saw his hermitage empty of his sons and again the tide of sorrow surged in his heart. He walked away from the asrama. Partha, Vasishta ranged over the Earth, dementedly, and one day, during the monsoon, he saw a river in spate sweeping away hundreds of trees and plants that grew on its banks.

O Kurunandana, the Muni bound his own hands and feet firmly with strong rope and cast himself into that cataract. Parantapa, the river loosened the knots of the rope and tenderly set him ashore. Rising, Vasishta called that river Vipasa, the knot-severer.

Restless with the sorrow which tore at his heart, Vasishta could never remain in one place. With no peace, he wandered along the banks of many lakes and rivers, through many deep forests and climbed more than one mountain.

One day, he came to the banks of the river that is called Hymavati, she who flows from Himavan. He saw huge and ferocious crocodiles and other sharp-toothed predators in the water, and once more threw himself into the river, hoping to be devoured. However, the river mistook the tejasvin Brahmana for a mass of fire, and in terror split herself into a hundred rillets and plunged away in every direction. Since, she has been called Shatadru, river of a hundred courses.

Vasishta found himself on dry land again and cried, "Ah, it is impossible for me to kill myself!" and he turned his face towards his asrama again. Back through many kingdoms, over mountains and through the forests of several countries, the Sage returned to his hermitage.

Unknown to the Muni, a daughter-in-law of his, Adrishyanti, had been following him all the time, hiding herself so that he never saw her. Now, as he neared his asrama, suddenly he heard from behind his back the Veda being recited in the most chaste and erudite tones, embellished with the six graces of elocution.

Turning, Vasishta asked, "Who follows me?"

His daughter-in-law said, "It is Saktri's wife Adrishyanti. Lord, I am chaste and ascetic, yet I find myself lost and without support."

Vasishta asked, "Daughter, who was just reciting the Veda and the Angas exactly in the voice and tone of my son Saktri?"

Adrishyanti said, "Saktri's son is in my womb. He has been there for twelve years, and it is his voice that you heard reciting the Veda."

Vasishta gave a cry of sheer joy, "A child of my race lives!"

Now, Partha, every thought of killing himself left the Sage, and he brought his pregnant daughter-in-law into his hermitage.

Then, one day, O Bhaarata, when Vasishta was out walking in the vana with Adrishyanti, he saw the King Kalmashapada, whom the Rakshasa Kinkara had possessed. The Rakshasa roared in rage, and rushed towards the Muni, to make a meal of him.

Adrishyanti cried in terror, "O illustrious, look, the savage Rakshasa rushes at us, with his cudgel raised. He comes to devour us, Holy One, and no one in the world can save us today but you."

Vasishta said calmly, "There is nothing to fear, my child. This is no Rakshasa but the great and renowned King Kalmashapada, who now lives in this forest."

The king possessed by the Rakshasa ran on towards them, and then Vasishta stopped him in his tracks by uttering a resonant humakara, a ringing *hummmm.* The Muni then sprinkled holy water sanctified with mantras over the king and exorcised him of the Rakshasa.

After twelve years of being possessed by Saktri's curse, even like the Sun being seized by Rahu during an eclipse, Kalmashapada was free. Now his natural lustre lit up all that wild vana, as the sun's rays do the clouds of dusk.

Regaining his mind and his senses, the king folded his hands reverently to the Rishi, and said, "Munisthama, I am Sudasa's son and I am your sishya. Command me, lord, I will do whatever you ask, give you whatever you want."

Vasishta replied, "I already have what I want. Go back to your kingdom now and rule your people. And, Purushottama, never insult a Brahmana again."

Kalmashapada said, "Never, my lord, shall I cross any Brahmana but worship them instead. However, Brahmanashreshta, greatest among all that know the Veda, let me be free from the debt I owe to the race of Ikshvaku. I beg you bless me with a worthy and splendid son, a prince of dharma to become king after me."

Vasishta answered that great archer and king, "I will."

Vasishta went with Kalmashapada to his capital, famed throughout the world, the city of Ayodhya. The people came out in crowds, in joy to welcome back their king; they were like the celestials of Swarga coming to receive Indra.

With Vasishta going before him, Kalmashapada entered his capital after twelve years in the wilderness. The people gazed at him as if he was the rising Sun, for so radiant was he and so handsome; his splendour filled Ayodhya even as the glory of the autumn Sun does all the sky.

Kalmashapada looked at his city, its streets swept and washed and bright with banners and arches, and he, too, was full of joy. O Prince of Kuru's race, yes, truly, Ayodhya seemed wonderful as Amaravati does when Devendra is in his heavenly city.

When the Rajarishi entered his palace, he ordered his queen to go to Vasishta. The Maharishi swore a solemn vow with her, and then he had congress with her. Shortly, she conceived and, having accomplished what he had come for and receiving Kalmashapada's reverences, the Sage returned to his asrama.

For a long time, twelve years, the queen carried her child within her. When she could not bear to wait any longer, she cut her belly open with a sharp stone and brought forth the Purusharishabha Asmaka, the Rajarishi who would one day found the city of Paudanya,' says the Gandharva."

CANTO 180

Chaitraratha Parva Continued

Vaisampayana said, "The Gandharva continues, 'In Vasishta's asrama, O Partha, when her time came, Adrishyanti gave birth to a son who was verily like another Saktri in every way. Best of the Bhaaratas, Maharishi Vasishta performed the sacred ceremonies for his grandson. Because that child was responsible for Vasishta abandoning his resolve to take his own life, he was named Parasara, he who gives life to the dead.

From the day he was born Parasara regarded Vasishta as his father and treated him as such. One day, O son of Kunti, the child called Vasishta, "Father", while Adrishyanti was present.

His mother's eyes filled on hearing his sweet voice say that word. Adrishyanti said tearfully to her son, "My child, do not call your grandfather 'Father'. My son, a Rakshasa ate your father in another forest. This holy one is your great father's father."

Hearing this, Parasara flared up in terrible grief and wrath, and cried that he would burn up all of creation. Then Vasishta Muni, son of Mitravaruna, greatest among the knowers of Brahman, forbade his grandson with these arguments. Listen, O Arjuna, to what Vasishta Muni said to Parasara to change his mind.

Said the Sage, "Once, there was a renowned king calls Kritavirya, and that Rajarishabha of the Earth was a sishya of the Bhrigus, who knew the Veda. After Kritavirya performed the Soma yagna, he gave immense wealth, grain past calculation and other incomparable gifts to those Brahmanas.

Later, when Kritavirya left this world and rose into Swarga, there came a time when his descendents became impecunious. Knowing that the Bhrigus were wealthy, the princes went to those best among Brahmanas, even as beggars.

Some Bhrigus buried their vast treasures under the ground; others gave it away to fellow Brahmanas, for they feared the Kshatriyas, while still others did give the Kshatriyas whatever they wanted.

Some Kshatriyas dug the earth all around the house of one of the Bhargavas and uncovered a great and rich hoard. All the Kshatriyarishabhas saw that buried treasure and they grew furious because of what they thought of as being deceit and treachery by the Bhrigus.

They seized their bows and slaughtered the Brahmanas in a hail of arrows, even while the Bhargavas begged for mercy. Why, those wrathful Kshatriyas wandered the Earth killing even unborn foetuses in the wombs of Bhrigu women. As they swept across the world, exterminating the very race of Bhrigu, many Bhrigu women fled to hidden fastnesses of the Himalaya.

Among these women was one who bore an embryo of terrific tejas in her thigh. However, another Brahmana woman, from fear, told the Kshatriyas about her. The Kshatriyas swarmed to the cave where she was, going forth to kill her unborn child and her as well.

Arriving at the cavemouth, the princes saw the woman ablaze with the splendour of her child. At that moment, the child came tearing its way out from her thigh. He was as refulgent as the noonday Sun and his light made the Kshatriyas blind. Sightless, they wandered, lost over those mountains for a long time.

At last, the stricken princes decided they must beg the sinless Bhrigu woman to help them. Like a fire that has burnt out, they came in great softness and anxiety to her.

They said to her, 'Be gracious to us, O lady, and let us see again. We will go back peacefully and never again sin. Most beautiful one, we kings and princes beg mercy from you and your child,'" said Vasishta Muni to his grandson,' the Gandharva says."

CANTO 181

CHAITRARATHA PARVA CONTINUED

Vaisampayana continued, "The Gandharva says, 'Vasishta went on, "The Bhrigu woman said to the Kshatriyas, 'Young ones, I have not taken your sight from you, and I am not wroth at you either.

However, this Bhrigu child is indeed wrathful at the massacre of his race. Princes, for a hundred years you killed even the embryos in the wombs of the Bhrigu women, and for those hundred years this child remained inside me.

The Vedas and their Angas came to my child even while he lay in my womb, so that one day fortune would return to the race of Bhrigu. He wishes you ill, Kshatriyas, and it is his cosmic splendour that has made you blind. You have murdered his sires and he wishes for your death.

Do not beg me, but this child for your sight. Pay him homage and appease his fury. Children, it is the only hope for you.'

The Kshatriyas turned to the thigh-born child, 'Forgive us, we seek your mercy.'

At once, the marvellous child turned merciful; the Kshatriyas had their sight back and returned to their homes. Because he was born from his mother's thigh, that splendid child is known as Aurva, thigh-born, throughout the three worlds.

His wrath unappeased, Muni Aurva of the race of Bhrigu decided that he would destroy the whole world, and every creature in it; he would give this as havis, a burnt offering to his murdered ancestors.

Aurva sat in terrible tapasya, and soon the heat of his penance began to scorch the Devas, the Asuras and Manavas, too. Then the Pitrs, his manes, learnt what the child of their race intended and they came down to him from their lofty realm.

The Bhrigus said, 'Child, Aurva, your tapasya has been stern and fierce, and we have seen your power. But turn kindly towards the three worlds; restrain your anger. Son, we Bhrigus did not allow ourselves to be killed by the Kshatriyas because we could not defend ourselves. The truth is that we grew weary of the interminably long lives given to us, and we wanted to die. Indeed, we subtly used the Kshatriyas to accomplish our own end.

We buried the treasure beneath one of our houses even so that the princes would discover it and become infuriated. Dvijottama, when we wished for Swarga, of what use could gold and jewels be to us? Kubera, Lord of Treasures, kept a great trove for us in Devaloka. But we found we could not die.

It is then that we decided to have the Kshatriyas kill us, for we could not kill ourselves, either, since no suicide ever attains to realms that are blessed. The Kshatriyas only helped us achieve what we wanted, and we are not pleased at what you now mean to do. It is a great sin that you intend, to consume all of creation in the flames of your tapasya.

Precious child, do not kill the Kshatriyas or burn the seven worlds; instead, quell your anger, which renders your penance sinful,' say his Pitrs to Aurva," Vasishta said to Parasara,' the Gandharva tells Arjuna."

CANTO 182

Chaitraratha Parva Continued

Vaisampayana said, "The Gandharva continues, 'Vasishta went on, "Aurva heard what his manes said and spoke to them.

Aurva Muni said, 'O my Pitrs, how can the vow I swore, even in anger, to consume the worlds go in vain? I cannot become one whose anger is impotent and his oaths hollow. For, if I cease my penance, my fury will devour me as fire does dry wood.

The man who represses rightful anger, provoked by grave injustice, becomes incapable of accomplishing the Purusharthas of dharma, artha and kama. The rage that kings use to conquer and rule the Earth is not a trifling thing; it keeps the evil in fearful restraint and protects good men of dharma.

Whilst I lay in my mother's thigh, I heard the screams of the Bhrigu women whom the Kshatriyas were slaughtering. O Pitrs, when the savage Kshatriyas began to murder the unborn children of our race, untold wrath filled my soul.

My mother and our other women, all heavy with child, and my terror-stricken father could not find anyone in the wide world to protect them. In panic, my mother lowered me into her thigh and held me there, so that her pregnancy would be hidden.

If there is justice and punishment for crimes in the world, then sinners hesitate to sin; if there is no chastiser, the numbers of criminals grow and their crimes become more terrible. The man who owns the power to punish and prevent crime but does not do so becomes a criminal and sinner himself; he shares in the sins of the sinners.

When the kings that could have saved my sires from the fury of the Kshatriyas did not do so, but remained immersed in their pleasures instead, I have more than just cause to turn my fury upon them. I have the power to punish these criminals. I wield absolute power over the worlds; I cannot do what you ask.

I must have revenge on the sinners, for otherwise they will again commit heinous murdering. Besides, if I do not burn them with the fire of my wrath, it will consume me instead.

Ah, my Sires, I know that all of you unswervingly wish for the weal of the worlds. Tell me what I should do, so that it benefits both creation and me.'

The Pitrs say, 'Cast the fire of your rage, which would consume the worlds, into water, and in water let it dwell, consuming water. That will benefit you and the worlds as well, for it is said that the worlds are made of water, why, the very universe has emerged from primal waters.

Brahmana, let the fire of your fury live in the Ocean, so that, sinless child, your vow is not proven false, so that you are not harmed by the fire, and neither the three worlds, or the Devas, Asuras and Manavas.'

The child Aurva cast the fire of his anger into the realm of Varuna, the Ocean. It lives there still, consuming the waters of the deeps, and there it has assumed the form of a great horse's head, so that those that know the Veda call it Badavamukha. It flames forth from its own mouth and ceaselessly quenches itself with the waters of the fathomless Ocean.

You, precious Parasara, wisest Muni, are like Aurva, a blessed one. You know the lofty realms of Swarga; it does not become you to destroy the worlds in anger," said Vasishta to his grandson,' says the Gandharva to Arjuna."

CANTO 183

Chaitraratha Parva Continued

Vaisampayana said, "The Gandharva continues, 'When his illumined grandfather Vasishta spoke thus, gravely, to him, Parasara controlled his anger and refrained from destroying the worlds.

However, that tejaswin Rishi, of terrific energy, the son of Saktri, performed a great Rakshasa yagna, and to avenge the killing of his father Saktri, he consumed Rakshasas, young and old, in the fires of his sacrifice. Now Vasishta did not attempt to restrain his grandson, because he did not want to force him to break a second vow.

Mahamuni Parasara sat before three blazing fires, himself like a fourth one. Saktri's son, bright as Surya emerging from behind clouds, poured copious libations of ghee into those tall flames and all the sky was lit up.

Vasishta and the other Rishis of the worlds saw Parasara ablaze, truly like a second Sun, and it seemed no one could stop his yagna. The compassionate Maharishi Atri came to Parasara's yagnashala. Parantapa, with him came the Devarishis Pulastya, Pulaha and Kratu, all to save the Rakshasas.

Bharatarishabha, when Pulastya Muni saw how many Rakshasas had already been killed, he said to Parasara aflame, "Child, I hope nothing hinders your yagna! But what joy do you find in killing even those Rakshasas that have nothing to do with the death of your father?

This is not the dharma of a holy Brahmana; it does not become you to take innocent lives. Peace is the highest punya. Parasara, make your peace, for you are a superior man and I wonder that you commit this dreadful sin.

How can you do this, who are the son of Saktri, who was a man of unswerving dharma, a man of peace? How do you kill any living creatures at all? Scion of the race of Vasishta, your father died because he broke dharma in anger and cursed Kalmashapada.

Saktri was taken to Swarga for his own fault. Parasara, no Rakshasa on Earth could kill the great Saktri, unless the Muni contrived his own death. Even Viswamitra was merely a tool in the hands of fate.

Besides, know that both your father Saktri and King Kalmashapada have indeed found Swarga, and enjoy every felicity there. Your father's brothers, Vasishta's other sons, are in heaven also, and finding untold joy in the company of the celestials.

Why, even you, Parasara, son of Saktri, son of Vasishta, are only a blind instrument of fate in this yagna of yours, which destroys countless Rakshasas. O be blessed, Parasara, and abandon your Rakshasa yagna. You have done enough killing."

Now Vasishta added his voice to what Pulastya Muni said, and Parasara ceased his fell sacrifice. He cast the fires that he had lit into the deepest vana north of the Himavat. To this day, that fire burns all year even in the dead of winter, even when rains lash the mountain, devouring trees and the very stones around it, and also any Rakshasas that come anywhere near its flames,' the Gandharva says."

CANTO 184

CHAITRARATHA PARVA CONTINUED

Vaisampayana said to Janamejaya, "Arjuna asks, 'Gandharva, why did the King Kalmashapada tell his queen to resort to Vasishta Muni, master of all the Vedas? And why did Vasishta, who knew all about dharma, agree to lie with a woman with whom he should not? Dear friend, did Vasishta not sin by what he did? I am full of dark doubt, and beg you to remove my fear.'

The Gandharva says, 'Irresistible Dhananjaya, I will answer your question about the Sage and the King. Listen.

Bharatottama, I have told you about how Vasishta's radiant son Saktri cursed Kalmashapada. With the curse falling on him, that king, who crushed all his enemies, left his capital with his queen. His eyes were red and spun in their sockets from anger. Kalmashapada wandered dementedly through the wild forest, the curse roiling him.

The vana teemed with deer and every other animal, and was thick with every plant and great tree. With hunger ravaging him, one day Kalmashapada ranged the jungle in search of food, uttering wild and terrible cries. Driven by hunger, he arrived in the very heart of the forest and suddenly came upon a Brahmana and his wife making love there.

Terrified to see the possessed and wild looking king, the couple jumped up and ran from him, with their desire unsatisfied. Kalmashapada ran after them, growling, and seized the Brahmana.

The Brahmani wailed, "Great King, the world knows that you are a sovereign of the Suryavamsa, devoted to your elders and betters, and a king famed throughout the world for his dharma. It does not become you to commit this sin, O invincible one, not though the Rishi's curse has robbed you of your reason.

I am in my season and was joined with my husband in desire. I am not satisfied yet; I beg you be merciful, O best of kings, set my husband free."

But Kalmashapada paid no heed to her pitiful entreaty and, ignoring her screams, devoured the Brahmana like a tiger does his prey. Her fury terrible, the tears of the Brahmani turned to drops of fire and burned up everything around her.

In that rage, in her grief, she cursed Rajarishi Kalmashapada, "Vile King, for what you have done I curse you that if you ever go to your wife again you will instantly die. Wretched Raja, also let your wife conceive and deliver a child by the Rishi Vasishta whose sons you have killed and eaten. And that child, O worst of kings, shall be the one that continues your race."

Having pronounced her curse, that chaste Brahmani of the race of Angiras, every auspicious mark upon her body, walked into the fire kindled by her tears and became ashes before the king's eyes. Parantapa, even as this happened, Vasishta knew about it with mystic intuition.

The years passed. Kalmashapada was freed from his curse, and taken with desire one night, the king went to his queen Madayanati. However, she reminded him of the curse of the Brahmani and would not lie with Kalmashapada. Bitter tears of regret that king shed; bitterly he regretted what he had done.

Purushottama, this is why King Kalmashapada asked Maharishi Vasishta to beget a son upon his queen,' says the Gandharva."

CANTO 185

Chaitraratha Parva Continued

Vaisampayana continued, "Arjuna asks, 'Gandharva, you know everything; so you tell us which Vedagyani Brahmana we should make our priest.'

The Gandharva replies, 'In this very vana there is a holy shrine calls Utkochaka. Devala Muni's younger brother Dhaumya performs tapasya there. If you want a priest for yourselves, you will find no better Brahmana than him.'

Delighted with their encounter, Arjuna gives his Agneyastra to the Gandharva, with the proper rituals. The Pandava says, 'Gandharvottama, let the horses that you wish to give us remain with you for a time, until we have need for them and then we shall take them from you. Be you blessed!'

The Pandavas and the Gandharva salute each other reverently and part ways upon the enchanted banks of the Bhagirathi. The Pandavas go to Utkochaka, to Dhaumya's sacred asrama, and ask him to become their Kulaguru, their family priest. Best of those that know the Vedas, the profound Dhaumya receives the sons of Pandu with offerings of wild fruit, succulent roots, and he does agree to what they ask of him.

When the great Dhaumya agrees to be their priest, the Pandavas and Kunti feel a stirring elation: they feel that that they have already regained their kingdom, as well as won the daughter of Drupada for their queen, at her swayamvara. Truly, the Bharatrishabhas feel that in Dhaumya they have found a powerful guardian of their future and their fortunes.

Dhaumya, Mahatman, knower of the true meaning of the Veda, knower of every law of dharma, becomes the Guru of the Pandavas, and he makes them his Yajamanas, his spiritual disciples. The Brahmana sees those Kshatriyas endowed with strength, intelligence and fortitude such as the Devas possess, and he also feels that they have already regained their rightful kingdom.

When Dhaumya has blessed them, by uttering holy mantras over them, they think it is time to set out for the Panchala kingdom, to the swayamvara of the Princess Panchali."

CANTO 186

Swayamvara Parva

Vaisampayana continued, "Those five Purushavyaghra brothers, the Pancha Pandavas, tigers among men, set out for Drupada's kingdom, to gaze upon that wonderful country, and especially its princess Draupadi.

As they go along, their mother with them, they see some Brahmanas on the way. Those Brahmacharis see the sons of Pandu, O Rajan, and ask, 'Where are you going? And from where do you come?'

Yudhishtira replies, 'Brahmanarishabhas, we five are brothers and this is our mother. We are coming from Ekachakra.'

The Brahmanas say, 'Take yourselves to the city of Drupada in the kingdom of the Panchalas, for there is a great swayamvara to be held there at which Drupada will give away great wealth. We are also going there and we can journey together.

Exceptional celebrations will take place there for Yagnasena has a daughter who is born from the heart of an agnikunda during a yagna. Her beauty is past compare, her eyes like lotus petals, her features flawless, her intelligence and beauty legend.

Why, Draupadi of the slender waist emanates a fragrance from her body, a scent as of a blue lotus, and it spreads around her a full yojana. Her brother is the mighty Dhrishtadyumna, who has been born to kill Drona. The prince is also born from the sacrificial flames, wearing natural armour and carrying a bow and arrows, and blazing himself like a second fire.

Yagnasena's daughter will choose a husband for herself from amongst all the Kshatriyas that have been invited to her swayamvara. And we are going there to witness the celebrations, which we believe will be like a festival in Devaloka.

Kshatriyas, munificent kings and princes from diverse lands who perform great sacrifices at which they give untold wealth to Brahmanas, will attend the swayamvara of Draupadi. They are handsome Kshatriyas, full of vigour, brilliance and learning, Maharathas and masters of weapons. Wanting to win Draupadi's favour, and so her hand, they will distribute great wealth, countless cows, wonderful food, and many other gifts to be enjoyed.

Taking all this and witnessing the swayamvara, we will depart Drupada's city and go our separate ways.

Many actors and bards, Sutradharas and Pauranikas, champion athletes, heralds, entertainers and performers of every ilk and hue, from across the length and breadth of Bharatavarsha, will come to the swayamvara. You shall see many marvellous sights in the city of Drupada, receive many rich gifts, and then go your way, as you please, or come with us.

Besides, you are all as handsome as Devas. Seeing you, perhaps the dark Princess Krishnaa will choose one of you for her husband!' And pointing to Arjuna, 'This brother of yours seems blessed with extraordinary fortune; he might well earn wealth past imagining in the city of Drupada.'

Yudhishtira says, 'Brahmanas, we will go with you to the princess' excellent swayamvara.'"

CANTO 187

SWAYAMVARA PARVA CONTINUED

Vaisampayana said, "O Janamejaya, the Pandavas go with those Brahmanas towards the kingdom of southern Panchala, over which Drupada rules. On their way, those Kshatriyas see the luminous and sinless Dwaipayana. They worship him, and taking his blessing, continue their journey towards Drupada's kingdom.

The Maharathas go slowly on their way, often lingering to admire the fine forests and shimmering lakes that they see. Finally, the devout, taintless princes enter Panchala lands and come to Drupada's capital, where they begin living in the home of a potter.

Still disguised as Brahmanas, they go begging for alms and no man recognises them for who they are.

Now, Drupada Yagnasena has always wanted to give his daughter Draupadi to the heroic Arjuna to be his wife. But he never speaks of this to anyone. O Janamejaya, thinking of Arjuna's matchless archery, the Panchala king has an exceptionally inflexible and stiff bow fashioned, which he thinks that no one other than Arjuna will be able to bend.

He also erects an unusual yantra, a device upon which he suspends an extraordinarily difficult target to shoot.

Drupada declares, 'The archer who can shoot the hanging target shall have Draupadi for his wife.'

Thus does the Panchala king proclaim his daughter's swayamvara, and every worthy Kshatriya in Bharatavarsha arrives in his capital. Countless Rishis also arrive, to witness the swayamvara, for it promises wealth and excitement.

Among the warriors that come, O King, are Duryodhana and the Kurus, and Karna with them. The highest born, most learned Brahmanas from every kingdom and land flock to Drupada's city. The great Drupada receives every king and Sage reverently.

Come the day of the swayamvara and the people of the city throng the tiers and platforms that have been raised around the arena for the swayamvara. The noise they make is like a sea roaring. That stadium has been erected upon a level and auspicious plain to the north-east of Drupada's capital. Fine mansions, set in their sprawling grounds, surround the majestic construction.

Lofty walls enclose the arena, as well as a deep moat circling it around, while fine archways at regular intervals lead into it, and a bright, many-coloured canopy covers the stands. The king enters the stadium through its north-eastern gate, to the resounding bass of a thousand conches.

The stadium is fragrant with the scent of black aloe, and with the holy water mixed with sandalwood paste with which it has been liberally sprinkled, and also with the extravagance of garlands made with every flower, hanging everywhere.

The lofty mansions that encircle it are snow-white and seem like the peaks of Kailasa that kiss the clouds. Their windows are filled by lattices of gold, their walls encrusted with diamonds, and priceless carpets of silk lie upon their gleaming floors. They are all adorned with garlands in every colour and of every fine fragrance, and they are indeed as radiantly white as the necks of swans.

The scent of aloe and the other redolences that those mansions exude can be smelt a yojana away. Each one has a hundred doors, each of these wide enough for a small crowd to enter through them at once. They are furnished extravagantly, beautifully, and they are like the peaks of Himavan.

The kings and princes, all the distinguished Kshatriyas coming from far-flung kingdoms, are housed in those seven-storied palaces. Invited by Drupada, each one has come to vie with the others for the hand of Draupadi, and they come wearing their finery and sparkling ornaments.

When the people of the Panchala capital and countryside come to the grand stadium of the swayamvara, they see those leonine Kshatriyas within the white mansions, all of them strong and vital, as great souls are. Those magnificent kings all wear the fragrant paste of the black aloe upon their persons. Liberal and majestic they are, worshippers of Brahman, invincible guardians of their kingdoms against every invader, and loved throughout the world for their dharma.

The Pandavas also enter the stadium, sit among the Brahmanas and see the unrivalled wealth of the Panchala king and the great and generous gifts that he gives. Lively troupes of actors, musicians and dancers perform daily, attracting more people, day by day.

Bharatarishabha, on the sixteenth day, when the stadium is packed to capacity, Draupadi bathes, puts on the most resplendent clothes and jewellery and she enters the arena carrying a golden chalice with the arghya in it and also a garland of wildflowers. The Kulaguru of the House of the Moon, a holy Brahmana who knows all the apposite mantras, lights the sacrificial fire and pours libations of ghee into the flames.

When Agni Deva has been appeased with ghee, the priest makes all the Brahmanas present utter auspicious mantras to bless the occasion. He raises his hand to stop the musical instruments that play all around the stadium and calls for silence among the people. When that vast crowd falls completely silent, Dhrishtadyumna takes his sister's hand, steps into the middle of the arena, and speaks in a voice deep as bass drums or thunderheads.

Sweetly, yet, he says, 'O mighty Kshatriyas, here is the bow, these are five sharp arrows and above is the target. Find the target through the aperture in the yantra, the device above which it hangs, and I solemnly swear, upon my lineage, my honour and my strength, that my sister Krishnaa shall belong to the archer who succeeds.'

Dhrishtadyumna turns to Draupadi and begins to recite the names, lineages and achievements of the great Kshatriyas of the Earth who have come to her swayamvara."

CANTO 188

SWAYAMVARA PARVA CONTINUED

Vaisampayana continued, "Dhrishtadyumna proclaims, 'Duryodhana, Durvisaha, Durmukha, Dushpradharshana, Vivimsati, Vikarna, Saha, Dushasana; Yuyutsu, Vayuvega, Bhimavegarava; Ugrayudha, Balaki, Kanakayu, Virochana, Sukundala, Chitrasena, Suvarcha, Kanakadhwaja; Nandaka, Bahusali, Tuhunda and Vikata are all the mighty sons of Dhritarashtra. My sister, these and many other valiant brothers of theirs have come to vie for your hand; and with them the indomitable Karna.

Many other great kings and princes, all Kshatriya bulls, have come for you. Sakuni, Saubala, Vrisaka, and Brihadbala, all sons of Gandhara are here. Aswatthama and Bhoja, best among masters of astras, are here, glittering in rare ornaments.

Brihanta, Manimana, Dandadhara, Sahadeva, Jayatsena, Meghasandhi, Virata with his two sons Sankha and Uttara, Vardhakshemi, Susarma, Senabindu, Suketu with his two sons Sunama and Suvarcha, Suchitra, Sukumara, Vrika, Satyadhriti, Suryadhwaja, Rochamana, Nila,

Chitrayudha, Agsuman, Chekitana, the mighty Sreniman, Chandrasena, powerful son of Samudrasena, Jarasahdha, Vidanda and Danda, father and son, Paundraka, Vasudeva, Bhagadatta of terrific vigour, Kalinga, Tamralipta, the Pattana king, Maharatha Salya king of Madra, and his valiant son Rukmangada, Rukmaratha, Somadatta of the Kurus and his three sons, all Maharathas and great Kshatriyas, Bhuri, Bhurisrava, Sala, Sudakshina, Kamboja all of the race of Puru, Brihadvala, Sushena, Sibi, son of Usinara, Patcharanihanta, the king of Karusha; Baladeva Samkarshana, Vasudeva Krishna, the matchless son of Rukmini, Samba, Charudeshna, son of Pradyumna, Gada, Akrura, Satyaki, the Mahatman Uddhava, Kritavarman, son of Hridika, Prithu, Viprithu, Viduratha, Ranka, Sanku, Givesshana, Asavaha, Aniruddha, Samika, Sarimejaya, the heroic Vatapi, Jhilli, Pindaraka, the powerful Usinara, all these Vrishnis, Bhagiratha, Brihatkshatra, Jayadratha son of Sindhu, Brihadratha, Balhika, Maharatha Srutayu, Uluka, Kaitava, Chitrangada and Suvangada, the most intelligent Vatsaraja, the king of Kosala, Sisupala, the awesome Jarasandha, and many more kings celebrated throughout the world, have come, my blessed sister, for you.

All of them are great archers. They shall all shoot at the target, and he that brings it down will have you for his wife.'"

CANTO 189

Swayamvara Parva Continued

Vaisampayana said, "The Kshatriyas, young and not so young, their earrings sparkling, each one feeling that he is mighty indeed, all brandish their weapons. Intoxicated with the pride of being handsome, powerful, learned, of noblest birth, wealthy, youthful and vigorous, they are like Himalayan elephants in musth, in the season of rut when their temples split open from an excess of ichor.

Seized by Kama, God of Desire, viewing one another with extreme contention, they all rise up at the same moment and roar, 'Krishnaa will be mine!'

The Kshatriyas gathered in that stadium look like the Devas of old did, when they gathered around Uma, the Mountain King's daughter. Kama Deva pierces them all, subtly, with his invisible flowery arrows, and they are without exception lost in a dream of winning the exquisite Draupadi. They stride into the arena and now favour even their dearest friends with glares of competition and animosity.

The Devas come to that stadium in their vimanas, with the Rudras and the Adityas, the Vasus and the twin Aswins, the Swadhas and all the Marutas, and Kubera with Yama at their head.

The Daityas, Suparnas, the great Nagas, the Devarishis, the Guhyakas, the Charanas, Viswavasu, Narada, Parvata and the main Gandharvas with the Apsaras are all there.

Halayudha Balarama and Janardana Krishna are there, as are the chieftains of the Vrishni, Andhaka and Yadava tribes, all of whom Krishna commands. Krishna sees the five Pandavas in disguise, like five elephants in rut drawn to Draupadi even as wild tuskers in season are to a lake blooming with lotuses; he sees them disguised as Brahmanas, covered with ashes, and he sees the great fires that those holy ashes conceal.

Krishna says softly to his brother Rama, 'Look, there is Yudhishtira; those are Bhima and Arjuna Jishnu; and there are the twins.'

Balarama sees the sons of Pandu and gives Krishna a look of great satisfaction. However, every other Kshatriya there, sons and grandsons of kings, their eyes bulging to see her unearthly beauty, many chewing their lips from intense desire, gaze only at the Princess Draupadi and see nothing other than her. The sons of Kunti and Madri's twins also look at Panchali, and struck by Kama's subtle shafts of love, they, too, see nothing else.

The sky is so crowded with Devarishis, Gandharvas, Suparnas, Nagas, Asuras and Siddhas, so fragrant with the scents of Swarga, with heaven's flowers cascading out of it, reverberant with deep conches, drums and the endless Pranava, the *AUM*, as well as softer, unworldly music from flute, lute and tabor, that the vimanas of the Devas find passage through those throngs difficult.

Now the trial of the swayamvara gets underway. Karna, Duryodhana, Salwa, Salya, Aswatthama, Kratha, Sunitha, Vakra, the king of Kalinga and Vanga, Pandya, Paundra, the lord of Videha, the chief of the Yavanas, and countless other Kshatriya princes—sovereigns of great lands, their eyes like lotus petals—begin, one by one, to display their prowess in order to win the hand of the princess who so obviously has no remote rival on Earth for beauty.

Yet, for all their fine crowns, necklaces, bracelets and all their ornaments, for their mighty physiques, their tremendous arms, bursting as they are with manhood, strength and vigour, most of those Kshatriyas cannot bend or string the great bow of the trial, not even in their dreams.

As they make their attempts, one by one, muscles bulging, veins standing out upon them, each according to his ability, the great weapon flings the best of them—who do indeed bend it a little—violently onto the ground, where they lie senseless for some moments.

Drained, their fine crowns askew, the garlands they wear ragged, panting, their ardour for the princess quickly cools; for they know that they can never hope to bend or string that dreadful bow. Mournful they are, those Kshatriyas, and give vent to their disappointment.

Karna, of the Sutas sees the crestfallen Kshatriyas. That greatest of all archers rises, strides up to the bow, picks up that awesome weapon effortlessly, bends it with no more effort, strings it, sets an arrow to the string and draws the string back so that the bow forms a circle.

The Pandavas look at that son of Surya, who is as bright as Agni, Soma or Surya Deva himself, and they quail, for they feel certain that the target has already been brought down.

Suddenly, the princess Draupadi cries, 'I will not marry a Sutaputra!'

Karna stops still. His lips curl in a sneer, he laughs bitterly and he flings the great bow down in disgust, in disdain, in anguish.

Now Sishupala, son of Damagosha and king of the Chedis, mighty as Yama, comes forward to string the bow, but the weapon brings him to his knees instead.

Jarasandha of Magadha, invincible king, walks up to the bow and stands before it like some mountain, as if to burn it up with his scrutiny. However, when he tries to bend it, the bow flings him down as well, on his knees. With a roar, he rises and stalks out of the stadium like a great wounded lion, to return to his kingdom.

Now the magnificent Kshatriya Salya, king of Madra, tries to bend and string the bow, and it brings him also to his knees. Finally, it is plain that none of the Kshatriyas present are up to the task, and a wave of snickers ripples through the crowd. Arjuna Jishnu, son of Kunti, feels that he wants to make his attempt to win the dark Panchali's hand."

CANTO 190

SWAYAMVARA PARVA CONTINUED

Vaisampayana continued, "When all the Kshatriyas have given up and sit down, frustrated and fuming, Arjuna of the lofty soul rises from the enclosure of the Brahmanas. The foremost among the Brahmanas see him get up, his skin the colour of Indra's banner, and they shake their deerskins and set up a loud noise: some of them are happy, while others shout their displeasure.

Among the most intelligent of them say, 'Brahmanas, how can a stripling of ours string the bow that the greatest Kshatriyas on Earth, men like Salya and the rest, equally powerful, and trained masters moreover in arms, failed?'

'If this callow youth fails, he will bring ridicule upon all of us Brahmanas. The Kshatriyas will pour scorn over us. He is vain and immature, which is why he even dares think of attempting the impossible task. He must be prevented from this rashness.'

But others say, 'No one shall mock at us even if he fails, and the kings will not be displeased.'

'Why, the handsome boy has a powerful physique, even like the trunk of some great tusker. He is as calm as Himavan. His gait is a lion's. He is formidably determined, and he appears to be as strong as a bull elephant in musth. It is quite possible that he will succeed!'

'He is strong and resolute. Otherwise would he dare rise up and approach the bow on his own? Also, remember that among all men it is the Brahmana who can accomplish anything to which he sets his mind. A Brahmana might not eat at all, or he might subsist on fruit and roots; he might become macilent and seem weak; but he will always be ablaze with the power of his own tejas.

Let him appear to be right or wrong, no one should ever underestimate a Brahmana or consider him incapable of accomplishing anything at all, great or little, any task, be it fraught with joy or sorrow.'

'Let us not forget how Jamadagni's son Rama vanquished all the Earth's Kshatriyas in battle, by himself. Agastya drained the very Ocean with his Brahma shakti. So let us all say in one voice, "May the youth bend the bow and bring the target down easily!"'

And many of the Brahmanas say, 'Tathastu, be it so!'

As the Brahmanas continue with their debate, Arjuna comes up to the bow and stands before it like a mountain. After a long moment, he walks solemnly around the great weapon, with his head bent in prayer to the Lord Isana, granter of boons, and then with a fervent thought of Krishna, he picks up the bow.

In a wink, effortlessly, Indra's son Jishnu, as strong as Indra's younger brother Vishnu, strings the weapon which so many mighty Kshatriyas like Rukma, Sunitha, Vakra, Duryodhana, Salya, and others could not manage to do though they poured every ounce of their strength into the effort. Quicker than the eye can see, he picks up all five arrows, in a blur, and shoots the target suspended above the yantra, so it falls onto the ground through the aperture in the uncanny device.

A moment's stunned silence, and then a huge shout from all the celestials shakes the sky, and the stadium reverberates with deafening cries and applause from the crowd. The Devas pour down a shower of unworldly blooms over Partha Parantapa.

Thousands of Brahmanas wave their upper cloths in the air, and shout for joy, while the Kshatriyas cry out in disbelief and agony. Flowers continue to pour out of the sky over the stadium and the arena. The musicians strike up a celebrant song, while bards and heralds sing and cry out praises of him who has achieved the staggering feat.

Drupada, slayer of his enemies, looks at Arjuna and is full of joy. If the need arises, he will deploy his army to help or protect this hero. While the uproar rises to a crescendo, the Brahmanas rapturous and the Kshatriyas furious, Yudhishtira Purushottama quickly leaves the stadium with the twins, to return to the potter's house.

The Princess Draupadi, Krishnaa, sees the target brought down, she looks at Arjuna who has found his mark, and joy sweeps through her. With a white silken robe and a garland of flowers in her hands, she walks up to the bowman as handsome as Indra himself.

When Arjuna, who could do the impossible, wins dark Panchali's hand, every Brahmana in the stadium rises to bow to him, to honour him. Like a lion, he walks out of the arena, with his newly won wife following him."

CANTO 191

Swayamvara Parva Continued

Vaisampayana continued, "Drupada rises to say that he will give his daughter in marriage to the Brahmana archer, when suddenly all the other Kshatriyas look at one another and are seized by wrath.

They say, 'Drupada dares treat us lords of the Earth like wisps of straw, and he will give his daughter, best among all women, to a Brahmana! Having planted a lovely tree he wants to cut it down when it is about to bear fruit. He has humiliated us and we must kill him.'

'He deserves neither respect nor reverence for his age; let us kill both him and his son, for they have insulted all the Kshatriyas of the Earth. He called us kings and princes here, fed us sumptuously, and finally he dishonours us. In this assembly of kings that is like a gathering of Devas, can the vile Drupada not see a single worthy Kshatriya, one that is fully his equal, that he gives Draupadi to a Brahmana?'

'The Vedas clearly say that a swayamvara is only for Kshatriyas and no Brahmana may be chosen for a husband during a swayamvara. O Kings, if this princess cannot choose any of us Kshatriyas to be her husband let us throw her into the fire along with her father and her brother, and return to our kingdoms.

But as for this Brahmana, either from arrogance or malice, he has indeed insulted us kings. Yet, being a Brahmana, he must not be killed, for our kingdoms, lives, wealth, sons, grandsons, and everything that we own exists because of and for the holy Brahmanas.

Yet, we must not leave him unpunished, so that never does another swayamvara end in such disgrace. We must teach him a public lesson that will be remembered for all time, a lesson that will keep the varnas each in their proper place.'

When they have spoken amongst themselves, the incensed Kshatriyas seize up their weapons, iron maces with spikes among them, and rush towards Drupada to kill him at once. Drupada sees the Kshatriya horde run at him in rage, with bows and arrows, and he seeks refuge in the Brahmanas.

Suddenly, Bhima and Arjuna stand between the charging Kshatriyas and Drupada, at whom they run like rut-maddened elephants. Raising their weapons in gloved hands, the kings turn roaring on the two Pandavas, now determined to kill them.

In a flash the tremendous Bhima, powerful as thunder, tears up a big tree from the ground and strips its leaves away. Bhima Mahabaho, son of Pritha, decimator of his enemies, stands next to his brother Narapumgava Arjuna; Bhima is like Yama, the Lord Death himself with his mace.

Jishnu wonders at his brother's awesome strength, and now, mighty as Indra himself, Arjuna also stands forth fearlessly, bow in hand, ready to face their host of adversaries.

Seeing them, Krishna Damodara of divine intellect, his deeds past understanding, murmurs to his brother Balarama, 'If I am Vaasudeva, O Samkarshana, that shura there, whose tread is like a lion's and whose bow is a full eight feet, is certainly Arjuna! The other hero who has torn up the tree to be his weapon is Vrikodara Bhima, for none but he can do such a thing.

And that other prince, eight feet tall, his eyes like lotus petals, who just left the stadium, his gait like a lion's yet full of humility, too, his skin fair, his nose prominent, is Dharma Deva's son Yudhishtira. The twins who also left, each one like another Kartikeya, I feel sure are the sons of the Aswin twins.

I did hear that Kunti and her sons escaped the fire that burnt down the house of lac.'

Balarama Halayudha, fair as rainless clouds, says joyfully to Krishna, 'My brother, how happy I am to hear that our father's sister and her sons escaped death!'"

CANTO 192

Swayamvara Parva Continued

Vaisampayana said, "Now all the Brahmana bulls there, those Dvijarishabhas, wave their deerskins and shake their coconut-shell kamandalus, and cry to Arjuna and Bhima, 'Fear not, we will fight the Kshatriyas!'

Arjuna smiles at them and says kindly, 'Stand aside and be spectators, dear friends, while I turn back these angry kings with arrow storms, just as snakes are with mantras.'

Arjuna raises the bow with which he has shot the target, and stands calmly beside Bhima; they are like mountains. Then, next moment, the brothers attack the Kshatriya host led by Karna, like two elephants charging as one.

Eager for battle, the kings roar, 'It is permissible to kill anyone who is bent on a fight!' and rush at Bhima and Arjuna disguised as Brahmanas.

Tejasvin Karna faces Arjuna, while the great Salya, king of Madra, lumbers at Bhima truly like a tusker in musth charging another tusker for the right to mate with a cow-elephant in heat. Duryodhana and some others give light, playful fight to the general throng of Brahmanas.

Arjuna sees Surya's son Karna advance upon him and pierces him with a lightning swift flurry of arrows, and Radheya Karna faints. Recovering quickly, Karna now fights Arjuna with greater intent. Fiercely, intensely, they duel, those greatest of all archers. Such is their speed and skill that they shroud each other in showers of arrows so both become invisible to the spectator crowd.

But what they roar at each is clearly audible: 'See the strength of my arms!'

'I have the answer for that!'

They say more, which is subtle, and only other great bowmen can fathom that exchange, full of the high secrets of archery.

Karna finds Arjuna indomitable and the Suryaputra raises his own exceptional archery. Arjuna looses shafts like thunder at him, and Karna roars and parries them. The Kshatriyas all applaud.

Karna cries to his opponent, 'Dvijottama, you are a matchless and tireless bowman, and your arrows are tremendous. Are you an Avatara of the Astrashastra? Or are you Parasurama, Indra himself, or his younger brother Vishnu Achyuta, come in the guise of Brahmana?

For I know that none but Indra or Pandu's son Arjuna Kiriti can face me in battle when I am roused.'

Arjuna, Phalguna, replies, 'Karna, I am not any Avatara of the Astrashastra, nor am I Parasurama of divine prowess. I am just a Brahmana but I am the greatest archer on Earth. Through my Guru's grace, I have the Brahmastra and the Paurandarastra, and I am here to vanquish you, O Shura, in a very short while.'

Karna lowers his bow and stops fighting, for that Maharatha knows that the Brahmastra is irresistible. Meanwhile, nearby, Salya and Bhima fight like two elephants in musth, striking each other with fists and knees. They shove each other mightily, flinging one another down, and hauling the fallen adversary face down along the ground.

Their blows are like granite blocks crashing together and the stadium echoes. After a brief struggle, Bhima Kurusthama picks Salya up bodily and hurls him down roughly, with enormous force, so that the crowd gasps. Yet, Bhimasena Purusharishabha flings Salya down subtly, too, so that he does not seriously injure the Madra king.

Seeing Salya supine and Karna lowering his bow in fear, all the other Kshatriyas become alarmed. Quickly, they throng round Bhima and say in placatory tones, 'These Brahmanarishabhas are certainly great warriors! We must know their gotra and where they live, for who can face Radha's son Karna in battle other than Drona, Rama or Pandu's son Arjuna?

Who can withstand Duryodhana except Devakinandana Krishna and Saradwan's son Kripa? Who also can hurl Salya down except the great Balarama, Shuravirya Duryodhana or the Pandava Bhimasena?

Let us not fight these excellent Brahmanas anymore, for however much a Brahmana offends he must be protected. At least let us first discover who they are, if indeed they are Brahmanas, and later consider fighting them with clear hearts.'

Having watched Bhima throw Salya down, Krishna is convinced that the two Brahmanas are indeed Kunti's sons. In his quiet but immediately arresting voice, he says to the Kshatriyas, 'The Brahmana has won the princess's hand fairly.'

He persuades the kings to abandon battle and to return peacefully, if amazed and wondering, to their kingdoms.

The other Brahmanas who have come to the event are jubilant. 'The Brahmanas have proved victorious and one of us has made the princess of Panchala his wife!'

They throng round Bhima and Arjuna, who wear deerskin, and now make their way with some difficulty through the rapturous crowd. Having been pressed hard by the Kshatriya enemy, blood upon them, the two shuras, those heroes, emerge from the milling crowd like the full Moon and the Sun emerging from behind dark clouds; Krishna follows them.

Meanwhile, in the potter's house, Kunti waits anxiously for her sons to return, for today they are late indeed. Her imagination conjures all sorts of fell happenings that might have overtaken her sons. One moment, she thinks that the sons of Dhritarashtra have recognised her princes and killed them. Next, she trembles to think that some powerful Rakshasa, with powers of maya, has slain them.

She even thinks, 'Ah, could Vyasa himself have been a victim of darkness of the mind when he told my sons to come to this city?'

Out of her love for her sons, Kunti's anxieties grow moment by moment. Then, in the stillness of late afternoon, Arjuna walks into the potter's house, like the Sun appearing from behind the clouds on an overcast day; following him comes a throng of festive Brahmanas."

CANTO 193

Swayamvara Parva Continued

Vaisampayana said, "Kunti's splendid sons come to the potter's house, bringing Draupadi Yagnaseni with them. Kunti is in the inner chamber when they call to her, 'Mother, come and see the alms we have brought today.'

From within, in great relief at their return, she replies, without seeing the alms that they mean, 'Share the alms you have brought and enjoy it equally.'

Next moment, she sees Draupadi and cries, 'What have I said?'

She clasps the lovely, ecstatic Panchali, but a shiver of fear runs through Kunti. Taking Draupadi's hand in hers, Kunti says to Yudhishtira, 'Your younger brothers called Drupada's daughter the alms they had brought home, and without seeing her I replied, "Share the alms you have brought and enjoy it equally."

Yudhishtira, Kururishabha, how can what I say not become a lie and yet no sin touch the Princess Panchali?'

Yudhishtira thinks for a moment, then puts his arm consolingly around his mother, turns to Arjuna and says, 'Phalguna, you won her at the swayamvara and it is only just that you should marry her. Parantapa let us light a holy fire and you must take her hand with all the sacred rituals.'

But Arjuna says, 'Rajan, do not make me commit this sin, for what you are saying does not conform to dharma. You are the eldest and you must marry first; then Bhima, then I, then Nakula and finally the youngest of us, Sahadeva.

Think well upon what would be the right thing to do, what would be just, honourable and also beneficial to King Drupada. Bhima and I, the twins and the Princess Panchali all wait for your decision. We will do what you say.'

Arjuna speaks with the utmost respect and affection. Now all the Pandavas turn to gaze upon the peerless princess, the dark Krishnaa; and she, in turn, looks at not just one but at all five of them. The sons of Pandu then look at one another, and they all sense one another's fervent desire.

They sit on the floor and are all plunged in a single absorption: of Draupadi, and her alone. Once they have gazed at her, Kama Deva easily captures their hearts, paralyses their senses, and fills them with one desire: easily, because Brahma himself has created this princess to be more beautiful than any other woman on Earth. Such is her beauty that she can enchant any man, why, any creature that lives.

Kuntiputra Yudhishtira looks at his younger brothers and clearly sees what is in their hearts. Now he remembers clearly what Krishna Dwaipayana, their grandsire Vyasa had said to him.

The bull among men fears that Draupadi will divide brother against brother unless he chose wisely for them all. Yudhishtira says quietly, 'The auspicious princess shall become the wife of us all.'

Such joy breaks out upon the faces of his brothers.

The great Shura of the Vrishnis, Krishna, now arrives at the potter's house with Rohini's Balarama. They see Yudhishtira Ajatashatru sitting there, his arms graceful, mighty and long; they see his younger brothers brighter than flames around him.

Krishna goes up to Kunti's eldest son, touches that Kshatriya's feet and says, 'I am Krishna.'

Rohini's son Balarama does the same. The Pandavas cry out in delight to see the divine Yadava brothers, who then proceed to touch the feet of Kunti, who is their father's sister.

Kurusthama Yudhishtira formally and lovingly inquires about the health of Krishna and Baladeva, and then asks in some amazement, 'O Krishna, how did you discover us when we are disguised as Brahmanas?'

Krishna says with a smile, 'Rajan, even if it is covered by ashes, fire can be known. Who among Manavas other than the Pandavas could do what Bhima and Arjuna did today? Parantapas, O sons of Pandu, the greatest good fortune helped you escape the fire at Varanavrata which Duryodhana and his conspirators lit.

Bless you! May your fortune increase like a fire that is lit inside a hidden cave and then spread out to cover the Earth. But now, lest we are seen here and you discovered, we must return to our own lodgings.'

Taking Yudhishtira's leave, Krishna, whose fortune never wanes, quickly leaves the potter's house with Balarama."

CANTO 194

SWAYAMVARA PARVA CONTINUED

Vaisampayana said, "When Bhima and Arjuna leave the arena of the swayamvara and make their way towards the potter's house, the Panchala prince Dhrishtadyumna follows them discreetly. He goes alone, dismissing his attendants, and hides himself in a dark corner of the potter's dwelling.

As dusk falls, Bhima and Arjuna return from their evening round of begging alms. They bring what they have received to Yudhishtira.

Kunti says kindly to Draupadi, 'Sweet child, take one portion of the alms, and having offered it to the gods, give it away to some Brahmanas. Give another portion to any other atithis, guests that have come to us to be fed.

Divide what remains in two halves. Give one half to Bhima, for this fair son of mine, who is as strong as an elephant king, this shuravirya always eats well. Divide what remains into six portions, my child, four of them for my other sons and one each for you and for me.'

Happily, Draupadi does as her mother-in-law asks, and those heroes eat the food that the princess serves them. Dhrishtadyumna watches from concealment as Madri's son Sahadeva now spreads a wide bed of kusa grass on the floor. Each brother spreads his deerskin upon the grass and they all lie down to sleep, with their heads facing south.

Kunti lies crosswise above the heads of her sons, and the princess Panchali at their feet. The lovely princess Krishnaa lies at the feet of the Pandavas even as if she is their lowly foot pillow, but she feels no shame or sorrow, and neither does a wrong thought of those Kururishabhas cross her heart.

Those shuras begin to speak softly among themselves, while Dhrishtadyumna listens avidly from his hiding place; he is intrigued and excited by what he hears, for those princes, each one capable of being a Senapati, speak of nothing but vimanas, astras, war elephants, swords and various kinds of arrows, and of battle-axes, too. He sees how his sister lies contentedly at the feet of the five.

With dawn the potter opens his front door and the Panchala prince slips out quietly and runs to his father to report everything he has seen and heard. Drupada is dejected because he does not know that it is indeed the Pandavas that have taken his daughter.

As soon as his son comes into his presence, he cries, 'Where is my Krishnaa? Who are they that have taken her from us? Has a lowborn Sudra or a deceitful Vaisya stamped on my head and made off with my precious child? O my son, has our fragrant garland of flowers been cast into a cemetery?

Or perhaps some noble Kshatriya or a Dvija has won her? Ah, has some mean fellow set his left foot upon my crowned head and taken my Panchali? Ah, my prince, I would not grieve at all but be so full of joy if Purushottama Arjuna had married my child today! Dhrishtadyumna, are Kurusthama Vichitravirya's grandsons alive? Is it indeed Arjuna who bent the bow and brought the target down?'"

CANTO 195

VAIVAHIKA PARVA

Vaisampayana said, "Dhrishtadyumna, best among princes of the House of the Moon, says to his father, 'The youth with long reddish eyes, who wore deerskin and is as handsome as a Deva, who strung that best of bows and shot the target, was quickly thronged by festive Brahmanas who all paid him homage for what he had done. He looked like Indra of the Vajra standing among the Devas and Devarishis.

As for Krishnaa, she held onto the youth's deerskin and followed him as joyfully as a she-elephant does the lord of a herd. When the incensed Kshatriyas advanced on them, another hero rose to stand beside the archer. He tore up a big tree and rushed at the kings and princes, smashing them down all around him even as Yama does all the living.

Rajan, the Kshatriyas stopped their assault and stood still, while the two shuras, who are like the Sun and the Moon, took Krishnaa with them and left the arena. I followed them discreetly to the house of a potter in the suburbs of our city. Inside the potter's house there sat a woman who is like a flame. I am sure that she is their mother, and around her there sat three other splendid heroes, each one like an Agni.

The two shuras touched the woman's feet and bid Krishnaa do the same. They left Panchali with the lady and went out to beg for alms. Returning, they gave what they had received to Draupadi, who offered one portion of it to the gods, gave away another as daana to Brahmanas, gave part of what remained to the noble woman, and divided the rest amongst the five young men. Finally, she kept a little for herself and ate when the others had all eaten.

O Father, when they had eaten they lay down to sleep and Krishnaa lay contentedly at their feet, even like a foot pillow. They lay upon a bed of kusa grass on which they spread their deerskins.

Before falling asleep the five spoke amongst themselves in voices deep as thunderheads rumbling, and from what they spoke about they are not Sudras or Vaisyas, nor even Brahmanas. I have no doubt that they are Kshatriyas, for they spoke knowingly of things that only bulls among warriors discuss.

Father, it does seem that our hopes have not been in vain, and that what we heard about the Pandavas having escaped the fire in the house of lac is indeed true. From the manner in which the youth strung the great bow and shot the mark, and from what I heard them say to one another in the potter's house, I am certain, O King, that these are the sons of Pritha disguised as Brahmanas.'

Drupada is overjoyed and he sends his priest to the brothers to discover if they are indeed the Pandavas. Coming to the potter's house, the priest lauds them, and delivers Drupada's message.

'Exalted ones, Drupada, most munificent king, has sent me to ask who you are. He saw the feat of this youth who shot the mark, and his joy was great. Tell us to which race, clan and family you belong, and trampling the heads of your enemies, complete the joy of the Panchala king and his kin, and mine as well.

King Pandu was a dear friend of Drupada, who loved him as he did himself. Drupada always wanted to give his daughter in marriage to a son of Pandu. Flawlessly handsome Shuras, Drupada has long wanted Arjuna of the long and mighty arms to marry Panchali by winning her hand at the swayamvara.

If that is what has happened, ah, nothing could be more auspicious or fortunate.'

Delivering his message, the priest falls silent and waits for their reply. Yudhishtira says to Bhima, 'Offer the Brahmana padya and arghya; he is Drupada's Kulaguru and deserves exceptional reverence and worship.'

Bhima washes the feet of the Brahmana and offers him arghya, while the priest sits there happily, at ease.

Yudhishtira then says to him, 'The Panchala king did not give his daughter away freely, by Kshatriya custom, but by a trial of skill. Drupada should ask no questions about the race, clan or family of this hero who won the princess's hand fairly. Let us say that his every question has already been answered by the stringing of the bow and the bringing down of the target.

This brilliant shura won Krishnaa amidst the gathered Kshatriyas and brought her away. After that, let not the king of the House of Soma entertain any regrets about what happened, for they will only serve to make him unhappy and not to answer any questions that he might have.

Let it suffice to say that whatever the king wished for his beautiful princess, who bears every auspicious mark upon her person, will come to pass. No one weak or lowborn, none that is not a great master of arms could have strung that bow or shot that mark. Once done, the feat cannot be undone either, not by anyone in this world.

It does not become the king to grieve for his daughter today, indeed to grieve over what is inexorable. Fate will take its course now.'

Even as Yudhishtira speaks, another messenger arrives hotfoot from Drupada and announces, 'The banquet is ready!'"

CANTO 196

Vaivahika Parva Continued

Vaisampayana continued, "The messenger says, 'King Drupada has prepared a grand feast for the bridegroom and his party. Finish your nitya karma, your daily rituals, and come quickly. The Princess Krishnaa's wedding will be solemnised there. Do not delay. Look, Drupada sends these chariots adorned with golden lotuses and drawn by the noblest steeds for you. Ride in them to the palace of the king of the Panchalas.'

Soon, those Kuru bulls send Drupada's Brahmana back. They help Kunti and Draupadi into one of the gleaming chariots and, climbing into the others themselves, drive to the palace.

Meanwhile, O Bhaarata, his priest brings back Yudhishtira's message to Drupada and that king prepares a subtle test of sorts to find out to which varna the five young men belong. He has fruit and sanctified garlands set out; he fetches shining coats of armour and war-shields, the keenest swords, fine horses and chariots, the best bows and arrows, and rare lances, battle-axes and spears worked with gold; he has carpets on view, fine bedsteads and other expensive furnishings and artefacts; and he also puts on show cattle, seeds for sowing and some farming implements.

Arriving at Drupada's palace, Kunti and her sons enter the king's inner chambers. Joyfully the women of the palace welcome her, with honour and worship. Rajan, Drupada, his ministers, his sons, his friends and attendants all look at the Narapumgavas, the sons of Pandu, each one with the gait of a lion, wearing deerskin, their eyes like those of great bulls, their shoulders wide, their arms long and powerful, hanging at their side like great and sinewy snakes, and the Panchalas are delighted.

They see how those shuras sit without hesitation and indeed with comfortable familiarity, upon the fine chairs to which they are shown, with silken footstools, in order of their ages at the king's high table. When they sit, liveried servants, male and female, bring fare of kings to them, wine in crystal decanters and rare delicacies steaming on silver and golden platters. They eat and drink with relish and discerning appreciation: the wine and every kind of meat as well, again with easy familiarity.

When they have dined, those young men look with keen interest at the weapons and the other warrior's things that Drupada has shrewdly put on display, ignoring everything else which might have attracted a Brahmana or a Vaisya. Drupada and Dhrishtadyumna see all this, as do their ministers, and they are certain that the young men, those sons of Kunti, are Kshatriya princes. The Panchalas' joy swells."

CANTO 197

Vaivahika Parva Continued

Vaisampayana said, "A beaming Drupada now speaks to Yudhishtira, in the form used to address a Brahmana.

'Should we know you to be Kshatriyas, Brahmanas, or as Devas who have disguised yourselves as Brahmanas to range over the Earth, and have come here to win our Krishnaa's hand? We are full of uncertainty and beg you to tell us the truth! How happy you will make us by dispelling our doubts.

Bane of your enemies, has fate been kind to us? Tell us the truth gladly, for the truth is better suited to Kshatriyas than sacrifices or the dedication of sacred tanks. Do not hide the truth from us any longer, O you who are as handsome as a Deva, O Parantapa. I must make arrangements for my child's wedding in accordance with the varna to which you belong.'

Yudhishtira replies, smiling, 'O King, let every anxiety leave your heart, and let it fill with joy. For your heart's fondest desire has come true. My lord, we are Kshatriyas, we are the sons of Pandu.

I am Yudhishtira, the eldest son of Kunti, and these are Bhimasena and Arjuna, who took your daughter from the swayamvara from amidst the gathering of kings. The twins and Kunti are with Krishnaa. Narapumgava, we are Kshatriyas, so banish the sorrow from your heart. O King, like a lotus, your daughter has only been moved from one lake to another. Rajan, you are our revered elder, our superior and our main sanctuary. I have told you the truth, the whole truth.'

Drupada is rapturous; his eyes shine and for some moments he is speechless for delight. Controlling himself with some effort, he finally asks Yudhishtira how they had escaped from Varanavrata. Yudhishitira describes their escape from the burning house of lac in detail. When Kunti's son finishes, Drupada has stern censure for Dhritarashtra, and he has warm reassurance to offer Yudhishtira. Drupada swears to restore the Pandava to his ancestral throne.

Drupada says that Kunti, the Pandavas and Krishnaa must live with him, and he shows his guests the greatest regard. The Panchala king then says to Yudhishtira, 'Mahabaho, let Arjuna marry my daughter on this auspicious day. Let us begin the wedding ceremonies.'

Yudhishtira Dharmaputra replies, 'Maharaja, I must also marry.'

Drupada says, 'Then you take my daughter's hand yourself, or let her marry any of your brothers that you choose for her.'

Yudhishtira says, 'O King, we shall all marry your daughter and she shall become the wife of all five of us, even as our mother says she should be. I am not married, neither is Bhima. Arjuna won your jewel-like daughter's hand. We have always shared every precious jewel that we have ever got; best of kings, we cannot make an exception for this the most priceless one.

Krishnaa will become the wife of us all; one after the other, each of us shall take her hand before the sacred fire.'

Drupada cries, 'O Scion of Kuru, it has been said that one man may marry many wives, but never that one woman can marry many husbands! Kaunteya, you are pure and you know the laws of dharma well. You cannot commit this sin, which mocks both common practice and the Vedas. O Kshatriya, why has your mind been darkened by this vile thought?'

Yudhishtira says, 'Rajan, dharma is subtle; we do not understand the course of fate. Let us follow the path that great men of bygone yugas did. My tongue has never spoken a lie, and my heart never turns towards a sin. My mother commands us to share Draupadi equally among ourselves, and my heart accepts it, as well.

Hence, O King, for me what I propose is consonant with dharma. Let us do this without any fear; no sin will accrue from it.'

Drupada says, 'Son of Kunti, let your mother, my son Dhrishtadyumna and you decide among yourselves what is proper. Tell me what you decide and tomorrow I will do what you say is dharma.'

O Bhaarata, even as Yudhishtira, Kunti and Dhrishtadyumna deliberate among themselves, Dwaipayana on his wanderings arrives in Drupada's palace."

CANTO 198

VAIVAHIKA PARVA CONTINUED

Vaisampayana said, "The Pandavas, the illustrious Panchala king and everyone else present rises and pays homage to the enlightened Rishi Vyasa. The Mahatman greets them in turn, asks after their welfare and sits on the floor upon a golden carpet. He, of measureless tejas, asks the others to sit, as well, and those best of men do so, upon their costly chairs.

In a while, Prihasta's son gently brings up the matter at hand with the Sage, regarding the marriage of his daughter Draupadi.

Drupada says, 'Muni, how can one woman become the wife of five men without sinning? Is this possible? I beg you tell me the truth about this strangest thing.'

Vyasa replies, 'Rajan, this ancient practice was discontinued since it is against both Vedic injunction and common custom. But I would like to hear what each of you thinks about it.'

Drupada speaks first, 'To my mind it is a sin because it is against both the Veda and custom. Dvijottama, I have never seen, anywhere, one woman having many husbands. The great men of ages gone by also never did such a thing. No wise man ever dares to commit a sin. I cannot countenance this in good conscience. To me it seems immoral and adharma.'

After Drupada has finished, Dhrishtadyumna speaks. 'Dvijarishabha, if an elder brother is a man of character how can he go to his younger brother's wife? The ways of dharma are always subtle, and we cannot fully fathom them. In the most obvious things, we cannot say with conviction what is dharma and what is not. Then, how can we agree to this unusual proposal with a clear conscience? O Brahmana, how can I say, "Let Draupadi become the common wife of five brothers?"'

Now Yudhishtira says, 'My tongue never speaks a lie and my heart never veers towards a sin. My heart approves of this, and it cannot be sinful. Also, I have heard in the Purana of Jatila, a woman of great virtue, of the race of Gautama, who married seven Rishis. Another Sage's daughter, born of a tree, married the ten brothers, all named Prachetas, all of them Mahatmas and illumined by great tapasya.

Best of those that know dharma, to obey one's elders and betters is always dharma. Among all elders and betters, there is none to equal one's mother. Our mother has told us to share Draupadi whom we brought to her as alms, equally among ourselves. Most of all, Dvijottama, I consider the five of us marrying the princess to be the highest dharma.'

Kunti says, 'I agree with my virtuous Yudhishtira. O Brahmana, I am terrified if what I say to my sons should prove a lie. Must I not be saved from the sin of falsehood?'

When they have all finished, Vyasa says, 'Truly, Susheela, how will you be saved from the sin of untruth? For truth is Sanatana Dharma. O Panchala Pathe, Drupada, I will not speak of this ancient practice before all of you, but to you in private. I will tell you when this form of marriage was established and why it is ancient and eternal. But this much I will say here: Yudhishtira speaks the truth and what he says is dharma!'

The great master Krishna Dwaipayana, the illustrious Vyasa, rises, takes Drupada's hand and leads him into a private chamber. Kunti, her sons and Dhrishtadyumna wait for them to return. Alone together in the other room, Vyasa begins his profound discourse to the great king on the subject of sacred polyandry, and why it is not sinful."

CANTO 199

VAIVAHIKA PARVA CONTINUED

Vaisampayana continued, "Vyasa says to Drupada, 'In the elder days, the Devas once performed a Mahayagna in the Naimisa vana. During that sacrifice, Vivaswat's son Yama, Death, was appointed to perform the animal sacrifices that were made as offerings.

Long that yagna lasted and while it continued Yama slew the sanctified beasts, but during all that time he did not take the life of a single human. Death, O King, left humankind alone and their numbers swelled greatly on Earth; their population was enormous.

Soma, Indra, Varuna, Kubera, the Sadhyas, the Rudras, the Vasus, the Aswin twins and the other celestial ones went in alarm to Brahma Prajapati, Creator of the universe.

They said to the Lord of Creation, "The race of Manavas has increased frighteningly on Earth, and we have come to you for protection."

The Pitamaha said, "You have nothing to fear from the humans. You are all immortal, while they are not."

The Devas said, "The mortals have become immortal; there is no difference anymore between us and them. We are unhappy; we do not like them to be equal to us. Make some distinction between the races of Swarga and Bhumi."

Brahma said, "Vivaswat's son is absorbed in the Mahayagna and that is why mortal men have stopped dying. But when Yama's part in the great sacrifice is over, men will die again. Infused with the power of all of you, he will sweep away millions of Manavas, weakened by time and unduly long lives."

Reassured by what the First-born God said, the Devas returned to the Naimisa vana, where the yagna was underway. Sitting beside the Bhagirathi, they suddenly saw a great many golden lotuses being borne upon the river, and were wonderstruck. Indra wanted to discover from where the golden blooms had come and he traced the river back to her source, from where the Ganga springs.

He saw there a woman as splendid as fire, bathing in the stream and all the while she wept. As her tears fell into the water they turned into golden lotuses. The Vajradhari went up to the woman and asked, "Who are you, beautiful one? Tell me, why do you cry?"

The woman replied, "O Sakra, you can only know who I am and why I am crying, if, O Devendra, you come with me. Follow me and you will know everything."

Indra followed her as she led the way. Soon, he saw a handsome youth and a young woman of great beauty sitting upon a throne and playing dice upon a peak of Himavat.

Indra, king of the Devas, said to the youth, "Intelligent boy, I am the master of the universe."

However, the young man was so absorbed in the dice that he did not respond to Indra, who grew furious and cried again, "I am lord of the universe!"

The youth was the Lord Mahadeva and only glanced at Indra and smiled to see him enraged. That momentary look froze Indra where he stood and he could not move but stood there like some stake.

When the dice game was over, Isana Siva said to the weeping woman, "Bring Sakra here. I will make sure that pride never enters his heart again."

As soon as the woman touched Indra he fell upon the ground. The glorious Lord Isana said to him, "Never be arrogant again, Sakra. You have great strength and vigour. Roll this stone away from the cavern that it covers; enter the cave and you will see some others there, all of them as brilliant as the Sun, all of them your equals."

Indra rolled away the rock and saw a great cave upon the breast of that king of mountains. Within the cave were four others exactly like him.

Seized by anxiety, Indra cried, "Shall I also become like these?"

Then the Lord Girisha glared at Indra, and said in anger, "You of a hundred yagnas, down into the cave with you! You have insulted me from your pride."

His limbs turning weak with shock, Indra trembled like the leaf of a Himalayan fig-tree at Siva's dreadful curse. His hands folded, shaking from head to foot, Indra said in a quivering voice to the God who rides the Bull, the fierce Lord of myriad manifestations, "O Bhava, you are the Lord of the universe!"

The God of terrific tejas smiled, "Those that are vain like you never find my grace. Once, the four inside the cave were all like you. Down into the cave with you and lie there for a while. All your fates shall be the same. You will be born into the world of men, where you will face untold hardship, and with much effort and after much travail, you will kill thousands and thousands of Manavas, and by that punya, you will return to Indraloka.

Yes, you will experience and accomplish everything that I have said and much more, besides."

Their glory lost, the four Indras in the cave said, "May we descend from on high to the world of men, where salvation is hard to gain. But let the Devas Dharma, Vayu, Maghavat and the Aswin twins become our fathers, and beget us upon our terrestrial mothers. We will fight the

Manavas on Bhumi with weapons of men and the gods, and reclaim Indraloka."

The Vajradhari said to Mahadeva, "I will create a Manava with an amsa of mine, a man of great tejas, to become the fifth of these to be born on Earth to raze the humans."

The first four Indras were Vishwabhuk, Bhutadhaman, Sibi, Santi, and Tejaswin was the fifth Indra of yore. And Siva Pinakin, from his great mercy, granted the five Indras their wish. He also declared that the woman of exceptional beauty, she who had been weeping, who was none other than the Devi Sri herself, would become the wife in the world of all five of them.

Taking the five Indras with him, Lord Isana went to Narayana of fathomless tejas, to the infinite, uncreated, eldest, eternal One, Soul of universes without limit or count. Narayana approved of what they meant to do.

The five Indras were born into the world of men. Narayana plucked two hairs from his body, one black and the other white; he sent the two hairs down the mandalas and into the wombs of two women of the race of Yadu: Devaki and Rohini. The white hair became Balarama and the black one Krishna, who was Narayana himself.

The Indras who had been sealed in the cave upon Himavat are none other than the sons of Pandu, of extraordinary energy. Amongst them Arjuna, who is Savyasachin the perfectly ambidextrous, is the amsavatara of Sakra.

Rajan, these Pandavas are indeed those same Indras of old, and your daughter of matchless beauty, Draupadi, born to become their wife, is the Devi Sri herself. Otherwise, how could she have been born as she was, so exceptionally, rising out of the very Earth at your yagna, lustrous as the Sun or the Moon, and the fragrance of her spreading for a yojana on every side?'

Vyasa Muni pauses, then suddenly says, 'Rajan, I now give you occult vision: see for yourself who these sons of Pandu actually are. See them in their sacred and unearthly forms of old!'

Vyasa of great spiritual power gifts mystic vision to the king and Drupada sees all five Pandavas in their pristine forms. He sees them with divine bodies of light, wearing golden crowns and unworldly garlands. Each one is an Indra, irradiant as Agni or Surya, shimmering with ornaments of heaven, ever-youthful and handsome past describing, their chests wide and great and all of them some twenty feet tall at least.

Incomparable celestial raiment they wear, the most wonderfully fragrant garlands. Drupada sees them as three-eyed Sivas, or Vasus, Rudras or dazzling Adityas. The Panchala king sees Arjuna as Indra himself, in amsa, and is enthralled, as well as wonderstruck and bemused by the deep and subtle mystery of what he sees: that manifestation of the power of heaven.

Drupada then turns to look, with mystic eyes, at his daughter, most beautiful of all women in the world, and now sees her truly as splendid as the Fire or the Moon, a Goddess; his heart knows beyond doubt now that she is indeed born to be the wife of the five Indras, for her beauty, her glory, and also her renown.

When he sees that vision, Drupada touches Vyasa's feet, crying, 'Maharishi, no miracle is beyond you!'

Dwaipayana continues merrily, 'Once, in an asrama there lived a Rishi and his daughter, who was chaste, accomplished and beautiful but she has not found a husband. The young woman worshiped the Lord Siva with a stern tapasya. Pleased by her devotions, Mahadeva Sankara, the benign, appeared before her and said, "What boon do you want?"

The young woman said over and over, "Lord, give me a great and worthy husband!"

The best of Gods replied, "Susheela, you will have five excellent husbands."

She said, "Sankara, I want just one husband, Lord, who owns every virtue."

The God of gods said, "Kanye, you said five times to me, '*Lord, give me a husband.*' You shall have five wonderful husbands: not in this life but in another one, in the future."

Drupada, this daughter of yours, of unearthly beauty, is that young woman, and the flawless Krishnaa born into the race of Prihasta, is destined to become the wife of five husbands. It is the Devi Sri herself, who performed intense penance for the sake of the Pandavas, who has been born as your daughter from the fire of your Mahayagna.

Because of her own karma, the peerless Devi whom all the gods and other celestials serve, will marry five husbands; indeed, Brahma created Draupadi just for this. Now I have told you all there is to know, Raja Drupada, and now you must do as you want.'"

CANTO 200

VAIVAHIKA PARVA CONTINUED

Vaisampayana said, "Drupada says, 'Mahamuni, I knew nothing of all this when I objected to my daughter marrying all five Pandavas. Now that I know, how can I go against the will of the Gods? I will do as you say, for the knot of destiny cannot be undone.

We do not decide anything that happens in this world, and while I had once thought that my child would marry one husband, she will now marry five. Draupadi herself said five times to Mahadeva, '*Lord, give me a husband!*' Siva himself gave her the boon of marrying five husbands, and He knows the dharma or adharma of this.

As for me, I cannot sin by doing what Sankara has ordained, be it right or wrong. I am content: let the five princes marry my daughter happily, with the appropriate rituals!'

Dwaipayana, the illustrious, comes to Yudhishtira and says, 'Today is an auspicious day, O Pandava, for the Moon has entered the Pushyami nakshatra. Marry the Princess Krishnaa this very day, you first and then your brothers as well.'

When Vyasa has spoken, Drupada Yagnasena and his son Dhrishtadyumna quickly make preparations for the wedding. The king brings out numberless priceless wedding gifts. He then fetches his daughter Krishnaa, who has bathed and put on royal finery and ornaments past value, to the kalyana mantapa.

All the king's well-wishers, friends, kinsmen and relations, his ministers and countless Brahmanas and the common people of his city, besides, come to the princess' unusual wedding. They are seated according to their respective stations.

Graced by that assembly of great men, its sprawling courtyard strewn with lotuses and lilies, striking lines of warriors standing mighty around and within, diamonds and every other precious stone sparkling upon its walls, King Drupada's palace looks like the sky with the stars shimmering in it.

Having bathed, putting on earrings, the costliest silken robes, smearing their magnificent physiques with sandalwood paste, the Kuru princes perform their daily religious rituals; then, with their priest Dhaumya, bright as agni, they enter the wedding hall, one after the other, in order of age, their hearts alight, like great bulls going into a cowpen.

Dhaumya, knower of the Veda, lights the sacred fire and, chanting the appropriate mantras, pours ghee as libation into the flames. First, he calls Yudhishtira and marries him to Draupadi. Taking each other's hands, the bride and groom walk around the fire.

When that ceremony is complete, Dhaumya takes his leave of Yudhishtira, jewel among Kshatriyas, and leaves the palace. After this, those Kuru Maharathas, richly clad and adorned, marry the Panchala princess, first among all women, one after the other, over the next four days, with Dhaumya as their priest for each wedding.

Rajan, the Devarishi Dwaipayana told me a most wonderful thing which happens to Draupadi during those five nights, each spent with a different husband—that she of the slender waist is a virgin afresh on every one!

When the five weddings are solemnised, Drupada gives those Maharathas, his sons-in-law, untold gifts and wealth. He gives them one hundred chariots with golden standards, each drawn by four horses of the noblest bloodlines, all of them with bridles of gold. He gives them a hundred elephants, all with the most auspicious marks upon their temples and faces, caparisoned richly, so they seem like a hundred mountains with golden peaks.

Drupada gives the Pandavas a hundred women to serve them, all beautiful and in the prime of their youth, all richly attired, bejewelled and wearing wildflower garlands. Yes, with Agni as the sacred witness to his gifts, the king of the House of the Moon gives those princes of unworldly splendour gold, the rarest, finest, costliest garments, and invaluable ornaments of antiquity, craftsmanship and brilliance past compare.

Having married Krishnaa, who is like another Sri, as well as incalculable wealth, the mighty Pandavas live happily, truly like five Indras, in the capital of the Panchala king."

CANTO 201

VAIVAHIKA PARVA CONTINUED

Vaisampayana said, "When the sons of Pandu have married his daughter, all anxiety and fear leaves King Drupada; why, he does not fear the Devas anymore. After the weddings, the noble women of Drupada's antahpura come to Kunti, and introducing themselves, telling her their names; one by one, they worship her by laying their heads at her feet.

Wearing resonant red silk, and the auspicious and ceremonial thread around her wrists, Krishnaa also pays reverence to her mother-in-law and stands happily before her, with folded hands.

Overwhelmed by affection, Pritha blesses Draupadi, of matchless beauty, who bears every auspicious mark upon her person, and has the sweetest nature and the noblest character.

Kunti says, 'May you be as precious to your husbands as Sachi is to Indra, Swaha to Agni, Rohini to Soma, Damayanti to Nala, Bhadra to Vasiravana, Arundhati to Vasishta, as Sri Lakshmi is to Narayana! Sweet child, may you become the mother of long-lived, heroic children, and may you have everything that will make you happy.

May fortune and prosperity always wait upon you. May your husbands perform Mahayagnas, and may you always be devoted to them. Let your days pass in welcoming and caring for guests and strangers that come to your home, holy men and the elderly, children and betters.

May you become Queen of Kurujangala in its capital, beside your husband King Yudhishitra Dharmaputra. My daughter, may you gift the whole world, subdued by your husbands of incomparable strength, to Brahmanas at an Aswamedha yagna.

Accomplished child, may the rarest gemstones on Earth, those of great virtue, come to belong to you, fortunate one, and may you be joyful for a full hundred years. Daughter-in-law, as I rejoice today to look at you wearing the red silk of your wedding, I will rejoice again when I see you become the mother of a son!'

When the sons of Pandu are married, Krishna sends them lavish gifts of golden ornaments set with giant pearls and lapis lazuli, black gems. He sends rare and priceless robes made in many kingdoms, as well as the softest, finest blankets and skins of great value, and precious carpets and expensive bedsteads and palanquins.

Hundreds of shining vessels, chalices, goblets, and other ware he sends, all encrusted with jewels. Krishna gifts them young, accomplished and beautiful women servants, thousands of them, also from diverse and far-flung countries: all these richly attired and wearing costly ornaments. He gives them masterfully trained elephants, all from the land of Madra, countless fine horses in golden harness, and chariots, too, with fine steeds, with large teeth, yoked.

Madhava Krishna, of fathomless soul, sends them gold coins, crores and crores of them, in separate piles. Wanting to please Krishna, Yudhishtira the just accepts all his gifts joyfully."

CANTO 202

VIDURAGAMANA PARVA

Vaisampayana said, "Now their spies in Drupada's city bring news to all the Kshatriya kings and princes who had come to her swayamvara of how Draupadi has married the five Pandavas. They tell their masters that it was Arjuna, greatest of warriors and archers, who shot the target, and that he who had dashed Salya to the ground and terrified the others with the tree he pulled up, who had stood utterly fearless facing them all, was Bhimasena, razer of enemy armies, whose very touch is enough to kill his adversaries.

The kings are amazed at how the Pandavas had managed to remain so long disguised as docile Brahmanas, and wonder how they are still alive for they have all heard how Kunti and her sons had been burnt to death in the house of lac. They even think of them as having returned from the dead.

The kings of the Earth remember again Purochana's vile treachery, and say, 'A curse on Bhishma, a curse on Dhritarashtra of the race of Kuru!'

When the swayamvara is over and they hear the news that Draupadi has married the Pandavas, the kings that still remained in Drupada's city set out each to his own kingdom. When Duryodhana hears that Arjuna of the white steeds has won Panchali's hand, he falls into dark dejection. His heart heavy, he sets out with Sakuni, Asvatthama, Karna and Kripa for Hastinapura.

Flushed with the humiliation of it, he says softly, feelingly, to his brother, 'If Arjuna had not disguised himself as a Brahmana he could never have won Draupadi. No one recognised him. My lord, I fear that Fate rules supreme; all our efforts have been in vain, my brother, and the wretched Pandavas are still alive!'

Cursing Purochana for his ineptitude, they arrive in Hastinapura, utterly defeated and depressed. Now they see that the mighty Pandavas have escaped with their lives and are also bound by their marriage to the formidable Drupada. They think of the prowess of Sikhandin and the fire-born Dhrishtadyumna and their hearts quail.

On the other hand, when Vidura hears that the Pandavas have won Draupadi and that Dhritarashtra's son has returned humiliated to Hastinapura, he is delighted. Vidura Kshattri goes to Dhritarashtra and says, 'Great fortune has come to the Kurus!'

Dhritarashtra also cries gleefully, 'Such great fortune, Vidura, such luck!'

Dhritarashtra orders fine ornaments to be wrought for Draupadi, and declares that Duryodhana and the princess must be received with unprecedented pomp and ceremony and festivity in Hastinapura.

When he pauses to draw breath in his fervour, Vidura quietly tells him that the Pandavas have won Draupadi for their bride; he tells Dhritarashtra that the sons of Pandu are alive and that they now live with great honour in the palace of Drupada. He does not fail to mention that all Drupada's powerful kinsmen and allies, every one the lord of a great army, and many other Kshatriya kings who had come to the swayamvara, have now aligned themselves with Kunti's princes.

Dhritarashtra says, 'Those children are as dear to me as they are to Pandu! No, they are dearer to me. Let me tell you why, Vidura. My heroic nephews are alive and well. They have garnered many friends and relations as allies, all these very powerful. Tell me who would not want the great Drupada and his kinsmen for an ally?'

Vidura says, 'My lord may your wisdom not change for a hundred years!' and returns to his own palace.

Then, Rajan, Duryodhana and Radheya Karna come into the presence of the blind king.

Duryodhana says, 'Lord, we can never speak freely in Vidura's presence. Now we have found you alone and shall speak our minds. We heard what you said, O King. What is this that you mean to do? Do you truly look upon the fortune of our enemies as if it was your own, that you spoke so lovingly and proudly to Vidura about the sons of Pandu?

Sinless, you do not do what you should be doing – everything in your power to undermine the Pandavas, to destroy them. O my father, we must confer and act quickly before the Pandavas devour us all, with our friends, children and kinsmen!'"

CANTO 203

VIDURAGAMANA PARVA CONTINUED

Vaisampayana said, "Dhritarashtra replies, 'I also want to do exactly as you would have me but should I betray my intention to Vidura by even a muscle twitching? That is why, my son, I praised the Pandavas and spoke affectionately of them. I would not betray what is really in my heart to Vidura, by the smallest sign.

Suyodhana, Vidura has gone, so now tell me what you think we should do, and Radheya, you also share your thoughts with me.'

Duryodhana says, 'Father, let us use subtle and cunning Brahmanas to create division between the sons of Kunti and Madri's twins. Or let us bribe Drupada, his sons, and all his ministers with vast wealth so that they abandon the cause of Kunti's son Yudhishtira.

Or let our agents persuade the Pandavas to remain in Drupada's kingdom, convincing them, individually and separately, how dangerous it would be for them to return to Hastinapura. Let the best of our spies create dissension among the brothers, by sowing the seeds of envy among them.

Better, let them incite Draupadi against her husbands; she has five of them, the task should not be difficult. Or let our secret men whisper such words that make the Pandavas displeased with Krishnaa; if they show displeasure, any of them, she will not be happy.

Best of all, let us send our finest assassins to kill just Bhima. He is the strongest of them; without him, the rest are nothing. Since we were young, they always depended on his strength to fly in our faces as they chose. If Bhima dies, they will not have the nerve to try to regain their kingdom.

My lord, Arjuna is certainly invincible in battle – as long as Bhima stands behind him! Without Bhima, Arjuna is not a fourth part of the archer that Radheya Karna is. If Bhimasena dies, the Pandavas will fear us and abandon every hope of recovering the kingdom.

Or if they do come here and prove to be docile, we will grind them underfoot. Else, we can seduce them with the most luscious women, and turn Krishnaa against them. Or let us have them brought here, and then kill them all secretly.

Father, choose whichever of these methods appears to you to be the best. Time flies, and we must strike quickly, one way or another, before their bonds with Drupada Rajarishabha grow even stronger, and their relationship with him takes deep root. Once that happens, we will not succeed.

Father, this is how I think we should deal with the sons of Pandu. You be the judge of the worth of my thoughts. And now, Karna, tell us what you think.'"

CANTO 204

VIDURAGAMANA PARVA CONTINUED

Vaisampayana continued, "Karna says, 'Duryodhana, I do not concur with your thoughts. O Perpetuator of the Kuru race, none of these methods will succeed against the Pandavas. Shuraveerya, haven't you tried such methods before and always failed to kill your enemies? That was when they lived here with you. That was when they were young and callow; and you still could not harm them.

Now they are far away; they are full-grown men. You cannot hope to bring Kunti's sons to grief with any of these subtle, underhand methods. This is my firm belief. It seems that Fate herself colludes with the Pandavas; they want to recover the kingdom of their fathers and no power in the world can hurt or stop them.

You will never succeed in dividing them against one another. How can five brothers who have married the same woman ever be divided? No agent or spy of ours can hope to turn Krishnaa against them; do not forget that she chose them for husbands when they appeared before her as indigents. Will she abandon them now when she knows who they are, now that they prosper again? Besides, women always want to have many husbands and Krishnaa has five. You can never turn her heart against them.

As for Drupada, the Panchala king is honest to a fault, and a man of dharma. There is no lust for wealth in him, or any greed. Even if you offer him the whole Kuru kingdom, he will not betray the Pandavas or turn against them. Drishtadyumna is no less than his father and has always been attached to Pandu's sons.

No, you cannot harm the Pandavas by any covert or cunning means in your power. However, Narapumgava, bull among men, we can attack them openly and kill them in battle when they are unprepared! We are stronger than the Panchala king; let us strike now when they do not expect us to. Let us strike and kill them all without mercy or scruple.

Son of Gandhari, Gandhareya, before they muster their numberless chariots and allies, and loyal clansmen, strike! Before the mighty Panchala king and his sons decide to attack us, attack them first! Before the Vrishni, Krishna, comes to Drupada's city with the Yadava host to help win back their kingdom for the Pandavas, my lord Dhritarashtra, strike! For there is nothing—wealth, every enjoyment, kingdom—that Krishna will not sacrifice for Pandu's sons.

The magnificent Bharata conquered all the Earth just by his own prowess. Indra won sovereignty over the three worlds just by his might. O King, prowess and valour are the ways of the Kshatriya; Kshtriyarishabha, might is the first virtue of a hero.

So let us immediately take our great army, with its four kinds of forces, to the Panchala kingdom, crush Drupada and drag the Pandavas back here, powerless. The Pandavas cannot be subdued by conciliation, gifts or bribes, or by cunning division. You must vanquish them in battle, and having done so, Duryodhana, rule this Earth unopposed.

I see no other means to achieve what we want.'

Dhritarashtra hears Karna out and praises him fulsomely. The king says, 'Sutaputra, you are not only a great warrior but have much wisdom, as well. Your view that we must take arms against the enemy suits you well, noble one. However, you both must consult Bhishma, Drona and Vidura, also, before deciding what must be done, which will benefit us.'

Dhritarashtra summons all those great ones and takes their counsel."

CANTO 205

Viduragamana Parva Continued

Vaisampayana said, "When Dhritarashtra asks Bhishma for his advice, the patriarch says, 'Dhritarashtra, I can never endorse a war with the sons of Pandu, for Pandu was as dear to me as you are, and Kunti's sons are as precious to me as Gandhari's. I must protect them exactly as I do your sons, Dhritarashtra.

I love the Pandavas as well as all the Kurus do; nothing should lead us into battle against them. Rather, make peace with Kunti's princes; bring them home and give them half the kingdom, for this is beyond doubt the ancestral kingdom of those best among the Kurus, as well.

Duryodhana, if you look at this kingdom as belonging to your father so do the Pandavas see it as being their father's. If Pandu's magnificent sons do not inherit this kingdom, how can you, or indeed any other scion of the race of Bhaarata?

If you think of yourself as having lawfully inherited this kingdom, I believe that they can also think the same, and before you. Quietly give them half the kingdom, keeping half for yourself. Narapumgava, this will be best for everyone. If you do otherwise, evil will befall each one of us, and you will cover yourself in shame and dishonour.

Duryodhana, a good name and honour are the very root of one's strength; do everything you can to maintain them. It is said that he who has lost his reputation lives in vain. Kaurava, as long as a man has fame and honour, he does not die. A man lives as long as his honour lasts, and dies when he loses his reputation.

Son of Gandhari, act in accordance with your noble birth; act as a Kuru should. Mahabaho, do as your ancestors would have done. We are fortunate that the Pandavas did not die, that Kunti still lives. We are fortunate that the wretched Purochana died himself but did not succeed in his vile attempt on their lives.

From the day that I heard Kunti's sons had died in a fire, Gandhareya, I was sick at heart and hardly able to meet or speak to anyone. Purushavyaghra, when the people heard that Kunti had perished they did not blame Purochana as much as they did you.

Now that the Pandavas have reappeared, obviously having escaped from the fire, Duryodhana, you must do away with your ignominy. And I say to you, O Scion of the Kurus, as long as Pandu's sons live, not the Vajradhari Indra himself can prevent them from regaining their rightful share in this kingdom.

The Pandavas are virtuous and united, and have been deprived of their birthright by adharma. If you want to make amends and do the right thing, seeking the welfare of everyone, yourself and your subjects, give them half of the kingdom.'"

CANTO 206

VIDURAGAMANA PARVA CONTINUED

Vaisampayana said, "When Bhishma has finished, Drona speaks. 'Dhritarashtara, Rajan, I have heard that a friend, asked for advice, should always speak truthfully, justly and in an honourable manner. My lord, I am entirely in agreement with the great Bhishma – a share of the kingdom must be given to the Pandavas. This is Sanatana Dharma.

O Bhaarata, send a well-spoken messenger to Drupada immediately, taking with him a treasure for the sons of Pandu. Let this man carry priceless gifts for the bride and her husbands. He must tell Drupada that you are pleased and proud that your power and glory have increased vastly after this new alliance, by marriage, with him.

O King, let your messenger tell Drupada how delighted both Duryodhana and you yourself are at what has transpired. Let him repeat this often to the Panchala king and to his son Dhrishtadyumna. He must say that the union is entirely agreeable to you and that you consider it as being fitting and a perfect and equal match.

Let your messenger repeatedly conciliate Kunti and Madri's sons. Rajan, order a bounty of the purest golden ornaments sent to Draupadi. Also, Bharatarishabha let excellent gifts be taken for all Drupada's sons. And when all these have been given and he has spoken sweetly to everyone, let your messenger propose that the Pandavas return to Hastinapura.

Once Drupada, mollified, gives them leave to return, Dushasana and Vikarna must go out with a handsome retinue to receive them. Once they enter Hastinapura, you must yourself welcome those Narapumgavas with the greatest affection. Then, Dhritarashtra, set them upon the throne of their fathers for that is what the people of the realm want.

This, O King of the House of Bhaarata, is how I think you should behave towards the Pandavas, who are like your own sons.'

When Drona finishes, Karna rises and says hotly, 'Dhritarashtra, you have lavished your wealth on both Bhisma and Drona! You have always thought of them as being your most trusted, closest friends and well-wishers. What could be more amusing, then, than to find them strongly urging you to act against your own interest?

It can never be wise to approve of counsel given by those whose true intentions are evil, if well concealed. In a time of adversity, no friend can either help or harm a man: each one's fortune or misfortune depends only on fate. Let him be wise or a fool, young or old, alone or with many allies – he will find joy and sorrow, alternately each in their season, regardless.

I once heard of a king of old called Ambuvicha, whose capital was Rajagriha and he was king of all the Magadha chieftains. He never attended to affairs of the state: his only exertion was breathing! His minister Mahakarni effectually ruled the kingdom, and in time became so powerful that he had scant regard for the king.

Indeed, the wretch took everything for himself – all Ambuvicha's wealth and even his queens. However, these did not satisfy Mahakarni but only inflamed his greed. Now he began to hanker after the throne. But, this he could not get.

Rajan, what else can we conclude from this other than that it was Ambuvicha's destiny to remain king though he spent his time just breathing the air? Hence, O Dhritrashtra, if Fate has willed that the Kuru kingdom will remain with you, undivided, and pass on to your son, then that is what will happen, even if the whole world becomes your enemy.

Equally, if fate has willed otherwise, whatever you do you will not keep your kingdom! Wise King, remember this when you gauge the sincerity or lack thereof of your advisors. Think carefully about which of them have spoken with evil in their hearts and which honestly, wishing your welfare.'

Drona retorts to Karna, 'As you are full of adharma, it is plain that you speak with evil intentions. You want to harm the Pandavas and that is why you dare point your finger at us. But be certain Karna, that I spoke for the good of all the Kurus. If you consider what I say to be ill intentioned or evil, let us hear what you would have us do instead.

I say to you that if the counsel that Bhishma and I have given is not heeded, it will not take long before the very race of Kuru is annihilated.'"

CANTO 207

VIDURAGAMANA PARVA CONTINUED

Vaisampayana said, "After Drona finishes, Vidura speaks. He says, 'Dhritarashtra, King, I have no doubt that what your friends say is for your good. Yet, I fear you do not like to listen to what they tell you and their wise words fall on deaf ears. What that greatest among all the Kurus, Shantanu's son Bhishma says is sagacious, excellent and will benefit you. But you do not listen to him. What Acharya Drona says is for your good, but Radha's son Karna does not seem to think so.

Yet, my lord, after deep thought I myself can think of no one who is a truer or wiser friend of yours than these two lions among men, old in years, in wisdom, and in learning, and always looking at you and at the sons of Pandu with equal eyes.

I have no doubt, O Bhaarata, that these two great ones are both no less than Dasaratha's son Rama or the great Gaya in their honesty and virtue. Have they ever given you evil counsel before? And you too, O King, have never done them any injury. Then why should these

Purusharishabhas, who never have truck with falsehood, now advise you falsely, especially since you have not harmed them ever?

My lord, these great and wise men will never give you evil counsel. They cannot be tempted by any wealth to offer you false advice, for they are both knowers of dharma. Everything they have said, O Bhaarata, is for your good and in your best interest.

Be certain, my lord, that the Pandavas are as much your sons as Duryodhana and his brothers. Those that urge you to harm the sons of Pandu do not have your interest at heart. If you nurture partiality for your sons in your heart, they that seek to bring it out do you no favour.

O King, these illustrious ones, these two splendid elders, have not said a false or evil word. Yet, you do not seem to realise it. What these Narapumgavas say about the Pandavas being invincible is the simple truth. Purushavyaghra, O tiger among men, do not deceive yourself for a moment that it is otherwise.

A blessing be upon you, my lord! Can even Maghavat vanquish Pandu's brilliant son Arjuna, who looses his arrows with both hands with equal ease and force? Can the Devas subdue Bhimasena, strong as ten thousand elephants in battle? Which man who values his life would dare face the twins, who are Yama's very sons, in war? And how can the eldest, in whom patience, mercy, forgiveness, truth and might all find their home, be overcome?

They that have Rama for their ally, Janardana Krishna for their mentor, and the dashing Satyaki for their friend have already vanquished all their enemies in battle. Drupada is their father-in-law; Drupada's sons, Dhristadyumna and the others born into Prihasta's race are their brothers-in-law: they are invincible, my lord.

Remember all this, Duryodhana, and that their right to the kingdom is before yours. Dhritarashtra, treat them justly. Already your name is tainted by Purochana's crime. Be kind and noble now to Pandu's sons and wash that stain from yourself. If you behave righteously and mercifully towards the sons of Pandu, what you do will bring great punya down upon us all, powerful blessings that will protect everyone who belongs to the race of Kuru, why, it will nurture all Kshatriya kind.

Once we fought against Drupada. If we can now make him our ally how much stronger we shall become. My lord, the Dasarhas are numerous and formidable; all of them will go where Krishna does. Also, know that where Krishna is, victory will certainly go. Dhritarashtra, only a man who has been cursed by the Gods would seek war when he can achieve his purpose and serve his best interest by conciliation.

The people have heard that the Pandavas are alive, and they rejoice and are beside themselves to see their princes again. My lord, you must do as your people want.

Duryodhana, Karna and Subala's son Sakuni are untutored in dharma; they are brash and sinful. Do not listen to them, I beg you. Virtuous as you are, O King, think back to what I said to you many years ago, that because of the terrible sins that would be committed by your son Duryodhana, the very House of Kuru and the people of this kingdom shall perish!'"

CANTO 208

VIDURAGAMANA PARVA CONTINUED

Vaisampayana said, "When they have all finished speaking, Dhritarashtra says, 'Shantanu's son, the great Bhishma, the illustrious Rishi Drona, and you, my brother Vidura, have indeed spoken truly and given me the counsel that is in my best interest.

By dharma, as Kunti's sons, the Maharathas, are the sons of Pandu and they are my sons, also. And just as my sons should inherit this kingdom, so, too, must the Pandavas. So, hurry, my brother, go and fetch Pandu's princes and their mother home; persuade them affectionately and kindly.

Bhaarata, also bring Krishnaa, whose beauty is not of this world, here. Ah, it is such fortune that Pritha's sons are still alive and greater fortune that the Maharathas have made Drupada's peerless daughter their wife. Surely, we have become stronger than ever before with this alliance, and it also our good fortune from which the vile Purochana died.

My resplendent Vidura, fortune has slain my grief and ended my mourning for my brother's sons.'

At Dhritarashtra's command, a joyful Vidura goes to Drupada Yagnasena and the Pandavas. Bhaarata, he takes a fair treasure of gold and ornaments and priceless jewels for Draupadi, the princes, and for Drupada, as well. Arriving in Drupada's palace, Vidura, master of dharma, master of court etiquette, greets the king formally, properly and with honour; and Drupada, too, receives Vidura respectfully and both ask after each other's health with every kindness.

Then Vidura sees the Pandavas and with them Krishna of Dwaraka; embracing them in joy, tears in his eyes, he asks after their welfare. The Pandavas and Vaasudeva Krishna greet Vidura, of measureless intellect, with every reverence. As for Vidura, he is overcome, O King, and repeatedly asks his nephews how they are, and says that their uncle Dhritarashtra also asks warmly about them.

Now he gives the Pandavas, Kunti and Draupadi, and Drupada and that king's sons all the priceless gifts that he has brought from Hastinapura, from Dhritarashtra and the Kauravas.

This done, the humble, soft-spoken Vidura speaks to the good King Drupada, in the presence of Kesava Krishna and the sons of Pandu. Vidura, of profound intelligence, says, 'Great King, listen to what I have to say, you, your sons and ministers, as well.

Overjoyed by this new alliance with you, my brother King Dhritarashtra repeatedly inquires after your welfare, and so do his sons and his ministers. Rajan, Bhishma the wise, son of Santanu, Drona, also of deep wisdom, the son of Bharadwaja and your dear friend, and also all the other Kurus ask after your welfare, in every particular.

The learned Drona says that he embraces you in his mind and hopes that you are well in every way. Lord of the Panchalas, let me say again that Dhritarashtra and all the Kurus consider themselves greatly fortunate and blessed by this alliance with you. Yagnasena, they are more happy than they would be upon acquiring a whole new kingdom! Now that you know all this, I beg you, allow the sons of Pandu to return to their home, the kingdom of their fathers.

Every Kuru is agog to see the princes again. These Narapumgavas have been away from Hastinapura for so long; I am sure that their mother and they must be as eager to see Hastinapura again as the people of the city are to see them. Also, all the royal Kuru ladies and the people are beside themselves to see the Panchala princess, the exquisite Krishnaa.

O King, I ask your leave for the Pandavas to return to Hastinapura with their wife. If you give your leave, I will send word back to Dhritarashtra through my swiftest messengers. Then, O Drupada, the sons of Pandu can set out with Kunti and Krishnaa.'"

CANTO 209

VIDURAGAMANA PARVA CONTINUED

Vaisampayana said, "Drupada listens carefully to what Vidura says, then he replies, 'Wise Vidura, everything is as you say and I, too, am greatly pleased by our alliance. I agree with you that it is only just that these splendid princes return to Hastinapura. However, it is not for me to force a decision upon them.

If Kunti's valiant sons Yudhishtira, Bhima and Arjuna, as well as the Purusharishabhas, the twins, wish to return to the home of their fathers, if Baladeva and Krishna, both of whom know every nuance of dharma, are of the same mind, then by all means let Pandu's sons return to Hastinapura. For, I do declare that the Purushavyaghras, Rama and Krishna, always have the best interest of the Pandavas at heart and always do their best for them.'

Now Yudhishtira says, 'O King, my brothers and I are your dependants and we will happily do what you tell us.'

Then Krishna says, 'I feel that the Pandavas should return, but we must do whatever Drupada decides, for he knows every aspect of dharma.'

Drupada says at once, 'I agree with what this greatest of all men feels. Pandu's great sons are now to me just as they are to Kunti, and I know that not Kunti's son Yudhishtira himself can decide what is good for himself and his brothers as well as this tiger among men, Kesava, can.'

Thus, with Drupada's leave, O King, the Pandavas set out with Draupadi and Kunti, with Krishna and Vidura for the city named after the elephant. On their leisurely way, they stop in many places of great beauty or sanctity, and take their pleasure as they please.

When Dhritarashtra hears that those shuras are nearing his capital, he sends the Kauravas out to receive them. O Bhaarata, Vikarna of the great bow he sends, as he does Chitrasena, Drona, greatest of warriors, and Kripa of the line of Gautama. Those five mighty heroes enter Hastinapura majestically, surrounded by these and others, all of whom enhance their glory.

Indeed, the entire city is radiant with the celebrant crowds that throng its streets to see the tigerish sons of Pandu return to them, and how they rejoice. All along their slow and triumphal progress towards the palace the Pandavas hear cries of affection from the people, who truly love their great and precious princes.

Some say, 'The Purushavyaghra of dharma who looks after us as if we are his nearest kin, has returned to us!'

Others cry, 'Ah, it is as if Pandu has come home from the forest today, bringing our lost fortune back with him! For sure he comes to do us great good.'

'What good remains to be done to us when Kunti's heroic sons have returned to our city? If we have given daana, poured libations of ghee into the holy fire, if we have any punya, may the sons of Pandu remain in Hastinapura for a hundred years!'

Finally, the Pandavas arrive at the palace and prostrate at the feet of Dhritarashtra and of Bhishma. They touch the feet of everyone else present who are elders and worthy of worship. They ask, individually, after the welfare of everyone there. When all this is done, at Dhritarashtra's command, they enter the apartments that have been kept for them.

When the sons of Pandu have rested, King Dhritarashtra and Shantanu's son Bhishma summon them to the royal sabha, the ancient court of Hastinapura.

Dhritarashtra says to Yudhishtira, 'Kaunteya, listen to what I have to say, your brothers and you. I want you to go to Khandavaprastha, so that never again does any dispute arise between your cousin and yourselves. If you live there, no one can or will do you any harm. Take half of the kingdom and, protected by Arjuna as the Devas are by the Vajra, live in peace in Khandavaprastha.'

The Pandavas accept what Dhritarashtra says, and paying him homage, those bulls among men set out from Hastinapura for Khandavaprastha, which is a desolate wilderness.

Arriving in that desert, those brilliant shuras, with Krishna at their head, create a new city in the desolation, truly like another Swarga on Bhumi. Dwaipayana helps the Maharathas choose an auspicious place; he performs the sacred rituals and measures out the land for their city.

When it has been built, some say by Indra's command to Viswakarman, the divine artisan, and at Krishna asking for Indra's help, that city has a moat encircling it, which is as wide as a sea. It has outer walls that touch the sky, walls white as rainless clouds or rays of the moon. Ah, the newly made city is as wondrous as Bhogavati in Patala, where the great Nagas dwell.

Palatial mansions it has; many gates lead into it, gates as great and wide as the outspread wings of Garuda, gates that are as formidable as massed thunderheads, and as lofty as the Mandara Mountains. So great are the walls and so well stocked with myriad weapons that no enemy army could even dream of ever breaching them or making any impression on them with any astras.

Those walls and gates are armed with thick banks of arrows and other missiles, narachas like twin-tongued serpents. The turrets along the walls are bursting with mighty warriors in superb condition and training; soldiers past counting line the entire length of those city walls.

Deadly sharp hooks, satagnis that can raze a hundred enemies in a blink, and other machines of war are planted upon those walls. Great iron wheels, which can be whirled down upon the legions of any invader also deck those ramparts. Yes, truly, with all these and more is that best of cities protected.

Within the walls, the streets are wide and excellently laid, so there is never any fear of accidents or collisions along their courses. And as numerous and so magnificent are the homes and mansions of the city of the Pandavas that it truly looks like another Amaravati on Earth, and some say that is why it is named Indraprastha.

In the most choice and auspicious precinct of Indraprastha, Viswakarman creates a majestic palace for the sons of Pandu. It is filled with every kind of treasure, and is so opulent that it is like the palace of Kubera, Lord of Heaven's Treasures, himself. Ah, it is like a great mass of cloud shot through with lightning.

O King, when the city has been built, a host of Brahmanas arrives there, all of them masters of the Vedas, and begin living in Indraprastha. Vaisyas from across the length and breadth of Bharatavarsha come to Indraprastha, and thrive in trade and earn great wealth in the city of fortune. Artists, the finest and of every kind, flock to Indraprastha, and begin living there.

Around the city are many enchanting gardens, with countless fruit- and flowering-trees – amras, amaratakas, kadambas, asokas, champakas, punnagas, nagas, kakuchas, panasas, salas, tola palms, tamalas, bakulas, ketakas with their fragrant blossom-loads. Great, gorgeous amalakas bend their branches down with the weight of their fruit; lodhras and akolas in bloom; jambus, pastalas, kunjakas, atimuktas, karaviras, parijatas, and many others all stand resplendent with flower and shining fruit, alive with birds and small creatures of every feather and species.

The green vanas ring with the cry of the excited peacock and the kokila in love. Myriad pleasure-houses, bright like mirrors, dot these woods and gardens, as do fine bowers of creepers, charming man-made hillocks, and of course crystalline pools and lakes brimful with water.

There are sparkling tanks perfumed by lotuses and lilies, jewelled with ducks, swans and chakravakas. The smaller pools are overgrown with water-plants, rare and exotic, and there are large ones, too, also of great beauty.

Rajan, the Pandavas live in that blessed, auspicious kingdom, peopled by pious men of dharma, and their joy waxes day by day.

And so it is that, because of the dharma shown them by Bhishma and also King Dhritarashtra, the sons of Pandu begin living in Khandavaprastha. With those five brothers living in it, each one equal to Indra himself, that best of cities truly resembles Bhogavati in Patala, the fabulous city of the Nagas.

O King, when he sees the Pandavas settled into Indraprastha, Krishna the magnificent takes their leave and returns with Rama to Dwaraka."

CANTO 210

RAJYA-LABHA PARVA

Janamejaya said, "O you possessed of ascetic wealth, what did those Mahatmans, my grandsires the Pandavas do when they had the kingdom of Indraprastha? How did their wife Draupadi serve and obey them all? Having one wife, Krishnaa, how is it that no dissension arose among those great Kshatriyas? O you of the wealth of asceticism, tell me in detail about how they are amongst themselves, after they marry Krishnaa."

Vaisampayana said, "Having gained their kingdom at the command of Dhritarashtra, those parantapas, the Pandavas, pass their days in great joy in Khandavaprastha, with Krishnaa. With his brothers beside him, Yudhishtira of tejas, always abiding by dharma, rules that kingdom. The sons of Pandu, endowed with wisdom, devoted to truth and virtue, and having vanquished their enemies, live there happily.

Sitting upon invaluable thrones, the Purusharishabhas discharge the duties of state. One day, as they sit together in their royal sabha, the Devarishi Narada, on his eternal wandering, comes to them. When he sees the Sage, Yudhishtira rises and offers him his own throne. When the Maharishi sits, Yudhishitra offers him arghya with his own hands, and the king formally tells Narada Muni about the state of his kingdom.

The Sage takes the offerings and is pleased. Showering his blessings on Yudhishtira, Narada asks him to sit beside him. The king sits and then sends word to the antahpura to Krishnaa, to inform her of the arrival of the illumined one.

Bathing, putting on fresh clothes, Draupadi comes reverently into the sabha where the Rishi is with the Pandavas. The chaste princess of Panchala worships the Sage's feet, and then stands before him with folded hands, her head bowed and her face veiled.

Narada blesses her many times with a variety of blessings, and then tells her that she may leave. When Krishnaa has gone, the Rishi speaks privately to just Yudhishtira and his brothers.

Narada says, 'The princess of Panchala is the wife of all of you. You must create a law among yourselves, so that disunity never rears its head amongst you. Once, there lived two Asura brothers called Sunda and Upasunda, famed through the three worlds, and so mighty that none could kill them unless they slew each other.

They ruled the same kingdom, lived in the same house, slept on the same bed, sat on the same throne, and ate out of the same plate. Yet, they killed each other for the sake of Tilottama. So, Yudhishtira, have a care to preserve your love for one another by making a rule for yourselves, which will keep you united forever.'

Yudhishtira asks, 'Mahamuni, whose sons were the Asuras Sunda and Upasunda? How did they fall out, and how did they kill each other? Whose daughter was this Tilottama for whose love the brothers killed each other? Was she an Apsara or the daughter of some Deva? O you whose wealth is tapasya, we want, O Brahmana, to hear everything that happened in detail. Indeed, we are agog to hear this story.'"

CANTO 211

Rajya-labha Parva Continued

Vaisampayana said, "To what Yudhishtira asks, Narada replies, 'Son of Pritha, listen, you and your brothers, to this olden tale; I will tell you everything exactly as it happened.

In ancient days, a mighty Daitya called Nikumbha, of untold strength and vigour, was born into the race of the great Asura Hiranyakashyipu. Sunda and Upasunda were the sons of Nikumbha, both awesomely powerful Asuras. Fierce were those brothers and their hearts evil.

They were as close as could be, sharing every resolve, striving together to achieve their common ends. They shared equally in each other's joy and woe. They were always together, and always spoke lovingly and pleasingly to each other. They were alike in every way, and truly seemed like one individual divided in two.

Slowly, they grew to manhood, and they had the same purpose – to conquer the three worlds. After being duly initiated, they went to the Vindhya Mountain and performed intense tapasya. Long they sat in penance, until, emaciated by hunger and thirst, their hair tangled in jata upon their heads and wearing valkala, treebark, they finally attained the ascetic power they wanted.

They had smeared themselves with dirt from head to foot, lived on just the air they breathed, stood on their toes, and from time to time cut off and threw pieces of their flesh into the sacred fire. Their arms were upraised, and their eyes stared unwinkingly at one spot, and long they stood thus, keeping their terrible vows unflinchingly.

While they performed tapasya, something marvellous happened – the Vindhya Mountain, at being heated by their rigours for so long, began to exude geysers of steam, from every slope and peak. The Devas watched the Asuras' great tapasya and were alarmed. They sought to obstruct the penance of the brothers with all sorts of interruptions.

Repeatedly, the gods tempted the Daityas, with the most enticing treasures and with the loveliest women. The brothers did not break their penance. The Devas now used their powers of maya, of creating illusions, on the brothers. The Asuras' sisters, mothers, wives, and other kinswomen, their hair, clothes and ornaments in disarray and askew, seemed to run towards them in terror, pursued and often struck by a Rakshasa wielding a long spear.

The women cried out to Sunda and Upasunda, "Save us! Save us!"

To no avail, for the brothers did not stir from their rigid postures of penance; and the mayic women and the Rakshasa vanished.

At last, the Pitamaha Brahma, the Lord who seeks the weal of all his creatures, appeared before the great Asuras and told them to ask for whatever boon they wanted. Now the mighty Sunda and Upasunda rose and stood with folded hands before the Grandsire of the worlds.

Together, they said to the God, "Pitamaha, if you are pleased with our tapasya and would grant us a boon, give us knowledge of all the astras and mahamayas, and power over them all. Give us enormous strength, and the power to assume any form and shape we wish. Finally, Lord, let us also be immortal."

Brahma says, "You will have all that you have asked for, but not unconditional immortality. Name any one way in which you can be slain, be it not so unlikely that you do indeed become equal to the Devas. Because you have performed your tapasya purely from desire for sovereignty I cannot grant you immortality. You did your great penance to subdue the three worlds, and for that, mighty Daityas, I cannot make you immortal."

Sunda and Upasunda said, "Then, Pitamaha, let no creature or creation of yours, mobile or unmoving, be able to kill us but just we ourselves, one the other. Let us fear no one but each other!"

Brahma said, "I grant everything that you have asked, and this last boon as well."

With that, the Pitamaha made them stop their penance and returned to Brahmaloka. With Brahma's boons, the Daitya brothers became invincible, and they returned to their home. Their friends and kinsfolk saw those matchlessly intelligent Asuras, resplendent with the boons they now had, and rejoiced.

Now Sunda and Upasunda sheared away their matted jata and wore golden crowns on their heads. Clad in priceless garments and wearing the richest ornaments, they were incomparably handsome. Why, the Moon rose full, nightly over their city, even when it was not his season to do so.

Abandoned and joyous celebrations erupted, with great feasts, flowing wine, with singing and dancing, and lavish entertaining in every home. One could hear loud revelry, with ringing laughter and the happy clapping of hands echoing throughout the city of the Daityas. Of course, they could take any form they chose at will, and indulged in every manner of sport and gaiety, never noticing the passage of time; why, a whole year passed like a day,' says Narada Muni in Indraprastha."

CANTO 212

Rajya-lahba Parva Continued

Vaisampayana said, "Narada continues, 'When that great and prolonged celebration ended, the brothers Sunda and Upasunda called a council of their greatest commanders, kinsmen and advisors, and then ordered their legions to be raised, for they wanted now to conquer the three worlds and have lordship over them.

With the assent of their friends and relatives, of the great Daitya elders, and of their ministers of state, the brothers performed the initiatory rituals of departure and sallied forth at night, when the constellation Magha was rising. They went with a teeming force of Daityas, wearing mail, armed with maces, battle-axes, lances and cudgels.

With joy in their hearts, the Daitya shuras set out with the charana bards chanting auspicious hymns that foretold their future triumphs. Ferocious and savage in battle, the brothers, who could go anywhere at will, flew straight up into the sky and arrived in Devaloka. When the Devas, who knew about all the boons that Brahma had granted them, learnt of their advent, they fled their realm and sought refuge in Brahmaloka.

The fierce and tameless Asura heroes quickly subdued the world of Indra, and vanquishing and killing myriad clans of Yakshas and Rakshasas, and indeed every creature that ranged the sky, they came away from on high. Next those Maharathas plunged down into the Patalas and quelled the Nagas of the under-worlds. Then they tamed all the races of the Ocean, and then all the Mlechcha tribes.

Now they wanted to conquer Bhumi, all the Earth. The inexorable brothers mustered their fell legions and issued this dire command:

"Brahmanas and Rajarishis, who make offerings of ghee and havis at Mahayagnas, swell the power and energy of the Devas, and their prosperity too. Those who perform these sacrifices are the enemies of the Asuras. So let us all band together and kill them all, wipe them from the face of the Earth!"

With that savage, ringing command to their legions swarming upon the eastern shore of the Great Ocean, the Asura brothers struck out in every direction with their terminal resolve. Anywhere they saw a yagna being performed, they instantly slew those engaged in the sacrifice and the Brahmanas who sat over them. The Asura brothers slaughtered them brutally and flew on again to their next quarry and prey.

Meanwhile, their soldiers doused the sacrificial fires in the asramas of Maharishis, great men who were masters of their souls. However, the fiery curses of those Sages did not affect the Asura brothers in the least, for Brahma's boon protected them.

When the Brahmanas saw that their curses had about as much effect as arrows shot at rocks, they scattered and fled in every direction, abandoning their yagnas and their vratas. Even the greatest Rishis on Earth, perfect masters of their emotions, men absorbed in samadhi, ran in terror from the Daitya brothers, as serpents do at the approach of Vinata's son Garuda.

The Asuras overran and trampled the holy hermitages. The sacrificial urns were smashed and their sacred contents rudely scattered on the ground. The universe appeared empty, as if a Mahapralaya had come and swept away all its creatures.

Rajan, when the Rishis all made themselves scarce or invisible, the two dreadful Asuras began to assume many different forms, for they were bent upon slaughtering the Sages. They became rut-maddened bull elephants, their temples cracked from a surfeit of, and oozing, the wild juice of musth; the demon pair rooted out the holy ones from caves in which they had hidden and despatched them to the land of Yama.

At times, Sunda and Upasunda would become lions, then tigers, then they would vanish – with all these, and other means, too, the violent twain hunted the Sages and massacred them. Brahmanas and Kshatriyas were extirpated, and sacrifices and study of the Veda ceased in the world. The Earth became devoid of yagnas and every holy rite and festival.

The people were terror-stricken, and screamed and wailed; all trade ceased, no one bought or sold anything anymore. The Earth was without religious rite and ceremony, and no marriages took place. Farming went to seed and nobody tended to their cows anymore.

Strewn everywhere with skeletons and bones, Bhumi assumed a dreadful visage. No sraddhas were performed for the Pitrs; nowhere was the holy sound of Vashat to be heard: all sacred observances fell into desuetude. The Earth became a fearsome spectacle, and Surya and Chandra, the Navagrahas, the Nakshatras, the Mandalas and all those that dwelt in the heavens watched the atrocities of Sunda and Upasunda; and they grieved much.

However, having violently subdued the three worlds, the Asura brothers began living in Kurukshetra, and nowhere had they any rival,' Narada says."

CANTO 213

Rajya-labha Parva Continued

"Narada continues, 'The Devarishis, the Siddhas, the Mahatmans of sthitaprajna, all watched the universal slaughter perpetrated by the Daitya brothers, and they mourned deeply. Their passions, senses and minds perfectly controlled, they went to Brahmaloka, for they were stirred by mercy for the universe.

Arriving, they saw the Pitamaha upon his throne, surrounded by the Devas, the Siddhas and Brahmarishis. Mahadeva, God of gods, was there, as were Agni, Vayu, Soma, Surya, Indra, all the Rishis that live absorbed in the dhyana of the Parabrahman: the Vaikhanasas, the Balakhilyas, the Vanaprasthas, Marichipas, Ajas, Avimudhas and other Yogins of immense tejas.

All those Rishis sat around the Pitamaha, when the Devarishis and the other visitors came sadly to complain to Brahma about the relentless savagery of Sunda and Upasunda. In gory detail, they described everything that the Asuras had done, how they had done it, and in what order. All of them implored the Creator that He must put an end to the Asuras' unholy reign of terror.

Brahma listened to everything that they said, and thought for a mere moment before deciding what he would do to destroy the Asura brothers. Summoning Viswakarman to him, the Pitamaha of absolute Brahmattva said to the divine artisan, "Create a woman who can enchant every heart."

Bowing down to Brahma, receiving that command reverently, the great artificer of the universe carefully created an Apsara. First, he gathered individually every exquisite feature of that celestial nymph. Those shone like a mass of jewels. When he had put her together with his divine art, she was the most beautiful woman in the three worlds.

There was no minute part of her, not the smallest portion, which was not so lovely that it could instantly fascinate anyone that looked upon her. She was like Sri herself; she stole the hearts of every creature whose gaze fell on her even for a moment.

Because she had been fashioned with the highest essences of every gemstone in existence, used in minuscule measure, Brahma named her Tilottama. As soon as the Pitama breathed life into her, she bowed low to Brahma, and with folded hands, said, "Lord of all creatures, why have I been created, what task do you want me to accomplish?"

The Grandsire answered her, "Tilottama, go to the Asuras Sunda and Upasunda. O Susheela, seduce them with your peerless beauty. Apsara, then do what you must to make the brothers fall out amongst each other, whenever they look at you."

She bowed to the Pitamaha, saying, "Tathaastu! So be it."

Then she walked in pradakshina around that divine congregation. Brahma sat facing the east, as did Mahadeva also; the Devas all faced north, and the Rishis in every direction.

As Tilottama walked around the gathering of the celestial ones, only Indra and Sthanu Mahadeva remained still. Yet, Mahadeva was also so intent on watching Tilottama as she circled around the assembly of Gods and Sages, that when she was at his side, he sprouted a second radiant face on the southern side of his body, and it was like a full-blown lotus. When she was behind him, another face appeared on the western side of the Great God; when she had crossed to his left a fourth face appeared, on his northern side.

Indra grew a thousand eyes, all large and reddish, all over his body. So it is that Sthanu came to have four faces and Sakra, the slayer of Bala, a thousand eyes. As for the rest of the Devas and the Rishis, they all turned their heads to watch Tilottama's progress, as she walked around them. Apart from Brahma, they all gazed avidly at Tilottama's body, and when she set out for the city of the Asura brothers, taking the shining wealth of her beauty, all of them felt certain that their purpose was as good as achieved.

When Tilottama had left, Brahma, First Cause of the Universe, sent away the Devas and Rishis,' Narada says."

CANTO 214

Rajya-labha Parva Continued

Vaisampayana said, "Narada continues, 'Meanwhile, the Daitya brothers had quelled the Earth and ruled without any rival. The tiredness of their exertions left them, and having the triloka under their sway, they felt they had nothing more to accomplish. They had brought home as spoils the greatest treasures of the Devas, Gandharvas, Yakshas, Nagas, Rakshasas and Kshatriyas and they began to live in sumptuous luxury and untold pleasure.

They had no fear of any enemy, and they lived in perpetual enjoyment, even as the Devas do. They gave themselves up to every kind of pleasure – indulging themselves in women, the finest perfumes, garlands, wine, rare delicacies of the table, and in every other conceivable object of desire.

In mansions, fine woods, great gardens, on hills and in forests, wherever they liked the brothers spent their time at pleasure, like the immortals. One day they went to please themselves to a tableland of the Vindhya Mountain. It was a place of rock, smooth and flat, with flowering trees growing all around. When they had indulged in everything they cared to, the brothers sat upon a fine throne, joyful and surrounded by handsome women. Music played, and the women danced for the brothers and sang countless sweet songs praising the indomitable pair.

Just then, wearing a single piece of red silk, which hid none of her charms, Tilottama arrived there, plucking wildflowers on her way. Slowly, she wended her way to where the brothers sat. The Asuras had drunk copiously, and with one look at the Apsara of unearthly beauty, were smitten.

Getting up quickly, they rushed to her: both stirred by lust, each wanted her for himself. Sunda seized her of the fair face by her right hand, and Upasunda by her left. Intoxicated with the assurance of their boons, with their strength, unhinged with all the power and wealth taken from every quarter, and with all the wine they had drunk, maddened by all these, and most of all maddened by lust, they knit their brows and spoke angrily to each other, for the first time.

"She is my wife and your superior," growled Sunda.

"She is my wife and your sister-in-law," retorted Upasunda.

Each said to the other, "She is mine, not yours!"

Quickly anger seized them. Mad for her beauty, they forgot their deep love for each other. Losing their reason from lust, they seized up their dreadful maces. Each roared, "I was first!" and they struck each other at the identical moment, each a thunderous blow.

Those savage Asuras fell on the ground, their bodies bathed in blood; they were like two Suns fallen from the sky.

Seeing this, all the other Asuras there and the women fled trembling and shrieking, in grief and in terror, and plunged down into the Patalas. Now the taintless Brahma came to that place, with him the Devas and the Maharishis. The glorious Pitamaha acclaimed what Tilottama had done and granted her a boon.

Before she could speak, he said, "Lovely one, you will range the realm of the Adityas, and so brilliant shall you be that no one will be able to look at you for long."

With that, the Grandsire of all the living returned sovereignty of the worlds to Indra and the others, and went back to Brahmaloka. So it was that the Asura brothers, always united before, killed each other in anger over Tilottama. So Bharatottamas, out of my affection for you, I say to you that, if you wish to do something to please me, have a care to make the most meticulous arrangement amongst yourselves, so that you five never fall out over Draupadi.'

The Pandavas take counsel among themselves and then lay down an inviolable rule with regard to Draupadi, in the presence of the Devarishi of measureless tejas. The covenant they make is that if any of them intrudes upon the privacy of another brother when he is alone and intimate with Draupadi, the intruder would spend twelve years in exile in the forest, as a brahmacharin.

When the good Pandavas have established that law amongst them, the great Narada is pleased. Blessing them, he leaves their city and goes his way. Thus, O Janamejaya, Narada Muni persuades the Pandavas to create a law among them about how they would conduct themselves with their common wife.

Indeed, this is the reason that no dispute ever arose among them over the exquisite Panchali."

CANTO 215

ARJUNA-VANAVASA PARVA

Vaisampayana said, "Having established the new code, the Pandavas continue to live in Indraprastha. By the might of their arms they bring countless kings under their sway. Krishnaa becomes the loving and obedient wife of all five sons of Pritha, those lions among men, of incomparable energy.

She is like the River Saraswati delighting in the great elephants that bathe in her – they repeatedly take their pleasure in her, and she from them. The sons of Pandu are men of exceptional dharma, and consequently, all the race of Kurus are sinless, happy and prosperous.

Then, when some time has elapsed, one day, some robbers lift the cattle of a Brahmana of that realm. As the thieves make away with his herd, the Brahmana, beside himself with anger, comes to Khandavaprastha and begins to berate the Pandavas in stricken tones.

The Brahmana cries, 'Pandavas, in your very kingdom, my kine are even now being lifted by vile brigands. Give chase to them. Alas, wretched crows are going to eat the sacrificial ghee of a peaceful Brahmana. The

Rishis have said that a king who takes a sixth part of the produce of his kingdom but does not protect his subjects is the greatest sinner in the world. A Brahmana's wealth is being stolen by thieves. Dharma itself is being injured. Ah, take my hand and help me, Pandavas, for I am plunged in grief!'

Kunti's son Arjuna hears the Brahmana sobbing bitterly and railing. At once, he reassures the man, 'Do not fear.'

However, at that time, Yudhishtira Dharmaputra is alone with Krishnaa in the chamber in which the Pandavas keep their weapons. So, though the Brahmana continues to wail and to beg him, Arjuna cannot go with him for he cannot intrude upon his brother's privacy.

The Brahmana sobs on, and moved to pity, Arjuna decides that he must wipe the innocent man's tears. He thinks, 'The Brahmana has come to our gates and weeps without let. If I do not help him, my apathy will bring sin upon the king. Our adharma will be spoken of throughout the kingdom and we will all find great sin for ourselves.

Yet, if I enter the room I will certainly insult my brother; also, I will have to serve a twelve years' exile in the wilderness. But now, I must not let that stop me from helping the Brahmana, not if I have to go into the jungle and die there. Dharma is higher than the body and it lives on after the body dies.'

Arriving at this resolve, Arjuna Dhananjaya enters the private chamber and speaks softly to Yudhishtira. He emerges with his bow and quiver, and says cheerfully to the Brahmana, 'Let us hurry, Brahmana, so the thieves do not escape. I will come with you and restore your herd to you.'

Armed with his bow, which the perfectly ambidextrous Arjuna uses with either hand with equal skill, wearing mail and riding his war-chariot that flies his standard, Arjuna gives chase to the cattle thieves. His arrows fly at them in a storm, and they instantly abandon the cattle and flee for their lives through the forest.

Arjuna brings the herd to the Brahmana, now beside himself with gratitude, and having won great fame, the Pandava returns to his city.

He pays homage to all the elders there, is applauded by everyone present, and finally comes before Yudhishtira.

Arjuna says to his elder brother, 'My lord, allow me to keep the vow that I swore. I saw you alone with Draupadi and I have broken the law we made for ourselves. I must go into exile in the jungle, for that is the covenant we swore.'

Suddenly hearing this, Yudhishtira is stricken and cries agitatedly, 'Why?'

He falls quiet for a while, then says sadly to Arjuna of the curly hair, who never swerves even by a hair's width from his vows, 'Anagha, sinless, if you consider me an authority worthy of your respect, then listen to what I have to say. Shura, I know why you came into my chamber and thereby did what you think of as being distasteful to me. But you did not displease me in the least.

A younger brother may always, without fault, go into the room where his older brother is with his wife. It is only the elder brother who causes offence by entering a room where the younger brother is alone with his wife. Mahabaho, so you must not think of going into exile. Do as I say, your dharma has not suffered in the least. You have not disrespected me at all.'

Arjuna replies, 'I have heard, even from you, one should not split hairs in discharging dharma. Truth is my weapon.'

Then, with Yudhishtira's leave, Arjuna prepares to go into exile in the forest, for twelve years."

CANTO 216

ARJUNA-VANAVASA PARVA CONTINUED

Vaisampayana said, "When Arjuna Mahabaho, who spread the renown of the race of Kuru throughout the world, sets out, Brahmanas who know the Vedas and the Vedangas, and are devoted to contemplating the Parabrahman, follow that great hero. Skilled musicians, many pious Devabhakta ascetics, masterly Pauranikas, and other narrators of sacred lore, all Brahmacharins, Vanaprasthas, other Brahmanas who told celestial Itihasas in mellifluous voices, and many other devotees, too, gifted bards from different varnas, go with Arjuna, and he journeys like Indra being followed by the Maruts.

O Bhaarata, the Bharatarishabha travels through many pristine and enchanted forests, pausing beside sparkling lakes, gushing rivers, endless seas, passing through several countries and kingdoms. Finally, he arrives at the source of the Ganga and feels that he will settle there for some time.

Listen, O Janamejaya, to something wonderful that happens while Arjuna lives there. In that holy place, Kunti's son and the Brahmanas who have gone with him perform countless Agnihotras, sacrifices of the sacred fire. O Rajan, because those devout, illumined and learned Brahmanas, who never leave the path of dharma, daily worship beside the holy river, because of their lighting their sacrificial fires with mantras, after bathing, because of the oblations of ghee they pour into the fires, the flowers they offer before the flames, that entire place for yojanas around blooms and becomes lustrous in every way and full of grace.

One morning, that Pandava bull goes as usual to the Ganga to perform his ritual ablutions. When he has finished, and has offered tarpana to his dead Pitrs, he is wading out from the water, when, suddenly, the Naga princess Ulupi, moved by Kama Deva, drags Arjuna down to the bed of the river, and indeed below it.

Under the riverbed, Arjuna finds himself borne helplessly into the wondrous palace of the Naga King Kauravya. There he sees a fire of sacrifice already lit for him to worship. Arjuna performs his daily rites with deep bhakti, and seeing how calmly and fearlessly that hero offers his worship into the Fire God's manifest flames, in the alien place, Agni is pleased with Arjuna.

When he has finished worshipping the sacred fire, Kunti's son sees the daughter of the Naga king, and says to her with a smile, 'Lovely one, what is this rashness you have committed? Bashful one, to whom does this beautiful realm belong? Who are you, whose daughter?'

Ulupi replies, 'There is a Naga called Kauravya born into the line of Airavata. O Kshatriya, I am Kauravya's daughter and my name is Ulupi. Purushavyagra, I saw you bathing in the river and Kama Deva pierced me with desire which snatched away my reason. Anagha, sinless one, I am not married and Kama torments me with love for you. Scion of the Kurus, give yourself to me today, gratify my desire.'

Arjuna replies, 'Susheela, gentle one, fettered by the command of King Yudhishtira, I have sworn to be a brahmacharin for twelve years and I am not free to do as I please. But, water ranger, I am still willing to please you if at all I can. I have never told a lie in my life. Naga

Kanya, tell me how I can do as you want and still not break my dharma or be guilty of lying.'

Ulupi answers him, 'O Pandava, I know why you are wandering the Earth and why your elder brother has told you to be a brahmacharin. Yes, this is the pact you made amongst yourselves, that he who goes into a room where his brother is alone with Draupadi must live in the forests as a brahmacharin for twelve years.

But your exile, Kshatriya, is only from Draupadi, and also your brahmacharya only with regard to her, and that dharma you are already discharging. By slaking my desire you will not break your dharma in the least. Besides, large eyes, it is also your dharma to assuage a woman in distress. By relieving my pang for you, what diminution will your dharma suffer?

Besides, Arjuna, even if your virtue does suffer some slight damage by satisfying my desire, you will find great punya for yourself by saving my life. Oh Partha, know me to be one that worships you, give yourself to me! My lord, the Rishis all say that a man must satisfy a woman who asks him to. If you do not come to me, be certain that I will take my life; so, Mahabaho, earn great punya by saving it.

Purushottama, I seek sanctuary in you. Kaunteya, you always protect those that are persecuted and masterless. Look, in tears I seek your comfort. I am full of desire, and I importune you. Do what I want you to; you must give yourself to me!'

Making dharma his motive, and the Naga princess is surely most desirable, Arjuna does all that she wants. The mighty Pandava spends that night in the palace of Kauravya, and with dawn the next day, he returns with Ulupi to the sacral pool of the Ganga, from where she flows down to the plains. The chaste Ulupi bids farewell to him there and returns to her under-world.

Bhaarata, before she goes she blesses Arjuna with a boon that he would be invincible in water, saying, 'You will be able to prevail over all creatures of the water and all creatures that dwell both in the water and on land.'"

CANTO 217

ARJUNA-VANAVASA PARVA CONTINUED

Vaisampayana said, "The son of the Vajradhari tells the Brahmanas what has happened and then sets out for the slopes of Himavat. He first comes to the place that is called Agastyavata, then continues and arrives at Vasishta's peak, from where Kunti's son goes on to the summit of Bhrigu.

Having purified himself with many rituals there, he ceremonially gives away thousands of cows and numberless homes to those Brahmanas and the others who have accompanied him; then, he goes on to the holy asrama calls Hiranyabindu. There, also, he performs ritual ablutions, and journeying, that Pandavottama sees many sacred places of unworldly beauty and sanctity. Finally, he comes down from the mountains, O Bhaarata, still accompanied by the Brahmanas, and that lord of men turns east, to see the realms that lay in that direction.

The Kurusthama sees many holy tirthas, one after the other. In the Naimisa vana, he is enchanted to look upon the river Utpalini, flowing with a denseness of lotuses, the Nanda, the Aparananda, the Kausiki of wide renown, and the mighty waters of Gaya and Ganga.

He bathes ritually in all those tirthas and gifts more cows to the Brahmanas. All the sacred fords in the lands of Vanga and Kalinga Arjuna visits, bathing in them all and giving away great wealth in solemn daana. Now, O Bhaarata, at the gates of the kingdom of Kalinga, all the Brahmanas who had followed Pandu's son, bid him farewell and turn back.

The valiant Dhananjaya, the son of Kunti, takes his leave of them and goes on towards the Ocean, just a very few servitors and companions going with him. The mighty warrior crosses the land of the Kalingas, and journeys on, passing through many kingdoms and countries, holy tirthas, seeing great and lovely cities and towns with their superb and varied mansions and palaces and homes.

He sees Mount Mahendra adorned with Rishis, and travels leisurely on, along the sea-shore, to Manipura. Having gazed upon all the sacred waters and other shrines and naves of worship in that realm, the Mahabaho son of Pandu finally comes into the palace of Chitravahana, king of Manipura.

This king has a remarkably beautiful daughter calls Chitrangada, and wandering through Chitravahana's palace, Arjuna sees her one day and he desires her. The Pandava goes to the king and says to him, 'Give your daughter to me, Rajan, I am a great Kshatriya's son.'

The king asks, 'Whose son are you?'

Arjuna replies, 'I am Dhananjaya, the son of Pandu and Kunti.'

Taking brief pause, Chitravahana says gently and sweetly to Arjuna, 'In our race, of old there was once a king calls Prabhanjana, who had no child. He performed a tapasya to have a child. Partha, he pleased Mahadeva, Umapati, God of gods, Paramatman, Pinakin, with the intensity of his penance.

The refulgent Lord blessed him that every scion of his line would have just a single child. Because of Siva's boon, one child is born into every generation of our royal House. All my ancestors each had a son, but I have only a daughter to continue our line. However, Bharatarishabha, I always look upon this daughter of mine as my son, and I have made her a Putrika.

If you marry her, one of the sons that you beget upon her must become the heir to my throne and the one to perpetuate my race. Bhaarata, that son is the dower for which I will give my daughter to you. Pandava, if you agree, you can take her on this condition.'

Arjuna agrees immediately, saying, 'Tathaastu, so be it.'

Making Chitravahana's daughter his wife, Kunti's son lives in that city for three years. Finally, Chitrangada gives birth to a fine son and Arjuna embraces the child lovingly. Then, taking his leave of Chitravahana, the Pandava sets out again on his wandering."

CANTO 218

Arjuna-vanavasa Parva Continued

Vaisampayana said, "Now, that Bharatarishabha journeys down to the holy southern Sea, her shore bejewelled with the Rishis that dwell there. Five great and holy rivers lie strewn in that realm, but the Sages shun all five. They are called the Agastya, Saubhadra, the most sacrosanct Pauloma, the greatly auspicious Karandhama, which yields the fruit of an Aswamedha yagna to those that bathe in her waters, and finally the Bharadwaja, ah, powerful washer of sins.

The Kurusthama sees the five rivers, and also that they are deserted, avoided by the hermits who live near them. With folded hands he asks those Rishis, 'Why O Sages, do the chanters of Brahman shun these holy waters?'

The Munis reply, 'Five great crocodiles live in the rivers and they devour any of us that dares bathe in them. That is why, Kurunandana, we do not go to the rivers.'

Arjuna Mahabaho hears this and says he will go closer to see the rivers. The ascetics try to prevent him, but he walks directly up to the bank of the great river Saubhadra, and the Parantapa plunges straight into her current. Immediately a huge crocodile seizes his leg in its jaws, but Dhananjeya Kaunteya seizes the crocodile in his mighty arms and drags it ashore.

No sooner has he hauled it onto land than the great lizard vanishes and a startlingly beautiful young woman, wearing unworldly ornaments and raiment, stands there in its place. O King, she is brilliant, her skin and her form shine!

Wonder-stricken, Arjuna asks her, in some joy, 'Lovely one, who are you? Why are you the water beast? What is your terrible sin?'

The beauty replies, 'Mahabaho, I am an Apsara who once frolicked in these woods. Kshatriya, my name is Varga and I am the beloved of Kubera, Lord of Treasures. I have four other friends, and all of us are beautiful and could go wherever we wished.

One day, we five were on our way to Kubera's home, when we saw a strikingly handsome and solitary Brahmana, a tapasvin, who sat immersed in studying the Veda. All the vana in which he sat was radiant with his splendour; he illumined the forest even like a Sun.

We flew down to where he sat, for both his fervid dhyana and his wonderful beauty drew us irresistibly. We meant to distract him from his tapasya. Saurabheyi, Samichi, Vudvuda, Lata and I approached that Brahmana, O Bhaarata, all together. We began to smile, sing and to otherwise tempt him.

Kshatriya, he was not to be tempted; not for a moment did his heart sway towards us. Purusharishabha the only gaze he cast in our direction was one of anger.

Glaring at us, he said, "Become crocodiles and swim in these waters for a hundred years!"' says the Apsara."

CANTO 219

ARJUNA-VANAVASA PARVA CONTINUED

Vaisampayana said, "Varga continues, 'Bharatottama, we were shocked by the curse and tried to mollify that Brahmana who would not swerve from his vows. We said to him, "Arrogant of our beauty and youth, and stirred by Kama Deva, we have behaved abysmally. O Brahmana, we beg you, forgive us.

Surely, it is our very death which tempted us to try to tempt you. However, the Sages always say that women must never be killed. May your punya swell, Brahmana, do not kill us, it does not become you. O, you know dharma well, and it is a Brahmana's dharma to always be a friend to every creature. Let what the Rishis say about Brahmanas be true of you: the superior man always protects those that seek refuge in him. We seek your protection; it becomes you to forgive us."

O Kshatriya, the high-souled and virtuous Brahmana, as bright as the Sun or the Moon, grew kindly towards us. He said, "The words hundred and hundred thousand all mean eternity. However, in this case I did not use the word hundred to mean time without end.

So, you will indeed become crocodiles and seize and feed on men for a hundred human years. When those years end, a great man will come and drag you out from the water, and you will have your true forms back. I have never told the smallest lie, not even in jest, and everything that I say must come to pass.

Once the hero delivers you five, the five sacred waters will be known the world over as the Naari-tirthas, the waters of the women, and the wise and the good shall know them as being holy and purifying."

We listened to what the Brahmana said, folded our hands to him and walked around him in pradakshina. Dejectedly, we left that place, thinking, "Where will we meet the great man who will remove the curse from us?"

At that moment, O Bhaarata, we saw the Devarishi Narada of measureless tejas and our hearts filled with joy. Saluting him reverently, Partha, we stood before him, with flushed faces. He asked us the cause of our grief and we told him everything.

The Rishi said, "In the plains that lie alongside the southern Ocean are five realms of water, enchanting and deeply sacred. Go there, and soon, the Purushavyaghra Arjuna, Pandava Nishkalankaatma will rescue you from your sad plight."

Shura, at the Muni's words we came here, and, Anagha, sinless, you have today delivered me from the curse. But my four friends are still bound by it and live in these rivers. Kshatriya, I beg you, save them as well.'

Rajan, that Pandavottama of untold prowess calmly does as Varga asks. Rising out of the water, the four other Apsaras have their true and beautiful forms back. Having freed the Apsaras from the curse and the holy rivers from the danger of the crocodiles, Arjuna allows the nymphs to go where they please.

His heart turns once more to Chitrangada and he returns to Manipura. Arriving in the city, he sees the child he has sired on the princess seated upon the throne, the prince called Babhruvahana. Having seen Chintrangada again, O King, Arjuna sets out for the place known as Gokarna."

CANTO 220

ARJUNA-VANAVASA PARVA CONTINUED

Vaisampayana said, "Now the mighty Arjuna sees all the holy rivers, lakes and shrines on the shore of the western Sea. Vibhatsu arrives in sacred and wondrous Prabhasa, in disguise. Madhusudana Krishna, however, knows that he has come and goes to meet his friend and cousin, Kunti's son.

Meeting, they embrace fondly and ask after each other's well-being. The two great friends, who are none other than the Rishis Nara and Narayana of old, sit down together.

Krishna asks Arjuna, 'Why, Pandava, do you wander the Earth, from tirtha to tirtha, shrine to shrine?'

Arjuna tells him all that has happened, and then the incomparable Vrishni hero says softly, 'This is as it should be.'

When they have spent some time at Prabhasa, Krishna and Arjuna go to the Raivataka Mountain, to pass some days there. Before they arrive, Krishna has the mountain adorned by countless fine artisans. At his command, a goodly amount of food is laid out there.

Enjoying everything, Arjuna sits with Vasudeva to watch the actors and dancers perform. Finally, the noble Pandava dismisses them all, with every courtesy, and stretches himself on a great and marvellous bed prepared for him. Lying there, he describes his travels to Krishna, telling him all about the holy rivers, the forests, lakes and mountains that he has seen.

As he speaks, O Janamejaya, lying upon that unworldly bed, sleep steals over him. At dawn, he awakens to sweet songs, mellifluous vina naadam, and the praises and blessings of bards. When he has finished his morning ablutions and worship, the great dark Vrishni comes affectionately to him.

Riding in a golden chariot they set out for Dwaraka, capital of the Yadavas. O Janamejaya, Dwaraka is brilliantly decked out, adorned to receive Kunti's heroic son. Eager to set eyes on Arjuna, the people pour out into the streets and highways, in thousands upon thousands.

In public squares and thoroughfares, countless women are out together with the men, in the teeming, milling crowd of Bhojas, Vrishnis and Andhakas. All the noble scions of those races welcome Arjuna reverently. He worships those that are his elders, receiving their blessings, and blesses those younger than him.

The young Yadava men receive him excitedly and warmly, and he repeatedly embraces those that are his equals in age. Slowly, they make their way to Krishna's marvellous palace, full of untold riches, rare gemstones and other indescribable treasures, replete with every object of enjoyment. Arjuna spends many days there with Krishna."

CANTO 221

SUBHADRA-HARANA PARVA

Vaisampayana said, "Best of Kings, a few days after Arjuna's arrival, a great festival begins upon the Raivataka Mountain, a festival of the Vrishnis, Andhakas and Bhojas, of all the Yadavas. During the mountain-festival, the Kshatriyas of those tribes give away untold wealth in charity, to thousands of Brahmanas.

Rajan, all around that massif stand countless magnificent mansions of wondrous beauty, all embellished with jewels, as are the artificial trees in livid and fantastical colours. The musicians strike up their lively song, the singers sing and the gifted dancers weave their lively rhythms. How glowingly handsome are the Vrishni youths, majestic and vibrantly strong, wearing fine jewellery, riding in chariots chased with gold.

Yes, the great citizens of Dwaraka turn out in hundreds of thousands, on foot, in fine chariots, with their wives and entourages. The Lord Balarama Halayudha is there roving where he pleases, inebriated with a surfeit of wine, his wife Revathi with him, and followed by numerous musicians and singers.

The awesome king of the Vrishnis, Ugrasena, is there, with his thousand wives, also followed by sweet singers.

Rukmini's son Aniruddha and Shamba are also there, both tameless in battle, also flushed with drink, wearing the costliest garments and garlands of supernatural beauty, wandering about like two Devas. Akrura, Sarana, Gada, Babhru, Nisatha, Charudeshna, Prithu, Viprithu, Satyaka, Satyaki, Bhangakara, Maharava, Hardikya, Uddhava, and countless others whose names are lost – all adorn the mountain festival on the Raivataka, each with his wives and with bands of singers.

When the festival of indescribable grandeur begins, Krishna and Arjuna range the place, arm in arm. As they roam together, gladly, they see Vasudeva's exquisite daughter Bhadra, beautifully attired and bejewelled, surrounded by her sakhis. Arjuna takes one look at her and Kama Deva pierces his heart fairly through.

Bhaarata, the Purushavyaghra Krishna sees Arjuna gaze adoringly at the princess, and says with a smile, 'Ah, how can this be? That the heart of a vanaprastha, a forest-rover, is shaken by Kama? That girl is my half-sister, Partha, and Balarama Sarana's sister.

Be you blessed, her name is Bhadra and she is my father's favourite daughter. So tell me if your heart is fixed upon her, and I will speak to my father Vasudeva myself.'

Arjuna replies, 'She is Vasudeva's daughter and Vaasudeva's sister; she is so beautiful, who could resist her? Krishna, if this sister of yours, princess of the Vrishnis, becomes my wife, I will truly find fortune in all things. Tell me, Janardana, how can I make her mine? I will do anything that a man can possibly do to gain her.'

Krishna says, 'Purusharishabha, for Kshatriyas the way of swayamvara is ordained. Yet it is uncertain, chancy, Partha, since we do not know the girl's mind. For daring Kshatriyas, the Sages advocate marriage by abduction. Arjuna, carry my beautiful sister away forcibly, for who knows whom she might choose at a swayamvara.'

Having decided, Krishna and Arjuna send swift messengers to Yudhishtira in Indraprastha, telling him what they intend. Yudhishtira gives his consent immediately."

CANTO 222

SUBHADRA-HARANA PARVA CONTINUED

Vaismapayana said, "Arjuna receives news of Yudhishtira's concurrence, O Janamejaya. He goes to Krishna's father, Vasudeva, and gets his consent as well. The bull of the race of Bharata learns that Subhadra has gone to the Raivataka and rides there in Krishna's mighty golden chariot, upon which rows of little bells ring, in which every kind of weapon is stored, which is as bright as blazing fire, whose wheels rumble like thunderheads, to which the magnificent steeds Saibya and Sugriva are yoked, which ratha strikes terror in the hearts of all enemies.

Wearing kavacha, carrying his sword, his fingers sheathed in gloves of leather, Arjuna sets out as if on a hunt!

Meanwhile, Subhadra has worshipped Raivataka, prince among hills. She has worshipped the Gods and made the Brahmanas say blessings over her; she has walked around Raivataka in pradakshina and is on her way back to Dwaravati, when all on a sudden, Kunti's son, shot through by the flowery shafts of Kama, swoops upon the flawless Yadava girl, hauls her into his chariot and flashes away towards Indraprastha, that tiger among men, with the girl of sweet smiles.

When Subhadra's armed guards see what has happened, and there is nothing they can do about it, they run shouting and crying out, back to Dwaraka. Arriving in the city, and rushing into the divine sabha, the Sudharma, hysterically they describe what has happened to the court's chief official, telling of Partha's inexorable prowess.

That man sounds his golden trumpet echoingly, calling everyone to arms. From every side, the Vrishnis, Bhojas and Andhakas swarm in response to the clarion blast – those that had been eating leave their food and come, they that had been drinking fling aside their goblets and fly to answer the sound for danger.

Those Purushavyaghras, irresistible Yadava warriors, fill the grand sabha and take their places upon the thousand golden thrones within the court, its floor covered by unworldly carpets, and its walls and seats sparkling with myriad jewels, with corals that blaze like red fire. Indeed, they take their places upon those thrones, like fires ablaze themselves, just fed with fresh faggots to burn more brightly.

When they all sit in that sabha that is indeed like a court of the Devas, the chief official of the sabha relates what Arjuna has done, while those standing behind him, who bring the news, add details. Almost all of them red-eyed at that hour with drink, the haughty Vrishni heroes rise as a man in rage.

Some cry, 'Yoke our chariots!'

Others say, 'Fetch our weapons!'

Others roar, 'Get our bows and our armour!'

Some of them shout commands to their sarathies to harness their rathas, while some are so impatient that they run out to do it themselves, yoking their fine horses caparisoned in gold to their chariots. Such a din they make, while their chariots, mail and standards are being fetched.

Fair and tall as the peak of Kailasa, wearing blue robes, colourful vanamalas of wildflowers from the forest, great, proud and drunkest of all, Baladeva, the mighty Balarama says, 'Fools, what are you doing when

Krishna sits silent? All of us rage and roar in vain until we know his mind. Let Janardana Mahatman tell us what he thinks we should do, and then do what he says.'

Immediately, the others all cry, as a man, 'Excellent! Excellent!' and then fall silent and sit down again in their places in the Sudharma.

Decorum restored, Balarama Parantapa says to Krishna, 'Why, Krishna, do you sit silently gazing? Achyuta, for your sake we welcomed and honoured Kunti's son, but it seems that the wretch hardly deserved our adorations. What honourable or well-born man would break a plate after having eaten from it? Even if he did wish to marry her, should he not have remembered how well we treated him, and not acted so rashly?

The Pandava has shown us and you his contempt today! He has dared outrage Subhadra: he has courted his own death. He has set his foot upon the crown of my head. Krishna, shall I bear this tamely? Shall I not resent it, even as a deadly snake does being trodden upon? Why, by myself I will rid the Earth of all the Kauravas today! I will not tolerate what Arjuna has done.'

To the last man, every Bhoja, Vrishni and Andhaka present approves of what Baladeva says: they roar all together, as reverberantly as a battery of deep drumrolls or thunderclouds."

CANTO 223

HARANAHARANA PARVA

Vaisampayana said, "When all the Vrishni heroes repeatedly echo Balarama's angry sentiments, Krishna speaks these words of true dharma, full of profound meaning.

'Arjuna has not insulted or dishonoured our clan by what he did, rather he has honoured us. Partha knows that we Satwatas are never mercenary. The Pandava also thought the outcome of a swayamvara was uncertain. Then, who could approve of being given a bride as a gift, just as if she were some animal? And what man on Earth worth his name would sell his child?

I believe that Arjuna considered all these possibilities, saw their shortcomings, and only then decided to abduct Subhadra, as is consistent with the highest Kshatriya dharma.

This is a proper and equal match. Subhadra is a well-renowned girl, and Partha also has great fame. Is it not possible that Arjuna thought carefully of all this before abducting her?

Who would not want Arjuna, scion of the race of Bharata and Shantanu, son of Kuntibhoja's daughter, besides, for his friend and ally? Other than the three-eyed Lord Mahadeva, no one in the three worlds, including Indra and the Rudras, can vanquish Partha in battle.

His chariot has much fame, and yoked to it are my own horses. As a warrior, Partha has incomparable renown; his lightness of hand is legend. Who will defeat him?

This is my opinion, and I think that you should go happily after Arjuna and bring him back to Dwaraka with conciliation. If he defeats us in battle and returns to his city, we will have lost our honour. But in conciliation there is no disgrace.'

O King, they listen to Krishna and do as he says. Accosted with respect by the Vrishnis, Arjuna returns to Dwaraka and is formally married to Subhadra. Adored by the sons of the House of Vrishni, steeped in every pleasure, in delight, Arjuna spends a full year in the Ocean city.

Later, he leaves with Subhadra and spends the final year of his exile in sacred Pushkarakshetra. When he has served twelve years in exile, he returns home to Khandavaprastha and first of all comes before the king, and worships his elder brother. He next reveres the Brahmanas of the court. Only then, does he go to Draupadi.

In the grip of jealousy, Draupadi flashes angrily at him, 'Why are you here, Kaunteya? Go to the Satwata princess! A second knot always loosens the first one.'

And Krishnaa sobs piteously. Dhananjaya pacifies her, repeatedly asking her to forgive him. He then goes back to where Subhadra waits outside the city, wearing red silk. Arjuna brings her into the palace dressed not as a princess but as a simple cowherdess. However, she only looks more regal and beautiful than ever in that humble attire.

Bhadra of great fame, of the big and slightly red eyes first goes to touch the feet of Kunti and have her blessing. Overwhelmed by affection, Kunti lovingly sniffs the head of the young woman of flawless features, and pronounces infinite blessings upon her.

Then Subhadra, her face like the full moon, goes to Draupadi and says straightaway, 'I am your daasi, your maid!'

Krishnaa jumps up and hugs Vaasudeva Krishna's sister to her in love, crying, 'May your husband be without an enemy!'

Delighted, Subhadra cries back, 'Tathaastu! So be it!'

From that time, O Janamejaya, those great Kshatriyas, the Pandavas, live in great happiness together, and Kunti, too, is happy.

When Krishna Parantapa, Nishkalankaatma, his eyes also pure as lotus petals, hears the Pandavottama Arjuna has returned to Indraprastha, he goes there with Balarama and other great shuras and Kshatriyas of the Vrishni and Andhaka tribes, and with his own brothers, sons and many magnificent heroes.

Krishna comes with a great army to protect him; with him, comes the most liberal and intelligent Akrura, Senapati of the Vrishni legions. Anadhrishti of mighty prowess, Uddhava of great fame and wisdom, Mahatman and Brihaspati's own sishya ride with Saurin Krishna, as do Satyaki, Salyaka, Kritavarman, Satwata, Pradyumna, Samba, Nisatha, Sanku, Charudeshna, Jhilli of untold might, Viprithu, Sarana Mahabaho, Gada, greatest among learned men.

These and many other Vrishnis, Bhojas and Andhakas come to Indraprastha, bringing wedding gifts for Arjuna and Subhadra, past counting. When King Yudhishtira hears that Madhava has arrived, he sends the twins out to receive him. Received by Nakula and Sahadeva, the glittering Vrishni host, flying bright flags and standards, enters Khandavaprastha.

The streets have been swept, washed, and decked with garlands and a profusion of flowers. They are again sprinkled with water mixed with sandalwood paste, which renders them cool and fragrant. The scent of burning aloe fills every corner of the city, which bustles with its healthy, happy people, with fine merchants and tradesmen.

Purushottama Kesava Krishna, Mahabaho, enters Indraprastha, with Rama and many other great Vrishnis, Bhojas and Andhakas, and is worshipped by the people, and by thousands of Brahmanas. At last,

Krishna arrives at the king's palace, which is like the palace of Indra himself.

Yudhishtira first welcomes Balarama, the eldest, with every ceremony. He then sniffs the top of Krishna's head and embraces him. Krishna, gratified, humbly worships Yudhishtira. He pays homage to Bhima, that great tiger among men. Kunti's son Yudhishtira now receives the other Vrishni, Bhoja and Andhaka chieftains with honour and appropriate ceremony: he reveres his elders and affectionately welcomes the rest as equals. In their turn, some of them worship him, while others greet him affectionately.

Now, Krishna of immense fame gives the clan of Arjuna, the bridegroom, lavish wealth; he gives Subhadra the gifts that her kinsfolk have sent. Krishna gives the Pandavas a thousand chariots of gold, adorned with fine rows of bells, each yoked to four pedigreed horses, and driven by the finest charioteers.

He gives them ten thousand cows from the land of Mathura, all of rich colouring and yielding copious milk. Happily, Janardana also gives a thousand mares, with golden harnesses, steeds white as moonbeams. He gives them a thousand mules, highly trained and obedient, and quick as the wind: these are white, as well, with black mane.

He of the lotus petal-like eyes gives the Pandavas a thousand young girls, skilled at drawing baths and pouring wine and at every other form of personal service, all of them virgins yet to have their first period, each one beautifully clad and wearing a hundred bits of gold around their necks, their skins like satin.

Janardana also gives them lakhs of draft horses from the land of the Bahlikas as part of Subhadra's opulent dowry. Krishna, best of the Dasarhas, also gives Subhadra ten palanquins of gold, blazing like fire, some purified and some still ore.

Balarama Halayudha, ever fond of battle and brave deeds, gives Arjuna a thousand war elephants – tuskers with ichor flowing in three streams[9] from their great bodies for a wedding gift. Each one is as big

---

[9]From their temples, ears and anus.

as a mountain peak, inexorable in battle, carrying fine thrones upon their richly caparisoned backs, adorned with golden ornaments, tinkling golden bells.

It is a tide of treasures that the Yadavas give as Subhadra's dower, and the fine silks, shawls and carpets are the foam of that great wave, the war elephants its crocodiles and sharks, and the banners and flags, its floating reeds! All these flow into the wealth of the Pandava ocean, filling it to the brim, so that their enemies grieve sorely.

Yudhishtira accepts those gifts humbly and worships all the great warriors of the Vrishni and the Andhaka races. The shining heroes of the Kurus, the Vrishnis and the Andhakas spend their days together in uninterrupted revelry and enjoyment, even as good men do in heaven's delights after they die.

The Kurus and the Yadavas amuse themselves variously, at times their loud shouts of joy echoing against the sky, and the clapping of hands, too. Many days they spend together, in sport and merriment of every sort, the guests being honoured and adored by their hosts, until at last the Yadavas turn home towards Dwaravati upon the Sea.

The great Vrishni and Andhaka warriors set out with Balarama at their head. They take with them the gemstones that shine with the purest rays, given them by the Kurusthamas. O Bhaarata, Krishna Mahatman remains in Indraprastha with Arjuna. They range the banks of the Yamuna together in quest of deer; Krishna hunts both deer and boar with Arjuna, piercing them with arrows.

In a while, Krishna's favourite sister Subhadra gives birth to a resplendent son, even as Puloma's daughter, Sachi, queen of Devaloka, brought Jayanta forth. The child has long arms, a wide chest, and eyes as big as a bull's. They name that little hero, that bane of his enemies to be, Abhimanyu, because he is both fearless and ferocious.

Arjuna begets the magnificent prince in the Satwata princess, even as fire from a sami twig by friction. When Abhimanyu is born, Yudhishtira gifts ten thousand cows and golden coins past counting to holy Brahmanas. From his infancy, the boy is a favourite of Krishna, Arjuna and his uncles, even as the Moon is of all Manavas!

When he is born, Krishna performs the rites of childhood for him, and Abhimanyu grows like the Moon waxing during the bright fortnight. Quickly, he masters the Vedas and the sastra shastra, the use of weapons both mundane and celestial, which has four great branches and ten smaller divisions, from his father Arjuna.

Endowed with great strength, the boy also learns how to counter astras loosed at him by others; his lightness of hand, and his fleetness of foot in every direction, forwards and backwards, sideways and all around, wheeling, are past remarkable. Abhimanyu is his father's equal in his knowledge of the Shastras and kriya-karmas.

Arjuna looks at his boy and is filled with joy. As Indra Maghavat would become joyful whenever he gazes down upon Arjuna, so does Dhananjaya become delighted when he sees Abhimanyu, who has upon his body every auspicious sign and mark, and who is invincible in battle, and can kill any adversary that comes before him.

He is broad-shouldered as a bull, great and wide is his face like a serpent's hood, and he is as proud and magnificent as a lion. He wields a great bow, and his prowess is like that of an elephant in musth. Ah, he is as handsome as the Moon when he is full; his voice is as deep as booming drums or rumbling thunderheads; why, he is his uncle, Krishna's, equal in courage and energy, in his sheer beauty and the perfection of his features.

Meanwhile, Panchali also has five sons, one by each of her husbands, and those princes are all exceptional warriors, invincible in battle, unshakable as hills. She bears Prativindhya by Yudhishtira, Sutasoma by Vrikodara, Srutakarman by Arjuna, Satanika by Nakula, and Srutasena by Sahadeva – she brings forth those five shuras even as Aditi did the Adityas.

Prescient and mystic Brahmanas say to Yudhishtira that because his son would bear the missiles of his enemies as the Vindhya Mountains do raindrops, he should be called Prativindhya. The son Draupadi bears

Bhimasena is born after Bhima performs a thousand Soma yagnas, and so he should be named Sutasoma.

Arjuna's son is born after his return from his exile, during which he performs so many legendary feats, so that prince is named Srutakarman, for his father's fame. Nakula names his son Satanika after an enlightened and great Rajarishi of yore, born in the line of Kuru.

The son that Draupadi bears by Sahadeva is born under the constellation Krittika, or Vahni Daivata, and he is named after the Senapati of the army of the Devas: the Lord Srutasena, who is more commonly known as Kartikeya.

Draupadi's five sons are all born a year apart, and they grow to be famous and devoted to one another. Rajan, Dhaumya performs all their childhood rites in accordance with the Shastras – the chudakarana, when their heads are first shaved, and the upanayana – the investiture with the sacred thread.

They are all princes of dharma, well behaved and of excellent vows; when they have studied the Vedas, they go on to learn archery and to acquire the astras, both mundane and celestial, from Arjuna. O Tiger among kings, the Pandavas see their broad-chested magnificent sons truly equal to Devaputras all turn into Maharathas, and they are filled with joy."

CANTO 224

KHANDAVA-DAHA PARVA

Vaisampayana said, "Living in Indraprastha, after having been sent there by the command of Dhritarashtra and Bhishma, the Pandavas begin to bring other kings under their sway. Their subjects live in the realm of Yudhishtira Dharmaputra as happily as a soul does in a body that bears every auspicious mark and has great punya.

Bharatarishabha, Yudhishtira lives by dharma, artha and kama, in due proportion, as if each of them is his friend dear to him as his own self. Indeed, it appears that these three purusharthas become personified on Earth, and King Yudhishtira shines among them as the fourth aim of life.

With Yudhishtira for their king, his people find a ruler who devotes himself to the regular study of the Vedas, one who constantly performs the Mahayagnas, and one who is the guardian of all the good. Through Yudhishtira's influence, all the kings of the Earth find unwavering good fortune; their hearts turn naturally in dhyana to the Parabrahman, and dharma swells in a tide everywhere, in every way.

And with his four brothers around him, and helped by and depending on them, that king shines forth as a great sacrifice does, when the four Vedas attend upon it. Countless learned Brahmanas, with Dhaumya at their head, each one like a Brihaspati, wait upon Yudhishtira, just as the Devas and other celestials do upon Brahma.

The people love Yudhishtira; their eyes and their hearts are full of him who is like a stainless full moon. They adore him not only because he is their king but for himself. On his part, he always does what is good for them, what delights them. Sweetly-spoken, intelligent and wise Yudhishtira never speaks a harsh word, nor a lie or anything hurtful or inappropriate.

That best of all kings of the line of Bhaarata, blessed with unflagging vitality, passes his days in joy looking after his people as well as he looks after himself. With their dauntless prowess, his brothers bring other kingdoms under Yudhishtira's power, and they also spend their days in blemishless happiness, without an enemy to threaten their peace.

One day, Arjuna says to Krishna, 'Summer is here, Madhusudana. Let us go to the banks of the Yamuna and sport there all day and return in the evening with our companions, Janardana.'

Krishna says, 'Kaunteya, my very wish! Let us go and sport in the waters as we please, Partha, taking our friends with us.'

With Yudhishtira's leave Arjuna and Krishna set out with many friends for the banks of the river. Arriving at a certain place, sylvan with tall trees, and with many fine and lofty mansions, furnished with rare food and drink, with dazzling garlands and scented with fine perfumes, all for the pleasure of Krishna and Arjuna, a place that looks like a city in Devaloka, the companions immediately go into the lavish apartments within, shimmering with precious jewels, and out of the heat of the day.

Once inside, they begin to take their pleasure as they please, O Bhaarata. The women, all with full round hips, deep bosoms and large bright eyes, unsteady on their feet from the wine they have drunk, begin to cavort exactly as Krishna and Arjuna direct them to.

Some women go into the woods and frolic there, others wade directly into the river, while the rest make merry inside the mansions. Draupadi and Subhadra, exhilarated with wine, begin to give away their costly robes and ornaments to those women, some of whom burst into joyful song while others dance in abandon; others joke and laugh loudly, all the while imbibing more drink.

Soon, some of them argue and quarrel among themselves, while others speak intimately together in soft voices. Those mansions and the woods all around are full of the enchanting music of flute, lute and quiet drums; ah, it is a place of delight and fortune embodied.

Things being so, Krishna and Arjuna go off by themselves into the nearby forest to another place also full of fascination. The great souled Krishna and Arjuna, conqueror of enemy cities, sit there upon two priceless thrones; they sit talking about many things, among these, of great heroes of the past and their legends.

Suddenly, a Brahmana appears before Krishna and Arjuna, sitting there like the Aswin twins of heaven. The Brahmana is tall as a sala tree; his skin is like molten gold; his beard is bright yellow and tinged with green; and his body great and wide in proportion to his height.

He wears jata on his head and rags upon his body, but he is as brilliant as the morning Sun. His eyes are wide and long as lotus petals and tawny; he truly blazes with splendour. Seeing this Brahmana coming towards them, Arjuna and Krishna quickly rise and stand respectfully, waiting for him to speak."

CANTO 225

KHANDAVA-DAHA PARVA CONTINUED

Vaisampayana said, "That Brahmana speaks to Arjuna, and to Krishna of the Satwatas, saying, 'You, who are so near the Khanadava vana, are the greatest Kshatriyas on Earth. I am a voracious Brahmana and I always eat a lot. O Vrishni, O Partha, I ask you to appease my raging hunger: give me enough to eat!'

Krishna and the Pandava say, 'Tell us what food you want and we will try to give it to you.'

The blazing Brahmana says, 'I do not crave ordinary food. Know that I am Agni! Give me food that I can consume. Indra constantly protects this Khandava forest, and for that reason I cannot devour it. Deep in this vana there lives the Naga Takshaka, with his brood and his followers, and he is Indra's friend.

For his sake, the Vajradhari protects the forest and all the other creatures that live in it. Ah, I long to devour the Khandava vana, but the might of Indra prevents me every time I try. Whenever I blaze forth in flames, Indra pours down torrents of rain that extinguish them. Many attempts have I made to consume this vana and always I have failed.

I cannot contain my hunger for this forest and I come as a supplicant to the both of you, who are masters of weapons. If you help me, I know that I can have the food that I want – this jungle. With your astras, keep Indra's rains from falling and prevent any creature that dwells inside the Khandava vana from escaping, when I begin to feed!' says Agni in his deep and crackling voice."

Janamejaya said, "Why did Agni want to devour the Khandava vana, full of all kinds of creatures and protected by the king of the Devas? Surely, there must have been some grave cause for him to want to do this thing. O Brahmana, tell me about it in detail. Tell me also, O Muni, how the Khandava vana was consumed of old."

Vaisampayana said, "Purushottama, I will tell you the tale of the conflagration that consumed the Khandava vana, as it has been told by the Rishis in the Purana. There was a king called Swetaki blessed with untold strength and valour, who was an equal of Indra himself. No one on Earth was his peer, in yagnas, in daana or gyana.

Swetaki performed the five Mahayagnas and many others, too, at all of which he gave bountifully to the Brahmanas present. That king's heart, Rajan, was always turned towards sacrifices, religious rites, and charity and gifts of every kind.

King Swetaki of great intellect undertook an endless sacrifice, until the Ritviks who performed the rituals grew weak with exhaustion, their eyes sore from years of being exposed to smoke from the agnikunda, and they left that king, never wanting to participate in his yagnas anymore. However, the king never ceased asking his priests to return, which they refused to do because of their sore and painful eyes.

Those Ritviks told him to ask other priests to complete the sacrifice that they had begun, which he did. After a short interval, the king wanted to perform yet another sacrifice, now one that would last a hundred years. But no priest could he find to help him with it.

Taking his family and friends with him, that famed king went and repeatedly implored the Ritviks, bowing to them again and again, praising them with the sweetest words, and with more munificent gifts. All of them refused to undertake to perform the king's grand yagna.

Now that Rajarishi flew into a rage. He said to those Brahmanas in their asramas, 'Brahmanas, if I were a sinner, or if I did not revere you properly or serve you as I have done, surely I would deserve to be abandoned by all of you, without scruple. But neither am I depraved, nor do I fail to pay unfailing homage to you. Brahmanottamas, it does not become you to abandon me and to prevent me from performing the Mahayagna on which I have set my heart.

Brahmanas, I seek refuge in you! Bless me, be kindly towards me. If you do not help me, it would seem to be out of enmity, and without just cause; and I will then take my service, my homage and my gifts to some other Brahmanas, and beg them to perform my sacrifice.'

With this, the king fell silent. Parantapa, those priests knew very well that they could not sit at Swetaki's yagna. So they pretended to be annoyed and said acerbically, 'Best of kings, your sacrifices are incessant and endless! By performing them for years and years we have become tired and weak: in view of this, it becomes you to spare us.

Anagha, sinless, you have lost your judgement and impatiently come to us again and again. Go to Rudra! He will help you with your yagna.'

Now King Swetaki became truly angry. He went away to the mountains of Kailasa, and sat there in tapasya. Rajan, keeping the sternest vratas, Swetaki worshipped Mahadeva Siva with fervid dhyana. For a long time, he ate only fruit and roots, at times at the twelfth hour, at others only at the sixteenth of the entire day.

For six months, King Swetaki stood in meditation, with his arms raised skywards and his eyes unblinking, like the trunk of a tree or a stone column planted in the ground. O Bhaarata, finally Sankara became pleased with that tiger among kings, and appeared before him.

The God spoke in a calm, solemn voice to Swetaki, 'Rajavyaghra, Parantapa, I am pleased with your tapasya. Be you blessed. Ask me now for the boon that you want, O King.'

The Rajarishi bowed low before Rudra of measureless tejas, and said, 'Most Illustrious, O you whom the three worlds worship, if you are truly pleased with me, Mahadeva, then help me perform my sacrifice yourself, O Devadeva.'

The God smiled and replied gently, 'We do not perform sacrifices ourselves, but since you have done such penance, Rajan, I will indeed help you with your yagna, but on one condition.

Rajaadhiraja, King of kings, if you pour libations into a sacred fire without pause for twelve years, with perfect devotion, being celibate all the while, then you shall have what you have asked for.'

King Swetaki did what Rudra said, and when twelve years had passed he came back to the Trisulin, to Maheswara. When Sankara, Creator of the worlds, saw the most excellent King Swetaki, he said at once, gratified, 'You have satisfied me, Rajottama, with what you have done. However, Parantapa, it is the Brahmana's dharma to perform yagnas. So, scourge of your enemies, I will not help you myself with your yagna.

On Earth, there lives a most pure and high Brahmana who is an amsa of mine. His name is Durvasa and that mighty tejaswin will help you perform your sacrifice. So, go and make all preparations.'

Swetaki heard what Rudra said and then returned to his capital, and began collecting everything he needed for his great sacrifice. When this had been done, he went again to Rudra and said, 'Devadeva, by your grace I have gathered everything needed for the sacrifice: all my preparations are complete. Let me be installed as the Sacrificer tomorrow.'

Rudra summoned Durvasa, and said, 'Durvasa, this is Swetaki, best among kings. Best of Brahmanas, at my command, you must help the king perform his yagna.'

The Rishi Durvasa said to Rudra, 'So be it.'

The mahayagna of King Swetaki got underway, with every proper ritual ordained, each in its proper season. Profuse gifts were bestowed upon all the Brahmanas present, and when, at last, the yagna was completed, the other priests who had come there at Durvasa's behest all went away, with the Muni's leave.

All the other Sadasyas, the resplendent guests who had been installed at the yagna, also departed. Now the noble king entered his own palace, adored by Brahmanas that were masters of the Vedas, and eulogised by panegyrics and warmly congratulated by the people.

This is the story of the Rajarishi Swetaki, who, later, upon his time coming, rose into Swarga, leaving behind incomparable fame on Bhumi, and also accompanied by the Ritviks and Sadasyas who had helped him accomplish his great sacrifice.

During Swetaki's own worship, Agni drank ghee, uninterruptedly, for twelve years, the clarified butter being poured in a constant stream into his mouth for that period. Having drunk so much ghee, Agni was so full and tired that he could not drink ghee from any other hand, at any other yagna.

Agni Deva became pale and wan, lost his colour, and he did not blaze as before. From that excess of twelve years, he lost his appetite, his vitality was sapped and he became sick. When he felt ill and weak, he went to the abode of Brahma, whom everybody worships.

Approaching the great Deity upon his throne, Agni said, 'Highest, I have drunk a surfeit of ghee at Swetaki's yagna, and I suffer from that excess even now. Lord of the Universe, my splendour and my strength both wane daily, and I need your grace to regain my original nature.'

Hearing Agni Hutavaha, Brahma Pitamaha said with a smile, 'Mahatman, you drank a ceaseless stream of ghee for twelve years, and you have become ill from it. But do not despair, O Agni, you will soon have your health back and your pristine nature, for I will cure you of your sickness, the time has come.

The fearful Khandava vana, home of the Asuras, which you once consumed with flames at the behest of the Devas, is now a home to myriad creatures. When you have devoured the fat of all those, you will have your glory back. So make haste, O Agni, consume the forest and all that live in it! That will be your cure.'

Hearing the Paramatman, Agni flew towards the Khandava vana. Arriving, he erupted, blazing forth in wrath, with his friend Vayu fanning his flames gustily. Seeing the forest on fire, those that dwelt within it strove hard to quell the conflagration.

Hundreds of thousands of elephants, thundering about in fear and rage, fetched water from rivers, lakes and streams in their trunks and tried to douse the flames. Thousands of many-hooded snakes, panic-stricken, spewed water on the fire from their countless mouths. So, too, Bharatarishabha, every creature that lived in the forest, each in its way, joined in the effort, and they quickly extinguished the inferno.

Agni flared forth again, and again the denizens of the jungle quenched his flames; yet again, Hutavaha burned, and yet again they put him out: all of seven times."

CANTO 226

Khandava-daha Parva Continued

Vaisampayana said, "Frustrated and raging, Agni Havyavahana, his ailment uncured, went bank to Brahma, and told the Pitamaha what had happened.

The refulgent God thought for a moment, then said, 'Anagha, I know how you can consume the Khandava vana even today and in Indra's very sight. The ancient Gods Nara and Narayana have incarnated in the world of men to fulfil a purpose of the Devas. On Earth they are known as Arjuna and Krishna Vasudeva.

At this moment, they are in the Khandava vana. Go to them and ask them to help you consume the forest. If they agree, you will succeed even if all the other Devas are arrayed against you. The two will surely keep the creatures of the Khandava from escaping, and even thwart Indra, if he comes to protect the ancient jungle. I assure you of this.'

Agni came speedily to Krishna and Partha. O King, I have already told you what he said to them.

Rajavyaghra, when Arjuna Vibhatsu hears that Agni wants to consume the Khandava vana, against Indra's will, he says to the blazing Deva, come as a Brahmana, 'I have countless great Devastras, enough to battle with many Vajradharins, but, Lofty One, I have no proper bow from which to loose my astras, no bow strong and powerful enough to bear the prowess with which I infuse my archery. Also, so quicksilver is my archery that I will need an inexhaustible supply of arrows.

My chariot, alas, is not mighty enough to bear the stores of shafts with which I would like to stock it. I wish for a chariot with the splendour of Surya, the thunder of whose wheels is like the roaring of stormclouds. I also wish for unearthly horses white as moonbeams, fleet as the wind.

Then, Krishna has no weapon to match his tejas, no shastra with which Madhava can kill the Nagas and Pisachas of the vana. Exalted, you must provide us with these instruments with which we can thwart Indra when he sends his downpour to put out your flames. Pavaka, we are ready to do everything that manliness and strength can achieve, but you must give us what I have asked for,' Arjuna says to Agni."

CANTO 227

KHANDAVA-DAHA PARVA CONTINUED

Vaisampayana said, "When he hears what Arjuna says, the smoke-bannered Hutasana wants to see Varuna, who is one of the Lokapalas, who rules the element of water and dwells in the deeps. Agni turns his thought to that son of Aditi. Immediately, Varuna appears before Agni.

The Fire God reverently greets the Lord of Seas, the fourth Lokapala, and says to him, 'I want you to give me the bow and quiver and the chariot that flies the flag of Hanuman, which you got from Soma the Moon. Partha will accomplish a great task with the Gandiva, and Krishna with the Sudarshana Chakra. So give both to me today, O Varuna!'

Varuna immediately says, 'Here, I do give them to you.'

He gives Agni the wondrous jewel of a bow, of incomparable energy, the bow that no weapon can withstand, which is the powerful enhancer of great deeds and renown. It is the lord of weapons, and the scourge of all the rest. It is equal to a hundred thousand other bows and it razes enemy armies. Brightly varicoloured is the Gandiva and it is the acquirer of kingdoms. Beautiful it is to behold, bejewelled, with no flaw, weakness or mark upon it anywhere. The Devas and the Gandharvas worship thc Gandiva.

Varuna also gives Arjuna two inexhaustible quivers, and a ratha, stocked with unearthly weapons, a chariot that flies a banner with a great Vanara upon it. Yoked to that chariot are horses as silvery as fleecy clouds, foaled in the realm of the Gandharvas, with golden harnesses, and as swift as the wind, why, even as the mind.

Every implement of war that ratha bears, and neither Deva nor Asura can arrest its careen. Dazzling is its sheen and tremendous the sound of its wheels. It is a delight to the heart of every creature that sets eyes upon it, for it has been made by Viswakarman, Architect of the Universe, one of the Lords of creation, after great and intense tapasya.

The chariot is as brilliant as the Sun, so that no one could gaze upon it for long. This is the very ratha, riding which Soma Deva had crushed the Danavas. Resplendent, glorious, it looks like an evening cloud reflecting the light of the setting sun. Golden and exquisite is its flagstaff, and the celestial Ape who adorns it is as fierce as a lion or a tiger. Flying high, he seems determined to burn up everything he sees.

Upon other flags on the great chariot are other large creatures, whose yells make enemy soldiers faint.

Accoutred in mail, armed with a sword, his fingers encased in leather fingerlets, Arjuna walks around that wonderful chariot in pradakshina; he bows to the Devas and then climbs up into the ratha like a righteous man does into the vimana that bears him into Swarga.

Seeing the celestial Gandiva, eldest of bows, created of old by Brahma, Arjuna feels a thrill of joy. Bowing to Agni, Arjuna the powerful picks up the awesome weapon and strings it forcibly. Anyone who hears the echoing sound of the Gandiva being strung trembles.

When he has the chariot and the bow, with the twin inexhaustible quivers, which well arrows ceaselessly, Kunti's son is glad and feels equal to helping Agni. Now Agni Pavaka gives Krishna a chakra, a fiery disc with a hole at its heart, and it would become Krishna's favourite weapon.

When he has the chakra, Krishna becomes glad and feels that he, too, can help Agni.

Pavaka says to Krishna, 'With this chakra, Madhusudana, you can quell even enemies that are not human. Wielding this weapon, you will be greater than Manavas, Devas, Rakshasas, Pisachas, Daityas and Nagas, and you will surely vanquish all these in battle. Madhava, if you cast this wheel at any enemy, it will slay him and then fly back into your hands.'

Varuna Deva gives Krishna a mace known as Kaumodaki, which would shatter any Daitya; and when hurled in battle, it would roar loud as thunder.

Joyful, Arjuna and Achyuta say to Pavaka, 'Mahatman, we now have the chariot and weapons with which we can do battle against the Devas and the Asuras combined. What then of just the Vajradhari, Indra, who wants to fight for his friend the Naga Takshaka?'

Arjuna added, 'Pavaka, when Krishna takes the field, chakra in hand, there is nothing in the three worlds that he cannot consume with it. With the Gandiva and these quivers, I, too, am prepared to conquer the trilokas. My lord, now blaze forth as you please, encircle this forest with your flames. We will help you accomplish your desire.'

When Arjuna and Krishna speak thus to him, Agni stands forth in his most incendiary form, and is ready to devour the vana. With his seven great flames he encircles the Khandava and begins to burn it, rather as he does the worlds in his apocalyptic form at the end of the yugas. Bharatarishabha, erupting in gigantic flames, which roar like thunderheads, Agni makes every creature of the jungle quail.

Quickly, O Bhaarata, the forest ablaze looks even like golden, resplendent Meru, king of mountains, when the rays of the Sun fall upon his sides and summits."

CANTO 228

Khandava-daha Parva Continued

Vaisampayana said, "Those two greatest among Maharathas ride to opposite extremities of the Khandava vana and, positioning themselves at either end, commence a huge slaughter of all the creatures that dwell in the forest, on every side. Wherever either sees any creature trying to escape Agni's conflagration, they flash towards them and cut them off.

Why, the two chariots might have been just one, and the two warriors in them a single person. As the forest burns, hundred of thousands of birds and beasts, giving vent to frightening cries, dash about in every direction. Some have a limb charred, others are scalded all over, skins steamed off by the heat, some run towards the forest's hem, while others just rush blindly from place to place in panic.

There are those that clasp their mates and children, their parents and siblings, serenely and in a surfeit of love, and die thus. Some beasts leap high into the air or scramble up trees but quickly fall spinning into the blazing element below. Birds try to escape by flying but the fire catches them inescapably and they fall onto the ground, feathers and wings burnt, eyes and feet frizzled, gasping, crying out.

All around, bird and beast die, quickly consumed. The lakes and pools in that forest soon begin to boil from the torrid heat, and the fish and tortoises in them perish. The burning bodies of the creatures of the vana look as if the very flames have assumed countless bestial shapes.

Birds flash up above the flames but these Arjuna brings down with unerring archery, carving their bodies in pieces in the air, and they fall into the maw of the fire, some of them screaming. The animals of the forest struck by his shafts also cry out or roar, while dying. The clamour they raise resembles that which is heard when the Ocean was churned, in elder days.

The towering flames reach into the sky, and the celestials are alarmed. The Swargavasis, the illustrious dwellers in heaven, go in a crowd to him of the hundred great sacrifices, the thousand-eyed, their king, that scorcher of Asuras.

The heaven-dwellers say to Indra, 'Lord of the Devas, why is Agni burning the creatures below? Has the time come for the world to end?'

Indra hears what the Devas say, he also sees what Agni is doing, and he who slew Vritrasura goes forth to save the Khandava vana. Indra Vasava, King of the Devas, fills the sky with banks and banks of thunderclouds, of every sort, and then lashes down awesome torrents of rain upon the burning forest. Hundreds of thousands of thunderheads pour down rain in streams thick as flagstaffs of chariots.

The searing heat evaporates those cascades in the air before they reach the forest's roof, or the flame-tips. Now Indra Namuchihara grows furious with Agni. An even greater mass of black cloud scuds into the sky at his command, and an even more copious and fierce rain flashes down on the burning forest.

Roaring, hissing, flames and rainshowers battle on high, and filled with smoke and rent by lightning streaks, that forest is terrible, dreadful to behold."

CANTO 229

KHANDAVA-DAHA PARVA CONTINUED

Vaisampayana said, "Arjuna, son of Pandu, summons his astras and, loosing them in a torrent at Indra's downpour, holds the rain aloft, at bay. Quick as thinking, unfathomable Arjuna covers all the Khandava vana ablaze with a mantle, a cupola of arrows, as the Moon does the sky in fog, and no forest creature can penetrate that dome of arrows to escape.

It transpires that, while the forest burns, the Naga King Takshaka is not in the Khandava vana at all, for he has gone to Kurukshetra. However, his mighty son Aswasena is in that jungle. Aswasena strives to escape Agni's conflagration, but Arjuna's dazzling archery prevents him.

His mother, daughter of a Sea-Naga, is desperate to save her son. She thinks that she will do this by swallowing him. She swallows his head first, then, continues swallowing his long body. As she does this, she rises up into the air and seeks to flee the fire. But Arjuna sees her, and cuts her head off with a razor-like arrow.

Indra is watching, and he wants to save his friend, the Naga's, son. Indra blows a sudden mighty gust of wind on the forest floor, from which Arjuna faints briefly. Aswasena escapes. Arjuna wakes from his swoon in fury and begins to truncate every creature that seeks to flee the forest, into two, three and, some, into several pieces.

Arjuna, Agni and Krishna curse the serpent who has escaped with trickery: 'You will never find fame!'

Arjuna thinks of how Indra made him swoon and, growing angry, covers the sky in a cloud of arrows, seeking battle with the thousand-eyed one. The King of the Devas sees Arjuna's fury and casts down fierce weapons of his own, also covering the firmament.

Raging, roaring winds, which make the Seas tremble, blow great masses of thunderheads into the akasa, and they are heavy with rain. The cloudbanks vomit thunder and terrifying gashes of lightning.

Arjuna looses the Vayavyastra, weapon of Wind, at those clouds; it scatters them and renders the power of Indra impotent. All the rain that the clouds bear evaporates, and the lightning that plays in them vanishes. In a moment, dust and darkness clear, and a fine, cool breeze begins to blow, while the Sun resumes his normal appearance.

Agni, who drinks ghee, becomes delighted, and dripping with the fat of the numberless creatures he has devoured, erupts in all his flames again. He assumes different flame forms and his roaring fills the very universe.

Suddenly, Eagles of the race of Garuda, richly feathered, see that Arjuna and Krishna protect Agni, and they fly down from the outer firmament, wanting to savage the two heroes with their wings like thunder, and their claws and beaks like daggers and swords.

Countless Nagas, also, spitting the most virulent venom, flash at Arjuna, who cuts them in shreds with arrows dipped in the fire of his wrath. The birds also he slaughters, and Naga and Pakshi fall into the blaze below and are consumed.

Now there comes a host of Asuras, Gandharvas, Yakshas, Rakshasas and Nagas, with terrific shouts and roars. Armed with uncanny devices that spew streams of deadly iron balls and pellets from their throats, catapults that hurl huge rocks, and fiery missiles, and propelled by their fury, these rush at Krishna and Arjuna.

They rain a storm of weapons over Arjuna, but he mocks them and strikes their heads from their necks with a dazzle of arrows. Krishna Parantapa massacres the Daityas and Danavas with his chakra. Asuras of mountainous stature and untold might Krishna's arrows pierce and his disc strikes deeply, and they are as still as little strays struck down by violent and mighty waves and stranded on a beach.

Finally, Indra, riding his white elephant, thunders at those shuras and, raising his Vajra aloft, his inexorable thunderbolt, prepares to cast it at them. The scourge of the Asuras cries to his Devas, 'These two are slain!'

Seeing the Vajra raised, all the Gods seize up their weapons. Rajan, Yama takes up his mace of death, Kubera his spiked cudgel, Varuna his legendary noose and the beautiful Varunastra. Skanda picks up his elegant and irresistible javelin and stands as motionless as Meru.

The Aswins stand with shining plant weapons in their hands. Dhatri stands with a bow and Jaya with a thick club. Tvashtri, the powerful, in anger draws up a mountain by its roots, while Surya has a brilliant dart, and Mrityu his axe.

Aryaman stalks the forest with a dreadful spiked bludgeon, Mitra stands forth with a chakra sharp as razors. O King, Pusha, Bhaga and Savitri dash enraged at Krishna and Partha, with bows and curved blades in their hands. The Rudras, the Vasus, the mighty Maruts, the Viswedevas and the Sadhyas, all splendent with their own lustre, and many other sky-dwellers, too, all armed with various weapons, run at Krishna and Arjuna, highest among men, to strike them down.

During the battle that ensues, marvellous omens are seen all around, even like those that appear during the Pralaya, making many a creature faint in fright. But Arjuna and Krishna wait calmly, bows in hand, fearless and invincible; then they beleaguer the Deva host with astras like thunder and lightning, routing them repeatedly.

The aerial legion flees to Indra, while the Munis who watch the battle from the sky are full of wonder to see the celestial ones beaten back effortlessly by Krishna and Arjuna. Indra is also pleased to witness the prowess of those two.

He flies into the fray, lashing down a thick storm of stones over Arjuna, whose ambidextrous archery he wants to test. In a flurry of furious shafts, Arjuna shatters every stone. Perplexed, disbelieving, Indra of the hundred yagnas hurls down another gale of rocks, thicker than before. But his son pleases his father again by smashing this hail into dust, as well.

Growing angry, Indra plucks a great peak from Mandara, with its stands of lofty trees, and flings it down whistling at Arjuna, who dissects it in a thousand slivers with his lightlike, fire-tongued missiles. The riven fragments of the mountain peak look like the Sun and the Moon dislodged from their places and falling to the Earth. Those still great pieces fall with a mighty reverberation, crushing numberless creatures of the Khandava vana beneath them."

CANTO 230

KHANDAVA-DAHA PARVA CONTINUED

Vaisampayana said, "Now the creatures of the Khandava vana, the Danavas, Rakshasas, Nagas, wolves, bears, other wild predators, elephants with rent temples, rut-juice flowing from them, tigers, lions with shaggy mane, deer, buffalo in hundreds, bird of every kind, and myriad other creatures fly in every direction from the falling stones and rocks.

The forest burns, and Krishna and Arjuna stand impassive and impassable with weapons in hand. Dreadful sounds fill that blazing jungle, and the fleeing creatures stand still, trembling. Looking at the towering flames and Krishna – both waiting to devour them they scream and roar in numberless different voices. The sky shakes at that frightful sound and with the raging of Agni as if with deep and portentous thunder.

Dark Krishna, Kesava Mahabaho casts his great and fierce chakra, burning with its own energy, at the denizens of the forest. It desiccates them, and they fall in pieces, Danavas and Rakshasas, too, into Agni's maw. Mangled by Krishna's disc, Asuras are painted with blood, smeared in their fat and look like clouds of dusk.

Bhaarata, the dark Vrishni flares through the vana as death, despatching Pisachas, Pakshis, Nagas and every other living thing, in thousands. The wheeling chakra that he casts at them again and again, returns each time into his hands, after claiming innumerable wild lives.

While he slays the Pisachas, Nagas and Rakshasas, the face of Krishna, soul of all that is created, is grim and terrible to look upon. None among the Devas gathered there can face Krishna or Arjuna in battle. When they realise that they cannot save the Khandava vana from burning, they withdraw, and, O King, Indra of a hundred sacrifices sees the immortals retreat and is filled with rarest joy; he applauds the two heroes of the Earth.

When his gods flee the battle, an asariri, a disembodied voice, deep as the sky, speaks to Indra, 'Your friend, the Naga King Takshaka, has not been killed, for he went to Kurukshetra before the fire began. Know, O Indra, no one can vanquish Krishna and Arjuna in battle. They are Nara Narayana, those Gods of old whose fame is still told in Swarga. You know their strength and their valour. They are invincible; no one in the three worlds can vanquish these best of all the ancient Sages. They are worthy of being worshipped by all the Devas and Asuras, by the Yakshas, the Nagas, Rakshasas and Gandharvas, by Manavas, Kinnaras and Nagas.

So, O Indra, leave this place with your celestials, for Fate has ordained that the Khandava vana will be consumed today.'

Leaving anger and envy, the Deva king returns to Devaloka; seeing him go, the other gods and their host follow. Arjuna and Krishna let out a lion's roar, which rings through the forest. They celebrate their victory over Indra and his Devas.

Having scattered the legions of heaven like clouds by the wind, the two now help Agni unhindered; countless creatures of the Khandava vana they slay with storms of arrows. Cut off by Arjuna's dazzling archery, no creature escapes the burning forest. Let alone attack him, they dare not look at him, not the strongest and fiercest among them, for fear of his inexorable barbs.

Flitting here and there in his chariot, at times he pierces a hundred creatures with a single arrow, then, shoots a single one with a hundred shafts. Dying as if felled by Yama himself, the birds, beasts and the rest fall into Agni's blazing jaws. They flee to riverbanks, to hilly zones of the forest, to burning ghats, but nowhere do they find sanctuary from the flames or from the two warriors.

Prides of lions roar in anguish. Elephant, tiger, deer and wolf scream and howl. The fish in the Ganga and the Sea hear that clamour and are afraid; Vidyadhara tribes living in the Khandava vana tremble. Mahabaho, it is true indeed that none of them could bear to even look at dark Krishna or Arjuna, so terrible are they.

A few times, bands of Rakshasas, Danavas and tribes of Nagas rush at Krishna, and he promptly despatches them with his chakra. Beheaded and truncated by the blinding disc, their huge bodies fall into the flames raging everywhere. Gratified by the streams of melting flesh, fat and boiling blood they feed on, the flames rise unimaginably high, and they burn smokelessly.

His eyes copper fire, his tongue a massive flame, his jaws agape, the hair on his head all fire, Agni Hutasana drinks what for him is that nectarine river of animal fat; he drinks because Arjuna and Krishna help him, and he is pleased indeed, he is delighted.

Suddenly, Krishna Madhusudana sees an Asura called Mayaa fleeing the wild palace of Takshaka, in the heart of the forest. Vayu is Agni's charioteer, and assuming a Form with jata on his head, roaring like thunder, the Fire God chases the Asura, wanting to devour him. Krishna sees Mayaasura and stands with his chakra raised, ready to kill him.

With Agni behind him and Krishna before him, Mayaa calls out, 'Arjuna, fly here and save me!'

Hearing his terrified cry, Arjuna calls back, 'Fear not!'

O Bhaarata, Arjuna's very voice gives life and heart to the Asura. As soon as Pritha's compassionate son speaks, telling Mayaa not to fear, Krishna of the Dasarhas no longer wants to kill the Asura, who is the brother of Namuchi. Agni, also, does not burn him anymore.

With Krishna and Arjuna guarding him against Indra, Agni Mahamatim, the Fire God of immense intellect, rages, burning the Khandava vana for fifteen days. When that forest burns down, only six that dwelt in it escape with their lives: Aswasena, Mayaa Danava and four birds calls Sarngakas."

CANTO 231

Khandava-daha Parva Continued

Janamejaya said, "Brahmana, tell me, when that forest burned, why did Agni not consume the birds called Sarngakas? You have told us how Aswasena and Mayaa Danava escaped, but not yet about the Sarngakas. I am amazed these birds escaped, O Brahmana, tell me about them."

Vaisampayana said, "Slayer of all your enemies, I will tell you why Agni did not burn those birds when the Khandava vana burned. O King, there was a Maharishi calls Mandapala, who knew all the Shastras, who was devoted to austerity and asceticism, his vows stern and inviolable, among the best of all good men. He was a brahmacharin, who drew, like Rishis of yore, his semen virile up into his body, had perfect control of himself and his senses, and dedicated himself to a life of study and dharma.

Having crossed the Sea of tapasya, O Bhaarata, he left his body and went up into Pitrloka, the realm of the Manes. However, there, he did not receive the fruit of his punya.

He asked the celestials who sat around Yama, King of the Dead, 'Why do the realms which I thought I had attained by my penance remain sealed to me? Have I not done enough punya so that the lofty realms become mine? Swargavasis, heaven dwellers, tell me what I must do to gain the fruit of my devotions.'

The celestials replied, 'O Brahmana, karma causes men to be born in debt. There is no doubt that men are born to perform yagnas, to study the sacred Shastras, and to beget children. The debts of karma are paid by these. You are a learned Yogi of great tapasya, but you have no children.

The higher realms are sealed for you because you are childless. So beget children, and you will inherit countless realms of untold felicity! The Vedas tell that only a son rescues his father from the hell called Put. Brahmanottama, strive to have sons.'

Mandapala listened to this and thought about how he could have the most number of children in the shortest possible time. The Rishi realised that among all creatures birds of the air are the most fecund. He took the form of a Sarngaka and mated with a female bird of that species, whose name was Jarita. He fathered four sons on her, all knowers of the Veda.

Leaving the mother and her sons in that jungle, the Khandava, while the children were yet to hatch from their eggs, the Sage went to another mate calls Lapita, with whom he now ranged through the vana. Jarita grew anxious and sad, but she did not abandon her sons, the infant Rishis still inside their eggs.

Later, as the Rishi ranged through the forest with Lapita, he saw Agni come towards the Khandava vana, to devour it. The Brahmana Mandapala knew what the Fire God intended, and for the sake of his unfledged children propitiated the blazing Deva, that Lord of the Universe, of terrific tejas.

The Sage said to Agni, 'O Agni, you are the mouth of all the worlds. You are the bearer of the sacrificial ghee. You are the purifier of every creature, latent and unseen inside each one. The wise speak of you as being One, and then again as having triune forms and natures. They make their offering to you, conceiving of you as having eight mouths.

The great Rishis affirm that you created this universe, O Devourer of the havis, and that without you the universe would cease to exist in a day. By worshipping you, Brahmanas, with their wives and children, attain to the eternal realms that they have earned by their karma and punya on Earth.

O Agni, the knowing speak of you as being like thunderclouds in the sky full of lightning. None can resist your flames, but are consumed. Splendorous One, you created this Universe. The Vedas are your word. Every creature, moving and unmoving, depends on you. Water depends on you, as does the Universe.

All offerings of ghee, every ritual offering of food to the Pitrs, are founded in you. O Deva, you are the devourer, you are the creator, and you are as wise as Brihaspati. You are the twin Aswins; you are Surya; you are Soma; you are Vayu.'

Eulogised by Mandapala, Agni became pleased with that Rishi of measureless energy.

The Deva said to him, 'What good can I do for you?'

With folded hands, Mandapala said to the conveyor of the havis, 'When you burn the Khandava vana, spare my children!'

Illustrious Agni replied, 'Tathastu! So be it.'

So it was, O Rajan, that he did not consume the infant Sarngaka birds, when he burnt down the Khandava vana."

CANTO 232

KHANDAVA-DAHA PARVA CONTINUED

Vaisampayana said, "When Agni blazed, licking up the Khandava, the little birds were terrified and, not seeing any escape, began to scream. Their helpless mother Jarita wept.

She cried, 'Ah, the terrible inferno, which lights up the universe and devours thc forest, flares towards us. My children are newborn and have neither feet not feathers with which to escape, and they are the only salvation of our dead ancestors. The tallest trees are consumed like wisps of straw and, licking up everything in his path with his great tongue of flame, Agni spreads fear on every side.

Alas, neither my children nor I can escape. I cannot fly with them and my heart will not allow me to leave them either: which of my sons shall I leave and which shall I take with me? What is my dharma now? What do you say, my little ones, what do you think? Oh, I will cover you with my wings and we will perish together.

When your cruel father left me, he said, "Upon Jaritari, my eldest son, shall my clan depend. My second Sarisrikka will beget children to further our race. My third, Stambamitra will be a Sannyasi and my youngest Drona will become the greatest of all knowers of the Veda."

But now doom is upon us, my sons. Which of you shall I take with me? What is my true dharma? I cannot see any way by which we will escape the dreadful flames!'

And she wailed and lamented.

The infants spoke to their stricken mother, 'Mother, sacrifice your love for us and fly to a safe place. For even if we die here, you can still bear other children. However, if you also die, that will be the end of our race. Your dharma is towards our clan, so fly! Your clinging love for us can destroy all of us and our hope, as well. But if you save yourself, our father, who is always anxious to attain the realms of heaven, can still have what he wishes for.'

Jarita said, 'There is a mouse's burrow in the ground near this tree. Go down into this hole at once and you will not need to fear the fire. Once you are inside, I will cover it with earth. I see no other way to save you from raging Agni. When the fire subsides, I will come back and uncover the hole again. You must do what I say if you are to save yourselves.'

The infant birds replied, 'We have no feathers and are just four balls of flesh. If we go into the hole, the mouse is sure to kill us. We, also, see no way to escape, so that our father's having begotten us might not be in vain, and our mother might also find salvation. If we go down the hole, the mouse will eat us; if we remain here, the sky-licking fire will consume us.

We prefer to die by fire rather than have the mouse eat us, for the first death is noble and endorsed by the Sages, while the second is vile.'"

CANTO 233

KHANDAVA-DAHA PARVA CONTINUED

Vaisampayana said, "Jarita listened to her sons and said, 'The little mouse came out from his hole and a hawk seized him in her talons and bore him away. You have nothing to fear in the hole.'

The young ones replied, 'We did not see the hawk take the mouse, besides there might be other mice to fear in the burrow. As for the fire, it might not come here at all, for we see the wind blowing away from this place, bearing the flames with it.

Inside the hole, we will surely die, while here there is some chance of escaping. Mother, it is better that we stay here. Your dharma is to escape, since if you live on you can have other children.'

Their mother said, 'Sons, I saw the great hawk swoop down and carry the mouse away. While he flew, I flew behind and blessed him for having taken the mouse from his hole.

I said, "King of hawks, you have taken our enemy the mouse away: may you live in Swarga with a golden body and without an enemy!"

Later, when he had eaten the mouse, I returned here, taking his leave. So, my children, enter the hole trustfully, you have nothing to fear. I saw the hawk bear the mouse away and eat him.'

But the young ones said again, Mother, we are not certain that the hawk took the mouse. We cannot enter this hole in the ground.'

Their mother said, 'I know for sure that the hawk ate the mouse. You have nothing to fear, sons; go down into the hole.'

The young ones said again, 'Mother, we do not say that you are lying to send us down into the hole. For no one can be held responsible for what they do when they are distraught. We have done nothing for you yet, why are you so keen to save us, at such cost to yourself? What are we to you?

You are still young and beautiful, and you will find your husband again. Go seek him out. He will beget more fine children on you. We will find heavens of felicity if we die in the fire. However, if the fire does not consume us, you can return to claim us.'

The mother bird anxiously left her sons in the Khandava vana and flew away to safety. Agni rushed along, blazing ferociously, to where Mandapala's sons were. The little birds saw the flames approach, and now the eldest of them, Jaritari, began to speak so that Agni heard him."

CANTO 234

KHANDAVA-DAHA PARVA CONTINUED

Vaisampayana said, "Jaritari said, 'The wise person is aware of death; when death comes, he feels no pangs. The deluded soul, who is not heedful of death, succumbs to terror when death arrives and does not find salvation.'

The second brother, Sarisrikka, said, 'You are patient and wise; the time has come when our lives are in danger. There is no doubt that only one among many has wisdom and courage.'

The third brother, Stambamitra, said, 'The eldest brother is the protector; he will save us from danger. If he can do nothing, what can the younger ones achieve?'

The fourth and the youngest, Drona, said, 'Seven-mouthed and seven-tongued, the voracious Fire God flares towards us, ablaze and licking up everything in his path.'

Having spoken thus to one another, Mandapala's sons now hymned Agni, with devotion. Listen, O King, to the praises they sang.

Jaritari said, 'O Agni, you are the soul of air! You are the body of the

Earth's plants! O Fire, water is your parent, just as you are the parent of water! Resplendent one, your flames are like rays of the Sun, extending above, below, behind and on every side!'

Sarisrikka said, 'Smoke-bannered Deva, we do not see our mother and we do not know our father. Our feathers have not sprouted yet. You are our only refuge. O Agni, we are infants, protect us! O Agni, we are distraught, protect us with your auspicious and gentle form; protect us with your seven divine flames. We seek sanctuary in you.

O Agni, you are the only one who gives heat. Lord, only you lend heat to the rays of Surya. We are infant Rishis, O Fire, save us. Havyavaha, bearer of the sacrificial ghee, we beg you, turn away from this place and take another path.'

Stambamitra said, 'O Agni, you are all things. This whole universe is established in you. You sustain every creature; you support the universe. You bear the havis, and you are the sacred havis.

The wise know you as being one and many. You created the three worlds, and when the time comes, you will destroy them, Havyavaha, swelling forth in tides of flame. You are the cause of the universe, and you are the essence into which the universe dissolves.'

Drona said, 'Lord of the universe, growing stronger within the bodies of living beings, you digest the food that they eat. So, everything is founded in you. O Sukra, you from whose mouth the Vedas emerged, you assume the form of the Sun and, evaporating and absorbing the waters of the Earth and every other juice of life, you send them back as rain that makes all the living grow.

From you, come these green plants and trees, and these vines. From you, have come these lakes and pools, as well as the great and always blessed Ocean. Fierce-rayed, our bodies depend on Varuna for life, and we cannot bear your heat. Be our auspicious guardian, Agni, do not kill us!

Coppery-eyed Deva of the scarlet neck, who leave a black wake behind you, burn along some other path, and save us just as the Sea might a house built on his shore.'

When Drona, chanter of Brahman, spoke thus, Agni was pleased by what he said. The Fire God remembered the promise he had made to Mandapala, and said, 'You are truly a Sage, Drona! For what you say is Brahman. I will do as you ask. Never fear, because Mandapala has asked me to spare his sons when I burn the vana. What he said and what you have just said carries great weight with me. Tell me what to do, Brahmanottama, for I am pleased indeed by your stuti. Be blest, Brahmana!'

Drona said, 'O Sukra, look at these cats; they stalk us every day. Hutasana, devour them in your flames, all their kind.'

Agni did what the Sarngakas asked him to. Janamejaya, he swelled in tidal flames and consumed the Khandava vana."

CANTO 235

KHANDAVA-DAHA PARVA CONTINUED

Vaisampayana said, "O Kurusthama, the Rishi Mandapala was very anxious about his sons, although he had spoken to Agni to spare their lives.

He had no peace, and spoke thus to his second wife Lapita, 'Lapita, my children cannot walk or fly, how will they escape the fire as the wind fans its flames into an inferno? Their poor mother will be terrified and grief-stricken, when she finds that she can do nothing to save them. Ah, I can hear her lament in my mind.

Oh, how is my son Jaritari? How are Sarisrikka, Stambamitra, Drona, and how is their helpless mother?'

O Bhaarata, stung by jealousy, Lapita said to the sobbing Mandapala, 'You need not worry about your sons, since you say they are all Rishis endowed with great powers and energy. What do they have to fear from fire? Besides, you spoke to Agni in my presence, and did the illustrious one not promise to protect them?

Agni is one of the sovereigns of the universe; he would never lie. You are not really anxious for your sons. I know that it is only because of Jarita that you have no peace. I am sure that you have never loved me as you do her. Oh, you so easily watch me suffer, but cannot bear to think of her in pain, for she dwells in your heart.

Why don't you go to Jarita, for whom your heart grieves so? As for me, I will wander alone from now, as my punishment for having given myself to a lustful, wayward man.'

Mandapala replied, 'I am neither lustful nor wayward. I only roam the Earth to beget sons. Even those that I have sired are in mortal danger, and the evil man is he who casts away what he already has for the sake of what he might acquire. The world disregards and insults him. I must go to my children, and you can do as you please. This blazing fire that licks up the greatest trees makes my heart quail and fills me with ominous thoughts.'

Meanwhile, after the fire had left the place where the little Sarngakas were, Jarita flew back to her children. She found all of them safe and well. Seeing their mother, they began to cry, and seeing them alive she wept as well – tears of joy. One by one, she hugged her sons in her wings.

Just then, O Bhaarata, the Rishi Mandapala arrived there. None of his sons showed any joy on seeing him. The Rishi spoke repeatedly to his sons and their mother, lovingly, but none of them made any reply.

Mandapala said, 'Which of these is my firstborn son, and who is second? Who is born third and which one is the youngest? I speak to you in sorrow, why don't you answer me? It is true that I did leave you all, but I was not happy where I went.'

Jarita said, 'What is it to you which of these is the eldest, or which second? What concern of yours is it who is third and who the youngest? Go to Lapita of the sweet smiles, lush in her youth, to whom you went, finding her better than me in all ways.'

Mandapala replied, 'For women, nothing shatters their happiness as when their husband marries a second wife, or when he takes a lover. Nothing inflames rage and anxiety in a woman as these do.

Even the gentle and chaste Arundhati, celebrated through the worlds, is intensely possessive of her husband, the great Vasishta, who is devoted to her happiness. Why, such is her jealousy that she once insulted that wisest of the Saptarishis, speaking harshly to him, and then she became a little star amidst the Seven Sages of the sky, at times bright and at others dim, like fire and smoke, and ominous.

I look only to you for children. Like Vasishta Muni, I never wronged you. Yet, you insult me even as Arundhati did Vasishta of old, out of your insane jealousy. Men ought never to trust women, not even their wives. Only when they become mothers, do women serve their husbands.'

Hearing what their father said, his sons came forward, one by one, to worship him, and he spoke kindly to them, reassuring them of his love."

CANTO 236

KHANDAVA-DAHA PARVA CONTINUED

Vaisampayana said, "Mandapala said to his sons, 'I spoke to Agni to protect you, and the blazing Deva gave me his word that he would not harm you. It was only because of that, and knowing your mother is virtuous, and also knowing the great tejas which is in you four, that I did not come earlier.

My sons, do not keep bitterness in your hearts towards me. You are all Rishis, and knowers of the Veda. Even great Agni knows you well.'

Having reassured them, the Brahmana Mandapala took his wife and sons, and leaving that charred forest, went away to another land.

This is the tale of how Agni blazed forth, and with the help of Krishna and Arjuna, devoured the Khandava vana, for the weal of the world. Having drunk many rivers of fat and marrow, Agni is pleased, and appears again before Arjuna.

Just then, Indra Purandara, surrounded by the Maruts, flies down from the sky and says to Partha and Kesava, 'No Deva could do what you both have done. Ask me each for a boon that no man can otherwise have, for I am pleased with you.'

Arjuna asks Indra for all his weapons, his astras. Sakra of untold splendour says, 'When illustrious Mahadeva becomes pleased with you, Pandava, I will give you all my weapons. Kurusthama, I will know when the time comes, and then for your stern tapasya you shall have all my astras of fire and of wind.'

Krishna asks that his friendship with Arjuna be eternal, and the king of the Devas grants that boon, and having given both those heroes what they asked, and speaking gently to Agni Hutasana, as well, Indra ascends into Swarga on high again, followed by the Maruts and the other celestials.

Gratified with his mighty feast, having burned the Khandava for fifteen days, with all its denizens, birds, beasts and the rest, Agni is becalmed: he blazes no more. Having gorged abundantly on the flesh of all those creatures, the pleased Fire God says to Krishna and Arjuna, 'Purushavyaghras, I am delighted with you. I bless you heroes that you will be able to travel wherever you wish.'

Agni now vanishes, leaving Krishna, Arjuna and Mayaa Danava. Those three wander along a little, then come to the banks of an enchanting river and sit beside it."

END OF ADI PARVA